STONE AND SCEPTRE

The Nifaran Chronicles Part 1

Books by John Howes

Fantasy

The Nifaran Chronicles

Part 1: Stone and Sceptre
Part 2: Vega Rising
(Parts 3 and 4 planned)

Science Fiction

Zero Magenta
Proxi

Please use the social media channels listed below for information on new releases and to engage with the author.

Social Media

Mastodon: johnhowesauthor@mastodonapp.uk
Instagram: johnhowesauthor
TikTok: johnhowesauthor
YouTube: https://www.youtube.com/@johnhowesauthor
Blog: johnahowes.blogspot.com
Twitter: johnhowesauthor

All information was correct at the time of publication. Social media channels are subject to change.

STONE AND SCEPTRE

The Nifaran Chronicles Part 1

JOHN HOWES

© John Howes 2023

This book is copyright under the Berne Convention. All rights are reserved. No part of this work may be reproduced or transmitted in any form, or by any means without the prior permission of the copyright owner.

Cover design by Damonza

Title page art by Lisa Howes

Map design by John Howes

Additional graphics by Gordon Johnson, Pixabay.com
Used under Pixabay license.

Radley font © 2011 Vernon Adams (vern@newtypography.co.uk)
Licensed under the SIL Open Font License, Version 1.1

Nymphette font by Lauren Thompson, The Font Nymph
(nymphont.blogspot.com)
Nymphont License v1.00

Proof reading and additional editing by Lisa Howes

First edition paperback: 2023

For the different who walk among us.

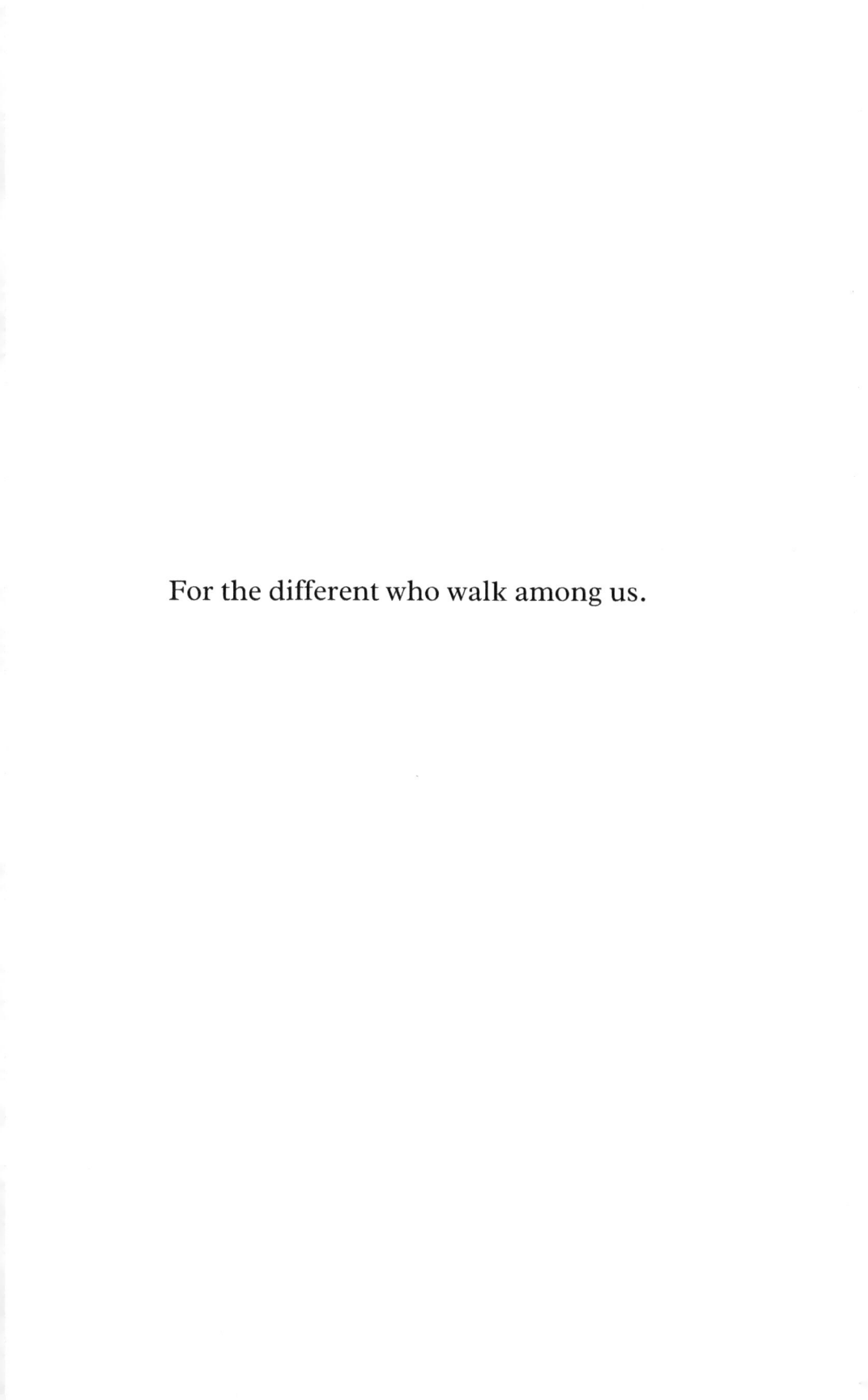

DETAIL MAP INDEX

Burland page 6
Caynna page 64
Deapholt Forest page 153
Alfheim page 225
Mirror Lake and Banafell page 253
Tudorfeld page 315
Stanholm page 393

1 THE GIFT

Sir Faege Aplite looked down at his mud-covered hands. Blood still seeped from the thorn cuts which wouldn't heal and mingled with the scabs and scrapes from three months in this despicable place. The pale, white skin above his black beard was almost lost beneath the grime, and raw, red streaks on his neck were painful to the touch.

The rain refused to stop, continuing to find its way through the tree branches above to tap, like slow torture, on his armour. Tears were welling in his eyes as he thought of Wena's soft embrace and their home together far to the east. The ghostly trees and thick, dank air sapped all hope of return.

As he sat staring into the grey at the shifting shadows, Sir Faege remembered how the squad of ten had first arrived, full of confidence despite grim warnings. Commander Gaelen Tonalite was sure they would reach their goal with a party of ten hand-picked men and a vital mission ahead. It didn't take long for the marshes to claim their first soul.

One by one, the men were lost. Most simply vanished into the gloom, but the company's guide was pulled into the bog by some unseen beast, his screams filling their hearts with blackness and leaving the men silent for many days.

After six weeks of unrelenting rain and misery, Commander Tonalite lost his senses. He claimed to see a naked, green maiden flitting through the trees and ran into the void to find her. The men gave chase, but after two days of searching, their commander was lost, along with another soldier who vanished during the search.

The last surviving knight, Sir Faege, reached into his sodden leather satchel to feel the creases of the two letters he carried with him. One to his wife Wena, and the other written to the parents of Gada Sonny Flint. Sonny was a brave, loyal lad to the last, and Faege had finally broken down when he found him gone in the morning. There were signs that something substantial and clawed had dragged him into the swamp.

He pulled out his sword, stained green from hacking at thorny bushes and snake-like roots. It had started to rust and rot like his damp feet and everything else in this forsaken place. Pulling the blade close, he inspected the jagged edge. Each notch had a tale to tell, but the briefest flicker of reflected, yellow light could mean his story had a final chapter.

Stone and Sceptre

Sir Faege whirled about and gazed past the tree into the thick wall of bramble and sedge beyond. All around him was nothing but darkness and menacing shadows. He looked around but saw no sign, not even a clue where the sun could be. He feared a trick, a phantom, one last cruel joke to send him running to his end like Commander Tonalite. He settled back against the tree and sighed; at that moment, his eyes caught sight of a glimmering light through the thicket.

His heart now racing, he poured all his will into concentrating his stare where the light had been. After what felt like an age, a faint glint flashed between the trees.

"That *must* be it," he said to himself. "Frea, give me strength."

Wearily he climbed to his feet and steeled himself for one last push to his goal or oblivion. Striding out into the putrid water, he kept his sword aloft, ready to clear a path or defend from unseen menaces.

It was tough going for Sir Faege, but he was familiar with this place now. The marshes sucked at his boots, threatening to pull him into the mire if he tarried too long, so he kept striding forward. Once again, a glimpse of light as the waters deepened to waist height, and he slashed at the low boughs blocking his path. Stumbling through the bog, he heard the splashing echoes of his toil behind, which became louder as he made for the thicket and the glow beyond.

Once again, he thought of Wena; her rose-tinted skin and strawberry hair, the lilt of her laughter, the beauty of her smile. Just maybe he could be back in her arms. He hacked and slashed through the tall reeds and lunged on through the gloom. His grunts of struggle and pain melded with the splashing water as if followed by a waterfall.

He stopped. All was quiet except for the wind in the trees and the rain on his armour. Then he heard it. There was no watery echo, but something splashed behind him, something big.

Sir Faege didn't turn to see what terrible creature pursued him. He mustered all his will and drove himself forward with all his remaining strength. Charging headlong into the bushes, pushing branches away with his gauntlets and ignoring the foliage whipping at his face, he barrelled blindly towards the light. The rain drove harder, and the air thickened, clawing at his throat as he gasped for breath.

His pursuer was getting closer; he could hear a snorting rasp as the water surged past him. "Hold fast!" he shouted, using up his last ounce of energy as the weight of the heavy armour took its toll. With one last effort, he pushed through a dense bramble bush. His boot hit something hard, and he fell, twisting onto his back. Hitting the hard ground, he yelped in pain.

He looked into the briar, but nothing came through, just the sound of water rippling as something unknown slunk away. Lying back, he looked up towards the sky, revealing nothing but impenetrable grey and the rain falling on his face.

After catching his breath, Sir Faege wearily climbed to his feet and looked around. He stood at the edge of a rough circle of solid ground, approximately thirty yards wide. At its centre, he could finally see the source of the light. The islet was dominated by a round, rough-built wooden hut containing a small arched door flanked on each side by small windows. A gnarled, stately oak tree grew through the shelter's centre, spreading its boughs past the hut's eaves. Vines and moss covered most of the outside, merging the building into the fens from a distance.

The dwelling looked centuries old, but the smoke rising from the small round chimney and flickering glow from the windows indicated a presence. A path of small, square-cut stone cobbles circled the hut and reached the land's edge in a few places, including where the knight stood.

Sir Faege made his way to the door and saw the shape of a small crescent moon carved into its centre. He stood beneath a short porch, giving a welcome respite from the never-ending rain. *How could anyone live in this place?* he thought as he raised his hand to give three knocks.

There was no reply or sound of movement. Once again, he knocked a little harder.

"Is there anybody there?" he said, in the clear common tongue, with the slightest hint of a Stanish accent, the product of a privileged upbringing.

There was no answer and no indication that anyone was home. Sir Faege pressed on the wooden latch, and the door swung inwards, creaking on its wooden hinges.

"Hello?" he said, gingerly looking around the door.

The knight was met by a warm blast of musty air which smelled of earth and damp moss. The same square stones continued into the home, bulging in places where tree roots had pushed them upwards. On the left was a table and single chair, above which were shelves containing several jars of various ingredients and animal skins hanging beneath.

Past the imposing tree trunk to the left lay a short wooden bed with rough sackcloth sheets and a homemade candle burning on a small table. Fully opening the door revealed the source of the light. A roaring fire blazed brightly in a hearth built from the same little square bricks as the floor.

"Hello?" Sir Faege repeated once more as he carefully walked around the tree trunk towards the back of the hut. Furs and clothes made from sackcloth hung from wooden pegs on the wall, along with a hat made from reeds. A large book cabinet was stuffed with well-worn volumes, but the book, which caught his eye, lay on a tiny table next to a small wooden chair. A thin, pale, weathered hand rested on the cover. A hand belonging to the chair's occupant.

"Come in and warm yourself by the fire," came a creaking elderly voice.

Sir Faege gradually took in the details of the older man sitting in front of the hearth. The man's head was bald with thin wisps of white hair over his ears, while a long white beard covered his sackcloth shirt and blended with a grey fur waistcoat.

"Thank you, kind sir," said Sir Faege remembering his manners. "I've come a long way."

"You have," replied the older man dryly. "Few make it this far."

As Faege moved around towards the fire, he saw the man's features for the first time. His face was thin and lined like parchment. He had a pointed nose and misty grey eyes.

"What brings a fair knight to the sunken isle?" continued the older man, looking Sir Faege up and down.

Faege shifted uneasily. He didn't know how much to say and wasn't sure how much of the story he believed himself. He had volunteered in blind patriotism, but it always felt like a fool's errand.

"I'm looking for a powerful man," he said finally. "A man who can help us."

"Just a man?" replied the older man, a mischievous smile creeping over his face.

Sir Faege watched him uncomfortably. He didn't want to say the words, they felt immature, but this was his best chance of finding the prize.

"A warlock," he said finally.

The man gave a rasping laugh and started to get up, his thin limbs shaking with exertion.

"Tell me, fair knight, how can this *warlock* help you?"

The knight finally felt his leggings and boots starting to dry in front of the fire, and perhaps the man might share some food. He could tell him the story, and maybe he could get help to leave this place.

"My name is Sir Faege Aplite, and I'm a knight from the House of Scoria. I'm a servant of King Ramon of Stanholm."

The man nodded and steadied himself by the chair. Sir Faege continued. "I'm the last member of a squad tasked with finding the warlock to help us retake the lands of Tudorfeld."

The man stared into the fire beside Sir Faege. "Go on," he said, caressing his beard.

"I have a gift for him if he agrees to help us. Do you know where he is?"

The older man seemed to ponder the question for a while as Sir Faege warmed himself by the fire.

"I might know," said the man finally. "Could you show me the gift?"

Sir Faege felt a strange calm falling over him. Maybe it was the room's warmth or the release of so much fear and frustration. His caution seemed to be easing away, and he found himself reaching into his satchel for the artefact.

The item was a short, silver-coloured metal rod about the length of a hand. It contained a tiny, silver metal ball at one end and a larger, translucent, round green stone at the top.

"May I see?" said the older man holding out his dry, creased hand.

Sir Faege handed him the item carefully and noticed the tiniest flash of green light in the rod's stone as it touched the man's hand.

The man scrutinized the item, and as he did, his voice changed; the rasp eased, and his words became clearer.

"Some people call him Jhakri," said the older man grinning, "and some call him Myrik; others call him the Scucca, while the Jakari people call him *Haldor Ma Kathyr Vizan*. I've not been called warlock in a very long time."

Sir Faege felt the calm lift, and a searing pain erupted in his chest. He looked down to see his dagger buried in his chest plate with his own hands on the hilt.

"Thank you for the gift," said the older man as the knight fell to his knees.

Life left Sir Faege. He held out his hands in a gesture of bewilderment. As his vision blurred, the man's image changed, as if his face and body were melting.

The long grey beard receded, and black hair appeared on the man's head. He grew in height, and his back straightened; the lines and creases dissolved in his face leaving sharp features, green, sparkling eyes and a cruel smile.

"Thank you, Sir Faege," said the man, with a menacing but youthful voice. "You may go now."

Sir Faege saw the world blur around him and heard the man laugh maniacally as life departed and the world turned black.

Sorry, Wena, my love.

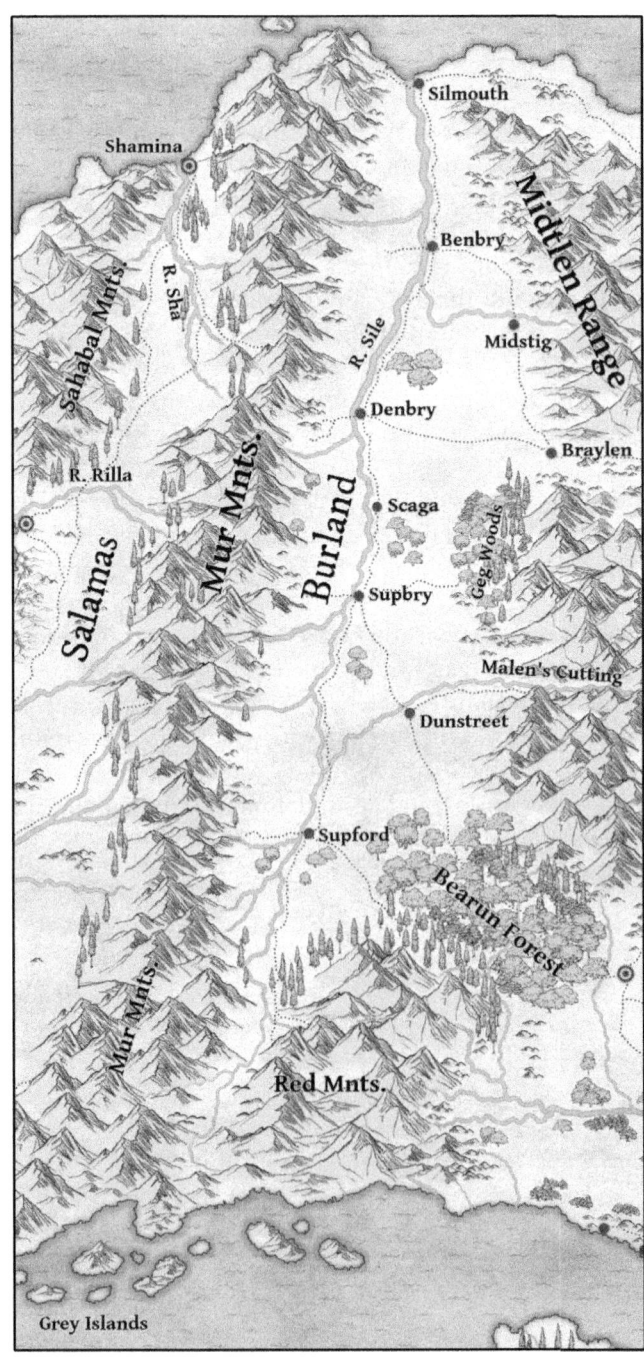

Burland

2 DANYA

Jem woke with a start to the sound of crockery smashing below. His heart raced, and the sheets clung with sweat.

"Another bad dream?" asked Aunt Ada; her face appeared at the top of the ladder on the mezzanine. "Come down now; it's time for breakfast."

Several chicken feathers slowly fell to the bed from the rafters above while Jem squinted through the shaft of sunlight coming through the curtains, pulled the covers aside and dragged himself out of bed. Just a short distance of squeaky floorboards existed between the box bed and a ten-foot drop to the floor below. Jem was so familiar with the tiny space he could navigate it with his eyes closed.

The home of Ned and Ada Poulterer was a small wooden barn containing just one room. The living space consisted of a dining area at the front, a large stone fireplace to one side and a sleeping area at the back. Humble in stature, it fitted perfectly with the other dwellings on the River Sile's east bank. Built from rough-sawn timbers and sealed with mud, it was draughty in the winter and as hot as an oven in the summer. Jem Poulterer slept on a wide mezzanine built at the far end, above his aunt and uncle's bed. A generous window poured light on his average frame; it sat in the centre of the roof's pitch, and he loved spending time watching the world outside.

The vision today was bright as the sun rose in the distant Braylen valley, a gleaming jewel between two sections of the snow-capped Midtlen mountain range. Jem often wondered what mysteries lay beyond the hills, having never passed the peaks or seen the ocean lapping the coast other than in his mind. The main island of Grenfold, along with Stanholm, Alfheim, and the sunken Brencan, made up the region known as Weorgoran, a title seldom used, as lands beyond the four were unknown.

Grenfold was split geographically into seven regions; however, the most significant divide was skin colour, and the Mur Mountains provided the dividing line. Humans to the east ranged from the light pink hues of the Stanish, Tudorfeldians, and Burlanders to the fawn lustre and dark hair of Caynna and Cultras. All these lands would unite in a shared distrust and fear of the Jakari people in the west. The land of Salamas lay beyond the Mur, and its people were seldom seen in the east. With a brown skin colour ranging from the nomads' deep umber to the city dwellers' golden ochre, it was easy for religion and power to mark them as different. Jem's fellow Burlanders called them demons; the Jakaris referred to easterners as white ghosts.

Jem's dreams were often of these alien lands. Unfamiliar people and strange languages populated nights of fantastical adventure. Sometimes his dreams would feature him with strangers, while other times, they were of life in far-away places, with strange folk, as someone else. One recurring dream featured a beautiful Jakari woman who spoke to him in a foreign tongue, but every time he reached out for her, she vanished, and he woke up.

He had always had such dreams, but recently their number had increased. Jem would find himself longing for sleep so he could escape to seek out the woman once more.

As Jem's gaze scanned down from the horizon, over the roofs of other Denbry residents, it rested on the small field behind the house. Full of compact, wooden chicken coops, it was the mainstay of the Poulterer's life and occupied most of Jem's time.

He felt his life wasting away here. Denbry wasn't a terrible place, but the thought of raising chickens all his life filled his heart with dread. In Denbry, your trade was your name, which you inherited from your father. A Blacksmith was born of a blacksmith, a Tanner born of a tanner, and a Poulterer was the son of a poulterer, but this chicken farmer was different. Even when he turned twenty-eight, the villagers would never accept him. An outcast, a mongrel.

Jem sighed as he pulled on his brown linen trousers and thin leather shoes. They were worn, and a small hole formed at one of the toes. Living was a bigger priority for his aunt and uncle, who'd toiled all their lives for their humble home. He grabbed a clean white shirt and backed over the mezzanine down the sturdy ladder permanently nailed in place. It creaked and wobbled, as did every board and frame in the grey, weathered barn.

A bowl of steaming porridge and a mug of milk awaited him on the table as Ada bustled about in her billowing day dress, cleaning away a broken plate with a willow broom.

"Your porridge is getting cold; come on, your uncle's already out," she said with a smile.

Jem forced a smile in return, then tried not to gag as he swallowed the lukewarm porridge and tepid fresh milk.

Ada had a caring face, lined with her advancing years and framed in grey-streaked hair tied back in a bun. She always smiled at the world, no matter how hard her toil became. "Frea placed me on this land to do my duty. I have no choice in that, but I can choose to be happy," she would often say. Jem couldn't help feeling that Frea intended more for him than just raising chickens.

Only once had he shared one of his dreams with his aunt and uncle, but so stiff was the rebuke that he never mentioned them again.

"Where's Uncle Ned?" said Jem, forcing down more tasteless porridge.

"Oh, he's at the Cartwright's. You can meet him there," she replied.

Jem finished up and bent low to kiss his aunt goodbye.

"Frea be with you," she beamed.

He towered above her with his six-foot frame, as with the other villagers, who were all much shorter. They also mostly had blonde or mousey hair and freckles. This jarred with Jem's short dark hair and his warm beige complexion. His face was rounded and even, with just the minimum of stubble giving him an intense, rugged look. He would be considered handsome anywhere but here. He cursed his father.

Jem walked along the main Burland Road, beside the burbling Sile River, towards the village centre. The village of Denbry sat in the heart of the Burland valley, which swept west to the imposing Mur Mountains and gently rose east to the Midtlen Range. The land was lush and fertile, with many farms along the river's path, but dwellings were always on the east bank. Jem loved to watch the sticks and leaves pass by on the current and wondered if they would make it as far north as Silmouth and the sea beyond. He often imagined stealing a boat and letting the river take him away to anywhere but Denbry.

Today he stopped for a moment and looked out over the Sile at the colourful patchwork of crops on the west bank. The fields only extended a couple of miles towards the Mur before they petered out, and the grey rock took over. No farmer would get too close to the wall of stone for fear of the Jakari people. Even though none had been spotted for many years, fear of the *demons* ran deep; the mysterious land of Salamas lay beyond the craggy peaks, but its secrets were closed to the superstitious valley dwellers.

The homes and shacks that made up the sleepy hamlet were all of a unique design but somehow coalesced into a whole repeated in every Burland village. The modest abbey, the shops and shacks where farmers' wares were sold, and dwellings of all shapes and sizes huddled close.

Continuing his walk, Jem passed the Cooper's stone house and its yard, littered with barrels and wooden off-cuts. Mik Cooper nodded to Jem as he emerged from his workshop but turned away abruptly and returned to the house. It was a similar story as he passed the Hwaetbur's farm shack, where Lyn Hwaetbur spotted him as she swept the porch and quickly looked away.

Jem looked through them as he did all the locals who shunned him daily. It made him loathe the sleepy hamlet and daydream of a better life wandering the lands east of the Midtlen Mountains. One day he'd be gone and never look back at the short, narrow-minded peasants. Only Mia Tunland had spoken to him, besides his aunt and uncle.

As Jem arrived at the village green, he gazed at the impressive stone manor house of Squire Hoy Tunland. It looked out onto the flat, wooden Denbry Bridge and dominated the village centre. A multitude of peaks and jutting bow windows peppered its steeply raked roof, with glass panes larger than any other Denbry house. The Tunlands owned most of the land in Denbry and most of the homes. It was said that the squire was the son of Earl Tunland, who had gifted Denbry to him and Lady Tunland as a wedding present. Jem couldn't begin to imagine such wealth or the ability to buy and sell a whole village.

Jem rubbed his eyes and wondered what Mia was doing right now. She was younger than him at twenty years, but being the squire's daughter put her out of bounds. If Hoy ever saw them together, Jem would be in serious trouble. She had the typical blonde hair and blue eyes of a Burlander, but her smile was infectious, and she never turned away when she saw him.

A year earlier, she'd grabbed his arm at the summer fair and pulled him into an alley behind the Plowright's home.

"I know all about you," she said, giggling. Her cheeks flushed rouge, looking beautiful in the summer sun. "I'm not supposed to talk to you, but I don't care."

Jem stared blankly at her, surprised that she would speak to a lowly peasant, especially one shunned by the rest of the village.

"I know the *real* you," she continued.

The real me? Jem thought to himself. He knew the story very well, having been told by his aunt and uncle many times.

Jem's father was Ben Poulterer, a peasant farmer who owned cornfields out on the village's far west. He married Ann, a sweet girl he'd met on a supply run to the village of Benbry in the north. They lived in a humble shack on the outskirts of Denbry, and although they were happy, Frea had not blessed them with children.

One day, after a hard day ploughing the fields, Ben was collecting his sandwich satchel and coat when he spotted something moving in the hedge between the fields. When he bent down and looked into the ditch, he found a young Jakari woman, dirty, shivering in the cold and looking scared and hungry. She wore a sky blue cotton dress, slit to her thigh, and her black wavy hair cascaded over a cleavage, obscene to the eyes of a Burlander. She was a pitiful sight, cut and bruised, with tear streaks trailing from her deep brown eyes.

The local tale maintained that from the moment Ben stared into her dark brown eyes, the woman had captured him with Jakari magic and was powerless to resist. Ben brought her home to his wife Ann, and they would give her a bed for the night, as any good Frean would. She spoke little of the common tongue but told them her name was Asmeen.

At midnight, Ben awoke and was driven by a strange compulsion to rise and leave the bed-chamber. He found Asmeen standing naked in the middle of the living room. Drawn to her as if in a trance, they lay together until the early hours. By morning she was gone.

Ben and Ann's life continued as usual, but Ben couldn't get Asmeen out of his head. He would often stand in the cornfields looking up at the Mur Mountains hoping to catch a glimpse. There was no sign of the woman until one stormy winter night over nine months later.

It was ten o'clock when a loud knock sounded on the Poulterer's door. The night watch found a Jakari girl on the bridge. She was soaked, exhausted, shivering and calling Ben's name. She was also heavily pregnant.

Ann wouldn't have the woman in their home, but no one else would help, so Ben insisted, and they lay her on blankets in front of the fire. The village midwife was called and reluctantly agreed to help. And so it was that on the stroke of midnight, Asmeen gave birth to a baby boy with beige skin and green eyes.

As the days and weeks passed, with Ann helping to look after the baby and Asmeen starting to learn a few words, Ben grew increasingly in love with the Jakari woman. He would walk through the village with her and ignore stares from the villagers. They spent time together in the fields and beside the Sile. All while Ann stayed at home and cared for the little one.

Over time, Ann became depressed and desperate. Confronting Ben one day, she told him that Asmeen and her son must go. One night Ann and Ben argued loudly and woke the whole neighbourhood. Ann told Ben that Asmeen and her baby must leave the next day, but in his blind love and anger, Ben snapped and shouted: "he's *my* son!"

Asmeen had gone when they awoke the following day, but the baby remained gurgling in his cot. Bewitched by the woman and not stopping to look back, Ben ran from the house towards the mountains, shouting Asmeen's name as he went.

Ann waited three months for Ben to return. On a bright midsummer morning, a farmer found Ann's body face-down in the Sile, caught in the west bank's reeds.

Most of the villagers believed Jem was either bewitched or a bad omen. Even Ned and Ada had only taken him in through a sense of duty. All the villagers shunned him except one.

"That's not it!" said Mia firmly.

"I don't understand," replied Jem dumbly.

Mia looked around to ensure they weren't being overheard. She pulled Jem down to her height and whispered in his ear.

"Do you remember anything in the village more than five years ago?"

Jem didn't understand and stared, open-mouthed.

"Do you remember the fire about eight years ago? It destroyed a barn and two houses. Remember?"

"What fire?" said Jem, shaking his head.

"*The* fire," replied Mia laughing. "The biggest fire in Denbry's history."

Jem shook his head, trying to remember the fire, his childhood, anything from the past. There were only shadows, no detail.

"Jem, you're special, very special," continued Mia. "You're a...."

"That's enough!" The commanding voice belonged to the imposing Lady Sen Tunland. She appeared behind the two dressed in a flowing, blue velvet gown and flanked by two of the household guards; she was in no mood for dissent. "Return to the green," she ordered Mia, "while *you*!" she said, looking straight at Jem. "Never speak to my daughter again!"

That was the first and last time he and Mia had spoken, although they had exchanged secret smiles on the few occasions they had passed in the village.

Jem looked up at the Tunland's home, hoping to catch a glimpse of Mia as he walked past, but all was quiet. He followed the Burland Road as it snaked away from the river and past the squire's manor before it doubled back towards the Sile. Twenty-two miles further north was the tiny village of Three Ways. Twenty miles on was the large village of Benbry, and thirty miles more was the port town of Silmouth. Jem would love to visit anywhere, but today he stopped on the outskirts of Denbry beside the Cartwright's home.

"It's about time," grumbled Uncle Ned as Jem's face appeared at the workshop door.

Ned was a typical Burlander with his short, stocky frame, no-nonsense manner and hard work ethic. Thinning grey hair and sagging skin might mark his age, but taught muscles rippled beneath. He could be very strict with Jem but never out of malice.

"Could have done with your help on the wheel," he continued, gesturing to the two-wheeled cart they rented from the squire. Ned and Jem used it to carry eggs to Denbry residents and others outside the village.

"The second one will need a new spoke," said Tom Cartwright as he appeared from behind the cart. "Oh, hi Jem," he added briefly as he spotted Jem leaning against the workshop door.

"Morning, Tom," said Jem, but Tom had already turned his back to talk with Ned.

The cart would be ready tomorrow, and the squire would pay as usual. Despite owning most of the village, the Tunlands were very fair. Rents were reasonable, and no one was chased for payment. The squire covered general repairs to buildings and equipment, so the villagers held their master in high regard.

"Jem, please take Flo home, then do the egg collection," said Ned referring to their cart horse tied up outside. "I've got more business with Tom, and then I'll be home for lunch."

Having walked across the village, Jem found himself walking back with Flo. He knew he had more to give the world than fetching and carrying; he felt trapped. After all they had done for him, he couldn't just leave Ned and Ada to fend for themselves. He sighed as he passed the tall wooden watchtower beside the bridge. Ever vigilant, watching for the advance of the Jakari invasion, which never came.

The days often blended: collecting eggs, delivering eggs, repairing coops, or running errands, all with no friends and no sign of a better future. After another sunrise-to-sunset cycle, Jem lay back on his straw bed and gazed at the thin blade of moonlight cutting through the curtains. That same moon shone on other lands with the promise of adventure. He hoped his dreams would take him there tonight.

The ocean's deep blue rolled into the beach's golden sands as the sun set directly ahead. Already it was bleeding its orange body into the water and lighting the clouds in hues of honey and gold.

Jem gave a long contented sigh and turned to see the alluring sight of a young Jakari woman at his side. She wore a short, sleeveless leather dress over her full figure, decorated with light blue and crimson red beads. Her dark hair was long and wild, with the same coloured beads woven into plaits. Her golden skin shone in the sunset, and Jem thought her perfect, even with the short scar on her left cheek.

The girl returned his smile and turned to pull him close. They kissed passionately, rolling on the sand without care. Jem felt the love they both shared for the first time, warming him more than any flame. She felt connected to him as if they were one person. Something in her smile and touch was so familiar.

"Alhum'la," she said, looking into his eyes.

Jem didn't recognize the language and only spoke the common tongue, but he found himself replying.

"Mafen'la," he returned. It made her smile, and she kissed him once more. Cradling her face, he continued: "dlen finst tu'vel aeon'tla."

He rolled onto his back and looked up as stars twinkled through the deepening blue. They lay there together for some time, just enjoying the warm evening breeze and the feeling of contentment, until something seemed to disturb her.

The girl sat up and looked around. She became agitated and started to scan the beach surrounding them.

"Quen?" said Jem.

She was on her feet now, and she looked scared. Her breath shortened, and her eyes darted left and right.

"Ven Ferdus!" she screamed suddenly.

Jem could hear the sound of a galloping horse approaching.

"Sil a'tlen," was the last Jem heard her say.

He turned to see a bright white light explode in front of his eyes, leaving only the faintest silhouette of a hooded rider before everything went black. A dark menacing laugh echoed in the void before morphing into the giggling voice of a—

"Danya!" shouted Jem, as his eyes flicked open to reveal the shadowy rafters above his bed, illuminated by the moonlight. Beading sweat made his body cling to the rough sheets.

Finally connecting with the strange woman in his dreams, her name tore through his mind as if he'd always known it. Now so clear, he could think of nothing else, the alien name was etched in his consciousness.

As Jem awoke and replayed the dream repeatedly in his mind, he didn't hear the horse and cart stop outside, nor did he see the hooded rider look up towards the rear where Jem lay with his heart racing.

After staring up at the house for a short while, the rider took the reins and steered the cart north towards the village centre, watched only by a second set of eyes, obscured by the Burland night.

3 THE STORYTELLER

Jem spent the morning surrounded by the sweet smell of linseed oil. It stuck to his fingers and fell from the brush onto his scruffy work trousers. It was an annual task protecting the hen houses from the ravages of rain and frost which would come to Burland.

Seasons were predictable in the valley. A short, pleasant spring was the planting season, leading to a fruitful summer, golden autumn and rainy winter. Frost and snow would sometimes reach down from the peaks of the Mur, but mildness marked the prevailing weather, as it did the people.

The brush strokes were slow this morning; Jem's mind was elsewhere. He couldn't stop thinking of the girl from his dream. He could still picture her inviting brown eyes and her alluring smile. Most Burlanders hurled insults toward the Jakari people, calling them demons, baby stealers, Jaks, or worse. Jem had never met a Jakari but couldn't understand the hatred; surely all were equal under Frea. His own appearance marked him as different; he was an outsider too.

Jem hadn't noticed Uncle Ned watching the lad daydream as long drips of oil rolled down the wood and fell to the stony ground below. Hands-on-hips, Ned leaned against the back of the house and shook his head.

"Jem! I need you to take Flo and fetch the cart." His uncle never asked, just barked orders. "Oh, and your aunt wants a loaf of rye."

Ned dropped a few coppers into Jem's hand and watched as he nonchalantly stoppered the linseed bottle and started walking towards the small stables.

"Just a minute, my lad," Ned continued sternly. "Your aunt and I work hard to look after you, so I don't want to see any more of this surly attitude."

"Sorry, Uncle," said Jem meekly.

"We knew what you were, took you in, and loved you like our own."

"I know," said Jem. "I just think there's a bigger world out there." He forced a thin smile and wandered off towards the village centre.

Ned watched him lope down the Burland Road, leading Flo until he disappeared behind the Coopers. Just like his mother, he thought.

The village green was the heart of Denbry. It was a rough circle, around fifty yards wide, marked by the gravel road. An ancient oak stood at its centre, under which was a wooden bench. The Tunland's house and the bridge marked the western end, while the circumference included The Crown Inn, the night stables and the bakery.

Today the green was busier than usual. A large group of villagers were gathered around the tree, with many children shouting and laughing. As Jem passed the inn, he overheard Jim Mason and Dan Barrick sitting outside, discussing the gathering.

"That witch shouldn't be telling those tall tales," said Jim.

"Aye," replied Dan. "Filling those youngsters' heads with all that rot ain't right."

"I'd ban her from the village, but she's thick with those Tunlands."

They continued to grumble as Jem tied the horse to the rail nearby and wandered over to see what was happening.

A woman dressed in black sat on the bench, surrounded by small children at her feet, older children and teenagers further back, and a line of parents and other villagers chatting and laughing behind. Jem felt himself smiling when the familiar woman was revealed through the crowd.

Lady Moranne, advisor to the king and a friend of the Tunlands, was a regular visitor to Denbry. Passing through the village two or three times a year, her origins were unknown, and her looks never changed. She had the appearance of a tall, middle-aged woman, perhaps in her mid to late forties, but her golden skin was as smooth as that of a teenager. The ageless looks, strange attire and tall tales had many Burlanders describing her as a witch, but none would dare say so to her face.

Long black hair framed a face capable of both kind smiles and smouldering looks of thunder. Moranne's high cheekbones and dark green eyes were alien to any part of Grenfold. Today she wore a long, black, sleeveless leather coat which gaped open to reveal slim black leggings and black leather boots. The arms of a clean white blouse emerged from the sleeveless jacket, and a thick, black leather waistcoat completed the look. More alarming was the slender sword, hung in a scabbard from a wide belt, which included many small pouches, bags, and a small dagger. The lady was equipped for the road, but today she held court in a humble village. Her clear, precise voice telling tales to amuse the children.

"Listen, children, I'll tell you the story of a brave boy."

She looked around to see the faces of the excited children and began her story.

"Once upon a time, long ago, in a faraway land, there lived a young boy named Shaja. He lived with his mother in a small village in the mountains. He helped the villagers by looking after the goats that grazed in the foothills of the nearby mountains."

"What kind of name is Shaja?" scoffed Guy Barrick. He was about the same age as Jem and considered handsome by the teenage girls of Denbry. He loved the sound of his voice and often made snide comments towards Jem and even about the Tunlands. His father owned a large farm estate at the north end of the village and employed many villagers. His power was slightly less than the Tunland's, and few would speak against him.

Moranne smiled but continued to look at the small children. "It's a Jakari name, of course," she said, ignoring the groans from some of the adults.

Jem thought of Danya, the girl from his dream. She must be Jakari, he thought. It had felt so real, like he knew this girl. His thoughts were disturbed as Moranne continued.

"Now, where were we? Oh yes! One day Shaja had taken the goats up the mountain to an especially high pasture, where the grazing was good. The goats wandered freely, and Shaja relaxed against a rock in the sun and fell asleep."

She leaned back against the tree and surveyed the expectant faces of the children before leaning forward once more to continue.

"Time passed, and the boy slept while the sun went down. He didn't hear the beating wings of a large dragon that had woken to hunt."

"Dragon? Pah! There's no such thing," spat Guy, laughing. He looked around to see his friends sniggering and nodding in agreement.

Moranne looked up for the first time and fixed Guy with her gaze. Jem thought he saw a tiny flash of bright green in her eyes before a sinister smile appeared.

"You know, our laughing friend here is right," she said, gesturing towards a puzzled Guy Barrick. "There are no such things as dragons."

Guy was grinning again, believing he had ruined the story, but Moranne wasn't finished.

"Men killed all the dragons. I should have said that a large wyvern had woken to hunt." She could see the question forming in the crowd, so she continued. "A wyvern has two legs, a barbed tail and vast wings. It can breathe fire over a great distance to burn a whole forest in one breath."

Guy started to form more words of ridicule, but Moranne cut him off.

"Oh, they exist, and once seen, they are never forgotten."

As she continued, more villagers were gathering, and even the teenagers were starting to pay attention.

"The wyvern roared as it landed in front of the frightened goats, and Shaja jumped to his feet. He grabbed his spear and ran in front of the goats to try and protect them. Wyverns will eat goats and small boys. The beast pulled back its head, ready to blast Shaja with fire or swipe him with its barbed tail. What should Shaja do?"

The children took this as a cue to call out with suggestions.

"Throw the spear between his eyes!" said an older boy.

"Run home," chirped a little girl.

"Fill his breeches," said Guy under his breath, giggling with his friends.

"Oh, no!" replied Moranne. "You can kill a wyvern, but you need a perfect aim, and you can't outrun a wyvern, for they are fast in the air. Shaja is just a small boy. No, I'll tell you what Shaja did."

She flicked the hair from her face and pulled up her sleeves.

"Shaja remembered something his mother had told him about wyverns. They're very intelligent, just as much as you or I, and they're quick to anger. With his mother's words in his head, he put down his spear and put up his hands."

"No!" shouted a little girl, as if she might cry.

"Well, I can tell you the wyvern's name was Aldnari, a mighty female over three thousand years old. In all her time, she'd never seen a human do this. She was puzzled and waited to see what this human would do next." The children looked puzzled, hanging on her every word. She bent forward and ruffled the hair of the little girl who had shouted out. "Shaja was thinking," she continued. "He knew the wyvern was hungry, but he needed to protect the goats. He surveyed the animals surrounding him and spotted an old billy with a damaged leg. He roped the old goat, pulled it until it was beneath the dragon, and tied it to a rock."

"The goat will be eaten!" screamed a young boy, head in hands.

"That's right," replied Moranne. "That's what Shaja wanted. He stepped back, and Aldnari the wyvern stared at him for a moment, then she understood. It was a peace offering. Aldnari took the goat in one great movement of her jaws, then flew away, never to be seen again."

"But the wyvern took the goat," whimpered the young boy.

"And the beast lived," added one of the adults from behind.

Moranne threw back her head and laughed. "By sacrificing one damaged goat, he saved himself and the rest of the herd. Few wyverns remain in the world, and killing one would be a crime. Not only was Shaja brave, he was also wise."

Some of those watching still looked mystified, so she spelt it out.

"Bravery without wisdom is another dead hero."

The story felt like one of Jem's realistic dreams; unusual names from faraway places. As the crowd started to disperse, he remembered his job and turned to get Flo.

Come with me.

Moranne's voice echoed through his mind. He turned quickly, but she was chatting with some of the children. *Just another daydream*, thought Jem as he shrugged and untied Flo from the rail.

He didn't see the dark green eyes follow him as he led the horse out of the village centre towards the Cartwright's. Nor did he see the bright green flash in those eyes that vanished instantly.

4 STEAK AND ALE PIE

Rana paced the grey stone room, shaking her head, while a dim light flickered in the breeze through the window.

She was in her early thirties and wore a bright white blouse over a short, black leather skirt with black leggings and tall boots. Short, black hair curved around her light, fawn, round face. It framed striking, large, feline eyes with deep green centres. Concern pinched her thick, black eyebrows as she begged.

"Aludra, please, please don't go. He's too powerful."

There was no answer from Aludra. She was sitting at the head of a large oak table in the middle of the room. Candles blinked in the draught, throwing ominous shadows against the stone.

"You're all I have," Rana continued, "Please!"

Aludra stared into the table centre. She looked a little older with tousled, dark hair draped over her shoulders. She wore similar un-Frean clothes; a short-sleeved, lace top over cross-patterned, black leggings. Emerald green eyes sparkled in the candlelight, leaking tears which ran down to her mouth and dripped slowly onto the oak. The rivulets glistened on a face which was lighter than Rana's with more of a pinkish undertone.

"We made an oath," she said solemnly, her eyes fixed on the woodgrain.

Rana stopped by the table with her hands outstretched.

"An oath? What about your promise to me?" She started to shake, and a bright flash sparked in her eyes. "You promised we'd be together. Ally, I love you. I've always loved you."

Aludra finally lifted her head, her face melting as she looked up at her beloved. "And I love you, Rana. I will love you until the land takes me, but I swore an oath to protect them, and I must help."

Rana cried, her eyes puffing as she clasped a chair to steady herself. "We owe them nothing; these people are simple savages. They curse the land which feeds them."

"I know," said Aludra, remembering the lynch mobs which met them. "You forget we owe Elara our lives. Without her, we'd be gone."

"Elara damned us all!" raged Rana, her brow creasing in anger. "She knew the price, yet you chose to pay it!"

"I won't abandon my friends," said Aludra calmly.

Rana nodded. She knew how much they had relied on Elara, how she'd found this place when all seemed lost. A promised land with its lush meadows, tall peaks and forests filled with foreboding.

"Then I'll be at your side, and we'll face him together," stuttered Rana.

The chair scraped over the flagstone floor and fell back as Aludra shot to her feet, embracing Rana and pulling her close. Their shadows became one as they sobbed in each other's arms. Aludra caressed Rana's hair and kissed her, but the moment was shattered by a knock at the door.

They both turned; Rana moved for the door, but the dream was already fading, and the women blurred to blackness.

Muffled voices continued and slowly became apparent in the darkness.

"Whatever you think, he's just a boy. He needs a stable home."

The voice sounded like Uncle Ned, and he was pleading with someone.

"We can protect him," chimed a voice Jem recognised as Aunt Ada. "Just one more year."

"I'm afraid you can't." It was a woman's voice, one Jem had heard before. "Just make sure he gets this note."

The front door slammed shut, and Jem sat up. His heart was beating quickly, and he was shaking. The image of the two women had shocked him, but it was the shape of the Jakari girl, Danya, which kept entering his mind. He was desperate to see her in his dreams once more.

"Is that you, Jem?" called Aunt Ada, "are you up?"

Jem leaned over the mezzanine railing and noticed his Uncle Ned was still at home. It was rare to see Ned at this time and stranger again to see his aunt without a beaming smile.

"Come down for breakfast, lad," barked Ned.

Jem quickly dressed and scampered down the ladder to the breakfast table laid for three. It seemed a special event today as it was precious eggs for breakfast rather than the usual tasteless porridge.

Ned said a short thanks to Frea then they ate silently.

Jem gazed out the window as they ate, wondering what Salamas looked like beyond the Mur peaks. Maybe he could find the beauty from his dreams on the beach where the sun seemed to shine so brightly.

He was so lost in thought that he didn't notice Ned and Ada finish eating. They were both staring at him.

"Erm, what's going on, Uncle Ned?" he said, finishing the last mouthful of toast.

Ned and Ada looked at each other, trying to decide who should speak first. Eventually, Ned cleared his throat and leaned forward.

"Jem, lad. We've always tried to be fair to you and treat you decent. We hope you know that."

"Of course," said Jem, wondering where this was going.

"We love you like our own," added Ada, her voice starting to break with emotion. She clasped Ned's hand, who continued.

"In the years ahead, we hope you will not think ill of us. We did the best we could."

Jem reached out and clasped both Ned and Ada's hands. "I love you both, and I know you've been good to me."

As his words ended, Ned smiled and produced a small piece of paper from his waistcoat pocket, placing it on the table in front of Jem. It was a small folded piece of parchment, sealed with red wax.

"What's this?" he asked, gazing at the article.

"It's your future, Jem," said Ned. "Open it, son."

Jem picked up the letter and examined it for a moment before splitting the seal and unfolding it into the sunlight.

Dear Jem.
Please meet me for lunch. Noon at the Crown Inn.
I have a proposition for you.

Kind regards,
Lady Moranne.

Standing on the village green, Jem had been gazing at the Crown Inn for several minutes. Uncle Ned often made it clear that he would not be welcome inside. A few patrons sat on the porch and eyed him suspiciously before turning to their friends and discussing him in hushed tones.

The coaching inn was a mixture of dark-painted wood and faded white render. It bore a small plaque above the door, which claimed it to be over four hundred years old. A few drinkers appeared as if they'd been attending the inn since the beginning, from the portly frames and slurred speech. A decked porch ran the width of the building with tables and chairs set outside for customers while Bev, the waitress, bustled back and forth with flagons of ale. She quickly disappeared back into the building when she saw Jem loitering.

He should be confident, having been invited by the great Lady Moranne, but he could feel the eyes on him. It was the familiar feeling he felt whenever he moved around the village. Jem longed to escape into his dreams once more and avoid the awkward stares. The inn's sign swung gently in the warm breeze. It showed a gold crown above a flying eagle. The emblem was the sigil of House Lenturi, which had ruled Grenfold for over a hundred years before falling to the House of Fierdman. *Be brave*, thought Jem, as Danya would be.

He clenched his fists and strode onto the deck and through the door. The bar was noisy with male laughter, shouting, mumbling, and the sound of pint pots hitting tables. All heard through a light haze of pipe smoke draped near the ceiling like mist.

Almost in unison, the men turned to see the newcomer, and the room fell silent. Bev dropped a tankard which clanged on the flagstone floor, but nobody moved. Those few seconds felt like an eternity, and Jem almost turned and ran, but a familiar voice saved him.

"Over here," called Lady Moranne, sitting in the corner near one of the front windows.

Jem made his way to her table while stares followed him, piercing the back of his head. It was awful. Sensing his discomfort, Moranne rose and looked out at the room, fixing the men with her alien stare until they turned, mumbling, and went back to their business.

"Thank you for coming, Jem," she said brightly. "Have a seat."

He sat down nervously and looked around to see most of the locals were now ignoring him. Moranne was less imposing in person. Her smooth skin had no lines, although slightly uneven patches around her mouth aged her a little and gave her character. The smile she gave Jem lit her whole face and looked genuine and regular from how her muscles quickly moved to form it. Her hair shone, and he wanted to reach out and touch it as it draped onto the clean white lace blouse.

"Let's deal with lunch first," she continued.

Moranne called for Bev, who reluctantly came to the table. She ordered a steak and ale pie for both of them and a small flagon of ale each. Jem never drank ale, but he didn't want to make a fuss.

"Now to business." She leaned forward and placed her hands face down on the table as if she'd played a winning hand of cards.

"Do you know what a gada is?" she asked, fixing her deep green eyes on his.

Jem shook his head, although he did remember something from a dream. *Sonny Flint*, that was his name.

"Well, a gada is a travelling companion or an apprentice if you like. Although a gada receives no wage, their food, clothes, board, and other expenses are paid for by their sponsors. They can sometimes become so highly favoured that they ascend into the higher levels of society," she explained, hands floating high into the air.

She watched Jem absorbing her words silently, but his brow was furrowed in puzzlement.

"Did you know, for example, that Squire Tunland's father was Benril Tunland, former gada to Earl Edwin Tunland of Tudorfeld?"

Jem shook his head, finding it difficult to remember all the new names.

"Hoy's family name is actually Grafan," she said, expecting some reaction from this revelation. Jem simply sat, taking it all in.

Bev arrived with two small flagons, then hurried away. Moranne took a gulp and then watched, smiling as Jem gingerly brought the mug to his lips. The initial taste was of water that had once contained an over-ripe cheese, but as he drank more, an earthy sour taste remained in his mouth. It was disgusting. Doing well not to cough into Moranne's face, Jem spluttered and choked on the brown liquid, much to the amusement of some of the men nearby.

"Taverns are the best places to learn stories," Moranne laughed, "but unfortunately, it does involve drinking."

"Anyway," she smiled. "My proposition is this: I would like you to be my gada and leave with me tomorrow for the capital."

Jem put down his ale and blinked. "What about my aunt and uncle?" he said. Others always came first, even as he was near leaving Denbry.

"They will be very well compensated. If you leave tomorrow, they'll be able to retire."

Retire? It sounded too good to be true. His dream was close, but it didn't seem real. "Why me?" asked Jem, still shaking his head.

Moranne's lips pursed into a thin smile, and she looked down at the grain in the table.

"You don't fit in here, and I don't fit in anywhere. I think you'll be a perfect companion, and you'll get to live your dreams."

Even as she mentioned his dreams, she looked away as if she had given away too much.

Jem was deep in thought, picturing the faraway places from his sleep world and how he might soon see those lands. Perhaps his dreams were leading him to a beautiful Jakari woman named Danya.

He was startled out of his daydream by a large, steaming plate of pie, potatoes, carrots and thick gravy, which almost landed in his lap. Moranne gave Bev a dark look, forcing a mumbled apology before she scurried back to the kitchen.

Jem looked up from the excellent-smelling food to see Moranne smiling.

"If you say yes, then lunch is on me," she said, laughing again.

While Jem *was* tempted by the steak and ale pie, he'd made up his mind to leave many months ago, and now he was desperate.

"I accept," he said formally and knifed into his pie.

Moranne leaned back, content and looked out of the window. She saw a long road ahead; much of it would be bumpy.

5 THE BURLAND ROAD

There was no sign of Moranne at the stables behind the inn, although Jem was on time; eight o'clock prompt. He had packed a few items of clothing in a kit bag but no tangible possessions as such. Aunt Ada had tried to give him food and even a blanket, but Moranne would see to all his needs. She just managed to thrust a few coppers into his hand as they parted. Uncle Ned had been as brief as usual, shaking hands and slapping Jem on the back. "Go and live your dreams, son," he said, maintaining his composure. Aunt Ada, however, wrapped her arms around Jem and sobbed into his linen shirt. Most of her words of wisdom were lost in tears, but she managed a weak "remember us" before Ned pulled her away and held her tight.

As sad as he was to say goodbye, Jem was excited to leave Denbry and the small-minded folk at its heart finally. Except maybe for one.

"Jem, Jem!" shouted a familiar, fair voice.

Jem turned to see Mia Tunland running across the grass in a pretty white dress. Her hair was tied back in a ponytail, bobbing from side to side as she ran.

"Don't you dare leave without saying goodbye, Jem Poulterer," she scolded, drawing to a halt in front of him.

"I thought you couldn't speak to me," mumbled Jem meekly.

"Oh, you know I don't care about that," she laughed as a cheeky smile crept into her eyes. "I'm so jealous. I wish I were leaving this backward hole with you."

"You'll come of age soon."

"Yes, and they'll send me to some town in Middcroft or Tudorfeld to find a boring husband. That's not what I want. I want to go with you on an adventure."

Jem was about to invite her but was interrupted by the sound of a horse and cart. It was being driven from the back of the stables. The small, two-wheeled carriage was drawn by a young grey, shaking its mane in the fresh, early air.

"Good morning, Jem, Miss Tunland," said Moranne, allowing the reins to slip through her hands to rest on the wagon's prow.

Jem turned back towards Mia and noticed her eyes were glistening in the morning sun as it rose above the timber stables.

"Remember me," she pleaded, as a tiny tear formed and ran down her cheek.

"I will," said Jem, starting to feel a real connection with her for the first time.

She quickly leaned forward, kissed him on the cheek, then abruptly turned and ran back towards the manor.

"Say goodbye to your parents for me," shouted Moranne after her, but Mia didn't turn and vanished behind the main gate.

Lady Moranne yawned and stretched before taking up the reins once more. "Right, Jem, climb aboard; we've got a long road ahead."

They set off through the village, heading south on the Burland Road. Jem had a strange sense he wouldn't see the place again. Some of the villagers watched him leave in the same silence he knew so well, but there was no sign of life as he passed the house which had been his home all these years. Only the low murmur of restless chickens emanated from the rustic building.

Moranne smiled as they passed the south gate of the village. She noticed Jem steal one last look before they were free of the hamlet and out in the wilds. "You'll see her again," she nodded.

The furthest Jem had ever travelled was the small village of Three Ways, north of Benbry. It marked a junction between the Burland Road and the trail to Midstig, a small hamlet in the foothills of the Midtlen Range. Uncle Ned sometimes took surplus eggs to the Three Ways market, and Jem would accompany him. He loved those rare trips, as he could talk with people who knew nothing of his past. It was like another life.

Now he set out into the unknown, having never been south. Every bump in the road was new, every tree a sight to savour, birds flying free above an unfamiliar landscape, and the burbling River Sile providing the music as they went.

"How far is the capital?" asked Jem.

Denbry had receded so far into the distance that it had almost disappeared, and he was becoming apprehensive.

"Oh, Cynstol is many days' ride. It'll be faster after Supbry, where I have two horses waiting," replied Moranne, her gaze focused on the road ahead.

"Horses?"

Jem had ridden, but not often. Moranne laughed, causing tiny creases to show in her smile before they vanished again. "You'll do fine; I know you can ride."

As the cart trundled on, Moranne explained his duties as her gada to Jem.

"You'll need to obey my orders," she said. "I may need you to run errands, get me things, pass messages and ensure my clothes are clean and pressed."

"No problem, ma'am," he replied. None of this would be different from his chores for Ned and Ada.

"When we arrive in Cynstol, we'll get you some clothes more befitting your rank. Part of my role is to teach you about the geography and history of Grenfold, so please pay attention."

Jem nodded. He didn't care about the duties as long as he left the village.

They reached the village of Scaga by early afternoon and made for the only inn called The Coracle. It was named after the small round boats that the locals used to fish and cross the River Sile. The inn was perched near the road, which ran straight through the small collection of crofts; it was similar to the Crown Inn but more modest. The Sile was a little further away here as the road had snaked inland. Its sinewy form could still be seen from the window as they sat themselves down for a late lunch.

Jem was accustomed to simple meals of soup or eggs. Another feast today was welcome; baked field mushrooms and mash was a local speciality. He was partway through chewing on an overly large fork-full when he noticed Moranne staring at him intently.

"Tell me about the dream you had two nights ago," she said, gazing into his eyes as if she might read his thoughts.

Jem quickly swallowed the ambitious mouthful to answer with another question. "How did you know I was dreaming?"

Moranne smiled. "I know everything," she said thoughtfully before cracking into laughter. "No, your aunt told me."

"I can't talk about it," said Jem shyly.

"And why might that be? Is it sordid?" she said with a mischievous grin.

"No, it's...."

"Go on; I'm a woman of the world."

"It's against the scriptures."

"The scriptures?"

Moranne was genuinely surprised. Jem was never allowed to go into the Denbry chapel, but he was aware of the teachings. They formed the fundamental morality of all Burland and most of Grenfold.

"Frea forbids it," he stuttered.

"Forbids what? As your mistress, I command you to tell me!" Her tone was light, but her eyes pierced him with the command.

Jem hesitated for a moment, then remembered his duties as her gada. He felt embarrassed and looked down as the memories returned.

"It was forbidden love," he said. Moranne nodded but didn't appear shocked. "Between two women," he continued. "They were kissing."

Moranne leaned back, slapped the table and roared with laughter causing other patrons to look over in curiosity. "Now you *must* tell me," she howled.

"I didn't know what was happening," replied Jem. "But for some reason, I knew their names. They were called Rana and Aludra; they had a strange look and wore strange garb for women. They dressed like you, ma'am," he continued before he realised he might have insulted her.

"Go on," she urged.

"They were crying and talking about someone called Elara."

Moranne's composure changed as soon as she heard the name. The smile dropped as she retreated into deep contemplation. Moments later, she raised her flagon of ale, took a sip and placed it carefully back down in front of her.

"That's not possible," she said eventually. *You weren't there*, she thought.

"Who are they?" asked Jem.

Lady Moranne was again lost in her thoughts as her mind returned to painful memories. She appeared to know Rana and Aludra, but Jem dared not ask of them further. He decided to try and lighten the mood.

"Err, is Moranne your family name or first name?"

She eventually looked up, but her reply was flat and factual. "I have no family name." She turned and looked out the window at the Mur in the distance. "I have no family."

"Oh," said Jem, and decided it best not to ask any more questions today.

They finished their late lunch silently and spent the rest of the day apart. Moranne said she wanted to be alone, so Jem was left to wander. He walked down to the river and sat on the bank, viewing the Burland valley and mountains beyond. It was a similar picture from Denbry, but now he felt free and would soon see sights other Burlanders would never know. He thought again of Danya, her radiant skin and beaming smile. One day he would know what lay beyond the mountains and walk on the warm sands of the beach, feel the sand between his toes. However, he kept this dream to himself.

As the sun sank below the tall peaks of imposing rock, casting long tendril shadows into the valley, Moranne stood naked before her bedroom window and stared at the orange glow in the west. No one saw the deep scars across her back from the flogging, which would never leave her thoughts, nor the simmering green smoke in her eyes that coloured her face as she looked up beneath her shining black hair.

Jem slept in the barn that night as the inn was short of rooms. Moranne lay awake, staring up at the stained beams of her room and counting to herself. "One, the gift of sight," she said. It was early, and he didn't know how to focus his skill. *Please give me more time*, she thought, then closed her eyes on another day in her long life.

Sir Torl Radborough scribbled his signature on yet another scroll, rolled it into a tube and sealed it carefully with red wax and his family seal. He tossed it into the outward-bound basket, leaned back in his chair and yawned loudly.

In the impressive Lyften Tower, his chamber was decorated in sumptuous crimson and gold drapes that matched his robes of office. The finest Caynna artisans had made his smooth, polished oak desk and all the other beautiful furniture.

He enjoyed the trappings of luxury, which came with his post as the king's chief advisor, but he found the minutiae of office very tedious. He stroked his short grey beard and picked up another scroll from the pile on the desk. Just as he held the paper open, there was a sharp knock at the door.

"Come," he said flatly, in the deep baritone voice he used to impress courtiers and underlings.

The door creaked open to reveal a short young man in his mid-twenties. Gada Tino Crayber stumbled awkwardly into the room and waited patiently in front of the desk for Torl to acknowledge him.

"Speak," he commanded, without raising his eyes.

Tino moved closer to the desk and held out a folded scrap of stained and dusty paper. "Sire, this was delivered to the gatehouse by a farmer who said it was from Stanholm."

Sir Torl took the note without making eye contact with the gada, and started to read. After a few seconds, he looked up. The regal robe swept the floor as he came to his feet, and the frown on his face emphasised the wrinkles and betrayed his advancing years.

"Where is Lady Moranne?"

Tino shook his head and backed away. "I don't know, sire; I think she went to Burland."

"Send a rider and bring her here immediately," snapped Sir Torl, still frowning.

"Yes, sir."

"And send messages to the generals. We're convening the full council."

He dropped the letter to the table, still staring at the words:

The Stans have a new weapon.
Soldiers are amassing in Gulward.

SM

6 THE FORTUNE TELLER

The road from Scaga to Supbry bent back towards the Sile as the darkness of Geg Woods reached out from the east. Although its name suggested a small woodland, Geg Woods covered a large area from the foot of the Midtlen Range to half a mile from the river. It was as dense and imposing as any forest. There were stories of strange creatures within its depths, and few Burlanders would venture closer than its thin outer reach to scavenge firewood. Tales that Moranne would describe as "ignorant rubbish."

"A Burlander's knowledge of the creatures and folk in its midst could be written on the head of a pin," she said, laughing.

Moranne was starting to share more of her knowledge as they continued south. Jem hadn't dreamt for two nights, which was unusual, enabling Moranne's teachings to take him on a different journey.

"Ma'am, could you tell me about the Jakari people?" he asked as they trundled beside the Sile. The image of Danya hadn't left his thoughts since he'd dreamt of her.

"What would you like to know?"

"Is it true that they're demons and use black magic?"

Moranne chuckled and turned to him with an eyebrow raised.

"This is what they tell you? Hmm, I refer you to my earlier comment on Burlander knowledge."

She passed the reins to Jem so she could teach him properly.

"The land beyond the Mur is called Salamas, and the capital city is Hurraj. There are few villages and towns, as the Jakari people are mostly nomadic. They live in tents and move around the country to find food. They believe that no man can own the land."

Jem was captivated. Burlanders only ever described the Jakaris as primitive animals.

"They have a god called Rajun and his goddess wife Aimran," she continued. "They say Aimran had a beautiful voice that enchanted the dragon god Stanin. He was so enchanted that he lay in wait for her one day and seduced her."

Jem thought of Danya's voice. *'Alhum'la'*. With each day, the sounds and images faded. He was desperate to dream of her again.

"Aimran became pregnant," Moranne continued, "and she bore a baby girl."

Stone and Sceptre

She paused for effect while Jem hung on every word. It was almost his story.

"The baby had fair skin, so Rajun knew that Aimran had been unfaithful. He banished the child to the lands east of the Midtlen and never trusted his wife again. She was banned from speaking outside his presence and stripped of her power of command. The Jakari people believe that the pale-skinned humans, east of the Mur, are the offspring of Stanin, the dark lord of dragons."

Jem understood the power of religion and those who wielded it. Adulterous women were shunned in Burland, yet straying husbands were seen as typical. As Moranne continued, it seemed his shunning was a trifle compared to the Jakari ways.

"Jakari women are not allowed to speak outside the home; they use sign language to communicate. They are also considered the property of their husbands and must do everything a man commands."

"That sounds awful," said Jem, suddenly feeling sorry for Jakari women.

"It is," said Moranne. "It makes Burlanders seem advanced."

"Do the women run away?" he said, thinking of his mother, Asmeen.

"Many try," she said. "Some of the things they endure are unspeakable, and I will not speak of them here."

Jem had not wanted to say anything, but Danya was so present in his thoughts that he simply blurted it out.

"I dreamt of a Jakari woman a few nights ago."

"Did you?" said Moranne, sounding genuinely surprised.

"Her name was Danya. Do you think she might be real?"

Moranne grabbed the reins from Jem and brought the cart to a halt. Her face had turned to thunder, and Jem saw a glimmer of green light flash across her eyes.

"No," she said sternly. "It was just a dream."

"But maybe..."

"I said it was a dream!"

It was a tone Jem had not heard before, and he began to understand why some people feared her.

"Ma'am," he said and faced forward, ready to resume the journey.

Too soon, thought Moranne as she pictured Danya once more.

"We must get to Supbry and rest the horse. We have far to go, and you have much to learn," she barked. Cracking the reins, Moranne signalled the end of that conversation, and they continued south, silent for the rest of the distance to Supbry.

The woods of Geg were left far behind, but the Sile was ever-present. Jem listened to the bubbling beck as it narrowed, and the cart bumped and thumped over the uneven road. They passed the occasional small croft, and farmers would wave them on their way. Crops slowly changed to herds of cows and sheep as the halo wealth of Caynna captured farms in its affluent glow. Passing carts increased in frequency, and the landscape took on a deeper green, proclaiming its connection to the capital.

Supbry was the largest of the Burland hamlets and was considered a town by many locals. It took some time to reach the centre, passing several inns and many smallholdings. Black-painted beams supported wattle and daub render, and some red, kiln-fired bricks were evident where properties had been modified or extended. The village population was too great for its size, and as a result, it felt squeezed. Homes had been built on top of homes, and taller dwellings leaned out into the street, almost touching across the divide.

Jem didn't like the sprawling village. It appeared dirty where Denbry was clean, and many villagers had a fell look as if they distrusted every traveller.

"We'll not be here long," said Moranne, steering the cart away from the centre, passing stalls and market traders.

"I've never seen so many folks," ventured Jem.

"Ha! Wait until you see Cynstol. Twice as dirty and a hundred times more crowded."

Jem wasn't sure he'd like that. Denbry had been very quiet, and Jem himself was a man of few words. Crowds were always noisy.

They eventually arrived at a sizeable stone-built coach house in a crescent of trade buildings. Moranne parked the cart outside and went inside to speak to the coach master.

Jem leaned back against the grey brick and looked at the sun passing its high point on its westward journey. *So Hurraj was the land where Danya lived*, he thought as his eyes followed the line to the Mur, just peeking over the wooden roof of a cobbler's workshop.

"Copper for your fortune, sir?"

Standing beside Jem was a young man in a wide-brimmed grey hat and dirty clothes staring up from his diminutive Burland frame. One of his eyes was blue, while the other was pale green. It was rare for street hawkers and fortune tellers to travel as far north as Denbry; Jem was taken by surprise.

"Err, I don't know," he stuttered, looking at the coach-house door for signs of his sponsor.

The young man smiled, showing his crooked teeth.

"Just one copper to learn your future, sir. I'm sure a young, good-looking gentleman such as yourself has a bright future. Would you like to know?"

Jem fumbled in his pocket and found a few coins that Aunt Ada had slipped him. The Grenfold currency had four denominations: copper coins, silver coins, gold coins and diamonds. Jem had never seen a gold coin or a diamond and doubted he ever would. Denbry had mostly survived on barter.

Moranne would doubtless frown on such nonsense, but few people had ever spoken to Jem outside of his aunt and uncle. The lad's crooked smile widened when Jem held out a coin and dropped it into his palm.

"The name's Huw, sir," said the lad.

Jem shook his hand and thought he'd just foolishly lost a copper.

"Sir, hold out your right hand with the palm facing upwards."

Jem did as instructed and watched as Huw placed his left hand above Jem's without touching.

"Now, I want you to close your eyes and remove all thoughts of the present. Think only into the future. Imagine yourself standing somewhere you know well, watching the world around you."

They both closed their eyes, and Huw chanted some incoherent words under his breath. Jem cleared his mind and tried to imagine where this adventure might take him, but all he saw was darkness.

Standing near the coach house wall, neither of the men noticed a slight green mist emerge between their hands or the tiny green lightning that sparked between them.

As Jem cleared his thoughts and tried to focus only on the future, he saw a dim flash of orange in his mind. He closed his eyes tighter and focused on the light. It slowly grew into a shimmering glow of yellow, dancing through his mind like a wave of autumn. The light faded to darkness, and Jem could hear the sound of shoes on stone. Someone was moving quickly and getting closer.

Huw appeared, running out of the darkness. His hat was gone, blood trailed down his face, and sweat poured from his temple. He was out of breath but kept running. The sky was night, but an orange glow lit the buildings and walls as he ran down lanes, through barns, and hugged the walls between houses.

He tripped and stumbled, whirling around to look behind, but nothing followed. The lanes split in three directions, and he hesitated. North? No. South? No. East? It was the only hope.

The sounds of battle were all around. Gut-wrenching screams echoed through the village but were silenced by the dead sound of metal on stone. Shouting in a language unknown could be heard as Huw ran into other villagers fleeing for their lives.

A snapping sound of timber bursting with flame grew louder, and the orange glow now danced around him. Licks of fire appeared above the house roofs.

Down the long lane, his eyes caught sight of the village edge and the void of the wild beyond. With one last push, he willed his aching limbs toward the black, ignoring the cries of terror behind.

"Come on, come on!" he shouted to himself, using every last drop of energy. His legs were near failing, and his heart was pulsing through his head.

He reached the end of the alley and stopped.

The figure standing like a statue in front of him wore dark loose robes, and a deep red scarf covered his head, wrapped around several times and draped over his chest. Only his severe brown eyes could be seen through a slit, along with a skin colour which identified him as Jakari.

Shaking, Huw slowly looked down to see the sword's cruel, curved blade, which had pierced his stomach. His blood was spreading from the wound, and he could feel his consciousness failing.

"Why?" gasped Huw, as tears welled in his eyes and the screams of battle approached from behind.

The hooded man remained silent. He pulled out the blade, and Huw slumped to the ground as his life cruelly ebbed away.

"What's going on?"

Jem's eyes snapped open to see Moranne walking through the coach house's main doors with a young lad leading two horses. Huw was still standing in front, but he appeared pale and shaky. He reached into his pocket and held out the coin Jem had given him.

"Jem, what are you doing?" said Moranne sternly. "I can't leave you alone for an instant."

"I was just learning my..." began Jem, but Huw cut him off.

"Nothing, my lady, nothing."

When Jem eventually took back the copper, Huw turned away and slowly walked back towards the village centre. His head was bowed, and Jem suspected he could hear sobbing.

"What did you do?" asked Moranne, as if probing his soul.

Jem saw the dark eyes of Huw's killer burning red in his mind. There was no remorse, no mercy; it was the look of hate.

I saw his future, thought Jem. "I did nothing," he said, looking down at his shoes.

Moranne nodded slowly and placed a hand on his shoulder. "Come. We need to eat, then be on our way."

Jem was reeling. It felt like one of his dreams, but it was real. How could a fortune teller reveal their own future? So many images now circled in his mind, but nothing seemed to connect them. Some were places he'd never seen and people he didn't know, others were friends and acquaintances, but a few were real people he'd never met. He wanted to share his thoughts with Moranne, but every mention of dreams seemed to vex her.

Strange questions and disturbing images haunted Jem's mind as they led the horses through the village.

Situated at the southern end of the hamlet, the Bridge Inn nestled beside the grey stone bridge over the Sile. The Supbry river crossing was the last bridge going south in Burland; the distant village of Supford was high in the foothills where the Sile was just a wide stream.

They led the horses to the front of the inn, where they were tied to a long bar above a watering trough. Moranne's horse was an impressive, all-black female named Bess. She'd owned her for many years, and there was a mutual affection; Moranne patted and calmed her with soothing words.

Jem's ride had been purchased just a week past. She was a slightly smaller bay with a prominent white blaze named Millie. Moranne had chosen her for her mild temperament and easy manners. Jem felt very grown-up as he tethered his horse, and they entered the inn for lunch. The bar was rowdy with locals who ignored the travellers as they found a table near the window. Moranne always liked to see the world from wherever she sat. Always on guard, her hand often fell to her sword when raucous men were nearby.

Jem inspected Moranne's face while she viewed the scene outside, lost in her thoughts. The bone structure was that of an attractive middle-aged woman, but no wrinkles troubled her skin. Her hair and skin radiated like a teenage girl on the first day of spring. She had no family and no husband. How did such a woman become an advisor to the king?

Grenfold was a male-dominated land where women made dinner, washed clothes and bore children. They didn't command the respect of noblemen or carry swords.

"Just ask me," said Moranne, still gazing through the window.

"Huh?" replied Jem.

"Jem, just ask me whatever's on your mind."

She gradually turned to face him with a weary smile spreading over her face. "Just ask," she said again.

"Ma'am, I don't know anything about you."

"Ah," she said, the smile turning to warmth. "Who in Frea's name am I, and why am I not like other women?"

Jem nodded, returning the smile.

"Alright, I'll tell you a few things about me, then no more questions for now."

"Of course, ma'am."

She took a bite from the pork pie which had arrived on the table and a swig of ale to wash it down. She leaned back and relaxed in the rough wooden chair, her long sleeveless coat swinging open to reveal the bright white blouse with ruffles down the centre.

"My title is Lady Moranne, and I am a travelling ambassador and advisor to King Pythar Fierdman, as I was to his father, King Tyborg III. I am a permanent member of the King's Council."

Jem's eyes widened as he realised her importance and the circles she moved in.

"I have a special insight which makes me useful to the king, and I can also go where other eastern humans cannot, such as Alfheim and even Salamas."

"You've been to Salamas?" gasped Jem.

"Yes," she replied, "and I can tell you that the Jakari are kind, friendly people. Nothing like the savages they are portrayed as."

It didn't chime with conventional perceptions, but it transported Jem to the beach again, where he lay beside a mysterious lover.

"I know many call me a witch," she continued. "Especially in Burland, but I don't make potions, eat babies, or turn people into frogs."

They both laughed, and even some of the locals nearby chuckled.

Jem noticed her hand was hovering over the hilt of her sword, the way it often did when she appeared to let down her guard.

"You'd like to know if I've ever used this," she said as Jem's gaze finally met hers.

He nodded and noticed some locals had stopped chatting and were hanging on her words. The same way she'd held court on that warm summer's day back on Denbry's village green.

"This blade was made in Hagall by Tropos Manlyn, the finest alviri swordsmith who ever lived."

In one smooth movement, she grasped the hilt and pulled the blade, near silently, from its scabbard. The crowd moved back and gasped as the light caught the polished metal, scattering bright beams around the room.

It was a little shorter than a broad sword and contained swirls and scrolls along its length. The blade looked sharp, with no sign of dents or scratches.

"There are those who say a blade should never be unsheathed without shedding blood," she continued. Her voice had become low and menacing, and the inn fell silent.

She lay the sword across the table, so all could see it.

"Yes, I've used this sword, and most do not walk the earth to tell the tale."

Jem was at once both impressed and intimidated. Making such bold claims in a room full of leery men would seem foolhardy, but none seemed ready to challenge her.

"Now," she said. "The person who took my purse has until I finish my ale to return it, or we'll see if Steorra is still... sharp."

A hush descended on the bar as Moranne clasped the tankard and brought it to her lips. Eyes only on her drink, she slowly sipped the bitter liquid as the crowd of fell-looking men dared not even breathe. She finally licked her lips and gave an exaggerated gasp of pleasure, bringing the empty vessel back to the table.

As the tankard struck wood, a black velvet purse landed next to it with the rattle of the contained coins. There was no visible sign of whence it had come, and all the men tried hard to look innocent.

"Wise choice," said Moranne.

She obviously knew the identity of the thief, but it was a point well made. The locals slunk back to their business, and Moranne's reputation remained intact.

"How did you know?" asked Jem, still trying to understand what had happened.

Moranne smiled as she slipped the purse back into the long black coat.

"Come, we need to be on our way. It's a long haul to Dunstreet, and we must be there before dark."

She left three copper coins on the table, and they departed the inn returning to the Burland Road.

Jem could only remember riding a couple of times, but the horse-craft seemed to come back quickly. They followed the road at a trot until they reached a fork at the edge of the village. An old wooden signpost showed Supford lay to the south and Dunstreet to the southeast. As they turned off the southern road, Jem realised he was leaving Burland far behind. From now on, everything would be unfamiliar. Although part of him was nervous, the promise of discovering his dreams brought a smile to his face.

7 DUNSTREET

General Cymel Marl was agitated and pacing from one side of Sir Torl Radborough's office to the other. He wore his full dress uniform of leather combat clothes etched with the king's insignia and a double-headed eagle. The long black cape of his office brushed the furniture as he moved.

"Damn that harridan, who does she think she is?"

Torl looked up from his desk, stroking his beard. His eyes were world-weary, and he grew tired of the continual spats with the king's generals.

"You know she has the king's ear, Cymel; he'll never act without her counsel."

Cymel stopped pacing and glared ominously at Sir Torl. He was a tall man with long dark hair, a pointed dark beard and brooding eyes, which pierced the unsuspecting. "We need to strike them now before they have time to prepare an assault!" he snarled, but the venom was reserved for Sir Torl. "And it's *General* Marl to you, Mr *Chief Advisor*."

Sir Torl didn't flinch at the reprimand and replied as if no blow had been struck. "*General*, I am as vexed as you at the news from Stanholm, and I have spoken to the king on this subject. He will not decide a course of action until Lady Moranne returns."

"So where is the bitch?" cursed Cymel.

"Be assured I've sent messengers to all the likely areas; she'll be here soon."

"She better," he snapped, before turning on his heels and slamming the door behind him.

Where are you, my friend? thought Torl as he looked down at the latest spy report from Stanholm.

> *Many troopships in Gulward harbour.*
> *SM.*

The foothills of the Midtlen Range loomed like silent watchers as Jem and Moranne made their way towards Dunstreet. They rode as fast as possible without tiring the horses, keen to see a homely, glowing fire before nightfall.

Jem could already observe the wide gap emerging between the Midtlen and the Red Mountains to the south, a chasm filled by the shadowy Bearun Forest.

Dunstreet marked the limits of Burland and the gateway to Middcroft through the valley known as Mallen's Cutting. It was also the only Dorbourne River crossing this side of the Midtlen. They reached Dunstreet just as the sun dipped below the Mur Mountains, casting its long, talon-like shadow to the gate where they dismounted.

"It seems very early to be closing the gates," said Moranne, brushing the dust from her coat. A man stood beside the tall panelled gates, almost lost in their shadow.

"Orders of Squire Scirmann, my lady," replied the gatekeeper. "There's been some strange folk about recently."

Immediately beyond the gates lay the small, grey-brick bridge over the River Dorbourne. Known to many as the Great River, it was narrow and shallow at this point, having split from the Sile some ten miles west. It would swell to become the most extensive and longest river in Grenfold and flowed east through the Midtlen, across Middcroft, through the forest of Deapholt and finally spewed into the Bay of Fayze.

Jem led the horses over the bridge toward the coach house, which was situated on the river bank. Dunstreet was more substantial, darker and built with much more stone than Denbry. It had a melancholy atmosphere, and Jem felt invisible eyes judging him as he walked with the horses.

"One other thing, my lady," called the gatekeeper, "The squire would like to see you as soon as possible."

It seemed strange to Jem that the local squire would know to expect them, although less and less would surprise him as their journey progressed.

Moranne nodded and looked across at her young gada. "Your first task, Jem: find us a suitable inn with a couple of decent rooms." She dropped a couple of silvers into his palm and pointed him toward the village centre.

She watched Jem amble ahead and pondered the last few days. His dreams were detailed, more detailed than even *she* remembered. *Patience*, she said to herself. She could help him, but too much could be uncovered, as it could in his increasing dreams.

Two swarthy men in military garb leaned nonchalantly against the side of a small house, and both nodded as she passed.

The impressive lodge of Squire Scirmann was a sprawling complex built from giant logs felled from Bearun Forest. The polished grey timbers shone in the light cast from oil lamps hung on posts surrounding the main three-storey building. A warm glow flickered through the large, gable-end windows.

Squire Wystan Scirmann was renowned in Burland for his tight stewardship of the large village. Dunstreet was a major crossroads from Middcroft and often attracted prostitutes, chancers and brigands from every region of eastern Grenfold. They didn't thrive long in Wystan's town. The squire had hired the best marshal from Caynna and many mercenaries from Cynstol, who made up a small militia, keeping the village in check.

"Squire Scirmann is expecting you; please follow me, my lady," said the butler formally, when the large oak door opened.

She knew the squire and his family very well, having visited many times over the years. The formality irritated her, but she always played along.

"Please wait here," added the butler.

He showed her into a lavish, double-height room where the exposed timbers were covered in family paintings and hunting trophies. A large fireplace dominated one wall, with a castle-like brick chimney reaching through the ceiling.

Moranne sat in one of the luxurious leather upholstered sofas and deliberately rested her boots on the low oak table at the room's centre. She was never impressed by ostentatious displays of wealth. Some people would never warm to her.

"Lady Moranne, it's so good to see you again," boomed the voice of Squire Scirmann as he entered the room from a door behind her. "It's been too long, my old friend."

His family were originally from Tudorfeld; he towered above his diminutive Burland staff. He had the broad, muscular frame of a Tudorfeldian, but good living had expanded his waist, and his expensive Cynstol robes now strained against his body.

As he sat across the table from Moranne, the light glinted off his bald head. Wisps of hair were cropped at the sides, and a short pointed beard that he loved to stroke flirtatiously, sat on his chin.

"You wanted to see me," said Moranne flatly. *We're not friends*, she thought as he smiled at her.

He shuffled uncomfortably and leaned forwards. Moranne always did like getting to the point.

"There are two things I want to discuss with you," he announced as if holding court. "The first is a message I've received from the capital."

"Go on."

"Your presence is required at court as soon as possible. Sir Torl Radborough is convening the war council."

That was bad news. It was too late to take Jem back to Denbry, and soon he'd discover the truth anyway. It would also take too long through Mallen's Cutting.

"Alright," she said finally, giving away none of her thoughts. "And the second?"

The squire stood and walked over to lean on the mantle below a portrait of his father.

"You know that I served as gada to Earl Greyhelm Linhold?"

Moranne was developing a sinking feeling; she knew where this conversation was heading.

"It was the greatest apprenticeship I could have had," he continued, looking wistfully into the distance. "You know that my eldest son Chadwick served in the House of Linhold, and he's now a knight in the Queen's Battalion?"

Please, no, she thought.

"My youngest son Hayden has just come of age and—"

Wystan couldn't finish as Moranne cut him off. "I can't take your son as my gada; I already have a lad from Denbry. He's booking my room as we speak."

The squire appeared stunned and returned to his seat.

"When did this happen?"

"His name is Jem, and he's coming with me to Cynstol." She didn't want a debate.

"Is he the son of an earl or a squire?" asked Wystan, desperate to spot a gap in Moranne's reasoning.

"He's my chosen companion; I know his family very well," replied Moranne decisively. "I'm not sending him home."

The squire visibly hardened at that comment, rising out of his seat to point an accusing finger at her.

"You owe me!"

"I owe you nothing," she replied impassively.

Squire Scirmann paced around the room with his face flushed red. He hadn't expected rejection.

"You really want all your sordid little secrets out in the open?" he said, baiting her.

A bright green light flashed across Moranne's eyes, and she sprang to her feet. Her hand hovered above her sword, and she looked up beneath her dark hair with a hardened look to match. "Don't ever think of threatening me," she snapped. "Utter one word to anyone about my past, and they'll be burying you in several pieces."

Visibly shaken, the squire took a step back and steadied himself against the hearth.

"Look, Moranne I—"

"This conversation is over!" she said briskly. "I'll show myself out."

Her long coat spun out from her body, slapping the table as she turned and strode into the hallway. She yelled out to the butler, who ran to the door and opened it just in time for her to plough through and out into the darkness.

"I told you she was dangerous," said Lady Carreen as she walked into the reception room. "I know Cymel is an old friend, but he asks too much." Her dark red hair gave away her Stanholm origins, but the lilt in her voice was pure Tudorfeld.

"We need allegiances, my dear," said Wystan wearily. "The general has powerful friends."

"Leave it to me," she replied, looking the squire in the eye before slowly bending forward to kiss him on the cheek. "I suggest you have some of the men watch her closely; she's not as pure as Torl thinks she is."

The Red Dragon Inn was considered the only decent lodging in Dunstreet. Jem managed to secure two good rooms on the first floor. The innkeeper had tried to turn him away until he'd invoked Moranne's name. The mere mention of which sent the man scurrying off to ready the inn's two most elegant bed chambers. He could be heard muttering: "of course, Master. My apologies, Master."

Jem tried earlier to send word to Moranne, but by the time he'd arrived at the squire's lodge, she'd already gone. He decided she'd deduce where they were staying, so he returned alone. It was still a novelty to relax in the clean, white sheets of a comfortable bed in a spacious, attractive room. The chamber was lined with wood panelling and had a window looking out onto the village square, known as The Cross.

He closed his eyes on another day away from Denbry, unaware that Moranne was enjoying drinks at the Burlander Tavern just a short distance away.

"Again!" she cried as she lost another game of shove copper (a game which involved tapping copper coins across a table).

"I think you've had enough, my lady," said the landlord nervously, but the green-eyed look she flashed at him sent him scurrying back to the bar for another flagon of ale.

"I'll tell you when I've had enough!" she blasted. "Now fetch me more ale and a round for my friends." The *friends* in question wore militia uniforms and exchanged wry smiles as she slurred her way through another game.

Another flagon of ale and a shot of the local poteen caused her to slump over the table. A shower of coppers rolled over the floor, and a slew of local men scrabbled after them.

"Danc, my love," she murmured, reaching a hand inside her coat before her mind clouded, and she passed out.

8 SQUIRE'S DEAL

A lone warrior emerged through the acrid smoke engulfing the battlefield. The sound of metal on metal rang about his head, punctuated by anguished shouts and screams of pain. The cacophony rose and fell in waves as the wind whirled, throwing the stinging fumes through the eye slits in his high-winged helm. The armour was splattered with blood, mostly of others; it ran in rivulets down his arm vambrace and the stained crevices of his gauntlets. His helm was cut, dented and damp, with sweat running from its base. The grisly stains trickled through the scales of a snake emblem engraved on his breastplate, mingling with the blood and mud already spattering his uniform.

With laboured breath and heavy legs, he clambered over the bodies of the fallen. Many were clad in similar armour bearing the same sigil. Other corpses were those of enormous terracotta-hued creatures with chains of wolves' teeth. Crude weapons such as spiked cudgels and blunt axes lay at their sides.

A few survivors cried out in pain. One poor soul crawled slowly across the warrior's path, dragging the remains of a leg severed at the knee. The warrior ignored them as his gaze fixed on a small hill ahead, bearing a lone, leafless tree. It was the perfect platform for a solitary figure standing tall at its peak.

The warrior stumbled onwards, using his stained and chipped broadsword to steady himself over the rough terrain of mangled bodies. Combining the strength of will and determination, he pushed himself to the foot of the hill, hauling his heavy armour to a stop where he could see the figure more clearly. With a commanding view of the battlefield carnage, a man stood with a gleaming sword in hand. He was tall with long black hair that cascaded over the shoulders of a black leather coat sweeping the ground. He wore no armour, and his clean-shaven visage was manifest in the dipping sun. A narrow face, sharp nose and wicked, thin smile looked down at the warrior and dared him to approach.

His lungs gasped as he filled them with air. The warrior stumbled on, climbing the hill with stuttering steps. As he closed in on his goal, the figure became more evident. His clothes showed no signs of battle, and his sword gleamed as though new. He held a short object in his left hand, which was topped by a round green jewel. The jewel shone brightly with fire from within. The man's smile widened as they drew closer, cracking into a slow, deliberate laugh.

"Finally, old man," he cackled; his youthful looks were at odds with the fallen men lying all around.

The warrior said nothing but continued his advance, strengthening his grip on the sword, which he turned, presenting its edge.

"Do you think your puny, human bag of bones is a match for me?" he continued, standing his ground as the warrior drew level. "You should have joined me."

Just a few feet away, the warrior could see a flash of bright green light in the young man's eyes. It pulsed in time to a glow emanating from the object in his hand.

With one last feat of strength, the warrior lifted his sword and rasped his last words. "I should have killed you at birth."

The sword swept upwards, aiming for the man's neck but didn't connect. Instead, it stopped just inches short. A bright green glow and cracks of green lightning danced around the tall man's body, running over his skin and reaching out into the air. His eyes burned green as he laughed coldly. The warrior froze, statue-like. His sword arm remained as if ready to strike, legs rigid and planted to the ground.

"Yes, you should have..." mocked the dark figure before adding a final word: "Father."

With one effortless movement, the young man brought his sword upwards in a circular motion and decapitated the warrior. His head fell to the ground, then tumbled down the hill, rattling inside the bloody helm.

The warrior's body remained still for a moment before crumpling to the ground with the sound of fallen armour ringing across the battlefield.

As the helmet stopped against a rock, the visor flew open to reveal the sun-blushed skin of a middle-aged, eastern man. His dark beard was clipped neatly, and his deep brown eyes glistened still. His mouth appeared frozen mid-speech as if calling a name.

"Master Jem, Master Jem, sir!"

Jem's body bucked beneath the sheets as the shouts jarred him from his nightmare.

"Master Jem, sir!" came the twanging voice of Don, the innkeeper, amidst furtive banging on the door of Jem's room.

Jem pulled on his breeches and opened the door revealing the rotund figure of the red-faced innkeeper, frozen, mid-knock.

"What is it?" asked Jem blearily.

"It's Her Ladyship, the Lady Moranne; the Marshal's locked her up for being drunk and disorderly."

Stone and Sceptre

Jem dressed quickly and followed the innkeeper's directions to the marshal's office, situated next to the squire's lodge.

The office was a small, two-storey, brick-built building with a broad iron gate, which opened, revealing a set of double wooden doors. It was unique in Burland as the only marshal's building to include a jail cell. It was here where Jem found Moranne pacing the small room, and she wasn't happy.

"Do you have any idea who I am?" she said again to Marshall Axton as he sat impassively across from the cell at his small desk. He was in his early sixties but lean and weathered. His garb was military and implied he'd seen service.

Moranne's eyes lit up as she saw Jem rushing into the room. "Jem, tell him who I am."

"Don't waste your breath, lad," replied the marshal as he reluctantly turned to see the newcomer. "I know exactly who she is, but the law is the law. Three days cooling your heels in the cell for drunk and disorderly conduct. That's it."

"I'm wanted in Cynstol urgently!" Moranne protested.

Fane Axton was unmoved. "It'll take at least three days to send word to the capital, and the Caynna laws don't hold much sway here. Three days and that's it."

Moranne slammed her hand against the railings and rattled them in frustration. Her hand hovered inside her coat, but she dared not use it here. "Jem," she commanded. "Go and see Squire Scirmann, and get me out of here!"

"Yes, ma'am," replied Jem, running out of the jail to the lodge next door.

Although wood-built rather than the stone of the Tunland's estate, the squire's lodge was an impressive site, dominating the skyline of sleepy Dunstreet. Peering up at the characterful structure, Jem realised for the first time he'd be moving in the same circles as his mistress. The world was getting much bigger for the village lad.

He was led into the same impressive room where Lady Moranne had crossed swords with Wystan the previous night, but it was Lady Carreen who entered and invited Jem to sit. She sat opposite with her hands gracefully resting in her lap.

Carreen Scirmann was a glamorous, middle-aged woman with flowing blonde hair striped with silver beads. Her long, red, crushed velvet dress draped perfectly over her shoulders and plunged provocatively, following the v of a silver necklace. Jem had never seen such a vision of beauty, although it instantly triggered memories of the fresh-faced Mia Tunland kissing him goodbye.

"Welcome to our home, young Gada Poulterer," she said, her silky voice caressing the room.

He could feel his cheeks flushing red as he heard his full title for the first time. He bowed his head and tried not to be distracted by her radiance. "It's a pleasure to meet you, Lady Scirmann. You have a wonderful home."

Her face lit with a smile. "Thank you, but please call me Carreen."

Jem nodded, feeling very nervous in her presence.

"Now, what may I do for you, Master Poulterer?" she said.

Lady Carreen nodded as Jem explained the situation and impressed the urgency of their journey. She brought her hands together and pondered for a little while as Jem looked around the room at wealth he'd never known in Denbry.

"I can help you," she said eventually and leaned forward to make a proposition.

༺༻

"No!" said Moranne firmly as Jem relayed Lady Carreen's proposal. "I told the old bastard last night that I wouldn't take his son. He should know better than to cross me."

"She said you could take him as far as Cynstol, then set him up in a noble house. That seems fair, ma'am." Jem could sense her anger and hoped it wouldn't be directed at him.

"Fair?" she screamed, causing the Marshall to turn in his seat. "They had me locked up!"

You *were* drunk, thought Jem, but he dared not say so. "I don't mind sharing," he added.

"I don't like being played!" she yelled. "I won't take orders from a fat fascist."

"Ma'am, you can always turn him into a frog when you return."

Moranne stared at him speechless for a moment before a gleeful smile spread across her face, and she roared with laughter.

"I knew there was a reason I chose you," she said, still chuckling. If only Jem could see how close to his father he was. "Tell Carreen I agree to the terms. Make sure their brat is ready to leave immediately."

Jem strode from the room, feeling pleased with himself.

You always did like a pretty lady in a red dress, thought Moranne as she saw Jem disappear.

༺༻

Young Hayden Scirmann met Moranne and Jem at the southern gate of Dunstreet. He was followed by Ham, his stable boy, who was leading two horses, one of which was loaded with provisions.

"I'm only taking one other," said Moranne irritably. Her head throbbed with impatience and hangover in equal measure.

Hayden was just twenty-one years old but liked to pretend he was ten years older. He held himself as Jem's superior and walked with a swagger, neither won in battle nor earned in deed. A little shorter than Jem, he sported his mother's blonde hair and the squire's swarthy frame. He dressed like a nobleman with a stiff white shirt and a black flowing cloak. The blue-eyed blonde with wavy, champion hair was considered very handsome by the village girls, who swooned at his passing. The broad sword swinging from his side made Jem regard his own empty belt.

"I need Ham at my side," complained Hayden.

Moranne was having none of it. "Split the provisions across our three mounts and send your boy home. That's an order!" she commanded.

Hayden looked down at his stable boy with regret in his eyes. "Sorry, Ham," he said.

Jem found himself gazing at the tall statue of an ancient king, standing just outside the gate at the crossroads between the Burland Road and the Bearun Path.

"That's the murdering King Malen Feorwelm," said Moranne with disdain.

"He's a hero in these parts!" shouted Hayden, still smarting from Moranne's rebuke.

"Very well, Jem, decide for yourself," said Moranne, thinking it was time for another history lesson.

Hayden looked uncomfortable, but he didn't interrupt.

"The kingdom where you now stand once had a different name. It was called Jakar," she said.

Why had no one ever told him this? thought Jem, as he realised for the first time why the Jakaris hated Burlanders.

"The Jakari people lived very happily here for a thousand years, free from conflict and free from dragons." The squire's son pulled a face at the mention of dragons, but Moranne ignored him and continued. "They traded freely with Caynna and Tudorfeld folk and even with the Stans and alviri. It was a peaceful time in Weorgoran.

Unfortunately, two things happened that changed the shape of Grenfold forever. Firstly, the Tudorfeld harvest failed three years in a row, and secondly, King Malen Feorwelm came to power. He immediately blamed the Jakaris for the failed harvest, citing their devotion to heathen gods. He ordered that a great road be built along the craggy course of the River Dorbourne, as Bearun Forest was much more extensive and twice as dangerous in those days. It took five years for three thousand men to build the road they now call Malen's Cutting, and then he marched his army through to Jakar."

Moranne looked to the east, where the arrow-shaped gap in the Midtlen marked the famous path.

"What happened?" asked Jem.

She sighed. "Twenty thousand Jakari men, women and children were massacred."

"That's a lie," mumbled Hayden under his breath.

Moranne ignored him and continued. "The rest fled over the Mur, through hidden passes to the land of Salamas, where a further twenty thousand died fighting the dragons that had lived in peace for millennia. The result? The near-extinction of the once majestic ancient beasts. Only two wyverns remain."

Hayden half-stifled a laugh as Moranne shot him a dark look. Before she could admonish him further, the gatekeeper appeared and opened the south gate.

"We're not going through the Cut?" asked Hayden, surprised.

"We're going through Bearun," said Moranne flatly. "The Dorbourne Path takes too long."

"Do you rave?"

Moranne turned her horse and trotted over to Hayden. With one swift movement, she kicked him in the side, sending him spinning off his mount into a crumpled heap on the ground.

"Contradict me once more, and you'll be wearing Steorra through your chest," she said, with her hand hovering over the hilt of her sword.

Hayden brushed himself off with a look of thunder. His stable boy Ham helped him back into the saddle.

In the corner of his eye, Jem noticed that Hayden held Ham's hand for the briefest moment, and the two seemed to share a look. In the same instant, it was gone, and Hayden sat upright and proud once more.

The squire's son said nothing as they set off, heading for the looming shadows of Bearun. He didn't turn to notice the lonely figure of Ham Grome watching him leave through the railings or the solitary tear which made its slow, painful journey down the young lad's cheek as his master disappeared in the distance.

9 BEARUN

While the party could easily reach the forest by nightfall, Moranne would not have them spend the night in its dangerous grasp. They would camp just outside, then cross Bearun quickly within a day.

The gap between the southern tip of the Midtlen Range and the tall peaks of the Red Mountains to the south expanded as they approached. The darkness of Bearun Forest filled the pass and spread high into the foothills of both ranges, where it turned to thin pines.

The Red Mountains were, in fact, a dark, granite grey. They earned their name from a mythical battle which took place a thousand years past between the humans of Caynna and a race of unknown beasts known as the Egessa.

"Beasts!" scoffed Moranne as Hayden recounted the story. "They were a peaceful hill clan whose only crime was being non-human. It was less a battle and more a massacre."

As Dunstreet and its outlying farms receded behind them, Jem decided to talk with Hayden. They'd gotten off to a shaky start, but it would be a few days before they parted, so Jem felt they should try to get along. Moranne led the party with Jem at her side, so he dropped back until he was level with the squire's son.

"Hi, we've not been properly introduced. My name's Jem Poulterer, and I'm Lady Moranne's gada. I used to be a chicken farmer, you know."

Hayden gave no response. He continued eyes-forward and ignored Jem's existence.

"I think we should all try to get along," continued Jem. "It's a long way to the capital."

Still no response, Jem decided to try one last time. "Have you ever used that sword?"

"You address me as 'Master'," said Hayden sternly, refusing to make eye contact.

For a brief moment, Jem thought of complying, then wondered what Moranne would do.

"I only have *one* mistress, and that is Lady Moranne." That could have been the end, but *she* would never leave it there. "I've been shunned most of my life, so another sulking idiot makes no difference to me."

With a click of his heels and snap of the reins, Jem urged Millie back to Moranne's side, where he found her smiling.

"He'll lose his saddle again before Cynstol," she said with a chuckle.

The landscape was changing quickly, with more trees now skirting their path. The road had narrowed into a dusty trail that snaked around small copses springing up amidst thickets of gorse and nettle. The woods grew denser, and small streams crossed their path, bridged by large rocks and felled trees.

It was late afternoon when Moranne called a halt, and they made camp in a large clearing surrounded by sparse woodland.

Jem prepared tents for himself and Moranne at her instruction while Hayden gazed at the heavy canvas and ropes at his feet with bemusement. Each tent was simply made by tying a rope between two trees and draping the sheet over it. The tarpaulin was then pegged into the ground through small metal eyelets. After watching for a while, Hayden tried to copy Jem's design, but he wasn't familiar with manual labour. Firstly his knots failed, then the rope wasn't straight, so the canvas slid to one end, and finally, both knots failed, and the sheet fell on top of him. Both Jem and Moranne howled with laughter, but Hayden was furious.

"Curses! Curse you, curse my father, curse my mother and curse this infernal place!"

"Would you like some help?" said Jem, sarcastically adding, "*Master*."

Hayden shot Jem a black look and stared back towards Dunstreet, muttering under his breath. Jem didn't wait for an answer and grabbed the sheet and rope, putting the make-shift shelter up in just a few minutes.

"Thank you," said Hayden grudgingly. He was well aware of his inexperience from the blazing lectures delivered by his impatient father.

Jem gathered firewood and prepared a small fire they would use to heat some cheese and onion pies. Along with hunks of stale bread, it made for adequate rations. Late summer in the valley was warm during the day, but a ground chill would quickly spread at night; the fire and shelters would guard against the worst of the cold and keep them in good cheer. The flames would also help to scare away wolves, bears and other predators which lived in Bearun.

"Are the wolves dangerous?" asked Jem, as darkness fell and they huddled around the fire. Wolves and bears rarely ventured near Denbry. Jem had seen neither, although he knew their shape from carvings in the village.

Hayden rolled his eyes, but Moranne was an excellent teacher as ever. "Wolves rarely attack humans, especially groups of humans. The wolves of Bearun are grey wolves, quite small and easily avoided. The black wolves of Deapholt? Well, they're a different matter."

"So what are the deadliest creatures?" asked Jem.

Moranne looked around and over her shoulder as if hiding the answers from threats unseen. Her eyes flickered with the fire's glow.

Stone and Sceptre

"A wyvern can kill you instantly, but they're large and easy to spot. Knifejaws are rare in these lands but deadly up close. A bunyip will creep up on you from a swamp or dark forest, but few are left. Man is the most dangerous beast on this land. Our biggest threat in Bearun is from bandits."

Hayden was laughing and shaking his head.

"What in Frea's name is a bunyip?"

Moranne gazed into the flames with a thin smile creasing her face.

"You will never know," she said. "You'll be alone in the forest and hear footsteps behind you. Turning, you'll see nothing, but the footsteps will continue coming closer and closer. You'll be mad with fear and running for your life."

Jem was hanging on her every word.

She looked across at both of them and raised an eyebrow.

"You'll be dead, with no sight of what killed you."

Hayden was still shaking his head as they settled down to sleep, but Jem believed everything she told him.

Jem's dreams were muddled that night. He saw a young boy with blonde curly hair running through a dark forest, chased by a large dark shadow lumbering from side to side. This image faded to reveal a pack of grey wolves running free across a plain, chasing a herd of deer. They isolated a straggler and brought it down, covering it with their number. Then he saw the eyes.

A green fire burned in the familiar eyes of a dark-haired man with sharp cheekbones and a wicked smile. His lips were moving, but at first, there were no words.

I should have killed you at birth.

Jem woke with a start to find Moranne's hand on his shoulder, waking him from his slumber.

"It's going to be a long day. We need to go," she said. Hayden was already awake and stripping down his tent.

The sun had yet to crest the treetops from the east, and there was a layer of fine mist over the ground, cut only by the statuesque trees. They quickly broke camp and returned to the Bearun Path, heading into the dense forest.

"We need to be through by sundown," said Moranne. "Nights in Bearun are too risky for a small party like ours."

As they followed the path, which became faint as the trees closed in, the darkness enveloped them. In some places, the trees were so dense that they resembled the bars on a prison window, an impenetrable jail where it would be impossible to fly from danger. The canopy began as a bright fern green, filtering the morning sun's rays, but as the party pressed further into Bearun's heart, the light dimmed to a deep jade. Brown and grey tree trunks transformed into sinister figures, row upon row behind them, forming a dark, foreboding wall.

"This was a mistake," mumbled Hayden.

Both Moranne and Jem ignored him as they concentrated on the path ahead.

Occasionally the bushes would rustle, and something unseen would scurry into hiding, or saplings further back would flex as a beast took flight. Dark birds would dart overhead, screeching as they went, and other strange eerie calls would echo through the forest. For every movement and sound, Hayden would reach for his sword, spinning in his seat to find the source. He was becoming agitated, his nerves shredding at every phantom.

"Calm yourself," said Moranne sternly. He was becoming a danger.

Jem was taking the forest in his stride. It felt familiar, like something from a dream. He felt a sense of calm as if he'd been here before, following the same path. Moranne stopped the party as Hayden reached for his sword yet again.

"Put your hand on your sword one more time, and I'll remove it." She looked up under her hair, something she did when the order was non-negotiable.

"We shouldn't be here," he replied, trying hard not to reach for the sword hilt.

"We shouldn't, but we are. The Cut would add two days, and my business in Cynstol is urgent."

She knew the sword was bravado; he'd never used it and probably didn't have the skill. Too proud to admit his fear, he would have been a poor gada ahead of Jem.

"Ride behind me," she continued. "Jem can take the rear guard."

"Of course, ma'am," said Jem proudly, already backing Millie to the rear. Although he carried no weapon, his senses were keen; he felt sure he could spot a threat.

They continued onwards in single file as the path narrowed. Hayden seemed a little less skittish riding close to Moranne, who pushed forward, hiding any fear she might have. Damp vines hung across the track. Moranne slashed at them with her sword, severing them instantly, the wounded ends staining their clothes with streaks of green.

"I think we're halfway through," said Moranne abruptly. She brought them to a halt. "We'll rest here and eat."

They dismounted and set up a temporary camp just off the path. There was no way to know the time from the sun. The canopy was thick, scattering the meagre light into occasional pin-prick shafts. They would be travelling blind come nightfall without stars or moon to navigate. Moranne was right to hurry them.

"I can't eat this!" spluttered Hayden, staring with contempt at his stale bread and soft apple.

The others ignored him, treating the travelling provisions as a necessity. Jem considered offering to chew Hayden's crust but remembered the advice never to poke an angry bear. As Jem finished his apple and tossed the core through the trees, he noticed that Moranne had stopped eating. She was still holding the dry bread but staring back along the path to some point beyond the bushes.

Jem felt it too. The hairs on his neck were tingling; he could sense something in his sight, like a blur or shimmy. He focused on the same point. The tingling spread to his arms and across his chest, causing him to take a breath as his heart fluttered. "How many are there?" he whispered.

"Two, I think," Moranne whispered in reply. "They've been following us for some time."

"Who has?" blurted Hayden.

"Hush!" whispered Jem.

"I don't know yet," Moranne replied. "Jem, keep your eyes open."

Jem nodded.

"What should I do?" said Hayden, trying hard to whisper.

Moranne looked at Jem with a wink. "Try not to get us killed."

They broke camp quickly and were soon back in the thick of the forest, making slow progress as they slashed their way through vines and bramble thickets. Jem was still acting as the rear guard, viewing Hayden's agitated body language ahead. He twitched and nervously looked around as his head filled with bandits, wolves, bears, bunyips, and other strange beasts. Gada Poulterer felt his skin tingle, looking back down the path at the ghostly shadows. They were being hunted for sure.

The sensation remained the same for the next hour while trudging through the darkness. Both Jem and Moranne kept a watchful eye while Hayden fidgeted and complained. Jem was convinced Moranne would kick him from his mount if it weren't for the danger.

Suddenly the path widened, and the vines vanished as they entered a large round clearing about fifty feet wide. The canopy thinned such that a single shaft of light pierced the centre of the clearing. It shimmered with dust and flies giving the area a magical look.

"Jem?" asked Moranne, growing in admiration for her young charge.

"Nothing I can see, ma'am," he replied simply.

"Be on your guard."

She made it through the blade of light without incident. Jem and Hayden slowly followed in single file, urging their mounts forward. The forest seemed quiet. Animal sounds were distant, and the bushes were silent. *Something's wrong*, thought Jem, and he suspected Moranne could feel it too.

A twig snapped behind them. Jem whirled around, but there was nothing. A rustle to the left, nothing there. Birds took flight to the right, with no sign of any danger.

"We need to fly now!" shouted Moranne.

It was too late.

"Move, and you all die!" boomed the voice of a towering figure on foot, appearing from the shadows and blocking the path.

Jem looked back to see another figure emerge to close off the exit. Two appeared to the left, followed by two more to the right. They were surrounded.

The men's features were gradually revealed as they advanced slowly into the light. All were large with long, tangled dark hair and unkempt beards. They were all eastern born, but their build was from all over the island. They wore military garb augmented with animal furs and leather straps. The man at the head stood over six feet tall and carried the most enormous sword Jem had ever seen. It was drawn, with the tip of the blade touching the ground.

The man behind Jem, glaring at them with gritted teeth, held a short, broad axe. Three of the four others had short bows, while the fourth pulled two curved swords from crossed scabbards on his back.

"We've got money!" shouted Hayden, his voice loud but uncertain.

"Thank you," said the large man with mock civility. "We'll have your money, your weapons, your provisions and your horses. Don't think of running. My archers are sharper than they look." He gestured to the three archers grinning in recognition.

"And one more thing," he continued. "We'll let you all live...."

Moranne looked around at Jem and Hayden, shaking her head. She knew the man wasn't done.

"...when we've finished taking turns with your woman."

She didn't flinch, holding her green gaze fixed on the hulking man before her. "Give me your names," she said as if meeting noblemen in the street.

"I am Skati," he said proudly, "and these are my friends: Wes, Bona, Bray, Gelic, and Drof the Axe."

Moranne nodded, smiling under her tousled hair. "My name is Lady Moranne of the King's Council, and these are my companions, Gada Jem Poulterer and Master Hayden Scirmann."

The six bandits looked at one another, shaking their heads and shrugging. "Never heard of you," said Skati, eliciting laughter from the others.

Moranne was still smiling as the men continued to chuckle. "I like to know the name of any man I kill. The man who touches me first dies first."

While the men laughed even harder, she turned to Jem, who had pulled near. "Watch for my signal," she whispered. "Protect Hayden."

Jem nodded. He had no idea what she planned or the signal, but he trusted her completely.

"Now get off your horses, *my ladyship*," said Skati, to the sound of further laughter.

Jem and Hayden followed Moranne's lead, dismounting as the men moved in closer. Jem put himself between Moranne and Hayden, whose hand shook nervously above his sword's pommel.

Follow my lead, Jem heard in his head.

Instinctively he answered it in the same way: *Yes, ma'am.*

With the sword still sheathed, Moranne closed her eyes and slowly reached into her long coat with her left hand. Skati saw it and readied himself for a knife while Drof twirled his axe with an evil grin.

Moranne blinked her eyes open to reveal two burning green orbs which reflected off Skati's face. He jumped back, the smile gone.

"What witchcraft is this?"

Pulling her hand from the coat, she held a short, silver metal stick with a glowing green sphere at its top. A shimmering green mist spread over her body, and Jem could sense the archers getting ready to let their arrows fly.

Now, Jem.

She swept her right hand high into the air, which now fizzed with crackling energy. She let out a mighty scream, and three streaks of green lightning snapped outwards from her hand, hitting the three archers and knocking them back.

Her hand dropped to her sword, which she drew with hurricane speed, sweeping the blade up just in time to parry a mighty blow from Skati. His claymore clanged harshly against her slender blade, sending sparks into the gloom.

Jem saw his chance and grabbed the hilt of Hayden's sword, pulling it from its home and carving it through the air to knock Drof's axe from his hand as he whirled it at Jem's head.

A windmill of twirling blades announced the approach of Gelic, who was rushing towards Hayden, cowering behind Jem. Moranne saw it from the corner of her eye. After parrying another strike from Skati, she ducked down low so that he missed with his next swipe and fell sideways with the weight of his blade. Facing Gelic as he aimed for Hayden, she quickly spun to the right and aimed a side kick, hitting Gelic in the ribs and sending him reeling in pain. With her sword outstretched for balance, she swiped Skati across the back, drawing a slash of blood.

Hayden watched Moranne in awe. She moved with a dancer's fluidity and fought with a craftsman's precision. Leaping and crouching to avoid Skati's swing, he became increasingly frustrated as she darted before him.

Thrusting madly, Jem had no sword training, but Hayden's knight sword seemed to become an extension of his hand. Drof, who now appeared fearful, was forced back.

Just as Moranne's eyes had erupted in green flame, so had Jem's. Two orbs of green fire blazed where his eyes had been, casting his face in a ghoulish light. Jem's face was hidden from Moranne and Hayden's view, but Skati's men could see, and cowered when he approached.

"The archers!" shouted Hayden. Wes had risen to his feet and was now targeting Jem.

Reacting instantly, Jem swept his sword to the right forcing Drof to lose his balance and stumble backwards. Jem ducked as Wes let his arrow fly; it struck Drof in the chest, who fell to his knees, clutching the wound.

Hayden finally noticed Jem's eyes and stumbled back. "What in Frea's name *are* you?"

"Stay behind me," ordered Jem, thrusting downwards with all his strength. He killed Drof as the man staggered around in bewilderment.

An arrow from Bona flew low past Jem, and he could see that Bray was back on his feet with Gelic running at them again.

"Take out your knife, kill that archer!" shouted Jem, pointing at Bray.

Hayden looked up at Bray in horror. He was going to die; they all were. At least his father would finally be rid of his despised son. It was time to muster his hate for the squire and channel it into one last selfless act.

"Curse you!" shouted Hayden into the gloom.

The squire's son did as ordered and sprinted towards Bray, who was busy pulling another arrow from his quiver. As fast as Hayden ran, he couldn't close enough distance. The archer was skilled. He readied his shot, pulled back the string, and took aim.

The sound of birch cutting the air streaked past Hayden, and a silver-coloured arrow struck Bray in the throat, killing him instantly. His own arrow flew harmlessly into the trees.

Hayden looked behind to see a slim shape running through the bushes and vanishing into the trees.

Jem was no match for Gelic, whose twin blades were a whirl of flashing steel. He backed away, parrying the attacks and keeping out of range. Moranne was overwhelmed by Skati as Bona and Wes scanned the thicket for any sign of Bray's killer.

Your father was a better man than you.

"What?" cried Skati at the voice in his head.

You fight like a little girl.

"Get out of my head, witch!"

Enraged, the huge bandit swung wildly, but Moranne jumped back as the slow, heavy blade cut the air.

Hayden could only watch the two brave souls battling against the odds. He stared down at the bloodless dagger in his hands and felt ashamed. *His father was right.* Stealing himself, he lunged back towards Jem, unaware that Bona was ready to fire and Jem was the target. Others saw the danger as Hayden did.

One silver arrow flew in from the south, hitting Bona in the chest. A second flew from the north, hitting him in the back just an inch from the first. He slumped forward, crumpling over his bow.

Your mother never loved you. Your father wished you dead.

"Curse you!" Skati screamed at Moranne and raised the sword above his head to deliver a crushing blow.

But the sword was heavy, and it took too long to lift. As Skati was poised to strike, Moranne thrust her light blade forward, embedding it into his gut, up to the hilt.

Skati cried in agony, cut short by the two silver arrows that pierced his chest in quick succession. He dropped flat on his face, and Wes appeared behind, two arrows already embedded in his spine. He fell to his knees for a while, open-mouthed and shaking his head.

Gelic saw the deaths but fought on, a manic rage in his eyes. He brought his swords together, capturing Jem's sword and yanking it from his grip.

"Now *you* die, little bastard!" shouted Gelic, bringing the two swords towards Jem's neck.

"You first!" cried Hayden as he thrust his knife deep into Gelic's back.

The bandit dropped one of his swords and reached back for the knife.

A silver arrow went through that hand, pinning it to his side, but the second pierced his eye. He crumpled to the ground, screaming. Hayden wasn't finished; pulling out the knife, he kicked Gelic onto his back. He thrust the knife into Gelic's chest, removed it and stabbed the dying swordsman over and over. Tears streamed down Hayden's face as the attack on the lifeless body continued. "Curse you, curse you!" he shouted until Jem held his hand back.

"I think he's dead."

Hayden dropped the knife and fell away sobbing. He pulled his knees into his chest and sat rocking while Moranne came over, exhausted from the fight.

"Is everyone alright?" she asked, looking down at the pitiful sight of Hayden crying with Jem's hand on his shoulder. Dead bodies littered the clearing, but other living souls remained nearby, watching. "Put the sword down, Jem," she said while looking to the east. "Thank you, friends. You're a long way from Alfheim."

10 FRIENDS IN THE FOREST

The sensation crossed his chest and pulsed down his arms, making his veins throb. It was like a headache that hammered his consciousness but then disappeared instantly. His narrowed eyes flashed green as he realised this could mean just one thing: *she* was still alive.

He smiled, causing his knife-like cheeks to rise into sharp peaks. As he settled to scan the horizon, a second wave of energy hit him, knocking him back against the boat's rail.

It couldn't be. There was another. Not as powerful; *yet*.

He returned to the main deck and looked again as the faintest silhouette of land sketched itself through the mist. Sir Faege's clothes hung loosely about his shoulders, and the boots were too large.

Soon he'd have anything he wanted. He caressed the bloodied slit in the tunic, just below the chest plate, the knife entry where Sir Faege had died at his own hand. He pictured Moranne standing over his own crumpled body, *his* gift glowing in her hand.

"You'll all pay the price in blood," he hissed.

He pulled the short, metal stick from the knight's satchel, grasping it tightly until a smoky green light writhed within the spherical stone at its top.

"I've imagined you dead every minute of every day, and soon I'll see your blood flow with that of your pitiful runt."

The clearing seemed to brighten, and an air of hope rose in Jem as he stood over the twisted body of Drof. A feeling of calm emanated from the narrow parting between the trees Moranne was facing.

"Please show yourselves; we are unarmed," she said, with her arms outstretched.

"And outnumbered," came the silky smooth reply.

Jem turned to see a tall, slim man striding silently through the trees. He had shining delicate features and aqua-blue eyes, but it was the bright white, shoulder-length hair which drew Jem's gaze. He looked to be in his middle years, and his features bore his wisdom. He wore tight-fitting leather leggings and a shirt which seemed to make him vanish as he moved through the brush. The bow which had claimed so many bandits was an ornately-carved longbow suspended across his back. The tips of pointed ears briefly showed themselves as his hair swept around his neck.

"An elf!" cried Hayden, jumping to his feet.

"I'm sorry about him, kind sir," said Jem quickly, throwing Hayden a disappointed look. "He's alviri," Jem whispered.

The alviri man laughed heartily, radiating warmth in a kind smile.

"You're well informed, *young gada,* unlike your companion," he said, still beaming.

"He makes so much noise we could have tracked him from the moon," came the sound of a dreamy second voice from the other side of the clearing.

At first, it appeared a young boy carrying a longbow was emerging from the forest, but as she strode past Moranne to stand beside her companion, the distinctive looks captivated both Jem and Hayden.

She was a little shorter than Jem but slender and lithe in her close-fitting leather. Her hair was dark but very short for a woman of these parts. It clumped into small tooth shapes that clung to her face, some pointing inwards towards her broad smile. She had slightly shorter pointed ears, but the most intriguing feature was her skin colour. She had the sepia hue of a Jakari but not as dark as the woman in Jem's dream. Yet, she was still darker than anyone Jem had seen in Burland.

"My name is Boran Berlain," said the white-haired alviri, "and this is my wife, Alize." They both bowed formally.

Jem nodded in respect, but Hayden was utterly enthralled by Boran, staring at his chiselled face while he wiped away his tears. "You're beautiful," he said, as if in a trance.

"He's had a sheltered life," interjected Moranne quickly, to save their blushes. "I am Lady Moranne of the King's Council, and this is Jem, my gada; the starry-eyed fop is Master Hayden Scirmann of Dunstreet."

"You are well known to us, Wickona," replied Boran. "We've been tracking your party since you entered the forest. Skati's bandits have been in this area for many months, but we don't usually concern ourselves with the business of humans. We know you as a friend to the alviri and wanted to help."

"Well, thank you once more, dear friends," said Moranne, taking Boran's hand in friendship.

"Wickona?" asked Jem, bemused.

"I have many names, not all of them as pleasant," replied Moranne with a wink.

Hayden dusted off his clothes and adjusted his belt to present himself gracefully. He extended a hand, not taking his gaze from Boran's bright blue eyes. "Thank you," he said, holding Boran's hand a little longer than necessary.

The alviri was unfazed, but his expression changed to one of concern. "Watch yourself in Cynstol, Master Hayden; there are those who would not accept your kind." Hayden wanted to ask about *his kind,* but he knew the answer before the question was asked. He nodded curtly and released Boran's hand.

"You're all welcome to spend the night in our camp," said Alize. "It's a short walk from here, and you'll be safe with us."

Moranne agreed. They gathered the horses and supplies and followed their new friends towards the north. She stopped at the edge of the clearing and turned to Jem.

"Gada, where's your sword?"

Jem was puzzled. "What sword, ma'am?"

She gave him a kind smile with which he was becoming familiar.

"You've earned it, my brave gada. Take a weapon and belt from one of the fallen. Choose well."

Jem surveyed the dead bodies of the bandit swordsmen. Skati's claymore was much too large and heavy, while Drof's axe seemed too barbarous. The only option seemed to be Gelic, who was a similar build. Jem removed the cross scabbard and fastened it across his back; it fitted perfectly. He practised sheathing and unsheathing the short curved swords; it felt almost natural.

"A good choice," said Alize beaming. "The Jakari blades suit you well."

Jakari blades, thought Jem, conjuring an image of Danya radiating in the sun. He would later discover they were short scimitars; they had a small cross guard, a leather-bound hilt and no pommel. Both blades were sharp and incredibly light; they felt good in his hands. They were plain but for an inscription near the guards of each.

"They are the names of Rajun and Aimran, the Jakari gods," said Moranne, translating them quickly.

Feeling very adult, Jem joined the group, and Boran led them deeper into the forest. The alviri made no noise as they gracefully weaved through the trees and gorse bushes. Their movement was deliberate and elegant, as if they were at one with the trees. Skipping over hidden streams and skirting fallen rocks, the group headed north towards the Midtlen Range's lowest reaches.

By mid-afternoon, the light faded below the roof of trees, and Alize announced they had reached the camp. "You can rest with us here," she said. "Please feel at home."

It appeared to Jem like a tiny clearing at first sight, but then the coarse thatched roofs of two small huts gradually came into focus. They were covered in moss and ivy, making them blend into the forest entirely. He remembered the round hut in the marshes from his dream, but these rough buildings were from a dream he had yet to experience.

"You live here?" he asked, as they stood in the clearing's centre and inspected the enchanted camp.

"No," said Alize giggling. "It's one of three camps we use when hunting. We have a larger home in the foothills of the Red Mountains."

"Where are your kin?" asked Hayden, trying not to stare at Boran.

"We live here alone," he said. "Wickona knows."

Moranne nodded in agreement. She knew there was a dark side to the alviri.

Boran and Alize emptied one of the huts, used as a storeroom, to provide a bed-chamber for the three, then started to prepare a fire. They produced a spit that hung over the makeshift fire pit and attached a small, skinned deer they'd caught that morning.

Hayden's eyes lit up at the thought of real food, and they all assembled around the flames as the meagre light faded into night.

The clearing took on a warm, safe feeling like the homely fire-lit room of a cosy cottage. Jem felt privileged to be in an alviri home. He'd heard many tales of the alviri, although most Burlanders referred to them as elves. The stories were of spells, magic and mischief. There was even a Burland saying: *I trust you as much as an elf*, meaning *I don't trust you at all*.

"And we trust *you* as much as an elf," said Boran smiling. He'd read Jem's thoughts as if Jem had shouted them across the forest.

Although Boran's handsome looks were striking, it was Alize who captivated Jem the most. She was bright and confident, holding herself with authority, the equal of any man. Hayden seemed busy with something, and while Moranne chatted with Boran, Jem took his chance to approach Alize. He moved around the fire to sit next to her, tossing a log into the flames as he settled.

Her face was round and tended naturally to smile, while her skin was smooth and free of marks, like a carefully crafted sculpture. Even her scent was sensual, like the sweet smell of freshly cut grass, melded with the freshest honey and brightest blossom.

"Do you mind if I ask you something?" he said nervously. "I've never met an alviri."

She tilted her head to the side, and the firelight shone in her cheeks and glinted from her dark eyes.

"You can ask me anything, Jem Poulterer, though I'm no alviri," she chirped. "However, there is a price."

How could she know his full name? Not an alviri?

"I don't understand," stuttered Jem.

She turned to face him and sat cross-legged on the mossy forest floor.

"I will tell you my story if you show me who you are."

Jem was desperate to know more about his enlarging world, and the others were preoccupied.

"It's a deal," he said, offering his hand. She shook it, beaming mischievously.

The first, faint moonbeams were breaking through the canopy, flickering off the moths which circled and flitted through the narrow rays. Bird song rang through the trees, and the air was moist and still. Alize looked around her as if gathering her memories, then leaned forward and told her tale.

"Once upon a time, many years ago, there lived an alviri male named Caltos Trenwane. He was the alviri ambassador to Jakar."

"You mean Salamas?" prompted Jem.

"I mean Jakar," insisted Alize. "Caltos' home in Alfheim had all the trappings of luxury, but he was sad. His wife had died many years before in an attack by one of the mountain clans."

That couldn't be, thought Jem. Jakar hadn't existed for hundreds of years. *Mountain clans?* Each story seemed to bring more questions. Burland started to look very small.

"While Caltos was in Jakar one day, the new emperor introduced him to Princess Zahrana. She had an exquisite beauty he'd never known before, and he instantly fell in love with her. The two were inseparable, and eventually, the king agreed they could marry and live in Jakar."

Jem couldn't help thinking of Danya and her deep, dreamy eyes as he listened to the story.

"They had many good years together, and Zahrana bore Caltos a little girl they named Alize. Alas, the tide was turning. The human king Malen was attacking Jakar from the east, so the Jakaris asked the alviri for help, thinking they were friends."

"The help didn't come," said Jem. He could predict the story unfolding before him.

Alize forced a smile. The young gada was bright. "All the alviri were banished from Jakar, so my father took my mother and me back to Alfheim in secret. Only pure-born alviri can live on the hallowed isle, you see." She looked out towards the west with a thin gloss forming on her eyes. "We lived secretly for many years; I even managed to sneak on and off the island using our boat. Father had a large estate on the bay; we were very happy."

"What happened?" said Jem, wondering what had brought her here.

"Human life," she said simply, holding her arms out with a shrug. "My mother died of old age. My father was depressed and started drinking. One day he became very drunk and told someone about me." Alize looked down, almost crying.

"It's alright," said Jem, "you don't need to—"

"I do; I want to," she insisted. "They came for me in the night."

Stone and Sceptre

"Who did?"

"The militia," she said, looking towards Boran.

"That's awful," said Jem.

"The militia captain put me on a boat and took me to Mirror Lake, a community of mixed race alviri. Unfortunately, even *they* wouldn't take me because of my brown skin. I'm half-human, but that half is Jakari. The captain took pity on me and tried to find somewhere for me to live, but we found nowhere." She looked across the camp at Boran, his white hair glowing orange in the firelight. "We ended up here."

Jem was baffled. "Boran was your captor?"

"We fell in love," said Alize, nodding. "I'm a dalfreni. A half alviri not even accepted by my dalfreni kin."

"Dal-freni?" repeated Jem, trying to form the unfamiliar word.

"It means 'dirty friend' in ancient alviri," said Alize.

"That's a sombre story."

"I'm happy," she said, the smile returning.

"There is just one thing," said Jem, still trying to piece things together. "How old are you?"

She laughed so loudly that the others stopped what they were doing and looked over. "You're a good man Jem Poulterer. I'm over seven hundred years old. I don't know exactly."

Jem stared open-mouthed at the revelation while there was further laughter behind.

"Sorry, I didn't tell you," said Moranne. "The alviri don't die of old age."

They continued to laugh and joke as Boran started to slice sections from the deer. Alize handed out hunks along with wooden mugs of a drink they called mapulder, made from maple tree sap. The dark liquid was sweet but had a kick like poteen.

The party enjoyed the hospitality of the Berlains. Jem wanted to stay as long as possible; it was the happiest of times since the day he decided to leave Denbry. It wasn't long before his vision blurred with the effects of the liquor, and he smiled openly at the delightful Alize.

"We have a deal, Master Poulterer," she reminded him, grinning.

Jem was struggling to form any words, so he just nodded while Alize held out her hands, palms upward. "Place your hands on mine, and clear your mind."

He dumbly complied and saw that nobody was watching them. Moranne was laughing with Boran while Hayden sketched something on a scrap of parchment.

"Close your eyes," she said.

Jem did as instructed. His blurred view immediately darkened. He could still see the glow of the fire dancing through his eyelids, but it was receding as if he were flying backwards. The dark image faded into the gloom while his mind flew high above the forest, and he darted across the land.

A tall castle loomed from the mist; bodies in silhouette were lit in orange at the window of a tall tower before it evaporated to grey. He flew low, skimming over an ocean, past a green pinnacle of land and small islands, before shooting back into the sky, whirling. The jagged teeth of a mountain range leapt from sheets of green. His vision sent him low through hidden passes and out onto a plain, which swept down to a shimmering beach with rolling dunes like waves in a sea of sand.

Danya stood alone, looking out to sea. Her dark hair clung to the perspiration on her shoulders. She turned and stared directly into Jem's soul.

"*He's coming.*"

"I'm sorry, Wickona, I didn't know," shouted Alize.

Jem snapped open his eyes and found himself lying on the ground, with Alize and Moranne standing over him.

"I'm sorry," said Alize once more as Moranne felt Jem's brow and brought a water pouch to his lips.

"Keep drinking the water," she said. "Mapulder is pretty strong for the uninitiated."

Jem spluttered on the cold water and blinked up at Alize. She took his hand and helped him stand, leaning close to his ear with a whisper. "I know who you are; be wary of her."

He looked her in the eye, but they said no more that night. Moranne insisted they get some sleep. Jem dragged his body to the hut where they slept beneath rough, hemp cloth sheets on a bed of dried moss and leaves. The musty, earthy smell of the camp filled his nostrils, and his dreams swept him away once more to the beach.

Be wary of who? Danya? Moranne?

Alize watched him from the door as his breathing slowed and his eyes fluttered beneath heavy lids.

"Goodnight, newcomer."

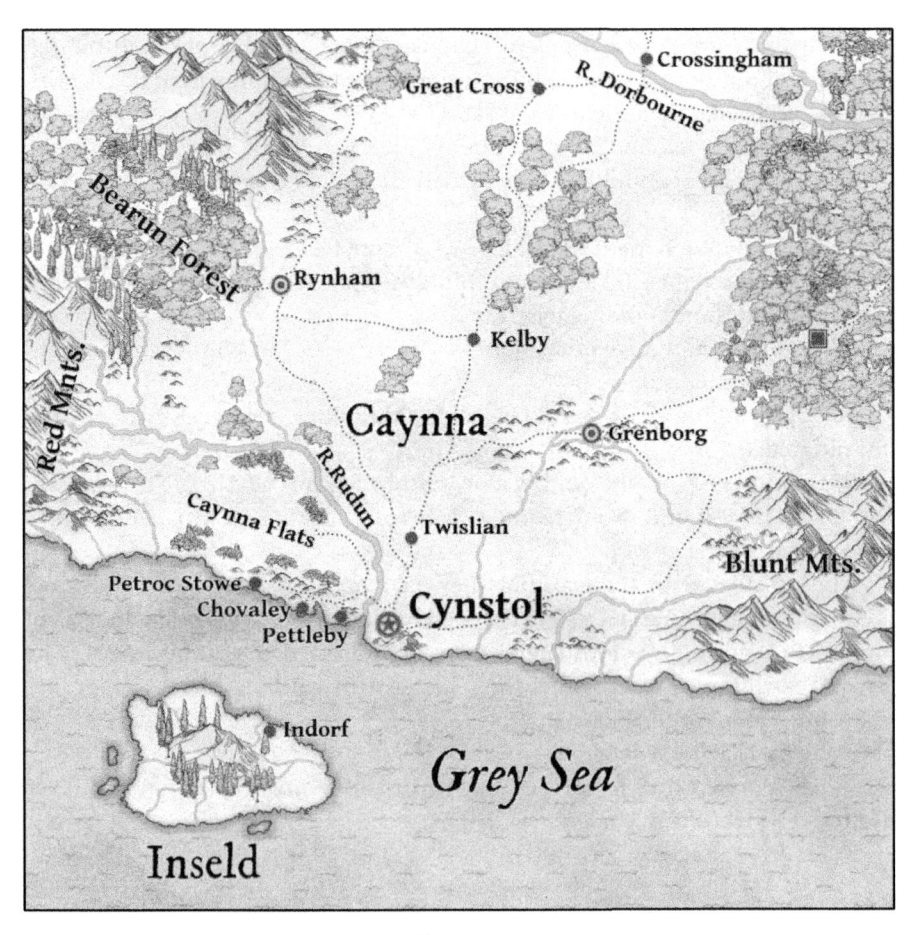

Caynna

11 THE FIRST SCEPTRE

"It's time you became a man. You can go with Lady Moranne, or I'll send you to the legion in Tudorfeld."

Hayden could still hear his father's words, infecting his dreams and haunting his days. He had no intention of ever joining the Queen's Battalion - only to play a distant second to his effervescent brother, Chadwick. He never wanted to leave Dunstreet and the carefree days spent near the river with Ham.

Seeing the knife in Gelic's back felt like he'd thrust the blade into his life, cutting ties to his father and everything he stood for. Boran, Alize; these were good people in a wider world. He'd saved Jem's life, a man with twice his bravery and an unholy gift for swordsmanship. A weapon he'd never used. He wanted to live at one with the world as Boran and Alize did. Although hundreds of years old, they still loved each other and the simple life in Bearun. Thinking of them, Hayden committed to finding his place in this world.

Hayden looked over at Jem and Moranne, who were still sleeping. The first half-light of the western sun leaked through the hut's door and moved up their bodies as they rested. Somewhere outside, the fair couple would be silently tending the camp.

Pushing the blanket aside, he stretched widely and stumbled into the clearing, where he found Alize cooking breakfast.

"Good morning, Master Hayden," she said sweetly.

An earthy-smelling pot of mushroom broth was bubbling above the fire, and she was tearing hunks of dark bread from a rough loaf.

"You're both so kind," replied Hayden, sitting near the fire to lift the morning chill.

She smiled coyly and gave him a bowl of broth, then sat next to him and looked about to ensure she wasn't overheard.

"Lady Moranne and her... Master Poulterer have an important destiny. There will be many dangers ahead; be brave, Master Hayden."

"I will," he said.

Hayden knew how special Moranne was, and he'd also seen the green fire burning in Jem's eyes. His father was wrong; there *was* magic in the world.

Jem and Moranne sleepily joined the breakfast party, and Boran arrived a little later. He'd been scouting the road ahead for bandits.

Hayden moved to the nearest hut and sat against the frame. He reached inside his cloak and pulled out a few pieces of crumpled parchment and a stub of charcoal from his pocket. His father hated his drawings, considering arts and crafts to be the preserve of peasants, something the unfortunate would fall back on when they didn't have the wealth of nobility. For Hayden, it was his real life. He'd wanted to be an artist from birth, drawing birds, trees and all the features of Dunstreet. He looked down at the creased image of Ham Grome smiling back at him. The long hot summer in Dunstreet, sitting on the banks of the adolescent River Dorbourne and sketching the young lad as they enjoyed the day.

It was his mother who discovered the stash of artworks showing the young stable boy, but it was his father who had ordered them burnt. Hayden had only one image remaining from that happy time. Shuffling the papers, he smoothed the wrinkles from his latest work and added some light shadow to the features.

"You're a man of hidden talents, Master Scirmann."

The smooth, reassuring voice belonged to Boran, leaning against the hut.

"I hope you don't mind," replied Hayden nervously.

The alviri laughed heartily and knelt to take a better look at the striking portrait. "I have never been drawn before; I'm honoured." The sketch showed Boran sitting by the fire, smiling as he chatted to Moranne. Hayden smudged the dust with his finger and held the drawing up to the light.

"It's yours," he said, handing it to Boran.

The tall alviri male was genuinely touched, taking the sketch and smiling at the perfect likeness. He leaned across and planted a kiss on Hayden's cheek. "Juldra protect you, my young friend."

The party was in good cheer when Boran and Alize finally led them back to the clearing where they had previously confronted the bandits. The bodies were gone, dragged away by forest creatures. A few bloody trails led off into the trees.

They were all sad to leave their new friends as they set off along the faded path towards the west. Boran had scouted the route, and it was clear, but Moranne knew the alviri would help them in an instant if they felt danger once more.

The partings were poignant. They all hugged and wished each other well, but the silent handshake between Hayden and Boran showed the deep bond forged in just one day.

"May Juldra smile on you all," said Alize, beaming her child-like beauty across the clearing.

Hayden looked down at a second, simple sketch of Boran before folding it carefully and stuffing it into a pocket. As the horses ambled into the gloom, he looked around from the party's rear. The alviri couple were already gone, but he knew they were watching.

Trees parted and thinned a little as they gradually moved away from the forest's heart. They were content, passing through the thin mist which carpeted the Bearun Forest floor. Bright yellow and crimson mushrooms clung to damp tree trunks, and delicate pale blue flowers emerged through tiny tufts of grass where the sun pierced through to the ground. The first chills started to bite as the cold autumn nights battled with the hot summer days. They would easily be through the forest in one day, but Moranne hoped to make the village of Rynham before night. It fell just west of Bearun, and she described it as "sleepy but nervous." It was away from any major routes, and few would risk the Bearun Path.

The party chatted lightly about their new friends in good heart as they travelled.

"Why are there not more alviri?" asked Jem.

"It's a long, dark tale," replied Moranne, "but you can lay the blame with your church. The alviri are an ancient, proud race from the age of galdur, but today they wane. Fear, jealousy and simple prejudice see them live only on the hallowed isle of Alfheim. You'll see very few in the wider world."

"How could anyone fear such fair creatures?" mused Hayden, unable to get Boran's handsome features from his thoughts.

"A long lifespan and the power of Juldra," replied Moranne. "They're also very bright and accepting of all life, which makes Burlanders very nervous."

Hayden didn't fully understand, but he was reborn since meeting them. "I owe you my life," he told Jem. "I'm sorry I froze."

Jem was having none of it. "You owe me nothing," he said. "I'm always ready to help my friends."

It was mid-afternoon when the forest thinned enough to see the thin clouds above, and the landscape widened to a lush bright green from the dim brown of the depths. Jem was riding alongside Moranne, who'd been lost in thought for a while. Jem too, thought of the last days. No one had spoken of Moranne's attack when phantom light had streaked from her hand, knocking back the archers. Now seemed like a good time to ask.

"Ma'am, the way you dealt with the bandits. Could you have struck them all?"

It was one of many questions swirling in his head. It felt wrong as he asked it. Moranne broke from her thoughts and pondered how best to answer.

"Earth power, young gada," she said as if he'd understand. "I can harness the power of natural things around me, but only so much. I could have hit one bandit and killed him or hit them all, but they would have barely staggered."

"I see," said Jem, not really understanding. "Why not hit them again?"

"Ah!" she said. "It takes a while to absorb more of the earth's power."

"Is that what your weapon stick does?" he blurted.

Moranne smiled and pulled the shining rod from her coat. The round, green stone was dull, but Jem knew what could happen if it burned brightly.

"I can use earth power any time, but this allows me to store and focus it for greater effect. I can do little without it." She showed it to Jem, who noticed some strange writing down its length. "It's called a sceptre," she said.

He saw the knight killing himself with his own blade and the lone warrior frozen on the hill. Without thought, the question spilt into words he couldn't take back. "Could you make a man take his own life?"

Moranne thrust the rod back into her coat and brought her horse to a stop. She grabbed Jem's arm and pulled him close. Her face had darkened, and a light flashed in her eyes.

"You've seen a sceptre before, haven't you? Haven't you?" She was shaking him as he grasped for the words.

"I... I..."

"Tell me!"

He nodded quickly as her gaze lowered to the same look she gave those about to suffer. "Where?" she said.

Her eyes were wild, and her lip quivered. Jem realised she was frightened.

"I saw a knight in my dreams," he stammered. "He met a strange man in a swamp and then killed himself with his own sword."

Moranne shook her head but said nothing and gestured for him to continue.

"And I saw another soldier die on a hill when a tall man killed him. He held a sceptre like yours."

Her demeanour changed immediately. Her grip on Jem's arm loosened and morphed into a warm squeeze of care. A single tear trickled down her cheek and dropped onto her blouse. She dismounted and walked slowly towards a shining birch. Leaning against the damp trunk, she looked west as dark memories swirled through her endless memories.

I'm sorry, Dane, my love. You were right.

"What's going on?" whispered Hayden, pulling his horse to a halt.

"I'm not sure," replied Jem cautiously as he realised he had seen something dangerous and significant in his dreams. They both dismounted and waited.

Moranne continued staring past the trees for some time as thicker clouds rolled in from the east. The air became heavy and humid, and the birds sang in shrill bursts as an atmosphere of foreboding descended on Bearun. Eventually, she returned to the others, wiping the trails of tears from her face.

"I'm sorry, Jem," she said, placing a hand on his shoulder. "I should have told you earlier." She was shaking her head and looked as if she could break down at any moment.

"You have a gift," she continued.

His dreams were real. *Danya was real?*

"You have the sight; you can see the past and the present; you may also be able to see a possible future."

"Those things were real?" he said, still focused on Danya's perfect smile.

She reached out to Hayden, holding his hand as the party came together.

"Yes," she said. "I'll need to teach you how to control it, but for now, try not to think about the man with the sceptre." *He may already know of you,* she thought. "We must ride quickly; I must get to the capital before they make the wrong decision."

Mounting again, they continued through the forest; the trees thinned and gradually gave way to small scattered copses and extensive gorse thickets. The path widened to a road, so they increased the pace to a trot with the sun dipping behind them. Soon they were riding past fields of potatoes, carrots, cabbages and seeding sunflowers.

It would be early evening when they reached the fortified village of Rynham. Luckily the gates were still open, and the gatekeeper recognised Lady Moranne. He waved them through without delay.

A tall wooden wall of Bearun tree trunks circled the village. Each log was sharpened to a point, and tall wooden watchtowers loomed above the barricade at regular intervals. The main gate was comprised of a pair of massive wooden doors flanked by even taller towers. An extensive bailey spread before them, with most dwellings nestled against the walls. Only a marshal's lodge and stables lay ahead of the gate before a shallow climb to the small fort behind a second gated wall. Barbican rings within concentric rings protected the village and did give a feeling of safety, but also of a trading post where people lived in continuous fear.

Jem noticed differences immediately. The folk of Rynham were taller and slimmer than their Burland neighbours. They had primarily dark hair, but their countenance seemed more severe and wary. Tall warriors walked the streets with long swords dangling or bows suspended on their backs. It felt as if the village was coiled to react to some unseen threat.

They left the horses at the stables, and Moranne walked them to the courtyard's centre. She pulled out the familiar velvet purse and handed coins to both Jem and Hayden.

"Jem, you're in charge," she said, looking over to Hayden, who nodded obediently.

He knew he was no leader and trusted his new friend thoroughly after the Bearun encounter.

"Hayden, I know you're good with horses," she continued. "I want you to sell your horse and buy a fast stallion for me."

Neither Jem nor Hayden knew what was happening, but they knew there was an urgency behind her instruction, and they trusted her judgement.

"One more thing Jem," she said. "You'll need to find an inn for two nights. Two rooms. I'll meet you both in the Red Bridge Tavern at eleven. I'll explain everything."

She turned and strode off towards the fort gates with orders issued, leaving the others looking after her in bewilderment.

"I'll never order you about," said Jem, while they both watched her dark form striding up the bank.

"And I'll never let you down again," replied Hayden, as he remembered freezing in the Bearun clearing.

Jem offered his hand, and they shook warmly. Jem had just made his first friend outside of the fleeting glimpses of Mia Tunland. They parted to complete their tasks as Moranne disappeared through the fort gates above them.

Jem secured rooms at a small boarding house opposite the Red Bridge Tavern, run by the stern-looking Mrs Scripen. Most of the buildings in Rynham were red brick, baked from the clay formed by the myriad of streams that fell from the Midtlen. It was an old village, but historical raids from Bearun bandits had taken their toll and left the villagers very distrustful of strangers.

Mrs Scripen had scrutinized Jem ruthlessly, including checking his ears, before she agreed to rent the rooms.

"No women and no funny business," she'd said when Jem handed over a night's deposit.

The door of the Red Bridge Tavern creaked loudly to announce Jem's arrival to the small number of locals gathered at the bar. They turned in unison and inspected the humbly dressed newcomer, still wearing Gelic's crossed scimitars.

Jem noticed that Hayden had retreated to a small table tucked in the furthest corner of the room and could be seen cradling a large goblet of red wine.

"At last, some civilisation. They have wine!" he said, as Jem sat down in the high wooden pew.

"Did you get a horse?"

Hayden lifted his goblet and nodded. "I have a swift horse named Demon, of all things."

Jem had no clue of Moranne's intentions, but he was too hungry to care. A serving lad hurried over to the table at Jem's signal, and they ordered pie together with Jem's first-ever wine. There was no sign of Moranne, leaving them to relax and chat about their former lives.

"So you're half Jakari, like Alize?" asked Hayden.

"Maybe that's where I get my green eyes," laughed Jem. "I've noticed that Lady Moranne also has green eyes. Do you think she's part Jakari?"

"Who knows? Who cares!" beamed Hayden in return.

They became merrier as the wine flowed, both revelling in the absurdity of their Burland lives. They didn't notice the thickset man at the bar watching them intently.

"So you really were a chicken farmer?" laughed Hayden.

"Oh yes," grinned Jem. "Collecting eggs, selling eggs, collecting more eggs, there was never a dull moment."

"And now you have a gift."

"Hmm," agreed Jem. "Although I don't know how to use it."

"Can you see my future?" asked Hayden, spilling wine as he used the goblet to gesture.

"I don't think it's always good to know our destiny."

Jem remembered Huw in Supbry and the possible dark future awaiting him.

"I like your swords, outlander." The voice was deep, with a rugged accent.

Hayden looked up to see a fell-looking man towering behind Jem. He had long dark hair, close-shaved at the sides, revealing swirling tattoos. His dark beard was platted with silver beads, and his ruddy, square face was crossed with numerous scars.

"Thank you," said Jem, keeping his eyes on Hayden.

The man grunted and shifted on his feet. "Those swords belonged to a good friend of mine," he said, building a tone of malice.

"Then maybe you knew *his* friends: Skati, Wes, Bona and Bray," countered Jem.

Hayden could see a pale green light start to swirl in Jem's eyes. He dared not speak as a hush descended on the tavern; all eyes were on them.

"Knew?" growled the man.

Hayden noticed the man's hand was moving towards the handle of a dagger concealed below his belt.

"My name is Gada Jem Poulterer, and this is my friend, Master Hayden Scirmann, the son of Squire Wystan Scirmann of Dunstreet. We killed your friends when they attacked us in Bearun. Now, who might you be?"

Although Jem was staring straight ahead, he could see the man reflected in Hayden's goblet, with his hand reaching for the knife. Only Hayden could see the bright green spots expanding in Jem's pupils.

"I'm called Stenic," said the man. His hand connected with his weapon, and he curled his fingers around it, ready to strike. "Gelic was my brother."

The hunting knife slid halfway out of the scabbard when it stopped.

Stenic stood still and upright as if rooted to the spot. The sharp point of a gleaming sword pricked the back of his neck and drew a small bead of blood, which trickled down beneath his collar.

"It would seem that your friends gained all they deserved."

The voice was well-educated and well-spoken, with the rolling lilt only found in Tudorfeld. As the owner of the voice gradually moved around Stenic, Hayden could see that he was dressed in elegant military garb that bore the crest of the Green Order, an oak tree in full leaf. He had a smooth, chiselled face and a finely trimmed short beard. His long dark hair was tied back in the style of a knight, and light mail showed beneath his engraved chest plate.

"Since we're introducing ourselves, please allow me," he continued. "I am Sir Caspin Linhold, son of Earl Normin Linhold, and these gentlemen are under my protection. Ultimately I am commanded by the king, so they are also under the king's protection."

Jem looked around for the first time to see the impressive knight smiling down at them.

"You have mere moments to leave this place and leave Rynham before I run you through. Drop the knife."

Stenic did as instructed and backed slowly towards the tavern entrance.

"See that he leaves," shouted Sir Caspin as Stenic backed into the Rynham marshal, who was waiting by the door. They bundled him out, and the tavern patrons slowly returned to their business, muttering about newcomers.

The knight grabbed a chair and sat down between Jem and Hayden. He looked between the two shaking his head.

"Lady Moranne told me you two would be in some kind of trouble. It seems to follow you." He had a natural charm and confidence which matched Moranne's.

"Thank you for your help, sir," replied Jem politely. He was starting to feel conscious of his humble rags compared to Hayden's clothes and the knight's finery.

"Please call me Caspin, and I will call you Jem and Hayden." He yelled for more wine and grinned as if smiling was so regular and casual that his mouth always settled that way. "I was sent to find Lady Moranne and heard she had come this way."

"The most dangerous route," grumbled Hayden.

"She fears nothing," agreed Caspin. "The strongest woman I know."

"Where does she come from?" asked Jem.

Caspin shook his head. "No one knows, and it's best not to ask."

While Boran's face had shone in the dark forest, Sir Caspin also had an aura of light which picked out his dark eyes and unblemished skin. Hayden couldn't help watching every tilt of his head and each laughter line as it appeared and disappeared with his smile. "Where do you come from?" he asked, unaware that he was dreamily staring at the knight.

"I've been stationed in Gosta for the last year," replied Caspin. "The Green Order has barracks all over Tudorfeld, but I've travelled to Cynstol with General Marl. He always likes to arrive with a large retinue."

"It must be exciting," said Jem.

"Not really," he shrugged. "We deal with bandits and border disputes. I've never rescued a damsel in distress. I serve at the king's pleasure."

"To the king!" cried Hayden, so loudly that some locals coughed into their ale.

The three raised a tankard to the king and slammed the table in mock patriotism. They were just raising a second toast when Moranne burst into the bar looking stressed. She refused a chair and stood at the table, clearly in a hurry.

"Jem, Hayden, did you do as I asked?"

They nodded, and Hayden slurred a description of the horse and where it was stabled.

"Now, I want you to listen carefully," she continued, while the two lads tried to stay focused. "Sir Caspin will be with you from now until you arrive in Cynstol. He'll help you to the city where I'll meet you."

"Where will you go?" exclaimed Jem.

"I can't explain. I'm leaving now. Things are more serious than I'd thought, and it can't wait. I'll be faster alone and on a fresh horse." She put a hand on Jem's shoulder and flashed them a quick smile. "I'll see you in a few days."

Saying nothing more, she strode out of the tavern, leaving the door to bang as she left.

Taking his duties seriously, Caspin decided it was time for them to turn in. They swayed from wall to wall as he led them to the boarding house, stumbling through the door and landing in a heap before Mrs Scripen. She was ready to scold them mercilessly until she saw the dashing Sir Caspin behind.

He apologised and gave her an extra copper for her trouble. She watched him go towards the fort where he was staying, then ushered Jem and Hayden to bed.

Jem's eyes closed when his head hit the rough, straw-filled pillow. Images of alviri, arrows and swords swept in front of his eyes as drink took him away from the day.

12 CASPIN

The knife and fork clanged agreeably on the fine porcelain plate when Penri Smolt leaned back in the oversized chair and sighed contentedly.

"Mrs Briwan, you have surely outshone yourself. That pheasant was a gastronomic delifance of divine insiference," he purred musically as she bustled to his table to gather the plate. He loved using impressive-sounding, made-up words, especially when conversing with the lower classes.

He carefully dabbed his chain of office with a napkin to remove any drops of gravy, then grasped the silver-plated goblet of wine to wash down another agreeable midmorning brunch. The Friar's Gate Tavern became too busy later in the day, and he preferred Mrs Briwan's personal service.

"Well, thank ye, Mr Mayor," she replied. A large woman with a perpetually red face and voluminous chest bulging over an impossibly tight corset. Penri always enjoyed the view as he dined.

Cynstol's mayor liked to think of himself as a man of the people, but in reality, he was either a hindrance or irrelevant to the city's smooth running. The castle was run effectively by the aristocratic Sir Torl Radborough, leaving the city below to Penri. Thankfully the city ran by itself for the most part; however, some of the bailey walls were running into disrepair, and brothels were keeping many fine folks away. They would be here to stay, and he certainly enjoyed taking his cut and fringe benefits.

He extricated himself from the chair and manoeuvred his ample body towards the door, waving goodbye to the buxom cook as he leaned against the frame. He gazed at the impressive grandeur of the mayor's palace over the road and remembered his humble beginnings as a gold dealer. He had, indeed, come a long way.

The mayor now enjoyed all the trappings of luxury and even a place on the King's Council. An anachronistic leftover of simpler times when the city was smaller and the mayor had absolute power.

It started spitting with rain as Penri's gaze lifted to the grey, imperious castle standing proud and high above the city. In times past, he would have made the steep ascent to its gates on foot, but nowadays, he would pay for a small carriage when summoned. Today he was meeting nearer to home.

A long shadow cast over him and blotted out the castle view. The tall shape of General Cymel Marl loomed over the diminutive mayor, and his voice boomed with authority.

"To business, Smolt."

The general always seemed agitated and close to anger whenever he spoke, but his troops held him in high regard. He was known as tough but fair, and he took the stewardship of Tudorfeld's Green Order very seriously.

Cymel ushered the mayor back into the tavern, and they sat face to face. He waited impatiently while Mrs Briwan brought more wine, then leaned forward to say his piece.

"You may know that the council is being assembled," he said as Penri nodded dumbly. "You may not know the reason."

He looked around to ensure the tavern was still empty, and Mrs Briwan was busy behind the bar. Lowering his voice, he pulled closer to continue.

"The Stans are planning an invasion of Tudorfeld, and they have a new weapon."

Penri tried to look shocked but merely seemed bemused. The island kingdom of Stanholm was very distant, and even Tudorfeld felt far away. Being situated in the far south of Grenfold always felt safe, especially behind the city walls.

"Oh, my," he said as if stumbling over a leaf.

The general flushed red and held his hands aloft in disbelief.

"Are you listening, Smolt? That wine you're drinking is from Tudorfeld, and your silk shirt is from Tudorfeld; all the gold in this city came down the Green Road to the city gates. The same road leads from the north shore to the south. The same road will bring a hundred thousand Stans to destroy the crumbling walls and slit your throat as you sleep!"

The mayor held his neck and swallowed a gulp of wine which seemed to stick in his gullet. "Do you think it will come to that?" he said shakily.

"I do. King Ramon is desperate, and desperate men make desperate plans."

"Are we sending the First Legion?"

Cymel leaned back in his chair. Frightening the corpulent mayor was too easy; now it was time to bring him into the plan.

"We are sending no one," he replied in resignation. "The king will not act without a council meeting, and Torl will not assemble the council without the witch."

"Then surely the king will act after the council meet—"

"Pah! You know the witch hates conflict; she'll whisper in his ear, bewitch him with her powers; we'll act too late."

"Lady Moranne *is* very persuasive," the mayor agreed.

"So that's where you can play a part."

"Me?" he said, reeling. Penri Smolt seldom played a meaningful role in anything, including the office of mayor.

"I have a vital role for you."

Penri couldn't know that General Marl had already bolstered the Green Order by cancelling leave and calling up reservists. He was also unaware that Cymel had colluded with Generals Benton and Lenturi to ensure the First Legion and Queen's Battalion were at full strength. It was close to treason; the stakes were high.

As the rain fell on the grey walls of the Friar's Gate Tavern, a casual passerby would see the two men huddled over a small table, talking intently.

"Just great!" moaned Hayden. His blonde hair was soaked, with rivulets of rainwater running down his forehead and seeping into his eyes. The rain began almost as soon as they left Rynham and had followed them relentlessly all day. It wasn't heavy, but the persistent drizzle had rekindled Hayden's whinging demeanour. It didn't help that Moranne's horse, Bess, seemed to dislike him, bucking and nodding as he wrestled with the reigns.

"We should have stayed longer," he continued.

"You know why we left early. If you rode as well as you complained, we'd be in Cynstol by now," laughed Caspin. His cheery tone was constant and seemed to antagonise the squire's son.

They'd tried to keep a low profile while spending the previous day in Rynham, but the eyes of several fell-looking men were on them. Caspin guessed they were other friends of Gelic and the bandits. He decided they would leave for Cynstol in the small hours.

The Caynna terrain was green and lush, with gently rolling hills cut by small streams from the Red and Midtlen Mountains. Many farms and small hamlets dotted the country. Far more than Jem had seen in Burland. The capital seemed to have a light which pulled folk towards it, like a grey stone candle.

"What's the capital like?" asked Jem. He did his best to lift Hayden's spirits, but with little success.

"It's a charming cesspit," laughed Caspin. "We can get you some decent clothes, and we can get Grumpy a hot bath. We can even get you both some unpleasant maladies if you frequent the wrong brothels."

Hayden wrinkled his nose at the thought of visiting any brothels and being described as grumpy.

"What else?" asked Jem, keen to learn as much as possible.

"Well, you'll see high fashion in the aristocracy and dreadful poverty in the Fourth Ward. The castle is impressive, and the royal family are splendid if you meet them. Unfortunately, the politics of Cynstol is the worst part. They think they make a real difference, but when was the last time you felt the reach of Cynstol in Denbry?"

"Nobody in Denbry speaks of the king," said Jem. "In fact, few speak at all." He remembered the stony silence whenever he walked into the village centre or shopped at the market. For a brief moment, he felt the warmth of Mia Tunland's kiss on his cheek, back near the coaching inn. He watched her svelte form running off into the distance and disappear into the drizzle.

"I hear you're leaving us in the capital," said Caspin towards the lagging Hayden.

He looked up and grimaced. "Hmm."

"We're not good enough for him," added Jem.

"Look, clowns. I didn't want to do any of this. My father wants me to be gada to some wealthy earl."

"Plenty of those in the capital."

"Earls?" asked Jem.

"No. Clowns," replied Caspin.

They both laughed heartily, and even Hayden smiled, although he immediately stifled it.

"My father wouldn't care who took me as long as I never returned home," he said. "An overstuffed aristocrat, or married to an ugly heiress. He wouldn't care."

"That's not true," replied Jem. "I'm sure you have friends back home."

Hayden had only one friend in Dunstreet, but every day took him further from that sweet embrace.

General Marl was expecting a full report on Moranne's activities, a deal struck with the squire. Despite being harsh at times, Lady Moranne had been kind to him; she understood him. Cymel Marl would need to find his spies elsewhere.

A gusty wind was starting to whip the rain into their faces, and the sky was darkening behind thick grey clouds. Progress was slow, but it had become glacial as even Caspin's will was tested. Finally, he stopped them near a small farm.

"I think we're done for the day, comrades," he shouted through the wind.

He led them off the road and towards the small croft, where a thin wisp of smoke climbed from the stone chimney of a compact, single-storey round cottage. It reminded Jem of something from a dream. *The Jakari people call him Haldor Ma Kathyr Vizan.*

Sir Caspin rapped on the door; the crofter and his wife soon answered it. Both were dressed in peasant folk's simple attire, and both were relatively young and not long wed.

"Good evening, fine folk," said Caspin, in a manner which instantly endeared him to anyone. "My name is Sir Caspin Linhold of the Green Order, and these are my friends: Master Jem Poulterer and Master Hayden Scirmann of Burland. We're on a journey to the capital and would ask if we could sleep in your barn tonight?"

The farmer's wife blushed at the sight of the dashing Linhold, and the farmer held out his hand.

"Tis an honour to meet a Knight of the Order, sir," he said as they shook hands. "Please come in, come in."

The couple welcomed them into their home and introduced themselves as Nyle and Dena Rowley. They'd been married for a year and inherited the croft from his late father. They both had a similar slim build and appeared to be natives of the area they called Feldseten, a collection of small crofts south of Rynham.

"We beg not to put you to trouble," said Caspin politely.

"Nonsense, sir," replied Nyle, "You'll sleep here as our guests." He gestured proudly to the tiny cottage surrounding them.

"I'm putting a stew on," added Dena, trying hard not to stare at the knight. "There'll be nuff for all."

Hayden was already smiling at the honest hospitality of the humble farmers. It gladdened his heart how people with so little could be so generous.

Rabbit, potatoes, carrots, onions and herbs went into the stew pot and filled the room with the earthy smell of home while the fire warmed their bones and dried their clothes. The cottage was a single, brick-walled room with a wooden, thatched roof and two small windows at the front. The walls were mainly adorned with tools and animal skins, but a little charcoal drawing interested Hayden.

"That's my mother," said Dena.

"It's good. Who's the artist?"

"Oh, just a travelling man."

They settled around the fire and enjoyed the stew with hunks of homemade bread. It reminded Jem of that night in the forest with Boran and Alize. The generosity of strangers.

"How's life in these parts?" asked Sir Caspin.

"We keeps away from Rynham, sir," replied Nyle. "There's thieves and other bad sorts movin' into that place. We don't see many fine city folks like yourselves."

"It's very quiet here," added Dena.

"Aye," said Nyle. "We're off the main path 'ere, but we do alright with the other crofters."

Hayden was busy sketching a portrait of Dena on his last scrap of parchment.

"We're trying for children," she said, smiling, "but no luck so far."

"You're very pretty; your children will be bonny."

She blushed at Hayden's comments as he sketched her round, smiling cheeks.

"Would you want to know if you'll bear children?" he said suddenly, remembering what Moranne had told Jem.

"Yes, of course," she replied, flicking her hair.

Hayden called to Jem, who came over to inspect Hayden's detailed sketch.

"That's really good," he said, putting his hand on Hayden's shoulder.

"Jem has the sight," Hayden told Dena. "He can see your future."

Jem was surprised. He was sure Moranne would counsel against trying to use his gift, as she called it. He'd never managed to control the skill, and the harrowed face of Huw in Supbry still haunted him.

"I'm not sure that's a good—"

"Oh, I'd love to know my fortune," she purred. "Please, Master Jem."

Every instinct told him it was wrong. He couldn't control the gift; it could be a lie. Caspin and Nyle watched as he stared at Dena, weighing up the risks. Maybe it would just come back to him, and he'd see Danya again; how could it hurt?

"Alright," he said, "but it may not work."

He asked Dena to hold out her hands, and he clasped them tightly.

"Empty your mind of everything around you," he said, unsure if it was the right thing to say. "Try to focus on your future here in the cottage."

He closed his eyes, seeing the flicker of the firelight filtered through his lids. There was nothing. He tried to clear his mind of all thoughts, but still, there was nothing. Finally, he cleared his mind once more and decided to focus on the cottage, floating in an invisible sea, sailing into the future. Dena's face appeared in his mind; she smiled and nodded as if spurring him on. The flickering light beams faded, and his mind became dark.

Jem opened his eyes to see the cottage still surrounding him. Hayden and Caspin were gone, but Dena was there with her back to him. Sun was streaming through the windows illuminating the dust which danced in its rays.

Turn around.

Dena turned on the stool to grasp a towel, revealing the tiny human life suckling at her breast. A boy with a tuft of dark hair and his mother's hazel eyes.

"Was that nice, Caspin?" she said, patting his back gently.

Jem felt the baby was staring into his eyes and boring into his soul, but no. The searching gaze stared through him to the weathered wooden door, splintered in places and warped after many winters.

"What can you see, honey?"

Dena followed the baby's gaze and looked at the closed doorway, standing solid against the world. "Who's there?"

The atmosphere was changing, the light dimmed, and the air became thick and acrid.

"Who's there?" she asked more urgently.

She held the baby closer and stood, backing away from the entrance.

"Please, who is it?"

A faint sound began. A distant thumping, getting closer and more urgent. It sounded like footfall, a heavy, running, pounding footfall coming nearer. Dena backed further from the door until she leaned against the far wall. She listened to the drumming sound as if it were in her head. It was coming still nearer; it was outside, at the threshold.

The door burst open, crashing against the wall and straining on its hinges. Nyle stood in the light. He was sweating, gasping for breath, and a bead of blood ran down his face.

"Dena, we need to go. Now!"

"Go where?" she said, clutching the young Caspin tightly.

"Just go!"

He turned to check outside, but something flashed behind the door, and he fell back against the door frame. His hand went to his throat, but nothing would stem the blood spilling from a wide gash.

Dena screamed and ran forward, but a dark shape appeared, standing above her husband's lifeless body. The figure wore dark silk robes, and a red scarf hung about his bare, dark chest. He was holding a curved blade dripping with Nyle's blood.

He looked Dena up and down, then walked casually into the cottage. Jem held up his hand, but the man walked through him. The screams told Jem the story he feared.

"Jem. What do you see?" said Hayden.

"See?" mumbled Jem. His eyes gradually adjusted to the firelight and focused once more on the friends surrounding him.

Dena was smiling, and Nyle's hand was on his shoulder. He looked at them both and wanted to hug them.

"Did you see, Master Jem?" added Dena, still holding his hands.

She'd seen nothing. Jem grasped for the right words; his mind still saw the dead body of crofter Nyle.

"I saw." He grasped her hands tightly and gazed into her questioning eyes. "You'll have a son. Soon."

Caspin watched Jem sink onto a stool with his head in his hands as Dena and Nyle embraced above him. He remained silent for the rest of the night while the others kept good company around him.

Moranne called it a "possible future." Could it be changed?

13 A SINGLE WOMAN

Running up and down two hundred and thirty-nine steps to Sir Torl Radborough's office kept Gada Tino Crayber fit. He stopped on the eleventh floor of the Lyften Tower and leaned against the door to catch his breath.

"Come!" boomed Sir Torl from within.

Tino stumbled into the chamber, still gasping, and came to a wobbling standstill opposite his master's desk.

"She's here, sir, at the North Gate," he said, stammering.

"Show her to the library and see she is comfortable. I'll be there directly."

"Yes, sir."

Gada Crayber turned on his heels, raced out of the office and galloped down the stairs to find the butler.

Torl pulled the velvet curtain from the small window near the door and looked down at the shining city below. It was too dark to identify any people, but somewhere beneath him, a solitary rider dressed in black was making the slow ascent up Castle Street to the castle above.

In a different life, my dear, he thought, catching the reflection of his wise elderly face in the window.

⁂

"Caspin," whispered Jem. He was trying to wake the young warrior without disturbing the others. The night had brought little sleep as images from the previous evening haunted every moment.

Eyes blinked open beneath the long dark hair and spied Jem with a finger held to his lips. Caspin was puzzled, but he remembered how Jem had withdrawn after reading Dena.

"Come outside," said Jem, as Caspin sleepily got to his feet.

They carefully manoeuvred around Hayden's snoozing body and slipped out the door into the fresh morning air. It was cold and damp, with yesterday's rain hanging over the land as a fine mist.

"What troubles you, my friend?" asked Caspin, rubbing the sleep from his eyes.

Jem looked back towards the cottage, struggling to find the words which captured the horror.

"I saw their future last night."

"Yes, she'll bear a child." Caspin was unsure why they were shivering in the half-light.

The thinnest smile creased Jem's face as he remembered seeing the baby. "Do you know she calls the child Caspin?"

"Really?"

Jem didn't want to utter the words as if saying them would manifest the carnage. His eyes moistened with the burden.

"They ..." The tears fell, adding to the saturated air. "They ..." He needed Moranne; he needed her guidance.

"What is it?"

"They all die." Jem's body convulsed with the pain.

Caspin wrapped his arms around his new friend. He knew it was true. He'd seen enough strange things in the land to recognize the truth. "At whose hand?" he asked calmly.

Jem was reluctant to name the race of his kin, the mother of Alize and Danya's people, but he saw it with his own eyes. No wish could mask the fact.

"The Jakaris."

Caspin grasped Jem by the shoulders and stared into his eyes, nodding. "We need to go."

They returned to the cottage to find the others were awake, and Dena was preparing toast for breakfast; she smiled as they walked in. The handsome knight and the seer who'd confirmed their dreams. Caspin wasted no time; he knew the words which must be spoken.

"All of you, please listen," he said, using the authority of his rank. It was the first glimpse of a man who could lead fifty warriors into battle. "We all need to leave as soon as possible. Master Jem saw something else last night, something serious he dared not share."

"What is it?" asked Hayden.

"War is coming," replied Caspin. He looked at the crofters with care in his heart. "It's true you'll be blessed with a son, but if you stay here, you'll all die."

"My love!" cried Dena. She embraced her husband and looked in horror at Caspin. "Where will we go?"

"We can't take you with us, but you must pack and leave today. Go to Cynstol and make for the quay, where you'll find a man named Keel Briman. Give him one of these." Caspin held out his hand, containing two shining gold coins. "He'll take you to Inseld, where you can find work with the fishermen. Don't return until the war is over."

Jem looked down, fearing that he'd brought trouble into the farmer's lives, but their reaction softened his heart. Dena flung her arms about him, and Nyle waited to shake his hand.

"Thank you, thank you," he said, gripping Jem's hand tightly.

"Get word to the other crofters," said Caspin, while Dena hugged him tightly.

"I hope you don't mind," she told him. "I'm naming my son after you."

Caspin cocked an eye and looked over at Jem, still buried in his thoughts.

After a hearty breakfast of hot buttered toast, they said their fond farewells and reluctantly departed the friendly cottage.

Dena watched as they disappeared over the hill, following the road west to Cynstol. She looked down at the crumpled parchment bearing her charcoal portrait. It showed her smiling in the firelight as she enjoyed Sir Caspin's company. "For your son," Hayden had told her.

The City Gate guards recognised the hooded figure, drenched in the late summer rain. They watched the exhausted horse plod mournfully past their station and the rider too tired to acknowledge them.

It was a steep, winding climb to the castle and she was too exhausted to take it. Dropping to the cobbles of Castle Street, she handed the reins to a stable boy and transferred, wordlessly, into a waiting carriage.

The rain was still falling, and it was getting late; few saw the small carriage pass as it trundled slowly up the main street of Cynstol. Moranne had seen the shops, taverns, inns and homes on many occasions and frequented all at some time. She would visit five or six times yearly, playing her part on the King's Council.

They rounded Tower Corner, where a tall watchtower sprang up on the left amidst the businesses and homes of the lesser dignitaries. The grey castle walls loomed up ahead. At fifteen-foot thick, they had never been breached, and an assault from the southern ocean was impossible. Precarious cliffs plunged vertically from the castle to the crashing waves below.

If Jem's visions were real, Cynstol could fall without losing a single brick or splintering a single door. There was little time to spare.

Two vast towers were built on either side of the mighty gates. Archers stood vigilant between the battlements, but they'd be little use against the foe Moranne knew so well. The gate was an unusual construction which rose slowly as a single structure through an ingenious design of cables, pulleys and wooden cogs. A large circular lawn filled the middle of the courtyard with a weathered statue of King Dane-Ale Donhalf at its centre. Moranne always gazed at the monument as she passed. It was a good likeness.

The carriage pulled up outside the doors of the imposing keep, which opened as she stepped out onto the cold flagstones. Several attendants were rushing down the steps led by a tall, grey-haired man with a large bald patch.

He wore a long jacket fastened with shining silver buttons and a silver brooch in the shape of a double-headed eagle.

"Lady Moranne, welcome once more to the seat of the king," he said, bowing low. "Your usual room is prepared, and I've taken the liberty of ordering you a bath."

"Thank you so much, Byrell, but I must speak to Torl immediately," she replied.

Edlin Byrell had been a servant of the royal house since he'd begun as a stable boy at just twelve. Moranne knew him very well and often used his first name when they were not in company.

"I had expected as such, my lady. Sir Radborough is waiting for you in the library. Refreshments will be sent as soon as possible."

Moranne smiled for the first time since leaving Rynham. "It's worth coming back here for some things. Thank you, Byrell."

He smiled in return and led her through the doors and into the hall of the keep. A sizeable marble-floored atrium was lined with artworks and sculptures depicting previous kings and historical events. All were lit by flickering oil lamps, giving the room a warm, inviting feel.

The most impressive feature was the sweeping marble staircase ascending to a small landing. This continued both left and right to a mezzanine forming the second floor. It was an excellent place to watch people come and go in the hall below.

Moranne drank in the familiar site while Byrell led her along the walkway towards the front of the building. He pushed the carved double doors open and stepped inside.

"Lady Moranne, sir," he announced.

The library was a long, cavernous room which spanned almost the width of the keep. Walls were lined floor to ceiling with colourful, bound books, and statues sprang from plinths dotted around the room. Three tall, stained-glass windows showed vivid depictions of tales from the scriptures, but tonight's darkness rendered them dim.

Several ornately-carved tables with chairs lined the centre of the library. In contrast, sumptuous upholstered chairs and sofas were arranged at either end, in front of the flames of flickering fires.

Moranne recognised the tall, grey-haired frame sitting before the fire and the swirl of his crimson robes as he rose to greet her.

"My lady, it's so good to see you again," said Sir Torl Radborough, in his rich, booming voice.

They hugged before she collapsed onto the soft sofa, chilled and soaked.

"You really should get some rest," he continued. "You look exhausted, my friend."

He poured them both a small glass of wine from a decanter by the sofa, and she took a sip of the soothing liquid.

"Have you arranged a council meeting?" she said, getting straight to business as usual.

"Tino is currently delivering messages to all the members. We'll meet at nine tomorrow morning."

"No, Torl! It must be now!" She was agitated and would have been pacing the room if she hadn't been so tired.

"Moranne, I love you dearly, but you must know that our best chance at the council is with clear heads. They would not agree to meet this late anyway. Please tell me your concerns so I may prepare for the meeting."

He was right, and she knew it. A snide remark from General Marl or Bishop Nesslor could quickly move her to fatigued anger, which would be counterproductive. She looked up at the swirling, patterned tapestry hung above the fireplace, pillaged from a Jakari home in other dangerous times.

Torl knew her history, one of very few souls who did, which is why he would see the truth when she uttered words not heard for almost five hundred years.

"Corvus has returned to full strength," she said, watching as the name triggered fear in Torl's eyes. "He has a sceptre."

As if in slow motion, the gleaming crystal glass slipped gently from his hand and tumbled gracefully towards the floor. The smooth marble floor flickered with the reflection as it fell. When it finally connected with the polished surface, it smashed into a thousand pieces, sending crystal shards across the room. A large spray of red wine reached across the floor and ran down tiny grooves in the stone towards Sir Torl's polished shoes.

14 THE KING'S COUNCIL

The sole woman on the King's Council needed no wake-up call to rise early; it was a habit long-held. She stood naked in front of the tall window and looked out over the Grey Sea to watch waves crashing against the cliffs below.

There was barely an inch of her flesh which wasn't scarred or pock-marked from a life in the wilderness. Each wound told a story, many she tried hard to forget.

The Lyften Tower had fifteen floors and stood as the tallest human-made structure in the known world. Each level had two rooms, except for the top, which contained one large round chamber opening onto a covered walkway circling the tower.

The Princess Femla Room was named after the daughter of King Tyborg I, who had ruled over two hundred years before. It was decorated with blue velvet curtains and a matching four-poster bed. The ninth-floor room had been Moranne's private retreat since joining the council many years ago.

She opened the large oak wardrobe and inspected the stash of clothes, always kept at the castle for her. She thumbed through the rack, checking the mostly dark-coloured garments. She needed to be taken very seriously today.

She picked out a short sky-blue dress and partnered it with brown linen leggings, a thin leather jacket fastened with leather laces, and knee-length leather boots. The outfit was pure alviri; it would cause a stir at court. She gazed into the full-length mirror and smiled at her audacity.

"A pox on you all," she said, turning to inspect the look.

Byrell personally delivered breakfast that morning and waited patiently to remove the tray after she'd enjoyed the hot buttered toast and sweet jasmine tea.

The council meeting was an hour away, so she sat for a while, looking out at the waves, cresting with white foam as the seagulls swept over the surface on the breeze. She felt the sceptre's hard metal through her shirt; every outfit included a hidden pocket for the strange artefact.

It felt as if time had become her enemy. Jem's news was moving things on too quickly, but his training had barely begun. He couldn't control his gift, which could ruin everything and place them all in great danger. She hoped the council would see sense.

"Time to go," she said to herself, striding out of the door and down the steep, winding staircase.

King Mylos Lenturi had built both the Lyften Tower and the entire east wing of the castle after he acceded to the throne. The Lenturi family reigned for over one hundred and fifty years; many of their descendants still held positions of power to this day.

Moranne admired the portraits which lined the walls of the east wing. All struck magisterial poses except for the last, which depicted a tall dark warrior holding a massive broadsword and cradling a battered helm. Dane believed in leading from the front.

"Good morning, my lady." Torl greeted Moranne in his rich baritone voice. He was already in the council chamber and seated at the head of the table. "You are looking refreshed and radiant, my friend."

The council chamber was dominated by a large oval table surrounded by eight ornately-carved chairs. The table was inset with exquisitely detailed marquetry outlining a map of Grenfold, Stanholm, Alfheim and Brencan. Torl sat at the Alfheim end, but the island was obscured by a large, closed, leather-bound book with crumpled and yellowing pages.

"Do try not to antagonise General Marl, my dear," continued Torl, with his elbows on the book. The two had a long history of arguments, caused chiefly by Cymel's hawkish tendencies.

"I'll be good as gold," she replied, taking a seat at the opposite end of the table. A large window directly behind cast her as a menacing silhouette.

"Some bedtime reading?" she asked, referring to the crumbling tome.

Torl simply smiled as High Bishop Namen Nesslor entered the room and took his traditional seat to the chief advisor's left. He nodded politely at Torl but avoided looking at Moranne. The Pillars of Freanism were often interpreted as banning women from meaningful work. "*Man shall provide for his family*" did not refer to women.

The Frean clergy wore plain, dark green robes, but Namen's attire was shining velvet, decorated with scrolls of gold on the arms that ran down the breast to a gold belt. He was tall, slim, and clean-shaven, with narrow blue eyes and short grey hair. Moranne hated his position on the council. He often derailed serious discussions with passages of mostly irrelevant scripture and never addressed her directly.

Next to arrive was the wheezing mayor. The three flights of stairs from the Great Hall left him breathless despite using a carriage to bring him from the mayoral palace. He nodded politely towards the assembled members and took a seat to the right of Moranne. His membership of the council seemed primarily symbolic. He played little part in the discussions other than nodding in agreement and making strained noises every time he moved in his seat.

Gada Tino Crayber hurried into the room with a jug of wine and poured a goblet for each seat. He almost ran into the broad torso of General Rune Benton as he left the chamber.

"Good morning," said the general in his soft, well-spoken lilt.

He was a diminutive man to wield so much power, but his bald head and small sharp beard gave him a stern but wizened appearance. The leather battle fatigues and gold-encrusted breastplate depicting the double-headed eagle, showed his stature as commander of the First Legion. A fighting force with the large Cynstol Barracks, dedicated to defending the city.

General Benton sat to Torl's right; he nodded and smiled at Moranne. On most occasions, he would be the sole military member of the council. The Queen's Battalion and the Green Order were too far north. Unfortunately, General Marl was in the city.

The Green Order commander barged into the room, crashing the door against the wall with a crack. Subtle entrances were not his forté and nor were manners. He took his place next to General Benton, acknowledging no one but his First Legion friend. He managed a brief scowl aimed at Moranne, who smiled back with her mouth alone. The council was complete but for one last member. They all stood and bowed their heads.

Prince Jarl's entrance was as slow and nonchalant as a petulant child forced to leave a favourite toy. As the eldest of the three royal heirs, the king insisted he take his place on the council, but Prince Jarl Fierdman had no interest in state affairs. At twenty-six years old, his handsome, clean-shaven, blue-eyed looks made him the darling of every royal ball, and he enjoyed the high life at all the stately homes in Caynna.

Shuffling behind the prince was the ever-present advisor known by most as Murmur. His real name was Sir Saul Runian, the descendent of a mighty Middcroft family. He was exclusively Price Jarl's advisor and seldom spoke to anyone else. His short, thin frame allowed him to disappear behind the dashing prince, but he was an ever-present whispering menace. When the prince took his seat between the bishop and the mayor, the snide advisor positioned his chair just behind the prince.

Moranne glared at him.

"Welcome all," began Sir Radborough, as the members were seated. "We are gathered here to review some disturbing news from the kingdom of Stanholm."

"We need to deploy now. We're wasting time!" blustered the impatient General Marl, aiming his comments squarely at the prince.

Torl ignored him and continued. "Word from our spy confirms that King Ramon is assembling troops in Gulward and that the Stans have discovered some kind of new weapon."

"*New weapon!*" mocked Cymel. "I can have a hundred ships ready to take Gulward inside a month."

"And I'm ready to send reinforcements from the legion," added General Benton.

Rune and Cymel had obviously been collaborating on a plan before the meeting and seemed to expect instant approval.

"How many men would be on those ships, General?" asked Moranne.

Cymel Marl grudgingly answered while staring into the table's map. "Eight thousand in the first wave."

"And what would you say to the families of the eight thousand dead soldiers?"

"How dare you!" he snapped, with anger furrowing his brow. "My men are brave, and they will endure."

"They have Frea on their side," added the bishop unhelpfully.

"You forget the weapon," said Torl, while Saul whispered something to the king's heir.

"So what is this weapon I hear of?" asked the prince. "A sword, maybe, or a spear?"

"A sceptre," said Moranne. "One of the five."

Cymel was laughing loudly, and Rune joined him. Even Penri and Namen were smirking at the woman in their midst.

"So a monarch's bauble is the Stans' great weapon?" teased Cymel.

"General, you know of the earth power some can wield," said Torl, trying to keep the meeting civil. He saw Moranne fidgeting in her seat and grasping something under her tunic.

"I know a tall tale when I hear it," chimed Rune on cue.

"Then know this!" shouted Moranne.

She whipped the sceptre from its secret pocket and brought it down firmly on the table. The spherical gem burst into a pulsing green light; it pulsed in time with a similar light shining in her eyes.

The men all pulled back in their seats, and Torl was horrified. *Be careful, my dear.*

"What witchcraft is this?" cried Bishop Nessler.

She stared directly at General Marl, her emerald green eyes fixing him as if in the sights of an archer.

"*This* is earth power, Frea's will, or whatever you choose to call it. I am one of very few who can wield this power. The man who now holds the fifth sceptre can ignite a thousand times the power I can. He will kill all of your forces, and then he will kill all of you."

"Impossible!" said Rune, gazing into the blazing orb before him.

"What do we do?" added Penri. He looked genuinely frightened.

Cymel was shaking his head and chuckling to himself. "Alright, *earth power wielder*, how do we beat this *man*?" His voice was dripping with vitriol, and he noticed the prince was amused.

Torl held a hand up to Moranne, willing her to moderate any response. The light in her sceptre faded, and she carefully returned it to the pocket inside her tunic.

She waited until the chuckling subsided, and all eyes were on her. Even Namen was looking towards the window behind.

"There are five sceptres, and the locations of three of them are unknown. Some idiot on Stanholm found one, and unfortunately, they knew what it was." The locations of some sceptres *were* known to Moranne, but she didn't share *all* her secrets.

"This is heresy!" Namen protested.

Moranne ignored him. "The Stans took the sceptre to the most powerful of us all, on Brencan."

General Marl shook his head once more. "There's nothing on the sunken isle; it's a death trap."

"This man now has the sceptre, and his power is returning to full strength."

"So?" prodded Rune.

"At full strength, he has three powers. He can locate any of us when we use earth power, and he can control any beast at any distance."

"And the third?" asked Torl helpfully.

Moranne remembered Aludra. The look on her face would haunt her forever.

"He has the power to control human men, to bend them to his will and force them to do his bidding."

"Rubbish!" shouted Cymel. "Must we listen to these lies?"

She ignored them all. They needed to know everything. "I don't know the exact number, but he can probably control between a hundred and five hundred men over fifty miles or so."

"No man has such power," protested the bishop. "The woman should be censured."

"His name is Corvus," she said flatly, ignoring Namen's insults.

"So how do we kill this, *Corvus*?" Rune repeated Cymel's words with further incredulity.

Now it was Moranne's turn to shake her head. *They would not like the truth.*

"You're not listening," she said. "Corvus can control any human *man*."

The copper hadn't dropped; they looked at each other, shaking heads and laughing in confusion. The bishop was first to make the connection and rose to his feet in consternation.

"That *is* heresy. The woman raves!"

"Please sit," said Torl.

"She's a witch; she defiles this room with lies!"

"I don't understand," said Penri.

The prince laughed as he leaned back in his chair and placed his feet on the table. "Women," he said, slapping his thigh in amusement. "Only women are immune to his power."

Moranne was nodding. "Along with the alviri and other fair creatures," she added.

"Manure!" shouted Cymel.

The table erupted into shouting from the bishop and much hysterical laughing from Cymel, Rune and even Prince Jarl. Namen was still on his feet and demanding to make an official complaint about Moranne. Mayor Smolt simply stared in bemusement.

Moranne remained seated, her eyes fixed on Torl while he stared down at the thick book in front of him. Arguing and laughter echoed through the castle halls, causing passing servants to stop and listen. Saul Runian furtively whispered into the prince's ear, but Jarl was far too entertained by the undisciplined rabble.

The room was silenced by the sudden sound of a heavy, dead weight hitting the table. The noise reverberated around the room, bouncing off the walls and reflecting from the window. All eyes were on the head of the table. A cloud of dust rose about Sir Radborough from the ancient parchment pages of the open book. Brushing the debris aside and holding down the creased leaves, he read aloud.

> *Striding as a colossus across sea and land,*
> *Jhakri smote every man with the power in his hand.*
> *They bowed their helms and held swords aloft,*
> *Until the command to kill, he gave.*
> *Man ended man, man ended woman, and man butchered child.*
> *From screams to lifeless bodies that saw no grave.*
> *Only Frea's daughters and faerie folk could stand against his will.*
> *They took his power and stayed his hand.*
> *He endures, still.*

Quiet remained as they all pictured this unstoppable force killing all in its path.

Moranne looked down into the table at the land of Salamas marked in the wood of different hues. The screams still echoed off the castle walls. The sound of steel on bone, the beat of boots on ground and the thud of bodies meeting earth. *They must understand,* she thought.

"What heretic penned this nonsense?" howled Bishop Nesslor, throwing an accusatory look toward Moranne.

They all hung on Torl's answer. "These are the annals of King Mylos Lenturi, penned in his hand." He waited for the men to absorb his words. "There are three other books in the king's library which mention this man. Two refer to him as Jhakri, while one calls him Bregu. The alviri have many tales that refer to this man."

Even Cymel seemed to be listening now.

"Corvus was responsible for the sacking of Grenborg, the destruction of the alviri village of Vindus and most importantly, the death of King Dane-Ale Donhalf at the battle of Crossing Fields."

"Frea, save us," whispered Rune under his breath.

"He *can* be killed, but only women and the alviri are immune to his controlling powers."

"You know the army has no women. There's no time to train them even if we could," grunted Cymel. The military planner in him was starting to take over, and he was frantically looking for answers.

"We need the Cempestre," answered Moranne, "and we need to ask the alviri for help."

"Who?" asked the prince.

"The Cempestre are a female warrior clan living in Deapholt," replied General Benton. "They have little to do with us."

"The alviri will never help us," added Cymel. "They hate humans."

In reality, most hate flowed from humans to the alviri, but Moranne wasn't going to start an argument with General Marl. "Maybe," she said. "We must try; we have few other options."

"And what about the Stans?" chimed Penri. He was finally beginning to grasp the situation.

Moranne stood for the first time while the midmorning sun shone through the tall panelled window and cast a long shadow over the table.

"I have a plan."

15 DARIAN FLYN

"It keeps getting larger, but we're still not there," complained Hayden.

Jem spotted the gleaming Lyften Tower before midday. After three more hours of travel, they entered the Fourth Ward. Not officially part of Cynstol, the ward comprised an extensive collection of small villages. These blended into one, outside the wooden barbican of the Third Ward.

Only Caspin was familiar with the poverty and squalor of the area. Dwellings were rough wooden shacks, thrown up tightly with a spider's web of alleyways connecting the districts. The roads were poor, potholed and streaked with deep furrows filled with mud and refuse. Two dogs ran in front of the horses and then bolted down one of the lanes.

"Why are so many people here?" asked Jem.

"It's a problem with big cities," said Caspin. "They come to find work and fortune. Unfortunately, they found the Fourth Ward."

"Someone should tell them," added Hayden.

"Oh, they try, but there are bandits in the wilds and strange creatures in the forests. Working the land is hard; many come seeking a better life."

They picked their way through the shanty towns filled with the unpleasant odour of open sewers and enticing smells of street cooking. It was an assault on the senses, and Jem was glad he didn't live here.

The castle dominated the skyline, sitting on a tall hill at the mouth of the River Rudun, which snaked from the Red Mountains in the west. The river couldn't be seen from most of Cynstol, but two bridges gave access to the rich pastures. One wooden bridge in the Fourth Ward and a much larger, three-span stone construction outside the Second Ward.

Barbican walls with numerous watchtowers separated each of the six city wards. These were wooden stockades in the outer wards and stone construction for the others. The city guard patrolled gates between the wards, and access was strictly controlled. Without Caspin, they would have needed a signed authorisation to travel.

The guards waved them through every gate as most men seemed to recognise the knight. Many were on first-name terms and exchanged jokes and anecdotes about the First Legion and life in the city. The streets became busier as they cleared each gate until they eventually saw a sea of bodies stretching up to the City Gate into the First Ward.

"This place is ridiculous," said Hayden, trying to prevent the bucking Bess from treading on any city dwellers.

They stabled the horses at the First Legion barracks and continued on foot through the City Gate.

"If you have any money, hold onto your purse," advised Caspin.

The broad Castle Street curved around to the right and stretched upwards at a steep angle. Every step was filled with shops, taverns, and businesses of all kinds, while street entertainers drew crowds to shows of juggling and conjuring. People shouted and jostled, crisscrossing the street to disappear into alleys or emerge from shops carrying new clothes or precious jewels.

Turning right to follow the cobbled main street to the castle, they discovered the reason for the large crowds. It appeared to be market day in Cynstol as the square outside the seat of power was full of colourful makeshift market stalls. There were exotic silks from Tudorfeld and plush hats from Cwen. Sparkling artisan jewellery and wooden toys for the children of the rich.

Hayden was drawn to the brightly coloured clothes and ran his hands through the fine silks while the store holders tried to entice him with special offers and discounts for the "young nobleman."

Even Jem was enthralled. It was unlike the humble market days in Denbry, where cheese and aged ham would be displayed. He scanned the stalls and noticed a bustling stand selling silk shirts and blouses. As he looked along the hanging garments, he saw the tradeswoman was staring at him. Her eyes were narrowed as if she was studying his features or trying to discern something about him.

She was middle-aged in appearance and had long blonde hair draped down the front of the aqua silk blouse she was modelling. Her blue eyes looked kind, and Jem felt for a moment that he should know her. Something about her was familiar.

"Darian?" she shouted suddenly.

Jem turned around, but no one acknowledged her call. She seemed to be calling him.

"Darian Flyn, is that you?" she continued, slowly coming from behind the stall and walking towards him.

Hayden was busy looking through a jewellery stall, but Caspin had noticed the approaching woman. He knew of the many thieves, chancers and tricksters who thrived in the city. "You're mistaken," he said.

"I'd know that face anywhere," she said. "You look the same; you haven't changed." She began to smile, remembering some past times.

"I'm sorry," said Jem. "I don't think we've met."

"It's me, Yuna!" she cried. "Yuna Lufest. I never married. You must remember Arlo?"

Jem blinked, shaking his head. In some strange way, he wanted to know her, but he had no recollection.

"I've never been to Arlo. I'm sorry, you have the wrong man."

Her face immediately dropped, and her eyes glistened. She looked down and clasped her hands in nervousness.

"I'm sorry, Master. Please forgive me."

She looked into his eyes once more, then turned abruptly and hurried back to her stall.

"What's going on?" asked Hayden, returning from his browsing.

"I don't know," replied Jem. The woman, Yuna, seemed so sure.

Caspin marshalled them together, and they proceeded to the castle gates, but Jem was still thinking about the market trader. He didn't notice she was still staring after him as the party entered the castle and the rolling gate closed behind them.

It had been a tough day working out the details, but both Generals Marl and Benton seemed to be on board. It was hard to be sure, as Cymel often had a personal agenda, but for now, they agreed. Along with Moranne and Torl, they had remained in the council chamber, poring over the map and discussing the logistics of a plan they hoped to put before the king. She was surprised at the collaborative tone of the two military men, which worried her.

After a cold lunch, served in one of the smaller dining rooms, Moranne climbed the tower to seek out Torl in his office.

"Come!" he boomed when she tapped gently on his door.

She entered the familiar room and draped herself over a crimson chaise beside his desk.

"That's very distracting," he said, watching her smile with mock ardour.

"You have a great room," she replied. "It's so much bigger than mine."

He leaned back in his padded velvet chair, with golden painted wood and intricate scrollwork.

"They say size isn't everything."

"What do they know," she laughed.

"I sense you're feeling pleased with this morning's resolution."

"Of course," she said, playing with her hair. "When can we see the king?"

Torl shuffled uneasily in his seat. She wasn't going to like the answer.

"Tomorrow morning."

"Tomorrow?" Moranne shot to her feet. "Did you convey the urgency?"

"I did, my lady."

"Are you sure?" she shouted.

Torl nodded wearily. Threats to the kingdom usually came from the north and were dealt with by the Green Order. The king was disinterested in conflicts and wars, preferring to enjoy the castle's luxuries.

"I'm afraid there's something else, my lady." The king had been particular; there was no way to sweeten the porridge.

"Yes?"

"You are invited to attend a ball tonight in honour of the king's guests, Earls Normin Linhold and Jonas Renshaw."

"Me?" she laughed. "Attend a ball? Have you been drinking poteen?"

He joined her in laughter at the thought of her attending any formal function.

"I'll be no one's arm ornament!" she bellowed. I'm not going."

"I'm sorry, my lady, but the king was precise. It will ease tomorrow's audience."

She knew he was right. King Pythar loved all the pomp and ceremony which came with his position, and he'd been trying to get Moranne to attend for many years. He'd seen his chance and struck.

"Well, If I'm going, you're taking me."

"I have not been invited—"

"I don't care. I'm not suffering this alone."

A familiar knock at the door saved Torl from further difficult discussions. "Come, Tino," said Torl, reverting to his formal, deep voice.

The young gada bounded into the room and stopped in his usual place in front of Sir Radborough's desk.

"Begging your pardon, sir," he stuttered.

"What is it?"

"Sir Caspin Linhold of the Green Order is in the hall asking for Lady Moranne, and he has two men with him who claim to be her companions."

Moranne left her old friend studying maps and logistic lists to follow Tino down to the mezzanine. Guards were posted at the double doors to the blue room, one of several reception rooms close to the library. It was a castle practice to guard any unknown visitors until a lord or lady could vouch for them.

The guards stood aside, and Tino pushed open the door revealing a glamorous room decorated with teal drapes and bright white plaster statues. The floor was a rich dark oak, and several teal upholstered chairs and sofas were arranged at the centre, containing some familiar figures.

"My lady!" exclaimed Jem, getting to his feet.

"As promised, my lady," said Caspin. "Delivered intact."

"You three look like you could use a bath," she said, smiling.

She sat with them for a while, and they discussed the journey and the incident at the croft. Moranne's expression changed at the mention of Jem's vision and the Jakari he'd seen. There was no point in hiding the truth from the lad.

"I believe there is a unique man behind these visions," she said. "A man you've seen in your dreams."

"Who?" said Jem.

"His name is Corvus. He's very powerful and very dangerous."

"What do you need from us?" asked Hayden.

"Well, Master Scirmann, you're staying here where Torl will find you a sponsor, and I will meet with the king tomorrow."

Hayden seemed deflated. He enjoyed the company of Jem and the gregarious Caspin. Although he wasn't brave, it seemed too early for the adventure to end.

"Byrell, the butler, will be helping the pair of you to find clothes suitable for a royal ball. I have some business in the city."

Caspin nodded and walked off to find the butler.

"A ball!" exclaimed Hayden. Maybe the castle wasn't so bad after all.

"Byrell will arrange rooms and food for you; I will see you both later. Try not to embarrass me," she said with a wink, then turned and walked briskly out of the room.

"I've never been to a ball," muttered Jem. He'd missed out on many social events as Denbry's resident pariah.

"You'll love it," gushed Hayden. "Can you dance?"

Jem stared at him. He was tired, hungry and haunted by the image of crofter Nyle Rowley being struck down in cold blood. *I'm not sure I feel like dancing,* he thought.

The light was beginning to fade, and a chilly wind was blowing in from the south when Yuna finally caught sight of the simple shack she called home. The cart, which doubled as her market stall, was only just wide enough to carry both her and her friend Billick. She paid him a copper a day to tow her livelihood to different spots in the city.

He unshackled the horse and helped her to push the cart back into the narrow shed beside her home. Trading had been brisk today, but she still couldn't afford a horse or a better home.

"Goodnight, Bill," she said and watched as Billick led the horse away, deeper into the Fourth Ward.

Tomorrow would be a repeat of today, as would every day until she could meet a kind man who would marry an old maid. Some women would settle for any man to act as protector and provider, but for Yuna, there was no compromise.

The battered wooden door opened with a creak to reveal a single room which contained her bed, a wooden chair, a low table and a small fireplace. She immediately lit a candle as the only windows were unglazed and shuttered.

The fire was soon crackling, providing a rich, warm hue to the simple abode. It was never meant to be a permanent home, just a short stop while she searched for her lover, but now the walls seemed to press inwards, and she loathed it.

She looked down at her cold, worn hands and remembered the young man who looked so much like Darian. In one instant, her heart had raced with hope, but in the next, it was crushed.

Yuna sat on her bed and gazed into the leaping flames while she cried.

There was a firm knock at the door, which sent the loose wood rattling against the frame.

She quickly wiped away the tears and ran her fingers through the tangled knots of her hair. It was probably just Billick or one of her neighbours asking for a favour. She brushed the day's dust from her long beige skirt and opened the door.

Her eyes opened widely at the sight of the tall, dark-haired woman before her, wearing an outlandish short skirt and exotic boots. Unsure how to react, she curtsied low and bowed her head.

"Lady Moranne!" she gasped.

The king's advisor smiled and placed a hand on her shoulder.

"Please," she said, offering her hand to help Yuna to her feet.

"Come in, come in," said Yuna. She held the door open and quickly ran around the hut, tidying things away and moving the chair near the fire.

Lady Moranne sat in the only chair and gestured for Yuna to sit on the bed. She did as instructed and sat fidgeting, unsure where to put her hands or how to address her ladyship.

"It's been a long time, Yuna," said Moranne, smiling broadly.

"You remember me?"

"Of course."

Yuna often remembered the long summers in Arlo and how Lady Moranne would hold court in the village square, telling tall tales to the children. They were the happiest days of her life.

"What can I do for you, my lady, ma'am?" she stuttered.

Lady Moranne removed a small velvet purse from a hidden pocket in her dress and emptied the contents into her hand. Five gold coins chinked together and sparkled in the firelight.

"I have a gift for you," she said, holding out her hand.

Yuna was puzzled. She hadn't seen the imposing woman for twenty years, and now she was offering money.

"I don't understand."

"You deserve a better life," replied Moranne, nodding. "I've made too many mistakes, and I need to make sure you live a happy life."

Yuna was shaking her head, still unable to comprehend.

"Buy a passage to Inseld where you'll have enough money to purchase a good home and live a good life."

"But—"

She didn't get a chance to finish. Lady Moranne held a silver metal stick with a green, pulsing gem; it lit the room with a strange glow, competing with the firelight. Her eyes burned with the same hue as she stared into Yuna's blue-eyed gaze.

The room pulsated with swirling light for several minutes while Yuna stared into those emerald green eyes. She couldn't move or speak.

Images were tumbling through her mind. She saw Darian standing on a cliff, high above the rushing water of the River Dorbourne. He smiled as she approached. They were relaxing together in a barn, their bare skin glistening in the light as they looked up into the rafters. He stood a few feet away this time, looking over her stall at the market. It *was* him!

She tried to grab the images and hold on tight, but as each vision passed, it evaporated in a blinding white light. Darian's features melted away, and even his name slipped from her consciousness. Finally, all the painful history ebbed away like a thawing frost until it was gone.

The light extinguished, and Moranne placed the gold coins on the table. "Remember my words," she said and departed, leaving Yuna to marvel at the shining money.

Yuna Lufest tried to remember, but all she could think of was the island of Inseld.

16 THE BALL

The castle servants' quarters were accessed through a winding staircase in one of the keep's four towers. The basement level contained few windows, but Jem's room was on the seaward side and had two small portals cut into the rock. The room was small but cosy and far superior to his mezzanine back in Denbry.

He sat in a deep, warm, iron bath, carefully shaving the road stubble in a mirror propped on a small table. A pretty maid named Tilly would bustle in and out with orders to "shave" or "clean your ears", all said in a no-nonsense tone. Jem initially protested when she'd ordered him to strip, but she told him she'd "seen it all before" - although he did catch her looking when he descended into the bath.

Denbry was two hundred miles away but felt like a million. He thought about Boran and Alize in the forest and the Rowleys near Rynham. His tiny world had expanded, and with his gift, it could take him anywhere.

He caught himself smiling in the mirror; then, he nicked himself with the razor.

"Curses!" he shouted, just as the door burst open.

A short, slim man with close-cropped grey hair marched into the room. Wearing a tightly fitted, long, red jacket with silver embroidery, the man had a breezy manner and seemed to hold his head perpetually too high for his slight frame.

"And best greetings to you, Gada Poulterer!" he replied sarcastically.

The man was carrying a pile of clothes that he deposited onto a chair, then turned to face Jem, almost standing to attention.

"My name is Jegun Seamestre, chief tailor to the king. I'm here as a favour to Lady Moranne. Now stop shirking and finish shaving. We have work to do."

Jem did as instructed while Jegun unfolded several garments and placed new undergarments beside the bath.

The following thirty minutes consisted of Jem getting dressed into various dress uniforms while Jegun eyed him from every angle, proclaiming "no", "maybe", or just "take it off!"

Eventually, he opened his arms wide and smiled for the first time.

"That is it!" he exclaimed.

Jem angled the small shaving mirror to inspect the look. He wore a brown suede tunic dotted with tiny silver studs over a matching brown shirt with ruffled sleeves. A pair of lighter brown leggings and tall black boots completed the look.

"Don't compromise any young ladies," said Jegun with a wink. He picked up the unwanted clothes and breezed out of the room.

A sturdy leather breastplate, leather wrist guards and a thick weapon belt remained, draped over a chair. Jegun had told him they were for "tomorrow" and left it at that.

Jem bent down to look out of one of the small windows, but he was interrupted by the door opening again.

"What now, Tilly?" he shouted before noticing Hayden standing proudly in a bright blue dress uniform.

"Tilly, eh? Something I should know?" smiled Hayden wryly. His room was on the second floor of the Lyften Tower as befitting his stature as a squire's son, while Caspin was staying in the officers' quarters of the First Legion.

"What do you want, *Mr Squire's son?*"

Hayden shrugged. He did need something but hated to ask.

"Are we friends?"

"We'll stay friends if you ever get to the point," Jem laughed.

"Look, I know you're close to Lady Moranne."

"What of it?"

Hayden could imagine his father's colour changing to crimson, his mother crying into her velvet robes and his brother laughing. He didn't care. "I want to come with you," he pleaded.

"Err, where to?" asked Jem. He was unaware they were going anywhere.

"I'm sorry you probably don't know," said Hayden. "There's going to be an expedition into Deapholt and beyond. I want to be on it."

"I'll do what I can." Jem wasn't sure of Moranne's plans, but he knew he'd be at her side.

"Thanks," said Hayden. "By the way, you smarten up well... for a farm boy."

Jem elbowed him playfully in the ribs and pushed him out of the door.

With just an hour to spare before he was expected in the ballroom, Jem climbed the keep's tower to the top, where he could look out over the city. A thousand flickering yellow lights spread out in the dusk as far as the eye could see, out to the Fourth Ward and beyond.

"Evening, sir," said a guard as he saw Jem surveying the land.

Jem noticed the course of the River Rudun for the first time as it bent gently to the west. Torchlight shimmered on its surface from the myriad of properties along its east bank. The city was busy and full of life, but the castle felt insulated, as if it rode above the people in height and stature. He *was* just a *farm boy* from a small town.

Two carriages arrived in the bailey below, and Jem guessed it was time to find the ballroom. He was supposed to be there before the guests arrived.

The castle was buzzing with excitement. Servants and footmen were hurrying through the corridors, and Byrell was shouting orders. The ballroom was situated in the east wing and accessed through tall, arched, double doors in the entrance hall. The doors opened onto a vast marble platform with several steps leading down to the main room. It was here where guests would wait to be announced by Byrell, before descending to parade their attire and wealth.

Jem stopped on the steps and looked out across the smooth marble floor. At its centre was a large depiction of the double-headed eagle of House Fierdman, made from thousands of tiny red-onyx tiles. The room was illuminated by three enormous chandeliers hung from the vaulted ceiling, each with over two hundred flickering candles. The glittering lights were lowered by pulley and then painstakingly lit by the servants.

He gasped at the opulence. A thousand glittering shafts of light twinkled around the room, and further light was cast from a host of oil lamps jutting from the walls. The entire hall was full of ornately decorated tapestries depicting ancient heroes and royalty from noble houses. *I must be dreaming,* thought Jem.

"Ah, Gada Poulterer," said Byrell, waking Jem from his reverie. "I have a job for you."

"How can I help?" beamed Jem.

It seemed that attending a royal ball came with strict etiquette, and Jem would be in the vanguard. "Guests arrive in a specific order," said Byrell. "The local nobility will arrive first, followed by local dignitaries, landed gentry, military men, the Privy Council and finally, the royal family. It will be your job to clap and smile when the early guests arrive to help them feel valued."

Valued? thought Jem; however, it was a simple task, and at least he wasn't collecting eggs. "I think I can manage," he replied dryly.

Familiar faces made up the early honour guard. Jem recognised a few of the castle footmen, some of the maids in clean, bright uniforms and even Jegun Seamestre, who bowed in recognition.

A small ensemble of musicians tuned up on a dais beneath a low section of the room. The lead lute player cleared his throat and counted his fellows in. Sounds of lyre, organ and tambour echoed off the cold walls of the sparse chamber as they played a calming melody to start the evening.

It wasn't long before the guests started arriving. Each couple or family stopped at the door where Byrell would read out their names; then, they strolled into the ballroom to rapturous applause. The room quickly filled with fine folk dressed in the latest fashion. Men wore plush velvet jackets and bright white shirts, while women dressed in colourful ball gowns that showed off plunging décolletage. All the ladies wore their hair high, tied in colourful ribbons, woven with jewels or dotted with flowers.

"Master Hayden Scirmann of Dunstreet and Miss Signy Torht of Cynstol," announced Byrell with a grin.

Jem looked up to see a smiling Hayden tarrying on the steps, arm in arm, with a charming, dark-haired young lady in a bright yellow dress. She seemed in awe as they slowly descended to the clapping Burlander.

"Well met, *Hayden Scirmann of Dunstreet*," he teased. "Who is your lovely companion?"

Signy blushed. Unsure whether to bow or curtsey, she did a little of both.

"This is my new friend, Signy," replied Hayden. "She's one of the maids servicing the Lyften Tower. I asked her if she'd accompany me, and Jegun leant her this dress to wear."

"You both look splendid. Don't worry, Signy; it's my first ball too."

"Thank ye, Master," she said, continuing to half curtsy.

They stood together by the steps, sipping wine as Byrell announced the guests. "High Bishop Namen Nesslor and Lady Corwen Nesslor."

The Frean church colours were instantly recognisable, but it was Lady Corwen who shone in white and gold. At less than half of Namen's age, it seemed an odd pairing.

"Mayor Penri Smolt and Mayoress Tulip Smolt."

The corpulent mayor was beaten squarely by the plump mayoress. She was wearing a corset dress which was so ill-fitting that it looked like she was barely concealing several bosoms. "Now that's a dance I'd like to see," said Hayden mischievously. Jem just managed to stifle his laughter and avoid spraying the guests with red wine.

The party was gradually increasing in stature, with the sound of chatter subsiding a little with each new announcement.

"Earl Normin Linhold, Lady Monenza Linhold and their sons, Sir Torbrand and Sir Caspin."

A buzz of excitement went around the hall as each name was uttered. Normin Linhold, the Earl of Faircester, remained impassive. The sharp family features lengthened his face and made him appear joyless; his short grey beard was a mirror of Caspin's. His wife echoed his stern looks. The dark, claret red of her dress was a bold statement in a room of bright summer hues. The family was imperious, but the sons set the young female pulses racing. Both Caspin and Torbrand were unmarried, but it was the eldest son who commanded the room. Sir Torbrand was a larger, more muscular version of Caspin. His face was fuller, his hair and beard darker, and his gait bolder as he strode confidently into the room. There were no smiles, just the determined self-assurance of a man on course to replace General Marl.

"General Cymel Marl, Commander of the Green Order."

Barely waiting to be introduced, Cymel marched into the ballroom, going immediately to speak with the earl.

Caspin flashed Jem a secretive grin and mouthed the words: *See you later.* He was doing his duty as the earl's son and seemed better suited to the role than his aloof brother.

"General Rune Benton, Commander of the First Legion and Lady Audhild Benton."

The ballroom was filling up quickly. There was a constant hum of chatter, which rose and fell as each new guest was announced. Each new glamorous ball gown added to the colour, which shone against the castle's grey walls while the players increased the tempo and volume.

"Sir Saul Runian, advisor to Prince Jarl, and Lady Elzbeth Dunn."

Hayden spotted Caspin through the crowd. He was still with his family, but the familiar smile had faded, and he looked bored. Taking Signy by the arm, they moved through the crowd towards the Linhold family. Every nobleman or lady they met on the way would smile and bow their head, which Hayden would return. The couple enjoyed the occasion, and even the castle maid was beginning to relax.

They found the family standing close to a raised platform at the far end of the room, including five large, royal chairs. Sir Caspin's face immediately brightened as he saw his friend with wine and a young lady in hand.

"Good evening, Master Hayden," he said politely.

Lady Monenza turned and looked down at the lad from Dunstreet, barely concealing the disdain with which she viewed the whole evening.

"Allow me to introduce my good friend, Master Hayden Scirmann," continued Caspin, presenting Hayden to his parents.

"Ah, Scirmann, you say," said Earl Normin, remaining closed and impassive. "I know your father, Wystan, the Squire of Dunstreet. A good man."

Hayden nodded politely. He wouldn't dispute the assertion that his father was a *good man*.

"And who is this lovely lady?" asked Caspin. Signy was blushing as the handsome knight smiled down at her.

"Allow me to introduce my friend. This is Miss Signy Torht," announced Hayden proudly.

Monenza looked her up and down with a quizzical look.

"Are you of the Langley Torhts?" queried the earl.

"No, I'm from 'ere in Cynstol, me lord," she said, curtseying low and awkwardly.

"She's a maid from the tower," blurted Sir Torbrand, who had re-joined the party from mingling with the crowd. His long dark hair swayed past his shoulder, showing the silver clasp which kept it back.

"A maid?" cried Lady Monenza. She looked down her nose at Caspin as if she'd detected an unpleasant odour. "*These* are your friends?"

"Hello, Your Ladyship," blurted Jem, who'd spotted his friends across the room and decided he'd fulfilled his clapping role for the evening.

"You must be the chicken farmer," said Monenza with relish.

"I'm gada to Lady Moranne, Your Ladyship," Jem replied.

"Hmm, so the witch has staff now."

Caspin was embarrassed by his family and looked away. The only reason for attending the ball was so his mother could marry him off to some young lady from the right family. His brother was already connected with several possible matches.

"Are you enjoying the capital?" asked Jem.

There was no answer. A hush descended on the room; even the musicians stopped playing. All eyes were drawn to two figures near the entrance.

The tall, grey-haired man wore a crimson and gold robe. It bore the king's crest and an ornate gold filigree pattern down the wide lapels. He confidently carried his statuesque frame and looked down proudly at the lady on his arm. She was the reason every soul was staring. She wore a striking blue, figure-hugging dress, which flared open to the floor, revealing a slender calf and silver shoes. Ornate silver stitching covered the entire gown cascading like a waterfall. A complete matching scarf was draped over one shoulder, and a silver necklace plunged to a hint of cleavage.

Lady Monenza gasped, but Hayden shook his head, smiling. It was like no ball gown anyone had ever seen. Although her eyes were lined with charcoal, the long black hair, high cheekbones and green eyes belonged to only one woman.

"Sir Torl Radborough, chief advisor to the king, and Lady Moranne, advisor to the king," Byrell announced clearly and loudly.

They slowly descended the steps and proceeded across the floor while the crowd remained silent. A footman quickly ran to the musicians and gestured for them to continue playing. As the music restarted, people gradually returned to their business.

"She's coming this way," whispered Lady Monenza to her disinterested husband.

"You look beautiful, ma'am," said Hayden as Torl and Moranne joined them.

"Thank you," she replied, smiling. "You're all looking splendid, and I must say, Signy, you do your family proud."

Signy was so nervous she was shaking. She curtseyed low and took Moranne's hand. "Tis an honour to meet you, me lady." Her eyes were glistening with the gravity of the occasion. "That's the most beautiful dress I's ever seen."

Moranne smiled, but Lady Monenza was unimpressed.

"Is it alviri," she asked dismissively.

"Thank you for asking, my dear," said Moranne mischievously. "It's not alviri."

"Oh, it must be Stanish," added Hayden unhelpfully.

Aware that many eyes were on her, Moranne's cheeks creased into a subtle smirk.

"It's Jakari."

Someone dropped a wine goblet behind, and a series of whispers raced around the nearby guests. Lady Monenza wrinkled up her nose and grasped for a pithy remark, but it was Earl Normin who released the pressure.

"You certainly know how to make an entrance, my lady," he said calmly.

Monenza was about to mouth a riposte when the music stopped, and the crowd turned to look up at the entrance, where Byrell was clearing his throat.

"Ladies and gentlemen, please be upstanding for the imperial ruler of Weorgoran."

The crowd moved away from the centre of the ballroom, leaving a corridor between the steps and the dais.

"His Royal Majesty King Pythar, Her Royal Highness Queen Mirin, His Highness Prince Jarl and Her Highness Princess Vena."

Two guards opened the double doors, and the royal family strode through.

Jem had envisaged the king as strong and powerful, but Pythar was tall and thin. The black tunic emblazoned with the double-headed eagle seemed too large, and the thick crimson cape, lined with white fur, swamped him. He appeared to struggle under the weight of his mighty crown, which shone in diamond-encrusted gold.

As the party walked through the room, guests bowed and curtseyed. Those near the front were almost scraping the floor in deference.

The queen was a large lady, but her tailored ball gown flattered her curves, and she glided across the floor. Only the queen and princess seemed to smile at the crowds as they passed. Prince Jarl was disinterested, and the king held an expression of sternness.

Finally reaching the raised platform, they ascended the steps and took their seats. King Pythar sat in the large chair in the centre, flanked by the queen and Prince Jarl. Princess Vena was seated beside the queen, but the far seat near the prince remained empty. Jem was about to ask Moranne about the empty chair, but she silenced him with a finger to her lips.

Byrell had followed the procession to the dais and now stood to the side. "Ladies and gentlemen, the king would like to welcome you all to the late summer ball. Prince Jarl, the Duke of Caynna, will lead the first dance."

The prince looked around and finally realised he had a job to do. Climbing wearily to his feet, he sauntered onto the floor, inspecting the rows of smiling ladies, fluttering their eyelids and tilting their heads, hoping to be picked. Slowly the prince paced down the one side, feigning interest, only to wander onwards. He shook his head and started to walk back to his family. His dark green tunic shone in the light, and the gold-encrusted black cloak billowed as he strode.

He walked past the area where Jem and the others were standing, then abruptly stopped. Slowly turning, he walked back until he was standing parallel to them.

"Oh no," whispered Moranne.

Prince Jarl was smiling mischievously. He knew exactly what effect it would have. "Lady Moranne, would you do me the honour?"

She smiled politely and moved through the parting crowd to face him. "Of course, Your Highness," she said, curtseying as low as the dress would allow.

He took her hand and bent close, whispering in her ear. "You're the only woman in the room."

The musicians struck up, saving her blushes and played a traditional couples dance known as the *lark's song*.

"Did you know she could dance?" whispered Hayden to Jem. They were both mesmerised by Moranne as she glided around the floor.

Eligible young ladies scowled in derision up and down the room, only faking a smile as the duo came near.

"I didn't think you could dance," laughed Jarl, as he spun Moranne out to arm's length, then whipped her back into his embrace.

"It's been a long time, Your Highness," she replied coyly.

Aware of the scandal he was causing, Prince Jarl smiled as they whirled about the floor. He had many friends in the capital, but his father disapproved of them, and they weren't invited. It was a small act of defiance, but he enjoyed it.

With a final flourish, they promenaded towards the king. The prince held her tightly and spun her around. She fell low into his arms just as the music stopped.

Hayden clapped without a care, and slowly the crowd responded by clapping politely at first, then whooping and calling as Jem and Caspin shouted for more. Much to the annoyance of Lady Monenza. The prince held Moranne while the applause echoed around the room, staring into her deep green eyes. He suddenly pulled her close with no warning and kissed her fully on the lips.

She dared not pull away and suffered the assault until he finally released her. Faking a smile, she hurried out to find Torl. The music started again, covering her escape, with the musicians playing a Carole which involved dancers assembling in a ring.

"Torl, you could have warned me!" she raged, her eyes flashing green with anger.

"I didn't know," he said honestly. "He was supposed to pick Lady Willonsa."

"If he touches me again, I'll—"

"Be careful, my dear," cautioned Torl. "You already have many enemies here."

Tomorrow would bring many challenges, and she'd need all her allies to help.

"You dance beautiful, me lady," said Signy.

Moranne acknowledged their praise, but she'd already had enough. It was a tolerable chore, but now she felt embarrassed and used.

"Make sure you speak with the king tonight," reminded Torl. She knew there was work to be done, so with the chief advisor in hand, they thanked Jem and Hayden and then set off to mingle in the crowd.

"Are you dancing?" asked Hayden, desperate to take Signy to the floor.

"I can't," answered Jem truthfully.

"Neither can Signy, but I'm going to teach her. Come on!"

Jem shook his head and wished them well, watching as they skipped off to join the dance. They were smiling and laughing while Hayden showed Signy the steps, her face shining like a summer bride. They danced around the room, and others smiled, watching them whirl around, the young maid screaming in delight.

Jem pushed through the crowds to the landing near the main entrance, where he could look over the floor and watch his giddy friends. They made a step to the right, then two steps to the left, before spinning to hold hands once more and circling round together. Hayden was right, it was a simple dance, but he was happy watching his friends have fun.

His lonely life in Denbry receded ever further into the past. Reality seemed more like one of his dreams; his aunt and uncle were mere phantoms from the past.

"Hello, Gada Jem Poulterer."

The perfectly spoken, soft female voice came from behind. Jem turned to see the effervescent Princess Vena standing beside him with two of her ladies-in-waiting.

"Your Highness!" exclaimed Jem, bowing low as best he could.

She chuckled lightly and begged him to rise.

Her features showed little resemblance to her family. She had neither her mother's round, full figure nor the king's tall, rakish stature. A pretty, slight girl, she had more in common with Signy, but how she held herself and pronounced every syllable exposed her privilege. Wearing a green ball gown decorated in gold, matching her brother's tunic, she was a delightful visage, and Jem found himself beguiled by the dark-haired princess.

"You look beautiful tonight, Your Highness," he said shakily.

She smiled back, shaking her head so that her gold tiara bounced on her neat, styled hair. "Oh, I think it is your mistress who wears the crown of beauty tonight," she replied, smirking.

Jem was desperate not to violate any rules of etiquette, so he just smiled politely.

"Tell me, Master Poulterer, what do they say of us in Burland?"

He knew there was little talk of the king in Denbry, and he didn't even know there were a prince and princess until tonight.

"Erm, I think the capital sometimes seems a long way away, Your Highness."

"You're right," she said. "I keep telling my father that we should try to visit the realm, but he doesn't listen."

Jem was developing a sinking feeling as if he'd just become embroiled in a family dispute. Luckily the princess could see he was nervous.

"Don't worry. You're not in trouble." She turned to the two ladies behind and ordered them to go, leaving her and Jem alone above the dancing crowd.

"Do you know why Lady Moranne chose you?"

Thinking back to that day at Denbry's Crown Inn, Jem remembered Moranne's words as they sat in the smoky tavern. *You don't fit in here, and I don't fit in anywhere.*

"I'm an orphan, Your Highness," replied Jem sheepishly. "I think Lady Moranne felt I would have a better life with her."

Princess Vena's demeanour softened, and her smile reassured him. "Did you ever know your parents?" she asked.

Jem shook his head slowly.

The princess looked around to see that they weren't being watched and noticed that all attention seemed to be on the dancers or the fawning queue of guests waiting to greet the king. Leaning forward, she whispered, "come with me," and led Jem to the corner, where a small door opened into one of the keep's square towers.

It felt wrong to run off with the princess alone, but he dared not refuse her. The stairs wound up for a long way until a door opened out to the wooden floor directly above the ballroom. They could hear the muffled sound of the party through the boards, which creaked beneath their feet.

The room appeared to be a small reception area with a large leather chaise, several upholstered chairs and a low table. A deep piled, crimson rug covered most of the floor and a small fire burned in a hearth against the front wall. Several doors led to other rooms, and an extensive collection of paintings adorned the outer stone walls and the inner dark, panelled wooden ones.

"You must promise me something," said the princess, stopping at the room's centre.

"Of course, Your Highness," replied Jem, feeling bewildered.

"Don't tell Lady Moranne about this."

Jem nodded in agreement, unsure what *this* was.

Princess Vena walked over to a tall, dark painting on one of the inner walls and gestured for Jem to look.

It showed a tall woman in front of one of the castle windows. She wore a long dark cloak, hanging open to reveal a silver belt, over dark leggings. A familiar, slender sword hung at her side. Her long dark hair cascaded over her face and rested over the collar of her white, ruffled blouse. The features were familiar, but the green hue of her eyes revealed her identity.

"It's a good likeness, don't you think?" commented the princess.

Jem had to agree; she looked the same as that day back in Denbry when she held court with the village children.

"How old do you think this painting is?" she asked.

Studying the aged brushstrokes didn't help; it couldn't be more than a few years old.

"Six years, Your Highness?"

She smiled and moved in front of the painting until he looked directly into her eyes.

"It's not six years old, Jem. It's not even sixty years old."

He looked back at the painting and then back to the princess. What was she saying?

"My dear gada, this picture was painted over three hundred years ago."

That can't be, thought Jem.

"It was a present to the child King Rygel Lenturi from the alviri on the day of his coronation. He idolised her."

She was aware that Jem was silently shaking his head in disbelief.

"Be wary of her young gada. She's not who you think she is."

Flashing back to the forest of Bearun, Jem remembered the dalfreni Alize saying the same. *Be wary of her.*

"Who is she?" asked Jem, forgetting the royal etiquette, but before Vena could answer, the tower door opened, and Byrell ran in.

"Begging your pardon, Your Highness. The king is asking for you."

She smiled at Jem's quizzical face and shook her head.

"Duty calls, Master Poulterer; remember what I said."

Jem bowed, then followed them back to the ballroom. Byrell led the princess into the crowd, where she was introduced to various noblemen. He saw Moranne near the front wall, the Jakari dress making her easy to spot. He passed the dancing to where she stood next to Sir Radborough.

"Ma'am!" he shouted through the noise.

She was discussing something with Torl and waved him silent, but Jem needed some answers. *Who was she?*

"Ma'am!" he pleaded again.

This time she whirled irritably towards him. "I'm busy, Jem."

"I need to ask you something."

"It can wait." Maybe the wine was getting to him, or the noise of the ball.

"I need to know now, ma'am."

Finally, she snapped and turned to him with a hand firmly on his shoulder. "What is it?"

Her green eyes flashed with bright sparks, and he remembered how she'd saved them all in the forest and plucked him from his miserable life.

"I ..." he stuttered.

He remembered the outskirts of Bearun when she'd cried, revealing the true nature of his gift. He couldn't know what suffering she'd endured in all those years.

"I ..."

She was his way out, and he owed her his loyalty. Maybe she was dangerous and still had secrets, but now wasn't the time to expose them.

"I wondered if Hayden could come with us on the expedition. I'll look out for him," he blurted finally.

She wanted to be angry with him, but his nature was kind, *just like his father*.

"Is that all?" she said, raising an eyebrow.

Jem nodded, and Moranne pretended to be pondering the question, with her forefinger and thumb caressing her chin.

"What do you think, Torl?" she asked.

"Well, my lady," he said. "You did promise to find him a sponsor in Cynstol, but you didn't say that sponsor wasn't your good self."

"Alright, Jem, I'll think about it. Now leave me in peace." She gestured for him to leave and continued her discussion with Torl.

Jem returned to the ballroom entrance, where he watched Hayden and Signy still dancing in circles. They'd been joined by Sir Caspin, dancing with Princess Vena. The four of them laughed and perspired in equal measure, and Jem wished he could be with them, but phantoms haunted his thoughts.

Hayden caught his eye, so Jem waved back to them. Feeling an uncontrollable pull, he then turned to ascend the keep tower stairs back to the reception area and that painting. He repeated his earlier steps over the creaking boards and plush carpet to the spot where the princess revealed the ancient rendering of Moranne.

It was gone. In its place was a painting which depicted a knight in full armour carrying a jousting spear.

In one of the castle's many dark cellars, Edlin Byrell carefully deposited a sizeable rectangular object wrapped in sackcloth. He propped it against a wall, then carefully moved several similar items and placed them in front.

As he was about to leave, he looked down at the nearest object. The small corner of a painting was jutting from a tear in the sack. He knelt down and carefully revealed the artwork. It was marked and faded in a few places, but he could still see the shape of a young man standing proudly in front of a horse. It was a little faded, but the likeness was unmistakable.

17 BY ROYAL DECREE

Someone was knocking; they kept knocking, or was it in his head? His mind was too foggy to tell.

"Go away!" shouted Hayden, pulling a pillow over his head.

The knocking continued, accompanied by a familiar voice.

"Master, I has mint tea and toast for ye. Lady Moranne says you're needed."

"Signy, is that you?"

She pushed the door open and placed the tray on a small table near the bed. Hayden reluctantly pulled himself up and sat staring at her in his bed shirt.

"Thank ye for last night, sir," she said, beaming. "I's never had so much fun."

"You're welcome."

Hayden was acutely aware that she could get into trouble or become too attached to him. His parents would be mortified if they knew, but the further away they were, the more he became his true self.

"I hope we can stay friends," he said, looking up with his lips pursed into a thin smile.

She tilted her head, and her face lit up. "Don't worry, sir, I's got a cousin just like you; just mind how you go."

Like me? he wondered. Both Caspin and Moranne had already said something similar. She might be a peasant girl from a humble background, but she was perceptive and loyal. With a last cheeky glance from the door, she disappeared up the winding tower stairs.

Hayden enjoyed his breakfast and pulled on his clothes just as the door burst open, and General Marl marched in. He came to an abrupt halt and stood, hands on hips, in front of the startled Burlander. The room was small and only contained a single bed, a small table and a tiny chair, but the mighty general seemed to fill it. He stared down menacingly.

"General!" exclaimed Hayden. "What can I do for you?"

Cymel forced a smile, but his brow remained furrowed and his eyes severe.

"How are your parents, Master Hayden?"

"Erm, they're fine, sir," replied Hayden hesitantly. He knew what was coming next and hated his father for it.

"Good!" boomed the general. "Now, tell me everything you know about the witch and her new apprentice."

Hayden furtively looked around the room, hoping for some inspiration. He must give the general something, but nothing which would hurt his friend and sponsor.

"There's not much to tell, sir, Jem was a chicken farmer, and she brought us here."

"Come on, lad, did she use her powers?" The general started to fidget, shifting his weight from foot to foot.

"No, not once," Hayden lied. "We met bandits in Bearun, but we fought them off."

"And what of the chicken farmer?"

The image of Jem reading Dena flashed before Hayden's eyes. Moranne called it a gift, but he wouldn't betray one of his few friends. Ham Grome was becoming a distant Dunstreet memory.

"I've seen nothing strange, sir, but he's very good with the sword." Mixing truth with lies could make the story seem more genuine. The moment Jem saved his life in Bearun, with eyes flashing bright green, was a turning point for the squire's son.

"Hmm, *good with the sword*, eh? Who trained him?" Cymel smiled mischievously for the first time, and Hayden wondered if he'd given too much.

"I don't know, sir, but he saved my life in the forest."

The general nodded sagely and put a large, gloved hand on Hayden's shoulder.

"Keep me informed!" he boomed.

With a stiff pat on Hayden's shoulder, the general turned on his heels and thundered out of the room, slamming the door behind him.

Jem sat alone, staring into the bright, colourful panes of the library's tall, stained-glass windows. The centre window depicted the winged goddess Frea, spear in hand, fighting the demon known as the Scucca. The evil creature was drawn with a man's body but a dragon's head and holding a flaming sword. Frean clergy used the brutality of the Scucca to frighten young children into belief, the assertion that naughty children would spend an eternity being eaten by the demon in the afterlife.

Moranne's gada knew that his mistress would call it rubbish. She'd never discussed her beliefs but seemed to view religion and superstition with disdain. It seemed strange to Jem that a wielder of earth power would be an atheist. What were these powers, if not a gift from Frea?

Who was she? It was a question he asked himself more each day. He'd woken early that morning from a nightmare that jolted him from slumber. The painting of Moranne had come alive, but as she stared from the castle wall with burning green eyes, the paint had begun to run. Three hundred years of age showed on her body as the paint dripped and cracked. It ran down the wall in shades of black and white, but as it pooled on the floor, it turned red. A pool of blood spread towards him while he backed away.

"Good morning!" shouted Hayden, striding through the double doors and allowing one of them to hit a bookcase with a loud crack.

"In Frea's name, Hayden! Do you ever knock? I was a thousand miles away."

Hayden collapsed in a chair beside the gada and emitted a sigh of contentment. Last night's ball and dancing with Signy had occupied his dreams. It was the first morning he'd woken without the dread of his father since Dunstreet.

"That's splendid armour, my friend; it suits you," he said, beaming.

Jem wore the leather breastplate with shoulder flaps and forearm guards over his dress uniform. The centre of the light armour included a large image of a snake burned into the leather. It was familiar, but Jem was struggling to place it.

"Thanks," he said flatly, "but I don't know what the snake means."

"It's the emblem of House Donhalf," said Moranne wearily. She stood by the doors, rubbing the sleep from her eyes. "Jegun made it."

Jem knew nothing of the royal houses, but it sounded impressive. "I hope I do it justice, ma'am."

You already have, she thought. Dane's kind-hearted smile still burned in her memory, as did the manner of his death.

"I need to speak with you both; this is important." She leaned forward, and they both sat up to attention. "I intend to take the two of you with me on a mission, but for you, Hayden, there is a condition."

"Pray tell, ma'am," said Hayden enthusiastically.

"I will make you my gada, but as Jem is already my ward, he will outrank you. You will obey any order given to you by Jem without question. I will arrange for you both to receive sword training on the journey. That is my condition. Do you both accept?"

They looked at each other, but both knew it was Hayden's decision. He'd seen Jem battling bandits, saving crofters and taking the lead. He was a squire's son by name, but Hayden knew he was no leader.

"I would be honoured to serve Gada Poulterer and Lady Moranne," he said formally. *As long as I never return to Dunstreet,* he thought.

"Good, that's settled," she said. "Now, the second matter. Your presence is required for an audience with the king at eleven o'clock. There are several things you must remember. Do not speak unless the king asks you a specific question, and if Prince Asger is present, you must be very careful."

"Prince Asger?" asked Jem. He'd heard mention of Prince Jarl and Princess Vena but nothing of Asger.

"Prince Asger is second in line to the throne, but he's seldom seen within or outside the castle. He was born with a malady that affects his movement and speech. His limbs are taut, making all things difficult. You must never mention his disorder, and you must not stare. If he speaks, you may struggle to understand. Don't finish his sentences for him, allow him to repeat himself, don't hurry him."

"Is he simple?" asked Hayden with genuine concern.

"Never use those words!" replied Moranne sternly. "His wits are sharper than the entire council combined, and he's twice the man his brother is. Don't let his ungainly ways distract you from his wisdom."

They both nodded their understanding.

"There is just one more thing." She smiled wryly, remembering her many arguments with General Marl and Murmur. "I have many enemies at court, and they may be unpleasant. Don't jump to my defence; I'm a big girl."

An ancient girl, thought Jem. One day he would ask her who she really was.

One day I'll tell you, rang through his head. He looked up, but she was telling Hayden where to find light armour like his.

The throne room was on the first floor, at the back of the keep. It was accessed through a set of large double doors, hand-carved with the familiar double-headed eagle. Guards stood on either side with long-handled broad axes and pointed steel helms. They glowered at Jem and Hayden before wordlessly pushing the doors open to allow the gada's entry.

A murmuring crowd had already assembled, including the familiar faces of generals Marl and Benton, High Bishop Nesslor and Mayor Smolt. Sir Caspin stood silently beside his brother, who was in deep discussion with Earl Normin Linhold and Earl Jonas Renshaw. Jem didn't recognise most of the assembled noblemen. All were eastern-born males; Frea's children occupied every position of power. Only one woman could be seen of the thirty or so souls in the room, and she stood directly in front of the king's throne. Wearing her familiar long coat and leggings, with the sword, Steorra at her side, Moranne stood her ground as well as any man.

Thick dust twinkled in the light cast from three tall windows behind the throne and the other minor seats of power while ornate crimson and gold drapes billowed in the draught. The flickering oil lamps reflected off Caspin and Torbrand's polished armour and picked out the gemstones in the cross guard of Cymel's mighty claymore. The army looked ready for battle.

The throne was a humble affair compared to other opulent furniture in the castle. It was carved from several large tree boughs, but in such a way that the tree's structure seemed to become the throne. Seats for the rest of the royal family were of a similar design. All were arranged in a line on a raised dais, with a door at each end, protected by two further axe-wielding guards.

"My lady," said Jem, as he pushed through the dignitaries to her side. She turned and half-smiled, her mind elsewhere. Moranne's demeanour was pensive and uncertain.

"Remember," she said. "Say nothing unless spoken to directly, and don't stare."

They waited while Moranne fiddled with her hands, and the throng behind whispered and conspired. Finally, the right-hand door opened, and Byrell strode to the platform's centre, holding a tall wooden staff with the double-headed eagle carved into the top. He banged the staff on the floor three times and addressed the crowd.

"Pray silence for His Royal Majesty, King Pythar, imperial ruler of Weorgoran and defender of the Frean faith."

First to enter was Princess Vena, who walked to the nearest chair and stood with her hands together. She wore a white and gold full dress with a purple sash fastened by a gold pennant. She looked straight ahead, holding herself with grace. Prince Jarl's swagger was in stark contrast; just three long strides took him to the throne's right, where he turned and smirked. His leather breastplate shone, and so did his polished sword, betraying its lack of use.

After a short delay, the king finally entered, followed by Sir Torl and Murmur, who shuffled to his place behind the prince. The king was also dressed in military finery, wearing a gilded breastplate and shoulder guards over shining silver mail. With thick black leather gloves and boots, he looked ready to lead an army.

He took the throne uncomfortably to the sound of scraping armour, prompting both the prince and princess to take their seats. Sir Torl, who stood just behind the king, cleared his throat.

"General Benton, could you please appraise the king of the current situation?"

King Pythar had already been briefed, but it was all part of the tradition and ceremony at court. The general began addressing the king, but he was interrupted when the left-hand door opened suddenly.

An older man, almost bald but with a few wisps of grey hair, walked cautiously into the room and stopped to bow low before the king. He was dressed similarly to Sir Torl, but his bones hardly filled the flowing robes.

"My apologies, Your Highness," he croaked, before backing gingerly towards the rightmost seat.

The king appeared agitated, letting out a sigh of disdain. He held out a hand to stop Rune Benton from continuing the brief.

They waited for what seemed an age, all looking at the open door left by the ageing Sir Annarr Radmond. Prince Jarl was drumming his fingers on the arm of his seat and rolling his eyes in irritation.

Eventually, Jem could hear a strange sound coming from the room beyond. It was like two objects being dragged across the floor, followed by two taps of wood on stone. Each tap echoed through the unseen passage, becoming louder as someone approached. After a while, he could discern the rasping sound of breathing behind the scrapes and knocks, then the grunting of exertion.

A hand appeared through the doorway holding a carved, wooden crutch that knocked on the stone dais and echoed off the wall; another followed it, and together they helped pull the body of a young man into the room. The toes of his shoes pointed inwards as he walked, dragging them into place, and his gait was forward and awkward.

Prince Asger was younger than Jem at twenty-five years, and unlike his brother, he wasn't dressed for battle. He wore a crimson velvet tunic emblazoned with the Fierdman insignia in gold stitch and black velvet leggings. His shoes were shallow and practical but scuffed where they dragged along the ground. His shoulder-length, dark hair flicked across his face as he moved towards his chair and tried to keep his head upright, battling against the unseen forces of his condition.

It sounded like he was trying to apologise and force the words out as clearly as possible. Sir Annarr took the prince's crutches as he flopped into his seat.

The king nodded and gestured for General Benton to continue.

"Your Majesty," said Rune bowing. "We've received word from our spies in Stanholm that King Ramon is readying a fleet of warships in Gulward. He intends to join forces with a powerful ally named Corvus, who wields one of the five sceptres of power. Lady Moranne tells us that Corvus has the power to control men's will."

The king listened patiently while Prince Jarl fidgeted, but both Asger and the princess hung on every word. The young prince twitched and contorted as he tried to hold the general's gaze.

Torl leaned down and whispered something in the king's ear, and the monarch spoke for the first time. He was gruff and severe, his eyes remaining fixed and emotionless.

"So, if I understand this tale correctly, King Ramon intends to invade Tudorfeld with help from a warlock we can't beat with an army of men?"

"That's what Lady Moranne tells us, Your Highness," replied the general.

Cymel Marl allowed himself a secret smirk at the mention of the *witch's* name. "We've sent scouts, Your Highness, looking for women able to fight," he said, just managing to suppress his glee.

"And?" asked the king.

"We found an elderly female archer, and there is talk of a swordswoman in Grenborg who performs with a circus."

Sir Torbrand couldn't contain himself, exploding into laughter. "You expect us to go into battle with a crone and a clown?"

"If I may, Your Highness," interrupted Moranne. "We need help from the Cempestre and the alviri."

The king smiled. She always spoke with sense and dignity when his generals called for war. "What do you suggest, Lady Moranne?"

She looked around at Jem and Hayden, who hung loyally on her words.

"I propose a small, mostly diplomatic company be sent to Cempess and then onwards to Alfheim, where we will try to recruit as much help as possible. We will go to Numolport and sail to the stone island, where we will try to reason with King Ramon before it's too late."

The king pondered the idea for a while but seemed unconvinced. "You know that the Stanholm harvest has failed again, and the Stans are desperate. How can we persuade them not to war?" King Pythar already knew the answer, but he didn't wish to say it or hear it. They all knew the solution.

"We give the Stans farming rights to part of Tudorfeld; there's plenty of spare land. They can pay taxes to the crown, and we'll avoid any conflict."

A murmur ran around the chamber with cries of *shame* and even *treason*. King Ramon had asked many times for farming rights, but the only reply had been that Ramon should surrender Stanholm to Grenfold and swear fealty to the king.

"Never," said the king, with a hint of emotion in his voice. "I agree to send an emissary, but the conditions are simple. If they surrender the island, they may have access to our pastures. The only question remains: who will accompany you as my representative?"

"I would suggest Sir Torl, Your Highness." She looked up at her old friend, who was shaking his head. She'd fallen into the trap.

"Your Highness!" shouted Mayor Smolt suddenly. "Should it not be someone of equal standing to King Ramon, such as a member of the royal house?"

Cymel had already discussed the choice of Prince Jarl with Murmur. He was so lazy that they'd never make it to Numolport, giving the generals chance to attack.

"Are you suggesting my daughter?" said the king sarcastically.

Penri shook his head quickly, but Princess Vena was already beaming.

"I would be honoured to go," she said, begging her father.

"It's too dangerous for a fair princess, Your Highness," added General Marl. "Might I suggest the prince?"

Prince Jarl almost fell off his chair. The thought of slugging through a dangerous forest and onwards to a barren rock was too awful to contemplate. He had parties to attend and deer to hunt.

"Err, I think I would be better utilised serving Caynna," he sputtered.

"Nonsense!" replied the king.

"Let me go, father," added the princess.

"The prince would make a fine ambassador," chimed Cymel.

"I... I... have too much to do here," howled the prince in desperation. He was standing now and pleading with the king to send one of his advisors. The scene descended into chaos; the royal family argued, and the generals tried to bend the choice towards Jarl.

Moranne shared a look of helplessness with Sir Torl. They knew what Cymel was trying to achieve: a military solution to the Stanholm problem. She needed to head the mission, but the king would never allow a woman to lead, especially with the pious Bishop Nesslor at his ear.

The crowd mumbled while the king lectured his languorous son, but Jem could see Prince Asger trying to speak above the cacophony.

"Allow me," pleaded the princess. "Sir Caspin can protect me." Even as Veena implored her father, Asger's voice was getting louder.

The young prince was shouting the same words over and over. "Oh weed, oh weed." His head flopped back and forth as he tried to wrangle the words into shape, but the king ignored him, preferring to lecture Prince Jarl on his royal duty.

In turn, Asger became frustrated, moving around in his chair until it rocked on its legs. "Oh weed!" he howled as the crowd was drawn to him, and princess Vena looked over with concern. Still, the king ignored him while Torl tried to intervene.

Prince Asger pushed against the chair arms with the sheer force of will and hauled his body erect, swaying on his wayward feet.

"Oh weed!" he shouted once more with all his might.

The king stopped hectoring Prince Jarl and swung to face his disabled son, with anger simmering behind his eyes. "What is it, Asger?"

Prince Asger stood silently for a moment, finally winning the king's attention. He wobbled on his feet, composing himself. "Oh weed, father," he said calmly.

At that moment, both Jem and Moranne understood the young prince. Bolder and braver than his able-bodied brother, he stood proudly as the king's son. The mission would be challenging for any man, but it would be doubly so for Asger.

I'll lead, father. The words echoed in Moranne's mind, and a smile formed, lighting her face. *Yes.*

"You?" said the king, forgetting his anger instantly. He despised his disabled son. It would put a weakling on the throne if anything happened to Jarl. That was no legacy he wanted. The queen loved him, but she wasn't there. "You make me proud, my son."

"Your Highness!" pleaded General Marl. "I'm not sure the mission is suitable for ...."

"A cripple?" bawled the king. "You'll watch your tongue, Marl."

The general bowed in submission and begged forgiveness, but in essence, the king was pleased. If Asger died on the journey, so be it. He asked who would accompany the prince. Both Caspin and Torbrand stepped forward immediately.

"Who will be your second in command?" asked the king.

The Linhold brothers stood proud with their chests puffed out, but Prince Asger lifted a wavering hand to point at the dark-haired woman standing before the throne.

"It will be an honour, Your Highness," said Moranne, curtseying perfectly.

Sir Caspin was smiling, but Torbrand looked like thunder. "I'll answer to no woman," he spat under his breath.

Moranne didn't want to take Torbrand, but he outranked his younger brother. She could only push the generals so far.

"Sir, with your permission, I would like to name Sir Torbrand as our military commander and Sir Caspin as his second. I will be taking my two gadas, and I suggest we find the old archer and the clown swordswoman," she said, eliciting chuckling from Prince Asger.

"I have sixty good men ready to go," added General Benton.

Moranne held up her hand. "You forget, General. A large party of men will not be allowed into Cempess or Alfheim, and men will be dangerous if we find Corvus. I suggest that Sir Torbrand and Sir Caspin choose a few good men to accompany us."

Caspin nodded, and Torbrand grudgingly agreed. Luckily for General Marl, the hapless mayor hadn't forgotten the plan.

"It might be prudent to have troops ready to act if the mission fails, Your Highness," said Penri, remembering his lines.

"I agree," said the king quickly. "Make the arrangements; you leave tomorrow."

18 THE GREEN ROAD

Daybreak brought a rippling orange glow to the waters of the Fayze Bay and cast long knife-edged shadows from the fishing boats making an early catch. The waves gently rolled onto the beach below and receded with the gentle hypnotic sound, making the hilltop villa a tranquil place in a turbulent world.

High Lord Nimmeral Andain leaned against the tree branches, which had been shaped into a rambling balcony. He sighed as he gazed beyond the sea to the razor points of Banafell some thirty miles north. Anyone looking up at his perch would see the sharp profile of his flawless face in silhouette against the sunrise. Long white hair was pulled back over his pointed ears and tied with a silver braid.

His full-length grey jacket gaped open, revealing a bright white shirt, upon which hung the silver star of his office, swinging back and forth over the rail. There had been peace in Alfheim for five hundred years; since the demise of Jhakri and the dominion of humans. The oni still raided the forest, but they mostly fought each other and never crossed the bay. So what vexed him so?

He'd woken that morning with a sense of foreboding, feeling a ripple in the earth, disturbing Juldra in her slumber. Something he hadn't felt for five hundred years, and it was building. The alviri were vulnerable and unprepared for war. It was his fault, but few would listen to the talk of dark days. With a lowering birth rate, their numbers dwindled. Soon the population would be near to that of the dalfreni, and with so much hatred, the outcast children could quickly return and bring lady vengeance with them. If he could feel it, his wife would indeed feel it more.

"Nim! What are you doing out there?" asked Lady Etherin from inside.

The double doors were open behind the high lord, exposing the opulent bedchamber to the late summer breeze. Etherin sat upright in the large bed, pushing back the bright white, tangled hair of the night. Her skin was porcelain smooth, and her eyes shone like stones of blue topaz. The thin, white nightdress draped over her chest, hinting at the shape beneath.

Nimmeral stood in the doorway, his eyes following the natural, unworked branches of the bed frame that bent and twisted. Two large boughs were pulled up behind the frame, meeting high towards the ceiling and tied to a point.

"I was just getting some air," he said, resting his weight against the doorframe. He knew there was something wrong. His wife could read Juldra's signs better than he ever could.

"I've seen it," she said sternly, waiting for him to confirm the vision.

"What have you seen?"

"She's coming; she's coming here."

He dared not ask *who*; he knew precisely who she meant. There wasn't a month that passed when he didn't see her dark hair and emerald eyes gaze up at him or crave the warmth of her hand as they walked through the forest. He stared at his beautiful wife and said nothing.

"If she sets one foot in this house...."

Etherin pulled back the sheets and stood gracefully. Her steps were silent as she glided across the room until she stood face-to-face with her husband, running her slender hands through his hair.

"...I will kill her."

The First Legion barracks were like a smaller version of the castle. Situated in the Second Ward, against the wall, it consisted of a small keep, a larger dormitory, stables and a generous training ground. Linen dummies swung from posts, and archery targets lined up against the ward's wall. A large area near the gate contained lines of tables and chairs where the soldiers and recruits would take lunch. It was here that Jem found Caspin, Hayden and many soldiers he didn't recognise.

"Good morning!" he chirped as he joined the group.

Sir Caspin shot him a disapproving look. "Gada Poulterer, you must address me as 'Sir' during the mission."

Jem was taken aback for a moment, then he realised that the other men would be expected to recognise rank, and there could be no exceptions. "Sorry, sir," he said quickly. He was rewarded with a wink and a wry smile from the knight, which none of the others saw.

The morning sun was just starting to peek over the wall when Moranne emerged from the Legion Keep with Sir Torbrand. They discussed something while a string of young hands fetched horses from the stables. Another party was also approaching from the castle.

Hayden and Jem stood out in this company. Their shining, new armour starkly contrasted with the scratched, dented, and tarnished battle dress of the eight soldiers who sat waiting. They all appeared hardened by conflict and a little weary. It would be just another mission for these seasoned hands.

Moranne stood before the men and nodded toward her two charges. "We're just waiting for the prince," she said, "and I think we're missing another."

"No, you ain't!" came the response from over Jem's shoulder.

He turned to see an older woman, with long flowing grey hair, beneath a wide-rimmed hunter's hat. She was lean and dressed in a light linen top with a plain leather breastplate sculpted about her body. Her black leather leggings were tight but crazed with extensive use. The skin was loose about her neck, and her face etched with lines, but the crow's feet showed character, and her hazel eyes twinkled with mischief. The bow slung over her back identified her as an archer.

"You should call her Ma'am and call me Sir," said Caspin, echoing what he'd told Jem.

"Should I?" said the older woman, raising a grey eyebrow. "You can call me whatever you like, but the day I calls you *Sir* will be the day I stops wiping my own arse."

Jem tried to stifle laughter; he could see Sir Torbrand's expression was thunderous.

Moranne was smiling. "I like her," she said under her breath.

"Me name's Brea, Brea Soytere. I was told to be 'ere, but I'm too old to care. So if you don't want me, I'll rag off back home."

"How old are you, Brea?" asked Moranne. "Where did you learn archery?"

Brea removed the bow from her back, allowing her hand to run over the wood as if she was caressing a lover.

"I has sixty-nine years, and twas me father who learned me the bow. He had no son and wanted to teach someone. I's been hunting deer west of the river since I had fourteen years."

"She'll snap her shoulder just pulling the string," said one of the soldiers dryly. He also appeared to be an archer from the bow propped against the table where he sat. He had shoulder-length black hair and a steely-eyed look, like a falcon spying its prey.

Brea threw back her silver hair and laughed through to her boots. "Well me little scroat, if you can hit the target's eye, I'll bend me broken back to kiss yer arse."

The bowman lifted himself slowly and pulled an arrow from the quiver slung over his shoulder. "Watch and learn, you old hag."

He spied one of the targets against the wall, around two hundred yards away, slotted the arrow into place and pulled back the string. It strained against the leather of his glove and vibrated as he drew it close to the kisser. With a loud thwack, it flew straight and true, shuddering to a halt as it hit the target just shy of the centre.

"Not bad for a scroat," said Brea, beaming, "but that wasn't the target."

With a graceful set of movements, she held the bow straight and set an arrow in place. She lined up the same target and pulled back the string. Her loose baggy skin became taught, and stiff sinewy muscles appeared under her shirt and down her neck.

She cocked one eye towards Moranne and winked. Just as the bow creaked at full stretch, she whirled around and let the arrow fly in the direction of the Legion Keep. The shot whistled through the air and hit something in the distance with a dull knock.

Jem and Hayden ran towards the building and found the arrow embedded in the wooden crest of House Fierdman just above the door. It was proudly waving from one of the eyes of the double-headed eagle.

"Old hag, eh?" She slapped the archer on the back and sat down with the other soldiers.

The sound of clapping stopped any further embarrassment, and the deep tone of Sir Torl Radborough echoed against the keep walls. "I can see we're in good hands," he said, from his perch atop a regal black horse.

Three other riders appeared behind him, all on thoroughbred mounts. Prince Asger sat proudly upright on a specially adapted saddle. It had a chair-like back and straps to hold him, but he had the reins and controlled the horse well. His battle dress was similar to Sir Caspin's, but small gold clasps held a crimson cape on his back, adorned with the Fierdman mark. The other riders were the prince's advisor, Sir Annarr Radmond and a bodyguard.

"Please can you speak with His Highness?" said Sir Annarr to Moranne as he dismounted. "I should be going with him."

Moranne noticed the prince looked displeased with the elderly Annarr. "This is no place for a civilian, Sir Annarr; the prince commands a good strong company. Have no fear."

No place for a civilian, thought Jem. He and Hayden were not battle-hardened veterans like the soldiers.

"Is everything in order, my lady?" asked Torl.

She'd known him long enough to detect concern in his voice. "We have horses on the way and two pack ponies. We also have some of the best soldiers in Caynna." The men stood up straight and faced the prince with pride.

"Allow me to introduce the men, Your Highness," said Sir Torbrand stiffly.

Each man stepped forward as Torbrand announced them and described their skills.

"The first archer you saw is Private Slitan Smite of the First Legion. He has already faced the Stans in Tudorfeld and is one of the finest bowmen in Grenfold."

Slitan nodded a perfunctory bow and smiled as if his muscles rarely pulled his face into such an expression. Little was known of the menacing archer, but he liked to drink with his comrades and use the Frean scriptures against anyone he disliked.

The nervous, clean-shaven archer at his side was his protégé, Gamin Boarman. At just twenty-three years, he was the youngest member of the company.

"He may be young," said Sir Torbrand, "but Private Smite assures me of his skills."

Gamin nodded several times and half-saluted until Slitan told him: "stop making a fool of yourself."

Private Cal Briman was already grinning as Sir Torbrand introduced the versatile soldier.

"He's served with the Burland Guard and Queen's Battalion as an expert in both the bow and sword."

Jem instantly recognised the look of a fellow Burlander. Originally hailing from Silmouth, the short, blonde-haired soldier bowed politely, exposing his short bow and the small knight sword at his side.

The following two soldiers were big, bald, thickset men with muscles honed wielding heavy weapons. Private Lunn Burndog stood at least six and a half feet tall and swung an enormous broad axe, almost as tall as him. His head looked square and seemed to vanish, neckless, into his body. Hailing from Gosta, he had a murky past, but gentleness lived behind his dark eyes.

"Your Highness," he said, in a deep baritone, almost shaking the ground as he bowed to the prince.

If Lunn was tall, then Private Gron Hamur was wide. Only a little taller than Cal, the Burlander, he was a square pylon of a man; his arms were almost as wide as his thighs. His bald head and thick beard made him look like an impervious blacksmith, but it was an appearance typical in the northern Midtlen. He pulled the heavy mace from his belt and rested it in his hand, bowing to the prince.

The tall Davill Hwaetbur had a farmer's name, but the mighty claymore hung from his belt, put him a long way from his birthplace, the village of Greydon. He was a man of few words and simply bowed when he was introduced to Prince Asger. He seemed interested in Jem's twin scimitars, as he was one of few soldiers to have seen Jakaris in the flesh.

Introduced by his nickname of *Knives*, Sax Stulor was a master of both the throwing knife and the long hunting knives hung from his belt. His long, thin face and sharp teeth echoed his reputation. Bowing low before the prince, his long coat billowed open, revealing a line of concealed short blades.

"Your Highness," he said, forcing air through his teeth like a hissing snake. His smooth skin might have marked him as handsome if it wasn't for the mop of unruly, thick black hair draped over his shoulders, often covering his eyes.

The last to be presented was Captain Biorn Fallon. He would be third in the line of military command behind Knight Commander Torbrand and Sir Caspin.

"Captain Fallon is a long-serving member of the First Legion," said Sir Torbrand, "and the only man I would trust to lead these men. His skills with the sword are a legend throughout the army."

Only Biorn's humble background prevented him from ascending to the rank of knight. He was in his late forties but still able to outfight any young pretenders, and he had the respect of his men.

"Your Highness, ma'am," he said stiffly and bowed perfectly.

Moranne introduced her two gadas and their newest member with a sweep of her arm.

"And, of course, you've already met our new archer. Brea Soytere, a hunter from Cynstol." Refusing to bow, she flicked the brim of her hat and winked at the young prince.

Asger turned to Sir Torl and said something that Jem couldn't immediately understand. It came to him later.

"I like her too."

With the introductions made, Moranne told the party of their mission to Stanholm.

"It's primarily a diplomatic mission," she said. "We must go to Stanburg to meet King Ramon and persuade him not to form an alliance with Corvus against us. We will try to recruit some alviri and Cempestre warriors to help us as we travel through Deapholt."

The mere mention of the dark forest sent a rumble of discontent through the soldiers.

"The forest contains many perils for the unwary," she said chillingly. "There are beasts and creatures in its black heart, which few have seen. The oni clans of Banafell often hunt in the lowlands, and they are fearsome warriors. We must all watch out for each other."

The words formed in Jem's mind, but Brea spoke them. "What in the name of horse dung is an oni?"

None of them braved the forest, not even the gallant Linhold brothers. Neither Torbrand nor Caspin knew of the clans.

"Sometimes known as the mountain men or the barbarians, the oni are an ancient race of cave-dwelling warriors," replied Moranne. "They are ferocious fighters, and they seldom take prisoners. I intend to avoid Banafell."

I agree, thought Hayden, who started to think volunteering for this mission might be a mistake.

"You should all be prepared," boomed Sir Torbrand. "Are there any other questions?"

The soldiers looked at each other, all with the same incomprehension, but only Captain Fallon dared to voice it. "Who is Corvus, sir?" he asked.

Sir Torbrand looked to Moranne, but even she struggled to describe the fantastical man in Jem's dreams.

"He is known by many names," she said. "For example, the alviri call him Jhakri, a word for shaman in their ancient tongue. Whatever name you hear, you should know that he has great power; he can use this to corrupt the minds of men. Thousands could die if we don't stop King Ramon from allying with him."

"What kind of man has that power?" asked Biorn.

"A warlock!" spat Private Slitan Smite, before Moranne could answer.

She stared open-mouthed at the impertinent archer, but in truth, it was a name which the men could most easily understand. Corvus was no warlock, but his powers would be magic to the simple, Frea-fearing folk of Grenfold.

"We leave when the supply ponies are ready," announced Sir Torbrand. "Make your peace with Frea, and saddle up."

It would be midday when they finally took the Green Road north after a small lunch of cheese and ham. Moranne insisted that Jem and Hayden ride behind her, as they should be at the rear by rank. Sir Torbrand began to argue, but he held out his hand in resignation when she flashed her green eyes.

Jem looked back over the company to the tall towers of Cynstol, receding into the distance. The Lyften Tower was visible for twenty miles and stood as a reminder that the safe, nurturing walls would become but a memory while they ventured into the unknown.

He found himself thinking of Mia Tunland back in oppressive Denbry. *If she could see me now.*

⁂

The small clipper pitched back and forth, crashing through the waves as it left Cynstol's quay. The castle walls stared down from the high cliffs, where foamy white surf crashed against the rocks, and the sky-scraping tower left a shadow which reached out to touch the boat's stern.

Yuna wrapped a shawl tightly around her shoulders as the stiff sea breeze raced across the bows and rattled the rigging. The ship mainly carried goods; passengers were expected to sit on the deck for the short journey to Inseld. People of all kinds paid for passage. Some were workers or family returning home, but a young couple on the starboard side caught her eye. They had the look of peasant farmers and were clearly in love. They huddled close and whispered affection.

Something tore at Yuna's heart, and she looked up at the grey city. There was somebody there, somebody she loved, but the body had no form, and the head had no face. She remembered the sun setting through the chasm of Malen's Cutting while the river cascaded over the rocks below. Why was she alone? A moment of panic took hold, and she slapped her head, but the memories wouldn't come. Something was lost, and she was leaving it behind.

She looked once more at the young peasants. As they kissed and smiled at each other, a small tear formed in the corner of her eye and ran slowly down her cheek before falling to the deck; it ran over the varnished timber and fell through the crack below, lost forever.

19 CAYNNA

The Green Road passed through the fertile lands of Caynna, scattered with smallholdings, crofts and the sprawling family estates of the landed gentry. Only Tudorfeld was more highly prized, with its crisscross of streams and tributaries providing natural irrigation. Many people were travelling on the broad route for trade or fortune in Cynstol or Numolport; they stared at the sixteen-strong company as they passed. Many recognised the royal emblem and bowed, but others whispered and grumbled. The royal family were often seen as distant and tied to the capital.

The company passed through the small village of Twislian in midafternoon, stopping only for refreshments before pushing north to the fork. Here, the wide Green Road continued for another two hundred and seventy miles over the River Dorbourne, the sparkling River Cwen and the rolling hills of Tudorfeld. There were many inns and taverns along the way, and it would have been good cheer to traverse, but that was not their path.

The Grenborg Road branched northeast. It was half the size of the Green Road, morphing from a broad, often gravel highway to a narrow dirt track. It swept through the undulating landscape bordered by drystone walls or rough wooden fences which marked the farms and crofts dotting the Caynna dales. Small woodlands edged the path, and rough clapper bridges, made from stone slabs, crossed the streams which trickled from the hilltops.

Jem spoke little as they travelled, noting that the soldiers were silent and obedient. Sir Torbrand also held himself severe and aloof; Moranne loathed talking with him. Only the prince made much sound, mainly from the exertion of holding the reins and steering his mount. Jem began to feel great respect for Asger. The Grenborg Road was the furthest the prince had ever ridden, and every step was a burden. In simply leading the company, he showed his steely character. Not once did he ask for rest or any special treatment; only mounting and dismounting required assistance from Lunn and Gron, who happily came to his aid.

The company's shadow was lengthening ahead of them, and a mild chill kissed their cheeks when Sir Torbrand called them to a halt near a small copse. He ordered them to make camp, which prompted the soldiers to unpack tents from the pack ponies and assemble them in a circle beside the trees. Jem helped and instinctively knew what to do. In contrast, Hayden stumbled about the clearing, dropping poles and tripping on guy ropes, much to the professional warriors' annoyance.

"Stick with me," said Jem, as he noticed Captain Biorn Fallon flash Hayden a dark look.

They sat in a circle around a stout fire, but the soldiers didn't relax. While some exchanged tales from the legion, others, such as Cal and Davill, rubbed oil onto their swords from rags they carried in their belts. Sax cleaned the day's dirt from his boots, and Gamin nervously inspected his bow.

Only the irreverent Brea sat smiling against a tree, with her legs outstretched, watching the dancing flames. "Keep rubbing that sword, and you'll go blind," she laughed.

Davill was unimpressed. "Quiet, hag," he snapped.

Biorn shot him a disappointed look, and Davill quickly looked away to continue his chores. It was clear that the soldiers disapproved of her.

Adherence to Freanism was patchy in Caynna, but few would openly blaspheme. The role of women was to bear children and support their husbands. While a woman like Lady Moranne was barely tolerated, with her exotic ways, unmarried women were generally reviled.

"You know I's seldom known by me name," said Brea, unfazed by the insult. "When I's young, they calls me wench; when I's older, they calls me whore, but now I sits with a bunch of kids only just out of nappies, they calls me hag. Tis funny."

"Hold your tongue," barked Biorn.

Brea smiled. "Or what, Captain? Are you going to strike an old woman? Do you not think these scars I has are proof I's already been hit enough times that makes no difference?"

Jem was sitting opposite the elderly archer and noticed the three scars on her face for the first time. They often became lost in the creases of her skin, but the flickering light picked them out.

"Who hit you?" he asked with concern.

Jem knew many men would hit their wives and used the Frean Pillars as justification.

"Men, of course," she said, allowing her eyes to flick upwards in disdain.

"Was it your husband?"

She shook her head. All eyes were now on the huntress while she gazed into the fire, and her mind rewound the years to times she'd tried to forget. "I's never been married."

The men mumbled with disapproval. It was inconceivable that a woman her age would be unwed in this culture.

"I came close," she said eventually. "Morris was a good man, the best I's ever met. I learned him to shoot, and we was happy."

"What happened?" asked Hayden. He loved romantic tales.

She gave a long sigh, and her gaze wandered south towards the hills and woodlands near Cynstol, where they hunted deer together.

"The stupid dung heap joined the Green Order for a two year tour. His first posting was Langley, where they were having trouble with bandits hiding in the forest. He took a sword to the chest on his first day, trying to save an idiot farmer living too close to the Deap."

"I'm sorry," said Hayden.

"So, who hit you?" asked Gamin shyly.

Slitan cast a disapproving eye towards his young apprentice and shook his head.

"Oh, a few," she said. "Usually, when they called us a slut or a whore."

Moranne and Asger had stopped talking, and even Torbrand was listening intently. Brea commanded the space whenever she spoke.

"There is one scar that runs deep," she continued. "Tis this one."

Brea pointed to a small scar near her eye, it was smaller than the others, but it seemed significant as it changed her mood.

"I was out in Cynstol having a drink at The Wheel Tavern. Twas a good night, and I took meself home with a fella named Bill Garrad. We has a kiss and a cuddle, and all was fine, but Bill, he wanted something else."

Moranne was stirring uneasily; she knew this story all too well. "Brea," she implored.

The archer wasn't done. "Well, he started hitting me, screaming and calling me a whore, but I still says no."

"Brea!" repeated Moranne, more urgently.

The huntress looked down so that the brim of her wide hat covered her eyes. No one would see them glisten in the light of the flames. "He took what he wanted anyway."

"I'm sorry, Brea."

"Don't be!" she snapped back. "Bill went straight to sleep, and I just lay there feeling wretched and filthy. I learned me a lesson that night, and I changed. When the sun rose, and a cock crowed, he woke up."

"What happened?" asked Jem.

"The last thing he saw was my face. I sat on top of him and slit his throat."

"I'm sorry," said the prince.

The mood in the camp had changed.

"Pay no bother, Your Highness," she replied. "It made me the woman I am and brought me to you sorry bunch of drain dogs. It also means I never sleeps without this in me hand."

With the mischievous smile starting to return, she held up a small hunting knife. It may have been the blade that killed Bill Garrad, but she'd never say. Brea stayed quiet for the rest of the night and finally retired to her tent ahead of the others.

"Do you think the story's true?" asked Hayden.

Jem nodded. "She's an old woman living in a world where men rule. I think she has more tales to tell." *She wasn't the only one*, he thought.

The look on Moranne's face told Jem she'd had similar experiences. Her words never betrayed her secrets, her real identity, her past or age. He could still see her standing in that painting, a three-hundred-year-old present to a long-dead king.

Moranne's mystery troubled his sleep that night. He wasn't transported to distant lands, but the faces of the living haunted him: the Supbry fortune teller, the Rowley crofters, and Alize in the forest. *'Be wary of her'*.

A set of glowing green eyes looked over Jem's tent as he tossed and turned. Brea's story reminded her to be brave and bide her time.

Jem woke with a start to see Lunn's enormous, grinning frame filling the tent entrance.

"Get up! Captain wants you."

He spoke with little detail and often just resorted to grunts and growls, but he always seemed to wear a disconcerting smile. Hayden proffered that he was dropped on his head as a child, but neither would dare joke to his face.

"That means now!" he boomed.

Jem and Hayden quickly dragged on their uniforms and ran out of the tent to see Captain Fallon waiting for them between some trees. The other men were also awake and busy taking down the camp or preparing breakfast.

"Next morning, I expect you both up by six," he said gruffly.

Giving a "yes sir" in unison, they stood before the grizzled captain and waited while he looked them up and down. He circled them, occasionally inspecting a strap on a breastplate, and checking that Jem's arm shields were tight.

"Well, you both look very pretty," he said, looking down beneath his thick, black eyebrows. "Can you fight?"

Hayden was tempted to answer but decided the question was both rhetorical and cynical. Jem gazed at the stoic soldier, trying to read the scars and creases which disappeared beneath a thick black beard.

"Lady Moranne has asked me to provide training in the sword, and I have decided to give the first lesson personally."

He was still pacing back and forth, but some of the other soldiers heard his words and started to pay attention.

Jem and Hayden were asked to remove their weapons, which Biorn inspected. A thin smile formed above his short, silver-flecked beard as he turned Hayden's knight sword in his hands.

"A Faircester blade and barely used, I'll wager," he said, holding the edge up to the light. "You carry a sword with no means to use it."

Hayden's usual arrogance evaporated in Bearun Forest when Jem snatched his sword as he froze. He bowed his head; the captain propped his weapon against a tree and picked up one of Jem's scimitars.

"Now, this blade is unfamiliar to me. A Jakari blade, I'm told."

Davill was leaning against a tree, watching proceedings and nodded in agreement.

"I took them from a dead bandit, sir," replied Jem, remembering the heated fight with Gelic and Hayden's desperate act of reluctant bravery.

"Well, you'll need to figure out the twin blades yourself. I will be teaching you both the knight sword."

He produced two swords from behind the tree and handed one to Hayden. The training swords had square edges and a blunt rounded tip, but they were the right weight and could still inflict a nasty bruise.

"You first, Gada Scirmann."

They moved away from the trees and stood on a flat area of rough ground. Most of the soldiers stopped their chores and gathered around the two men.

"Attack me!" barked the captain.

Hayden held the sword at his side and looked stunned. He had no desire to hit the captain, but some soldiers sniggered. He could hear Cal taking bets.

"I said, attack me!"

The young gada lifted his sword towards Biorn, but even before it reached waist height, the captain parried the attack sending the sword flying across the clearing, leaving the tip of his training blade resting on the top of Hayden's breastplate.

"Again!" shouted Biorn.

The words rang in Hayden's head as the captain shouted them continuously over the next half an hour. Every time he lifted the sword, Biorn would send it spinning across the ground, sometimes causing the men to duck out of its path. Other times, the young gada would manage to hold the first attack, only to find the tip of Biorn's blade against his body or resting beside his head.

Jem started shouting words of encouragement such as "strike from above" and "lean back", but Hayden grew tired and embarrassed. With anger swelling inside, he held the blade high and pushed it down with all his strength; once again, Biorn swept the sword away. This time Hayden had committed so much energy that he fell forward, crumpling into a heap at the captain's feet.

Lunn's rumbling laughter joined the other men, who clapped and whooped in amusement. Even Prince Asger smiled as he steadied himself on his two walking sticks.

"Enough for today," said the captain gruffly, as he retrieved the sword from a gorse bush.

Crestfallen, the young Burlander wandered towards the remnants of the camp, where a grinning Davill slapped him on the back.

"Don't worry; he's just putting you in your place. I'm taking your next lesson."

It was little consolation. Hayden sunk to the ground and stared back towards the clearing where Jem held the same sword and stood opposite the harsh captain, waiting for the order.

"Attack m—"

The words barely escaped Biorn's lips; Jem was already striking down from a height, causing the captain to reel backwards and only just parry the blow. His eyes widened, clearly surprised at the gada's confidence. He countered late, but Jem was already wheeling the blade around, throwing Biorn sideways and causing him to duck as the tip skimmed past his ear.

Cal recoiled, gasping, and the other men let out calls of "oh", sucking air through their teeth. Moranne stood beside the prince smiling with pride. *Just like his father.*

Biorn collected himself and thrust confidently at Jem's chest, but the gada was already countering and pushed the cross guard close to the captain's face. It was there that Biorn saw the green fire burning behind Jem's eyes.

"Frea!" he cried, pulling back. "Who are you?" He quickly turned so that Jem's back was to the men, hiding the lad's wild green eyes.

They fought on, exchanging blows and using every inch of the area, but finally, Jem tired. His lack of practice showed, and his breath started to labour. With a final counterstrike, the captain brought his blade down heavily and stopped it just an inch short of Jem's neck.

The men were clapping and whistling. "The lad can fight!" shouted Cal, handing coins to the winking Sax.

Brea sat against a tree, sipping soup. She threw back her head, and her silver hair spread across her shoulders. "You show him, kid," she said, smiling mischievously.

"Who taught you?" asked Biorn.

Jem shook his head. "No one," he replied meekly.

"I will train you myself, be here early tomorrow."

Jem nodded curtly and slotted the twin blades back into the crossed scabbards on his back.

Caspin was still clapping when Jem returned to the camp. "You are a man of many hidden talents, Master Poulterer." He gave a quick reassuring wink. Jem's other gift would remain secret for now.

Back at the clearing, Biorn stood looking out at Gada Poulterer while the other soldiers congratulated him and slapped his back in turn.

"Do not speak of it," said Moranne quietly, as she appeared behind him. "The others need not know."

The captain's gaze remained fixed on Jem and the menacing blades crossing his back. "What is he?"

For a brief moment, she remembered another man holding a mighty broadsword, the same way Jem had held the blade before bringing it down towards Biorn. It was a long time ago. "He's exceptional," she said finally. "That's all I can say for now."

Biorn nodded; the mysterious Moranne was well known to the men, who called her a witch behind her back. She was tight with the crown; the captain would do as she bid, for now.

It didn't take long to break camp; the men were well-drilled and efficient. The last pony was loaded with tents, and the soldiers prepared for the saddle. Everyone was ready, but Brea stood beside the same tree she'd sat against the previous night, gazing back along the trail.

"Are you alright?" asked Hayden, leaning against the opposite side of the trunk.

"Why wouldn't I be?" she replied, lost in her thoughts.

Hayden loved spending time with women and sharing their stories. They often talked about their feelings, and he felt relaxed in their company. "I wondered if you're thinking of the story you told us last night."

Her demeanour changed immediately. Turning quickly to face the squire's son, she grasped the top of his breastplate and dragged him forward, pressing her face against his. "Never ask me," she said, her voice deepening with menace. "I'm no victim. I'm a survivor."

He nodded quickly, and she released him. "I'm sorry," he blurted, but he could see she already regretted her harshness.

"You're a good lad, Gada Hayden. Just watch what you say to the men."

Captain Fallon was barking the order to mount before Hayden could ask Brea what she meant. He wanted to say more, but instead, he simply smiled at her and returned to his horse where Jem was waiting.

The Grenborg Road snaked through the Caynna dales, past fields of complaining cows, braying sheep and tall lines of late-harvest corn. Jem was riding a little taller after his morning lesson, and the men were starting to include him in their jokes and banter.

Lunn wouldn't talk about his past but enjoyed laughing at the others. His baritone voice could be heard across the whole company.

"He's from Fiske," said Gron of his best friend. "It's a fishing village on the north coast. Nothing there."

"It's a hole," rumbled Lunn in agreement.

The stocky Gron Hamur hailed from the town of Cealdwater, high in the Midtlen Range, perched on the banks of the icy Lake Brantmere. "We're all big in my family, with plenty of muscle," he said.

"You should see his sisters," laughed Lunn. He slapped his friend hard on the back, but Gron's frame was so solid he barely moved.

"Passengers," moaned Slitan.

"Civilians," agreed Cal referring to Jem and Hayden.

"The lads are alright!" boomed Lunn protectively.

Cal ignored him. "This ain't no mission for babysitting the witch's lapdog or his girlfriend," he chuckled.

Moranne didn't hear the insult, but she could see that Hayden's graceful ways had been noticed by soldiers who followed traditional Freanism. Slitan and Cal had started to refer to the squire's son as "Lady Hayden." He could be in danger if it continued. She decided to have a quiet word with Captain Fallon, who'd seen it all before.

"I'll do my best, but if he doesn't prove himself soon, the men will turn, and I'll have trouble stopping them."

Biorn didn't seem reassuring, prompting Moranne to ride beside Jem for a short while and remind him to watch Hayden's back.

"I will, ma'am, don't worry," said Jem. He knew Hayden was no soldier, but he'd saved his life in Bearun and wouldn't see his friend harmed.

It would be early afternoon before the company's shadow finally pointed to the distant towers of Grenborg.

20 THE WALL

"I will not enter the town!" said Moranne once again.

Sir Caspin and Sir Torbrand had been trying to persuade her for almost half an hour. The party waited, sitting astride their mounts, just outside the tall wooden gates to the walled town of Grenborg.

"It's only for one night," said Caspin. "Then we'll be on our way."

"My word is final!" she replied, becoming increasingly agitated. "I will be staying at the Gatehouse Inn. Find the swordswoman. That will be all!"

Moranne was already leading Bess towards the inn's stables, leaving the Linhold brothers to command the company.

"What's wrong with Lady Moranne?" asked Hayden.

Jem was just as puzzled. He knew better than to question the mysterious woman and her strange ways.

Grenborg lay in a natural dip between the surrounding hills, making it easy to approach unseen. It was placed to benefit from the three small streams which crossed it, but the town fathers realised the defensive weakness and built a twenty-foot wall to circle the town, dotted with small watchtowers. The Grenborg Road passed through the West Gate and ran straight through the High Street town; it exited the East Gate and became the Deap Path to Deapholt Forest.

In centuries past, the town functioned as a valuable trading post and overnight refuge for the alviri; now, it catered only for the local farmers and travellers from Deap Gate's direction. Few locals remembered seeing the fair folk, and sightings of the Cempestre were rare. The walls' cold grey stone was pockmarked and weathered, with signs of repair. It had stood for six hundred years and had witnessed many empires come and go while protecting its people.

Torbrand exchanged a few words with a guard leaning from one of the gate towers. The tall, heavy doors soon swung inwards on creaking, rusty hinges.

The town air rushed through the opening, blowing Brea's hair and startling the horses, which whinnied and bucked on clattering hooves. Scents of mature cheese, aged ham and the sweet flavour of toffee and fudge swirled from the town's market.

Jem could detect something else in the air, something foul and something from a dream, but what was it?

Folk on the High Street stopped to stare at the varied company, especially the young prince. Few knew of Prince Asger, and fewer knew of his disability. He met it with good grace, waving to the curtseying housewives and saluting wall guards. The party dismounted near the Green Man Tavern and proceeded towards the town square, pushing through the busy crowds.

Fly, my love.

"Who was that?" shouted Jem.

Hayden cocked his head in surprise. "What's wrong?"

Jem seemed agitated; he looked around as if trying to identify a face in the crowd. The air was thick, and the overpowering smell was causing him to gag. He loosened his collar and felt the sweat pouring down his neck.

Torbrand and Caspin were asking after the swordswoman, and locals were pointing towards the centre of town. Jem started to stumble, pushing through the crowd and cowering as faces loomed close, taunting him.

Please, no, please!

"Where are you?" shouted Jem.

"We're here," said Hayden. "What's wrong?"

Somebody was calling to him, but the voice came from everywhere as if it echoed from the shops and homes with their grey walls and roofs of blood-red brick.

Something's wrong.

"Yes, ma'am?" blurted Jem as he spun around, trying to find the speaker.

It was a woman's voice, but Moranne was outside the gates. His temple pounded, and his vision blurred as he staggered between the buildings, searching for the voices. He left Hayden and the others, separated by the market day crowds.

Fly, my love.

This time, the voice was louder, causing Jem to stagger back as the words rang through his head. It was familiar, like something from a dream. It reminded him of Denbry and those last days in its green, rural prison.

Through narrow passages, he stumbled past a pigsty and under damp linen washing that hung across the alley. He could hear the High Street noise and wondered where his friends were, but something was tugging at him and pulling him towards the wall. The ill smell invaded his senses until his eyes ran, and he begged for it to stop.

Finally, like a lifted veil, he saw it: a lone warrior walking through a green sea of twisted, dead bodies. It was all around, thick and cloying like the mist over the battlefield. It was the smell of death.

"What happened here?" he shouted.

When the answer came, it was so loud that he fell forward onto stony ground, cutting his hand.

We made an oath!

"Who are you?" he cried, dragging himself upright, but his foot gave way, and he barrelled forward towards the town's grey wall. He thrust out his hand at the mossy bricks, but as Jem touched the cold stone, a jolt of pain pulsed through his arm; it leapt across his shoulder and into his head. A piercing, bright white light scorched his eyes, and he felt himself becoming weightless.

Slowly an image formed. Starting with bright blue and vibrant green, the colours swirled together until they coalesced into hard grey edges and floating white clouds. The smell of roasting meat permeated the air, and a gentle breeze caressed his skin. The town gates looked different, just as tall, but the wood was more ornate with bevelled panels and shining square-headed bolts. Jem's vision followed the woodgrain, skimmed the rough grey stone and flew over the wall. It revealed the same cobbled Grenborg High Street, but some buildings were different, and this was no market day.

Soldiers filled the western end of the street. Some were spit-roasting a pig, while others cleaned their weapons or chatted. Make-shift tents dotted the square, hung from simple wooden frames. A few of the men sheltered, nursing bandaged wounds.

Captain Keylenn Domliff strode through the camp, nodding to soldiers, encouraging them to "be ready" and "stay sharp."

The men's loyalty pleased him, and the trust kept them tight. Fighting hadn't yet troubled the walled town; however, they'd taken in many of the walking wounded.

Women, children and the elderly were sheltered at the east end of the town at the lady's insistence. She was particular, giving orders like a general since she'd arrived a week ago with her friends. He railed against it at first, but her forthright nature won him over, and now he looked forward to the precious moments they spent together, flirting.

He ducked through the entrance of one of the gatehouse towers and climbed the spiral stairs to the wall top. Keylenn was already smiling as he emerged into the light. She was leaning over the battlements with her short-haired friend.

"Lady Moranne," he said, striding confidently towards her. "Is everything to your liking?"

She scanned the horizon, gazing at the hills which surrounded the town.

"Not really," she said stiffly.

"This place is a death-trap," added another vaguely familiar voice.

Standing on the opposite side, the short bobbed hair of Rana barely moved in the gentle breeze. She continued to gaze along the horizon, fully aware that her and Aludra's presence was causing much consternation among the Frean faithful.

"These walls have stood for three hundred years," said Keylenn. "We're quite—"

"Safe?" she protested. "Ally is down there treating the wounded because he beguiled the oni. His power can cut through any wall. We're too exposed here."

Keylenn was about to defend himself, but his secret love cut him short.

"Rana is right," said Moranne. "We need to get out of here."

"Where would we go?"

Moranne looked out to the south, and just for a moment, she glimpsed a shadow on the hill; when she looked again, it was gone.

"South," she said finally. "We go across country to the coast and make our way to the capital."

"That's rough terrain," replied the captain.

He didn't want to admit it, but he knew she was right. The roads would be watched.

"Something's wrong," said Rana, turning to Moranne. "I can feel it."

Lady Moranne was pacing along the wall, trying to see the shadow again. "Get your men away from the wall, Captain."

"Why?"

"Just do it!" she snapped.

Captain Domliff gave the order that rippled around the wall. Men stepped away from the battlements in a cascade, circling the city.

"What's going on?" shouted a tall, dark-haired woman who stood beneath their position in the square.

"Something's not right, Ally," replied Rana. She peered down at her partner and shook her head.

Aludra paced back and forth a little while Moranne and Rana continued to check the terrain, and then she stopped and looked back at the gate.

"He's here," she said solemnly.

Moranne strode to the captain and placed a hand on his shoulder. "Get the men inside." Their eyes met for a moment, but she couldn't tell him what was coming. She pulled him close and kissed him on the lips. She knew how he felt.

"I'm sorry, Captain; you need to go."

As Rana looked at the undulating Caynna hills, she saw the shadow first. A vast dark shape poured into the creases and crevices of the hill's body and folded over each summit. It jinked left and right, but its path was absolute. It was heading for the town.

"Please, no, please!" she gasped under her breath.

"You need to go now, my friend," shouted Moranne to the young captain. "Get the men inside."

"It's too late," said Rana.

The shadow's owner was a flock of starlings dancing in slow sweeping curves as it approached the town.

"I see nothing," said Keylenn, peering at the horizon.

"Get off the wall, and get your men inside. Now!" shouted Moranne. She pushed him towards the tower door, then thrust a hand into her jacket to grasp the cold metal of her sceptre.

"We need to go," said Rana. She put an arm around Moranne and started tugging her along the wall, but her friend's gaze was on Captain Domliff as the shadow crept over him.

His eyes filled with incomprehension as he felt his right hand reach for the sword hanging from his waist. He didn't see Moranne matching his moves and grabbing for the hilt of Steorra. She pulled it free of the scabbard with a warrior's smooth, practised movement.

For the slightest instant, the captain's eyes widened as he swept his sword towards her head, with might he didn't possess. The incomprehension was cut short by the blinding sweep of Moranne's blade glinting in the corner of his eye and the searing pain in his chest breaking the bond.

Through tears, Moranne watched the life leaving his body at the end of her sword, with no knowledge of what had passed.

"I'm sorry," she cried.

He slumped to his knees, open-mouthed, before falling flat onto the cold stone.

"Ally! Run!" shouted Rana. She peered over the wall at her love while soldiers became possessed all around her. "Get out of there!"

As one, they ran through the town towards the East Gate. Moranne and Rana sprinted along the wall while Aludra ran through the centre of town, pursued by possessed soldiers with swords aloft and fear in their eyes.

Rana held the sceptre before her, and charged, head-down with her eyes blazing green. A soldier emerged from a tower ahead, with cruel knives in both hands, running wildly towards them. With a flick of her wrist, Rana swiped the air forward, and a bolt of green energy pulled the soldier off his feet. The blast sent him flying to the cobbles below, where he crashed in a sea of broken bones.

Moranne sent her own bolt behind Aludra, knocking the soldiers back, but still, they persisted, jumping over the fallen and racing madly towards her.

"There are too many!" shouted Rana. "We'll never make it."

The gate was open, and the women and children streamed through as they saw their husbands and lovers charging toward them with weapons drawn.

Women, unlucky enough to emerge from buildings on the street, were mowed down instantly and hacked to death where they fell. Screams of terror from the lost merged with the terrifying anguish of men killing their wives and daughters with hands which weren't their own.

More soldiers made the wall, both behind and in front. Moranne cut them down with no mercy, while Rana's power flattened them against the stone or threw them down.

"Come on!" shouted Moranne. She could see the gate ahead; Aludra would make it before them as they cut their way through the men.

A young boy swiped at Aludra as she ran past, cutting her side, so a streak of blood fell into the cobbles, becoming lost beneath the boots of her frenzied pursuers.

"I'll hold them!" she shouted, while Rana threw another poor soul to the earth, and Moranne decapitated the sergeant who'd greeted her with "good day" just hours earlier.

As she reached the open gates, Aludra turned to face the horde with her hand already holding the sceptre aloft. Its orb pulsed with a faint green light, but as she lifted it high above her head, it snapped and crackled into life. A dancing emerald flame poured forth as if cascading over an invisible dome, spreading out so that it filled the entrance and dipped to touch the ground. The surface blinked and stirred as it wrapped around Aludra, forming a shimmering barrier. She bowed her head and watched as the soldiers threw themselves forward.

Gada Sam Tanner, the shy apprentice from Supford, couldn't grasp why he'd just killed Eveline, the lovely maid who smiled at him daily. He'd cut her throat with no mercy, then joined the stampede towards Aludra. The image wouldn't leave him. Sam couldn't cry or stop running while the unseen power forced him onwards. He wanted it to end and soon got his wish; the first man to hit the shimmering wall of light, his body was engulfed in an explosion of white and green sparks. He was thrown back into his brethren with a mighty force, scattering the soldiers on either side. His lifeless body hit the cobbles, his heart stopped, and the puppeteer was gone from him.

Wave after bloody wave of screaming men piled into the wall of light. The first ones fell instantly dead; others were knocked back, concussed and bewildered; still, they charged forth.

Moranne reached one of the East Gate towers just ahead of Rana, chased by a wild-eyed sergeant. With the last of her sceptre's power, she lifted him from the ground, his legs still spinning as he tried to scramble towards her. She held him for a few seconds knowing the evil which lurked behind his eyes.

"I'll come for you. You'll pay!" screamed Rana to the hapless soldier; then, she threw him down towards Aludra's barrier. His body writhed in green flame, and the force sent him flying into the tower wall.

"Move!" shouted Moranne. She grabbed Rana by the arm and pulled her down the spiral stairs. The carnage echoed from below as the soldiers threw themselves against the barrier. The writhing green light cut through the stairway, but the women passed through it unscathed.

Aludra's power was great, second only to Corvus himself, but as she poured all her will into the barrier, it started to fail.

"Ally, come on, we need to go!" shouted Rana, emerging through the tower doorway.

Moranne summed up the situation first. The doors were opened on the wrong side of the barrier. They couldn't be closed without leaving its embrace; if Aludra lowered the protection, they would all die. She put a hand on Rana's shoulder, with a sick feeling in her stomach and tears already flowing.

"Rana. We need to go."

Even as she grasped the situation, Rana wouldn't accept it. She threw her arms around Aludra and hugged her tightly, sobbing into her dark, tousled hair. "I'm not leaving you; I'm never leaving you!" she sobbed.

Still grasping the sceptre as men continued to rebound from the crackling veil, Aludra stroked Rana's glossy black hair and kissed her gently. "You've given me the best days of my life, and I would change nothing. Just do one last thing for me." Tears were cascading down her smooth cheeks, but her voice never broke.

"Anything. I'll do anything for you!"

Aludra glanced at Moranne, who couldn't bear to watch, then fixed Rana with her gaze while stroking the tears from her cheek.

"Live."

Rana convulsed as grief took her, her chest was heaving, and her breathing stuttered. She squeezed Aludra tightly, but her lover dropped her hand, leaving Rana clinging to her body.

Moranne noticed the barrier start to shimmy and blink; Aludra's power was waning. It would only take a few soldiers to kill them all. Time was running out. She grasped Rana by the arm and tried to pull her away.

"You go!" insisted Rana. "We'll be right behind you."

"No!" insisted Aludra. "This is me, *my* powers; this is *my* choice."

"I'm nothing without you!"

"And I have failed if your journey ends here." Aludra shook her head and pushed Rana to the ground. "Go with Elara, and I will follow; trust me."

They knew it was a lie, but Rana had always been in Aludra's power. Almost as if hypnotised, Rana peered up at Moranne and took her hand.

With a last look at Aludra, Moranne helped Rana to her feet and dragged Rana through the gate. She pulled back and strained to see her love until the will to live took over, and they both ran. They could see other women in the distance, heading into the gorse and scrub which marked the south. Even if they got clear, they would struggle to lose the chasing pack.

Just as they reached the first thicket, Rana stopped and turned to look back.

"Don't," said Moranne.

Rana gazed back at the walled city and the flickering green halo surrounding the love of her life, a love which had stood for over a thousand years and would stand for all eternity.

The barrier was flashing now. Aludra poured all her strength into it, but her power reserves were spent. She turned to look out towards Rana and Moranne. The adventure was coming to an end. She smiled broadly; only her two friends would hear her final words echoing through their minds.

Fly, my love.

She dropped the sceptre, and the light blinked out. Her visage was lost immediately in a sea of frenzied bodies, crushing their brethren and stabbing wildly at the spot where she'd stood. So great was their number that they filled the gate, blocking it with their mass until a wall of bodies sealed the East Gate.

Rana dropped to her knees, fixated on the spot where Aludra had fallen. Unable to believe her soulmate was gone, she trembled, wept and convulsed in anguish. She tried to blink away the memory as if it were a dream, but the image wouldn't change.

"Ally..." she sobbed. "My Ally..."

Moranne, too, was in tears, but her focus was on survival. "I'm sorry," she said; her voice was trembling. "We must go."

"My Ally," wept Rana.

"Rana, we must go now!"

"Then go!" screamed Rana. Her eyes blazed like green suns, and her forehead wrinkled into a terrifying scowl.

"Not without you."

"Leave me be! It's your fault she's gone! You've taken the only good thing in my life!"

"Rana, please," implored Moranne.

Rana turned back to look at Moranne's ashen face. "After we kill him..." she began, but her grief couldn't form the words of hate circling her mind.

Watching, through the starling's eyes, safely out of reach, a tall man with sharp features and a sadistic grin chuckled to himself. "And now just two remain. I found you once, and I'll find you again."

The image of Aludra smiling just as she fell was burning into Jem's consciousness, and the evil words echoed as if in a great chamber. *I'll find you again. I'll find you again.*

"Jem! Are you alright?" The voice was different; it seemed familiar. "We've found her. Wake up!"

The images were fading, and a new blurry image was forming. Jem could see many faces staring down at him as if he'd sunk into the underworld.

"Master Jem! Please wake up!"

Gradually the familiar voice matched the friendly face of Hayden kneeling over a bruised Jem lying on the cobbles beneath a section of the wall. Some of the townsfolk stood around, watching the drama.

"How long have I been gone?" asked Jem, rubbing his eyes.

Hayden took his hand and helped him to his feet. "Not long," he replied. "I'm guessing you had another vision?"

Jem nodded; he was in no mood to relive the carnage he'd just witnessed. At least one thing had been resolved; he knew why Moranne was staying outside the town.

"We've found the swordswoman," said Hayden excitedly. "Come and see."

The town wall loomed over Jem as he looked up into its grey, cold heart. It stood silent now, but the sounds of death still haunted his thoughts. He saw Aludra vanishing beneath a tsunami of frenzied bodies and Rana's pain etched across her furrowed brow in rage. Moranne seemed strangely detached from her supposed friends, but more worryingly, who was Elara?

21 THE CLOWN

Raffus Hildebill wanted a son. He'd been very close to his father, a sergeant in the Queen's Battalion. They would hunt together, where his father taught him the bow and later taught him the sword. He would follow in his father's footsteps by joining the Queen's Battalion as a gada; however, he would never equal his father's rank, reaching only corporal by the end of his commission.

He needed a son to continue the family line and surpass his stature. His caring wife, Shenti, bore him just one child; a daughter.

From birth, he could barely look at her, and in adolescence, he ignored her. Laying on his deathbed when she was just twenty-one years of age, his last words would haunt her forever.

"Marry a soldier," he said, before closing his eyes for the last time.

Ellen pulled the buckles tight on the tan leather bustier, which barely passed for armour. Birger assured her the sight of cleavage would bring more customers, and it did seem to encourage the local male low-lives to take a chance. She spotted herself in a mirror, propped against the tent's walls, and sighed. Her dark, strawberry blonde hair was pulled back into a ponytail and held secure with an alviri silver band; her light blue eyes were lined in charcoal, making her look demented. At twenty-seven years, she should have a husband in Frean eyes, but none were worthy.

When Windrass taught her the sword, she had high hopes of joining the Green Order or even the Burland Defence, but men's laughter sealed her fate. A touring sideshow and fighting off the advances of drunken fell men; that was her life.

The crowd outside were clapping, which meant she'd soon be passing the curtain for her star turn. She pulled on the leather cuff guards and reached for the two splintered and marked wooden swords at the heart of her act. She listened for Birger to start his introduction.

"And now, ladies and gentlemen, my lords and Your Royal Highness, let me present to you the star of our show. I warn you to prepare yourself for what you're about to see. There are no tricks, simply the devastating power of the wild woman reared by wolves and trained by bears in the forest of Deapholt.

You may call her an abomination, but we call her Torvixen, the angel of death."

She took a deep breath, tensed her shoulders and pushed through the curtain to find a familiar reception.

The laughter was immediate, rippling around the crowd and echoing from the surrounding buildings.

"Raised by wolves?" yelled one man. "She's more like a mouse."

"Our scullery maid has bigger muscles," shouted another.

"And a bigger chest!" mocked a third.

At barely five and a half feet tall, she was average height for a woman in these parts, but Birger made her sound like a giant. He insisted it was all part of the act, which usually led to a change in atmosphere as the performance progressed.

"This is a joke," said Torbrand under his breath. The men were assembled at the front of a small gathering in one corner of the town square. The previous act was an excellent juggler; this seemed like a poor choice for the finale.

Moranne gave Torbrand very explicit instructions to recruit the swordswoman, but he wasn't taking orders from a woman. He would be the judge of her worth.

"She seems quite small for a warrior," agreed Sir Caspin.

"And female," quipped Captain Fallon.

Sir Torbrand had already decided he wouldn't take her, but he needed a convincing story to persuade Moranne.

"Don't be fooled by her stature, for beneath the exterior of this slight woman beats the heart of a demented killer," shouted Birger from the bright red box where he stood. His coat was a patchwork of brightly coloured velvet, and he wore a dark blue velvet hat which seemed to perch on his large ears. He stroked his long grey beard and smiled, ignoring the jibes.

"We're more interested in what's beneath the armour," shouted a man from the back of the crowd.

"I'll give you two coppers for an hour, love," bawled another big man sitting on a nearby bench.

Ellen ignored the hecklers; she'd heard it all before and much worse. The song of bravado would soon change.

"Step up, gentlemen," continued Birger, "The end of the wooden sword has a blue paint mark. Score a hit, and you'll win a real gold coin. Just two coppers to prove yourself."

Ellen held the wooden swords aloft, showing the painted blunt ends.

"Let's get this over with," said Biorn as he loosened his sword belt and stepped forward.

He was about to part with his money when Torbrand held up a hand.

"I'll do it," he said. "Fetch the practice blades."

Jem arrived in the square with Hayden to see a smiling Birger, an impassive *Torvixen* and the soldiers laughing and joking. "What's going on?" he asked. Sir Torbrand was pacing back and forth, swiping the air with one of the practice swords.

"My lord," implored Birger. "We feel that the wooden blades are safer for everyone."

Torbrand finally stopped pacing and held out his hand containing a bright gold coin.

"I'll give you a gold coin and another two if your wench lands a blow."

The faintest flash of anger creased Ellen's face before her expression returned to impassive indifference.

Birger gazed at her with a plea in his eyes. She looked Torbrand up and down, and a thin smile creased her lips. A single nod sealed the deal.

"A copper says he breaks her arm," said Slitan.

"Two says she puts him on his arse," answered Brea.

"Done!"

Torbrand handed Ellen a practice sword. He could smell the jasmine in her hair as she leant forward to take it.

"I don't want to hurt you," he said.

She remained mute, weighing the blade in her hands. Torbrand had never hit a woman and didn't intend to start today, but she seemed unfazed and treated him with contempt.

"Very well," he continued, "proceed...."

Torbrand had barely finished speaking when she swept the sword upwards with breathtaking speed, slashing towards his chest. He leapt backwards, the blade missing his breastplate by just an inch, bringing gasps from the soldiers.

Torvixen didn't wait for him to recover. Twirling the blade in a show of confidence, she thrust forward at his chest. Torbrand parried the attack, but she countered immediately with a hidden cut that almost connected with his neck.

"Frea!" he gasped. The woman had skill.

"Come on, sir!" yelled Gron. "Teach the wench a lesson."

Sir Torbrand composed himself and moved back to find some space. The square was bordered on three sides by buildings, including an inn called The Green Man, where Gron, Lunn and Sax flanked the prince. All were sitting, enjoying the spectacle.

"Give her a spanking," continued Gron, chuckling to himself.

Ellen flashed him a dark look, then readied herself for the knight's attack, which came swiftly. He cut down towards her shoulder, but she countered quickly, ducking back with impossible speed. They fought around the square, trading blows aggressively. They were very evenly matched. Torbrand's strength powered massive swings, but Ellen was fast and agile, ducking below his strikes and leaping sideways to counter at his rear.

She was pushed back towards Gron, who held out his hands as if caressing her rear. Taking one more step, she raised her foot and stamped on Gron's boot with all her might. He screamed in agony and rose to his feet, cursing, but the swordswoman was already dancing away.

The fight was taking too long, and Torbrand felt foolish. She was running rings around him and was clearly well-trained. She didn't fight like a bear; she was like an alviri. He needed to finish it.

Deliberately stumbling, she took the bait and came in close. Torbrand drove the blade away, and she lost her footing for an instant. He pushed her in the stomach with his boot and sent her reeling over a table into the crowd.

For a moment, Torbrand thought he'd gone too far until she emerged with a trail of blood from the cut lips of a broad smile. *Finally, a worthy opponent,* she thought, shaking her head from side to side and brushing the dust from her arms.

From a slow walk, she launched into a sprint directly at the tall Middcrofter. He readied to counter, but at the last second, she ducked down and slid over the pathing to swipe his legs. Noticing just in time, Torbrand leapt to avoid the blade but landed awkwardly and fell on his back.

Brea winked at Slitan, thinking the bet was won, especially as Ellen was on the knight, aiming the sword for his chest, but steel struck stone when Torbrand rolled away. He swiped at the fixed blade, knocking it from her hand across the square. Jumping to his feet, he grabbed her bustier and pulled her close, the tip of his sword resting beneath her chin.

"You lose," he said, with laboured breath, through the whoops and cheers of his men.

Still, without words, she slowly shook her head, with a wide grin lighting her natural beauty. She nodded down, gesturing for Torbrand to look. His eyes followed the gesture over the curve of her chest, down the creases of her armour, and to the cuffed hand near his stomach; the hand holding a small hunting knife pressed against his leather breastplate, ready to pierce his gut.

Everything which made Torbrand Linhold an aloof, difficult disciplinarian melted away for a short moment when his stony face cracked into a smile for the first time in many months.

"My name is Sir Torbrand Linhold of the Green Order. I have a proposition for you."

Torvixen cocked her head to one side, and the smile shifted from triumph to mischief. "And I have one for you," she said, speaking for the first time. Her voice was deep and hypnotic. Nothing like the giggling girls of court or the eligible ladies Torbrand's mother tried to match.

Torbrand held out two gold coins, but she took his hand and closed it.

"Keep your money, Sir Torbrand. I will join your company on one condition."

He looked around to see Caspin standing behind him and the soldiers re-enacting the battle with hilarious embellishments.

"Name it," he said, staring into her mysterious blue eyes.

"I want a commission with the army. Any legion."

He knew what the men would say, and he could sense his father's disdain at the mere thought, but he was in charge, and Moranne expected results.

"Granted," he said finally, holding out his hand.

She reached out and found his large, masculine grip immediately relaxed as she took his hand.

"My name is Ellen. Ellen Hildebill."

Although dawn cast its light against the East Gate, it was filtered through grey clouds spreading from the north and creeping over the landscape like a mourning veil.

Jem slept uneasily in the small barracks. The image of Aludra falling under the onslaught was plaguing his thoughts and filling his heart with dread. He'd watched the fight between Ellen and Torbrand but felt detached, as if time had stopped around him. Hayden woke Jem early and dragged him through the town to the rally point outside the East Gate.

They stood near a large stone obelisk, weathered and crossed with moss and lichen. It bore the simple phrase: "In honour of all those who lost their lives in the battle of Grenborg."

Jem knew there was no battle. He'd lived through every moment of the massacre and couldn't cast the memories aside. They piled onto the images of the Jakaris he'd seen at the croft and the dead bodies of Skati's men in the forest. There was so much death.

"No sword training today," said Captain Fallon as he joined them with Torbrand and Caspin in tow.

The group slowly assembled around the monument, tightening armour, readying the horses and complaining about the barracks food.

"Mornin' scumbags," joked Brea as she emerged from the gate with Ellen. The two had spent the night in the Green Man at Torbrand's insistence. It was to save Ellen from unwanted advances rather than protect Brea's honour.

"The crone and the clown," mocked Slitan, leaning against the stone while he waxed his bow.

Ellen gave him a thunderous look, but Brea laughed. "You can rub it all you want, but you still can't shoot for dung."

Stone and Sceptre

The soldiers laughed, and even Torbrand hid a secret smile when Moranne joined the group. She'd walked around the wall with Bess, and even now, she kept her distance from the gate.

"I hear you're all in fine spirits," she said warmly. "Please introduce me to our newest member."

"This is Ellen Hildebill," said Sir Torbrand stiffly, "and this is Lady Moranne. The leader of our mission."

After the formalities were satisfied, Moranne took Ellen aside to tell her of the mission and the critical role she could play. While she didn't understand Corvus's power, she was honoured to be involved and assured Moranne of her loyalty.

As the group readied to leave, Jem found Moranne standing gazing at the obelisk. Her brow was furrowed, and her eyes glistened in the half-light.

"I know what happened, ma'am," said Jem cautiously. He knew how painful it must be and wasn't sure she would share her secret.

"I knew you'd see it; the echoes are powerful here. I feel them too." She continued to stare for a while, lost in her long history.

"Were you close to Aludra?"

She raised her eyes to meet his at the mention of that ancient name. Countless years passed, but it felt like yesterday.

"Ally was my best friend. We grew up together." It was all she could say to stop the torrent of tears which would come if she continued. With every answer came more questions, and she could feel them bubbling in Jem's consciousness. *Grew up where?*

While Jem knew Aludra's fate, the image of Rana faded with despair and anger.

"What happened to Rana?" he asked, conscious that every memory wounded her afresh.

Moranne looked back towards the city walls and into the distance where the mighty Lyften Tower stood beyond sight.

"She's gone."

There would be no more questions today. Moranne mounted her horse and signalled to Caspin that they should go.

Jem looked back at the grey walls of Grenborg with its streets of hidden blood. A threshold had been passed, and innocence was forever lost in its cold stone heart.

Moranne stared straight ahead until the walled city was lost behind the hills, which blanketed the Caynna dales.

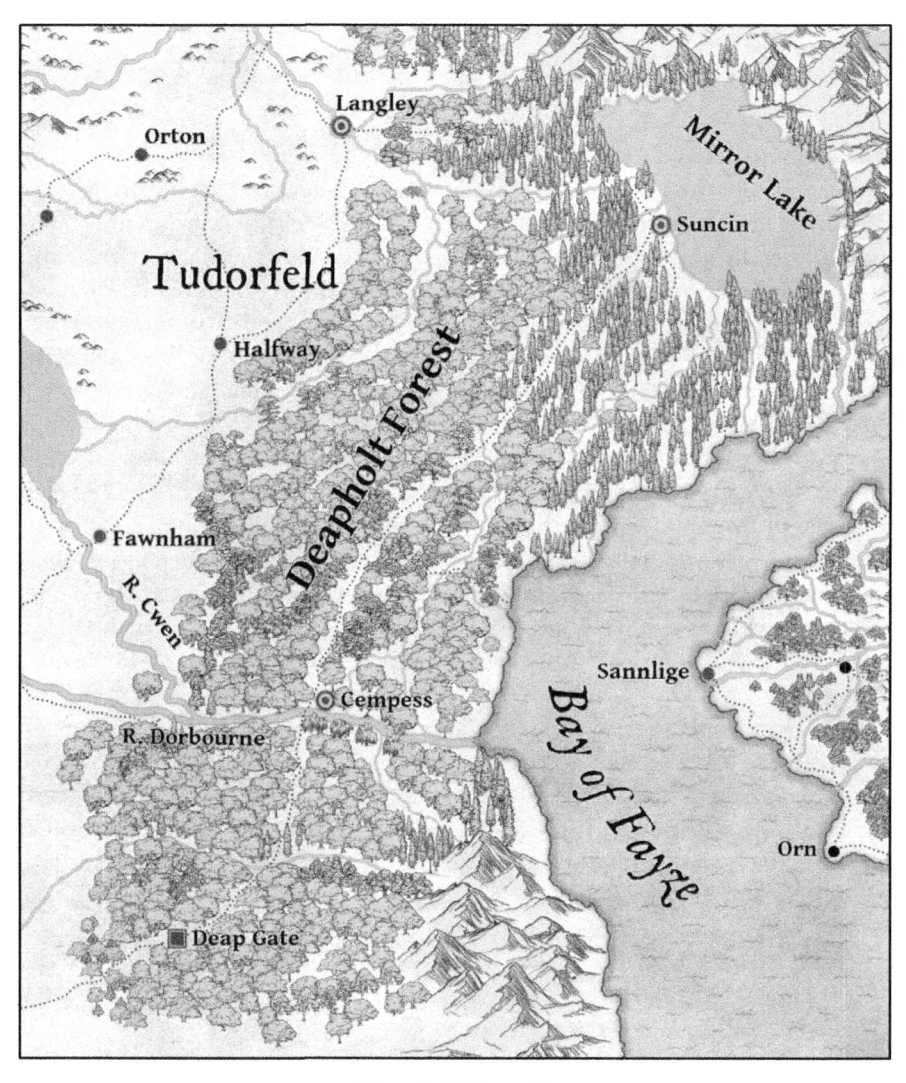

Deapholt Forest

22 RED CAP

Few humans remembered the Deap Road as a bustling artery connecting the alviri, and later the Cempestre, with Caynna and Middcroft. The path through Deapgate and onwards to Cempess and Alfheim had been wide and busy, dotted with inns and small villages. The fair folk of Fayze traded freely with the humans and travelled across the land into Salamas unhindered. Alliances were formed, and the children of both races played together in the streets.

There may have been tolerance, but humans were always wary of the alviri acceptance of varied sexual relationships and their strange prescient power, a power they channelled from the earth mother, Juldra. Human religion was more diverse and unfocused. It consisted of folklore and faerie tales, different in every village, passed down from mother to child. No single faith pulled men together or tore them apart until one day, when everything changed.

A peace of sorts had continued for thousands of years when a preacher, wearing sackcloth and carrying a staff, arrived in the west from lands unknown. He was eloquent and forceful, speaking with clarity and calm to the poorly educated villagers of the middle lands. The message was simple, and it resonated.

There was only the goddess Frea; all other gods were false.

His name was Lygen or Father Lygen to his followers, and his words spoke to the simmering prejudice lurking in the crofts and hamlets of the green lands. Fell words muttered in the village taverns or crossed between workers in the fields. It was a set of rules which morphed into the scriptures and the eight Pillars of Freanism:

> *Man shall lie with a woman*
> *Man shall defend his home*
> *Man shall provide for the weak*
> *Man shall provide for his family*
> *Man shall fight the forces of darkness*
> *Man shall not steal*
> *Man shall not kill man*
> *Man shall not suffer a witch to live*

The role of women in Grenfeld had always been low, but the pillars cast females as subservient in every way. However, it would be the alviri and Jakari who would pay the greatest price. The people of Jakar were immediately cast as *the forces of darkness*, and the alviri were associated with witchcraft and *unnatural* sexual acts.

So began a low level of prejudice spreading out from Middcroft like a cattle-born plague. It first permeated the smallholdings and villages but eventually made its way to the cities and islands. It started with dark looks and whispers, then name-calling and slammed doors, but the Langley incident cemented hatred in hearts and minds.

Father Lygen was spreading his word through Tudorfeld with several followers when bandits attacked them near the town of Langley. Lygen and most of his people were killed, but one young boy survived. He dragged his wounded body to Langley, where he lived long enough to describe his attacker as "bewitched."

The alviri Forlyn family were enjoying a late supper when the mob arrived. Snawfel Forlyn, his wife Lunniss and their young son Mercen were dragged into the street. They pleaded for their lives, and a few villagers tried to help, but the mob had their way; the family were stoned to death.

Within a month, no alviri were left in any of the open lands of Caynna, Middcroft or Tudorfeld. High Lord Khazri Andain declared Alfheim an independent country, and the alviri never again ventured past the boundaries of Deapholt without using their stealth powers to avoid detection.

The Deap Road decayed when the traffic slowed, and the forest advanced once more; locals stayed clear for fear of alviri wrath or worse. There were tales of strange beasts wandering the Deapholt margins and the ever-present threat of attack from the mountain clans. Caynna folk retreated; the last farmhouse was fifty miles from Deapgate Castle. Few would venture further.

Morning broke to the familiar sound of steel on steel as swords clashed and men grunted with exertion in the damp air behind the farm's large barn.

Davill sparred with Hayden while Captain Fallon was training Jem and beginning to realise the young Burlander had the makings of a master swordsman. He seemed both composed and experienced. Jem's reactions were fast, and his counterattacks were instinctive.

"Give him what for!" shouted Brea unhelpfully. She sat on a hay bale with Ellen, who was entranced by Jem's skill.

"Who taught him?" she queried.

Brea shook her head. "No one knows, and 'tis best not to ask."

The other soldiers quickly lost interest in the gifted gada, preferring to ridicule the squire's son at every opportunity.

"He's not your dancing partner!" shouted Cal, as Hayden ducked and dived from Davill's attacks. He continued to laugh, and some of the others joined in.

"Leave the lad alone," mocked Slitan. "It's only young love."

Hayden stopped to look up at the smirking archer, but Davill's sword was still in flight; it hit his upper arm, sending him flying over a milk churn and into the barn door, clutching his bruised limb.

Gron and Lunn laughed loudly, and even the ordinarily quiet Sax stifled a chuckle. Only the young Gamin Boarman stayed quiet, lost in his thoughts.

"Leave him be!" yelled Ellen.

It was the plea of one outsider for another, but the hecklers simply turned their attention to her.

"Don't think he's interested, love," howled Cal.

"Hear that, Lady Hayden?" laughed Slitan. "I think the clown fancies you."

Ellen stood with a hand hovering over the hilt of her sword.

Brea grabbed her arm. "They're not worth it," she said sagely.

Jem helped Hayden to his feet and patted him on the back. "Pay them no mind," he said. In reality, he was becoming concerned by their hostility. He could use his standing to protect his fellow gada, but he couldn't be there at all times.

"Time to break camp," announced Sir Caspin; he emerged from the creaking farmhouse with Torbrand, Moranne and Prince Asger.

The Pandel family had been happy accommodating the royal party, but they warned against going further west. Farmer Liam Pandel told them of "strange goings-on" and "dark forces," which now inhabited Deapgate and the surrounding forest. He urged them to turn back, and his wife nodded in agreement.

Unfortunately, the path was set; getting a boat from Cultras would take too long, and the course of the River Dorbourne through Deapholt was just as dangerous. Deapgate was the only viable route to Cempess.

The men scurried about the barn, gathering their kit and some supplies that the Pandels had kindly offered. Hayden packed two training blades on his horse and noticed a shadow looming behind him.

"Come to me if you need some training," said Ellen under her breath. She smiled quickly and returned to her horse.

The squire's son looked after her for a moment before dragging himself wearily into the saddle. She seemed fair and kind, unlike the brutish sword wielder he'd expected. She reminded him of the sweet maid, Signy, back in Cynstol and how they'd danced through the night. That happy time receded into the distance, and the reality of the daily taunts wore him down.

Ellen patted the bay's flank; Sir Torbrand had personally picked the horse for her, insisting that it was his duty. Pulling herself into the saddle, she glanced up to see the tall knight looking at her. He nodded politely and turned back towards Moranne and Caspin, discussing the route.

"He's a mystery, that one," said Brea, pulling her mount alongside. "His mother, the old bag, has been trying to wed him off, but he's havin' none of it."

"He doesn't say much," agreed Ellen, "but none of the men speaks to me much."

Brea chuckled, exposing the deep lines in her cheeks. "He warned them off you."

"Really?"

"Oh, yes. The general might be as dull as a puddle, but he's a gentleman."

Ellen glanced back towards the leaders, but they were still in discussion. "The men don't seem to like him," she ventured. They would laugh and joke with Biorn and Caspin, but the older Linhold brother was always alone.

"He's not one of the men like Caspin," Brea agreed. "He don't eat with them or drink with them. Sir *Tor-bland* thinks he's better than everyone else like he's got a gold coin up his arse."

They both laughed at Brea's irreverence, but Ellen glanced back once more to see the knight deep in discussion.

"You heard what he said," pleaded Caspin, recounting the warnings of Farmer Pendel. "The road becomes difficult, and Deapgate's dangerous."

"There are no other routes to Cempess," said Moranne plainly.

"Is it worth the risk?"

Sir Torbrand remained impassive, listening to the arguments and waiting for his moment.

"We only have two women soldiers," Moranne replied. "We need an army."

Caspin shook his head. Few from the legion had been this far west in many years, and it seemed the area had become wild.

Moranne looked up at the square-jawed Torbrand, who seemed lost in his thoughts. "Can we do it?" she asked.

Sir Torbrand looked back at the men, most of them in the saddle, and the lithe Ellen Hildebill laughing with Brea.

"We can handle any bandits on the road or beasts in the forest," he said firmly. "We go to Cempess and onwards to Alfheim as planned."

They broke camp and headed west, waving to the Pendel family as they passed. The men were mostly in good cheer, but the mood would change as the day progressed.

The road continued for a few miles, worn passable by Liam Pendel's cart, tending his fields, but it soon shrunk. It became a narrow track which snaked its way over fallen tree trunks and tiny streams. The pastures of Caynna gave way to coarse brushland, with clumps of gorse and groves of blackthorn or hawthorn, all tied with strings of spiky bramble.

Thick briar would often block their path, so Lunn and Sax would be dispatched to clear the way. Lunn would wield his axe, slicing through stems and small trees, while Sax swung a heavy machete which he carried on his back. *Knives* appeared to possess a blade for all occasions.

The sound of men carving through the thorny wall sent rabbits and other small creatures scampering for shelter while crows squawked loudly overhead and sparrows chirruped their disapproval. Brea and Slitan managed to shoot a few rabbits, which they hung from their saddles like trophies.

Jem slowly learned more about his companions during the lengthening pauses. Many of the men now included him in their banter and swapped stories from old campaigns.

Lunn Burndog barely knew his family, but what little he knew was never discussed. They were killed by a gang of bandits when he was seven, but the same bandits made him their own. "They used him as a slave," said Gron quietly. Later they trained him as a killer and gave him the name *Burndog*. He escaped his bonds aged sixteen when the bandits killed a young family of farmers. He went berserk and killed every one of the twenty bandits in the gang.

The axe wielder just grinned from the thicket while Gron recounted the tale. Most of the other men had simple backgrounds, but Sax remained a mystery. He never spoke of his past and uttered little of the present. Mainly communicating through nods and a raised eyebrow, he was an enigma. The men agreed he was deadly with a knife, but none were close to him.

Grey clouds had followed them since Grenborg, deepening as they rolled in from the north. The path became treacherous as the light faded, and the green bramble cut out the light. It was mid-afternoon when the first raindrops landed silently on their armour. It was light at first but gradually thickened to a misty drizzle which seemed thin but soon soaked through their clothes and soured the mood.

"Onwards!" shouted Captain Fallon. They needed to be at Deapgate before dark.

Jem noticed Hayden riding at the back, his head was down, and drops of rain trickled through his hair and fell onto his saddle. He looked tired and miserable. Taunts from the men never stopped, especially from Slitan; it was beginning to weigh on him.

"Ignore them," said Jem. He knew how it felt to be an outcast. You needed to learn self-preservation.

Hayden said nothing. His thoughts were back in Dunstreet, sat on the riverbank, running his fingers through Ham Grome's short hair. With Jem and Caspin, it seemed like an adventure, but the soldiers reminded him of his place in Grenfold, a place with no future.

"Leave him be," said Brea gently. "He needs to find his path in this world. I'm watching his back, don't worry."

She seemed to be watching many backs, thought Jem, but he was happy she was with them.

Dusk was falling when they came across an incredibly thick section of brush. The party pitched in with knives and swords; even Sir Torbrand dismounted to hack at the twisted spiny barrier. Prince Asger watched contentedly, seeing the men acting as one against nature's enemy.

With a final swing of his axe, Lunn broke through the centre. He dropped the weapon to the floor, and it clanged against stone. Few things scared the giant axeman, but he stepped back, allowing the others to widen the hole while he stared through.

One by one, they led the horses through the rough opening and onto a wide paved square. It was cracked and broken in places where trees forced themselves through small fissures, and roots pushed the stones out; they stood like cairns of rubble. Moss and green lichen carpeted large areas, and a dank smell filled the air.

The square directed their eyes to a dark grey wall, almost lost in the gloom. It was crisscrossed with vines and roots. Large parts were missing and almost appeared to crumble before their eyes. Two large towers, wrapped in green ivy, rose from the ground, and the remains of a tall wooden gate, hung splintered and rotting to one side.

Deapgate barely stood before them, but what remained was like a nightmare. Lines of trees abutted the wall disguising the castle's actual size, and every stone was weathered and streaked with green. The battlements were wrecked, and few of the ramparts remained. Large sections were lost or lying in mounds of grey stone, riddled with nettles and spiky bramble.

"Nice place you've found us," said Brea playfully.

Sir Torbrand didn't flinch. He surveyed the scene taking in every detail.

Four large crows sat along the left wall and looked down at them as the company approached the gate. Moranne eyed them suspiciously and held her hand close to the hidden sceptre.

Jem could feel something was wrong. Something lay ahead, something ancient.

"What's wrong?" said Caspin.

"I don't know, but there's a presence here," replied Jem.

They all felt something, and some of the men had drawn swords.

"Be on your guard," said Captain Fallon, unsheathing his blade and holding it low.

The light dimmed further as they passed through the decaying gate into the outer courtyard. Vines clung to every wall, and dead branches hung down from the walkways.

Captain Fallon led the party and gestured for the men to fan out, taking positions along each side.

"Hold there!" yelled Lunn. He quickly reached out and snatched at Biorn's belt just as the captain stepped out into the air.

Peering into the gloom, they saw that a large floor section was missing. Jem could make out the shadows of large stone arches below, which would have been the dungeons or storerooms. These were covered in ribbons of thick bramble and creepers which twisted about them as if strangling a serpent.

"What happened here?" said Hayden. His sword hand was shaking, and he felt a chill run down his spine.

"The clans took it," replied Moranne. She held a hand flat to one of the walls as if trying to read the distant echoes.

One building leaned against the wall and appeared to have a watertight stone roof. A wide arched doorway gave access to a rectangular room crossed with tree roots and the scattered remains of pots and barrels. Several rusting swords were propped against one wall, and a tarnished helm lay in one corner. The fireplace on the outer wall was unblocked, as part of the chimney had collapsed outwards, exposing the rain-soaked sky.

"Is it safe?" asked Caspin.

Biorn shrugged. The captain felt uneasy, but they couldn't see any dangers.

"We'll camp here tonight," announced Sir Torbrand.

Captain Fallon ordered the men to make a fire, and they roped the horses into the far end of the room. Lunn and Gron helped Prince Asger from his mount, and he sat against a large stone opposite the fire.

"Not in the city now," he said, smiling up at Brea, who was skinning some rabbits for supper.

She smiled in return and sat beside him for a moment. "Your Highness, can I ask you something?"

Asger nodded, still smiling.

"Why did you come?"

He stared into the flames for a short while, pondering the question, then put a shaking hand on her shoulder. "Things much harder for us. King wants me dead. Prove myself by living."

Brea laughed after deciphering his words. "It's a wonder I'm still alive; this trip could end us both. At least we see's us some lovely sites," she said, gesturing to the crumbling walls around them.

"I hope she's not bothering you," said Caspin, sitting to dry himself by the fire.

Brea and the prince chuckled together and stared into the flames.

Captain Fallon had organised the men to keep guard. Slitan and Gamin would take the first watch, followed by Lunn and Gron, Davill and Sax, Hayden and Brea, and finally, Jem and Ellen.

The men had a hearty meal of rabbit, fresh bread and roasted carrots before they wrapped themselves in rough field blankets as the light failed and the room's doorway became a black abyss. Moranne used one of the tent sheets, packed into a ball, to sleep upright opposite the opening. There was something out there, she knew it, but it was too late to find anywhere else. One by one, they fell asleep, leaving Slitan telling tall tales to Gamin to keep them both awake.

Jem closed his eyes, and a deep black flooded his thoughts. It rolled over the death of Aludra and blanketed the sight of Hayden knifing the lifeless body of Gelic in Bearun. A mist swirled in his thoughts like the slight rain which plagued their day; it parted to reveal the dark eyes of a face only remembered in dreams. "A'tlen. Ven Firdus," said the voice before the eyes of Danya faded, and Jem found himself back at the castle yard, looking down at one of the stone arched dungeons. A light flickered behind one of the openings, and gentle tapping could be heard, like rain falling on a windowpane.

After a short while, a second tapping sound started in his dream, and another flickering yellow light burst into life behind another distant arch. More fires flickered in low corners, and the tapping echoed off the walls until it seemed to come from all around. Fires reflected off every stone, and other fires started higher on the battlements.

The tapping continued, but now it was joined by another sound, like metal scraping on stone. It was coming nearer and joined by more screeching, which blended into high-pitched guttural laughter, ending in a rasping wheeze.

Danya's voice was pleading now. "A'tlen", it said over and over until Jem wanted to will himself to wake; the dream wouldn't let him leave.

Suddenly the fires were extinguished, and the noises were silenced. Jem's mind was plunged into darkness. Danya's eyes appeared once more, but as he gazed into the beautiful brown lakes, they changed in front of him. They narrowed, and the colour changed, first to burnt umber and then to a deep blood red, which shone like a demon's ruby. A cackling voice pierced his heart.

"Wake up, Jem!"

He resisted, but the voice was insistent.

"Wake up, Jem!"

He was tired; he needed to sleep. Jem ached to be in the arms of Danya once more.

"Jem! Get up!"

His eyes opened while his heart pounded through his chest. Moranne was kneeling over him and shaking him by the shoulder.

"Jem, we've been drugged!"

Shaking the sleep from his eyes, he looked over to see Gamin and Slitan slumped on either side of the archway, fast asleep.

"Witchcraft?" he whispered.

"No! It's bohun upas. Somebody is burning it."

Jem had no idea what bohun upas was, but it sounded unpleasant. They both crept slowly to the snoozing Captain Fallon and managed to wake him after much shaking. He instinctively went for his sword until he saw Jem with his finger to his lips.

"What is it?" whispered Biorn.

"Dunters, replied Moranne.

The captain nodded in agreement as Jem mouthed *dunters* without comprehending what that meant.

"Redcaps," said Biorn. "I knew it."

"How many are there?" Moranne asked Jem.

He was puzzled until he realised Moranne knew he'd seen them in his dreams. Going by the number of fires, there were many. "Maybe a hundred?" he said helplessly.

"Frea!" cried the captain. "Help me raise everyone."

They carefully worked around the camp and woke everyone as quietly as possible. Biorn left Slitan to last and woke him by slapping him full across the face. He fell sideways and reached for his sword but stopped when he felt Biorn's blade against his breastplate.

"What's your advice, Captain?" asked Sir Torbrand sleepily.

All the men were gathered around the seasoned warrior as he pondered their situation.

"The last time I came across redcaps, I lost seven men. We need to leave now, as quickly and quietly as we can.

"What's a redcap?" said Hayden, asking the question they were all thinking.

"Dunters," said Moranne. "They live in caves or move into old castles or other buildings. They're very dangerous."

The men quickly broke camp, loaded the horses, and carefully crept through the archway towards the gate. They were led by Moranne, holding a small flaming torch.

As the last man, Gron passed through the door. A slow tapping sound began ahead. Another joined it to the left and another to the right. More joined until a slow, rhythmic tapping was all around.

"We're done for," said Gamin, his hand shaking on his wet bow.

"Hold your nerve," ordered the captain.

It seemed too late as the tapping was joined by scraping and a vicious, giggling laugh. The sounds were all around, even emanating from the building they'd vacated. There was nowhere to go; they were trapped in the dark as the clinging rain swept through them.

Moranne halted the men and held up her hands.

"We didn't know you were here," she said into the night. "We mean you no harm. Please let us pass."

The tapping and scrapes stopped, but a single, high-pitched voice chuckled in the darkness. It was stilted and harsh, savouring every staccato syllable.

"Trespass," it hissed.

"We didn't know," repeated Moranne. The men nodded in agreement, but the laughter returned from behind this time.

"Toll you must pay."

That didn't sound so bad, thought Hayden.

A different voice continued on the right. "Blood toll," savoured the unseen foe. A chorus of "Yes" hissed around the party and descended into cackling laughter.

"Show yourself, dunter!" ordered Moranne.

The cackling stopped, and a furtive whisper echoed from the walls. It was too quiet to hear clearly, but the men were anxious and held their weapons ready. All they could see was blackness, but there seemed to be some movement ahead of Moranne.

A pair of deep red eyes blinked open just a few feet from the ground, followed by a grin filled with razor-sharp teeth. Light glinted from the dented blade of an axe dragged along the stones. Encrusted with blood and rust, it belonged to spindly hands with sharp talon fingers.

The dunter stepped out into the light and cocked its head at the sight of so many humans. Its skin was creased, pale grey, and it had a dirty white beard draped over a rough sack-cloth shirt and leather leggings. It resembled a twisted quarter-height man, but the small pointed ears and red eyes marked it as an ancient creature from the age of galdur. A tapered, long red cap covered tufts of white hair and one side of his face.

"You are known to us, Wickona," he said, moving his head back and forth, like a bird sensing danger.

"I would know your name, sir," she said formally.

Jem remembered the confrontation with Skati's bandits in Bearun, which seemed to follow a similar pattern. Surely there were too many for the same trick.

The dunter laughed, and others joined him around the ruins. "I am Roban, and you must pay the price."

Stone and Sceptre

"What price?" asked Moranne; they all dreaded hearing what a *blood toll* was.

There was more sniggering and tapping before Roban delivered his demand. "You must give us your youngest."

As one, the men looked at Gamin, who had begun whimpering like a child.

Moranne leaned towards Jem while Roban was chuckling and whispered into his ear. "Hold onto my sceptre when you see it; think of me and only me. Run up to the battlements when I give the order." She sighed at the final message. "Leave the horses; they're lost."

Bess had been with her for six years, and they'd developed a strong bond, but it was time to say goodbye.

"Whispers, whispers," hissed Roban. He shifted his weight between his bowed, skinny legs. "Toll must pay."

Moranne glanced at Biorn, who nodded.

"We'll pay no toll, you foul creature," shouted Torbrand in defiance. "You'll have the edge of our swords."

The dunter was cackling, but Torbrand was already raising his sword, with Caspin shadowing his move.

"Now!" shouted Moranne.

Sensing the soldiers' stand, dunters started appearing around them on all sides, swinging short axes, sharp sticks and pikes. One took flight at astounding speed, rushing into the centre and swiping his blade at Gamin, but Slitan kicked him, sending the dwarf screaming into the darkness.

Moranne pulled out the sceptre and held it in front as more dunters started running from the shadows. She grabbed Jem's hand and wrapped it around the bottom of the rod. Her eyes were already blazing green when she ordered the gada to "Hold tight!"

He felt his limbs become rigid as a tingling sensation began in his legs, then moved to his chest and buzzed down his arm to the metal. Moranne pushed the sceptre upwards and let forth a mighty scream; her body was bathed in a dancing green mist. A jolt of energy pounded through Jem's taught body, forcing the air from his lungs and throwing his head back. He yelled with agony, and his vision blurred as he, too, sparked with a green glow.

A final pulse held them both rigid, and then a wave of bright green light burst from their bodies and leapt outwards like a shimmering wall of destruction, passing straight through the soldiers. It threw the dunters back with a force so massive that many fell into the pits or were smashed against the castle wall, leaving sprays of dark red blood. The nearest redcaps died instantly, but the furthest were stunned as the wave lost its power.

"Follow me!" shouted Jem instinctively while Moranne stumbled with the exertion.

Captain Fallon was next to see the chance and turned, yelling at the men. "Lunn! Carry the prince. Everyone else form a protective ring."

Still holding the sceptre, Jem pulled Moranne towards him and dragged her forward to the wall. A broken, stone staircase led up to the battlements, and he pulled her onto the steps, then turned to see the others running towards him.

"Come on!" he shouted, then reached behind to grab the grips of his twin blades. In a move he'd now practised many times, both scimitars slid from their scabbards and appeared upright and ready in his hands.

The party scrambled onto the ramparts when a cacophony of screams rose below, gnashing teeth and the sound of metal on stone.

Moranne and Jem led the soldiers running along the wall. Lunn carried the prince on his back, followed by Slitan, Gamin, Brea and the others. The two knights held the rear with Ellen and Gron, who swung his mace.

"They're coming!" shouted Caspin.

A swarm of tiny bodies poured from the depths; more appeared through wall gaps in all directions. They moved so quickly it looked like a wave breaking over the stones. The first of them scaled the wall and sprinted along the battlements with blades held aloft. Eyes blazed crimson with hatred.

"Get down!" shouted Brea.

Hayden flattened himself against the stone as three arrows flew over him from the archers ahead. Three dunters fell dead, then Gron sprang to his feet and swept the hammer left and right, connecting with a dunter on each swing. Heads and bones shattered as they flew into the wall or onto their brethren below.

Several started to run down the walkway towards them. Moranne pulled out her sword, but Jem pushed passed, with blades twirling. "I've got this!" he said. Every swipe cut one of the redcaps or clashed with a sword as he pushed onwards through the melee.

Dunters were now climbing the walls, hanging onto vines and appearing in their midst.

"Don't let them through!" shouted Biorn, swinging his blade over the edge of the wall, decapitating several or pushing them over.

"There's too many!" said Cal, fighting several at once. A snarling dunter jumped from the wall and landed on his back; it raised a knife to stab him in the neck when a small dagger flew out of the night and pierced the redcap's back. Cal turned just long enough to see a smiling Sax give him a salute.

Caspin moved up to protect the prince while Lunn lumbered towards the end of the wall, carrying the prince, who flopped from side to side with every step. Torbrand and Ellen remained as the rear guard, fighting as one. Their blades flashed in the half-light and carved lines of spray in the drizzle.

The dunters seemed fearless, throwing themselves forward in a frenzy of anger. They snarled and spat curses but couldn't break through.

Jem would never know how Moranne knew there was a way out. Maybe she felt it, or perhaps it was just a guess; the wall was broken ahead, and a tumble of smashed bricks had spilt out, making a ramp at the back of the castle. Captain Fallon saw it too, and ushered the archers ahead.

Gamin didn't see the scarred dunter hiding in the wall behind him, but he felt the knife as it found a gap in his armour and pierced his side. He howled in agony, but the redcap held tight and prepared to stab him again. The blade of Hayden's knight sword was in flight and cleaved the redcap in two.

The young archer stumbled and fell to his knees, but Hayden grabbed his arm and dragged him up. Davill appeared behind; the two men took Gamin's arms and pulled him forwards.

Blood was dripping from a cut on Torbrand's cheek, and Ellen could feel where a spike found her arm, but they fought on against the wall of hatred before them.

"Come on!" screamed Moranne. She stood above the broken cascade and ushered the men downwards into the forest.

"You first, ma'am," said Biorn.

Moranne had other plans. "Get all your men clear; I'll be last. *That's* an order."

He did as instructed and led the men down the broken bricks. Some stumbled and fell, picking up bruises to join the cuts.

Moranne stood defiantly on the top of the wall while the remaining Torbrand, Ellen and Gron held the dunters back long enough for her to pull out the sceptre once more.

With her last breath of energy, she summoned the earth power to send a short blast of green lightning along the wall, knocking the leading enemies down like falling stones. She collapsed, unconscious, into Sir Torbrand's arms.

The strong Middcrofter cradled her tightly and carried her carefully down the stones, with Gron and Ellen watching their retreat. The dunters seemed to stop on the wall, unwilling to leave the castle's cover. They cursed and spat in anger, but the party was free.

The horses were gone, along with most of their supplies. They were wet, cold, bruised and cut. But they were alive.

23 DEAPHOLT

Moranne stared into the bright blue, watching the clouds drift by, merging and swirling in the gentle breeze. Her hands clenched the warm grass on either side as she lay on her back, ripping up small tufts and letting the blades fall through her fingers. She sighed contentedly and looked out from the hill towards the little stone cottage nestling on the opposite side of the shallow dell.

The happiest home she'd known since those last tranquil days in the old world. It was a real home, close to the capital but distant enough to escape prying eyes and whispers; a humble abode but a cosy cottage. It was a place to hide and a place to think, but more importantly, a place to love.

"What are you thinking of?"

The voice was deep and comforting. It cascaded over Moranne like a blanket and wrapped around her, making her feel safe. The owner appeared in silhouette above her with his hands on his hips. A broad smile appeared above his trimmed beard.

These moments made the loss bearable and kept her sanity alive. Dane was her rock and the only true soulmate to share her heart since tragedy scarred her life.

"I was just thinking how happy I am right now," she said, reflecting the sun's warmth towards her tall knight.

Dane sat beside her with his hand on his knees and matched her gaze towards the humble building. He struggled to spend much time here, but these small moments made his burden bearable. One day they'd be together, and nobody would come between them.

"There's one other thing," she continued, while Dane looked down with his melting brown eyes. "I'm..."

The dream vanished, and her heart pounded; Moranne awoke violently into the gloom.

"Ma'am, are you alright?" pleaded Jem. He was leaning over her with concern creasing his face.

First light glinted through the green canopy scattering narrow rays into the forest. The trees were dense, and in some directions, the trunks seemed to form a grey, impenetrable wall. An occasional drop of water plunged from the leaves above, a final testament to last night's rain; the area smelled of wet leaves and bark.

Moranne was sitting in the natural armchair of a large tree's exposed roots, looking out at a makeshift camp. Most of the company sat on tree roots and rocks around a smoky fire, all except for Gamin, who was lying in a mossy hollow, attended by Brea.

"How's the lad?" said Moranne, ignoring Jem's concern.

Jem looked over at the pale archer and shook his head. "It's not good. The wound's not deep, but Brea says it looks infected."

Moranne sighed and climbed to her feet, despite Jem's protestations.

"I didn't know there were dunters," she said flatly. "I haven't been this way for many years." Frequent visits to Alfheim were usually by boat from Cultras or Cynstol, but she knew the dangers of Deapholt had grown.

"I trust you are rested, my lady," boomed Sir Torbrand. The slash across his cheek still looked fresh, but at least it was healing.

Moranne nodded. She was unaware that the knight had carried her from the walls of Deapgate, then a further quarter of a mile into the forest, before collapsing with exhaustion.

All the men were tired, damp and hungry after a rough, rainy night sleeping on the ground. Most were sporting cuts and bruises from the escape, rubbing their eyes and groaning from strained muscles. The atmosphere was dour, but they were too fatigued to dwell on their situation.

"We came off the castle's south side, so I would guess the Deap Path lies to the northwest," said Moranne.

Torbrand nodded in agreement. "We need to go quickly for the sake of the young archer. I'll have Brea and Slitan hunt for food as we travel."

Jem stared in awe at Moranne. He didn't know many women who could compose themselves so quickly and command a group of soldiers. At least not in Burland, where they were housewives and barmaids. He could still feel a faint vibration through his hand where he'd held the sceptre. *What happened?* The list of questions was growing, but it never seemed the right time to ask. He sat beside Hayden on a mossy, fallen tree trunk and shook his head. "What's happening to me?"

Hayden was still reeling from the escape. He and Davill had dragged Gamin this far, but there was no knowing if the lad would live. "I don't know what happened last night," he said, turning to his friend, "but whatever you did, saved our lives."

Gada Jem Poulterer wanted to share his thoughts with the young squire's son, but Captain Fallon was standing in the middle of the camp and clearing his throat to demand attention.

"Steel yourselves, men. We're around a mile east of the Deap Path, so we need to move. We'll catch our supper today, but we'll soon be dining in Cempess. Onwards!"

The men obediently rose to their feet and formed a column, following Torbrand, Caspin and Moranne into the trees. Brea, Slitan and Sax had crafted a simple sledge from tree branches and Prince Asger's cape, which they used to drag the wounded Gamin. The prince propelled himself with the help of a crude staff made by Gron.

It was slow going, negotiating thickets of dense, shoulder-high ferns, fallen tree trunks and clinging vines hanging from distant branches. Dewy, luminous moss covered everything and filled the air with an earthy smell; large plates of fungus clung to tree trunks inviting the unwary to take a bite. The background beyond always appeared lush and bright, but they never seemed to reach this verdant land.

Jem slipped and stumbled over the damp ground and scratched his hands on rough bark as he reached to steady himself. He'd envisaged the area much like Bearun, but Deapholt made the smaller forest seem like a copse in the centre of a field. *The Deap,* as most soldiers called it, had no rules or order. Occasionally a few shafts of bright summer light would break through the canopy, but mostly the green roof was the only visible light. Bushes rustled as unseen creatures fled from their feet, and birds screeched overhead, warning their kin.

If the path was a mile, it was a long mile. Lunn almost slipped into a muddy stream, dragging the pale Gamin with him, but Gron caught his arm and yanked him upwards. Slitan had no luck hunting as he struggled to keep his footing, but Brea managed to take several pigeons and a couple of rabbits, running for their bolt-holes.

"Wait!" said Moranne, suddenly holding up her hand ahead of the column. She looked forward, scanning the tree line, but no movement was visible.

"What is it?" asked Caspin. He'd known Lady Moranne long enough to understand how perceptive she was.

"Bandits?" ventured Torbrand.

Bunyips? thought Hayden.

She turned to Sir Torbrand without looking directly at him and lowered her voice. "Straight ahead of me, there's someone there."

He peered through the trees but saw nothing but the green and brown of Deapholt. He didn't see the bright brown eyes suddenly snap shut and the body melt once more into the forest.

"Hmm," chuckled Moranne, smiling. "It's nothing." She knew what followed them: another ancient creature from the age of galdur. "Onwards," she said, striding through the trees.

"What was it?" asked Jem. He tried to feel the presence, but his abilities revealed nothing.

"Of no concern. They will not show themselves while I'm here."

Whatever *they* were, Moranne was in no mood to teach the young gada. He returned to walk with Hayden at the back of the group.

It took an additional hour of bruised shins and sodden boots to reach the Deapholt Path if that was what they'd found. A narrow track, no wider than a rabbit run, snaked into the distance, vanishing behind bending trees, almost daring you to pass.

"We'll rest for a moment," called Sir Torbrand.

Gamin groaned when Gron and Lunn laid the makeshift stretcher across the path. He was deathly pale, and a sheen of sweat glistened on his forehead; his eyes remained closed. Brea leaned over him and felt his brow; he was burning up.

"How is he?" asked Moranne. She knelt beside him and held his clammy hand.

Brea shook her head. She'd seen similar fevers before, and this one was advanced. "He won't survive the night; there's nothing I can do."

Moranne knew there would be casualties, but Gamin was too young. She looked over at Jem and Hayden. *I shouldn't have brought them,* she thought.

"Please keep him comfortable, Brea; I'll ask Torbrand to pick up the pace."

"I've given him so much khat he don't know where he is." Brea's supply of hunter's weed was running low, but the lad could have it all if it eased his pain.

Sax *"Knives"* Stulor watched the two women looking over the wounded gada. He knew as well as they did that Gamin wouldn't see the dawn. It would be a risk, but he couldn't stand by and do nothing.

"Gather yourselves, men!" boomed Captain Fallon, "we need to move."

They assembled as a column led by Torbrand, Moranne and Caspin, then headed north along the winding Deap Path. It circled fallen trees, dipped beneath twisted tree roots hugging the rocks of a long-dead range, and crossed streams with stepping stones or rotting timber bridges.

It was hard to understand how the path could endure when they met no one on their journey and saw very few beasts which didn't scurry for boltholes. Brea told Jem it was "best not to ask, " implying that many strange creatures used the path but were hiding in the shadows. Moranne often stopped and peered into the gloom before shaking her head and returning to the leaders.

It was later that morning when Jem first felt they were being watched. There were several sets of eyes but no clue to the owners. They weren't human, and it was a different feeling than Bearun. They were not alviri and not human.

"You're making me nervous," said Hayden, when Jem stopped and looked around again.

"No bunyips," he replied with a raised eyebrow. Hayden countered by elbowing him in the ribs.

Scanning the treeline was all the two gadas could do, but most of the others had jobs to keep them busy. Brea and Slitan circled out wide to hunt for wood pigeons and rabbits. Sax and Ellen followed Caspin as part of the vanguard, Davill and Cal covered the rear guard, Gron and Lunn carried the pitiful Gamin in the centre, and even the prince found a role.

Conscious he was setting the slow pace, Prince Asger made it his job to keep spirits up and get to know the troops. He moved up and down the column, spending time with each soldier.

"Why soldier?" he said to Davill as they picked their way through a dense area of nettle together.

The seasoned warrior from Greydon was reticent at first, but denying the prince could be disrespectful, so he reluctantly told his story.

Both of Davill's parents died from the pox when he was a child; he was raised by his aunt and disciplinarian uncle. He fled his home in Greydon on the stroke of his twenty-first birthday and made his way to Silmouth, where he joined the Burland Guard as a humble gada. He was a natural with the sword, and it wasn't long before he became a regular soldier patrolling the Burland borders. He made his way to the Green Order when his Burland Guard commander transferred him.

"Transfer?" asked the prince.

"The commander didn't like me," said Davill looking down. A painful memory resurfaced and creased his forehead into a frown.

"Tell. No trouble," said the prince.

The swordsman had told the tale to no one, but a prince had never asked him. It was time to free himself.

"We were on patrol in the foothills of the Mur, just south of Silmouth. I'll always remember the day. It was warm, but grey clouds were coming in from the east, and it felt like a storm was coming. There were ten of us in the squad; it was just a routine tour."

"What happened?" prompted Asger.

Davill collected his thoughts. "Well, Your Highness, we saw smoke rising behind one of the hills, so we investigated. We'd never seen trouble in the Mur other than the odd group of bandits, so we weren't expecting too much hassle.

From a ridge above, we could see a fire in a dip below. There were three round tents, and we saw three families with children sitting around the blaze." He paused to catch his breath, and his eyes glistened. "They were all Jakaris."

The prince nodded. Like most, he'd never seen a Jakari, but he'd heard the stories.

"The captain took us down. We walked into their camp, and they didn't even try to run. They offered us food and tried to talk to us in a foreign tongue.

My stomach was turning, I knew what would happen, and I could see it in the captain's eyes."

"Happen?" asked the prince.

He had the answer from the tears falling down Davill's weathered face. "We butchered them all. Men, women and children, then we burnt the bodies."

"You?"

"I refused," said Davill. "I tried to stop them, but they just said they were dealing with *dark forces*."

"Did all you could," said the prince, trying to reassure the swordsman.

Davill would never forgive himself. "I didn't try hard enough. The faces of those children will haunt me forever."

Prince Asger stopped briefly and placed a hand on Davill's shoulder.

"You, right man for mission."

Davill embraced the prince, breaking all royal etiquette, and sobbed into his silks. Twenty years of guilt wouldn't leave him so quickly, and neither would the lie.

Night fell quickly in the forest, signalled by the bats which swooped overhead, hunting the midges dancing over the streams and stagnant pools.

Biorn called the company to a halt near a broad stream spanned by a mossy clapper bridge. Moonlight was breaking through the canopy and shining on the bubbling water, which disappeared into the twilight. Cal and Sax made a fire, which they used to cook some pigeons supplied by the archers, but the flames would also serve another essential purpose.

As all the soldiers found space around the fire, the sound of trickling water and crackling wood was drowned by a distant howl which rose until it echoed through the forest and gradually fell to silence. Moments later, another answered it, much further away this time. The gathering was quiet for a moment until Biorn broke the silence.

"Keep that fire stoked!" he barked.

A chorus of "Yes, sir" didn't make Hayden feel any safer. "This place is a death trap," he said, shaking his head.

"Don't worry about them wolves," answered Brea, "It'll be the clans who gut you in yer sleep."

"Thanks, Brea," said Jem. He remembered how nervous Hayden had been in Bearun. They all needed to keep calm. He looked out at the grey body of Gamin near the fire. His breathing was shallow, and he occasionally twitched as delirium took hold and his body lost the fight. When Jem closed his eyes that night, he hoped there'd be no dark dreams and that Gamin would see the morning.

The dunter's eyes burned like a smith's furnace, and its jagged teeth ground together, muting an angry snarl. It stood on the castle battlements, staring at the shaking Gamin, waiting for him to die.

Drizzle ran down the young archer's face, merging with his tears. He sat on the cold stone surrounded by the gnashing menace cursing him to oblivion. Unable to move, he shook in the cold and tried to think of happier times, but none would come.

He'd never known the sweet caress of a woman; her smile, the lilt of her voice as she laughed or the creases of her body in the warm sun. Too shy to smile at the barmaid in Orton and too proud to bed the whore in Gosta, it was too late.

The dunter laughed; it knew he was finished. It crept to his side and stretched out its clawed hand to press against the knife wound, but there was no pain. Gamin's side buzzed with a warmth that spread over his side and through his body.

His eyes blinked open, adjusting to the darkness of The Deap and the dark figure bending over him. The figure looked up, revealing the chiselled face of Sax Stulor.

"Shh!" said Sax, putting a finger to Gamin's lips.

Sax held his hand just above Gamin's wound, and a pale light danced in the gap. The lad's whole body tingled, and he felt warm and relaxed. His eyes closed again to darkness, but no redcap troubled his dreams. As sleep took him, he heard some final soothing words.

"Our secret."

24 WARRIOR CREED

"Me lady, you need to see this," said Brea, tugging at the arm of Moranne's blouse.

She shook her head to clear the sleep and tried to focus on the lined face of the Caynna huntress. The sun peeked through the canopy, and flies danced through the tiny shafts of light, hovering above the dew-covered moss.

"What is it?"

The others stirred when they heard Brea's unsubtle tones. Arms stretched, eyes were rubbed, and Lunn's booming yawn rippled through the camp.

"The lad," said Brea. "Come and see."

Wearily Moranne dragged her limbs across the glade to the rough stretcher where Gamin lay. His breathing was deep but steady, and the shaking was gone; the most significant change was his face.

Moranne looked open-mouthed at Brea, then back at Gamin's coloured cheeks. The sweat was gone, and a thin smile creased his lips as he slept.

"The fever's broke," said Brea, shaking her head. "I's never seen nothing like it. I thought he was a goner."

The news soon spread through the company and immediately raised the spirits, bringing smiles to every face. Gamin still slept, but he seemed peaceful and stable. Gron and Lunn lifted him with lighter hearts that morning, exchanging insults as they navigated the narrow path northwards.

"I asked Frea to spare him last night," said Cal.

Davill and Slitan nodded in agreement, but Sax hid a knowing smile as he took up the rear guard.

"I blame the fornicator in our midst," he continued, looking in Hayden's direction.

"The squire's son?" asked Davill. "He's alright."

"He's wrong, and we all know it."

"Given me the eye he has," added Slitan. "He's bringing bad luck. Have you seen how he fights? He's going to get us all killed."

"Mind your tongue!" bellowed Biorn. "I'll have none of that talk."

Slitan bowed his head, but he continued grumbling to himself as they picked their way through a dense area of elm, struggling to follow the route.

The pace seemed faster, even with Gamin asleep and Prince Asger stumbling with his staff. The day also appeared brighter and warmer. Birds scattered in their path, and Brea even managed to kill a small deer which leapt in front of her. It was bound to a tree branch so she and Ellen could carry it to their next camp.

"It's about time the clown made dinner," laughed Slitan.

"The clown will slit your scrawny throat," said Ellen under her breath.

Brea gave her a sharp look but said nothing. The young warrior woman had much to learn.

The path gradually widened and showed some signs of use; a broken twig here and a partial boot print there. These were the signs of Cempestre hunters, ranging from home. Brea identified the site of a recent kill. "Probably a deer," she said.

"It'll be good to meet some *real* women," said Slitan; he eyed Ellen, hoping for a reaction.

"You're joking!" spat Cal. "I hear they're all as big as Gron but with more hair."

"And beards," added Lunn.

They all roared with laughter.

"Makes kissing a bit hairy."

"You're kissing them in the wrong place," chirped Slitan, who seemed desperate to ignite the simmering Ellen.

"They'll welcome some real men. I hear their husbands are all simpering twigs like Lady Hayden," added Cal.

Ellen saw Hayden bow his head and felt her arms tensing, ready to grab her sword. The hairs had risen on the back of her neck, and a thin veil of sweat was forming over her brow, causing her dark red hair to stick in streaks.

"Real man?" she barked. "I'll let you know when I see one."

Looking smug, Slitan finally found his reaction. He opened his arms as if including his comrades in the observation.

"The clown finally makes a joke!"

Ellen reached for her sword and was about to pull it free when a shallow voice stopped the entire party.

"What joke?" came a feeble voice from the stretcher; Gamin looked up into the canopy with tired eyes.

"Gamin!" shouted Jem. Everyone rushed to see the bleary-eyed archer as Gron and Lunn gently laid him on the ground.

Brea felt his brow and noted the fever had gone. His breathing was stable, and he seemed merely tired.

"How are you?" asked Moranne, kneeling by his side. She felt the burden lift from her shoulders.

"A spirit came to me," replied Gamin.

"Must have been Frea," said Cal briskly.

"No, it was a man."

"What man?" asked Moranne.

Gamin shook his head weakly. "I don't know."

"It don't matter," said Brea, smiling to reveal a fan of laughter lines on her cheeks. "You're back with us, and I'll thank all the gods for that."

Sax placed a hand on Gamin's shoulder and looked into his eyes. There was recognition for a brief moment, and then the lad smiled and nodded. If he knew, then he was keeping the secret.

"We'll rest here a short while," said Sir Caspin. He and Torbrand were hoping the young archer would be able to walk, to quicken the pace. Neither of them wanted another night in the forest without blankets and shelter.

Brea and Sax cooked the deer on a makeshift spit, and the party gathered around the fire in high spirits. Gamin sat up, and they talked of their escape from Deapgate, trudge through the forest, and how some kind of forest creature was following them. He remembered nothing after the dunter attack, just dreams and nightmares.

"Right, men!" shouted Captain Fallon. "I've heard some fell talk of the Cempestre from you lot, and that must stop. Lady Moranne has something to tell you."

Slitan and Cal grinned, showing no remorse, but both bowed their heads when Moranne scowled at them. She sat in the centre of a fallen tree trunk and addressed the group. It seemed like the time she told the tale of a wyvern back on that warm, sunny day in Denbry.

"What I tell you is true, but you must never discuss this with a Cempestre. They are strong, proud people who will not share their secrets with outsiders."

Sir Torbrand watched Ellen across the fire. The flames seemed to leap through her hair, throwing her cheeks into shadow and making her eyes burn ominously.

"We need to go back nigh on seven hundred years when there was a small village in the forest known only as Haven. The people were humble peasants living on the land, trading with all the folks of Caynna, Middcroft and Tudorfeld. They lived a simple but happy life and wanted for nothing.

Unfortunately, the king of Grenfold wanted something else. A war was raging with the Stans, so the strongest men in Haven were conscripted into the army. The women begged the king, but the men were taken by force and sent to the front line."

"So they had no protection?" asked Davill.

Moranne shook her head. "The mountain oni clans are a warring ancient race from the time of galdur. The clans are constantly at war, as an oni can only prove himself in battle. Most of the time, they stay in Banafell, but occasionally they send scouting parties into the forest. It would be the fearsome Lysu clan who would test Haven's defences and find them wanting."

"What happened?" asked Jem; it didn't sound like a happy tale.

"The elderly and disabled men? The oni killed them all. Every child was butchered, and every grandmother was shown the knife."

Davill winced. He could still see the eyes of the little Jakari girl as she pleaded for her life.

"Only the younger women were spared. They were shackled and chained to be dragged to Banafell to be enslaved. Haven was burnt to the ground."

"That's sickening," said Ellen. She didn't notice Torbrand nodding slowly across the fire.

"I will not utter the unspeakable cruelty dealt to those women, nor will I detail how the group of over fifty dwindled to less than twenty over five wretched years. I will tell you that the oni are simple creatures with limited intellect and that they underestimated the resolve of those brave women."

"I'm sure there's a point to this story," grumbled Slitan.

"Quiet!" shouted Biorn. "You *all* need to hear this."

Moranne's eyes flashed bright green for a moment, but she nodded curtly to the captain and resumed her tale.

"The clan became so familiar with the Haven slaves that they used them for all the domestic tasks, such as cleaning and cooking; this was their first mistake.

One of the women was exceptionally brave and managed to gather leaves from the bohun upas tree. She devised a plan to poison their guards by dropping the chopped leaf into the guard's food. Her name was Lena Cempess."

"Did they get away?" asked Gamin, sitting up and listening to the story like a young lad.

"Over twenty guards lay dead. The women took the shackle keys and escaped. They ran through the dangerous passes of Banafell, careful to avoid other clans, and followed the mountain streams to Mirror Lake.

The women were tired, bruised and hungry. Three more died in the escape, falling to their deaths or succumbing to fatigue. The seventeen were lost in the forest, pursued by oni, wolves and other dangerous creatures. Lena did her best to lead them towards Numolport, but they were weak and making slow progress. It seemed that all might be lost, but they were found by a pair of kind eyes scanning the forest for danger. The eyes belonged to the experienced alviri warrior, Calima Freond. She led a squad of soldiers through Deapholt, ensuring the oni didn't settle west of the mountains. She took pity on the Haven women and insisted that they come with her back to Alfheim."

"I thought humans weren't allowed on elf island," shouted Cal.

Moranne flashed him a dark look, and for the briefest moment, he thought she might strike him down. The afternoon sun glinted through the trees behind her, marking her frame in silhouette. Only her bright green eyes twinkled under her matted dark hair.

"Normally, that's true," she continued, "but such was Calima's compassion that the alviri elders agreed to make an exception, and they allowed the women to stay in Veorn until they were rested.

The women of Haven had never seen female warriors, and they were impressed by the sword skills of the alviri. Lena asked Calima if she would teach the women to fight. At first, she was reluctant, but she was so inspired by the Haven survivors' bravery and endurance that she agreed. Over the next seven years, the women lived in Alfheim. They learned the ways of the sword and the bow and even adopted the alviri earth goddess, Juldra, as their own. The alviri made them gifts of unique light swords and bows with range and accuracy. An oath was sworn between the followers of Lena Cempess and the alviri, which stands today. They are friends and allies. They will always come to each other's aid.

The ladies of Haven could have stayed in Alfheim for the rest of their days, but Lena had other plans. The women started to go out into Tudorfeld, Middcroft and Caynna, looking for kindred spirits. Women who longed for a better life away from male-dominated servitude, and men who saw women as equals, not wenches and whores."

"These men weren't simpering twigs," she continued, scowling at Cal. "They had pure hearts but were big, powerful, muscular men. They had the skills to build a great town out of the ashes of Haven and the strength to plough fields and construct the defences of the forest home they unanimously chose to call Cempess.

The town had its rules decided by the surviving seventeen women who founded it here in Deapholt. Never again would the women rely on men for their protection.

Only a woman may become oretta, ancient alviri for a warrior.

Only a woman may lead the Cempestre.

A woman and her bonda, or husband, are equal in all other respects.

Any man or woman who does not wish to obey the laws can leave anytime.

Cempess has stood for nearly seven centuries. They live in peace and harmony with the forest and don't recognize the Grenfold monarchy. Sorry, Your Highness."

Prince Asger smiled. Many had heard of the Cempestre, but few had met them. He thought they sounded fascinating.

"What happened to clan Lysu?" asked Jem, who was hanging on every word, as he had with the story of young Shaja and the wyvern.

"Oh, someone's listening," said Moranne, smiling at Jem. *Remember all my words.* "The oni's second mistake was to think that the founders of Cempess would forgive and forget what they did.

Ten years after the first stake entered the ground of the women's new home, at the age of fifty-seven, Oretta Lena Cempess led a fifty-strong group of female warriors against clan Lysu in Banafell.

All fifty warriors returned, leaving every member of clan Lysu dead in their wake. The clan was wiped off this earth and serves today as a warning to any oni clans thinking of taking on the most fearsome warriors in these lands."

The clearing was silent as the men pictured a small group of women destroying an entire clan of massive, powerful beasts. It didn't seem possible.

"Horse dung," muttered Slitan under his breath. "A bunch of sword-wielding clowns butchered a whole clan?"

He'd barely uttered the last syllable when a sword flashed in the half-light. It carved the air with the sound of a whip and settled onto the skin of Slitan's neck, drawing a thin crack of blood which trickled from one end.

"Private Hildebill!" shouted Sir Torbrand, rising to his feet.

The sword was stiff in Ellen's hand as if she'd hacked into an invisible wall that held it motionless. Her eyes were narrow, and her furrowed brow glistened with sweat.

"Put it down, love," said Brea, placing a hand on her shoulder. "He ain't worth it."

Gradually she lowered the sword and bowed her head towards Torbrand, who seemed to be showing the faintest concern beneath his tough exterior.

"Sorry, sir," she said humbly.

"That's what happens when you give a sword to a woman. Very dangerous once a month," snorted Slitan.

His mirth was short-lived. Biorn punched him square in the jaw, sending him flying onto his back, dislodging one of his crooked teeth, which he coughed up in bloody drool.

"I've had enough of your lip. One more word, and it'll be *my* sword that splits your head from your worthless body."

"Men!" commanded Caspin. "You must heed Lady Moranne's words."

"Thank you," replied Moranne. "The reason I've told you this tale is to warn you. The Cempestre are very proud people. They may not let us enter Cempess, but if they do, be careful of what you say or do. Don't show any disrespect, regardless of your beliefs. We need their help."

"This should be fun," stated Brea mischievously.

The men nodded, except for Slitan, who sat staring into the trees. A rage simmered behind his eyes. The son of a Kelby whore had been kicked and spat on all his life, but no more. He discovered Frea when he ran away from home at fourteen. A home to which he would never return. *The sinners and fornicators would all pay.*

"Is everything alright, Mr Smite, sir?" asked Gamin, who was now managing to stand with the aid of a tree branch. Slitan had taken the young archer under his wing when they were stationed in Faircester, but the lad didn't seem to need him any longer.

"Go play with your new filthy friends!" spat Slitan. "Leave me be."

Gamin watched his back for a moment, then turned to join the others.

Throwing the venison carcass into the trees, the company set off northwards once more. Moranne estimated they had just a couple of hours' travel remaining to reach Cempess, but some of the men's attitude was beginning to worry her. She asked Caspin and Biorn to watch Cal and Slitan especially closely. The mission hung on a knife edge and relied on Cempestre help. It had been years since she'd passed this way, but they parted on good terms the last time. *But would they help?* There was no way to tell, and an aggressive mood in the men could undoubtedly ruin any chance.

"Ma'am?" asked Jem, dragging her from her thoughts. "How can the Cempestre fight so hard when women are the weaker sex?"

She smiled down at the young man with hidden gifts. "Anyone can fight if they have something to fight for."

Jem nodded, but it didn't mean much to him. What was his motivation to fight?

"You'll discover a reason to fight before our mission is out," said Moranne, reading his thoughts.

He returned to his place in the column beside Hayden and pondered her words as they tramped through the greenery.

Alliances had begun to form in the group, some old, some new and some unlikely. Moranne, Torbrand, Caspin and Biorn led the party into the gloom. Although the eldest Linhold brother was aloof and economical with his words, he always seemed to listen to the counsel of the others. He did not know Deapholt and seemed happy to let Moranne take the lead. He wasn't the boorish brute she'd imagined, and with his brother Caspin, they made a formidable team.

Brea and Ellen had bonded immediately, as Torbrand had hoped. He relied on the uncouth Caynnan to look after the swordswoman and keep groping hands away, but now it seemed he was protecting the men from her. Every day he found his eyes wandering in her direction, but it couldn't be. *It mustn't be.*

While Jem and Hayden were already friends, an unlikely gang emerged, including Gamin, Lunn and even the menacing Gron. Gamin was so grateful for Lunn and Gron's help that he refused to leave their side, and together with the two Burlanders, they became a happy group, exchanging insults and jokes, mainly at Gamin's expense.

"Next time there's trouble, we'll just throw you at the enemy," said Gron.

"Yea, I'm using you as a shield," rumbled Lunn.

His miraculous recovery was a mystery, but they seemed ready to accept it was Frea's will.

Sax and Davill were happy to be alone, but Cal and Slitan could be seen on the fringes of the column discussing the others in hushed tones. The names Lady Hayden, the hag and the clown could sometimes be heard; then, they would lower their voices once more to conspire in secret.

"Can I offer you some advice, me dear?" said Brea, as she and Ellen walked together just within earshot of the whispering men.

"Do I have a choice?" countered Ellen.

Brea took everything in her stride. "You always has a choice, love. You can choose the easy way or the hard way. I always chooses the easy path, cos it takes a lot less energy, and I prefer to stay alive."

"Alright," said Ellen. "What's your advice, oh great sage?"

Brea looked at Cal and Slitan, who were sniggering together, no doubt sharing some jokes at her expense. "You need to *own* the insults; otherwise, they'll just use them to grind you down 'til you snap. If you think Sir *Tall Boring* is gonna save your skin, think again. He don't know you, and neither does the captain. They'll side with the men if it comes to it."

"So I should roll over and let them call me *the clown*?" said Ellen incredulously. "After all you've been through yourself?"

Brea stopped and grabbed Ellen by the arm, and looked straight into her eyes. "I'm still here *because* I knows when to fight and when to let it go. I'm a better archer than any of these dim wits, and you're one of the mightiest swordsmen I's ever seen. You almost had Sir *Smug Breeches*. Don't let them call *you* the clown; call *yourself* the clown. Own the name before they do. We needs to win the battle before we wins the war."

Brea was right; it was a man's world with men's rules. Being twice as good as the men wasn't enough; she needed to be five times as good. She smiled at the grizzled huntress, who slapped her on the back.

"Come on, clown; we're gonna find us some big, butch warrior women."

25 CEMPESS

After pausing for food, an unlikely group of humans and strangers trudged through the forest once more. Twigs snapped underfoot, and some of the men muttered continuously. The loud group was easy to track. She blinked in the half-light, spying the party through a tangle of bramble and tree branches caked in luminous moss. Her colours blended perfectly so that none would see her, none except for the dark-haired woman. Her powers were strong. Quiet, light footsteps had followed the group since they escaped from Deapholt, and the young one had been hurt, but now things seemed urgent. If they entered the place of women, would they return?

"We should kill her," came a silky female voice from the shadows.

"No," was her simple reply. "The man is also strong, and you forget the healer."

"We must kill her and the other two."

"The Cempestre men seldom leave the village, and other human men die at the hands of dunters, oni or tunnbroccs. We can't afford to let these men slip away."

"The tall one is mine," announced another silky voice.

"Red has him," said the second.

"Patience, my loves," said the leader. "They will not stay with the warrior women. Our chance will come when *she* leaves them."

"You are sure?" asked the second voice.

"I've seen it."

The dream showed the mysterious dark-haired woman leaving the group at the fork, but from there, the vision fractured and became uncertain. She didn't know if the younger one would fight them or if he could be brought under the spell. It was a risky strategy, but she'd allow no further bloodshed even in their darkest need. Too many lives had already been lost.

As the blonde-haired lad, the tall large man, the short, stout man, the wounded lad and the stranger disappeared into the forest, she closed her eyes and vanished into the bushes.

"Begging your pardon, ma'am," said Biorn stiffly, "but where exactly is Cempess?"

"Quiet!" snapped Moranne.

The sound had been getting louder all morning, but now it was unmistakable. Water was thumping against stones and splashing over rocks. It trickled through tiny crevices and burbled against unseen banks.

"Is that water?" asked Caspin.

Moranne smiled broadly and urged the men onwards.

The path widened, and the forest gradually changed from tall, dense trees to shorter, lush foliage. The huge spade-shaped leaves of paulownia soon covered the pathway, providing a bright green roof. Bear claw leaves of the tetrapanax arched in the shade to swipe the men as they passed.

"I's never seen nothin' like it," said Brea.

Many of the plants only thrived in this area and would not be found in any other part of Grenfold. Birds sang in the spindly branches, and small creatures darted across their path. The sound of water became a cacophony as they drew near.

Moranne eventually gestured for the company to stop. They tentatively followed her forwards until the path opened onto a wide, wooden bridge fifty feet long. It spanned a foaming, muddy-brown river which snaked through the trees. The watercourse eventually became lost behind the overhanging branches and bushes which sprouted from small islets in its centre. It seemed odd that such a large river could sit within a dense forest, but such was Deapholt's density that it seemed to wrap around the waters and claim them for its own.

"The River Dorbourne?" ventured Captain Fallon. He knew it flowed into Deapholt, but no boatmen ever returned. Now he knew why. It was unnavigable.

Moranne nodded and noticed the other men looking over the waters in wonder.

The bridge was well maintained, with recently repaired planks and stripped wooden railings. It still bore the orange hue of new wood and glistened in the sunlight.

"We must be near," said Brea.

Sir Torbrand led them warily across the bridge. His soldier's training told him this was an exposed position, but nothing befell them as they crossed, staring into the burbling depths.

The opposite banks were different. The trees thinned on the left, but a tall thicket of woody shrubs, gorse and creeping vines towered on the right. They spread along the north bank to the east until the overhanging trees blotted out the river as it disappeared towards the Bay of Fayze.

"Where is this *Cempess*?" asked a puzzled Torbrand. He'd expected to find it on the river, but the forest seemed more impenetrable than ever.

"Follow me," said Moranne.

She strode along the path leading away from the bridge. The party plodded for another half a mile until the sound of the River Dorbourne retreated to a constant gurgle.

"Never trust a woman with directions," grumbled Slitan.

"Yea, they get lost in their kitchens," agreed Cal.

Moranne held up a hand, signalling the men to stop. The path bulged out into a circle at this point, but there was still no sign of the town.

"Remember what I said. Hold your tongues, and show respect." She turned to Prince Asger, who was wearily propped on his makeshift walking sticks. "Please, may I borrow a stick, Your Highness?"

The prince looked puzzled, but he shakily handed over one of his supports while the baffled men looked on.

Moranne gratefully took the stick and walked over to the wall of foliage. She studied the mass of green for a moment, then with a careful, deliberate movement, she pushed the stick into the thicket, followed by her arm until she was at full stretch. She pressed firmly and was rewarded with a knock which sounded like the echo of a wooden box. Withdrawing her arm slightly, she pushed forward three times to make three loud knocks which echoed from deep within the bushes.

There was silence except for the distant river and birdsong in the canopy.

"Don't think anyone's at home," joked Slitan.

Moranne pushed the stick back into the green and was about to knock again when a deep, commanding voice bellowed from above.

"Who knocks on the gates of Cempess? Identify yourselves."

Moranne looked at Torbrand, who was shaking his head.

"My name is Lady Moranne of the King's Council, and I bring His Royal Highness, Prince Asger, on a diplomatic mission. We respectfully request an audience with the prime oretta."

There was a short pause, and the gruff voice boomed out once more. "You are known to us, Wickona. How many are in your party?"

"Fifteen," shouted Moranne. It was a large number. Not *too* large, she hoped.

"How many men?"

"Twelve."

"More like eleven," whispered Cal, grinning at Hayden.

There was another pause, much longer this time. Moranne looked at Caspin and Torbrand. The Cempestre were wary of men and could easily turn them down.

"You may not pass," came the reply.

"What now?" asked Caspin.

Torbrand stepped forward until he stood beside Moranne. "Sir! I understand your caution. I am Sir Torbrand Linhold, son of Earl Normin

Linhold and military commander of this mission. I swear an oath to you that any of my men violating your rules will see the sharp edge of my sword; furthermore, we will leave all our weapons at your gate. We need your help, and we have nowhere left to go."

They looked at each other, and Moranne smiled at the tall knight. He grew in stature in her eyes with every step.

The deep, commanding female voice took them by surprise. "Sir Torbrand, I am Oretta Tiam Brimwulf, Commander of the Cempess protectorate. Will you swear your oath to me as one commander to another?"

The men all looked shocked, especially Cal and Slitan, who stared at the tall knight, daring him to treat a woman as an equal. The Pillars of Freanism closed in on Torbrand like the bars of a prison. He could almost feel the contempt from his father at the mere thought of a woman as commander. If Normin ever discovered the commission he'd promised Ellen, there could be consequences. Torbrand found his eyes settling on the lithe form of Ellen. Her red hair shone in the low light, and her eyes seemed to twinkle just for him. *She* would never accept him as her master.

"Oretta Brimwulf, as the military commander of this mission, I swear to you that my men will behave in accordance with your laws and that I will punish any man who disobeys."

No other voices sounded through the brush, and there was a deathly wait. Slitan and Cal muttered ill words, and the others looked at each other. Torbrand's shoulders slumped, and he held out his hands in defeat.

"I tried," he said, looking north along the path to their next challenge.

The sudden sound of heavy metal bolts sliding in metal latches echoed in the clearing. A loud creaking sound occurred as if a large piece of wood was sliding. The bushes moved.

At first, it was as though the brush was falling inwards, then pulled aside. Dust whirled in the air as the doors scraped across a dry pavement and opened inwards to reveal a bright light unfiltered by a tree canopy; it was like the entrance to another world. The bushes were attached to two large, heavy doors, and the ivy had been allowed to grow over them, disguising them entirely from the casual passerby.

The doorway revealed a wide passage formed by tall, spiked timber walls. It included a high walkway and opened out to reveal the wooden buildings of a town beyond. It was called "The Neck" as it resembled the neck of a bottle and acted like a funnel to control entry to the secret city. *An excellent defensive design,* thought Sir Torbrand.

The dust settled to reveal a line of some twenty female warriors barring their way. Around half were archers with bows drawn, while the others held their hands over their shoulders, ready to draw slender swords from back-mounted scabbards. Their dress was light armour with sculpted breastplates, lapped skirts over tight brown leggings and lightweight boots, all in deerskin leather. Each breast bore the marking of two interlinked circles.

A gruff male voice barked at Torbrand from behind. "I am Bonda Olaf Brimwulf; your men will each come forward and drop their weapons."

Olaf was a large man, almost as tall as Lunn and nearly as wide as Gron. He held a heavy broad axe which he fingered as his eyes met Torbrand's.

"You heard the man," said Biorn. He stepped forward boldly and removed his sword belt, placing it in front of Bonda Brimwulf.

Each man followed suit until it came to Slitan, who stood rooted to the spot. "I'm not..." he started to say, but Biorn shoved him so hard that he fell forward, landing at Olaf's feet.

"Not what?" said Olaf staring down at him.

"Nothing," muttered Slitan getting to his feet. He removed his bow and threw his hunting knife down in disgust; it bounced off the cobbles and came to a rattling halt.

He sheepishly returned to the ranks while Biorn eyed him with a furrowed brow.

Ellen was already removing her sword and striding forward when Olaf held up his mighty hand. "The women may keep their arms."

Slitan took a step forward, but Captain Fallon threw his arm across the archer's chest. "Don't," he said gruffly. "Put one foot wrong, and a broken tooth will be the least of your troubles."

The warrior at the centre of the Cempestre line stepped forward with a broad smile, and her hand extended towards Sir Torbrand. Her long black hair was braided with coloured beads, and a long scar ran from her left eye to the corner of her mouth. At around forty years, she matched her husband, not only in age but also in stature.

"I am Oretta Brimwulf. Welcome to Cempess."

As the commanders shook hands, the archers lowered their bows, and the swordswomen dropped their arms, but they all remained alert.

Torbrand introduced his brother and the captain before presenting the prince. Asger dragged himself before Tiam and bowed as low as possible without falling from his crutches.

"You don't need to bow, Prince Asger," said Tiam with a grin. The royal protocol demanded that she address him as *Your Highness,* but the Cempestre would never recognise the crown.

"I honoured meet you, Oretta Brimwulf," he said formally. "Long wished to meet proud people."

Tiam was smiling broadly and shaking her head. "The honour is ours. You're the first prince to grace our home." She turned and gestured to the town beyond. "My warriors will escort your men to a dormitory where they can relax, and I will take you to meet the prime oretta."

The men would be watched closely, as Moranne expected. She trusted Caspin and Biorn to keep them in line, but they'd hate being caged for too long.

Cempess was designed in the shape of a bottle. The Neck opened out into a wide curved shoulder, where the street branched evenly and followed the wall in a ring known as The Pendant. A broad oak stood at the branch, bowing low over two paths which led to the prime oretta's residence opposite The Neck.

Tiam led Moranne, Torbrand and the prince into the large log-built Prime Lodge while the others were taken along the southern Pendant Path. The Cempestre stopped to stare at the strange newcomers. Some shook their heads, and husbands gathered their children and ushered them inside. Most women wore warrior garb, but the men were equally impressive. Broad and strong, they pulled barrows, chopped wood, built cabins or tended to livestock and crops. The inverted society was strange to Frean eyes, but the people seemed happy. Little girls played with wooden swords, while boys made forts and treehouses from sticks and log off-cuts.

The warriors led the men past rows of neatly built homes with bright flowered gardens. Trees filled all the other spaces, except for a vast area in the centre which spanned the whole city. It was split into a livestock paddock with cows and goats and a cultivated area growing all kinds of crops.

The fields were separated by a large, square, wooden built keep which the Cempestre called The Last Stand. More fortified than the rest of the town, it acted as both a final defensive position and the oretta training school. The party was led through its tall double doors into a recruit dormitory which was being hastily cleared for them. Every wall was made from smooth, oiled log beams with precision-crafted joinery. There would be no escape if the women used it as a prison.

Jem looked around at the soldiers polishing swords, practising against straw dummies, or manning the wooden plinth clung to the walls. There were no Cempestre men within the keep's sturdy confines.

A stocky woman with dark, grey-streaked hair stood at the bailey centre with her hands on her hips. Her eyes were a piercing grey-blue, and her mouth slowly creased into a smile as the group arrived.

"Welcome!" she shouted, surveying the weary soldiers. "My name is Tarn Tarben; I am the Chief Oretta Instructor; please feel at home. As a precaution, the gates will be locked tonight, but you are free to leave at any time. My warriors will show you to your quarters."

Caspin was invited to Tarn's office while Biorn went with the men to ensure they caused no trouble. Brea and Ellen were invited to stay with the recruits in a higher part of the keep.

Tarn Tarben's office was situated in a low building that sloped from the keep's east wall. A short deck stood in front of the door containing racks of training weapons; thin swords, no more than an inch wide, with long, gently curving blades, extended grips and no prominent cross guards.

"We call it a katana," said Tarn when she saw Caspin staring at them. "It's an alviri weapon. Very effective."

Tarn's quarters were simple by Cynstol standards. The wooden furniture was made from small, whole branches, oiled and polished the same way as the buildings. More katanas hung behind the desk, where Tarn took a seat. The blades arched above her head like a rainbow.

"Please sit, Sir Caspin," she invited him cordially.

Caspin pictured the dressing-down he would often get from his father in Faircester or General Marl at the Green Order barracks in Numolport. While he was familiar with Lady Moranne's lead, the sight of Tarn sitting across from him with her hands clasped was unnerving.

"Relax, I'm not going to bite," she continued smiling. "I just want to know about your men."

"How can I help?" he said, fidgeting slightly in his seat.

"Who should I watch?"

She was forthright and immediately to the point. Tarn knew some of the soldiers would have fundamentalist views, and she tested his honesty. He knew how much they needed the Cempestre help; he decided to be true. "Cal, the short Burlander, comes from a devout farming community, but Slitan is the most outspoken. I will discipline the men; please be assured."

"I am assured, Sir Caspin, and thank you for your candour, but I'm afraid it's your men I'm concerned about. My warriors will strike them down immediately if they violate our laws. Be sure they understand."

"I will," said Caspin, standing. They shook hands and nodded in respect.

His men were unarmed and outnumbered by highly trained, sword-wielding women. He would need to ensure that Slitan didn't bring ruin upon them all.

The Prime Lodge was a large building which also doubled as the parliament for this single town state. Eschewing the opulence of the capital, the log construction made it feel more like a Burland village hall than any Tudorfeld mansion. Large, colourful rugs covered the wooden floors, and candles burned in holders, illuminating the walls in a warm glow.

Polished farm implements stood on short plinths, and swords hung on the walls serving as a testament to this close-knit community's self-reliance. There was no throne room or ceremonial chamber. Moranne's party was shown into a broad lounge, where a low fire crackled in the centre. Smoke spiralled into a central stone chimney which also acted as roof support. The light danced in the vaulted ceiling; the room had an earthy, warm quality which made Moranne, Torbrand, and the prince feel safe and relaxed.

A door swung open at the far end of the room, and a tall woman strode forward confidently to greet them. Her weathered, pale features were revealed as she stepped from the shadows and beamed at the three representatives.

"It's been a long time, Wickona," she said, aiming her warmth at Moranne.

The prime oretta's hair was the same streaked grey as Brea's, but it was strung into tight braids filled with blue and orange beads. The slightest puff beneath her eyes showed her age. Otherwise, she was muscular and strong, towering above all but the statuesque Torbrand, who she fixed with a twinkling grey gaze.

"Too long, my old friend," replied Moranne. They embraced while Torbrand, Tiam and the prince looked on.

She gestured for them to sit, and they did as instructed, reclining onto a sizeable upholstered bench which ran around one side of the fire. It was good to feel relaxed again after sleeping on the damp forest floor for many days.

"This is Freca Holthand, the Prime Oretta of Cempess," said Moranne, introducing her old acquaintance. "May I introduce Prince Asger of House Fierdman and Sir Torbrand Linhold of the Green Order."

They all bowed in recognition while a thin man entered, carrying a tray of food and drink.

"Things must be serious if a prince comes to call on *the wenches*," said Freca wryly.

Moranne recounted their mission from Cynstol, the flight from Deapgate and the intelligence from Stanholm, which prompted them to seek Cempestre help. Freca listened intently without comment until Moranne finished the story, and then she relaxed back in her seat, leaning on clenched hands, deep in thought.

"So how does this affect the Cempestre?" she asked eventually.

Moranne looked to Asger and Torbrand, but only *she* knew the evil which came their way. "Corvus believes he is the rightful ruler of Grenfold. He will not allow you to rule your affairs if he snatches the crown."

Freca nodded, although she seemed unconvinced. "We are small and insignificant; we pose him no threat."

"It's your duty to help," blurted Torbrand unhelpfully.

Freca took no offence. "Hmm," she laughed. "Where was your Green Order when the clans attacked, and where was a hand of friendship when our harvest failed? Where is our seat on the King's Council?"

"Sorry," said Asger. "Offer seat."

"Those are kind words Prince Asger, but in reality, we don't need any help. We've learned to help ourselves, and in troubled times we turn to the alviri." She looked at Tiam, who was nodding sagely. "When my people last fought in a war which was not of their making, it brought us to ruin. I cannot ask my warriors to risk their lives for the sons of men."

"You don't understand," said Torbrand in desperation. "Thousands of innocents will die."

She looked down and nodded solemnly. "I *do* understand, dear knight, but those lives will not be Cempestre."

"Please, a few brave warriors?" asked the prince, holding out his hand in pleading.

"I'm sorry, but I will not ask my warriors to die for your cause."

Torbrand was about to rise to his feet, but Moranne laid a calming hand on his shoulder. "Thank you for seeing us, Freca," she said humbly.

Freca stood and gestured to Tiam, who stood to attention.

"You are free to remain here until your strength is restored, and you will have rooms within this lodge as befits your stature." She clasped Moranne's hands, and their eyes met in understanding. "I'm sorry, Wickona."

Leaving them in the hands of Tiam Brimwulf, Freca strode to the far end of the room and vanished through the same door she had entered. Her exit echoed around the chamber, leaving the three in stunned silence.

"This is your friend?" grumbled Torbrand.

Moranne was lost for words.

"May I speak alone?" asked the prince.

Tiam shook her head, the audience was over, and her leader had spoken. "Hadwin will find you some rooms." She gestured towards the tall, thin man who had brought refreshments. Only later would they discover that he was Bonda Holthand, Freca's husband.

They were led to simple, spacious chambers in the north wing, with views over some of the tiny houses below.

"What now, ma'am?" asked Torbrand loitering in her doorway.

She had no simple answers. Although she'd expected a difficult conversation, it was shorter and more final than her friendship with the Cempestre would suggest. Maybe it was the presence of the prince or so many soldiers.

"I'll try again tomorrow," she said finally. They were all tired and needed to regroup. If the Cempestre wouldn't help, it was unlikely the alviri would. That left only one option, and it was one she feared to take.

"Get some rest," she told Torbrand. *We need to be focused.*

26 SWING

His breathing was urgent and laboured, stumbling through the forest. Thorns tore at his clothes, and vines whipped his face, threatening to drag him down into its path. Jem spun around, but there was nothing there, though he could hear it thrusting through the bush and swiping branches aside like twigs.

He was lost and alone. Where were Moranne and Torbrand? Where was Hayden? The path was lost, and Jem was lost. There was too little light to tell north from south, and he'd lost his bearings in the blind flight. He could hear the beast's breath like the snort of a mighty bull and the scrape of its long claws slashing through the foliage like machetes.

"Come on!" he said to himself, running blindly forward once more. If he ran far enough, he could reach the Bay of Fayze or Tudorfeld. There was even a chance he could find the path.

He wiped the sweat and blood from his forehead and then pushed onwards. The crashing sounds receded. Maybe the creature was tired from the chase. It was large, but the dark, hulking shadow was too distant to make out its details. Jem took a breath and listened for a moment. No, it was still coming.

A twig snapped in front of him, and he looked up, but it was too late. A massive black beast with white striped markings reared out of the bushes. It had shining white curled tusks and cruel, sharp teeth in its slender snout. Its front legs were poised above him, and its razor-sharp claws stood ready to tear him to shreds.

It plunged forward, and Jem cowered in a ball with his arms wrapped over his head. It was the end. He screamed as the beast's body blotted out the remaining light and its jaws opened to devour him.

"Jem! Jem!" shouted a familiar voice. "It's just a dream!"

Jem opened his eyes to see the concerned face of Hayden looking down at him.

"Where am I?" asked Jem. He could feel the sweat running down his brow and soaking the sheets around him.

"You're safe, my friend. We're in Cempess."

His eyes adjusted to the morning light streaming through the window and spied the wooden barrack walls with rows of bunks where the others slept.

"It was no dream," he said solemnly.

Hayden nodded. Only he and Caspin knew of Jem's gift. "What did you see?"

Jem pushed himself up and leaned against the wall; he could see the others had already risen, except for Gamin, who slept peacefully.

"There are dangerous beasts in the forest."

It seemed obvious to Hayden, but this was something specific, and Jem looked scared.

"We need to tell Lady Moranne," he said.

Jem washed in a bowl of water by his bed and dragged on his clothes. He followed Hayden into a large mess hall where the others ate a breakfast of eggs and fried beans. They were served by a small number of Cempestre men who bustled in and out with trays and mugs of warm mint and nettle tea.

"How's your boyfriend?" said Slitan, as Hayden took a seat at the long table opposite Jem.

"I'm fine," answered Jem without hesitation. "How's your mother?"

Slitan rose to his feet, and his hand reached for the dagger, which wasn't there. He glared at Moranne's gada until Biorn's stern expression had him sinking back to the bench, scowling at both Jem and Hayden.

Lunn's chuckling baritone broke the atmosphere, and there was too much good cheer to let the mood linger.

Cal and Slitan sniffed at the male attendants who served them, but the others seemed less concerned and accepted the Cempestre society more readily.

"Don't you feel ashamed?" asked Cal as one of the Cempestre men took his plate. He didn't become angry and simply appeared bemused.

"Sir, I would only feel ashamed if I treated my wife as less than equal. I am happy with my work. More tea, anyone?"

Gron laughed so hard that he sprayed his warm drink across the table, and Davill fell back in his chair, holding his sides. None of this soothed Slitan's simmering rage as a fissure opened up between the fundamentalists and the others.

"Did I miss something?" asked Brea striding into the hall with Ellen.

"Just Cal and Slitan being idiots," said Sax in his quiet, straightforward way.

"A normal day then," said Ellen. Along with Brea, she took a chair near Biorn.

Sir Caspin slept in an annexe to Tarn's office as his rank befitted and had breakfast with her earlier. He entered the mess hall in a buoyant mood and stood beside the captain at the head of the table.

"I have some good news, men," he said, smiling. "You will be allowed freedom of the town until we leave." There was a low cheer, but Caspin wasn't finished. "I must remind you to behave honourably at all times and do not attempt to fraternize with the Cempestre women. They will not be interested, and you will likely lose your head. Get as much rest and food as possible; we aim to leave tomorrow."

"Couldn't we have an extra day?" asked Davill, echoing the thoughts of many of the men.

"We have a mission," said Caspin, "and we're behind schedule."

There was a slight chill in the air as autumn knocked on the door of summer, but the sun streamed over the city wall to illuminate the fields planted with wheat, rye, corn, carrots, potatoes and many other blossoming crops. Two streams crossed the town from the north to join the River Dorbourne in the south. The larger of the two ran through the arable fields for irrigation, while the smaller was used for drinking water. They were both unsullied and fed from Mirror Lake and the glaciers high in Banafell.

A large set of gates on the city's south side opened to a protected landing on the River Dorbourne. Wide nets caught a variety of small fish, while a mill with its wooden wheel ground corn and rye for making the bread. Heavy-built Cempestre men toiled hard in the fields and on the river, hauling large sacks of grain and repairing the fishing nets.

The mission's guide was a woman named Ranka, who didn't appear to be a warrior. Her garb was similar but made of cloth rather than the light leather of the orettas. She showed them the storehouses and the fortified wall with its high walkway and numerous watchtowers hidden under the ivy. Thick scrub and creepers encircled the town; these had been cultivated to mask Cempess from all but the most determined foe.

"Who are your enemies?" asked Davill, looking up at the spiked walls.

"The clans test our walls every few months, but they don't like to stray too far from Banafell. It also helps to keep out some of the more dangerous forest creatures such as the dryads and tunnbroccs."

The men looked at each other, but none were brave enough to ask what these creatures were.

"Take no offence," said Davill shakily, "but what makes the men stay in a town where they do not rule?"

Ranka smiled. "Fear not; I'll not take your head for speaking your mind. I am a teacher by trade and answer such questions daily. We have a strong bond between man and woman, a promise of fealty and a common goal of life and love. We serve no squire and no king; we work only for the good of our town. There is no money, no poverty and no hunger; every Cempestre has a place."

"What if a man or woman doesn't want to live that way," asked Jem.

"Cempess is no prison; we need some people to leave so that numbers remain manageable. A few leave each year, and we escort them to a town of their choice. All who remain have chosen this life."

"Are all orettas married to a bonda?" asked Hayden, with thoughts of Ham Grome back in Dunstreet.

"No, sir," she replied. "Juldra doesn't dictate a marriage or nay. Both men and women may be bonda, but only a woman may be an oretta."

"Heresy," muttered Slitan. The nuance was lost on most of the men.

Hayden nodded and smiled at the fair Cempestre. She knew what he asked.

"I only have one question, if you please," asked Gron, leaning on a spade handle as the others looked out at the river.

"Ask it, sir."

"Do you have a tavern?"

She looked around at some of the Cempestre men watching the tour. All were grinning.

"Of course we do."

⁂

"Do they not knock in Cynstol?" Freca Holthand sat at a broad, ornately-carved desk poring through long lists of stores to ensure they had enough food for the winter.

"They wouldn't let me see you," replied Moranne. She stood against the doorframe with her arms folded.

Freca continued to total the figures for a while and added ticks against the rows already tallied.

"You're hoping to change my mind."

"I'm hoping to try," confirmed Moranne.

The prime oretta put down her quill and leaned back in the rough-hewn chair. "Do you know how often we've asked the capital for help?"

Moranne shook her head. Sir Torl Radborough didn't keep her appraised of all royal business.

"None," said Freca, resting her hands behind her head. "We're whores, abominations, fornicators in the eyes of the realm. Freans would rather see us dead than lift a hand in our need."

"You're right, but would you see thousands die? Many will be Freans; some will be dalfreni, some alviri or Jakari, and it may touch your kingdom. Will you not help?"

Freca stood, walked around the table where she sat, and picked up the ledger.

"We have just enough food for the winter and just enough warriors to protect us from hungry clans and desperate creatures. Our life here balances on a knife edge. I know you care for these humans, but it's not our fight. We will give you provisions and all the help we can. You have our best wishes but not our warriors."

Moranne slumped into a chair and gazed through a window at one of the watchtowers.

"There is one more thing," continued Freca. "Our doctor has examined your young lad, Gamin. Not only is he making a full recovery, but the knife wound is disappearing."

"Disappearing?"

"We've only seen the alviri cure a wound this way."

"Hmm," mused Moranne. "Thank you for the information."

"Now go to your men and enjoy a drink as our guest. I believe they've found the tavern."

A large community hall and school lay behind the Prime Lodge. It was used for celebrations and other collective purposes. It also functioned as a parliament of sorts, hosting meetings of the Cempestre to discuss work and any issues in the town. All the buildings had the same simple log construction, with thick glass windows and thatched roofs.

Just north of the centre was a large grassy area on the banks of one of the streams. This location was of more interest to Moranne's men as it included the town's only tavern. It served mead, mapulder, a cloudy cider and mixed berry wine. Rough-built benches and tables were scattered over the area, and it was here that Moranne found some of the men enjoying the local brews.

"The mead is excellent, ma'am," gushed Gron, sitting with Jem, Lunn, Hayden and Gamin. They told the lads some of their adventures with bawdy tales of the young women they'd known. Barrack's talk didn't chime well with some Cempestre warriors who sat opposite and shook their heads in disgust.

"Watch how much they drink, Captain," said Moranne, sitting down with Biorn and Caspin.

"It does them good to relax a little, ma'am," replied the captain, sipping his cider.

"This place is paradise," added Caspin, as his gaze caught a young Cempestre warrior. He was very popular with the ladies of Tudorfeld until they discovered his brother, and then they used him to meet Torbrand. Even now, they all knew that Ellen only had eyes for his taller brother.

"Could you denounce the Pillars of Freanism?" asked Moranne.

"What pillars?" he said, laughing.

Sir Torbrand sat alone, staring at the table where Brea and Ellen were relaxing with berry wine. He wanted so much to say something, but women usually came to *him*. He couldn't bear it if she laughed at his words. It couldn't happen. His mother would find him a nice Tudorfeld girl from the right family; they'd live a privileged life and produce beautiful children. He sighed, watching as Ellen flicked the hair from her face and laughed at one of Brea's dirty jokes.

Sax also sat alone; he watched Cal and Slitan try to get the attention of a group of Cempestre warriors while becoming very drunk on the unfamiliar mapulder. He smiled to himself, but something felt wrong. It wasn't a strong feeling, but something deep and ancient was near. He scanned the area, but all he found were the townsfolk going about their business. It must be nothing.

Over the stream, across a small wooden bridge on The Pendant road, was a large field which held livestock and horses in separate sections. Davill looked across the nearest field at a proud stallion standing silently at its centre. It nodded its head almost as if acknowledging a fellow loner. He strolled by, sipping his mead and enjoying the quiet.

Passing a low hedge, he came to another small open green; a children's play area. It included a climbing frame built from sturdy logs and a swing made from more forest wood. A little girl, no older than five, pushed herself back and forth, swaying gently and imagining herself in some fantastical world.

A line of terraced houses backed onto the green, all with their own small garden and different coloured curtains showing the slightest individuality in this communal town. Davill sat on the climbing frame and watched the girl smiling contentedly. Her bright blue dress billowed out when she swung forward before she leaned back to propel herself once more. He took a swig of the potent, sweet drink, but no alcohol would wash his sins away.

If only he could roll back time to that moment when they discovered the Jakari camp. The innocent eyes of the little Jakari girl filled with tears at the sight of her butchered mother. Moments before, he raised his knife and killed her too. He'd lied to the prince. It haunted him every day, and he hated himself. They told him it was his duty, but it was murder. He thought it would help to volunteer for the mission, but the scar was too deep.

The swing creaked as the girl arched back and forth, giggling while she pushed her legs forward to gain height. Just as she thrust forward once more, Davill felt a vibration through the climbing frame. He looked into his drink, and a little pattern of waves pulsed across the surface.

He looked around, but people walking past seemed unaware, and the little girl laughed more loudly. It came again, but this time it was accompanied by a loud thump which rattled the swing.

"In Frea's name?"

Still, the little girl swung back and forth, and another loud thump shook the earth and caused a thin smoke of dust to rise above the path. A man appeared from one of the terraces and called to the little girl, Marta; she was oblivious.

The next thump was so strong it shook the houses, and the climbing frame rocked. People stopped, looking around for the source. Davill saw it first.

The ground cracked between the climbing frame and the swing, and part of the swing's frame sank suddenly into the ground. Marta fell forward into a heap, crying out in anguish, just as the A-frame collapsed on top of her.

"Frea, no!" cried Davill, racing to the broken swing. The logs were heavy, but he used all his strength to pull them upwards. He could feel more ground giving way behind him and a scrabbling sound beneath. "Come on!"

Holding the main beam with his back, he pulled the sobbing girl free and held her close as the frame crashed to the ground. At that moment, his leg gave way when the land subsided, and he fell to the earth, still clutching Marta.

"Throw her to me," cried her father as more earth moved and a large shadow emerged behind Davill.

The swordsman looked into Marta's eyes as if she was the little Jakari girl back in the Mur. "I'm sorry," he said and threw her with all his might towards the waiting arms of her father.

As she left his grasp, a vast dark shape erupted from the ground behind him. He turned to see a sleek black and white snout, tipped in two curved tusks like the horns of a boar, and lined with razor-sharp teeth. It reared on its hind legs, as tall as five men, and bore down, snatching him in its jaws and dragging him backwards. Despite the pain tearing through his legs, Davill reached out to grasp rocks and roots as the beast tugged on his body. He scrabbled wildly, snatching for any hand-hold, but the creature was too strong, and it dragged him into the crevasse.

Davill's screams were lost in the ground as a second creature emerged beneath the end-terraced house. Broken wood and splinters exploded outwards, and it stood in the wreckage shaking the debris from its coat.

"Frea's teeth!" shouted Lunn. He was the first to his feet and ran wildly towards the beasts. He spied an axe left on a wood chopping block and ripped it free as he barrelled past.

Brea and Ellen were still armed and chased Lunn, while Sax ran into the tavern and ransacked the kitchen until he grabbed a cook's knife. Gron smashed a table with his bare hands and took one of the planks. The rest of the party just ran to help as they could while Cempestre warriors jumped from the walls, and men came from all over the town with axes and pitchforks.

The first beast returned as they drew near, its snout red with Davill's blood. It reared up and roared in defiance, summoning a third creature which burst from the paddock beside the road.

"What in Frea's name?" said Torbrand, as the three beasts pulled themselves free of the rubble and looked around for easy meat.

"They're tunnbroccs!" yelled Moranne. She held the sceptre, gathering the power to wield it. "Giant badgers from the time of galdur!"

The nearest beast crashed through the paddock fence and turned to face Sir Caspin, who was closest. He dived beside the road as it lunged and one of Brea's arrows whistled overhead, catching it in the flank. It roared with pain and whirled to find the archer.

"Oh, bugger!" cursed Brea. She turned and ran towards one of the watchtowers in the wall. The tunnbrocc galloped after her, but she made the tower entrance just before the beast's snout smashed into the rigid structure.

Ellen slashed at one of its rear legs, and it bellowed in agony, kicking her across the road. It turned to kill her, but it saw a blinding flash as a ball of green energy flew from Moranne's hands and hit it between the eyes. It swayed for a moment, then fell stunned onto its side. A group of Cempestre warriors jumped onto its body and thrust their slender swords into its head.

"You distract it!" shouted Lunn towards Gron, facing the blood-soaked tunnbrocc.

"Distract it? What with? Shall I dance?" He waved the table plank, daring the creature to come for him. It swayed back and forth warily until it decided he was easy prey. It bounded towards him at great speed, but Gron stood his ground. It didn't see Lunn running in from the side with the axe held high. He brought it down with all his might, and embedded it in the tunnbrocc's side.

It howled in anguish and thrashed in a circle, trying to see the weapon still cutting deep, but it eventually spied Gron once more and ran straight towards him.

"Get down!" shouted Sax.

Gron hit the grass just in time to see a cook's knife flying over his head to embed itself between the beast's eyes. It fell to the ground, ploughing to a halt just short of Gron's outstretched body.

The final creature was the largest, an alpha male they'd learn later. It shook itself free of the house debris and was snarling at the surrounding warriors, who only succeeded in making it angry with their arrows.

Jem had no weapon but wanted to help; he kept back, looking for any chance to strike. The Cempestre had no such fear; their katana-wielding warriors ducked in and out, trying to slash its flanks as it circled in anger. Each oretta would dive towards its hindquarters and swipe before tumbling away to avoid its kick. It was an elaborate dance, but they made it look effortless.

Unfortunately, one of the younger warriors seemed less experienced and mistimed her run; the tunnbrocc kicked her hard, sending her crashing to the ground; she was dazed with a gash to the forehead. Sensing a victory, the beast turned to devour her, but Jem was already running.

It was suicide, and he'd never know why he would give his life for a stranger, but the reaction was automatic and instinctive. There was no time to drag her out, as the animal was already widening its jaws to kill them. Jem wrapped his arms around the young warrior and turned his back to the beast.

"I'll protect you," he said and closed his eyes.

Everyone but Jem and the girl saw the ball of intense green light swirl instantly about them, and the jaws of the tunnbrocc snap onto the pulsing sphere. It screamed in pain and fell onto its back, creasing the ground with the force.

Twenty oretta warriors jumped onto its belly and tore it to shreds before it could muster, leaving large pools of dark blood running down the road and into the large holes left by the creatures.

When death didn't come, Jem opened his eyes to see the deep brown eyes of the Cempestre girl smiling up at him.

"Thank you," she said and leaned forward to kiss him on the cheek.

"I don't know what you've got, young Jem, but I'd like some," said Cal, holding out a hand.

Besides a few cuts, bruises, and one broken arm, the only fatality was Davill. The men stared down into the wide tunnel where he met his end.

"I didn't really know him," said Gron, and the others agreed.

"He was a brave soldier, and that's all we can ask of ourselves," added Biorn.

The Cempestre gave them space as they stood silently with clasped hands and prayed to their gods.

The men thought Moranne had used her power to save Jem and the Cempestre woman, but she knew it came from him. He was strong, maybe the strongest. To summon the shield of protection required skill and experience the lad didn't possess; to invoke it with no sceptre was impossible. Not even Corvus himself had that gift.

She watched Jem staring down into the burrow with the others and felt a nervous pang she'd not experienced since the handsome, chiselled, dark-haired boy became a mass murderer. It was fear. Jem could become a potent weapon in the wrong hands.

Ellen blinked her eyes open and felt the pounding in her head where she'd hit the road; a pair of dark, concerned eyes were looking down at her.

"Are you alright...private," he stumbled. Sir Torbrand cradled her head in his lap and pulled back the hair from her bloody forehead.

"I am now," she said before the throbbing overwhelmed her, and she passed out.

Oretta Tiam Brimwulf's home was no different from any of the humble timber dwellings of Cempess. Its size was modest, and it was situated near the neck, where its only view was of the Prime Lodge across The Pendant. Olaf had felled every tree and honed every log with his own hands, and even now, he continued to make improvements each year.

The tiny crib had been a work of art, which now cradled the baby of another oretta; the extra room had been completed a few years ago, and now it was Lanika's haven. Hunting trophies adorned the walls, but no bright dresses hung in the cupboards, and she had little time for boys. Muscular and stocky in her father's image but beautiful in her mother's teenage years, Lanika Brimwulf was rapidly approaching womanhood. She was desperate to join her older friends at The Last Stand. Oretta training began at fifteen, and Lanika was eager to start. The braided beads would not adorn her dark hair, and nor would she bear the ivy tattoo until the day she stood proud as an oretta. The emblem of Cempess was a pair of interlinked rings, but it was traditional for orettas to bear the ivy tattoo in honour of Kalima Freond.

"Lani?" called her mother as she appeared through the door. Gone was the leather armour, replaced by a short linen dress; she carried a katana in its scabbard, which she placed on a low dresser. Olaf had cooked a root vegetable stew, which they usually enjoyed with heavy, sourdough bread; its earthy smell wafting through the open door.

"I wish I could have helped with the tunnbrocc," replied Lanika. "I hear the newcomers acted with honour."

"They did," agreed Tiam. She sat on the edge of the small bed and put her arm around her daughter. "They were fearless, even without weapons."

"I can't wait to begin my training."

"I know," smiled her mother, "and you will very soon."

Lanika's eye was drawn to the sword, which she immediately recognised as her grandmother's. The braided leather handle was worn, but *Clansbane* was light, sharp and fabled in the hands of its former owner.

"It's yours," said Tiam.

"Mine?" gasped her daughter. "But—"

"I have a new blade. I wanted you to have this for your training."

Lanika leapt from the bed and lifted the sword. The katana slid easily from the well-oiled scabbard and felt perfectly balanced in her small hands. The edge was polished to a fine edge, but there were still dents and scrapes where the alviri steel had clashed with the rusting cudgels of rampaging clan warriors.

"I can't...."

"Your father and I are very proud of you," said Tiam. "The sword will always pass to you, but I decided it should be now."

"Why?" queried Lanika. Her mother's demeanour had changed, and a serious expression had wiped the smile from her face.

Tiam placed a hand on her daughter's shoulder and looked directly into her glossy, brown eyes. "There's something I must do."

27 HONOUR

The sun was setting over The Neck, sending the long shadows of the walls deep into the town, but Moranne still sat above the spot where the experienced swordsman had died. She passed a small, polished stone pendant between her fingers, watching the light scatter from its dark surface. They found it in the hole and guessed it was Davill's.

"We don't know if he had any family," she remarked to Prince Asger, sitting beside her. "We only know he hailed from Greydon."

"A good man," added the prince.

"I'm told the tunnbroccs would have been digging for weeks. It was the most deadly attack anyone could remember."

The strong Cempestre men had already started to fill the holes with rocks from the riverbed. They would add clay and mud to pack the breach solidly over the coming days.

"Going to presentation?" asked the prince.

Moranne slowly nodded; she was in no mood to socialise, but it would be good for the men to commemorate Davill's sacrifice. She sighed and lifted herself from the bench, looking back at the spot for one last time.

"Many more will die before Corvus is stopped," she said.

The prince nodded. He could be one of them.

It was a short stroll west along The Pendant, past the field with the hastily repaired fence and the tavern where they relaxed earlier, to the large communal hall. They entered through the north door into an atrium used as the school, then along a close-panelled corridor into the main hall.

The cavernous square chamber had a high vaulted roof and hundreds of candles mounted on its four walls. The flagstone floor was laid out with long lines of wooden tables, where a sizeable proportion of the Cempess population had assembled for a special presentation.

Tiam Brimwulf met Moranne and the prince to escort them to a raised dais on one side of the hall. It consisted of another long set of tables draped in a red linen cloth, where Torbrand and the others were already seated. The prince sat beside the prime oretta, and Moranne sat between Sir Torbrand and Oretta Brimwulf. As Moranne took her seat, Freca Holthand rose, and the room fell silent.

"Women and men of Cempess, we are gathered today to honour Private Davill Hwaetbur of the Green Order. He gave his life to protect us against the forest beasts, and we will be forever grateful. Marta Sumars-Dag will live to become a Cempestre like her mother and father because of Davill's selfless act of heroism." She looked across at Moranne's company with a smile. "The strangers in our midst are strangers no longer. Their immense bravery and selflessness has saved lives and won them our eternal thanks. You are all free to visit Cempess at any time as friends of the Cempestre."

A deafening roar rose from the crowd, accompanied by the banging of tables and stamping of feet.

"I would especially like to thank Prince Asger's soldiers who didn't hesitate to help, despite the risk to their own lives. I will see all your weapons returned to you," she said, addressing the men directly.

Moranne nodded along with the others as Freca continued.

"Please enjoy a feast in your honour."

When she finished speaking, a string of men appeared from the atrium carrying long planks of steaming roast meat and pots of fresh vegetables. Two of the tunnbroccs had been butchered for the feast; however, Davill's killer had been burnt on rough ground. The tough tunnbrocc meat had been perfectly cooked, and with the local mead, it made a satisfying feast which brought cheer to Moranne's party.

"To Davill," chimed Caspin, raising a tankard.

The party stood and took a long draught in his name.

As the night progressed, warriors formed a line to the dais to meet the soldiers. One woman made straight for Jem and clasped his hand. She was a middle-aged warrior with long dark hair split by a seam of grey.

"How can I repay you?" she said. "My name is Shina Horpen; you saved my daughter's life with Juldra's power."

Juldra's power? thought Jem. He stared at the woman, unable to form a coherent response.

"Her name is Keela; she's only twenty years old."

He still didn't know what had happened or how he'd conjured a barrier. "You're welcome," he said. "I hope Keela is well." He knew his response was underwhelming, but he couldn't think of anything to say.

"She is, thanks to you," said Shina. She squeezed his hand tightly, then hurried back to her friends with tears in her eyes.

By the night's end, the Cynstol mission and the Cempestre had mingled across the room. Gron and Lunn swapped war stories with some orettas while the prince chatted to Tiam Brimwulf. Sir Torbrand also tried to maintain a conversation with her husband, Olaf, although his mind was elsewhere.

Ellen lay in the Prime Lodge with a bandage around her head. She was conscious but weary; Brea mopped her brow to reduce the headache she suffered.

"Sir Torby wouldn't leave your side until I told him to rag off to the party," said Brea with a wink.

"No future," wheezed Ellen.

"Well, who knows what these snobby inbreds get up to. He don't have eyes for any other unless he's staring at *me* across the room."

Ellen smiled for the first time since the attack and closed her eyes, thinking of a tall knight striding to greet her.

⁂

Caspin led the men from The Last Stand at just past eight o'clock in the morning. It should have been earlier, but the mead-induced hangovers had affected everyone, including him. They met the rest of the party in The Neck, where the Cempestre had supplied them with four pack ponies and a horse for Prince Asger, complete with a modified saddle prepared overnight. The air was cool, and a fine mist rose from the ground, helping to clear their heads.

A line of Cempestre waited along one wall, and they stood to attention when they saw Moranne, Torbrand, Ellen, and Brea arriving with Tiam and the prime oretta.

"At ease," ordered Oretta Brimwulf.

"There's no need for another honour guard," said Moranne as she clasped Freca's hand.

"Ha, that's no honour guard, my friend; these are volunteers."

"Volunteers?" blurted Torbrand.

"They came to me last night and offered their service. I counselled against it, but my warriors were insistent. Maybe not the army you wanted, but one of my orettas is worth ten good men," she said, grinning.

Moranne embraced her old friend, and genuine warmth flowed through them for just an instant.

"There is one condition," she continued, "and I'm not sure Sir Torbrand will approve."

"Try me," said the knight, inspecting the orettas.

"A Cempestre warrior cannot take orders from a man; Oretta Brimwulf will be going with you."

Torbrand was becoming familiar with compromise, and he didn't flinch. "I can work with that," he proclaimed and offered his hand to Tiam in partnership.

"Allow me to introduce my warriors," said Oretta Brimwulf. She stood to the side ahead of her soldiers and barked their names. As each was called, they stepped forward for inspection.

"This is Brenna Gunborg," she began, introducing a very imposing figure.

The oretta stepped forward and met Torbrand eye to eye. Thick dark eyebrows matched her long dark hair, and a scar crossed her face marking her as a true seasoned warrior. With thirty-seven years, she'd seen plenty of action against the oni, and her alviri blade had the notches as proof. She wore a tattoo, high on her right arm, of the two interlocking rings, wound with intricate detail of verdant green ivy, which twisted past her elbow and finished on the inside of her forearm.

"There are few better with a sword," said Tiam.

"Unless you count *my* blade," said Sefti Regenherd. She stepped from the line beaming. Her slight frame seemed too brittle for combat, and Tiam could see it in Sir Torbrand's eyes.

"Don't let her slight build fool you," said Tiam. "She may not be as strong, but there are none faster or as fearless."

Both Cuyler Blodsuster and Yuka Bowhand were archers in their mid-thirties and also seemed to be good friends.

"Two of my best," said Tiam. "They were keen to join."

Cuyler had short black hair and brown eyes, while Yuka had lighter long hair and sparkling grey eyes. They moved together, and something unspoken passed between them.

"And this is Isen Stanhamur," said Oretta Brimwulf. The tall, muscular warrior took a long step forward and almost collided with Sir Torbrand. Her jawline was square, and her eyes small and narrowed in suspicion. The bulging biceps exposed below the arms of her leather tunic were as thick as Biorn's.

"Lunn, is that your sister?" joked Gron.

She was the same height as Lunn and wielded a long, bearded axe and a round wooden shield which she wore on her back. Her thighs were almost as thick as Gron's, and she had wide black eyebrows to match her tousled dark hair.

"No," replied Lunn under his breath. No one heard him; some things were never a joke.

"I thought there were no male warriors," said Slitan, sniggering. Isen shot him a dark look and moved back into file." She didn't notice Gamin gazing at her in awe.

"And finally, this is Bresne Fixen," announced Tiam. "She's one of my most experienced warriors and taught me everything I know."

The fifty-year-old oretta bowed to Sir Torbrand, exposing the orange beads woven into her grey hair.

"It's an honour, sir," she said, before moving back into line. Her status was very high in the Cempestre ranks, and she'd often been feted as Freca Holthand's successor.

"The honour is mine, ladies," replied Torbrand. "You'll take your orders from Oretta Brimwulf, but I expect us all to act as a team. Together we'll stop Corvus."

And so it came to pass that the twenty-one-strong party, consisting of eleven men and ten women, left Cempess and headed north.

They were followed by three ancient creatures and a tiny sparrow circling in the canopy.

28 THE FORK

Corvus stood atop a pinnacle of grey rock while the wind whipped about him, throwing his cloak into the swirling beat of a crow's wings. Motionless, feet apart, he remained welded to the mountain as if retained by an invisible force.

His gaze was to the south but not to the land below. He spied the world from above through the eyes of a tiny bird swooping through the yellowing canopy of Deapholt.

Women won't save you, he grinned to himself.

Settling in the branches of a tall tree, the sparrow lifted its tail and looked down.

Lots of grubby soldiers on their way to die, led by the witch and...

His concentration dropped, and the bird flew off, trying to find its kin. Corvus held his chest, remembering the jolt he felt when Moranne used her power in Bearun. He knew there was another.

"So we have a runt," he said into the wind. "Runts are already dead; they just don't realise it."

The northern branch of the Deap Path from Cempess was broader and more regularly used than the southern portion. Four could easily walk abreast, and the vines and bramble kept clear of their way. Streaks of brown were starting to appear in the trees, and yellow leaves would drift slowly across their path as summer melted into autumn.

Cempess seemed far away now, but the loss of Davill still weighed heavily. Gamin was back to full strength, and Ellen had removed the bandage revealing a cut which would scar, something which pleased her.

The nine Cempestre women marched through the forest with seemingly endless stamina while the men struggled to keep pace.

Slitan joked that it "wasn't a race," but Tiam Brimwulf insisted they were going as slow as they could.

The terrain rose, and grey rocks dotted the landscape, flung from the ancient eruptions of an extinct Banafell volcano. Clear, cold streams followed the path, trickling south to join others, eventually flowing into the River Dorbourne.

"I've never seen such impressive women," said Hayden, marvelling at the Cempestre's stature.

"Not sure you've seen many unimpressive ones either," laughed Cal.

"Leave him be!" blasted Jem. He was starting to loathe the backward Cal and nasty Slitan.

"Didn't mean to offend your girlfriend, Jem," added Slitan.

Jem was unfazed and ignored them, but Slitan's anger was simmering. His tongue felt the edge of the broken tooth he earned from Biorn, and his gaze darted towards Ellen, chatting with Brea as usual. He decided there would need to be changes, and the snivelling Dunstreet dandy would be the first to go. Lunging forward, he struck Hayden in the back. The lad stumbled for a few paces and then fell forward into the rough path.

"Tripped on your skirts?" asked Slitan.

"You pushed me!" shouted Hayden. He dusted himself off and stared wildly into the bowman's eyes.

"Calling me a liar?"

"No, I am!" said Gamin, standing at Hayden's shoulder.

"Keep out of this, lad; he'll infect you with his perverted poison."

The others turned, and soon, Lunn and Gron stood behind the squire's son.

"I didn't peg you two for lovers of the forbidden," continued Slitan.

"He's one of us," said Gron.

"He's brave just being here," added Lunn. "Leave him be."

"What's going on?" stormed Biorn. The column had now stopped, and all eyes were on Slitan. Jem stared at the whore's son, fixing him with his gaze.

"Nothing!" he said, "just a disagreement."

"You can fight on your own time," said the captain. "Any more disruptions, and I'll have you bound and dragged behind one of the ponies."

Moranne watched the angry Kelby man muttering under his breath as Captain Fallon sent him to the back of the column. He was becoming dangerous and unpredictable. She needed to change her plans.

The sun twinkled through the canopy, dimming the light as the day wore on, and a cool breeze whistled through the forest, causing crusty leaves to fall like snow. The prince tightened his cloak, and the Cempestre women pulled high-waisted coats from their packs. Everyone felt the chill, but their unseen pursuers were accustomed to the cold.

The party made camp some thirty miles north of Cempess, and Moranne took the opportunity to talk with their new comrades.

"Do you know we're being followed?" she asked Tiam Brimwulf.

"Of course," replied the swordswoman. "They've watched Cempess for months and follow us when we go hunting."

"Have they ever attacked?"

"Not in living memory," she said, "but I think they're becoming desperate, and they could be unpredictable."

"How many are there?"

"Just a handful now. The clans killed many, and they're dying out anyway."

Moranne stared back along the trail where a slender creature with green and brown skin watched them from the bushes, unseen by all but the most experienced trackers.

"Don't hurt them unless you must," she said.

Tiam bowed in agreement and put her feet up before the fire. "It's going to be a tough winter."

The chilled evening air turned their breath to steam which dispersed in the fire's warmth. The company pulled itself close and stared into the flames.

"Does the lad know his powers?" continued Tiam. "I can see the questions in his eyes, and no one missed the spell he wove during the tunnbrocc attack."

Moranne shook her head. Jem wasn't strong enough to know, and she wasn't strong enough to tell him. His power was mighty, and he needed to understand how to guide it, but the dangers were immense.

"He'll need help," said Tiam.

"I know," replied Moranne. "There's too much at stake right now."

Tiam kicked a stick into the fire and leaned back, fixing Moranne with her stare. "If he endangers any of my warriors...."

She watched the flames leaping from the fire, whipping into smoke as they vanished into the fluttering canopy above. The experienced oretta had seen too many young warriors die at the hands of the oni or forest beasts. She'd see no more die for the cause of ancient witchcraft.

Moranne said nothing more that night. Lost in dark thoughts, she watched Jem as he laughed with his new friends. *Don't become too attached,* she thought. Many would not survive.

She carried the same silent burden through the night and the following morning when they continued to push north. It was a lonely life with no one to share the long-buried secrets or intimate moments when this world showed the beauty of its nature. *His* smile still entered her dreams and wrapped her in warmth, but the memory of his death soured the image and sent the brief moment reeling from a cliff.

It was midday when they reached the fork. A wide, well-trodden path reached westwards to the shores of Grenfold and the Bay of Fayze, while a narrower, darker trail continued north, almost ninety miles, to Mirror Lake and the mountains of Banafell.

The group broke out rations and sat around the junction, unaware that Moranne was standing at its centre, waiting for her moment.

"Men, women, I have an announcement," she said formally. "We will be splitting the party here."

They looked at each other in puzzlement. Moranne hadn't shared this plan with either of the knights, the prince or any of the Cempestre.

"I thought we were heading west to Alfheim," said Sir Torbrand. Both Prince Asger and Caspin nodded. All were in the dark.

"I'm sorry. The alviri will never allow such a large party of men onto the hallowed isle. I will go with Sir Torbrand, Prince Asger, and Orettas Brimwulf, and Regenherd. I will also take Hayden and Sax."

Sax was resting against a tree branch as Moranne spoke and almost snapped it when he heard his name.

"I'm not going there!" he exclaimed.

"Watch your lip," warned the captain.

Moranne eyed him suspiciously. "And why are you *not going*?"

The *Knife* looked around furtively, searching for a plausible excuse. "It's... er...."

"Spit it out," said Biorn. His patience was running thin at the insubordination in his ranks.

"...full of dirty elves."

"Well, I won't force you," said Moranne with one eyebrow raised. Sax was lying. "I'll take Oretta Yuka Bowhand instead. We'll meet again at Mirror Lake."

Captain Fallon gave Sax a disapproving look, but *Knives* had soared in Slitan's estimation. "Didn't take you for an elf hater," he said, smirking.

Sax stared into the trees. To see Alfheim once more was just a dream.

"Caspin!" called Moranne. "You'll meet the dalfreni near the lake. Try to persuade them to join us; you'll have better luck before I arrive."

Without explaining, she turned to Jem, who would miss her guidance. "You're much stronger than I could have hoped, and your prescience is growing. Trust your instincts and watch for trouble from Slitan." *You've been here before.*

The words rang in his head, but he dared not ask the question which woke him every day. *Who are you?*

He threw his arms around Hayden and hugged his friend, ignoring the whistles from Cal and Slitan. "Look after yourself," he said. "Don't pick up any stray elves," he whispered.

"Try not to kill any more giant badgers," grinned Hayden in return.

"I'm moving on to bunyips," laughed Jem.

There were many more fond farewells as the party split, but one partnership was conspicuous by its distance. Sir Torbrand stood along the Alfheim trail, looking at the dusty path which wound its way to the sea. He didn't see Brea appear behind to place a veined hand on his shoulder.

"Say goodbye to her," she said, "anything can happen out 'ere."

He turned to gaze at the radiant Ellen, busy hugging Hayden and laughing with Lunn.

"Look after her," he said impassively.

Brea shook her head and sighed loudly. "You're a big strong bloke with the whole world at your feet, but you're still an idiot."

He knew she was right, but a wench like Ellen could never feature in the future mapped out for him by his parents. Maybe time away would help. *Take care, my noble warrior.*

It was just past midday when the party split. With one last fleeting look back from Hayden, Moranne's group vanished into the trees.

"Alright, men," said Captain Fallon gruffly. "We've got a long road ahead. Let's get to it."

29 THE BAY

The clear waters of Cwenmere lapped gently against the bank while bright white swans glided serenely over its surface. A calm breeze blew through the spring air, causing the daffodils to bob gently as early bees buried themselves in the bright yellow trumpets and buzzed loudly as they scampered to leave.

Propped against his favourite tree, at his favourite time of year, sat Torbrand Linhold. He smiled and even laughed as he watched a young woman dancing along the bank. She skipped and spun, throwing out the vibrant blue dress until it resembled a giant flower bobbing beside the lake.

Ellen's laughter filled the small world where they were alone. Gone was the tight ponytail and leather armour as her hair whipped about her face and flared in the wind. He wanted to reach out and touch her, to take her in his arms, but instead, he sat watching her pirouette past, filling the air with her sweet jasmine perfume.

He could watch her forever, but a shadow crept over them from behind, and a chill wind bit at his neck. Torbrand turned to see a thick blanket of dark clouds rolling in from the west, and a mist of rain seemed to be pouring over the mountains beyond. He stood and watched the clouds blacken until her call pulled him back.

"Tor!"

She faced him now with fear in her eyes and a wide, curved blade above her neck. A tall figure dressed in colourful silks held the knife and fixed Torbrand with deep brown eyes.

"Ing ra'dren," said the man without emotion; he cut Ellen's throat with one rapid movement.

"No!" cried Torbrand. As he lunged wildly for the Jakari warrior, the vision splintered into a thousand glittering fragments, and he found himself sitting in a shallow bunk, sweat pouring from his brow.

"Bad dreams?" asked Tiam. She stood over his bed with a mug of steaming nettle tea.

He nodded, still waiting for his heartbeat to steady.

"You'll have more as we get closer to the island," she said. "Juldra is powerful here."

He looked around the room, seeing it plainly for the first time since they'd arrived in the twilight yesterday. It was a long wooden cabin with bunks lining the walls and a large table at its centre where the Cempestre sat eating warm porridge. He could just make out the sound of water lapping a stony shoreline under the women's banter.

"Where are we?" he said blearily.

"This is our boathouse on the bay. I think you were too tired yesterday to take it in."

"You went out like a candle flame," added Moranne, appearing behind him.

He dragged on his boots and stumbled to the door, which creaked open to reveal the magical Bay of Fayze in all its splendour. It spread out in a vast green arc of trees on each side but turned dark grey in the north, where Banafell slid into the waters. Even over a hundred miles away, the snow-capped peaks dominated the landscape; they curved eastwards in a line that faded out in the morning mist. The Blunt Mountains to the south occasionally revealed themselves in the haze, but clouds hid the peaks.

The Scinslo Hills of Alfheim were mere pimples in comparison and just peaked above the horizon sixty miles to the east. These grey silhouettes marked the far edge of Grenfold and the kingdom of King Pythar, although no member of the Fierdman family had ever set foot on the island's mythical soil.

"Beautiful, no?" said Prince Asger, sitting on a large pile of rocks at the water's edge.

"Hmm," replied Torbrand, "but how do we get there?"

The question was soon answered when Tiam took him to the side of the dormitory, where a thick layer of shrubs and vines covered another, larger building. The Cempestre had used the depth of rock to create a natural mooring, and they'd built a large boathouse shielded from prying eyes by well-planted shrubs and creepers. The oni damaged it from time to time, but the men of Cempess kept it in good repair, and it looked solid and safe.

Tiam, Sefti and Yuka pulled on two hidden handles, opening a pair of large double doors at the water's edge. They revealed a cavernous boathouse which contained a vast sailing boat with a folded mast.

"Very impressive," said Sir Torbrand as the women pulled out the vessel and erected the mast.

The boat was some thirty-five feet long with a symmetrical design like a giant eye. It was broad in the centre, where pens were situated for livestock, but it narrowed to a point at each end. The prow was crowned with a carved dragon's head which stared out into the bay with bulging eyes.

"You're now going to tell me you're also expert sailors." The knight shook his head.

"We'll get you there in one piece!" shouted Sefti, tugging on ropes to secure the mast.

Prince Asger watched them in wonder. A hard-working society that didn't need or want a monarch. They were together because they chose to be.

"I hope you don't get seasick," said Tiam, slapping Hayden so hard on the back that he almost stumbled into the water. He'd never been on a boat; he just watched them on the River Dorbourne in Dunstreet as they made their way towards Arlo.

"No one is being sick," said Moranne. "We don't have time."

The boat was readied quickly, and the women carefully led Prince Asger's horse and the single pack pony into the penned area at the centre. Moranne, Torbrand, Tiam and the prince took positions on the prow while the other women unfurled the two sails, and Yuka took the tiller.

Sailing conditions were good, with a light westerly breeze and calm waters. They quickly set sail and launched out into the bay, making fast progress skimming through the still waters. Moranne stood at the prow, steadying herself against the hull. She watched as the island slowly grew. In all shades of green, red, amber and yellow, it exploded like a shepherd's sunrise, a golden land amidst the Grey Sea.

Nimmeral knew she was coming, she could feel his glassy blue eyes watching every move and his nerves shredding in anticipation. *Don't come to my home,* she heard loud and clear as if he'd shouted it into her ear.

You know why I come; I have no choice.

There were always choices, however, and many were wrong. Leaving Jem with Caspin protected him, while Hayden's presence was to take him from Slitan's reach. Like moving the pieces on a board game, every move was a risk, but the reward was life.

As Deapholt retreated to a green band behind, Alfheim grew to a colourful haven before them. The purple-topped Scinslo Hills stood dripping in the green of thousands of pine trees, while flashes of red dotted the lower hills where rare groves of cercis spread out to form a blanket.

They passed alviri fishers, reaching twenty miles out from the island. They waved in friendship until they saw the strange men amidst the Cempestre crew.

Hayden sat astern, close to Yuka, who was steering the boat with a calm experience. "I can help," he said. "Just tell me what to do."

Yuka handed him the tiller with no hesitation and relaxed beside him. "Have you ever crewed a boat?"

He shook his head. Taking a small rowing boat on the River Dorbourne and the Sile hardly counted, but it took his mind back to the simple, warm summer days spent in Burland.

"It's pretty easy," she continued. "What's your role in the mission?"

Like a bolt to the heart, her question opened up his self-doubt. Why *was* he here?

"I'm gada to Lady Moranne, it's like an apprentice, and I'm supposed to be learning about the world."

"So what have you learned, young gada?"

He glanced back to the thin line which marked the edge of Deapholt, where Slitan, Cal and the others would be pushing north.

"I've learned that there is no place in Grenfold for a man like me."

She laughed heartily, to his surprise, while he stared at her, dismayed.

"What's so funny?"

"There's no place for a woman like me either."

"Nonsense!" said Hayden. "You're a good-looking woman; you'd be fine."

"A good-looking woman, eh?" she snorted. "But a good-looking woman on the arm of another good-looking woman?"

"You mean—"

"Yes! Cuyler, the short-haired archer with Sir Caspin's party. She is my partner, my love."

"But I thought—"

"We all needed to have husbands and children?" she laughed. "Juldra doesn't judge us the way Frea judges you, the mean-spirited bitch who insists that every woman is shackled to a man."

It was blasphemy, and Hayden had never heard anyone speak of Frea that way; he was impressed. The oretta was open, and no one cared. Her comrades didn't judge her. *Juldra* didn't judge.

"So you know about me?" he asked, dreading the reply.

"Of course we do. You wear it like a pennant."

He was crestfallen, dressing like a warrior, holding himself tall and proud, and even dancing with Signy at the ball. Nothing disguised his true nature; everyone knew. Jem knew but was still his friend.

Yuka could see how saddened he looked as tears welled in his eyes. She reached out and placed a warm hand on his arm. "Juldra has a purpose for *all* of us. You may never know what it is, but your life will touch every life in the world like today it touched mine. Be yourself, my young friend."

Hayden felt a smile creep over his face as he realised for the first time that he wasn't the abomination so hated by his father and some of the men. There was a place for him.

"Tell me about Juldra."

"I'm no expert, so I'll do my best," she giggled.

While Hayden steered a steady course through the tranquil waters, Oretta Yuka Bowhand did her best to relate the story of Juldra and how it linked closely to the lives of the alviri.

Unlike the Freans, who believed Frea created the world, the alviri believed that the earth was created in a giant cosmic explosion and that Juldra burst into life simultaneously. Juldra was the earth mother and the spirit who flowed through every tree, animal, rock and grain of sand. She was most potent in living things and coursed through every creature as a living power. The alviri could harness this power for prescience and healing, but some, like Moranne and Corvus, could channel the energy to protect or destroy.

There was no scripture to follow nor rules to endure; the alviri merely understood that every life was connected. If you chose to live a life helping others or a selfish life doing little, Juldra would never judge you. She wouldn't tell you who to love or how to love, and whatever your nature, her life force ran through you and supported you.

"So Juldra is the world around us," said Hayden.

"Exactly," grinned Yuka. "Freanism is about control, but Juldra gives you freedom."

It was late afternoon when the boat neared Alfheim, and a large, golden vessel, with five billowing, red sails glided across their path. The warship's deck was lined with alviri archers in bright silver mail, all with their bows trained on the little boat.

"Let me do the talking," said Moranne.

30 SEDUCTION

The broad-leaved deciduous trees changed to fresh-smelling pines, and the forest floor changed from compacted earth to a springy carpet of brown pine needles. Spotted deer and imperious elk ran freely through the slender trunks while speckled owls flew overhead, searching for the tiny rodents which scampered for cover. The party were in black wolf country.

"They won't attack such a large party," said Bresne.

Sir Caspin had been worried since leaving Moranne, and every time they heard wolves howling in the distance. He'd only seen grey wolves running in packs through Tudorfeld, but tales told of the aggressive, giant, black wolves of Deapholt. Few survived to pass on the stories.

"I hear the black wolves are more dangerous," he said.

"That's true, but they still avoid humans. There is plenty of deer for them in wild parts of the Deap."

Free of his severe and imposing brother, Sir Caspin liked to foster a lighter mood with the men and women. In Tudorfeld, he would eat and drink with them, join their rowdy parties, and even frequent the same brothels, but Torbrand frowned on such camaraderie. He insisted the men would never respect someone who would get drunk with them. Perhaps he was right, but it wasn't Caspin's way. Initially, he tried bonding with Bresne, but she was almost as severe as his brother. Instead, he found Jem a perfect companion; thus, the two walked together with Ellen and Brea at the group's head. Oretta Fixen led the Cempestre, and the other men took up the rear guard.

Slitan was still grumbling, but the presence of the Cempestre stopped him from making any comments. The men hadn't yet mingled with their new comrades, and an uneasy stand-off had developed where neither would speak first. The young Sefti Regenherd was the prettiest oretta in the men's eyes; her sunny demeanour endeared her to all she smiled upon; however, it was Isen Stanhamur who caught Gamin's eye.

Isen was the same height as Lunn, but she held herself so well that she towered above the man from Fiske. Her arms were thick, and her thighs were like tree trunks. The slightest hint of a double chin and a square jaw gave her a touch of masculinity, but her dark hair cascaded over her shoulders in waves. The young archer watched her from behind and wished he had the courage just to say hello. The twenty-three-year-old Gamin usually kept himself well-groomed, but a fluff of stubble now clung to his upper lip and made him look very young and inexperienced.

After a full day's march, they camped just off the path. Dinner was rabbit again, expertly prepared by Cuyler and Brenna, but the men and women still said nothing.

Gron took the first watch, and it wasn't long before the camp was asleep, with Lunn gently snoring as the dimming fire embers crackled and popped, casting an orange glow on the sleeping bodies. Gron Hamur was a long way from the glacial Lake Brantmere and wondered what his parents would think of him on a vital mission with female warriors. He smiled to himself. Just at that moment, something caught his eye, movement in the trees.

A thin tree branch sprang back and forth, set free by something tall, but nothing was there. No restless deer or night owl was flying from its perch. Gron's eyes struggled to focus in the remaining firelight; he tossed another few branches into the smouldering embers. A twig snapped, behind him this time. He whirled around, but again there was nothing.

"Who's there?" he whispered. "Is that you, Lunn?"

The tall axe wielder breathed deeply and added the occasional snort as if he was about to snore.

Gron looked past the fire as it slowly grew, casting a warmer light against the pines. Like statues, the pine trunks circled them and stacked into the distance, throwing long finger shadows into the gloom. Without sound or warning, something moved between two tree trunks. It was tall and deliberate. Gron was on his feet with the mace in his hand.

"Who are you?"

He tried not to shout; it could still be a trick of the light. His pulse was racing, and he could feel a bead of sweat forming on his forehead. The fleeting answer made his heart skip a beat.

A friend.

The voice was female and sensuous, but it was in his head. It seemed to come from all directions at once.

"Show yourself."

He scanned the tree line, but the woman must be hiding. The fire flickered into more life, throwing its warm glow further out until it picked out trees deeper into the forest.

From left to right, there were ten trees; from right to left, there were ten trees, but when Gron looked again, there was another tree-like form. He spun left to see a slender shape emerging between two of the pines. It gradually turned from behind a tree to reveal the profile of a face. Gron's eyes followed the figure's contour flowing down to a thin neck and a gently sloped breast. A beautiful female form was etched, in silhouette, against the forest's darkness.

"Don't move," he said.

She ignored him. With the stealth and precision of a cat, she stepped silently into the light, revealing a smooth, silver female body. She was naked except for a narrow leather belt which held a small wooden contraption. Streaks of brown wrapped about her arms and twisted across her stomach like binding tree roots; splashes of light green dotted her breasts, face and legs like tufts of luminous moss. Her silver hair was streaked with green and smoothed back, but it was the deep brown eyes that hypnotized the man from Cealdwater.

"What do you want?" asked Gron. A strange calm was settling over him. He wanted to feel her skin beneath his fingers.

"Come with me, Gron Hamur," she said, in a silky smooth voice, as if she was caressing his mind.

She lifted her arm with the same grace and poise to offer him her hand. As if in a trance, he reached out as she came closer, revealing the detail in her skin like the bark of silver birch.

"I shouldn't..." he started to say.

Sound from behind broke the spell.

"Gron! Who are you talking to?" Lunn was standing near the fire, rubbing the sleep from his eyes.

"There's a woman..." began Gron.

He gestured into the forest, but when he turned, she was gone, vanishing like a phantom into the night.

"A what?"

"There was a woman here, right here! She was silver and green and...."

"What's going on?" said Sax, who was always a light sleeper.

"Lunn saw a naked, silver woman!" boomed Lunn.

"Fell asleep on watch more like," added Brea, who was now sat up, warming herself by the fire.

"All of you back to sleep!" roared Biorn. "We have a long road ahead. Lunn, take over the watch, and don't let me hear another sound."

"I know what I saw," mumbled Gron.

The rest of the night was uneventful, but Gron couldn't get the woman's image from his head. Her luring brown eyes haunted him, and he could hear her voice in every quiet moment as the party pushed north once more. He didn't mention his encounter again.

The coniferous terrain became dense, and the air thin and chilled as lichen-caked rocks dotted their path. Still, the five Cempestre women kept their council while Cal and Slitan mocked them in secret. Despite his best efforts and well-known prowess with the women, Caspin couldn't get Bresne to engage in any conversation, which wasn't a simple yes or no answer. He decided the situation needed to change when they made camp that evening.

Cuyler made a large fire, and Caspin ensured that the whole party was sitting around. They were in good spirits, having enjoyed tonight's venison, shot by Brea and expertly cooked by Brenna.

The Green Order knight stood up and threw his arms out as if to embrace the camp. "Everyone. We've come a long way, and we have far to go. I think it's time we knew more about each other. In turn, I want you to introduce yourselves, tell us if you're married, a little bit about your home and one thing you like."

Slitan rolled his eyes, but the Cempestre seemed most horrified by the prospect. "Is this necessary?" asked Bresne.

Caspin was in no mood for compromise. "We are living together, and we may yet die together. I want to know a little about those I'm fighting with. To make it easier, I have a cask of mapulder, which Oretta Brimwulf packed for me here."

"Now we're talking," said Brea, grinning.

"I'll start," continued Caspin.

"I love me a good story. Is it a happy ending?"

Even some of the Cempestre were smiling at Brea's irreverence. Caspin ignored her.

"My name is Sir Caspin Linhold, son of Earl Normin Linhold of Faircester. You already know my older brother, Sir Torbrand; I'm a knight of the Green Order, and I'm not married."

"Hear that, ladies?" laughed Brea.

"...and I'm not engaged, he continued with a wink. "My favourite thing is enjoying a drink with my comrades." He took a swig of the sweet drink and passed the small cask to Brea."

Brea examined the cask for a moment, then took a generous swig.

"Well, me name's Brea Soytere, I'm good with a bow, and I ain't ever getting married."

"No one would have you!" cried Slitan, but she wasn't finished.

"Me favourite thing is making loud-mouthed archers look stupid," she said, grinning.

Slitan shot to his feet, but a hand from Biorn had him sinking back into his space, grumbling. "Damn hag," he muttered under his breath.

Brea tossed the cask to Lunn, who caught it in one of his massive hands. He inspected it briefly and then addressed his story to the stiff leather container. "My name's Lunn Burndog," he boomed. "I'm from Fiske, but that's all I'll say of my history. I ain't married, but one day I'd like to meet an honest woman and have a big family." Uncharacteristically he didn't take a swig but passed the drink on to his friend Gron.

"You all know me," said Gron cheerfully. "My family is in Cealdwater, and I have two sisters. There's no woman in my life, but I always has time for my best mate." He threw his arm around Lunn, and the pair resembled drunken sailors.

"Very sweet," simpered Slitan.

Gron offered the cask to Bresne, but she hesitated. She scanned the expectant faces of her warriors until her gaze rested on Caspin, willing her on. *What do I have to lose*, she thought, taking the mapulder from Gron's hand.

"I am Oretta Bresne Fixen; I have been a Cempestre all my life. My bonda, Gunnar, died three years ago; he was a good man. My favourite thing is watching our young women become the brave warriors you see today." The pride cracked her voice, and her warriors smiled and nodded in recognition. She took a deep swig and passed the drink on to Jem.

He hesitated momentarily, remembering the last time he drank mapulder in Bearun Forest.

"Go on, lad," prompted Brea. Some of the others started shouting words of encouragement.

Jem scanned their expectant faces, then took a brief swig of the sweet liquor.

"My name is Jem Poulterer, and I'm gada to Lady Moranne. I have no one special." He thought of Mia Tunland's sweet smile, but Danya's image rose quickly to cast the little Burland lass in shadow. "My favourite thing is being right here with my friends."

He tried passing the cask to Sax, but *Knives* held up his hand in denial. Brenna grabbed it next.

"I'm Oretta Brenna Gunborg. I've got no time for a man because I'm too busy killing oni."

"My kind of woman," laughed Lunn.

"More like a man," quipped Cal.

No one but Slitan laughed, and Biorn shot them both a disapproving look.

"I also have no time for a man because my love is Yuka Bowhand," said Cuyler defiantly. "How do you like *that*, you thick Burlander?"

"Who are you calling thick?" protested Cal.

Caspin's bonding session seemed to get out of hand as Cal and Slitan started trading insults with the Cempestre.

"That's enough!" shouted Biorn. He took the cask from Cuyler and stood in front of his men. "I will have an end to the disrespect, and I will have it now. One more word from either of you, and I'll have you both tied to a tree and left to rot." He turned to the Cempestre and held out his hand. "Please accept an apology for the behaviour of my men; we are lucky to have you with us."

"Thank you, Captain," said Bresne, nodding as one leader to another.

"I'm Captain Biorn Fallon, and I'm married to Nina. We have a seven-year-old daughter named Brenni; my son is also named Biorn; he's twelve. My favourite thing is to be at home with my family." He took a short drink and passed the cask to Ellen.

She expected the usual jibes from Slitan and Cal, but the two cohorts were silent. She decided to stand and winked at Brea as she climbed to her feet.

"I'm Ellen Hildebill, the daughter of Corporal Raffus Hildebill of the Queen's Battalion...." She hesitated for a moment before turning to Brea with a wink. "...but *you* can call me the clown."

"About time!" screamed Brea, as the men collapsed in laughter and Jem, clapped loudly.

"You're *our* clown," laughed Caspin, while Brea slapped her on the back.

"I always wanted to be a soldier, so I'm living my dream right now," she giggled. "There's no one special in my life."

"Cos he's an idiot," added Brea, to further laughter.

Ellen tilted her head in resignation. She hadn't realised how obvious her affection was towards Caspin's elder brother.

"Me next!" shouted Slitan.

Biorn ignored him and gestured to Ellen, who passed the cask to the stoic Isen. She hesitated for a moment, then took a long draught of mapulder as her fellow warriors spurred her on.

"My name is Oretta Isen Stanhamur, I'm the daughter of Oretta Svell Stanhamur, and I have no partner. My favourite thing is to watch the River Dorbourne running past our home."

There was a chorus of "ahh" from her comrades; she sat down quickly, looking very embarrassed.

The last man to hold the near-empty cask was the slim Gamin, who climbed to his feet while others shouted, "Gamin, Gamin, Gamin!" stamping their feet and punching the air.

"Alright, let the lad speak," said Biorn, trying to calm them. Mapulder was strong, and just one swig was enough to make most grown men drunk.

The young archer tried to control himself, but he couldn't help gazing at the statuesque Isen staring into her hands.

"I'm Gamin Boarman, an archer in the Green Order. I was born in Braylen to a family of bowmakers." He took a last swig from the empty cask and looked straight at Oretta Stanhamur. "There's no one special in my life now, and my favourite thing is just to be here with my friends."

He sat down but immediately stood once more as if an invisible string was yanking him to his senses. "I think watching the river is beautiful," he stuttered.

The company erupted in a chorus of "ooh!" Gron elbowed Gamin in the side, and Brenna put her arm around Isen and kissed her cheek.

"Well done," said Bresne to Caspin, relieved his plan hadn't backfired.

Slitan and Cal played no part in the banter, and Sax was content to watch, but all the others started exchanging war stories and getting to know each other. Isen was too disconcerted to say much but couldn't help smiling when her friends gently ribbed her.

Captain Fallon also congratulated Caspin for improving morale, but he'd reached a decision regarding Slitan.

"I'm cutting him loose when we reach Numolport. He may be a good archer, but I must admit Brea is twice as good," he said decisively. "I've not decided on Cal; he might be manageable without Slitan."

"I leave these matters in your capable hands," said Caspin. "I trust your judgement."

The jokes and banter gradually subsided as drink and fatigue took their toll. Gamin found himself still awake, taking the first watch. He knew he'd made a fool of himself and embarrassed Isen, but he still couldn't take his eyes from her long, sleeping form. She had her back to him; Gamin imagined snuggling up and kissing her neck. He shook his head and slapped his face. "Be professional," he said to himself. He'd looked up to Slitan for many years, but now the bitter bowman was an embarrassment. He disrespected all of Gamin's new friends, including Brea, who'd nursed him day and night, and Isen, the most impressive woman he'd ever seen.

"I don't need you anymore," he said into the night.

The night answered:

You do need me.

"Slitan? Is that you?" whispered Gamin, but the voice was feminine. Deep, but definitely a woman.

He could see everyone from his vantage near the fire. Nobody was missing, and everyone was asleep. Peering into the trees revealed nothing, not even a breeze through the branches.

Gamin decided it must be the mapulder, but he still sat with his back to the fire, gazing into the shadows. It had been another long day, and they were still only halfway to Mirror Lake. He felt the lids heavy over his eyes and starting to droop. They closed slowly until just a slit remained, a narrow window onto the world.

Something moved right in front of him; his eyes snapped wide open.

"Who's there?"

The forest was silent except for Gron's heavy breathing and Lunn's snores.

"Show yourself!" he commanded.

Is that what you want, Gamin Boarman?

"This isn't funny!"

The clearing was empty; he turned to scan the party once more. They were all still asleep. He could feel his heart pound in his chest and sweat form on his hands. He reached for his bow and slotted an arrow, pulling it to half stretch.

I'm behind you.

Whirling, he let the arrow fly. It twanged from his bow and flew straight and true, embedding into a tree on the edge of the clearing.

"Not very friendly," came the deep, smooth voice, which seemed directly ahead.

Gamin watched nervously as a deep orange hand slowly emerged from behind the tree and grasped the arrow. It was gracefully followed by the arm entwined with green lines like ivy, then a body mottled in patches of brown and green like lichen.

A shapely leg stepped out of the shadows, and the naked body of a young woman followed it, uncoiling like a serpent.

He remembered how Slitan encouraged him to bed a whore in Gosta and how he'd run when she removed her clothes. It wasn't right; he wanted it to be special.

"Don't come any nearer," he said.

Slowly she stepped into the light. Her body was like autumn maple; a burnt orange leaf wrapped in brown swirls and a green hue ran into her hair and circled her brown eyes.

"You won't hurt me, Gamin Boarman," she purred, dropping her gaze to look up at him under her ivy-green brow.

"I don't want to, but I will."

"You've never been with a woman; do you think Isen will ever love you?"

She advanced with stealth, placing her naked feet between twigs in slow circular movements like ripples on a calm pond.

"What are you?" he gasped.

"I'm the answer to your dreams," she whispered, just a few yards away.

She was right, he couldn't kill her, but this was wrong. He turned to the camp and shouted as loud as he could.

"Jem!"

"What in Frea's name!" shouted Biorn.

"Look!" cried Gamin, but she was gone even as his voice echoed through the forest.

"What is it?" asked Jem. "What's going on?"

"There was a woman right here. A naked woman."

"The lad can't take his mapulder," said Cal, stretching.

"I'm telling the truth!" protested Gamin. "She was here," he said, pointing to the spot where she'd stood.

"Nonsense," said Captain Fallon.

Bresne put a hand on Biorn's shoulder and shook her head.

"It's true," she said. "We're being hunted."

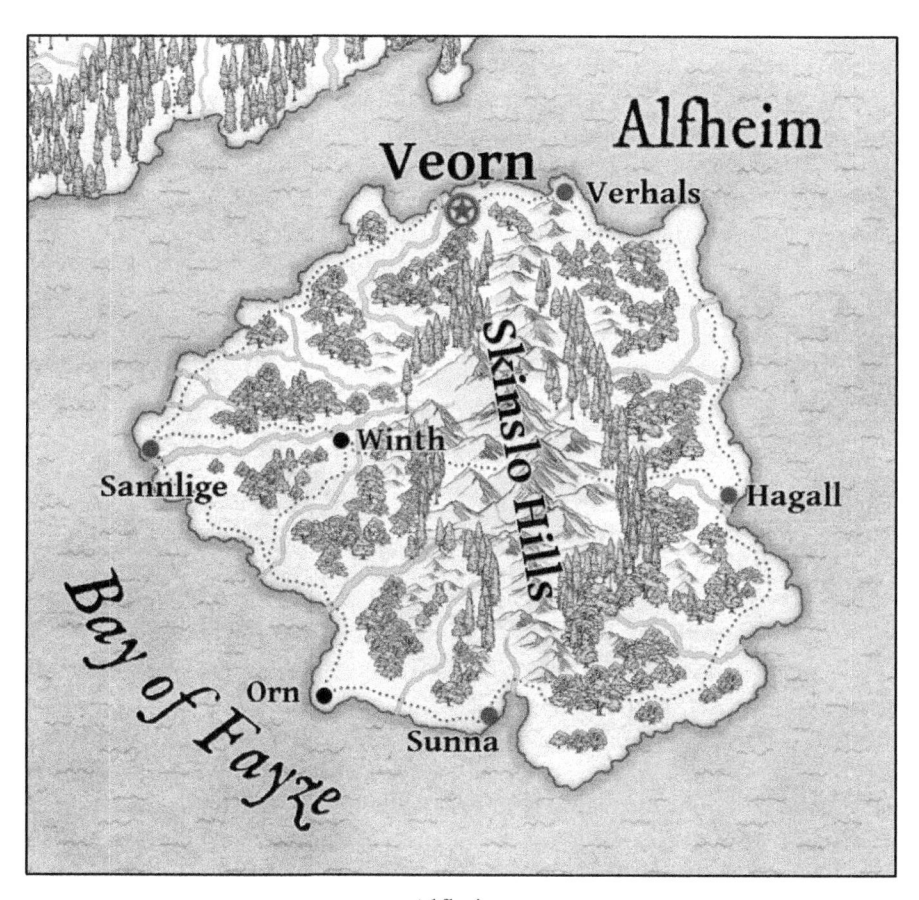

Alfheim

31 ALFHEIM

Large fish circled the quay, ducking under the boat keels and sweeping back and forth in great shoals. The fishers of Sannlige could land all they needed just yards from the harbour in the bay's abundant waters.

Sannlige was much like any small fishing town in Grenfold with its square, stone harbour, and brick-paved streets; however, the design of its buildings was very different. Humans usually favoured the local stone for construction, but the alviri preferred wood. Businesses and dwellings, from one to four-storey, bordered the harbour and swept gently upwards inland. The rounded, lacquered logs stood proudly on display, as did the craftsmanship of the alviri engineers. The whole quayside also made for an excellent holding area, walled off from the rest of the town; access was gained through one set of thick oak doors.

Hayden kicked his feet back and forth, dangling over the harbour wall. He'd given up counting fish, and now sat spotting barnacles on the glowing alviri vessels. There weren't many blemishes on the impressive ships.

"Any word?" asked Yuka.

"None," replied Hayden sullenly.

Moranne and the other leaders had been locked in the harbour master's office for over two hours, arguing with the local garrison commander. It seemed apparent that they weren't going to be allowed to stay.

A ring of near-identical soldiers surrounded Hayden and the other Cempestre. All had long white hair with a stark, almost white complexion; the silver mail and polished round helms made them look like lightning bolts.

Yuka had tried to engage them in conversation, but they remained rigid and impassive. "They're normally very friendly," she said, "I don't understand what's going on."

Moranne knew, but it was unexpected. She walked into the setting sun as it blazed across the bay, throwing shadows of tall masts over the harbour and the town beyond.

Just days before the arrival, Commander Cirren Dorrel had received a letter from Lady Etherin Andain. It ordered him not to allow passage for Moranne and her company. While receiving a command from the high lord's wife was unusual, the local military leader wouldn't risk ignoring the order.

"I'm afraid we're stuck here tonight," she said, walking over to the waiting group.

After sustained arguing, Commander Dorrel eventually agreed to confirm the orders by sending a rider to Veorn.

A stiff corporal led them to an inn on the docks, where they were each given a room. Taking late supper on a high veranda, they viewed the town as thousands of oil lamps burst into life, marking the streets which wound upwards and into the distance.

Alfheim rose from the bay on all sides, climbing in a series of small hills to the centre. The Scinslo hills were patterned in every hue of green with streaks of yellow and large pools of red. The shades were mirrored in the town by brightly coloured roofs and coloured lights strung from the balconies of tall wooden buildings. Every home was rough-hewn as if the forest had tumbled into the quay, forming a town which straddled the narrow Sayle River.

"I'm not in Dunstreet now," said Hayden.

"Or Cynstol," added the prince.

"The alviri have an eye for style," laughed Yuka. "It makes Cempess look like a bunch of sticks."

They found themselves back on the same vantage twelve hours later, but the view's allure was fading, and Tiam was pacing back and forth like a disturbed dog. "I've been here many times; this is insulting!" she said.

Everyone was restless except Sir Torbrand, sitting alone at the front of the inn, watching the ships come and go. It was good to be alone, with no one expecting anything from him.

"Sir Torbrand, please come with me," said a guard.

He was led outside to the front of the inn. It was right on the harbour in a row of similar buildings used for trade and storage. The others soon joined him, all escorted by shining guards with trailing ponytails of bright white hair.

"Well, that's it," said Tiam. "Looks like they're sending us back."

Prince Asger was the last to join them, tapping on the cobbles with the crutches made for him by the Cempestre. Alviri guards soon appeared, leading his horse and the pack pony.

"Send back?" he asked Moranne.

The king's advisor was deep in thought; she'd been here just seven years past and left on good terms with the high lord. Something had changed; it could only mean one thing: Etherin knew.

"There's a rider coming!" shouted Sefti.

High in the town, a horse galloped through the streets at great speed. Its hooves clattered on the stone with no sign of a slip or slide. The road zig-zagged down the hill towards the harbour, and they could hear the rider tugging on the reins to change course. The horse whinnied and spluttered with the exertion. It was near and coming their way, but the guards stood still like silver pylons, making no movement and barely blinking.

Stone and Sceptre

Finally, the tall harbour doors swung open, and a blinding white colt burst onto the quay, galloping with grace at full stretch towards them. The rider was clad in the same silver mail top with dark grey leather leggings and shoulder protection. A black ash bow was slung across his back, and a quiver stuffed with arrows.

He slowed just feet from the party, and the alviri soldiers stiffened and stood to attention. In one smooth movement, he dismounted though the horse was still moving and brought it to a stop in front of Moranne.

Hayden gazed, open-mouthed, at the young alviri. Boran Berlain had impressed him, but this horseman shone luminously in comparison. His white hair was centre-parted and shoulder-length, feathered so that it swept forward over his neck. His skin was porcelain white, with just the lightest pink in his cheeks.

He strode towards Moranne confidently, but on the final step, his lips creased into a broad smile, and his emerald green eyes sparkled into life.

"Wickona!" he said, embracing her.

"Cierzon, you look well," she replied, beaming back. *What's going on?*

I'll tell you later, flowed through her mind as he winked.

"This is my good friend, Lord Cierzon Andain," said Moranne, introducing the rider.

"Please call me Cierzon," he said. "I'm so sorry for the delay. I'm here to escort you to Veorn."

"And you may call me Asger," said the prince, doing his best to bow on his crutches.

"The honour is mine. I am pleased to welcome you all to our homeland. Please join me for refreshments while horses are readied."

He led them all to the harbour master's quarters, where they were treated to a lavish meal of fried john dory with roasted vegetables and fresh olives. Even the quiet Sir Torbrand leaned back in his chair and thanked his host for the feast.

After lunch, while the women continued to enjoy their wine, Moranne took Cierzon aside and asked him about Lady Etherin.

"She gave the order to send you back," he confirmed. "Father is furious and sent me here immediately. What have you done, Wickona?"

She knew exactly, but it was another secret to hide. "Nothing that I know of," she lied.

The alviri could read the minds of the weak, but she'd always guarded her thoughts on the hallowed isle. Someone had talked. Too late, it was done. Etherin would be crushed, and she had every right to hate. Moranne would need to take care as alviri vengeance could be swift and permanent.

The thoroughbred alviri horses were tall and elegant, trotting through the streets of Sannlige while the townsfolk looked on. They stood out against

Prince Asger's humble mount and the tiny pack pony. Veorn was fifty miles to the northeast; they would easily make the capital by nightfall and still enjoy the colourful Alfheim countryside.

A coastal road ringed the island and acted as the main route joining the large towns of Sannlige, Veorn and Hagall on the east coast, home to the famous alviri swordsmiths. The road delved close to the rocky shore in places and then climbed once more into the Scinslo foothills, where alien trees overhung the path and vegetables grew on expansive terraces.

Even the birds and beasts seemed content. Swallows dived towards the group before darting upwards and spinning with their friends. Deer skipped along the path ahead of them. Everywhere the people smiled and nodded as they saw Lord Cierzon leading the foreigners with cheer and wit. He was acting as a guide, describing his home to the newcomers.

"Our climate is unique," he said. "We seldom see frost on the lower slopes, so we can grow all manner of crops you couldn't attempt in Caynna or Tudorfeld. The soil and flora are so rich they provide us with all the earth power we need."

"What can you do with the earth power?" asked Hayden.

"Many things," replied Cierzon. "We can read minds, see the future, plant thoughts in the feeble-minded, heal some ailments and even appear invisible, blending into our surroundings."

Hayden was fascinated, hanging on Cierzon's every word, but he quickly noticed very few children or even younger alviri, such as the high lord's son. Content to stare at the iridescent lad, Hayden said nothing for a while until, eventually, his curiosity spilt over, and he blurted out his question. "Why are there so few children?"

The Cempestre women were immediately silent, and Moranne threw him a disapproving look.

"Did I say something wrong?" he stuttered.

Cierzon's smooth features remained bright, turning to the young gada with a wink. "Do not worry, my friend; you were not to know." He pulled on the reigns and steered to Hayden's side, putting a reassuring arm around his shoulder. "It is the biggest blight on our idyllic lives here. The alviri birth rate is very low and getting worse. An alviri woman may only have one child in five hundred years, and there are many reasons why children do not survive."

"I thought you were immortal," said Hayden.

Cierzon laughed, whipping back his head so that Hayden could see a pale white, swirling tattoo running down his neck.

"We do not visibly age much past a thousand years, but we're not immortal. Illness, war, accidents, and suicide can kill us like you."

"May I ask how old you are?"

"Don't be impertinent!" snapped Moranne.

Cierzon held up his hand. "I don't mind answering. I'm over six hundred years old. The alviri don't celebrate birthdays, and we don't count years, so I can't be accurate."

Over six hundred, thought Hayden. *I must seem stupid to you.*

"You're not stupid," said Cierzon, "but you do think loudly."

Oh no! You must know how much I admire you.

I do, replied Cierzon, projecting into Hayden's mind. *Fret not; I'm flattered.*

The alviri grinned, causing his whole face to shine with warmth. He rode high and proud in the saddle, but his manner with the party was easy and unforced, belying his position as the son of Alfheim's leader.

"Trouble on island?" asked Prince Asger. He was impressed by the clean roads and the happiness he saw in the islanders' eyes as they rode past.

Cierzon pondered the question for a moment, trying to understand the context. The edge of Deapholt marked the furthest he'd travelled from home; he'd seen none of the poverty and squalor in parts of Cynstol or Numolport.

"There is little crime on the hallowed isle," he said. "The oni will not cross the bay, and few humans brave the forest. I wish we could travel freely over Grenfold, but life here is very good."

While no laws denied alviri access to the green lands, the persecution they met from Freans meant they would seldom breach Deapholt's border. Before Mallen's time, they would trade with the Jakaris by sea, but that moment had gone. The island was dying as the population decreased and more folk left for new lands. Cierzon and his father knew it, but prejudice was hard to overcome.

The road was fair, crossed with many small streams and waterfalls that crashed beside it before rushing under small bridges to the sea. Low tree ferns spread over the land, and tetrapanax trees with huge bear-claw leaves dipped over the path. Villages and small towns sprang from nowhere, suddenly appearing between the trees. Any fields of corn or vegetable terraces were small and scattered. The alviri favoured the natural habitat above all other things.

Resting at many rustic inns, the party relaxed into drinking the potent mapulder and watching birds and animals wander past, unperturbed by their presence. Hayden became so drunk that he almost fell asleep on his horse. It was only later that he discovered the alviri had a high tolerance for alcohol.

As the sun arced into the west and the horses slowed, they could hear water spilling over stones and crashing into rocks. The River Skyr tumbled from the Scinslo hills and poured its clear waters into the natural harbour on the city's west side. It wasn't long before they could see the city's natural elegance stretching out into the sea as if it were melting into a forest. It was ringed by a deep, golden beach dotted with long wooden landings and a few grand homes jutting out on stilts.

The only trees felled in Veorn were the giant redwoods which supported the sturdy bridge crossing the Skyr. The timber of the dwellings was moved from other parts of the island. In this way, the city appeared to grow inside the woodland. Some trees grew through the homes with branches bursting through the roof, while others supported large treehouses linked by precarious rope bridges. The whole city looked like it was borrowing space from the trees, so Hayden was shocked to hear that Veorn was over seven thousand years old.

The Alfheim capital continually morphed as older buildings were replaced and trees grew; it was a living, breathing mass of nature with the alviri living as one. The column slowed on the bridge, trying to take in its grandeur. Although the Cempestre had been here many times, they, too, smiled in admiration.

"There are no defences," pondered Sir Torbrand. He always had a mind for the military implications in any situation.

"That's true," chirped Cierzon. "The alviri don't believe in walls."

"So, how do you protect yourselves?"

Cierzon grinned with pride. The city had always been his home, and he was happy to answer any questions.

"Invaders?" he asked rhetorically. "The oni will not cross the bay, and humans will not brave Deapholt. If we were to be attacked, we would go into the hills. When the invaders felt comfortable, we would return to the trees and kill them all."

Of course, thought Torbrand. No one knew the city like the alviri, and no human could match their speed and agility in the trees.

"I hope you don't try to conquer us too soon," laughed Cierzon.

It would be a while before Torbrand and the others realised their thoughts were not secret on the hallowed isle.

Cierzon led them over the bridge to a small building with a green sedum roof. Another silver-clad guard walked out to greet them.

"This is where I leave you," said the high lord's son. "The guard will take you to your quarters near the palace, and I will see you all again tomorrow."

"I need to speak with your father urgently," said Moranne.

Cierzon had his orders. "Get some rest, Wickona, and enjoy the city," he said.

With barely a nudge of heel nor tug on the reins, the gleaming horse galloped off towards the city and disappeared through the trees. Hayden stared into the distance where Cierzon had vanished. He could feel his heart racing and a warm feeling in his chest.

We'll meet again, young gada.

32 THE PACT

Captain Fallon set two guards on rotation for the rest of the night and insisted that everyone should try to get some sleep. None of the night's watch reported any further incidents or sightings of strange naked women.

"Smells like dung to me," said Brea as she munched on some dry toast.

A thin veil of morning mist hung over the pine floor as each soldier emerged to take breakfast. The Cempestre had packed enough rye bread to see them to Mirror Lake, but it didn't go down well with the men. Cal described it as "floor sweepings", while Slitan thought it was like "tree bark".

Brenna squared up to the trouble-making archer, fixing him with a dark stare, but Bresne called her off, shaking her head at Slitan's poor manners. "Save your fists for the oni," she said.

"Oretta Fixen, what can you tell me of last night's events?" asked Sir Caspin. He always seemed bright and alert at all times of the day. He called Bresne and Biorn to discuss the sightings. "You said we were being hunted."

"Yes, sir," she replied. "I think they've been on us since Cempess, at least."

"Who has?" asked the captain.

"The dryads."

"Dry-ads?" mouthed Caspin.

"Succubus; demons who seduce men then kill them," said Biorn.

It seemed too fantastical to believe. Caspin stared open-mouthed at the normally rational captain.

"That's not quite true," said Bresne. "Dryads are tree nymphs. They've lived in these forests since before the alviri."

"Are they dangerous?" asked Caspin, still struggling to believe the tale.

"Not usually to women."

Bresne continued to tell Sir Caspin all she knew of the dryads while he gazed at her, still struggling to believe it.

"In the time of galdur, there were both male and female dryads, and they lived a happy, simple existence in the forests of Grenfold. Unfortunately, for reasons unknown, the female dryads stopped giving birth to male offspring. The alviri claimed it was a punishment from Juldra for their nakedness. Still, the real reason is a mystery."

"When the male population dwindled to zero, the remaining females tried to continue by forming unions with the alviri, but all the babies were stillborn. It was thus that they turned their attention to humans. A dryad-human partnership resulted in a full dryad female child; this, therefore, seemed like a perfect solution, but the Frean church branded the dryads as demons. Many were murdered, and the survivors fled back to the safety of the forests."

"Now they wait for human men to wander into the forest. They use hypnosis and seduction to lure the men to a safe place where they lay together. When the men awake, they find the dryads gone and end up lost and alone in the forest. Many men die trying to find their way home or go mad, trying to find their lover."

"This is true?" asked Sir Caspin, still struggling.

"I've heard the tales," confirmed Biorn, "and I trust Oretta Bresne's experience."

The endorsement surprised the Cempestre, and she smiled.

"Are they dangerous?"

Bresne weighed the question for a while before answering. The Cempestre had few problems with the tree nymphs, but she knew their numbers were dwindling. "They are becoming very few, and I think they're getting desperate," she said. "They may try to kill my warriors."

"To remove the competition," added Biorn.

"Right," said Caspin. "We'll have a rotating, two-hour watch of four. Two men and two women."

Biorn and Bresne shook hands in agreement, but Bresne followed the captain as he left to talk with the men.

"Captain, I'm surprised at your willingness to treat me as your equal, given the views of your men."

"Ah," he replied. "Well, I know what I know and what I don't know. You know these woods. I'd be a fool to ignore you."

"You're a good man."

"So my wife tells me," he said with a wink.

Jem pulled his collar tight, but the cold air still found its way to his skin. The temperature dropped as they pushed north towards the foothills of Banafell. They could see the distant, snow-capped peaks of the formidable mountain range, where only the oni made home.

The consensus amongst the men was that both Gron and Gamin had dreamt of the nocturnal female visitors, but the Cempestre knew better. They became extra vigilant, looking out into the forest for any sign of movement.

"Do they still follow?" asked Caspin. He wasn't expecting much enlightenment, but Bresne's answer surprised him.

"Ask Gada Jem," she said. "He has the sight."

Jem's instincts were usually excellent, but he couldn't detect the dryads. He did, however, feel the presence of something larger and more dangerous.

"The clans," said Brenna. "They're near. I can feel them too."

No one else felt anything or heard anything other than rodents scurrying through the undergrowth or crossbills calling in the trees.

Bresne guessed they had just one more night before they'd reach Mirror Lake, which immensely pleased the men. They were tired and bored of the forest. It was fortunate that they had no idea what lay before them or how Deapholt would keep them prisoner for many more days before seeing Tudorfeld.

All the men had lost some girth, with Gamin looking exceptionally pale. His brush with death had left him weak, and fatigue slowed him by the day. He tried to catch sight of Isen when she wasn't looking, turning away quickly when she looked up, but his interest was evident to the whole party. The formidable oretta ignored him, but Cuyler and Brenna had begun to tease her and gave him the nickname of "twig."

"You could snap him in two," said Bresne, loud enough for some of the men to laugh.

Isen remained severe and focused. She didn't respond to the taunts or look in Gamin's direction. The only worthy man was a strong Cempestre man.

The light faded early as the nights drew in. Captain Fallon found the party a small clearing just off the path where they endured another rabbit stew, courtesy of Brea's hunting and Ellen's cooking.

The Cempestre were especially nervous that night, and Biorn didn't want any trouble caused by an itchy bow finger. He decided to post a large watch consisting of Ellen, Brea, Slitan and Jem for the first three-hour shift.

The group huddled at the clearing's centre around a fire stoked high for a chilling night. Crisp, dry pine branches cracked and popped, sending yellow sparks into the moist air like fireflies dancing against the green backdrop. Brea was the last to fall asleep, keeping Ellen company, until her eyelids started to droop and sleep took her in a wave that passed over her tired body.

"So it's the clown and me, eh?" said Slitan, grinning.

Ellen had other ideas. "I'll be over there with Cuyler," she said. "Just cry like a baby if you see anything."

Jem couldn't help smiling. As formidable as the Cempestre were, Ellen was their equal.

"What are you laughing at?" grumbled Slitan.

Jem simply shrugged.

The women took up position at the north end of the camp while Jem and Slitan sat back-to-back against a small tree to the south.

Jem pulled out one of his twin sabres and gazed at the ornate text on the blade, just above the hilt. He knew this sword as Aimran, the Jakari goddess of beauty, grace and talking too much. He couldn't imagine the radiant Danya, unable to speak. *Ven Ferdus* pierced his mind and sent a shiver to his heart.

The thought of Danya smiling in his dreams sent him back to the mezzanine in Denbry. Shadows of the Midtlen Range would reach through the small farmhouse window and beckon for him to breach their icy peaks. His home was far westward, and he didn't miss it. The world was hazardous and mysterious, but every day was an adventure and a gamble with his life. He barely knew Davill Hwaetbur, but the man seemed honest and genuine. If Frea was real, she took the best lives first.

"So, who's your favourite?" blurted Slitan, waking Jem from his thoughts.

"My favourite?"

"Which of the women would you—"

"What?" interrupted Jem. He barely tolerated the Frean archer after he bullied Hayden and disrespected the Cempestre. He knew what Slitan was trying to say and didn't want to hear it.

"I'm thinking of Sefti, the young blonde girl with Lady Moranne," he continued, unfazed by Jem's disinterest. He started to describe some of his ideas graphically. Jem put his hands over his ears and tried to picture Danya once more.

"What are they talking about?" said Cuyler. She could see Slitan gesticulating and chuckling to himself on the edge of the clearing.

Ellen shook her head in disinterest. There were men in this camp she respected, but Slitan and Cal were not in that group.

"Brea told me you're soft for Sir Torbrand," continued Cuyler. "He's big and strong. Would make a good Cempestre."

"Brea talks too much," replied Ellen. "Torbrand barely notices me."

"But do you like him?"

Ellen looked up at the Cempestre archer with resignation in her eyes. "It doesn't matter," she said. "He's a knight, and I'm a clown."

"Rubbish!" said Cuyler. "Do you know I was born in Gosta?"

"I thought you were a Cempestre."

"I am now, but before, I was just a Frean wife."

Without sadness or regret, Cuyler told Ellen her story. Her puritan parents pressured her to marry a local man with a large farm and high standing. She was young and carefree, and her father worried her "path to the pillars" might be jeopardised.

Her new husband showed his true colours within the first month of marriage. He came home late from working the fields to find that she hadn't finished cooking his dinner. She was beaten so severely that he left her unconscious on the kitchen floor while he went out to the tavern.

She told her mother, who instructed the young Cuyler to: "take her punishment and please her man."

After a year of beatings, exacerbated by her failure to conceive, she packed a few belongings and set out towards Deapholt to find the mysterious

Cempestre. It was a challenging journey through the forest alone. Hunted by wolves, oni and other creatures, she wandered the woods for a month, living on berries and stream water.

When a Cempestre hunting party found her, she was starving and close to death. They took her in, where a young Cempestre apprentice named Yuka Bowhand nursed her back to health and taught her the bow.

"You could have died out there," said Ellen.

"I would have been free," she replied. "Now I have my sisters around me and the person I love more than any in the world."

"You're married?"

"No," she laughed. "Yuka is my lifeblood and my soul. I will never leave her."

"But—"

"Frea had no time for me, so I have no time for her. Juldra doesn't judge. In Cempess, I can be myself. In Cempess, there is no *forbidden love*."

The story could have ended very differently, but Cuyler was strong, as were all the Cempestre. Ellen was humbled by them and proud to serve beside them. Her eyes rested on a clump of nettles, throwing mottled shadows in the firelight. Something large moved behind them.

"Did you see that?" she whispered.

Cuyler shook her head but reached for her bow and silently slid an arrow from her quiver. "It may have been a badger."

Ellen stared at the spot, but there was nothing. She looked towards the men and noticed that Jem was slumped against the tree, sleeping, while Slitan whittled a stick.

"Psst!" she whispered, but he couldn't hear her.

Slitan's eyes were on the sharpening point of the stick, smoothing the ridges and starting to pare back the bark along with the imaginary stake. He saw the bedroom door closing as another man was led into his mother's bedchamber. Then the knocking would start. Slowly at first, then faster and louder until it suddenly stopped.

He felt the sharpness of the point on his finger and imagined thrusting it into his mother's chest.

You deserve better, my love.

"Who said that?" he gasped, spinning around to check on the clearing.

Jem was still asleep, and the women seemed to be whispering at the north end. There were no such things as dryads, just women who couldn't help themselves.

We choose wisely. The voice was silky, like the wind blowing gently through green leaves on a summer's day. It blew through Slitan's mind pricking the hairs on the back of his neck.

"Show yourself!"

"I am... *Slitan Smite*."

There were trees everywhere, just trees. Brown statues stood still into the distance. Every one with rough, wrinkled bark, weeping orange sap and twisting vines that spiralled into the darkness above. Every trunk, but this one.

Slitan's eyes bulged wide, and his heartbeat skipped. His gaze was captured by the slim grey hand, mottled with brown lines, wrapped around the terracotta tree trunk just a few yards away. The fingers of another hand slowly crept around to meet the first, rubbing suggestively.

Slitan laughed. "Is that supposed to entice me?"

The dryad's face appeared against the tree; her white hair was flecked with green, framing a long silver-grey face cut through with brown tendrils. Her grey lips pursed into a smile which spread to her brown eyes.

"I'm not your mother," she said, pouring her voice over him like an icy stream.

"How dare you!"

"I dare."

A slender knee appeared, revealing a shapely thigh and a gently arching calf.

"You expect me to go with you," said Slitan. "You'll get nothing from me. Whore."

The dryad didn't flinch and continued to unwind her body so that her sculpted naked form lay against the tree. She didn't take her eyes off him.

Slitan wanted to hate her, but a wave of calm spread through his thoughts.

"I know what you want, Slitan; take my hand." She held out her mottled arm and gradually moved towards him, shifting her hips in exaggerated circles.

"What about *him*," he whispered, gesturing to Jem, who was fast asleep.

"Hmm," she laughed. "Jem is not who you think he is."

Slitan raised his hand and reached out as she uncoiled her body to stand directly in front of him. Her dark eyes peered into his soul and weren't repulsed. She wanted him.

"Don't move, dryad!" shouted Cuyler. Her bow was at full stretch and aiming for the shining nymph.

The dryad flipped her gaze to the archer and hissed, baring her teeth. "He's mine!"

"You can have him," chimed Ellen.

She just saw the flash from the corner of her eye and turned to see a spinning dart fly from the forest darkness and clip her hair before it embedded in a tree behind.

"Don't touch it," yelled Bresne, awake with a sword in hand. "The darts are poisoned."

"What's going on?" said Jem yawning.

"There's a dry—" began Slitan.

The strange woman with forest skin was gone.

"They'll be back," continued Bresne, "and next time, one of us will be dead."

The whole camp was awake and discussing the latest encounter.

"I was luring her into a trap," said Slitan, to nods from his cohort, Cal.

"Trap, my arse!" joked Brea. "We should have let them take you."

Cuyler saw most of the affair, but she decided not to contradict Slitan's account. Jem tried to keep up, but the consensus seemed to be forming, which involved trapping and killing them. He sought out Bresne, leaning against a tree, pondering their situation.

"Are they strong fighters?" asked Jem.

She nodded sagely, remembering another time when the Cempestre crossed paths with the forest folk. "When they're desperate, they're deadly."

"Have you ever spoken with them?"

"Me? No, they don't like the Cempestre women. We guard their men."

I need to talk with Caspin, thought Jem, but it would need to wait until dawn. They were all exhausted. The next watch would be Cempestre at Bresne's insistence.

The sun was barely breaking through the trees when Jem awoke and made straight for the sleeping Caspin. A casual observer would have noticed the two men deep in conversation, with lots of nodding from the knight. Warming rays shone through the camp when he arrived back in the centre with the smiling commander.

"I hope you know what you're doing," said Sir Caspin, as the two stood near the fire. A breakfast of dry toast was on offer once again.

Jem shook his head. It was a gamble which might not pay off.

"It's your idea, so I think you should execute it," continued Caspin.

Jem shook his head again, but the knight was already addressing the party.

"Gada Poulterer has an idea, and I think it's worth a try. We need as much help as possible, and we don't want to fight a battle with creatures who are not our enemies. Do as Gada Poulterer says." He moved away, leaving Jem in the middle of the clearing with all eyes on him.

"Go on, lad," said Brea, smiling.

Jem composed himself and watched the expectant faces around the camp. Only Slitan was pretending to ignore him.

"We can't fight the dryads; we'll risk casualties on both sides," he said.

Bresne and the other Cempestre warriors nodded and muttered together in agreement.

"I suggest we attempt to reach out to them in the spirit of friendship," he continued. "We should give peace a chance before we get into a fight which no one will win."

"Wimp," cursed Slitan under his breath.

The others were nodding in agreement.

"Whatever happens next," said Jem. "Please keep your weapons down."

Captain Fallon gestured towards his men, and they stood at ease. With the agreement all around, Jem strode to the southern end of the camp. The others followed behind at a respectful distance. He stopped and looked around at Caspin; the knight winked, just as he had back in that smoky Rynham inn before Jem knew of dryads and tunnbroccs. *You can do this,* Jem told himself.

"Dryads!" He shouted into the forest. "We want to talk. We will not harm you."

"Has he been drinking?" whispered Gron.

There was no answer or movement in the woods, so he tried again.

"We want peace; please show yourselves."

Jem waited, but the leaves seemed static, refusing to bend in the wind. For one last time, he yelled into the trees.

"Please speak with us. We mean no harm."

Still, there was no reply. Jem peered around at the camp with his arms outstretched. He walked back towards Sir Caspin when a voice jarred his mind awake.

Speak, and we will listen.

Jem stopped and scanned the faces around him, but no one else had heard the voice.

They need to see you, he said in his mind, hoping that the Dryad would hear it.

"See me now," came the response from behind.

A single dryad appeared just ten yards away. She stood in clear view on the edge of the Deap Path. Her naked form was mostly in mixed hues of green which cascaded over her body, intertwined with twisting brown lines like the stems of aged ivy. Her eyes were deep brown, and her brunette and green hair swept back from her face as if dipped in glossy sap. Her only clothing was a thin leather belt about her waist, and a tiny crossbow hung with a quiver of darts and some leather pouches.

Some of the men instinctively felt for their swords, but Jem raised a hand to stay them. "We don't want to fight you," he said.

She stood with her hands on her hips and her legs apart. The men were captivated, straining to see past the gada. "We listen," she said plainly. Her voice was like a warm caress, without the sharpness or the battle-hardened tone of the Cempestre.

"We both need something." continued Jem. "You need human men, and we need help against a formidable foe."

"Myrik is no enemy to us," she replied, reading his thoughts correctly.

Jem would later discover that Myrik was the dryad word for any deadly disease spreading through a forest, killing their beloved trees. It seemed an appropriate name for Corvus.

"Our shared enemy is time," he retorted.

The dryad flicked her head back and forth, trying to force out the shouts of her sisters. They knew Jem was right, and the desperate instinct to reproduce was tugging on them like an addiction.

"To whom do I speak?" continued Jem.

She was deep in thought but snapped out to answer him. "I am Chakirris, and with my sisters, we are the last of our kind in this forest."

"I think you know who *we* are," said Jem, guessing they'd been watched since Cempess.

"We know *you*, Jem Poulterer, and we know Sir Caspin Linhold and Oretta Bresne Fixen. We know *all* your secrets."

"We want to offer you a pact," said Jem.

"The answer is no!" she snapped back.

Even as she uttered the words, her sisters shouted in her thoughts.

Listen to the lad, said one, *you know that his heart is pure. We are too few,* added a second, *they will kill us if we continue.*

"Alright!" cried Chakirris, silencing the voices. "Speak your *pact*."

Slowly and steadily, Jem described the idea he had proposed to Sir Caspin.

"Here is our proposal. If you join us to fight Corvus and do not attempt to seduce any of the men, Prince Asger will agree to provide you with willing men, in a safe environment, for as long as you wish. We will be meeting the prince at Mirror Lake. If the prince does not agree, or you change your mind, you'll be free to go without harm from us."

"You want us to risk death for you?" said Chakirris.

"You already risk death," replied Jem, "but you could also save thousands of lives."

She pondered his words and conferred mentally with her sisters. Their vote was overwhelming, but she was the leader and would act cautiously.

"There has never been a pact between dryad and human," she said. "We will meet again when the prince joins you. Until then, you have my word that we will not approach you."

"What worth is the oath of a fay creature?" said Slitan.

When Jem turned back towards her, Chakirris was gone.

If you lie, I will kill you, Jem Poulterer.

33 THE ANDAIN DYNASTY

The small fishing boats left long, weaving furrows on the beach where the Veorn fishers had tugged them into the water for the early catch. Wide nets were thrown into the shallow waters to reap the rich bounty in these parts.

Moranne sighed, breathing in the cool, pine-scented morning air which blew into her room from the north. It was the same chamber she always used when visiting the hallowed isle. The Cercis suite covered half of the fifth floor of the Palace Lodge. An ornate guest residence which joined the palace from a long winding walkway on the tenth floor.

The palace was built high in a group of mighty redwoods; parts were suspended like giant treehouses. Other sections were built upon rocks which spilt out into Fayze Bay. There was nothing like it anywhere else in Grenfold, but the alviri had left their engineering mark in many places since claimed by the ungrateful humans.

Wickona could peer over the balcony all day, just watching the alviri go about their simple, earthly lives, surrounded by richly coloured trees - but there was work to do. The room was filled with richly stained oak beams; the bed was like something from a dream. Branches spiralled around upright beams to form a nest-like structure adorned with dark blue drapes and a matching bedspread.

Moranne smiled at her reflection in the polished mirror. Her white blouse was clean and fresh, and a sturdier brown leather pair replaced her tight black leggings, a gift from the lodge. She threw her arms into the black leather waistcoat and pulled the dark hair over her shoulders. She'd not seen Nimmeral for many years, but she knew what he liked.

Winding stairs spiralled around the tall redwood trunk, piercing the lodge's centre and took her to the covered walkway. It emerged from the building, supported on gently moving boughs of other nearby redwoods. Walking on the swaying paths was a strange experience forming the heart of alviri life. They were at one with the forest and all life around them.

The walkway ended in a high chamber that clung to another redwood's side. It acted as a reception room, where Moranne found a smartly dressed clerk who asked her to take a seat while he went to see if the high lord was ready for visitors. He returned after a few minutes and escorted her onwards, down another spiral staircase and a further walkway that arched at right angles to the first. Suspended on ropes from branches in the redwood canopy, it led to a broad, ornately-carved doorway in the side of the main palace. The clerk opened it and led her inside.

She'd walked the long corridor many times, but it was still a marvel of expert craftsmanship. In essence, just another covered walkway that joined many different buildings and chambers. The wooden panelled walls were lined with paintings depicting alviri leaders and great warriors of old. There were no depictions of great humans, but then alviri images were absent from Cynstol. The divisions in Grenfold couldn't be starker.

With large stag carvings outside, a set of double doors opened to reveal a long chamber boasting generous glass skylights in the high vaulted roof.

"Please," said the clerk. "Your party is waiting for you."

My party? thought Moranne. She'd intended to meet Nimmeral alone.

Her heart sank when she strode into the room and saw that Sir Torbrand, Oretta Brimwulf and Prince Asger were already waiting. They sat on a collection of carved benches backed with an array of thick, aqua-blue cushions in the middle of the room.

"Morning," said Prince Asger, smiling. He was very impressed by the majesty of Veorn and struggled to tell every member of the household staff how thrilled he was.

"So you all made your way here?" asked Moranne.

Torbrand confirmed they'd been summoned quite early. Nimmeral didn't want to be alone with her. It was obvious.

"Welcome to Veorn!" exclaimed a rich, well-formed voice from the room's far end.

High Lord Nimmeral Andain strode confidently into the chamber, followed by Cierzon, a young alviri woman and an older man dressed in grey, carrying a large book. Nimmeral wore a long black jacket embroidered with swirling silver filigree, and his long white hair was tied back behind his pointed ears in an unapologetic statement of his race.

"I trust you all slept well," he said, smiling. "You know my son, Cierzon, but may I also introduce my daughter, Mistral and my highest commander, General Typhon Surlain."

Tiam and Torbrand rose immediately to their feet and bowed formally, but Prince Asger struggled to get up from the soft cushions.

"Please," said the high lord, gesturing to the prince.

Asger ignored him and pulled himself erect on his sticks.

"Pleasure meet you, my lord," said Asger.

"Likewise, Your High—"

"Just Asger," insisted the prince.

Asger knew his father and brother would expect deference and respect as the self-appointed rulers of all Weorgoran. However, the prince respected the graceful alviri too much. He would never show superiority in their lands.

Nimmeral smiled and cocked his head in surprise. The humans wanted help and were willing to bow to him to get it.

Sir Torbrand offered his hand to Typhon, but the serious alviri eyed him coldly. Noting his rudeness, Lady Mistral pushed in front of him and curtseyed low, then offered her hand to the knight. He kissed it and gazed into her glittering sky-blue eyes.

"Enchanted, my lady," he said, lowering his voice in embarrassment.

Her hair was the same shimmering white as her brother's, but it was long and gently curled, draping over her bare shoulders to rest near her breast. She wore a strappy blue dress, perfectly matching her eyes and the blue gem twinkling low on her forehead.

She showed no such protocol when greeting Moranne, throwing her arms around the woman in black to hug her tightly.

"You've been away too long, Wickona," she effused.

"You're even more beautiful than I remember," replied Moranne, exuding genuine warmth.

"Lady Etherin sends her apologies," interjected the high lord.

Moranne knew it was a lie; she could see it in his eyes.

A servant bustled quickly into the room and deposited a tray of sweet pastries and a large ceramic jug of wine. They sat in a circle with the high lord in a tall, padded chair; the alviri eschewed the formality of royalty, preferring the democracy of a republic.

"I know why you're here," began Nimmeral, pressing his hands together as if praying. "Jhakri has returned to strength, and you ask for our help."

"Corvus is joining the Stans to invade Tudorfeld," confirmed Moranne. "You know he will not stop there."

Nimmeral pondered her words, but General Surlain was dismissive. With no inflexion, his words sounded final. "He does not threaten us. We have no part to play."

"If he defeats the king, he will not permit you to rule yourselves," said Moranne. "You must know this."

"We pose him no threat," retorted Typhon.

"You would deal with his evil?" gasped Sir Torbrand.

Moranne could feel the atmosphere changing. Nimmeral was using his general to refuse them utterly. Cierzon, too, was surprised by Typhon's tone. The relationship with Moranne had always been good, and he had no negative experiences with humans.

"Father, can we not offer some help?"

"We should build bridges," added Mistral.

Nimmeral waved them aside and sat forward. "My children are ignorant of the world beyond these shores. They've not seen the alviri spat on and stoned in the street and know not of King Pythar's refusal to help us control the clans."

"I change this," retorted Prince Asger.

The high lord was already shaking his head. "I sense you're an honourable man, Prince Asger, but your father does not favour our kind."

General Typhon opened his large dusty book, removed a single parchment piece and passed it to Sir Torbrand. "Five years ago, we received this letter from your father ordering us to swear a vow of fealty to the Crown or risk invasion. It's signed by General Cymel Marl and King Pythar Fierdman."

Torbrand nodded and handed the note back to Typhon with a heavy heart. Cymel had set him up to fail. There was no chance of taking Alfheim, but the threat alone would guarantee hostility from the alviri.

"I'm sorry, my lord," said Torbrand humbly. "I had no knowledge of this."

Nimmeral's smile was thin with regret, but his hands were tied. "We are unable to help you. I'm sorry."

"We can't let them die!" cried Cierzon. "We're better than that!"

"I am sorry, my son, but my first duty is to the alviri. I will not see our kind die in defence of humans." He turned to Prince Asger and sealed the decision. "You will leave Alfheim by midnight tonight, and our borders will be closed to all humans except our friends, the Cempestre."

"This is wrong," said Mistral.

Nimmeral ignored her and climbed to his feet. "My assistant will see that you have supplies for your journey, and I wish you good luck."

"Am I not a friend to the alviri?" called Moranne.

The high lord was already sweeping from the room, leaving his son and daughter looking on.

"I'm sorry, Wickona," said Cierzon.

His father hadn't even embraced his old friend, just dismissed her as he would a peasant farmer.

"I will speak with him," assured Mistral.

Moranne knew it was in vain. "Thank you, my lord and my lady, but your father has great responsibilities. I hope we meet again." She embraced them both once more and then watched as they followed Nimmeral through the door beyond; it shut with a slam which echoed through the tall chamber.

"That went well," said Tiam unhelpfully.

"We should go as soon as possible," added Torbrand. "We're wasting time."

"Have enough?" asked Prince Asger.

None of them could answer. The company had just ten female warriors, but Corvus could control hundreds of men.

Lord Cierzon found Gada Scirmann lying on the beach beneath the palace. He was propped on his elbows, watching the tide ebb and flow while Banafell loomed large in the distance. A tide line of wet seaweed ran along the beach where he rested his feet, allowing the stringy green threads to fall through his toes. Cierzon sat beside him and followed his gaze towards the dangerous mountains where the oni clans ran free.

They sat for a while in silence, enjoying the sun and the cool northerly breeze until Cierzon broke the calm.

"I don't agree," he said, fixing his stare on the horizon.

"Your father is right," said Hayden. "Humans are narrow-minded, prejudiced creatures who like to be told how to think." He couldn't help picturing his father and how he worried more about appearances than his son's welfare.

"I don't care what my father says; there is a place for you here. I'll hide you if I must."

Hayden turned to gaze into Cierzon's green eyes and saw the same glint which had sparkled in Ham's face on the banks of the River Dorbourne.

"That's very kind," he said, "but my place is with Moranne, Jem and the others who helped me escape from Dunstreet. I owe Jem my life."

"Lady Moranne is a good woman," agreed Cierzon, "and Jem sounds like a good friend."

"I've killed a bandit in Bearun, met a beautiful dalfreni, danced in the ballroom of Cynstol Castle, seen women fight as hard as men, and gazed at the beauty of your hallowed isle. My life has been bigger in a few weeks than in all my years, and I have the good lady to thank."

Hayden reached out a hand and touched Cierzon's arm. "And I'll never forget you, my friend."

Slipping past the guards was too easy. Torbrand was right; the defences were lax. The high lord's private chambers were situated high in the branches of a giant redwood linked to the main palace by another precarious, suspended walkway. It swayed a little with every footfall, but the alviri engineers made structures which weathered any storm and withstood immense weight.

The door opened silently, swinging inwards to reveal a generous, panelled chamber surrounded by large, arched windows. A wide oak desk stood at one end. Nimmeral had his back to the door as he watched his people below.

"I expected you sooner," he said without turning.

"I had to wait for one of your guards to spend a copper," replied Moranne, standing in the doorway.

"Should I call for them?" he joked, turning to face her. His expression bore no malice.

"I just need to know," she begged. "Then I'll be gone."

Nimmeral walked around his desk and sat on the edge with his arms folded. She'd seen him age, but every mark on her face and every line in her smile seemed the same as the first day they'd met.

"You know, there was a time when I thought of abdicating. Running away from Etherin and giving myself to you?"

"I didn't know that," she said.

"Even when Cierzon and Mistral were born, I still craved your touch." He sighed and looked past her as if he was gazing into their past. "Things have changed."

"I know we can't go back, but please don't punish the humans. They're weak, and they need you."

He held out his hands, taking hers, caressing them with his thumbs.

"I loved you," he said, "but I've discovered I love my people so much more. I will not desert them."

"I still care for you, Nim."

He released her hands and sat down behind the desk. "Etherin knows everything."

"How?"

"I told her," he said. "I couldn't hide it any longer, and she deserved the truth. I'm sorry, Wickona, but you're no longer welcome here."

"But—"

"Please leave."

He picked up a large scroll and started reading, leaving Moranne stunned, with her hands still outstretched. She stared at the man she once called *my love* and felt alone once more.

Corvus was too strong, and they had insufficient warriors. The war could already be lost. He'd come close before, but this time he'd know better. With five hundred years to plan his vengeance, many would die.

She paused on the walkway and looked west. Something was different. Jem was still alive, walking through the forest, but he wasn't alone. Earth power surrounded him, watched him and believed in him. "Clever boy," she whispered to herself.

34 CLAN MORP

"We should be nearing the junction soon," said Bresne, striding along the path with such gusto that Caspin struggled to keep up.

There had been no sight or sound of the dryads since morning, but Bresne knew they were out there. Could they be trusted to keep their word? Only time would tell.

As the trees and bushes blurred past, she thought of Gunnar; his big, dumb smile always made her laugh, and his thick, muscled arms were good to fall into after a hard day in the forest. She knew instinctively that something was wrong when her hunting party returned to Cempess one cold winter's evening. They found a group of friends waiting for her at the gate. Gunnar had been unshackling a horse and plough when someone had seen him stoop suddenly onto the wooden tool before falling to the ground clutching his chest. His last words were, "tell Brezy I'm sorry."

Since that day, she'd dedicated her life to training the orettas and always felt a pang of pride leading them into battle.

"Stay sharp, people!" she shouted. "We're bordering clan country here."

Although the oni clans were based in Banafell, they hunted across the entire northern end of Deapholt, from the mountains to the sea. They ranged from seven to ten feet tall and were twice the width of an average man. Their natural skin colour was a rough terracotta, but the sharp horns and curving fangs made them the spectres of nightmares.

The number of enemy kills determined the status of each oni warrior. Destroying other oni clans was highly prized but killing alviri, humans, or dryads was the greatest victory.

"Oni clans," grumbled Slitan. "Horse dung and old wives' tales."

"See this scar?" said Brenna, pointing to the deep gash across her face. "That's what you get for staring an oni in the face."

Jem knew they were real; he could feel a massive menace growing, the deep breathing of something big tramping through the trees somewhere ahead.

Tell them, came the now familiar voice of Chakirris echoing in his head.

They won't believe me, thought Jem; however, they'd all seen him against the tunnbrocc, and Captain Fallon had witnessed the green fire in his eyes.

They will believe and trust your instincts.

They were Moranne's words spoken by a dryad in his head. Almost pinching himself, Jem looked around at Gron, Lunn and Gamin, his travelling companions. He felt the tunnbrocc attack before it happened and said nothing, and now Davill was dead.

"Captain!" he shouted, making his way to the front of the column where Biorn kept pace with Caspin.

"Gada?" chimed the captain.

"I know this will sound mad, but I can feel trouble ahead."

Bresne overhead Jem's words; she pushed behind Sir Caspin and grabbed Jem by the collar. "What kind of trouble?" she asked.

"Speak, lad," added Biorn.

Jem looked at one, then the other; they appeared to believe him.

"Something big," he stuttered. "I can't see properly, but it's breaking branches and coming this way."

"A war party," said Brenna, who was listening intently.

The pine trees followed the coast up to the foothills of Banafell, allowing a thick canopy of maple, oak and elm to crowd the north path. Thick, glistening moss clung to fallen trunks, and shining ivy wound around every branch and hung in their faces. Little could be seen beyond the path, making the Cempestre tense, trying to peer into the green.

"Hands on swords!" shouted Bresne.

"Stay alert, lads," added Biorn, forgetting Brea and Ellen, who smiled between each other.

Lunn took the axe from his back and allowed it to swing at his side; Gron pulled the mace free of his belt and felt the weight in his hand; the archers took arrows from their quivers and slotted them in readiness.

"I hope you're wrong," said Caspin, "but from what I've seen...." He tailed off, thinking of the crofters near Rynham and the baby who would bear his name. "I'll need this," he continued, pulling the sword from its sheath.

Bresne and the other Cempestre adopted a slight crouch as they walked forward, coiled as if ready to act, and the others were warily following their lead.

"I'm hungry," complained Lunn.

Gron ignored him; he was listening to something distant from the right. "Do you hear that?" he asked.

"Yeah, it's my stomach rumbling."

Gron shook his head and noticed that Brenna and Isen could hear it too.

The group were approaching a short, broad, planked bridge crossing a narrow stream. Further ahead, Bresne spotted the junction on the right.

"We'll stop here," said Captain Fallon.

As his boot landed on the bridge, and the knock echoed through the trees, they all heard the sounds.

Something significant splashed through the stream to the right of the bridge. Branches snapped and flicked aside, and water hurled against the trees, absorbed by the mossy cushion. A shadow moved behind the leaves, following the stream's winding course towards them. Its knotted, musclebound arms tossed saplings aside, and it snorted with exertion through its wide wrinkled nose.

"Oni!" shouted Isen.

The colossal beast burst through the trees and started to climb the bridge. His large, gnarled hands grasped the wood to pull himself up, raising his massive head to snarl. Eyes were sunken, mustard yellow in a broad, pock-marked, red face. His hair was long and black, whipping water and sweat about his body, but it was the long, twisted horns on his head that Jem stared at in horror. One was broken, and the other was stained red.

"Humans, die!" he growled, pulling himself to full height.

The party scattered around him, and the pack ponies bolted northwards.

The clansman was bare-chested, except for a wide leather sash patterned with beads, carrying an array of knives and animal teeth. His red, muscle-bound body was scarred, and his knee bulged from thick leather shorts, where it had broken and set poorly.

"There'll be more!" cried Bresne, grabbing Biorn by the arm.

Brea didn't hesitate, letting an arrow fly from the back of the column; she threaded it past the men, whipping past Brenna's ear by just an inch to embed in the oni's shoulder. It roared angrily; a long club appeared in its right hand, studded with sharp metal shards.

"Between the eyes or in the heart!" shouted Cuyler, pulling the archers to the left.

The oni swung the club in a wide arc as he stomped across the bridge, but the party just managed to jump out of reach. Ellen dived beneath the barbs while Bresne, Caspin and Isen regrouped to swipe at the eight-foot behemoth. They couldn't get close enough to hit him as he rampaged towards them.

Biorn was backing towards the junction and almost didn't see a second oni storming towards him from the Alfheim road. It was painted bright blue, denoting a warlord, and swung a giant, rusting iron sword. The captain ducked in time, inertia almost toppling the grunting beast as its swing missed.

The ground shook with the thunder of heavy boots. Branches snapped and flew across the path as more oni appeared behind.

"Fall back!" cried Biorn.

The warriors could barely hear him amid the melee. Cuyler, Gamin and Brea let forth a flurry of arrows against the first creature, but none could hit home as it whirled, trying to swat the humans like flies. Luckily the Cempestre had fought the clan creatures many times and knew how to tackle them.

Bresne led Caspin, Brenna and Lunn to goad the oni, allowing Isen to sneak into his blind spot. Brenna managed to lunge at his left arm, slashing a deep cut. The beast whirled to face her, baring its yellow fangs.

"Die, bitch!" it sneered.

Isen was already swinging her gleaming axe at its calves with the crunch of steel on bone. He fell forward, howling in agony; Isen leapt onto his back and buried her axe in his vast head.

"You first," she said, wiping the blood from her forehead.

Gamin gasped, watching her stand on the oni's back, impressive *and* formidable. She would never care for a lean bowman from nowhere.

There was no time to celebrate with movement everywhere. Biorn was struggling to counter the heavy blows of the oni warlord.

"Come on!" commanded Bresne, urging the warriors to help the captain. More oni appeared from the forest.

Jem and Lunn were the first to Biorn's aid, while Bresne and Caspin tried to lead another brute, swinging a club from the right. Still, more were piling in from behind. There were too many.

Brea could see the danger and took Cuyler to the west edge of the path; here, they could fire rapidly over the swordsmen's heads, although it was hard to find a clean shot.

Another oni joined the attack on Bresne from behind. Gamin saw it and loosed an arrow that pierced the beast's cheek, sending it roaring into the trees. Cuyler hit the other in the chest moments later, but it managed to stay upright, pounding the ground near Caspin with so much force that the shockwave knocked him off his feet.

The hulking oni were now pouring into the junction, but their bulk made it difficult for them to swing their cruel clubs without hitting each other. They formed a kind of queue behind the first three who were battling the swordsmen. Jem's twin blades were a blur of steel, but the green fire burning in his eyes caused the oni leader to back away.

"Elf magic!" he bellowed.

Arrows were flying everywhere, but Brea was concentrating on the closest threats. As a ten-foot oni raised its massive club to crush Bresne, she hit it square between the eyes, killing it instantly. The hulking body crashed into the junction, but more stomped over its corpse.

Biorn was forced further up the road over another stream. The blue chieftain's sword was so large it swept across the whole road. Both Lunn and Jem were forced to battle another two red demons who appeared behind them. In a scissor movement, Jem's sharp Jakari blades severed a finger, and Lunn swung his axe to gash the creature's leg, but it only seemed to enrage it further.

Bresne, Brenna, Ellen and Caspin attempted to form a protective arc against most of the horde while the archers fired over their heads. However, the group were gradually forced back. One brave oni managed to blunder through the barricade to swing his club wildly towards Gamin, but Cuyler saw it, and an arrow pierced its club hand, forcing it to drop the weapon. Isen seized the opportunity, running at the creature's torso to bury her axe in its chest.

"Thanks," stuttered Gamin. He was rewarded by his first smile from the impervious Isen.

Cal stood at the south end, trying to find a good shot in the melee, while Biorn still ducked from the warlord's attacks, and the others fought bravely at the junction. No one saw the slow, grinning oni, with only one horn, emerge from the bushes behind him.

Cuyler caught it in the corner of her eye, but her hand had no arrow ready.

"Behind!" she yelled, but the nine-foot creature was already mid-swing.

The rough club hit Cal in the side, cracking ribs and sending him flying off the bridge into the icy stream below. The oni followed him, bounding over the planks, to jump down towards the stranded Burlander. Cuyler fumbled to help, but another colossal creature leapt out of the bushes swinging towards her with a dull sword.

There was a click, followed by the whistle of wind, and the oni slapped its arm like swatting a gnat. It started to shake, stumble, and then crumple onto the bridge. It was dead.

Cuyler looked up to see the smooth, green and brown shape of Chakirris smiling down at her. She held a miniature wooden crossbow in her right hand and offered her left in assistance.

"Need some help?" she purred.

It was too late for Cal. The Burland archer lay in a crumpled heap across the stream while the snarling oni trod slowly towards him, relishing the fear in Cal's eyes. He chuckled, raising the spiked club high above his head as his shadow blotted out the light casting Cal in darkness.

"Please!" screamed the hapless soldier; it was his last word as the club came down.

The other dryads started to appear around the junction, flashing between the trees, despatching two more oni quickly. Chakirris herself spotted Cal's killer climbing back onto the bridge with his bloodied club and lifted the tiny crossbow in readiness.

"Green elf, I will eat your—"

It started to taunt her, but with another poison-tipped bolt, she shot it in the throat; it collapsed dead in front of her.

Another oni jumped from a stream near the junction and lunged towards Bresne, forcing her back, but Sax spotted an opportunity. He'd already circled the area using stealth skills, waiting for a chance to strike. Jumping on the oni's back, he thrust two knives deep into its throat. Gurgling in agony, it stumbled forward onto Bresne's sword.

Even with help from the dryads, the battle was far from won, as fighting raged all over the clearing. One of the dryads shot at an oni but missed,

Stone and Sceptre

causing it to leap towards her, but her sister managed to kill it as it grabbed her ankle.

Wearily flailing his sword from left to right, Biorn was exhausted; sweat poured from his brow, and his breathing was shallow. The large blue oni could sense his difficulty and raised its sword for one more blow.

"Brave fight, little human," he laughed. He swung the sword towards the captain with eyes of malice, but the warlord's grip failed, and it flew from his hand into the trees. He looked down at the silver arrow embedded in his chest.

"Elves," he growled, then fell back across the bridge.

Silver streaks now swished overhead; arrows were flying in from somewhere in the north.

Oni warriors were dropping to the floor all over the clearing. The party had begun to beat them back with concentrated fire from the archers, dryads, and the three strange master archers emerging from the north.

Seeing that all was lost, the one remaining oni turned on his heel and ran back to the forest. A hail of arrows followed him, but the long strides took him away quickly, and he vanished into the green.

Biorn dusted himself off and looked up to see a dark-haired woman and two dark-haired men, who all had short, pointed ears and the smooth skin of the alviri.

"Thank you, whoever you are," said the captain, struggling to stay on his feet.

The woman had shoulder-length, dark hair streaked with grey, although she looked no more than twenty years older. She had high cheekbones and deep green eyes, which seemed to be probing him for weakness. She reminded him of someone.

"My name is Carina," she said with a cultured voice. "They may return. We should go."

⁂

Pag collapsed onto a fallen tree trunk and gazed at the cedar-wood arrow protruding from his shoulder. He grasped the shaft and pulled it from his arm, grimacing as he remembered seeing Rak murdered by the elf girl.

Clan Morp would learn of this dishonour, and they would kill every last human, elf and green bitch in the sacred forest.

He looked back down the trail, but no one followed. Steeling himself against pain and hunger, he turned towards Banafell and pushed on with giant strides to the land he called home.

Mirror Lake and Banafell

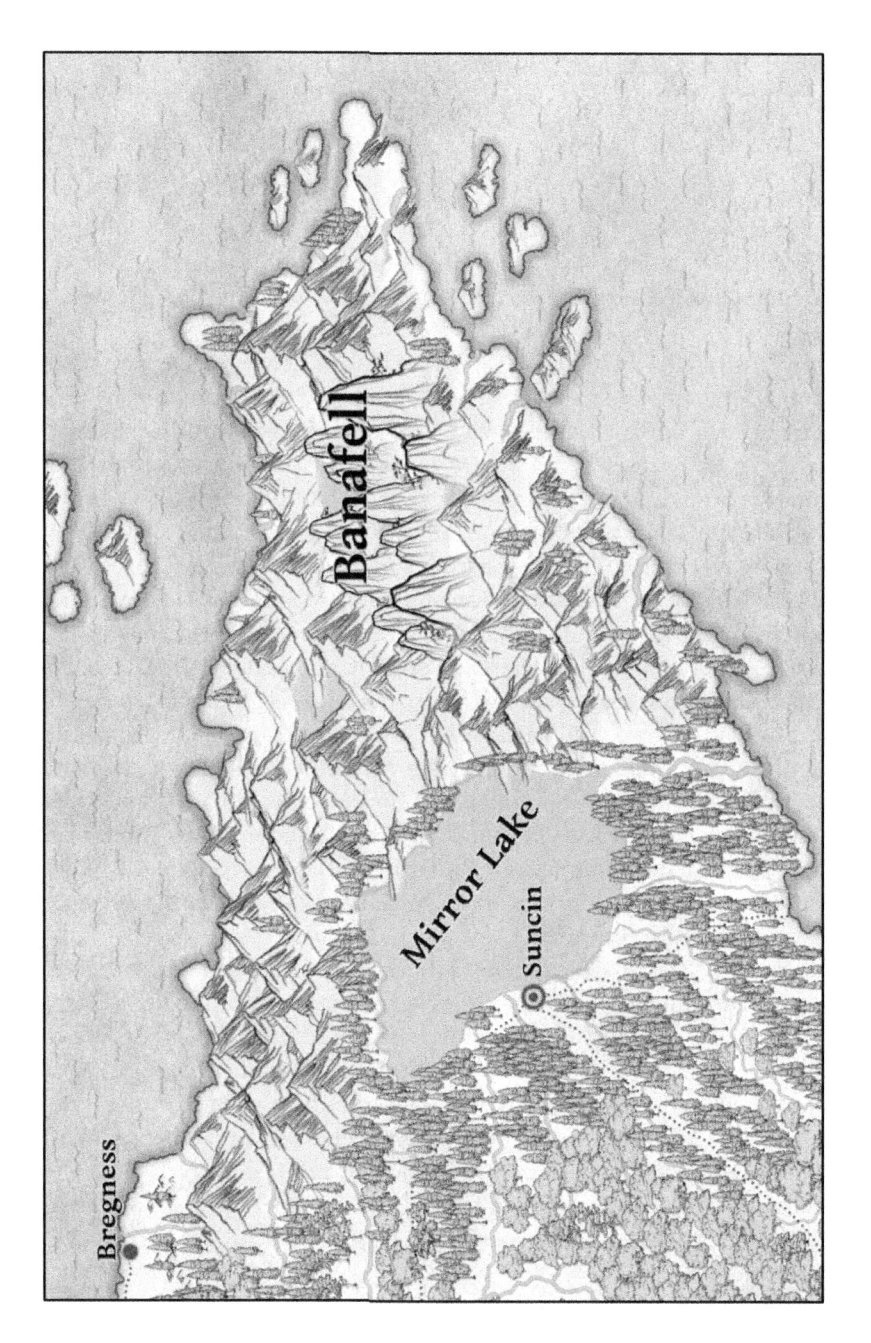

35 REFLECTIONS

No guards were posted at the gates of Verhals, and the gardeners hadn't seen her, but Moranne was wary. Lady Etherin had extraordinary perception; she could see much more than most alviri. She might already know of Wickona's presence.

The impressive villa was a short horse ride east of Veorn, nestling on cliffs overlooking a long, unspoiled beach. The frontage was accessed from a steep, stone staircase winding back and forth across the hill and running through garden terraces along the way. Moranne gazed up at the house she knew so well. So many parties and happy times spent with the Andains.

Passing the steps, she quietly moved towards the beach and followed the rough pathway eastwards. Vegetable gardens and beds of fragrant roses were scattered on each side, but the small stone hut, at the far end of the beach had her full attention. It was round, with a tiny window and a short, arched door. She looked around to ensure no one was watching and pressed the latch.

The door swung inwards, revealing pots, gardening equipment, boxes of seeds, and bags of charcoal. A sizeable old chest stood against the opposite wall, with drawers of tulip and daffodil bulbs. Moranne held it by the corners, testing the weight, and then she pulled it from one side; it scraped over the slabs like an opening doorway. The empty spot revealed nothing of interest, but she knelt on the floor and felt over the rough, flat stones. One was more significant than the others; she ran her fingers along its edges until she could get a grip, then pulled it upwards.

The stone tipped back, revealing a shallow pit containing a rusting metal box. Moranne carefully removed it and carried it to a small potting table under the hut's window. With considerable effort, she prised the lid from the box so that it flipped off the table and clattered to the floor. Like the presentation of a hero's prize, she removed a leather package from the box and laid it on the table. Moranne gazed at it for a moment, then pulled on the rotting string as the crusty leather unfolded, revealing two shining sceptres.

Touching the strangely warm metal, she remembered handsome Sheratan and sweet Porrima. They simply wanted their own peaceful life until it was ripped from them.

"I knew you'd come here."

Moranne looked up to see the silhouette of an alviri woman standing in the doorway. It was a voice she knew well, which once belonged to a friend.

"Etherin."

Lady Etherin glided gracefully into the small room and faced Moranne with the cold, serious gaze of her glassy blue eyes. Her smooth pale skin and white straight hair, combined with a crystal white dress, gave her the appearance of a ghostly spirit of doom. The sharp, polished knife in her right hand marked her intent.

"Once, I considered you my best friend," she said. "Always spending time with us, regaling us with your tall tales. I never thought you'd betray me."

"I'm sorry," said Moranne, backing away.

"Do you know how I knew?" asked Etherin, still moving slowly towards her.

"Nimmeral told you."

Etherin was already laughing. "Is that what he told you? Ha! I ripped it from his ungrateful soul." She let her gaze wander through the wooden slats of the tiny shed as she remembered the moment. "The last time you were here, we had dinner, and for one moment, I saw the look you two shared; that was the moment I knew."

"I'm sorry—"

"You could have had any man in Grenfold, but you took my husband. Did you think he loved you?"

It hit like an arrow. Nimmeral did love her, he told her.

"He loved you *so* much," mocked Etherin. "So much that when I threatened to leave him and embroil him in a scandal, he renounced you."

"Scandal?" said Moranne.

"An alviri and a human? They would have run him out of Alfheim."

"I'm not hu—"

"You're a selfish, lying witch, leading good people to a doom of your making."

Moranne looked down at the knife, limp in Etherin's hand.

"Are you going to kill me?"

Etherin finally stopped and looked down at the dull blade, turning it in her hand. She'd envisaged this day many times, but the sight of her old friend did not trigger the hate she expected to feel.

"You'd blast me with your power instantly," she said blankly.

"I would never harm you," replied Moranne.

With her gaze fixed on the alviri blade, Etherin slowly lifted it and placed it on the table, then she turned and walked to the doorway, where she paused against the door frame.

"Take your weapons, and don't ever return."

Without looking back, she walked away towards the villa. Tears welled in her eyes and dropped to her breast, disappearing beneath the floating, white gown.

The stream was clear and cool to Slitan's hand as it searched the silt and pebbles for the perfect size. He lifted the rough granite stone, about the shape of his fist, and wiped the water onto his sleeve. Only the endless trickle from the slopes of Banafell broke the silence. He carefully carried the precious rock, watched by his fellow soldiers with their heads bowed.

With a clock maker's care, Slitan gently placed his prize on top of the cairn, marking the spot where his friend's body rested. Ellen was crying despite Cal's harsh words, and Lunn took a deep breath to hold back his heart. Slitan said nothing; he stared at the pile of water-washed stones.

"Cal was a real soldier," said Captain Fallon solemnly. "Born to goddess-fearing farmers near Silmouth, Cal never wanted the sleepy Burland life. At eighteen, he tried to join the Green Order, but the snobs wouldn't have him, so he found a home with the Queen's, where I met him many years later."

Caspin nodded in agreement. He preferred the company of down-to-earth warriors rather than the toffs in the Order.

"I knew he was special," continued Biorn. "When we were dealing with bandits near Braylen, six came out with their weapons lowered, but Cal spotted the archer high in a tree. I only saw him when he hit the earth with Cal's arrow in his chest."

Brea smiled. That was her kind of soldier.

"Farewell, my friend, and may Frea take you to her bosom and guide you through the afterlife."

"So be it," said some of the men, holding hands over their hearts.

They stooped to touch the cairn one by one before turning north behind three new friends. Even the dryads paid their respects but hung back behind the column. Biorn asked them to hide their nakedness until they could find some clothes. The pack ponies were found alive and unharmed, just north of the junction.

Carina and her male companions, Tyde and Mykil, were dalfreni from the settlement of Suncin on Mirror Lake. They'd been tracking the large oni group for several days, expecting them to attack. Fighting off the clans was a constant chore for the lake folk.

"Thanks for your help," said Caspin as they walked. They were lucky to lose only one. Without the dryads and dalfreni, things could have gone very differently.

"We have few visitors," she replied. "We thought we better keep you alive."

Her smile was infectious and it seemed familiar. She wore a short green tunic over a pair of tight leather leggings cut with a pattern which swirled about her legs. A light leather tunic and arm guards completed the look of a huntress.

Her colleagues wore similar garb but were different in all other ways. Tyde had short hair and a thin moustache, while Mykil was tall with straggly grey hair. They all looked to be in their twenties, but Caspin knew their appearance could be misleading.

"Now tell me, Sir Caspin, what brings a group of Caynna soldiers, Cempestre and forest folk to the lake?"

"I'd prefer to speak with your leader first," he insisted.

"My leader?" she laughed. "The dalfreni have no leader."

"So, how do you arrange defence and keep order?"

"Suncin has a council," she replied, still smirking. "If you have something big to say, you'll be saying it to anyone who wants to know."

Great! thought Caspin. He wasn't as eloquent as Moranne and only knew of Corvus through her.

There was little talk amongst the men and women as they watched Banafell grow above the trees. The loss of Cal weighed heavy, even more so than the death of Davill, who was less well known. With the dryads moving silently behind, the women outnumbered the men, a fact not lost on Slitan. The bowman said nothing, but he silently seethed with anger. He blamed the witch for bringing them here, he blamed the Cempestre for marching them into a trap, and he hated the dryads for their immodesty. They were marching into a pit of filthy elves, and he found his hand hovering over the hilt of his knife.

Other soldiers kept their distance and didn't see his darting eyes and soundless muttering. His mind combined his mother and the surrounding women into a grotesque, single evil. He paid no attention to the terrain, which rose gradually, becoming jagged and rocky, or the trees becoming tall and broad.

It was early dusk when they crested a hill to see the magnificent Mirror Lake filling the expansive valley below.

"There's a sight," gasped Brea. Most of the others also stopped for a moment to marvel at the beauty.

Thousands of lights lined the south bank and followed the lake's edge eastwards until they ended in a wall of trees marking where Banafell sloped into the water. Foaming waterfalls cascaded from the glaciers, depositing turquoise blue water into the expanse, some fifty miles long and thirty miles wide.

"Not much of a mirror," grunted Gron, seeing only the firelight reflected on its surface.

"That's not where the name comes from," corrected Cuyler. "The alviri believe that the pure of heart will see the face of Juldra when they look into the water."

"That rules Gron out," joked Brea.

The path sloped downwards, weaving around outcrops of rock until they could see a tall, stockade wall running half a mile from the shore. It hung between tall trees like a curtain, with watchtowers nestling in the branches above.

A pair of wide gates swung open silently as they approached, and the dalfreni led them inside. The scene meeting them was an immediate assault on the senses. They expected to find the fair folk in elegant wooden houses, singing and dancing joyfully. Instead, they discovered a cramped, creaking city so overcrowded that many of the tiny lean-to dwellings seemed to pile one against another.

The road from the gate was rough and furrowed, with pools of stagnant water; a stench of open sewers drifted on the air from the grey water which ran into the filthy edge of the lake. The dalfreni sat on tiny porches in high-rise shacks or crisscrossed the road, giving wary looks as the company passed. The town teamed with furtive and suspicious life.

Children played in the mud with sticks, and merchants sold forest fruits from carts on either side of the road. A high balcony caught some of the men's attention.

"Three coppers for a good time, boys," bawled a dark-haired dalfreni woman dressed in a short leather skirt.

"Two for the girls," shouted another, laughing.

"Eyes on the road," said Biorn gruffly.

There were no large, ornate dwellings to be seen. The tallest buildings were split into small apartments, brothels, taverns or gambling dens. Tiny alleys branched from the road, disappearing under the overhanging buildings and smoke from a thousand fires. Sax led the pack ponies behind the group and hid behind them from passers-by.

"This is a death trap," grunted Gron.

Lunn nodded in agreement.

"What happened here?" asked Caspin, trying to shield his nose from an open latrine.

Carina sighed. She felt the same despair whenever she returned from a hunting trip and saw the overcrowded slum.

"Our birth rate is a hundred times that of the alviri," she replied. "Most of those you see are at least tenth generation."

Children ran through the lanes or cried for their mother's milk. With his face streaked in mud, a young lad stopped to look up at the tall knight and smiled.

"But why stay here?"

"Where would we go?" she laughed. "The Tudorfeldians would kill us in our sleep, the alviri won't allow us on the island, and the oni rule Banafell and roam throughout the north. We're trapped here."

"I'm so sorry," said Caspin, unsure if he was apologising for himself or all humans. "I had no idea."

The dalfreni hunters led them down to the lakeshore, where the road continued out into the lake as a wide boardwalk. Dwellings sprang up on either side, supported on stilts and surrounded by narrow jetties with hundreds of fishing boats. The buildings were more prominent than those on the land and seemed in a better state of repair.

"The posh end of town," laughed Tyde.

"Merchants live on the water," agreed Carina. "Trying to escape the stench."

They stopped at the end of the walkway where a large, comprehensive, three-storey building stood in silence. Carina asked them to wait while she disappeared inside. One of the dryads spotted a tear running down Lunn's broad face. The sight of ragged, dirty children playing amongst the filth was too much for him.

"Right!" shouted Carina when she emerged in the doorway. "Most rooms are unoccupied, and the owner has agreed to let you all stay here. Please choose your room."

"It's an inn?" asked Jem.

"No," replied Mykil. "It's a newly built brothel."

Slitan stopped and stared up at the freshly cut timbers. There was an empty spot where a gaudy sign would entice the men.

"I'm not sleeping here," he said flatly.

Biorn was in no mood for a confrontation. "Do as you please," he said and followed Caspin and Carina into one of Suncin's few clean buildings.

The brothel had ten rooms on each floor, but it was currently only inhabited by the owner. Some of the varnish was still wet, loose sawdust piled up against the walls, and only the top floor rooms had furniture. The men took what they needed from the pack ponies, and Carina sent Mykil into town to find clothes for the dryads. Everyone was tired and sore.

Jem's room looked along the boardwalk to the grimy town covering the west bank. The overcrowded squalor made the Cynstol Wards seem palatial. The dalfreni deserved better. He closed his weary eyes to the sound of dalfreni life, but his dreams were troubled by hulking dark shapes, beating the life from his friends.

36 IN STRENGTH

The torches flickered against the rock, throwing dancing shadows against the cave walls, but Zonta's eyes were fixed on the task. Her hand was steady, working slowly over his broad, leathery back, darkening the blue with every stroke of the thick woad solution. Only *she* could apply the sacred colour, for only a warlord's mate could be touched by the hue of death. Her hand dripped with indigo, which ran down her arm and spattered the granite plinth.

At just seven feet tall, his nine-foot frame towered above her; oni females were consistently smaller and slimmer than the hulking males, and they knew their place. When Kagel was unhappy, he would beat her; if she failed in her orders, he would beat her and should she ever deny him? She dare not think of the consequences.

Her horns curved upwards evenly, and her skin was smooth, while her incisors were knife-sharp, gleaming white. The females did not grow the long, curving tusks of the square-jawed males. She scrambled over Kagel's back, dressed in a blue stained cloth tied into shape by a series of leather straps wrapping the material around her cub-bearing hips. Her hair fell into dark ringlets, which she kept at shoulder length. It would be woven with beads in battle, but today it bounced free.

She was considered the most beautiful of all the females and a high prize. Other warlords had killed trying to win her, and Kagel himself had murdered her former mate. Now she'd feel the back of his hand if she even blinked at another male or dared to answer back. Zonta longed for release. With luck, he'd die in combat, or she would.

The cave naturally formed three rooms and was the largest of Clan Morp. Although three warlords vied for the leadership, Kagel held the green stone and the perks that went with it. His horns were long and straight, and his arms bulged like oak trunks. The reign of a clan leader was often short, but he'd ruled with an iron fist for three miserable years.

"Sir!" boomed the voice of Vrass, who'd appeared in the doorway, trying to look as humble as possible. He might be Kagel's second, but he had no designs on the stone.

"What?" grumbled Kagel. He hated being disturbed at home.

"Soldier from Deap. News."

Kagel pushed Zonta off his back; he knocked over the dye so that it splashed over her chest and ran through the cracks in the floor.

"Bring," said Kagel.

The oni had never developed a language; instead, using simple grunts and gestures in the time of galdur. However, when they first enslaved humans, they were captivated by the cultured language and took it for themselves. Now they used it sparingly, lacking the patience or intellect to form sentences longer than a few words.

Vrass yelled something out of the cave, and a young warrior soon appeared, bowing his head in respect.

"Speak!" yelled Kagel.

The warrior knelt and kept his stare at the ground. He dared not look Kagel in the eye, and if he glimpsed Zonta, it could be the last sight his eyes would see before Kagel gouged them out.

"I Pag," he said shakily. "Rak dead."

Kagel lifted himself to full height and roared. Rak was the closest thing he had to a friend and a warlord who would never threaten him. If he allowed this outrage to go unpunished, he'd lose face.

"How?" he bawled, grabbing Pag by the top of his sash and lifting him such that his feet barely touched the cave floor.

"Humans, elves!" he spluttered.

"More!" growled Kagel, pulling Pag close so he could taste his foul breath.

"Females, lake elves, green elves," he replied, referring to the Cempestre, dalfreni and dryads.

Kagel threw the warrior to the wall, where he cowered in fear. He could hear the Scucca's words in his head again, plaguing his dreams and disturbing his thoughts. *Join me once more.*

"War!" he cried at his startled second.

Vrass knew what to do and hurried from the cave, dragging the hapless Pag with him. They would need trackers and the best warriors available.

The warlord turned to Zonta, staring at him with thin, yellow eyes. He felt like hitting her smooth, beautiful face, but she dared to speak.

"I fight," she said, holding herself tall and straight.

For a moment, he thought of punching her so hard that her horns would crack, but then he remembered how the others coveted her. They could take her while he fought.

"You fight," he agreed, then stormed from the cave, leaving his mate with the first glimmer of hope in a tortured life.

The alviri vessel was longer and broader than the Cempestre boat, with room for Moranne's party and six crew. The bay was smooth when they set sail, with only the slightest ripple on the clear waters.

No one had come to bid them farewell, just a retinue of guards to ensure they left. It was the saddest parting she'd endured, but there was no time for regret. Corvus would be in Stanholm, and the attack would come any day; they could already be too late.

Moranne sat astern by herself and watched as Torbrand discussed tactics with the prince. Oretta Brimwulf spoke with her warriors, and young Hayden pined for the fair lord. Banafell stood like an impenetrable wall ahead of them, and the forest looked dark. She longed once more for the warm embrace of her love, of Dane, of Nimmeral, of any worthy man to share her lonely life.

Tears slid silently from her face and dripped to the deck, where they rolled between the timbers and plunged to the hull below, a small, cramped space where a stowaway smiled at his audacity and waited for landfall.

Caspin didn't sleep well; there was too much noise from the lakeshore, where the townsfolk folk didn't seem to stop for breath. He used a bowl of ice-cold water to wash, then descended the creaking pine stairs to find the others awake and waiting for him in the bare lounge. He almost stumbled on the last steps when he spotted the five dryads near the door.

"In Frea's name!" he gasped while the men chuckled.

"We tried to tell them," said Biorn, "but they reckon they get too hot."

The dryads were only slightly more covered than the dalfreni whores, leaning out from the brothels. Most of the nymphs wore a one-piece, figure-hugging, leather bustier with long matching leather boots, but Chakirris had an ornately decorated two-piece which emphasised the forest patterns on her midriff. All had lightly armoured leather shoulder pads and daggers hung from slender belts.

"Well, it's a look," said Caspin smiling.

"Do you not approve?" asked Chakirris, who seemed genuinely shocked.

"It's not as modest as I'd hoped."

"Looks fine to me," laughed Gron.

The dryads looked at each other, but the concept of modesty was alien.

"We can remove them," she said, starting to peel off her top, but Caspin held up his hand and told her it was fine.

"There is one thing," he said, shaking his head. "I don't know all your names."

Chakirris smiled and nodded. She was still wary of the humans, but they seemed harmless, except perhaps for Slitan, who'd slept on the porch.

"These are my sisters," she said. "Jilliad and Sondrin."

They each bowed in turn, and Caspin tipped his head in response.

Sondrin and Jilliad looked like an autumn day in red, orange and brown hues. The silver in Sondrin's hair was like the striped bark of a birch tree, and the twisting pattern of green in Chakirris' arms shone like ivy. They all moved with the fluid grace of prowling cats and watched the men with glistening brown eyes.

As Sondrin bowed low, the door opened, and Carina entered with a tall, male dalfreni wearing a long, green velvet gown.

"This is Geltus, a local merchant," she said.

He smiled broadly and opened his arms in a gesture of welcome. "I have arranged for breakfast and then a meeting with the council," he beamed.

He was tall, with a short pointed beard and a bulging belly, indicative of his prosperous life. He smiled continuously, but it was shallow and false, something he used when selling his wares.

The party of twenty followed Geltus to a large inn where they enjoyed breakfast, and then Caspin, Jem, Bresne and Chakirris accompanied him with Carina to the town meeting. Biorn told the knight he was no good with politics and suggested that Jem had better instincts. There was no dissent, but Slitan glared at the gada as he disappeared with the leaders.

They followed the shoreline as it snaked back and forth, past numerous jetties where fishers readied for the first catch, and fish merchants shouted at busy workers. There were people everywhere: running from doorways, shouting from windows, haggling on market stalls and gossiping in the alleyways. A few sniffed warily as they passed, but most folks paid no heed.

"Do you have marshals?" asked Caspin, seeing many opportunities for crime.

"We have the militia," replied Geltus. "It's funded by the merchants and protects our interests."

"But what about everyone else?" blurted Jem.

"They fend for themselves," said Carina. "Crime is terrible in this terrible place."

Geltus shot her a dark look, but he didn't argue.

Half a mile along the shore, the merchant led them back up the bank a short way to a wide-open area with a large round tent at its centre. The tepee structure was formed from twenty enormous tree trunks. The stiff animal hide exterior stopped ten feet from the floor, so the entire cover was open all around. They could see that many folks were already sitting on the dusty floor, gathered about a central wooden dais.

Geltus showed them to their seats on the dais, then took his own besides an array of other merchants and traders. Fruit merchants, brothel owners, seamstresses, carpenters, and many other skills and professions were represented. They waited while more folk piled into the tepee, and others came to stand outside and watch. When at least four hundred souls were assembled, the brothel owner stood and called for quiet.

"Friends, for the benefit of our visitors, my name is Mylten, and I chair the town council."

His garb was similar to Geltus', but his waistline was broader, causing his gown to billow out like a jar. He cleared his throat and continued. "We are joined today by Sir Caspin Linhold of the Green Order, Gada Jem Poulterer, Oretta Bresne Fixen of the Cempestre and Chakirris of the forest folk."

There was laughter at the dryad's name, but she didn't flinch.

"Sir Caspin would like to address the council," Mylten continued. "Please give him your attention."

Caspin gulped. Why had Moranne not warned him? He didn't know what to say or how to say it. He thanked the merchants and stood, looking out at the expectant faces.

"Speak up!" shouted a voice from the back.

"Erm, you know of the Stans," he said shakily. "Well, they're—"

"What of them?" bawled another voice in the crowd.

"They've allied with a man named Corvus, and he—"

"Who?"

The crowd shouted and jeered. Some asked who these people were, while others wanted to discuss fishing rights or the noise from a brothel. Caspin looked at Bresne, but she had no answers. Lady Moranne would be furious. He had let her down.

The fracas continued for several minutes while Mylten tried to restore order. The chance seemed to be slipping away until an ear-splitting scream blasted from the dais and silenced everyone in the room.

Chakirris stood at the edge of the stage with her hands on her hips.

"You will listen," she ordered. "Then you may return to your tiny lives."

"Or what?" shouted a tall, grinning man, leaning against one of the tent supports.

"Or she'll slit your throat in your sleep," came the reply from behind.

He turned to see the silver-haired Sondrin placing a brown-stained hand on his shoulder and smiling with malicious intent.

"Enough!" shouted Jem, who now stood beside Chakirris. They only had one chance, and threats wouldn't help. "I will tell you our story, then do as you will."

Chakirris nodded and returned to her seat. Sondrin had vanished.

"There is one thing to know," continued Jem. "Jhakri has returned. He has the power to control human men, to make them do his bidding. He will use them to destroy humans, the alviri, and all of you. He is the embodiment of hate."

There was silence.

"Only women, the alviri and the dalfreni are immune to his power. That is why we ask for your help."

"Are the alviri helping?" asked a woman near the front.

"We hope they will," said Caspin. "Lady Moranne is meeting us here, and hopefully, she has alviri with her."

"Wickona is coming here?" exclaimed Carina. She was leaning on a support post close to the dais and stood statue-straight at the mention of Moranne.

"You know her well?" queried Tiam.

The huntress was already striding from the room. "Know her?" she snapped without looking back. "How dare she, how dare...."

Tiam, Jem and Caspin exchanged puzzled looks.

"Do they have a history?" whispered Caspin to the brothel owner, but Mylten simply shrugged.

"So we need your help!" shouted Jem, aware that they needed to push the crowd.

There was much mumbling and chatter but no whoops of support or pledges of allegiance. Some said it wasn't their fight, and many were scathing of the prejudiced humans, but one name seemed to bubble above the muttering; the militia.

Caspin turned to the merchants, but they were already shaking their heads.

"We can't spare them," said one.

"We need the militia for protection," said another.

"From the oni?" asked Caspin.

Mylten's gaze pointed outwards to the assembly.

Jem looked at the unruly crowd of fishers, carpenters, market traders, tinkers and others scraping an existence in the streets. They were poor, hungry and lacking hope. *Desperate people do desperate things*, like invading Tudorfeld.

"They fear their people," said Tiam.

No hands went up in the crowd, and no one stood. The dalfreni of Suncin might have little to lose, but they also had nothing to gain. Caspin slumped into a seat, and Tiam slowly sank to his side, leaving Jem alone on the stage with his arms outstretched.

There were moments when Jem felt a heavy weight on his shoulders; the entire mission somehow hinged on these moments. He could almost see a future where the choice would be his to make.

As he gazed at the pale faces, he noticed a nearby knocking sound. It was getting louder, and some of the dalfreni also noticed. They turned where they sat, and Jem surveyed the hall, but no one could see. Eventually, it became so loud that the commotion stopped, and all eyes seemed to be on a spot in the middle of the crowd.

A dark-haired, dalfreni man looked down while he mashed the end of a long staff into the floorboards. He looked up only when he had the full attention of the gathering and slowly rose to his feet, letting the smooth staff slide through his fingers.

"I will fight with you," he declared in a soft, mellow voice like the rumble of distant thunder.

His long dark hair was platted into three tails. The widest ran down the back of his dark blue robe, which was patterned with golden scrolls, while the smaller ones draped either side of his long face. His skin was unblemished, while his eyes were dark, thin, and sharp.

"You're too valuable," insisted Mylten.

The dalfreni man didn't flinch. "I make my own way," he said flatly. "I resign my position."

There was panic on the stage; merchants started shouting over each other while Mylten attempted to establish order.

"What is your name?" asked Caspin, trying to shout over the melee.

The man let his staff swing outwards so that his robe parted, revealing a bright white shirt over black leggings and long boots; a short dagger hung on his left hip.

"I am Ostro Vildeen," he proclaimed, bowing slightly. "Former commander of the Suncin militia."

His sharp cheeks puffed into a smile, which Caspin couldn't help returning. "Welcome, friend," he said, holding forth his hand.

⁂

After troubled sleep from the dryad encounters and tragedy in the ranks, Captain Fallon felt it was good to allow the men some relaxation before they pushed onwards to Numolport. Breakfast consisted of humble but filling, seeded pancakes. His men appreciated the honest food.

"Don't go too far," he said gruffly. "I'll count you all before sundown."

He thought of warning them away from the painted ladies but decided to leave them be. It was Slitan who troubled him. Gone were the pithy comments and dark murmurings, replaced by a sullen sentinel, furtively glancing into every alley, viewing every dalfreni with suspicion. He was wound tight, like a bowstring ready to snap; he was dangerous.

The Kelby archer remained still when the others left to wander the streets, so Biorn decided to stay with him. He ordered them both a tankard of mead, but Slitan barely sipped on it and refused to make eye contact.

Biorn leaned back in his chair to think of Nina and how she'd throw her arms about him when he returned. She was the constant in his life and the reason he was here in this stinking place. The sun was still creeping through the clouds, but a westerly chill was blowing through his beard. Slitan would leave them at Numolport; his mind was made.

Both the Cempestre and Biorn's men walked up into the town, following the road from the inn, which curved parallel to the shore. They browsed the traders' cart stalls, brimming with colourful clothes and fine, alviri-style jewellery. They tasted sweet pastries and cured meats. Every stallholder smiled politely, but despair lurked just behind their eyes.

"Where are the green girls?" asked Gron when he realized the dryads hadn't followed.

"Probably seducing the locals," grinned Lunn.

"I trust them," proclaimed Gamin. "They fought hard against the beasts, almost as hard as the wenches." He nodded towards the Cempestre just as Isen examined a silver bracelet on one of the stalls.

"Aye, they're strong," agreed Lunn. "I've never seen the like."

"Ahem!" interrupted Brea, who was following with Ellen.

To her surprise, Lunn stopped and held out his hand.

"I saw you both as we battled the ogres. I'd like to shake you both by the hand."

Expecting some kind of joke, Brea looked at Ellen, but the swordswoman was equally baffled. The two women tentatively offered their hands and shook Lunn's huge, shovel-like hand in bewilderment.

"You're still the clown and hag," he said in his deep baritone, and they all laughed.

"We sound like an inn," replied Ellen.

"So, Mister Boarman," said Brea formally. "When are you going to speak with Isen?"

Gamin flushed red and looked away from the tall oretta. He'd seen her fight, and it was the most impressive sight of his life.

"I'm not worthy," he replied.

Gron put his thick arm around the young archer. "You're a brave lad," he said. "She'd be lucky to have you." Neither noticed Brea striding towards the Cempestre with mischief in her heart.

"Oh, no!" cried Gamin.

It was too late. Cuyler smiled, and Brenna dragged Isen over to where the young bowman stood shaking.

"Right!" said Cuyler. "Brea tells me you want to know if you're worthy of the Cempestre."

"Erm, I didn't—"

"Don't be shy," chirped Brea.

Gamin didn't know where to look. He wanted to gaze at the wondrous Isen, but she scared him.

"Leave the lad alone, you mean bunch," said Ellen.

"I think it's a fair question," added Brenna. "What do you think, Ice?"

It was the first time Gamin had heard her nickname, and he liked it. *Ice Stanhamur*.

Without a smile, she looked him directly in the eyes. Her thick, dark eyebrows and iron jaw made her look fierce, like she was about to lock heads.

"You fought bravely," she said flatly. "You're a good soldier."

Gron elbowed Gamin, and Brenna hugged the tall oretta while the others teased them.

"Why don't we all find a tavern by the lake," said Cuyler.

"Now we're talking," laughed Lunn.

37 SHORE LEAVE

The passage behind was twisty and narrow, with barely enough room for two men to pass. His chest heaved as he caught his breath and looked down at the fetid water trickling down a gully to the lake. He hadn't been seen and wouldn't be missed. Sax looked up towards the thin, tall building between two narrow lanes. The walls converged almost to a point, making it appear like a leaning wedge. The slim wooden chair still stood on the balcony, looking out over the smoke and grime to majestic Banafell beyond, but no eyes would see that view today. Alert to every voice and every whip of wind through the high strung laundry, Sax crept to the narrow entrance and silently slid inside.

A winding stair climbed past the two lower floors and ended in a short landing with a low, arched door. Sax glanced downwards to street level, then gently tapped on the cracked wood.

"I have nothing to steal," creaked a voice from within. It was slow, frail and female, like a late wind through autumn leaves. "It's not locked."

Sax pushed on the door, slowly swinging inwards on worn, wooden hinges, and crept forward into a small, narrow room. The right wall housed two large, rotting doors leading to the balcony, while the left was adorned with shelves of dried food. However, It was a rocking chair at the room's centre that drew Sax's attention.

The human woman's long grey hair cascaded untidily over her shoulders and covered her cream blouse. It wafted back and forth as she rocked, uncovering glimpses of her lined, weathered face. Her eyes were milky white and darted left and right as if trying to see the man before her.

A smile emerged, revealing the creases around her mouth.

"I knew it was you," she said, bringing the chair to a halt.

Sax said nothing and silently moved closer. Six years ago, she still had some sight, but now it was gone.

"You always sneaked around the house," she continued, "but I always caught you."

He found his hand trembling, afraid to break the moment which transported him back to more innocent days.

"Is Denny looking after you?" he asked, crouching to her level.

Her smile broadened, and she reached out to touch him.

"Don't worry about me," she said. "I'm just glad you're here."

"I can't stay."

Her mouth sagged, and the light slid from her face.

"I'm sorry, mother, I need to get back."

"At least let me *see* you," she pleaded. "Let me hold you."

Reluctantly he leaned forward so she could touch his face. She felt the contours of his chin, the sharpness of his nose and the smoothness of his skin. Her hands were soft, feeling through his hair.

"You've grown so much, I hardly recognize you. But at least this."

She stopped, with her hand cupping his ears. Sax pulled away and stood up.

"What have you done?" she demanded. "What have you—"

"I've got ten silvers here for Denny," he said, interrupting her. "I'll leave them on the side."

"Marin, what have you done?"

"I need to go," said Sax, backing towards the door.

"Don't be ashamed of what you are," she cried.

Her words cut him more than any of his knives. He stopped and fixed her with all the hate which burned deep within.

"I know what I am," he said flatly. "It's my father who was ashamed. Remind me again how long he stood by you."

"He had no choice; you know that."

"I know you always excuse him for leaving us in this scum hole," raged Sax. He hadn't come for a confrontation. It wasn't what he wanted.

"Marin, the hate will eat you!" she begged, almost pushing up from the chair.

He opened the door and looked back as his mother placed a hand on her chest, trying to hold in tears.

"I use that hate daily, so I can do what must be done."

Sax slammed the door and stood on the landing alone once more. Leaving as quietly as he arrived, he stole across the junction and disappeared down a narrow alleyway, heading to the lake.

A pair of bright, brown eyes saw him leave and hurry silently away. The woman seemed to blend into the scenery even though a leather bustier covered her green and orange skin. Sondrin looked up at the balcony where an elderly, blind woman struggled to hold herself upright against the rail. They all had secrets.

The Fell View tavern stood half on the shore and half over the lake, supported on sturdy stilts. It resembled a rough, wooden shed from the front, but the rear overlooking the water opened onto a deck with chairs and tables. The bar was inside, but the wide-open double doors gave the inn an outdoor feel.

Several local fishers sat on tall stools at the bar, but the arrival of the soldiers and Cempestre transformed the sleepy tavern into the barrack's bar. They sat at a long table overlooking the turquoise lake and the steep slopes of the mountains beyond.

"Come sit on my knee," shouted Gron, with Cuyler in his sights.

The archer's sparkling hazel eyes didn't blink.

"Beware, you don't wear an arrow in your back," warned Bresne.

Gron was unbowed. "You need a man to make you smile," he grinned.

"That rules you out," laughed Brenna.

Lunn banged the table, jogging his flagon of mead, so it splashed onto the wood. Even Cuyler broke into the slightest smile before it disappeared in a snap.

The fight with the oni had brought the group closer, although none would discuss the battle or the loss of Cal. Unlikely alliances started forming as their real personalities emerged from tough exteriors.

Brea formed a friendship with Cuyler after the Cempestre saw how well she marshalled the archers against the clan. They also shared a similar background, although the details were too dark to air with the rest. Equal respect had grown between Ellen, Gron and Lunn. They openly called Ellen 'the clown', but she now wore it as a badge of honour. Although Gron's humour was still sexist and risky with the Cempestre, he secretly admired the strong women in their midst.

The closest bond had formed between Oretta Fixen and Captain Fallon. He didn't know if he could ever admit his respect to other ranks, but Biorn's admiration for Bresne had grown dramatically since the skirmish in the forest. She was fast, strong and brave. He was a natural leader who often felt his captaincy was a fraud. When he appeared at the table, a smile and a nod were all they needed.

"Mead for the captain!" boomed Lunn.

A young dalfreni waitress scurried from the bar with a tray of flagons, brimming with the sweet, potent liquor.

"Is there enough to spare?" asked Caspin, emerging through the bar with Tiam, Jem, and a dalfreni man. Chakirris was nowhere to be seen.

"Of course, sir," said Biorn.

They all stood, but Caspin begged them to remain seated.

"As you were," he commanded. "You've earned a day's leave, so please enjoy your time here. I fear we have more challenges ahead of us."

The men banged the table in agreement, and Tiam nodded to her warriors. They would *all* enjoy a day's rest.

"May I present our newest recruit," continued Caspin. "This is Ostro Vildeen. He will be answering directly to me."

The men raised their flagons in salute, and Ostro smiled in return.

Although Slitan had followed Biorn to the bar, he refused to sit with the others. He screwed up his face at the mention of a dalfreni joining them and continued staring into the wall ahead. Dark paths filled his mind with dark, hulking beings and toxic thoughts.

As the waitress bustled out to them once more, with copper flagons clanking, Jem found himself standing at the head of the table with his drink in hand. He'd seen death in his dreams many times. The lone knight at the hand of Corvus, crofters, killed by a Jakari, and Aludra beneath a torrent of raging bodies, but real deaths were weighing on his mind. He wasn't close to Cal, but Davill had been his swordmaster and seeing the bonds emerge around him, it was sad that the men were gone. He could feel the tension through his body, his soul still trying to hold onto each of his new friends. Some would not survive.

Since learning of his gift, Jem avoided touching anyone for fear of seeing a vision of their end. It could be the cruel cut of a blade or the heart-tearing thud of an arrow.

"Before we take the rest of this day to relax, can we take a moment to remember?" he said shakily.

"Speak, lad," replied Biorn solemnly. They all felt the same thing in their hearts.

"To Cal and Davill," he proclaimed. "Part of our mission to the end."

He raised his drink as the others echoed his words and stood to attention. They took a swig and a moment to remember fallen comrades. Even Ostro paid his respects as one warrior to another.

They sank back into their seats, still thinking of the perils ahead, until Gron decided to lighten the mood.

"Anyone for a game of dice?" He fumbled in his pockets and produced two carved bone cubes painted with black dots.

"I'll play," replied Cuyler, to everyone's amazement.

Jem didn't join them and didn't drink as much as the others. He still had too many questions to ask, and now they were filling his head. He wanted to ask Carina how she knew Lady Moranne, and he wanted to ask his mistress many other questions. He knew he had powers but couldn't control them. They ruled him and broke his sleep, sending his mind into a fantasy which could be a deadly portent or a glimpse into the past. *I need answers, ma'am.*

Chakirris knew, but it wasn't her place to tell him.

All species of the fair folk could harness the earth's power, but the dryads derived most of their gifts from trees' energy. Telepathy and prescience allowed them to probe the enemy for weakness or weave a hypnotic spell, luring a man to his doom. Knowledge and cunning had kept Chakirris and her sisters alive when other Deapholt dryads had perished. She was suspicious of their new comrades, but her sisters were openly distrustful.

The dryads eschewed the crowded town and retreated to the forest; they sat in a dense woodland area, almost invisible against the twisted vines and thorny bramble. They ate the raw flesh of a recently killed boar and sipped the clear mountain water from a nearby stream.

"When they have used us, they will kill us," hissed Sondrin.

"They hate our kind," agreed Jilliad.

Chakirris listened intently to her sisters. She, too, had seen humans slaughter her kind, burn them as demons or drown them as witches. This time it seemed different; it felt like a chance. "What would you have me do?" she asked. "Take their men to give us daughters? What then? See our precious offspring dead at the hands of the oni, or fail to find a mate because few humans will come here?"

"It's the only way," replied Jilliad. "We will never be accepted."

"When has a human ever held out the hand of friendship? I say we hear the prince and take a chance."

"You've led us this far," said Sondrin. "I will follow you to the end."

"I, too," agreed Jilliad. "Although it could be *the* end."

The dryad leader sighed and reached out to her sisters. They'd been through so much together, but nothing would break the bond. "I will make you a deal, my loves. If the prince offers us good terms, we will go with them to Numolport; if we don't trust them at that point, we'll take what we need and return here."

Agreed, they chorused without making a sound.

The second day in Suncin was much like the first. Sax had re-joined the men but said nothing. Caspin tried again to find warriors to join them but to no avail.

The morning began with a winter chill, and grey clouds were bubbling towards them from the west. Winter would soon be knocking on autumn's door, and they needed to be on their way. None of this bothered the men and Cempestre women, who enjoyed the rest, but Caspin was nervous. The soldier within longed to fight; the leader worried their force was too small. He tried to find Carina, but no one had seen the huntress, and Ostro couldn't persuade fellow militiamen to join them. They needed to leave, but Moranne was still absent. Without her, they were lost.

Absent, too, were the dryads, but Jem assured Caspin they were still around. Chakirris had startled him while he took breakfast when her words burst into his mind. *We wait for the prince,* she said, with no clue of their whereabouts.

The youngest Linhold brother sat on the main quay, watching the fishing boats come and go through the thin mist hanging above the surface.

"May I join you?" asked Oretta Gunborg, sinking to his side to let her legs dangle over the water.

"I fear the Stans are already invading and I'm sitting here waiting," said Caspin solemnly.

"I feel the same way," she agreed. "Fighting covers the things I wish to forget."

He looked over and noticed the green ivy tattoo that spiralled around her arm until it hung from the interlocking hoops below her shoulders. She was attractive when she smiled. Small creases emerged near her mouth and forehead, betraying her age and spirit.

Caspin never forgot he was number two to Torbrand's magnificence. With the sword, on horseback or with the ladies, Caspin's brother surpassed him in all things and his father never tired of telling him so. "Do you know my family sees me as a disappointment? My brother is everything I'm not. I'm only a knight because my father called in favours."

"You have a job to do, sir," Brenna chided him. "Do your job. Let others worry about nothing."

He laughed at her clarity and followed the scar on her face, which disappeared under her long dark hair. He'd not been with a woman since the last Faircester Ball when his mother tried to pair him with a succession of dizzy suitors.

"You're right," he replied, putting his hand down so that it covered her own.

She pulled away quickly and shot to her feet.

"I, er, need to return to the others," she stuttered.

Nodding curtly, Brenna rushed away.

"I'm sorry," said Caspin, but she was already striding from the dock.

Captain Fallon found the knight gazing into the water as the sun faded. Together they strode back towards the brothel, with the last orange hues of the day, on their backs.

38 PORRIMA

The wind blasted the cliff, flattening the grass so that it rippled over the ridge like a den of snakes. The smell of ocean spray was thick in the air, mingling with the mist of rain that fell from clouds, billowing over the land like a moving blanket.

A tall figure stood facing the wind, wearing a blood-red cloak that swirled and bucked. A mighty gust tore the hood away, exposing the dark, flowing hair of a middle-aged woman with the appearance of a Jakari. Her face was stone against the wind. Tears were lost in the rain, which clung to her smooth skin, glistening in the half-light, as her green eyes fixed on a nowhere point, far beyond the clouds. Her face was chiselled like Moranne's, but the faint lines at the corner of her mouth betrayed her playful nature.

The sceptre in her right hand pulsed slowly with a dull green light, blurred by the whipping rain. She was cold and scared, but her will was resolute. Opening the cloak, she revealed a matching red dress billowing in the gale, showing lithe legs that were sculpted and muscular.

She looked down at the sceptre, which glowed brighter, but something made her look back toward the rising hill. A figure dressed in black was running down the hill and screaming into the wind. The figure stumbled and fell, rolling in a sodden cloak, then running again until the words could cut through the maelstrom.

"Porrima!" she yelled. "Stop! Let me help you."

I don't blame you, thought Porrima, *but you can't help me*.

The cloaked woman finally drew close and threw back her hood, revealing the high cheekbones and smooth, tan skin of Lady Moranne. Her eyes sparkled green as she looked up and stared into Porrima's dark soul.

"I'm sorry," she said. "We all loved him; he was so gentle."

"And too trusting," added Porrima.

Moranne held out her arms, but Porrima moved back towards the cliff edge. "Come with me," she pleaded. "We can fight him together."

"You'll kill him?"

"We'll stop him."

Porrima's eyes narrowed, looking into her old friend's heart. Moranne brought them here, saved their lives and fought for a life worth living, but these simple creatures could never understand a life eternal.

"No," said Porrima flatly. "My path is ending."

"It doesn't need to be that way. We can rebuild, start anew," begged Moranne.

Porrima was already shaking her head. "Sheratan was my world. I have nothing left."

"Please!" gasped Moranne.

Porrima was already raising the sceptre, holding the flashing orb against her chest.

"Goodbye, Elara."

She took a deep breath and screamed out with all her might. The end of the sceptre fizzed with energy, and then a massive bolt of green lightning arced from the tip, ripping through Porrima's chest and into the earth behind. She stood for a moment in a rictus of pain, then crumpled to the ground, dropping the sceptre, which rolled to Moranne's feet.

Moranne looked down at the silver rod and watched the green light at its tip slowly fade and extinguish. Her tears were lost in the storm.

"Porrima, no!" cried Jem.

The room was empty. Jem's eyes scanned the bare timber walls of the brothel chamber and looked to the window, where the sky was pitch black, and stars still twinkled between the gathering clouds. *Moranne is Elara, or Elara is Moranne?* he thought. His mind was too cloudy to think straight, and he returned to a stormy sleep of further questions.

❦

Carina's home was just inside the stockade wall and formed mainly by a cave in an outcrop of granite rock. The cave section at the back formed the bedchamber and main living area, while a wooden frontage included two windows and a narrow porch. It was one of the oldest dwellings in Suncin, and she'd always resented needing help to buy it.

Caspin's news had upset her balance, and she hadn't been sleeping well. She lay in the rough, straw bed, looking up at the grey cave roof illuminated by a low flickering candle. Sometimes she wanted to flee far from here in any direction, to know wide-open oceans, green rolling plains and the valleys between distant mountains. The daily toil in this cramped, dirty town was all she knew. She hated it.

Someone was outside. Carina sat up, pulled on her clothes and grabbed the hunting knife she kept stashed by the bed. Her alviri side provided excellent intuition; as with Caspin's men in the forest, she could feel events before they happened.

Three short knocks echoed around the cave walls and shook the door's hinges in its frame. Carina knew that knock. The weight of it, the style and the hand which made it. She pictured the person standing outside and shuddered.

Although she knew the identity, something still made her reach for the handle and tug it open.

"Hello, Carina," said Moranne, standing alone on the porch.

They watched each other warily until Carina broke the silence, mustering as much venom as she could in her tired state.

"What do you want?"

"We need to talk," replied Moranne in a conciliatory tone.

Carina was still angry and unwilling to allow her mood to drop. "I have nothing to say to you," she spat.

"Corvus is coming—"

"What of it?"

Moranne sighed. Her list of mistakes was long, and she couldn't begin to atone for all she'd done, but Carina must be made aware.

"You're in great danger here," she argued. "You don't understand."

"I can look after myself," said Carina, closing the door.

Moranne quickly shoved her boot in the gap and pushed the door open.

"You don't know him as I do. To get to you, he'll kill every person here and raze the town to the ground."

"And why will he come after me?" she said, placing her arm across the doorway like a bar.

"If he can't get to me, he'll kill my daughter."

Carina wearily shook her head and walked back into the cave, leaving the door open behind her. She sat on one of two small wooden chairs under a table made from packing crates and pulled a jug of wine towards her.

Her mother watched the young girl in her lonely, humble life and pangs of regret welled in her stomach.

"Why should I believe you?" hurled Carina.

Moranne slowly entered the room and stood near the window.

"It's the truth—"

"Truth?" she retorted. "Everything you say is a lie; every time you speak, it's more lies."

"I've never lied to you," said Moranne meekly.

"Then who is my father?" she spat.

The lights of Suncin flickered in the darkness, shadowed by the local folk and serenaded by the bawdy sound of the nearby brothel. Moranne looked out into the night and tried to hold back the tears.

"You know I can't tell you," she said finally.

"Liar!" shouted Carina, thumping the table with such force that a small bowl tumbled to the ground and smashed on the cave floor. "Where do you go when you leave me for years? Who is my father? Who in Juldra's name are you?"

"I'm your mother," she replied, almost whispering.

"My mother?" Carina lifted the jug and poured herself a mug of bitter, elderflower and nettle wine. "I have no mother."

Moranne pulled out the second chair and sat with her hands clasped over the table. Carina poured her a glass of wine without a word.

"I'm sorry, my love; you're right. I've failed you."

Carina stared into her mug. She'd told her mother never to return when they last spoke, many years ago, tired of the half-truths and secrets. She wanted to be free of this place, to wander the lands and never think again of her torrid childhood.

"Before I leave," continued Moranne, "would you allow me to give you just one truth, which might help you understand?"

"Why not?" snorted Carina. "What's another lie on a bed of lies?"

The mug was cold in Moranne's hand as she brought it to her lips and took a sip of the dry, bitter liquid. It left a sour taste, symbolising the broken trust between a mother and daughter. She fingered the sceptre beneath her cloak, wishing her powers could turn back time. A tiny Carina played with a cooper's hoop, running down the bank to the lake, gambolling into the water. She jumped up and ran to Moranne with her arms outstretched and love in her heart.

"Corvus is the most powerful of his kind," began Moranne. "He can see far through the eyes of beasts and birds, and he can see into the minds of the weak. I have the power to withstand his gaze, but you do not."

Carina continued to sip from her mug, giving no indication that she was listening. Moranne continued.

"If I tell you the truth about my life and your father..." she began, letting the hypothesis hang in the air. "Corvus will kill everyone I care about; he will kill your father, his wife, and his children. He'll destroy Alfheim and Suncin and burn Deapholt to the ground."

Carina finally lifted her head and locked Moranne's brown eyes in her gaze.

"Why does he hate you so much?"

Moranne sighed and leaned back in her chair, trying to straighten her weary back.

"With my two best friends, Aludra and Rana, we took his power and defeated him. They paid the ultimate price, and I stand vigil, guarding against his return."

"He was captured?"

"He escaped," said Moranne, hanging her head in regret.

"So if he's coming for me," wondered Carina. "What can I do?"

Moranne reached across the table and took her hand, holding it tightly even as Carina tried to pull away.

"Come with me," she said. "I'll answer all your questions, tell you every secret, and...."

"And what?" prompted Carina.

Moranne seemed to be thinking of something long forgotten. "...I'll give you your birthright," she said, her voice dropping to a whisper.

"What birthright?"

Deep within a second hidden pocket, two slightly dull metal rods were wrapped in a rotting leather square. Moranne freed one rod from its bind and placed it on the table in front of her daughter. It was stained in places, and some of the shine had receded, but the crystal sphere was unmarked.

"Your sceptre," said Carina.

Moranne shook her head. "It belonged to a good friend of mine. Now it's yours."

Carina gazed at the tarnished surface and remembered all the times she'd seen her mother wield its power. She reached out but dared not touch it. Her hand hovered over the rod as if it might reach out and sting.

"Take it," urged her mother. "It won't hurt you."

Gingerly Carina's hand clasped the metal and found it warm to the touch. A gentle fizzing sensation made her fingers tingle as the sceptre started to pull its power through her. She gently lifted it from the table and found it almost weightless.

"What metal is this?" she asked.

Moranne smiled. It was made of a material not found in *these* lands.

"Each of us has several gifts, like your power of sight. The sceptre can increase that power and also reveal new powers, like the ability to smite your enemies with the flare."

As she continued to hold her new prize, Carina noticed the room seemed to change. The moth's flight around the candle had slowed; she could see every sweep of its wings in fine detail. The wall's texture revealed itself as all the fine cracks and blemishes stood out like giant canyons. She almost dropped the sceptre when she turned back to face her mother.

Moranne's body pulsed in a green halo which danced above her, like the firefly's glow through an evening mist.

"Moments become hours, and hours become days," said Moranne. "You can use this ability to target your enemies effectively."

"How do I use it?" asked Carina, becoming excited.

It was the first time in many years that mother and daughter had shared a moment that wasn't punctuated by shouting and tears. Moranne smiled, looking at her daughter as if she was that pretty eight-year-old playing on the lakeshore.

"Be careful, my dear. Emotions govern the amount of energy released. If you release too much energy, you could pass out; it could be many hours before you have the strength to use it again."

"Show me."

High on the creaking balcony of a brothel in the centre of town, a lone dalfreni girl snuffed out the oil lamps one by one. It was a nightly ritual when the customers had left, and she could relax for the remaining dark hours. She blew on the last wick, which extinguished, leaving an orange glow and a waving hand of smoke.

Something glinted in the corner of her eye. She looked out across the rooftops towards the stockade wall. A flash of green light flared in the distance and then disappeared. She continued staring at the same spot, but there was nothing more. Shaking her head with a wry smile, she went inside to rest before her daily routine reset for the new day.

39 THE FAY LEGION

His mind floated in the mid-space between sleep and reality, where the echoes of his dreams still played like disparate fragments of a story. Porrima stood on the cliff tops while the wind swirled about her, and Elara, or Moranne, cried in vain. A distant thudding began and seemed to draw nearer. Like the tramp of oni boots on the Deap Path, it grew to a cacophony that finally ended in a mighty crash.

Jem sat up in bed with his heart beating so hard it made his body shake. He looked up to see a smiling Hayden standing near the door. "Do you ever knock?" he yelled, clutching his chest.

"Never!" joked Hayden.

Jem climbed wearily to his feet, but Hayden was already launching himself at the Burlander.

"I have so much to tell you," he gushed, as they embraced. "Alfheim is beautiful; I could stay there forever."

"Did you meet a handsome alviri?" joked Jem.

"Maybe."

Moranne's party had arrived late the previous night, and they'd been given lodgings in a merchant's house near the gate. The journey from Alfheim had been uneventful, and they were in good spirits, despite failing to persuade the alviri to help them.

"And have you had any adventures?" asked Hayden, grinning.

"We've been joined by a group of strange forest creatures called dryads," said Jem, "*and* we encountered the oni."

"What are they like?"

"They're the largest, most fearsome beasts you'll ever see," he replied solemnly, shaking his head.

Hayden placed a hand on his friend's shoulder, and they sat together on the rough bedding.

"Cal's dead," said Jem.

Mixed emotions swirled in Hayden's mind. Cal and Slitan's bullying had made the forest a miserable place, but he would never wish death on anyone.

"I'm sorry," he said, "I sometimes forget we're soldiers. How's Slitan taking it?"

"Very badly. He's barely spoken, and I think Biorn will leave him in Numolport."

"That'll certainly make my life easier," sighed Hayden.

He wanted to spend time telling Jem about his adventures in Alfheim, but Captain Fallon was rousing the troops, yelling orders up the stairs. "Everyone up. We'll meet on the shore in ten minutes."

Hayden looked out the window at the grimy town beyond the boardwalk. The contrast with Alfheim couldn't be more stark. It was little wonder that the dalfreni had such a dim view of their island cousins.

"I'll see you and your new tan at the shore," laughed Jem. "Now get out!"

Hayden hurried out of the room, chuckling as he careered down the staircase. It would be good to have the whole mission together once more, thought Jem; he quickly pulled on his leather armour and hurried to meet the others. He met Lunn and Gron on the boardwalk, and together they marched towards the muddy shoreline.

On the other side of town, in one of the few stone dwellings, another member of the mission awoke from a deep sleep. Sir Caspin was more restrained than the boisterous Hayden when he knocked on Prince Asger's door and waited respectfully for the prince to rise.

The prince's room was on the ground floor of a local moneylender's plush home. It wouldn't have been Asger's first choice, but they were exhausted when they arrived on the cusp of nightfall. He was coping much better with the terrain than even *he* thought possible, and he loved being away from the stuffy chambers of Cynstol. His father would never allow him to leave the castle for fear people would laugh at his disabled son. The monarchy was all about appearances. Not once did his father spend time with his subjects or venture much further than the stately homes of Tudorfeld.

"How dare wake me," he joked, making his way into the expansive lounge.

He refused any help in dressing or negotiating doors. His old advisor, Sir Annarr, would rush to his aid, but his mother taught him to stand on his own. "You can do anything," she would always say, "It will just take you a little longer."

The assembly all rose as he entered, but he gestured for them to sit as he manoeuvred into a tall chair laden with velvet cushions.

Moranne, Sir Torbrand, Sir Caspin, and Oretta Brimwulf were all present, along with the robed figure of Borgend, the moneylender. One other figure was also present, but the prince didn't notice her at first. She seemed to emerge from the shadows and preferred to stand. His eyes followed her shape from her slick brown and green hair across her face's green hue, her ivy arms, and the enchanted forest of her midriff and legs.

"Your Highness," said Caspin stiffly. "I present Chakirris of the forest folk."

She walked gracefully to stand in front of the prince. Every step was carefully placed and seemed to cause her whole body to bend like a blade of grass in the wind. Her gaze locked onto his and peered into his soul. There was no curtsey, bow, or any other formal acknowledgement.

Caspin eventually broke the awkward silence. "Chakirris and her two sisters helped us fight the oni in the forest. More of us would have died without their bravery."

Prince Asger's smile could sometimes be involuntary as he struggled to form his words, but the look he gave this beautiful creature was genuine. "Thank you," he said and was rewarded by the slightest nod and the first flicker of recognition in her deep brown eyes.

Sir Caspin cleared his throat and tried to assemble a narrative in his mind which might sound plausible. "We proposed a deal with the dryads," he said, shakily. He then described how they'd met the three nymphs and proposed a pact where they would join the Stanholm mission. "It's at your pleasure, Your Highness," he said. "We didn't know what else to do."

The prince pondered Caspin's words and was about to speak when Chakirris finally broke her silence.

"What is your malady?" she asked bluntly.

Caspin was horrified, but Moranne chuckled at the dryad's lack of deference.

The prince was unfazed. Most people assumed he was simple, but Chakirris knew it was merely a physical disability.

"Palsy," he answered simply.

Without even a flicker of recognition, she held out her hand while staring deep into his eyes. "Take my hand," she commanded.

"My liege!" protested Caspin, jumping to his feet.

Asger gestured for him to wait; he reached out and took Chakirris' mottled hand. It was smooth, soft and warm. Warmth spread up his arm and through his body, igniting a tingling sensation on his skin. The tightness in some muscles eased, and a sense of calm flooded his body.

After a short while, Chakirris blinked and released him. "We accept," she said abruptly.

"Accept what?" he retorted, trying to understand what had just occurred.

She bowed curtly for the first time and acknowledged the puzzled faces in the room.

"Your word," she stated, finally taking a seat near Sir Torbrand.

The prince watched every turn of Chakirris' body, from toned legs to gently curving chest. The eurythmic proportions were captivating. *You're the most beautiful thing I've ever seen*, he thought.

Torbrand, Moranne and Tiam discussed the journey ahead, but Asger couldn't take his eyes off the woodland nymph. She seemed to be listening but then slowly turned her head and gave him the first genuine smile. *Thank you,* rang through his head like a spell. His heart skipped. Entering his thoughts would breach royal etiquette, but he was excited.

Can you read my thoughts? he formed the question in his mind.

We are bound, she answered.

Her voice had a dream-like quality which made him want to recline and close his eyes.

"What do you think, Your Highness?" interrupted Torbrand.

"About?" stammered the prince, pulling himself back to the present.

"We have two recruits," added Moranne, "and I believe that's the best we can do. We plan to leave immediately."

He looked around the room at the expectant faces and nodded his agreement. His father had neglected these proud people and the alviri of Alfheim. It was a vain hope that they would offer their lives to protect those who persecuted them. When he returned home, he resolved to use every ounce of his power to help the fair folk.

∽

The soldiers and Cempestre assembled on the shore under Captain Fallon and Oretta Fixen. They returned to the same large tavern for breakfast before Biorn marched them through the town towards the gate.

There were warm embraces between the Cempestre, especially Cuyler and Yuka, who were rarely separated. Slitan eyed the pair with disdain, still seething with a deep hatred of all around him.

"Unnatural," he mumbled under his breath.

The usually calm Yuka clenched her fists and readied herself to confront the bowman when Cuyler stayed her hand. "We lost Cal," she whispered. "They were friends."

"We've all lost someone," retorted Yuka. "He has a dark heart that will get us all killed."

Her eyebrows slanted into a frown as she stared at Slitan, but his eyes were down, tracing the cracks in the rough road.

"Anyway, forget him," she continued. "I want to know all about the battle."

Cuyler told Yuka how they'd come across the oni and engaged them at the junction. Isen had been fearless, killing two massive brutes herself, and then the dryads and dalfreni had come to their aid.

"What of the others?" asked Yuka.

"They are all brave souls," said Cuyler. "Brea is an exceptional archer, but the captain is most impressive. He tackled a warlord on his own."

"I should have been there. Alfheim was a waste of time."

"I didn't expect them to help," Cuyler sighed.

"Neither did I," agreed Yuka. "But there was more. There was bad blood between Wickona and the high lord."

"Any idea of the cause?"

"No, but Lady Etherin wouldn't see us and even tried to get us thrown off the island."

After two days of rest in Suncin or on the beaches of Veorn, most of the company was in better spirits. The sky grew dull with thickening grey clouds, but they arrived at the town gates in good cheer. The mission leaders were all present, along with the dryads, Ostro, Carina and the fully laden pack ponies.

"Good to see you all once more," shouted Moranne as they approached. "I trust you're well-rested and ready for the push to Numolport."

There were smiles and nods from most of the throng, but Slitan scowled and kicked a pile of stones into the stockade wall.

"I should announce some new mission members," added Sir Caspin. "Please welcome the forest folk; Chakirris, Sondrin and Jilliad. We owe them greatly for their help with the oni. Please also welcome our new dalfreni friends, Carina and Ostro."

Jem was the first to step forward, offering his hand, but the others followed suit. They all embraced their new comrades, except for Slitan, who pulled away when Ostro tried to shake his hand.

"I didn't come this far to join the Fay Legion," he cursed. "Keep your dirty elf hands to yourself."

Ostro shrugged in resignation, but Brea was laughing heartily.

"Fay Legion!" she cried. "That name's perfect."

Before Torbrand could intervene, she ran before him and marshalled the company.

"All those in favour of calling us the *Fay Legion,* say aye!"

The dryads were bemused, but the others cried *aye* so loudly that many of the locals stopped to see what was happening.

"Great," grimaced Torbrand.

Moranne was laughing. "Cheer up; it could have been worse."

Slitan didn't react, continuing to look away from his new comrades. His mind was dark, filled with evil thoughts and chilling designs. The Pillars of Freanism were just a prop to support his hatred. He could hear the familiar knocking behind the door pulsing through his head. They would all pay, one by one.

Yuka and Sefti were surprised by the camaraderie between the men and the other Cempestre; the fight against the oni and two days in Suncin had sealed a mutual bond. Gamin still stole secret glimpses of Isen's rugged frame, but the hefty axe-wielder no longer scowled in derision. She turned to Sefti and smiled when she noticed Gamin looking away quickly.

"Is there a tale to tell?" asked Sefti.

Isen shook her head. "He's brave, but just a boy," she maintained.

Secretly she'd grown fond of the slight archer. None of the Cempestre lads had ever looked at her that way, but he was too timid for her, too slight to be a Cempestre man.

Jem watched the men and women smiling and joking together. When the mission started at the barracks in Cynstol, he couldn't believe that the rough soldiers would ever form friendships with *fighting wenches* and *evil elves*. He saw Yuka and Cuyler holding hands and thought once more of the love between Rana and Aludra. The painful image of her sinking under the bodies in Grenborg always surfaced whenever he thought of the strange women from Moranne's hidden past.

He shook the thoughts from his head and found the dalfreni girl standing in front of him, with her hand outstretched.

"I'm Carina," she said politely.

Most dalfreni looked like eastern humans, except for the ears; however, Carina had a darker look, similar to Moranne. Her wavy dark hair was marbled with sections of white, which cascaded to her shoulders, parting where her pointed ears emerged. The smile emphasised her high cheekbones, and something in her green eyes seemed familiar.

Jem reached out and took her hand, but as he clasped it, a jolt of power pulled his hand to hers, locking them together. The pulse of energy coursed through his muscles, jolting them into spasms. A bright light burst into his mind and yanked his consciousness from his body.

Trying to fight it led to searing pain, so he relaxed and allowed his mind to reel. Jem's vision blurred and Carina's face melted before his eyes. Something was lifting him; Suncin receded beneath him. Jem's vision was thrown southwards, brushing the treetops of Deapholt before skimming low over clear water.

His sight focused on a bright dot coalescing into a gleaming, tall villa perched high on imposing cliffs. The force didn't stop. It yanked at him, dragging him further towards a small arched window that looked out onto the beach. The vision pawed and tugged him through the glass; he felt dizzy as he was thrown around the room until the picture steadied.

The room was simple, with two small arched windows and two wooden chairs, but at the centre, on a simple plinth, was a baby's cradle. Made from woven birch twigs, the crib was deep and lined with sheep's skin.

Jem's sight looked over the high sides and down into the bright green eyes of a newborn baby. It had a small tuft of dark hair, a few strands of white, and the fair folk's slightly pointed ears. Baby Carina giggled, almost as if she could see Jem looking down at her. An argument behind the door drowned out the gurgling voice.

"You can't bring her here," said a strong male voice. "She must go to the lake."

There was no reply, but a woman was sobbing.

"I'm sorry, but she'll never be mine," continued the man.

A blinding flash seared Jem's vision, but gradually the dowdy colours of Suncin seeped back across his eyes until he could see the ashen face of Carina, staring at him, open-mouthed.

"What are you?" she said shakily. "What have I seen?"

Becoming more familiar with his gift, Jem didn't hesitate.

"I have the sight," he said, "but I don't know what happened to you."

"The man's voice. I need to see him," she pleaded.

Jem wanted to help her, but he couldn't focus his visions.

"I'm sorry, but that's all I saw."

Her eyes searched him for a moment until a fragment of truth filtered into her mind. The tears were her mother's but the voice? Moranne had promised to reveal the whole story at the journey's end, but the price was patience and silence regarding her true identity.

"Please tell me if you see anything else," she said humbly.

Jem nodded in agreement.

Carina studied the visage of Suncin for one last time. It had been her home for three hundred years, and with luck, she'd never return to the cursed town. Its smoke, noise and putrid stench were familiar, but the cruel poverty and barricade walls made it a prison to cage her spirit. Her essence would fly far from here, at her mother's side. She *would* know the truth.

The town gates were pulled open by a pair of fell-looking horses. The cracked wood doors creaked wide, exposing the dark, ivy-infested forest beyond. For many, it would be dark and full of foreboding, but for Carina, Ostro and the dryads, it was home.

As Jem stepped onto the Deap Path once more, a solitary raindrop hit his cheek. He looked up into the swelling, dark clouds and felt a tremor through his heart. A shiver caused him to rub his arms, but it was an uneasy feeling that worried him. Something was out there waiting for them.

40 RAIN

In a blur of red fur, the tiny squirrel leapt from tree to tree and scampered up the long oak branches. It scurried over twisting vines and ducked under crossing boughs, with its bushed tail bobbing for balance. Bright eyes were fixed on its quarry, but it was no tree of nuts or tempting seeds. The burning green eyes followed a group of humanoid shapes tramping along the path below. They would be easy meat for dark friends further north.

"Sir, we've found something."

The voice invaded the squirrel's tiny brain, and it lost focus. How had it come to this place; why was it here?

"Sir," pleaded the same voice once more, and the bond was lost.

Frightened and bewildered, the little rodent darted into the canopy and disappeared beneath the leaves.

Corvus opened his eyes slowly and deliberately. The bright green light dimmed, but it still flickered in his peripheral vision. He stood on an outcrop of rock, looking across the ocean to the gathering storm above Grenfold. Beginning as a swirling maelstrom in the west, the clouds had converged over Tudorfeld, and now they readied to spill their power. It had taken three hours of concentration to find a creature near Moranne's party and all his strength to steer his puppet to follow them. He looked down at the sceptre in his hand and squeezed it in irritation.

"Captain Kimberlite, I said I wasn't to be disturbed," he sneered, turning gradually to face the two soldiers, standing to attention.

They both wore leather armour and high gleaming helms engraved with the sign of a cut diamond.

"I thought—" began the captain.

His words faded, even as they echoed in his head. He looked down to see his hand reaching for the dagger hanging in a short scabbard on his left. His fingers slowly grasped the hilt, gradually drew it from the sheath, and pointed it towards Corvus' heart.

Words wouldn't come, and he couldn't stay his limbs. His hand slowly rotated the blade until it was aimed toward his own chest. He tried to cry out and beg for mercy, but Corvus was grinning a wide, sickening smile, savouring every moment.

Slowly the dagger moved, inching closer to the soldier's chest until the tip met his thick leather breastplate. Corvus' smile broadened to an impossible width, and he winked his malice. The knife continued to move as Captain Kimberlite drove his dagger slowly into his own body. There was no scream or pain while Corvus held utter control over the blade.

Captain Kimberlite's soul could only watch in horror as his heart pumped its last drop of blood, oozing down the blade and staining the leather. His life was gone, and the bond was broken. He slumped to the ground.

Corvus rubbed his hands as if shaking off the trail dust and turned to the other soldier, visibly shaking.

"Now, what have you found, *Captain* Arkose?" he said, grinning.

The newly-promoted captain looked down at his former leader and gulped. Kimberlite was a good man; the king had brought them in league with the darkness.

"I'm waiting," said Corvus. "You don't want to keep me waiting."

"We've found the entrance," blurted Arkose.

With an eyebrow raised and a wry smile, Corvus looked back towards Grenfold, where the weak humans scurried through the forest.

"Show me."

Throughout the morning, they could hear the rain pattering on the canopy above, but it ran down the leaves and gathered in small pools until it became too heavy. It fell in large, heavy globules which hit a body with the weight of a stone.

"My axe is rusting," huffed Lunn.

"I think my bones are rusting," chimed Gron.

The Deap Path, north of Suncin, was little used; it was narrow and crisscrossed with brambles and ivy slowing their progress. Stopping to hack and slash their way through was wet, tiring work, sapping both strength and will.

"We can't camp here," said Moranne. "This area is full of clan-hunting parties."

"Hmm," nodded Torbrand, "but at this rate, we won't break the forest by nightfall."

Captain Fallon bellowed his orders to the sodden unit, but they were already working as hard as they could. Biorn slashed at the thick bushes with Jem, Sax, Brenna, Sefti and Ellen while Hayden and the archers carried the dripping debris away. The rain strengthened as if the forest gods tried to slow them down and imprison them in its barbed embrace.

"Great!" grumbled Hayden, tossing more dripping ivy on the side of the road.

The rest could only watch as the rain dripped down their sullen faces. The path was too narrow for them to all work. Frustration was mounting, but the sight of Jem and Sax's whirling blades was a wonder.

Carina stood with Ostro watching *Knives* Stulor at work. He'd been avoiding eye contact with her or the militiaman; he kept to the periphery when they were on the move.

"Do you think they know?" whispered Ostro.

Carina looked at the shivering, wet soldiers and the Cempestre with matted, drenched hair.

"They don't see what we see," she replied. "I expect Moranne knows, and possibly the nymphs, but the others?" she shook her head.

It had taken them five hours to journey just eight miles, and they were exhausted. The small streams crossing their path had become gushing torrents; they were wet and caked in mud. The trail was slowly curving westwards towards Tudorfeld, but the trees were still dense and wreathed in shadow.

Jem's soaked leather hung heavy, dragging him down into the sucking mud while Hayden reverted to his grumbling petulance. Only the dryads seemed unaffected, basking in all the elements Juldra threw at them. They skipped over the streams and darted through the sodden undergrowth like leaping deer.

"This is hopeless," sighed Sir Torbrand. "We should have turned back."

"Too late for that," chimed Oretta Brimwulf. She strode just before him, using her katana to sever the vines hanging in their faces.

"We must at least make the edge of the forest," shouted Moranne.

Bresne was shaking her head. "It's too far; we're in the jaws of the storm now."

Prince Asger wishing he could help, sat astride his mount. At times like these, he felt dependent and longed to be of service. The queen would tell him that "every man has his moment," but he saw the men scrabbling in the mud and wanted to rush to their aid.

"The men have maybe an hour's march left, but then we'll have to make camp," said Biorn.

The others agreed, but there would be no comfortable resting places in this torrent. They needed a small clearing with just enough trees to hang the tents, but the thirty-strong mission was challenging to accommodate. Some of the men would find little shelter.

Plodding on slowly, they made little further progress and were forced to stop when Caspin collapsed. The tall knight had been faithful to his reputation as one of the men, lugging heavy branches and slashing at the tough bramble while the rain trickled down his back and blurred his vision. Ellen cradled him in her arms as Sir Torbrand rushed to his brother's side.

"That's it," he ordered. "We'll camp here as best we can."

Jem, Gron, Lunn and Brenna were also spent, slumping against trees to sip from their water flasks. The others pulled the linen canvases from the pack ponies and erected the simple tents, hanging a rope between two trees and draping the canvas over. Gamin, Torbrand and the Cempestre made light work, but Hayden couldn't find a suitable place to tie the rope.

One end would appear tight but slip down while he tied the other, and then a gust of wind would take the sodden sheet and whip it into his face. He remembered Bearun forest and how Jem had teased him.

"Curse this place, and curse you!" he screamed, throwing the canvas across the path.

"Do you need some help with that?" It was a strangely familiar voice coming from the trees behind.

Hayden turned to look at the speaker, but it was the piercing green eyes he saw first, shimmering in the rain. They were as bright and sparkling as the last time he saw them on the beaches of Veorn.

"Cierzon!" he cried. "What...how...where?"

The others looked to see the unfamiliar alviri lord standing in their midst and embracing Hayden as a best friend.

"Just what we need," seethed Slitan. "Another elf."

Gada Scirmann felt all his troubles fade like the rain running off his blonde hair as Cierzon's warm heart beat against his chest. *I'm so glad you're here*, he thought.

As am I, came the reply.

Most of the Cempestre recognised Lord Andain, while the others were bemused. However, Moranne's face was darker than the storm above.

"What are *you* doing here?" she jabbed, dispensing with any pleasantries.

He gave her the same cheeky, broad smile as he did that day back in Sannlige.

"Good day, Lady Moranne," he replied, bowing low.

"Enough of that," she snapped back. "Why are you here?"

He leaned forward and held her arm. He could see the green sparks dancing deep within her feline eyes.

"My father is wrong not to help you, so I offer my services. I'm of age, and it's my choice to be here."

"You know your father will be furious."

"Yes," he shrugged. "I left a note; they know where I am."

"And what skills do you have, *elf*?" spat Slitan.

Unfazed, Cierzon bowed low to the miserable archer and gave him an extensive smile. "Well, I know how to pitch a tent," he replied, to laughter from Carina, *and I'm a better shot than a dumb yokel*, he spoke into Hayden's mind.

"Honoured to have you," added Prince Asger.

Cierzon introduced himself to all the company members with strict instructions not to call him *Your Lordship*. When Brea told him they were now to be known as the Fay Legion, he threw back his head and laughed. "Another thing for my father to hate."

The alviri lord was like a force of nature; no rain could quench his enthusiasm nor dent his good humour. He helped Hayden set up his tent, then assisted Jem and the others who could barely lift their limbs.

"I've heard much about you, Gada Poulterer," he said.

Jem could only muster the slimmest smile. His eyes were heavy, but the constant drip of rain on his face was like ticking torture.

"I'm told you have the sight," continued Cierzon. "Very rare in a *human*." He knew exactly what he was saying.

Jem's sight blurred for the merest instant, and he saw the alviri lord standing before a gnarled, twisted tree with grey clouds on the horizon. Fear marked his expression, and he tried to speak, but the vision was too brief, fading into the forest's darkness. The image made no sense. Jem shook it from his mind.

Four tents were pitched on each side of the path. Most of the party shared with three others. Despite his protestations, the prince had a tent to himself, and Slitan shared with Sax.

Hayden bedded down with Cuyler, Yuka, and Cierzon. The two Cempestre women immediately snuggled together. Hayden found himself alone, staring into the alviri's emerald eyes, until sleep and inviting dreams led him away.

The dryads had volunteered to take all the watches that night. They didn't need shelter and were naturally light sleepers. Biorn didn't completely trust them and was about to protest, but he was too tired to argue. The tree nymphs also benefited from good night vision, which was lucky as it was impossible to make a fire. The forest was pitch black, without even the stars to provide a distant light.

The background noise of a million raindrops hitting a million leaves echoed through the forest, but the sound of large droplets hitting the canvas mesmerized Ellen. Staring up at the cover revealed nothing in the darkness. Only the sound of Brea's deep, rasping breath let her know she wasn't alone. She longed to be at Torbrand's side, but the knight was sleeping in the nearest tent with his brother, the captain, and Ostro. He hadn't spoken to her since Suncin, and she knew there was no chance in her heart. "Curses!" she whispered to herself.

The constant drip and patter of rain in muddy puddles had worked its evil spell. The call of nature could be denied no more. Carefully she scrabbled out of the tent and stood in the deluge.

A distant sound caught her attention for a moment. It rose and fell like a battle bugle, then vanished with a low echo. *Just the wind,* she thought, counting her steps away from the tent.

Prince Asger also struggled with sleep; his dreams were full of his disapproving father. He was constantly wincing when the prince struggled to walk in a line or stumbled over his words. Asger knew the stories; he'd heard the castle servants talking often.

His father wanted him left to die when his condition surfaced at three years. Taken out into the wilds and given into Frea's arms. If the rumours were true, his mother saved him when she threatened to kill the king in his sleep should he harm her son. The dreams were always the same, ending when he took his dagger and cut his father's throat.

"What's that?" he exclaimed, waking suddenly.

Even in the black of night, he could see the starry sheen of two brown eyes studying him from the end of the tent.

"Wolves," said Chakirris, pouring the word over him as water covers a stone.

The prince propped himself on his hands and watched as she blinked slowly. A faint shaft of light filtered through from the crescent moon and flashed between the clouds of black.

"Raise others?" he asked.

Chakirris cocked her head as another distant call echoed through the Deap.

"We should be safe," she replied. "They will not attack such a large group."

She crept slowly into the tent without invitation and sat cross-legged at his side. Her scent was like freshly cut grass and the first rains of autumn. Asger found himself reaching out to touch her; she took his hand and clasped it between hers.

"I will protect you," she said

The prince found himself leaning back and returning to sleep, with her warmth coursing through his body.

Jem could see it all as if day were night but from somewhere high in the trees. In black, white and grey hues, he glimpsed the dryads holding station around the tents, Ellen traipsing through the clinging, damp ivy, and another person following the sound of her path.

A wolf howled, much nearer than the last, and Jem could see a large shape in the north. He wanted to shout out, to raise the alarm, but sleep held him prisoner and wouldn't let him leave.

"Oh no," sighed Ellen.

The wolf cries were coming nearer, and she was cold, wet and lost. Spinning desperately, she'd lost her direction and was beginning to panic. Her father appeared in the shadows, wearing the same look of disappointment

Stone and Sceptre

which had haunted her life since he died. He never held her in his arms, touched her, or wiped away her tears.

Maybe he was right, she thought. Married to a soldier, she could have had everything she needed: a cosy home, good clothes and female friends. The pursuit of happiness had only brought her despair and a constant feeling of failure. "Stupid, stupid, stupid," she cried, leaning back against what she thought was a stout tree.

A rough hand slapped her mouth shut and yanked her head back while another brought the cold steel of a blade to her throat. Instinctively she tried to cry out, but the muzzle was too tight, and the blade pulled closer, almost choking her as it drew blood.

"You think you're so clever," spat Slitan, "but you're just a whore like the rest."

She could feel his hot breath on the back of her neck, which turned her stomach. Slowly she reached down towards the hunting knife at her side, but Slitan was wise to her.

"Touch that blade, and I'll slit you right here. Don't make a sound. Don't even breathe."

Slowly he took his hand from her mouth and reached down to remove her knife from its small sheath. Her mind raced, trying to plot an escape, but every route ended in death. She'd welcome that end before she'd let him defile her.

"Sister!" whispered Sondrin, appearing at the end of Prince Asger's tent. The orange glow from her skin and the silver sheen of her hair shone luminously in the sparse light.

Chakirris released the prince's hand and spoke wordlessly to her sister as Asger blinked his eyes open. They conversed for a short while before the green nymph looked back at the prince with real fear in her eyes.

"What?" asked Asger, propping himself up and reaching for his cloak.

She shook her head slowly, struggling to comprehend what Sondrin had told her.

"The wolves," she said slowly. "Five packs are converging on us. It's not right; packs don't hunt together; I don't understand." As if to punctuate her words, a loud howl slowly built in the north, followed by another to the south, and an answer to the east.

"Wake others," commanded the prince.

The howling was so loud that it drowned out the rainfall and tore through the tents like an alarm. The men and women were blundering from their tents, struggling to see anything in the darkness.

A bright green light flashed into existence, and Moranne held her sceptre aloft. It cast its ghoulish light some thirty yards out, leaving a deadly veil of darkness beyond. "Has anyone seen Ellen or Brea?" she shouted.

The party was too busy trying to dress and locate their weapons. The wolves were howling all around them now. What first appeared to be echoes now revealed themselves as many packs coordinating an attack.

"Everyone, stay together!" commanded Biorn.

Tiam marshalled her warriors to form a protective ring, with swords ready and bows straining, while Caspin led Gron and Lunn to take up posts at each end of the path.

"It's Corvus!" yelled Jem. He had no doubt the puppet master was pulling the strings and watching from nearby.

Moranne whirled at him and grabbed his arm.

"You're sure?" she retorted. She knew Jem was right. *Corvus is with us.*

The wolves snarled and whined, circling the camp, looking for a weakness. A twig snapped, and the bushes shook as unseen shapes shot past.

Gamin's bow was taught, and his bow finger was aching, but he dared not lower his guard. He shook so violently that his aim was blurred, and his muscles spasmed. A calming hand took his shoulder and held him still. Oretta Stanhamur looked down at him. She said nothing, but Gamin visibly relaxed under her touch.

There was movement everywhere, with dark shadows flashing around them. Slitan didn't care. He'd pushed Ellen to the ground; he sat astride her with his dagger dangling above her breast and malice in his eyes.

"Slitan, it's not too late. Let me go; let's return to the others," she pleaded.

"Shh!" he gestured, holding his finger to his lips. "You and I are going to become *very* well acquainted."

He slowly moved the blade to her side, where her thick, leather breastplate was laced with thin strips of softer leather. Carefully and deliberately, he cut through the chords so that they popped, revealing a thin white blouse beneath. He laughed and sat up.

"I see you wear virginal colours," he sneered, grinning to reveal his broken tooth. "A strange choice for a whore—"

His words were snatched away in a blur of leaves, splinters and mud as a heavy branch smashed into his head. It sent his lifeless body reeling into the glistening bushes.

Ellen scrambled backwards, expecting a giant wolf to leap from the gloom, but they were familiar weathered hands which grabbed her arm and pulled her upwards.

"Come on, love!" yelled Brea.

Ellen wanted to throw her arms around Brea and sob into her hunting leather, but the snarling, howling beasts were all around and closing in. She pulled out her sword and blundered after her friend, who seemed to know where she was going. The mud sucked at her boots, and dripping ivy whipped at her legs, but Ellen barrelled onwards towards a flickering green glow. With every step, there was sound until she could make out the footfall of something running towards them at speed.

She looked back just in time as a vast, slavering, black wolf burst through the undergrowth. Its eyes burned green, and its jaws snapped in readiness for her flesh. With Brea stumbling behind, Ellen arched backwards to avoid the razor teeth and threw up her sword, decapitating the rabid creature in a single movement.

"Run!" she screamed, not waiting to see the carcass fall. The bushes beyond were moving as if possessed.

Dark shapes crossed their path ahead or flashed behind the trees, but they didn't stop running. Soon they could hear shouting and the voice of Captain Fallon trying to maintain order.

"Don't let them in!" he bawled as Brea and Ellen burst through the undergrowth and onto the path.

Without thinking for a second, Sir Torbrand grabbed Ellen by the shoulders and stared in relief.

"Are you alright?" he cried.

She was unaware of the broad streak of wolf blood covering half her face or the mud caking her back and leggings. *I am now*, she thought, too terrified to answer.

Arrows were already flying at fleeting shadows, and Lunn was whirling his axe in readiness when Moranne called on the archers.

"Keep a lookout for any birds or beasts in the trees above. It doesn't matter how small the creature. If it moves, kill it."

Tiam ordered Cuyler and Yuka into the centre, protected by Sefti, as the archers scanned the branches for anything moving, anything controlled by Corvus.

"They're coming!" warned Sondrin. Her excellent night vision could discern at least thirty wolves bearing down on their position. The pack ponies were whinnying in fear and stamping their hooves in the muddy puddles.

"Hold fast," ordered Sir Caspin. His shining sword was held high like a talisman.

A brief moment passed while the company waited in a wide circle. Prince Asger and the archers stood positioned behind sword and axe wielders while Moranne stood near the centre, holding her sceptre aloft. Ostro looked over to Carina, winking, and they both smiled at Lord Cierzon with his polished katana held flat. Raindrops skittered from its slippery surface, reflecting the single moonbeam breaking through the canopy.

"More fun than Suncin," chuckled Ostro.

His mirth was short-lived as the trees erupted around them with flying, snarling black fur. The first wolf leapt from bramble before Bresne, sending her reeling backwards, but Cuyler's bow twanged in the same instant. The arrow swept over the warrior's shoulder and pierced the beast's throat. It landed dead at Bresne's feet.

Others were testing the flanks, trying to find a weakness. They scurried quickly inwards but stayed just out of range of Lunn's axe. He swung it in a wide arc, scattering the wolves back into the shadows, where they regrouped to probe once more.

Be ready, Chakirris told her sisters. The dryads and wolves seldom crossed paths and usually respected each other's territory. It pained her to kill any forest creatures when not for food, but the black beasts were possessed.

"I needs more light," moaned Brea, trying to pick out the emerald eyes lurking in the bushes.

Then they came.

Five snarling black wolves burst through the south's bushes while another three ran in from the north. Others still joined from the brush behind them.

Ostro shrugged off his cloak, which fell, revealing breast armour made from crisscrossing leather straps. His arms were bare but for leather cuff guards, and a waterfall tattoo cascaded from his shoulder. He twirled his staff with an indulgent flourish, and then his hands burst into life, moving the stick with poise, grace and deadly accuracy. Two wolves were knocked away, and a third was stunned long enough for Tiam to skewer its flank. More emerged from the shadows, barking their defiance.

"Jem!" yelled Hayden. A giant wolf was jumping towards his friend.

The gada was ready; turning on his heels, Jem pushed the twin blades forward. The wolf was on him, but its momentum and weight carried it onto the Jakari blades. The impaled body pushed Jem to the ground, where it pinned him against the mud. Its last gasp of foul breath emptied in Jem's face. He turned away in disgust and watched his friends hacking at the beasts in a blur of flashing steel and twanging bowstrings.

Brenna, Caspin, Torbrand and Ellen formed a vanguard, hacking limbs and severing heads, while Brea, Cuyler and Carina covered them. Most of the others gave support, with the dryads picking off stragglers just out of reach from the swordsmen. Ostro was a one-person army, taking the whole area for his own. He brushed off the attacks and sent fur flying through the bushes with every spin of his staff.

If Ostro was proficient, Isen matched him in ferocity. Her axe dripped in blood, and more streaked her arms and face. It diluted in the rain and ran in streaks down her neck. She welcomed the fury as wolves leapt at her two at a time, but for each one she killed, Gamin downed another. His aim was the sharpest it had ever been; each arrow killed a further black beast. A partnership born in blood emerged in Jem's eyes.

"Move!" yelled Sax, waking Jem from his reverie.

Two wolves had spotted him pinned beneath the carcass, and they headed for him with burning green eyes.

The whip-cracking sound of a throwing blade pierced the air; the first wolf was dead, but Sefti's sharp katana decapitated the second. The head rolled rapidly through the camp and into the mud.

Jem struggled to his feet and surveyed the carnage. At least thirty dead or dying wolves were scattered about the path, but more were coming, and the rain wouldn't ease. A deep rasping howl rose from the undergrowth, followed by another nearby and more behind them. The attacking wolves disappeared into the bushes leaving the Fay Legion looking on.

"They've given up!" shouted Gron.

Some of the others smiled and looked at one another in relief. The dryads maintained their guard.

"No," corrected Chakirris. "They make way."

Slowly and without fear, three enormous shapes pushed through the bushes, with heads down but eyes fixed on the disparate company. They snarled and slavered while the men and women stood transfixed.

"Somebody shoot!" commanded Biorn, but the pack leaders were already sitting back on their haunches to attack. An arrow from Carina hit the lead wolf on its flank, but it ignored the strike like a cow ignoring flies.

The three launched towards the centre with a growling bark, where Moranne stood with the glowing sceptre. Other wolves poured in behind. The party was overwhelmed.

The giant leader barrelled into the Cempestre, barging Brenna and Bresne aside. It snapped at the end of Ostro's staff, ripping it from his grip, and launched itself towards Moranne. She struggled to pull out her sword and maintain the light, but the wolf was bearing down on her, angling its jaws to rip out her throat.

Just two feet from snatching her; she recoiled from the wolf, covering her face; the wall of black fur stopping short. A blur of leather armour and steel threaded through the party and decapitated the pack leader with a single strike of his katana.

Cierzon placed a hand on Moranne's shoulder and felt her shaking. Any last hope that she and Corvus could once again speak in peace was finally gone.

Wolves were now among the company, snapping at their legs and grabbing at any loose clothing. One beast sank its fangs into Isen's arm before she hacked off its paw with her axe. Another managed to yank on Prince Asger's robe, pulling him into the mud. Ellen skewered it, plunging her double-handed sword into its back. She stood to see Torbrand taking on two at once; something hit her from behind, sending her head-first into the sodden filth.

Squirming in the mud, she turned, expecting to see sharp teeth dripping in death, but it was the deadly grin of a crazed man pinning her down.

A deep gash ran down the side of his head, covering half his face and clothes in thick, dark blood. He squinted through the rain with one good eye, as the other was red and swollen, making his face almost unrecognisable. Grabbing her around the throat, he pulled her close so she could taste his fetid breath. "I counted every man entering that room and saw them laughing at me when they left. I vowed to be free of you one day," spat Slitan. "Time for you to die, *mother*."

Ellen's eyes widened in terror; she tried to scream, but his hands clasped around her throat and squeezed. She attempted to shout for Torbrand as she kicked and struggled to reach for the knife, but it was gone. She couldn't breathe and felt her life hanging by a thread. Her father lay on his death bed with disappointment creasing his face. Ellen swiped at Slitan with flailing arms and kicked her legs in panic, but he was too strong. His glee was sickening as he crushed the life from her.

Oblivious to the melee around them, Slitan didn't see the large, dark shape of fury running directly at them. The wolf snapped at Slitan's arm, cutting to the bone and dragging him off the gasping swordswoman. He cried in anguish and kicked the beast away, but another took him by the leg, pulling him back into the mud.

"Help me!" he cried.

Ellen strained for breath and saw the wolf trying to drag him away, and the shadow of someone running through the mayhem behind.

Hayden grabbed Slitan's hand while he fumbled to bring his sword into play.

"Hold on!" he shouted and looked to Ellen for help. She sat impassively while the wolf sank its teeth deeper, and Slitan screamed in agony.

At that moment, Hayden realised what had happened. He scanned the path for help, but all the others were busy fighting off the wolves and saving each other. He looked at Slitan's broken face, twisted into a grimace of pain; more dark shapes still exploding from the forest.

Another wolf appeared from the shadows and tore into Slitan's ankle. He screamed as the two beasts pulled on him while Hayden tried to hold on. Ellen was shaking her head.

Hayden looked back into Slitan's eyes and deep into his dark heart. "I'm sorry." He released his hand.

The two wolves dragged Slitan's writhing body into the bushes, where his screams reverberated through the clearing until there was silence. Ellen and Hayden stared into the darkness until a shrill cry alerted them from the centre of the camp.

"An owl!" yelled Cuyler.

The weak, grey light of dawn gradually filtered through the rain and gloom to illuminate leaves high in the canopy. With his keen archer's eye, Cuyler could see the shadow of a small, tufted-eared owl sitting on a broad branch directly above them. The tiniest flash of green sparked in its dark eyes for a moment. Her arrow was straight and true, hitting its target in a flurry of leaves and feathers. The bird fell dead at her feet.

The attacking wolves changed immediately. They lost focus, looking to the two alpha males for guidance. They became nervous and wary of the shining swords, too afraid to run in and attack. The green fire was gone from their eyes, and the spell was broken.

Spotting the change, the Cempestre warriors started chasing them away, and the archers kicked out at them. They scampered into the bushes whining and howling in defeat.

Jem sank to his knees in exhaustion. A small section of the path was littered with dead wolves, mingling with the blood of both man and beast. Moranne collapsed, and the green light blinked out.

A tall figure stood, legs apart, at the clearing's centre. Tears cascaded down Isen's face and onto the lifeless body of Sefti Regenherd. She held the slight warrior gently in her arms. Sefti's eyes were closed in an image of serenity at odds with the blood dripping from a deep wound on her leg and mud caked in her blonde hair.

41 THUNDER

The rain still pattered on the tents, dripping from leaves into muddy puddles and forming a background cacophony. All else was silent as the exhausted camp slept into the dim morning light.

Sir Torbrand had ordered everyone to get some rest after the midnight ordeal. Moranne had used all her energy maintaining the light, while Gron, Brenna, Isen and Sefti had all been bitten. Sefti's wound was so painful that she'd passed out. The others were bruised and tired, and the leaders all agreed it would be madness travelling in such a state. Only the dryads seemed unscathed.

Chakirris wouldn't leave Prince Asger's side, despite Biorn's orders, and Brea wrapped the shaking Ellen tightly in two blankets. Exhaustion and infection would now be the most significant challenges (or so they thought). The short twenty-five miles to Langley would feel like fifty.

Sax Stulor had killed many wolves and saved Jem's life, but his dreams were turbulent. He saw his mother sitting alone in a humble apartment. She naively thought his father would return one day, but Sax knew well that a muscular young alviri man would have no time for a wrinkled, blind, single mother. Suncin loomed over him like a threat. It made him feel sick, thinking he could be confined in its walls again. The dread increased until it burst into his consciousness and broke him from sleep. He looked up to see three shadowy figures leaning over him.

"What do you want?" he cried, reaching for a knife.

"Relax, we just want to talk," said Carina.

She stood with Ostro and Cierzon at the end of the tent. They seemed calm, with weapons stowed, but they wanted something. One by one, they entered the tent and crouched around the stunned soldier.

"There are people who need your help," said Cierzon.

Sax looked bewildered and sat up, leaning against the tree stump which split the tent. He looked down at the space left by Slitan.

"I couldn't save him," he stuttered.

"He was lost before last night," replied Carina. "That's not why we're here."

"You're a healer," stated Ostro, coming straight to the point.

Sax thought of denying it, but they had him. Ostro recognized him from Suncin, and the others could easily read him.

Stone and Sceptre

"Will you tell anyone?" he asked.

"We won't break your secret," replied Cierzon, shaking his head, "but Sefti will die if you don't help her."

"Gron, Brenna and Isen are also in need," added Carina.

Sax looked out at the other tents, flapping in the wind and battered by the torrent.

"You're a good man *Marin,*" said Ostro. "Your true identity is your own business. If you help, we'll do all we can to keep you safe."

He knew he had no choice. Luckily none of the wounded soldiers was billeted with the human leaders. Only Tiam slept with Isen, but she was a friend to the alviri..

"It must be tonight," he said. "Let's go."

They made their way to Sefti's tent first, where she slept with Brenna. Luckily she was asleep near the side, with her damaged leg extending towards the end of the tent.

Sax used stealth to carefully reach out and place his hand over her bandaged wound. He closed his eyes and concentrated, forcing the earth power from his head and down his arm. It buzzed in his hand, and a dim white light sparkled between his palm and the wound. He held steady for three minutes, then carefully retraced his steps back to the others.

"Is she cured?" whispered Carina.

Sax shrugged his shoulders. "Hard to tell," he said. "The wound is deep. We can only ask for Juldra's mercy."

Ostro placed a hand on his shoulder, and Sax flinched. After spending so much time amongst the humans, he'd learned to despise the dalfreni and the imperious alviri.

"Can you help the others?" asked Cierzon.

Sax answered with a nod; the others could be helped without the risk of disturbing them. He crept close to their tents and held his hand against the damp canvas. Anyone awake would have seen a sparkling, white light permeating the air inside, finding its way to any cuts and gashes.

After dealing with Lunn, he stumbled back into the arms of Ostro and Cierzon, completely drained. They helped him back to his tent and laid him gently down.

Carina leaned over and placed a kiss on his forehead. "Thank you," she whispered, and they left him in peace.

A thin, green snake slithered along the broad, damp branch, trying to wrap itself under the bough to avoid the fat raindrops. Its life was short but cut shorter as a hulking blue shape smashed into the branch and trampled it under a giant, rough leather boot.

The two long, straight horns were a constant annoyance, catching on branches or becoming trapped in vines. A gnarled, wide fist splintered trees into twigs and tore down the vines, throwing them into the brush. Kagel always teetered on the brink of anger, but tramping through the muddy forest brought it simmering to the surface.

His acolytes dared not speak; Zonta wouldn't even look at him. The battle armour was heavy, and she struggled to keep up with his long strides; she dared not slip back. He could crush the life from her with one hand.

She wore thick leather shoulder guards, cuffs and a protective, layered skirt over her light leather leggings. Less protected was her body wrapped in a simple, soft blue cloth draped to knee length. It was tied with wide leather straps that lifted her breasts and accentuated her curves. Kagel loved showing her off to the other warlords. The chieftain mate's look was completed by a short axe at her side, a rusting sword on her back and a sculpted steel helm from which her smooth, curving horns protruded.

Zonta stumbled in the mud and almost fell, but she quickly picked herself up, to disapproving grunts from her master. He'd killed over a hundred humans, alviri, dalfreni and other oni. His prowess was legendary, as was his barbarity.

Favouring traditional clan weapons, he carried a vast spiked club still spattered with his enemies' blood. Chunks of rotting flesh hung from some of the spikes. His armour was primitive, consisting of two thick iron plates which covered his front and back and a wide-brimmed, rusting iron helm. Eschewing the rough, loose trousers of most oni males, he wore the dark brown hakama of a leader. The wide, pleated trousers were stained with ivy and tied at the top with a wide leather belt.

Suddenly he stopped. The warriors behind him stretched far into the forest, leaving a path of trampled bushes and dead wildlife that snaked over the northern tip of Mirror Lake and upwards into Banafell. Every member of Clan Morp stopped at once. Sixty brutal clubs, iron cudgels, or blunt, rusting swords hung ready for action.

Kagel sniffed the air, tasted the rain and stared to the west. He knew the column of humans was travelling through Deapholt, and there was only one path. They would ambush them out of Suncin or catch them on the way to Langley. Either way, they were dead meat.

They've turned the corner, said the voice of the Scucca in his head.

He looked down at Zonta, dutifully averting her gaze. Neither of the other warlords behind him had brought their mates, as none matched Zonta's beauty. He smiled to himself and swung the massive club onto his shoulder.

If he killed this band of humans, they'd sing songs of his name through all of Banafell, and Beadu would smile on him.

Without a word, he took a mighty swing at the nearest sapling, shattering its trunk into fragments, and kicked it from his path. Once more, they marched onwards as the murky sun rose behind them.

⁂

Jem sat bolt upright, his heart pounding hard in his chest. The rain was still falling hard, but a grey light now permeated the camp; he could just see the sleeping outlines of Lunn, Gron and Gamin. "Oni!" he yelled.

Gron sat up so quickly that he hit his head on the canvas. "What's going on?" he said, rubbing the sleep from his eyes.

"The oni are coming!"

"Where?" added Lunn. His voice was deep, like rolling thunder; it was almost unintelligible as he woke.

"Who's yelling?" barked Captain Fallon, leaning into the tent.

Jem scrambled from the blanket and out into the morning rain. Most of the Cempestre were already awake, munching on soggy bread, and he could see the Linhold brothers deep in conversation.

"Lady Moranne!" he shouted, running to her tent.

She was already awake, looking over the injured Sefti. "Calm yourself," she said. "Now tell me what you've seen."

He realised how hysterical he must look and took a few deep breaths before telling Moranne his dreams. She listened intently and nodded as he described the warlord and his small army.

"Are you sure this is happening now?" she said, knowing that Jem's visions came from the past, present and future.

"It was raining, and the sky looked as it does this morning," he replied, looking up through the gaps in the canopy.

Moranne decided to tell everyone together. She marshalled the company in the centre of the camp. Her hair was so wet that it clung to her face in strands, and she shivered as cold drops ran down her neck.

They would pack and leave immediately. Gron and Lunn would carry Sefti on a stretcher made from one of the tents, Prince Asger would lead the column, and the best warriors would form a protective rear guard.

"Why are the oni so bent on killing us?" asked Hayden. The heart of Banafell was a long way east, and it seemed madness to risk such a journey for a few humans.

"You don't understand the clans," answered Brenna. "They live for war. They considered it an insult when we left one alive at the junction. We couldn't be bothered to kill him, so now they're going to wipe us out."

"That's insane."

"That's the oni," added Cuyler.

With the threat at their door, the Fay Legion mobilised quickly. They were ready to move within fifteen minutes, with Asger leading the way. Rotting wolf corpses littered the path, but it would take too long to deal with them, and the experienced oni would read the signs either way.

Slitan's remains were near, but no one volunteered to look, and nobody spoke of him.

Sir Torbrand asked Brea what had happened to Ellen, but "try asking *her*," was all she would say.

The rain eased as they set off, and the occasional shaft of light found its way to their backs, but the ground was so saturated it sucked at their feet like a bog. Lunn and Gron felt pulled by the mire as they toiled with the makeshift stretcher. Sefti drifted in and out of consciousness and murmured with every stumble.

"Careful with her!" yelled Isen, oblivious to her wound. She felt herself looking at Gamin as they stomped through the mud. Something had changed in the slim archer. He'd come alive next to her last night, and now he carried himself with more assurance and fewer furtive glances in her direction. They'd shared less than five words, but a bond was struck when they fought together.

The path was crisscrossed by vines, bramble, tall ferns and fallen trees, making progress painfully slow. Few humans or dalfreni travelled north of the lake, and the dryads only ventured into clan country if the southern hunting was poor. A myriad of small streams flowed northwards, where they would eventually join the River Hiwness or pour directly into the sea.

"I feel them coming," said Jem to himself.

Jilliad was listening. "I feel them, too," she added. Her hair was red, like autumn maple, and shone as the light touched it, but her voice had been unknown. The men, and some of the Cempestre, speculated that she might be mute.

"You can speak!" exclaimed Jem, immediately feeling impolite; Jilliad simply smiled.

We talk if you care to listen.

Their ability to delve into minds was unnerving, but Jem's gift of sight was no less invasive. He wished he could scan the horizon to find the oni, but all he felt was looming malice creeping up on them from behind.

The rain ceased entirely by midday, allowing the sun's rays to penetrate to the mossy forest floor, raising a thin mist that wove between the trees. The brightness would have lifted their spirits, but something was spooking the horses.

"The oni," said Sondrin flatly.

"How far?" asked Biorn.

Chakirris gathered her sisters, and they conferred silently. When she finally turned to the nervous captain, her face was ashen.

"Maybe five miles," she guessed.

"Five miles?" gasped Caspin. "We'll never make it."

"Yes, we will," proclaimed Sir Torbrand, shooting his brother a look of disappointment. "Your Highness, you need to ride ahead to Langley. Try to get some help." He looked around at what they had, then summoned the men to him. "I want you to strip everything from the pack ponies and drop everything you don't need. Brea, you'll use the two ponies to take yourself, Yuka and Cuyler just outside the tree line. We'll need you to cover us when we break through." He looked to Tiam, but she nodded in agreement and came to his side.

"Orettas!" she cried. "We know the clans like no other; how they run, how they fight and how to kill them. I will take charge of the rear guard, and I'm relying on you to pull us through.

Brenna smashed her fist into her palm. "About time!" she cheered.

Everyone started to move, carrying out their orders, but the prince remained still on his horse.

"Sir, you need to go," shouted Torbrand.

Asger shook his head. "Not without Sefti," he stammered.

The knight was about to complain, but the prince ignored him and turned directly to Lunn and Gron. "Tie her to my back," he commanded.

Sefti's colour had lifted since Sax had helped her, but she was still fragile and barely conscious. The prince knew they couldn't escape the oni with her on a stretcher, and he was pleased to be of use finally.

"You heard the prince!" yelled Biorn, nodding curtly.

Within a few minutes, Lunn and Gron, with help from Isen and Bresne, had managed to tie Sefti to the prince using the tent ropes. It was time to go when the archers were ready on the ponies.

"Frea be with you," said Sir Torbrand.

"With Juldra's strength," added Tiam.

"Come on, girls," joked Brea, at the prince's expense. She mustered the party, which included Cuyler and Yuka sharing the other pony.

"Look after him," she shouted to Ellen, standing just behind Torbrand. With a kick of her heels, the ponies lurched forward; they picked their way through fallen trees and then disappeared along the path.

"Move yourselves!" boomed Biorn.

Leaving packs, tents, and food behind, they set off quickly westward. The forest edge was still some ten miles away, with the town of Langley a further five into Tudorfeld.

Tiam estimated that the oni would reach them before leaving the forest, knowing how quickly they could push through the trees. Their only hope was to draw the beasts into open ground where their large hulking shapes made wide archery targets.

Orettas Brimwulf, Gunborg, Fixen and Stanhamur took positions at the rear of the column along with Gamin, who ignored Isen's scowl. Gron and Lunn took the vanguard, using the mace and axe to quickly clear any obstructions while Jem and Hayden positioned themselves behind. Sax, Carina, Cierzon and the leaders were just ahead of the Cempestre. Chakirris gave her sisters a scouting role. They took the flanks and watched for any sign of rogue clan members coming from the north or south.

Everyone was nervous but tried to remain calm and maintain a steady pace. Sir Torbrand was content to let Captain Fallon keep them all moving with some colourful language. Only Brenna seemed happy, a manic grin creeping over her face. From the terrible spring day fifteen years ago, when an oni scout had crushed the life from her sister, she'd hated the ancient creatures. "The only good oni is a dead oni," she'd often say on hunting trips out of Cempess.

"They draw near!" shouted Chakirris.

Jem could almost feel the vibrations through his boots as the oni flattened saplings and crushed branches under their giant feet.

"Pick it up, lads," called Biorn.

They broke into a jog, but the tree roots made it challenging in the mud. Hayden stumbled, cursing, and many of the others fought with the spiky bramble and clinging ivy. It wasn't long before Lunn and Gron were starting to labour. The big men were powerful and fast over a short distance, but with heavy weapons, the constant pace pulled them back.

"Give me your axe," shouted Jem, but Lunn hugged it like a new-born. He'd never allow a chicken farmer to carry his prized weapon.

"Come on, lads," chided Brenna, "you don't want to be beaten by a bunch of wenches."

They stumbled onto a narrow stone bridge layered in spongy moss and bright lichen. It spanned a thin stream which transformed into a raging torrent by the rains. Lunn and Gron slumped onto the bridge walls, but as they sat, a nearby horn sounded a long deep note of doom. The tone echoed through the woods like thunder. All eyes scanned the eastward path, but nothing stirred.

"Three miles," said Chakirris confidently.

"We can't stop here," chimed the captain.

"No!" agreed Tiam. "We need to go now!"

Biorn grabbed Lunn by the shoulder and dragged him to his feet.

"The next fry-up is on me, so move it!"

Brenna didn't wait to ask this time and grabbed the axe from Lunn's hands while Bresne wrestled the mace from Gron.

"If you can catch me, you can have it back," laughed Brenna, running ahead.

Oretta Gunborg now set the pace, jumping over fallen trees and sprinting along the path.

"We're not going to make it," whispered Bresne to Biorn. He nodded as they ran together. There was no plan other than flight, and they had too few archers at the tree line to make a real difference.

"We may need a miracle," he agreed.

The horn sounded again, even closer this time. The oni enjoyed taunting their enemies and making them run. The chase made conquest even more satisfying.

All attempts at an ordered column had gone as the company ran blindly through the trees. Carina, Ostro and Cierzon ran gracefully and effortlessly, barely breaking a sweat, in sharp contrast to the men who struggled to keep up.

Hayden noticed a pale green light start to flicker in Jem's eyes as his body summoned the earth power to course through his limbs. Moranne, too, gathered her strength with her hand, ready to grab the sceptre. She leapt over a tree stump and reached Carina's side.

"You know I asked you not to use it," she gasped.

Carina nodded; she knew what her mother was implying.

"I'm ready," she replied, unaware of the green sparks igniting in her own eyes.

The bellowing sound of the oni horn blasted through the forest around them. It seemed to emanate from somewhere to their left.

"They've spread out," said Tiam.

"Trying to cut us off," agreed Bresne.

Hayden tripped and fell sprawling over gnarled tree roots, but Jem caught him and dragged him to his feet. They weren't dying today or any day. His eyes were burning bright, and the others could see it now.

"What is he?" asked Ostro.

Sax was shaking his head. Moranne wouldn't say, and no one would ask her.

The next horn blast was all around them. The trees were starting to thin a little, and they could see further into the forest on all sides, but there was no sign of danger.

Brenna stopped ahead, waiting for the others to catch up; she peered back along the trail. In the far distance, she could just make out a ripple moving in the canopy. Birds flew from their perches, and leaves fluttered in the branches.

"They're coming!" she shouted.

Sir Torbrand turned to the company and shouted his orders.

"Archers and dryads, fan out at the front; everyone else, stay tight."

"Keep up with Brenna," added Tiam. "Don't let her out of your sight."

They still couldn't see their pursuers, although they were no more than a mile away. The air was thick with tension as the Fay Legion mustered for a final push to safety. They were sprinting and struggling to stay together.

Lunn, Gron and Hayden were trailing at the back, but Bresne and Isen wouldn't leave them alone, spurring them on against their heaving chests and rasping breath.

Jem could feel the beat of oni boots pounding the ground and the swipe of their clubs, splintering trees and crushing small animals. Their burning yellow eyes scorched his consciousness, trying to frighten him into a mistake; the power throbbing in his mind was taking over and driving him on. Soon he was stride for stride with Brenna and starting to pass her.

There was a crash behind them and the sound of cracking wood. Sixty pairs of rugged boots crushed everything in their path, spreading out in an arrowhead with the warlord at its tip.

"Don't look back!" snapped Tiam. "Be ready."

The party scrabbled wildly against the mud; adrenaline pumped, pushing them onwards into the trees. There was still no sign of the forest edge, Brea, or the archers. Hayden was starting to panic, as he did in Bearun, but Jem was determined to save his friend. His thoughts cast back to Denbry, and his uncle, who always said: "there are many kinds of bravery, lad."

Sax held a throwing knife in his palm, Moranne clasped her sceptre, Isen pulled the axe from her belt, and Tiam swept the katana from her back. A cacophony of guttural shouting and grunting rose behind them, with a low rumble, like a cattle stampede.

"Run!" shouted Biorn.

Jem reached back, pulling the twin blades from their sheaths. The steel clashed as though he was sharpening them for the attack. He looked over at Hayden and Gamin beyond. They were young and full of life. Gamin was born again, grasping his bow as he stole a glance at Isen. The young archer had a reason to live and someone to protect, but who did Hayden have?

"You're my best friend!" shouted Jem. "I'll watch your back if you watch mine."

Hayden nodded, clasping the hilt of his sword tightly.

None of them looked around, but the oni were no more than three hundred yards away. The clans never mastered the bow, relying on close combat, but they were still too far for a clear shot.

"Archers, ready!" shouted Torbrand.

Gamin barrelled onwards with his bow in one hand and an arrow ready in the other. Carina was at his side, but Isen held his gaze. He wanted to shout and tell the world before it was too late, but he respected her too much for that. *I love you,* he thought.

Sondrin heard it and smiled. There was hope for them.

"On my command," continued Sir Torbrand.

The oni were so close that their breathing joined the thunder of boots, clash of weapons, and snarl of hatred. A wall of death was sweeping towards the fleeing warriors. They could smell victory and started to break ranks, running ahead of Kagel, oblivious to his wrath. Zonta struggled to keep up due to her shorter frame, but her face was frozen in a rictus of anger, and her short fangs gleamed in a demented grin. It would soon be over.

"Steady!" shouted Torbrand, praying for an end to the forest, but the trees still came. They were dotted further apart now, and tufts of prairie grass started to appear, but still, the forest held them in its grasp.

"Stay wide when you attack!" added Tiam. "Go for the legs."

The Cempestre had developed a sophisticated strategy for defeating the oni, which played on their weaknesses, but Oretta Brimwulf had never engaged so many.

"Now!" cried Torbrand.

Gamin and Carina turned and dropped to one knee, steadying their aim. Carina let fly, hitting one brute mid-stride, but the sight of so many twisted beasts took Gamin's breath away. Their broad, rough shoulders powered them forward, head down. They resembled charging bulls with curled or damaged horns and wide flared nostrils.

Stealing himself, gamin loosed an arrow on the nearest oni, hitting it clean between the eyes. It stumbled sideways and crashed into another before falling dead beneath more pounding boots.

While the two archers stood, Chakirris screamed silently at her sisters. As one, they spun around and released a volley of poison darts. Three oni swayed and stumbled until the bohun upas penetrated their hearts, leaving them dead in the mud.

Running once more, Gamin struggled to keep up; Jem hung back and grabbed him by the collar.

"You're not going to make fearsome warrior babies if you're dead," he laughed.

Carina and Gamin grabbed another arrow on the run, then repeated the attack, sending another volley with the dryads. Two of the beasts went down this time, while Gamin's arrow hit a large, rough oni in the shoulder. He roared in defiance and ripped the arrow from his flesh, snapping it between his fingers.

"They're too close," shouted Caspin.

The archers had thinned the oni vanguard, but the nearest was now only fifty yards away. Once the party engaged, the rest of the creatures would swamp them.

"One more volley!" shouted Torbrand. "Thin them out!"

Gamin looked across at Carina with her eyes blazing green. Her aim was perfect, and her reflexes were twice his. She nodded, and it was time. They dropped together, pulled back the bowstrings and loosed their arrows together. Two more oni sank to their knees, and it was time to run.

Carina was away, but when she looked back, Gamin had fallen. His foot caught on a tree root, and he scrambled to get up as a giant oni bore down on him with a studded club.

"Gamin!" cried Isen, but she was too far from him.

Sax saw the situation unfolding and stopped, running back for the archer. "Get down!" he shouted.

Gamin crouched just as the oni swung his club back, ready to strike, but as he looked down at the cowering human, a small knife struck him in the throat. He reached up to grab the handle while his blood sprayed. He staggered and fell forward, just missing Gamin as he escaped.

"Three groups!" bawled Tiam.

Three groups of four warriors would tackle each oni before continuing to run. This tactic would keep them moving while reducing the threat from the clan vanguard. The archers and the dryads would cover them. The oni bloodlust was so great that they seldom coordinated and often charged blindly forward into a trap.

"Now!" screamed Tiam.

She stopped with Torbrand, Cierzon and Gron to tackle the first oni. He wasn't expecting them to fight and almost fell, trying to stop his charging bulk.

He flailed wildly, swiping at them with his rough club, but Tiam rolled beneath it and cut a gash in his ankle. Stumbling sideways, he tried to swipe back, but Cierzon cut across his back. He roared in pain, but it was cut short when Gron leapt towards him and buried his mace in the creature's skull.

They were thinning the numbers, but the main body was still solid and coming at them quickly. Tiam spotted the warlord and directed the archers to take him out, but there were too many others around him. They managed to kill another three, but any closer and they'd all be dead. There was only one plan left. They needed to run.

The trees were thinning quickly; Torbrand could finally see the tree line, but their foes were on them. Just a few feet now separated them from the swinging clubs, dotted with spikes, rusting nails, and chunks of rock. There was no sign of Brea and the archers.

"Where are you, Brea?" mumbled the knight.

Sax threw another knife behind without even looking, taking out the nearest oni as it tried to swipe at him with a metal cudgel.

With time running out, it was Moranne's turn; she stopped in her tracks while the others ran past her, and she turned to see the army almost on her. With a mighty scream, she held the sceptre aloft. It crackled into a spike of green lightning, then blasted out towards the host like a shimmering wave of power, knocking back every creature in its path. The thirty nearest beasts fell back, dazed, but the others piled forward. At least it had bought the company some time.

Moranne pocketed the sceptre and ran, but Kagel had seen her. The Scucca warned him about a witch. She was the one; she must die. With Zonta at his side and his best warriors around him, he gave a mighty roar and doubled his speed.

The plains of Tudorfeld curved upwards from the forest and onto the northern hills, but a narrow hollow dipped down just outside the woods, where Brea lay in wait. She knew they couldn't be seen from Deapholt. The afternoon sun shone overhead and would light up anything cresting the ridge to make a perfect target.

Lunn and Gron were spent, and Moranne kept up by the sheer force of will. They were done, and Torbrand knew it. He turned to Ellen, about to spill his true feelings when they crested the ridge.

"The archers!" shouted Brenna.

Partly running and partly gambolling, they hurtled down the hill with the oni at their backs.

"Get down!" yelled Brea, as four arrows shot through the air, skimming above their comrades and hitting four oni between the eyes. The giant, pock-marked bodies rolled and slid down the hill to rasps of hatred from the survivors.

"Again!" commanded Brea.

The women were crack shots; all hit their marks except for Yuka, who hit her target in the cheek. He sprinted down the hill with the arrow protruding from his face.

When Gamin and Carina reached the bottom, they lined up with the others, ready for another volley. Six arrows flew, and five more beasts crashed to the ground in death or agony.

The odds were getting better, but there were still too many, and Kagel was alive. With all her hunting experience, Brea ordered the archers to scale the opposite incline to allow them to shoot down, once the hand-to-hand combat started. They didn't have long to wait.

Kagel flew into their midst, aiming his club at Moranne, but Ostro twirled his staff to strike the warlord on the side of the head. He turned, roaring, as blood ran down his face and charged towards the dalfreni. Ostro was fleet of foot and quickly jumped clear.

"Behind you!" cried Hayden. A lumbering, single-horned beast loomed behind Jem, carrying a blunt, rusting axe. The killing blow never came; the oni's body crashed to the ground nearby, with Isen's axe in his back.

Another five arrows flew overhead, and each found its target, but Carina stood near the bottom of the hill holding a glowing sceptre high in the air. She took a deep breath and screamed with all her might, squeezing the metal rod with every fibre.

A wide bolt of green lighting flew from its glowing tip and skewered three oni in a row. They stood rooted to the spot by the writhing green beam and then dropped to the ground. Each one had a foot-wide circular hole in its chest, smoking with the stench of burning flesh.

Some of the oni stopped, and a few turned back. Those that fled felt the sting of a dryad dart. Another stream of arrows streaked overhead, and more clan beasts fell in agony. Less than twenty remained, but they weren't giving up.

"Die, fighting bitch!" screamed Zonta, whirling her axe towards Brenna; the katana flashed across her vision and parried the strike. She spun around and struck again, but Brenna was too fast.

More arrows and darts streaked past, but swords and clubs now clashed in desperation. Isen and Sax took on two for themselves. *Knives* used his athleticism to weave between them while Isen hacked at them, then rolled beneath their clubs. Biorn, Bresne and Caspin managed to kill two who were wildly swinging their clubs, and Ellen slashed the warlord across his back as he lunged at Ostro.

With only eleven oni remaining, they were starting to flee.

"Don't let them go," shouted Tiam, over the melee.

Cierzon decapitated two trying to climb the hill, and another hail of bolts and arrows saw four more hulking bodies slam to the ground.

Five became four, and four became three. Tiam and Isen combined to finish a tall, broad oni carrying a long, metal pike. Isen jumped over the pole and slashed its legs, and then Tiam drove her katana through its chest. She stood on top of the carcass and pulled her blade free.

"He's mine," said Sir Torbrand, squaring up to the wounded warlord.

"Pah!" spat Kagel. "Little human, die screaming."

He lifted his filthy club high to crush the little knight but didn't see Ellen running to his side. She thrust her sword deep between Kagel's ribs.

He screamed in agony and lashed out, grabbing Ellen by the throat, but Torbrand was already in motion. Crying with emotion, he swung his broadsword in a wide arc and decapitated the blue-painted oni in a single movement.

Stone and Sceptre

The head bounced across the grass to stop just a few feet from the spot where Zonta and Brenna still fought.

"It's over," yelled Sir Torbrand.

"It's over when one of us is dead," replied Brenna.

Zonta snarled in defiance and reached for her short sword. With the rough axe in one hand and blade in the other, she jumped and rolled from Brenna's long reach, savouring the last moments of her life.

"I said that's enough," bawled Torbrand again, but to no avail.

Shaking his head, Ostro decided it was time to rest. With one well-placed twirl of his staff, he hit Zonta on the side of her head. She fell sprawling backwards, dropping both her weapons, which were quickly collected by Gron and Bresne.

Spitting in anger, Zonta climbed to her feet and wiped the blood from a cut on her forehead.

"End it!" she growled.

Brenna lifted her katana and brought it down on Zonta's shoulder, but there was no thud of metal on flesh or ring of the blade striking bone, just the clang of two swords locked in defiance.

Jem stood in front of the snarling oni female holding Brenna's blade between his twin sabres. He looked around at the piles of dead oni bodies and shook his head.

"There's been enough killing," he said. "We'll not execute this female."

"Out of my way!" howled Brenna.

"We don't leave oni alive," agreed Tiam, soberly.

Ostro nodded in agreement; he knew to his cost of their bloodthirsty barbarity.

Torbrand looked at his brother, then across at Ellen, who was shaking her head. "It's not our way," he said finally.

"It *is* ours," added Isen. "If we let her go, they'll return in greater numbers."

Sir Torbrand looked to Moranne. In the absence of Prince Asger, the mission was under her authority, and she knew it.

Gazing at the defiant Jem made her think of Dane in his shining armour. He was honourable and loyal. No man had ever been better. She smiled at her young gada, unable to contain her emotion. He was everything she'd dreamed of and more.

"Tie her up," she said. "There's been enough killing."

There were howls of consternation from the onlooking Cempestre, but the decision was made.

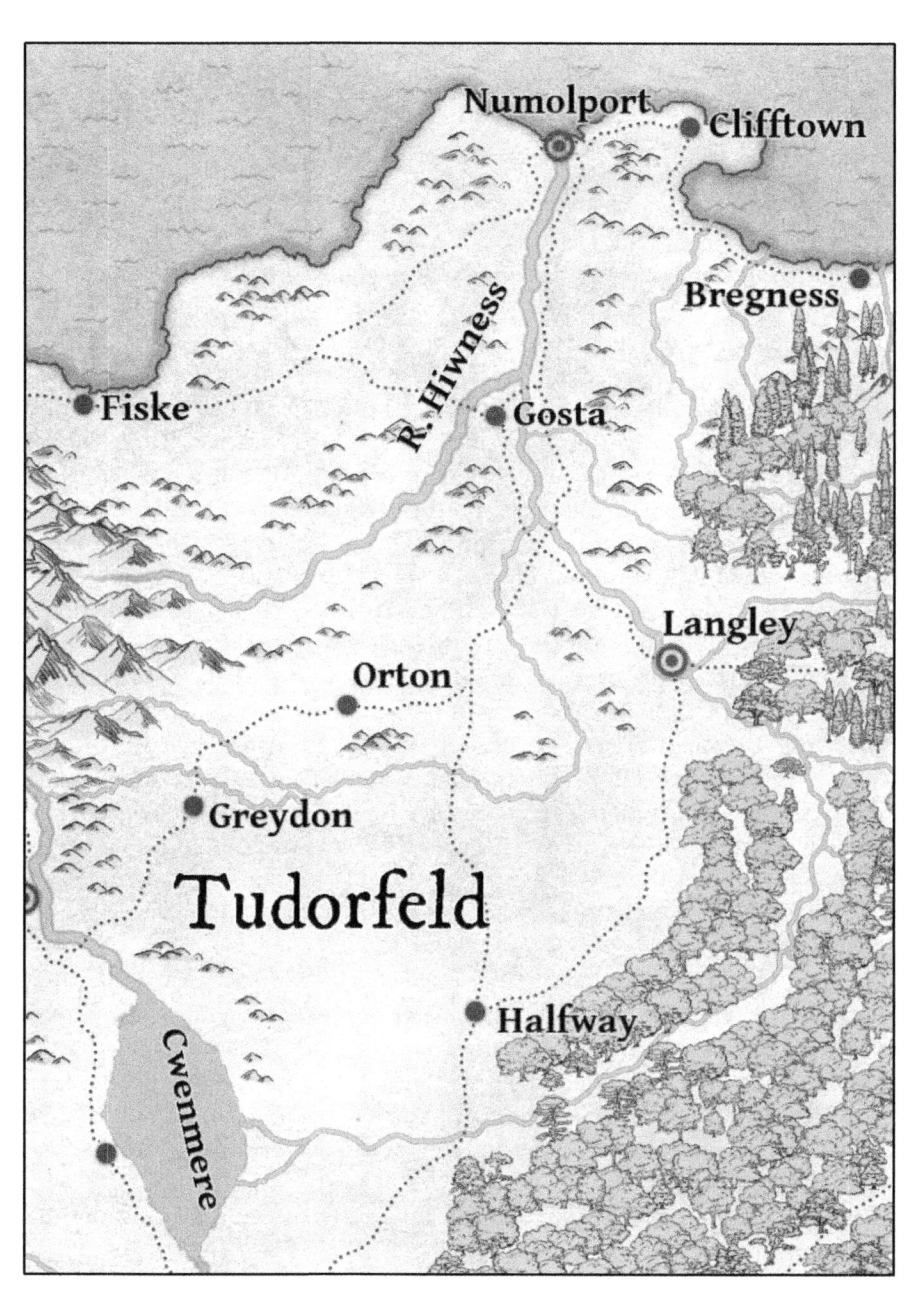

Tudorfeld

42 LYGEN'S MEMORIAL

The sun dipped in the west, throwing a wide shadow down the western side of the hollow. It gradually approached the exhausted warriors, but its foretelling of the night would not quickly raise them from fatigue.

Jem lay on the spongy, damp grass gazing into the blue above. He watched the clouds morph into brave knights riding shining steeds before melting into wide, gruesome oni with impossibly large clubs. After so long under Deapholt's shadow, seeing the sky again warmed his heart. It was a miracle that they'd lost no one to the clans and their bloodthirsty charge.

He looked over at Carina, stretched out on the bank with the bow at her side. She wouldn't speak of the power she wielded nor why she held a sceptre, and nobody would press her. Ostro ventured to ask what a dalfreni was doing with a sceptre of power, but "I'm no dalfreni," was all she'd say.

The dryads appeared as if they'd just enjoyed a brisk stroll, but the Cempestre were as drained as the men. They were relaxing against the west bank, but Brenna still seethed over Moranne's decision to spare the oni female. She continued to rant until Tiam eventually ordered her to be quiet. Zonta herself was tied tightly near the pack ponies and watched by Lunn and Hayden. They sat quietly, recovering energy, when Moranne appeared before them to interrogate the prisoner.

"Give us some time," she told the men. Wearily Lunn and Hayden relocated to Jem's side.

Zonta hissed through her teeth and scowled at Moranne as she sat cross-legged before her. She looked away, refusing to make eye contact.

"We won't hurt you," said Moranne.

The oni female twitched and writhed inside the ropes. If they set her free, she'd return to Banafell and bring more warriors back with her until the clan was no more, but if they took her to Numolport, the inhabitants would treat her like an animal.

"I have a problem with you," said Moranne. "I can't let you go, and I can't take you with us."

"Kill me!" spat Zonta. "Cowards!"

Moranne shook her head. There would be no executions in her mission.

"What's your name?"

Zonta hesitated, but there was no harm in telling her the truth. "Zonta, Kagel mate," she said flatly, before adding "witch," with venom in her gruff voice.

"You know me?" asked Moranne, puzzled.

"Scucca know you," she grunted.

Corvus had many names, but that one was reserved for the clans. The oni worshipped Beadu, the god of war and believed that Scucca was his son, returning to end the dominion of men and help them win in battle.

"You speak to the Scucca?" said Moranne.

Zonta grunted with disdain. "Speak to Kagel," she said.

It was strange that Corvus would try to enlist the oni once more, given how their lack of discipline had cost him so dearly. However, teaming with the Stans would mean opening a conflict on two fronts.

"What happens if I free you?"

Zonta seemed bemused by the question. The humans were strange and weak, but they'd just killed Kagel and his army.

"I..." she stuttered, not knowing if she should kill the witch, return to Banafell or roam the lands alone.

"Would you return to the mountains?" prompted Moranne.

"Not..." continued Zonta, still struggling with the concept of freedom. She should be dead by now. She shook her head, struggling to grasp the idea. "Not know," she blurted.

Moranne reached out and placed a hand on Zonta's leather-bound leg.

"When you're ready, tell me what you want," she said tenderly. "My name is Moranne, and no harm will come to you; we will not kill you."

Zonta watched Moranne return to the tall warrior who seemed to be the leader. She watched them talking and looking toward her. They might still kill her; it was hard to see.

"Sir!" yelled Captain Fallon, trying to get Sir Torbrand's attention.

The dipping shadow had cut across the middle of the hollow. However, there appeared to be several spikes on its edge, which shifted and shimmered.

Torbrand peered upwards to see a line of figures on the western ridge silhouetted against the sun. He squinted in the light and noticed they wore shining armour and sat astride regal horses.

"It's the Green Order," announced Sir Caspin.

Slowly the mounted soldiers picked their way down the bank until their polished breastplates and tall helms could be seen engraved with the Green Order crest, an oak tree in leaf.

The nearest warrior wore the same garb, but the image on his armour was marked out in green copper, and a green ribbon trailed from the top of his helm. He steered his mount to stop a few yards from Sir Torbrand and dismounted, stowing the helmet under his arm.

"Kane!" exclaimed Sir Torbrand. His face exploded in an uncharacteristic smile, and he threw his arms around the tall warrior.

"It warms my heart to see you, old friend," he continued. "This is my good friend, Captain Kane Megendade. We came through the ranks together." Kane was a similar height and build to Sir Torbrand, but his dark hair was shorter, and a wide scar cut across his face from a long distant bandit skirmish.

"It seems you didn't need us," replied the captain, surveying the red bodies of over a dozen Oni scattered around the hollow.

"I have my archers to thank for that," said Torbrand, winking at Brea.

Kane nodded, but something in his demeanour had changed. "You have fighting wenches and elves, I see."

Tiam and Bresne bristled at the mention of "wenches," and the smile vanished from Cierzon's face.

"We're on a special mission," explained Torbrand. "The Cempestre, dalfreni, alviri and forest nymphs have joined us and served with great bravery."

"Hmm," mused the captain, not wishing to countermand a superior officer. "You'll be pleased to know that the prince is well and your woman is being attended."

He was clearly uncomfortable with the racial mix, but his orders were to bring the company to Langley. He strode across to Zonta and looked down at the bound oni, shaking his head. Few humans had seen the clans, but fewer had ever met a female.

"You have a pet," he remarked, watching Zonta screw up her face in anger.

"We have a prisoner," corrected Moranne.

Remembering his manners, the captain bowed curtly and kissed her hand. Moranne was well known in Tudorfeld and stayed in Langley many times, but her tall tales didn't always chime well with the pious town fathers.

"We have food and water for all," boomed the captain. "Let's see you all refreshed; then it's just an hour's walk to Langley."

The thirty Green Order warriors dismounted and broke out rations of bread, cheese and aged ham. They distributed the fare between the men and the Cempestre, but they wouldn't go near the others. Lunn was incensed, angrily gathering armfuls of provisions with Gron and distributing them to all the others, including Zonta.

"This could be tricky," whispered Moranne to Caspin. The full scale of the challenge would be revealed later.

Suitably revived, the party assembled behind the shining warriors and began the short walk to Langley.

Tudorfeld was known for its sweeping, fertile farmland, which blanketed gentle rolling hills in a patchwork of varying crops, but only stout grassland filled the space around Deapholt. Langley residents wouldn't stray near the Deap and feared all the dark creatures under its trees.

A wide path gradually became visible, rutted with cart tracks and hoof prints. The remnants of the once busy Deapholt Path faded out near the forest through lack of use, but here there was life. It pushed through a field of bright, late-flowering poppies, reflected in the red sky forming ahead.

"I'm looking forward to a real bed," sighed Hayden.

"And real food," agreed Lunn.

They were both ready to drop when the tall spires of Langley appeared like black needles against the setting sun. There were no farmhouses on this side of the town and no trees. They'd all been cut down to give a better view of approaching threats.

Langley sat on the convergence of two broad streams which formed Foaming Brook. A narrow cutting diverted the water to a moat around the town, crossed by three permanent wooden bridges. Sharp and angular were the grey stone walls, dotted with tall lookout towers, each manned by uniformed archers. The battlements were in excellent repair, and the whole town was substantial as if ready for an attack at any time.

"Please wait here," said Captain Megendade. His horse plodded across the short bridge, and the tall double doors opened and shut behind him. As they did so, his remaining men shuffled their mounts to form a barrier between Moranne's mission and the town.

"Charming," sniffed Brea.

She wasn't the only one unimpressed by the lack of hospitality. Sir Torbrand was seething, clenching his fists and tapping his boots on the rough ground.

Kane returned on foot after a few minutes and headed directly for Torbrand. His expression didn't inspire confidence.

"Can I talk to you privately?" asked the captain.

Torbrand shook his head. The mission was Moranne's; Caspin, Biorn, Tiam and Cierzon were all of leadership rank.

"Sir," continued Kane. "I can escort you and the wench… I mean women, into the town, but the others can't be admitted."

"On whose orders?" stormed Torbrand.

"The mayor's."

Torbrand aimed to grab his old friend by the collar, but thirty gauntlets reached for their swords. He stopped and looked along the line of Green Order soldiers in horror.

"I'm sorry, please don't make this difficult," said Kane, before he remembered who he was addressing and added: "sir."

"I want to see Mayor Grignys," ordered Moranne. She knew the pious town leader of old, but he wouldn't usually risk insulting the crown.

"That won't—"

"Lady Moranne of the King's Council is *not* asking!" raged Torbrand.

Reluctantly, the captain returned to the gate and waited while they were opened once more.

His comrades had started to murmur and whisper, but Jem already knew of Langley's dark past. The images were so vivid that he saw them all around him, like grizzly apparitions. Mercen Forlyn was screaming at the mob, but the stones kept flying until his mother lay dead in the town square. Her blood trickled between the cobbles as the alviri light faded from her eyes.

Jem didn't want to see it, but the town needed to confess its diabolical sins. Nowhere in Grenfold was Freanism more fanatically followed and encouraged by a priesthood bent on power.

When the mayor finally appeared, his false smile and patronising manner did nothing to ease the mood. Accompanied by the captain, the two men ensured the gates were shut once more before they spoke.

Drodel Grignys was a tall, balding man with thin dark eyebrows and a fresh complexion. He wore a smile which stopped at his cheeks and made him look like an assassin. Dressed in a dark green tunic over a black and green gown, Drodel's colours echoed the garb of the priesthood.

"Lady Moranne," gushed the mayor. The words fell from his narrow lips like the slow pour of fetid water.

"Drodel, what is the meaning of this?" she blasted, coming straight to the point. "Do you dare defy the king?"

"The king is a devout Frean, as you know, my lady," he purred, ignoring her anger. "In this most devout of places, we cannot permit fay creatures to enter."

"All Frea's creatures!" shouted the familiar voice of Prince Asger, struggling across the bridge. He'd made his way through the town when the mayoral staff had failed to help him.

"Ah, Your Highness," cooed the mayor. "I'm sure some elves are perfectly decent, but we can't take any chances. They might use their magic accidentally, and we have the children to think of."

"I'd like to accidentally kick his arse," mumbled Brea under her breath, causing Cierzon to burst into laughter.

The prince was angrier than anyone had seen, and both Carina and Sondrin were shouting. Captain Kane took the opportunity to pull Torbrand aside for a quiet word.

"Sir," he began, "I've been here for a year, and I know the townspeople well. If your friends enter the town, there'll be a riot."

Sir Torbrand knew he was right. Spending so much time with the Cempestre and their new fair friends, he was beginning to forget how most of Grenfold existed in a state of terror. The constant threat from Jakaris, mysterious alviri powers and strident women. The Frean church worked hard, peddling half-truths and total lies.

"King will hear of this," said Asger.

"We should have led the oni horde to your door, you ungrateful inbred," yelled Tiam.

"This is wrong," added Sir Caspin.

Mayor Grignys smiled politely through every jibe. Sir Torbrand knew it was a lost hope and raised his hands in defeat. "So be it," he said. "I will stay with our fair friends outside the wall while the others rest in the town." He hoped that would end the debate, but a tall, muscular human had other ideas.

"Forgive me, sir," boomed Lunn. "If you stay with our new friends, so do I."

Fiske's axe wielder was the last person Torbrand expected to show loyalty to the forest folk, but Lunn bonded with every person who joined the mission. If they fought together, they were brothers in his eyes, and he wasn't alone.

"As do I," added Captain Fallon.

"The Cempestre are with you," stated Tiam.

"Who needs a warm cosy bed," laughed Brea.

Every member of the Fay Legion pledged their loyalty until Prince Asger stood alone by the grinning Drodel.

"Room for one more?" asked the prince.

Chakirris broke into the first genuine smile since joining the team, and Sir Torbrand opened his arms in welcome. "Of course, Your Highness."

The first flicker of disquiet registered in the mayor's demeanour as he realised that the prince had snubbed his town. "Your Highness," he babbled, "you don't need to sleep with these—"

"Elves?" chimed Cierzon.

"We're the Fay Legion," said Moranne, "and we'll keep you safe in your cosy beds despite your ingratitude."

"Let us at least dispose of your creature," continued the mayor, gesturing towards Zonta. She spat at him and snarled in defiance.

"We'll take care of the prisoner," snapped Moranne. "Now, take me to see Oretta Sefti Regenherd before I *really* lose my temper."

Drodel bowed uncomfortably and showed Moranne, Tiam and Isen into the town while the others took the circular path along the moat to the West Gate.

The central road through Langley was wide, clean and lined with attractive shops and dwellings. The town had been built on a simple grid; the affluent lived along its centre and the poor near the walls. Sewage gutters ran along the spur roads to the outer edge, saving the well-heeled from noxious fumes.

An uneasy calm descended on the three women who strode through the town. The people gave furtive looks and whispered to their friends.

"Never seen a woman?" shouted Tiam.

A tall, imposing abbey stood at the town's heart, surrounded by an expansive, open courtyard. It acted as a memorial to Father Lygen, even though his body was never recovered from the site of the bandit ambush. Langley was a place of pilgrimage for all good Freans, and many townsfolk prospered from their visits. The inns were always full, and shops made a brisk trade in religious relics and anointed garments.

The mayoral palace was almost as large as the abbey, with four tall spires at its corners. It doubled as the bishop's residence and housed a religious school and an alms-house, where Sefti was being treated.

Moranne stopped by the door and looked into the long room. There were tall, stained-glass windows on each side depicting the white-haired Father Lygen staring in awe at Frea's winged beauty. The tall, vaulted wooden roof made their footsteps echo as they entered. Thankfully, Sefti was easy to find. There were no other patients.

"She's awake," gasped Tiam.

Not only was she conscious, but she sat upright, gazing into the light. Her straggly blonde hair seemed luminous, and her face was bright and vibrant. Isen ran to her side and flung her broad arms around her friend, sobbing into her shoulder.

"I'm alright," she said softly, hugging Isen tightly.

Moranne and Tiam pulled out chairs and sat beside her as a middle-aged woman joined them. She was dressed in a long green robe with a white headscarf and seemed to be one of the nurses.

"When was she hurt?" asked the woman.

"Last night," replied Tiam. "We were attacked by wolves in Bearun, then fled from a clan attack." She was surprised to find Sefti awake, having feared the worst.

"I need to show you something," said the woman.

She pulled the bedclothes back and revealed that Sefti was dressed in a long, white smock. Carefully folding the smock to one side, she showed the warrior's right leg with no bandage or dressing. A deep red scar ran for a foot from mid-thigh to just above her knee. Its edges, where the wolf had torn at her, were ragged, but the gash had closed entirely. There was no open wound, showing the bone below and no sign of infection.

"That's impossible," gasped Tiam.

"No one heals that quickly," agreed Isen.

The woman was nodding as she replaced the covers. The wound was so well healed it couldn't have only just happened.

"Witchcraft," she whispered out of Sefti's earshot. "The girl is a witch."

Moranne pulled Tiam close and whispered into her ear. "We have a healer in our midst, but these backward yokels will have Sefti burned at the stake if we leave her here."

"Agreed," said Tiam. She turned to the woman in no mood to be questioned. "Fetch her clothes and weapons; Sefti's coming with us."

The Frea's Cup Inn sat just outside the town on the northern bank of Foaming Brook. It was a large, rustic, grey stone building with an adjacent set of stables. The town gates were closed each night at nine; travellers arriving after this time were forced to stay at the inn. Warm yellow light flickered in its small windows, and the smell of home-cooked stew drifted from the chimney.

"I can't guarantee they'll let you stay," said Captain Megendade as he led Sir Torbrand and the others to its door.

"I don't intend to give them much choice," stated the knight.

A few weeks earlier, he would have sneered at any suggestion that he would consort with the alviri, dalfreni, or warrior women of Cempess. He watched Ellen as she wearily stumbled beside Brea. Without words, she judged every one of his actions, and without embrace, he felt his heart expand when she smiled in agreement.

"I need one night's lodgings for at least twenty-four and stable space for a prisoner," boomed Torbrand as the wide inn door creaked open.

Cade Milton, the innkeeper, was short and round with a red, flustered face and hair that seemed to be the same length around his head.

"Erm, we're full," he stuttered and tried to shut the door quickly.

It bounced off Sir Torbrand's foot; he grabbed the opening and forced the door wide open. "Tonight's your lucky night," he said, smiling. "Captain Megendade has agreed to let all your customers into the town, so you'll have plenty of space."

Cade was fumbling for another excuse, but Sir Torbrand's company was already following him into the bar and slumping into its chairs.

"Frea, save us!" cried one of the customers, as Ostro and Carina strode into the room.

The innkeeper looked at Kane for support, but the captain shook his head.

"I only has twelve rooms," said Cade. His wife Daisy had now appeared behind the bar and looked horrified. She had almost the same shape and hue as her husband.

"We'll make do," said Sir Caspin.

"Do something!" shouted Daisy to her hapless husband. "Think of the children."

"Oh, I like my children roasted with a honey glaze," laughed Cierzon.

Torbrand shot him a disapproving look, but the rest of the party were already laughing.

"I do the jokes, sunshine," chuckled Brea.

"We'll be here for just one night," said Torbrand, trying to soothe the worried Miltons. "You have my word as a knight of the Green Order and the word of Prince Asger that we'll not harm you or your family. There are three gold coins in it for you."

Daisy's demeanour changed immediately when Sir Torbrand mentioned money. She held out her hand and tilted her head with the other hand on her hip. "In advance," she demanded.

Captain Megendade couldn't provide horses for the whole group, but he agreed to have three pack ponies delivered with enough provisions to get them to Numolport, along with a suitable mount for the prince.

The inn was a humble affair with few home comforts, but it was warm, and the beds were soft and well-laundered. Most of the company shared two or three to a room, but the prince and Moranne relaxed in their own chambers. The dryads chose to sleep under the stars in a small copse just a few hundred yards to the west.

Sleep took most men and women quickly, although the last day's events were burning bright in some dreams. Hayden was twitching in his sleep, but Jem lay on his back, gazing at the vaulted ceiling; too many questions swirled through his mind. Who was Lady Moranne? Why did Carina possess a sceptre? He could see the past or future of those around him, but why had he never seen his parents? Even Aunt Ada and Uncle Ned never appeared in his dreams. The dryads seemed to steer clear of him and even to fear him at times.

"Who am I?" he exclaimed aloud. Hayden barely stirred.

Eventually, the fatigue closed his eyes and drowned him in a sleep so deep that no dreams would trouble him that night.

―※―

An occasional thump would echo through the rough planks as half-sleeping horses bumped against their stalls. Otherwise, the stables were quiet. The oni had exceptional night vision in common with the dryads, picking out features and landscapes with only the slimmest shafts of light. It made them fearsome night hunters. Her bright yellow eyes were like lamps in the darkness, tracing the waving line of woodgrain in the rafters above as it swirled around dark knots and vanished into dovetail joints. Any oni would find themselves assessing their environment for an advantage in war, but Zonta's mind was elsewhere.

Kagel was dead. His broad, rough hands would no longer strike her, and his hot, putrid breath would be gone from the back of her neck. Escape had occupied every waking thought since her pairing with the warlord, but now there was a void where free dreams failed to grow; she was nothing without him. Returning to Banafell would bring the rest of clan Morp to their doom, and she'd be mated to another hulking brute. If she stayed in the dales, it could only be as a prisoner or freak show. Neither option offered a final escape.

A door creaked somewhere ahead, and Zonta knew she wasn't alone. The oni was tied tightly to one of the stable supports giving no chance to wriggle free. She remained still, focused on the bars of her prison.

The light flickered against the ceiling and shone into the small, straw-strewn space where she sat. A hand clasped the stall latch and carefully pushed on the gate until it swung inwards, and the narrow area was flooded with light.

"Finish me," said Zonta. Her voice was calm and filled with resignation. Gone was the bravado and defiance of earlier. She was tired and craved release.

Brenna Gunborg lowered herself to sit opposite the oni female, taking care to place the candle holder where it couldn't catch the straw. She studied the terracotta-hued creature for a while, taking in the shining, curved horns, the sharp fangs and the tiny blue beads sewn into dark, wavy hair. "I'm not here to kill you," she said finally.

"Then go," replied Zonta, turning her head away.

Brenna had no intention of leaving. The same question swirled in her thoughts since that moment in the hollow.

"My sister, Catia was beautiful," she recounted. "Fair of face and warm of heart. Every young man in Cempess wanted to be hers. She loved life so much, but not just her own." Brenna stared through Zonta into the distance, summoning the painful memories once more. "She would have spared your life in an instant... but me?"

Zonta heard every word, but she didn't flinch.

"It was just a hunting trip north of the village. I'd been that way a hundred times, but this time Catia wanted to come too. She was average with the bow and terrible with the sword, but I would protect her."

Even with her limited intellect, Zonta knew where these stories led.

"Five of your kind came at us from nowhere," said Brenna, with the glistening of tears beginning to well in her eyes. "I ran as fast as I could, but all I could do was watch as a large male crushed her slender neck with one hand."

The tears ran slowly from each eye, connected with the corners of her mouth and continued dripping from her chin.

"I killed the beast, and I wear this scar to remind me of that moment every day."

She gestured to the deep scar across her face that split her lip. She wiped the tears on her white blouse and pulled back her hair.

"Why tell?" said Zonta. It was a sad story, but war was war.

"I've fought and killed many of your kind," said Brenna. "Each and every one has wanted me dead. Every one but you."

"Wanted you dead," protested Zonta.

"You wanted me to kill you," corrected Brenna.

Zonta scowled at her, screwing up her face into a grimace. There was no way a human woman could understand the clan life of an oni female.

"Have no honour," she spat.

"Do you want me to kill you?"

The oni shuffled in her bounds and looked away.

"Do what you want," she sighed.

Brenna sat for a while, following the candlelight as it danced over Zonta's solid body. Her skin was smooth and attractive in its warm red hue, but thin lines marked her face and arms. They were no battle scars. She seemed pitiful, bound tightly and deflated; Catia would have shown compassion to this wounded creature.

"Who hit you," asked Brenna.

Maybe the human wasn't as stupid as she looked, but Zonta did not share her story with a simple wench.

"Kill or leave," she snapped and said no more.

43 THE MAD DUKE

"I thought the dalfreni hated us," said Cierzon. He sat at the Frea's Cup bar with Carina enjoying a humble porridge breakfast and a mug of nettle tea. Most of the others were awake or just emerging from the landing at the top of the stairs, but the fair folk were light sleepers and usually rose first.

"Not true," replied Carina. "We hate our alviri parents for abandoning us here and the elders for banning us from Alfheim."

"I would change the law if I were the high lord," said Lord Andain. "You're our blood."

"And what will you do about that," she said, gesturing to the far end of the bar.

Poppy, the innkeeper's daughter, was leaning on the bar, supporting her head in her hands. Her eyes followed Cierzon as he descended the stairs and hadn't strayed since he sat on a stool with Carina. She was a sweet fourteen-year-old who hadn't yet developed her parents' rotund looks. She twirled her blonde hair through her fingers when she saw Cierzon look her way.

"You have an admirer," teased Carina.

Cierzon smiled, lighting his entire face. His white hair shimmered as he turned and beckoned to the young girl.

"What would you like to know?" he said.

She looked around as if Cierzon was addressing someone else, but slowly she crept along the bar, hypnotized by his light.

"My father says you're dangerous," she said, trembling.

"I promise not to turn you into a frog," laughed Cierzon. "At least not until I've finished my breakfast."

"You be teasing me," she said coyly.

Cierzon smiled and held out his arms in apology. "Ask me whatever you want to know."

She smiled, blushing, but her parents weren't around, and few of the original guests had stayed. Thus, she decided to venture the question foremost in her mind. "Does it all…"

"What?" replied Cierzon.

She looked away, but curiosity got the better of her. "Does it all work the same way?"

Carina almost spat her tea across the bar, but the alviri lord took it all in his stride. "Last time I looked," he said, smiling.

Poppy grilled the alviri lord for a further half-hour until she learned that they didn't live forever, couldn't do magic and despite what the priests told her, they never summoned demons.

"That's a shame," joked Brea, emerging down the stairs. "We could do with a good demon."

The others congregated around the bar to hear Cierzon's stories. The innkeeper, his wife, and both of their children were enthralled. All the assembled races laughed together for just a moment until Captain Megendade burst into the room.

"I'm afraid you'll need to leave. Now!"

"What's the meaning of this?" demanded Moranne. Sefti was still unsteady on her feet but healing quickly, and the whole company was tired.

Kane quickly took Sir Torbrand to one of the inn windows to show him what awaited. A line of townspeople stood quietly in front of the inn. Further rows echoed into the distance, and more seemed to be joining from the city.

"I don't understand," said Torbrand. "We've kept our distance."

"I'm sorry," he replied. "News of the girl's miraculous recovery has spread across the town. They think she's a witch, and they also want the ogre."

"The eighth pillar," said Poppy. "They mean to burn her."

"You'll protect us," said Sir Torbrand.

The captain shook his head. "I don't have enough men; I can't fight the clergy."

"Will you at least stand by?"

Kane pondered for a moment, then nodded in agreement. His men wouldn't take up arms against the Fay Legion.

"Nobody will touch Sefti or the prisoner," announced Oretta Brimwulf.

"They'll need to come through my axe," rumbled Lunn.

"It won't come to that," added Moranne. "Leave it to me."

The company prepared quickly and crept into the stables from an interconnecting door. Three pack ponies were ready as arranged, and Zonta was awake.

"Don't harm the locals unless they strike first," ordered Moranne.

Lunn pushed open the stable doors to be greeted by the murmuring crowd. With Moranne at its head, the party emerged to form a wide protective ring around Zonta and Sefti, walking with an improvised crutch.

"Stand aside!" shouted Moranne.

The crowd didn't move. A tall, thin man dressed in the green robes of the Frean church strode confidently from the mob until he was just yards from them. He removed a wide parchment scroll from his belt and read two passages aloud.

"Man shall fight the forces of darkness; man shall not suffer a witch to live."

While smiling thinly, he rolled up the scroll and placed it back in his belt. Bringing his hands together in piety, the priest stared into Moranne's green eyes.

"Firstly, I'm not a Frean," she said, "and secondly, I'm Lady Moranne of the King's Council, and this is Prince Asger Fierdman. We are commanding you to stand aside."

Still smiling, the priest looked down on her as if he were addressing a child. "We practice the law according to the scriptures, so your status has no bearing. Leave the witch and the ogre with us, and you may leave with your elves."

"Who is ogre?" roared Zonta, drawing attention to herself. Some of the crowd gasped as they noticed the red oni struggling behind Moranne and the others.

Moranne looked across at Torbrand. There were too many people to fight through; it would be a bloodbath. There was only one way. Moranne strode to meet the priest face-to-face but spoke loud enough for all to hear.

"If you take my warrior, you must also take me, for I, too, am a witch."

In the well-practised movement honed over thousands of years, she took the sceptre from her cloak and held it aloft for all to see. Her eyes burned a bright emerald green, and lightning sparked from the sceptre's orb, snapping into the air. The priest moved back, and the crowd gasped. A few stragglers stopped in their tracks, and others backed away.

"A crude trick," said the priest, smirking with a slight quiver in his voice.

"You dare to test me!" she said in a low menacing tone.

A bright lightning bolt flared from the sceptre and arced into the ground just ahead of the mob. It blackened the earth and sent dust flying into the air.

A few of the women screamed, and some of the men yelled out. Many fell in panic and hysteria as the townspeople fled towards Langley. A couple even threw themselves into the moat, scrabbling to get away. Even some of Kane's men ran away, but the priest stood his ground.

"You'll burn for this," he seethed.

Moranne was in no mood for compromise. With the fire still flickering in her eyes, she grabbed his high collar and pulled him close.

"You'll not be here when I return," she said menacingly.

"We need to go," barked Torbrand. Moranne looked as if she could strike the priest down where he stood. The party needed to get moving before the crowds returned in more significant numbers with weapons.

"Cross-country, ma'am," added Biorn.

Tudorfeld had a significant population, and adherence to Freanism was widespread. Traversing its sweeping dales on the Green Road would be difficult without attracting too much unwanted attention. Torbrand was shocked by the level of small-town prejudice, but as Caspin reminded him: "that was you once." Their parents still held unpleasant views.

The dryads joined the column at a small wood just off the road. Together once more, the company turned northwards and headed cross-country into the heart of Grenfold's prime farmlands. More wheat, corn and other crops were produced in these fertile lands than anywhere else in Grenfold.

Large country estates spread out in every direction; wealthy lords in grace and favour mansions and retired generals on pilfered land for military services rendered. The Frean church kept restless peasants in check while landowners grew their wealth on the backs of cheap labour and ever-rising croft rents.

Numolport lay some sixty miles north, and the route would take them through busy farmland and ostentatious estates. Sefti was walking with difficulty, Zonta was bound, and the men were tired. Three to four days of travel was too much, and Sir Torbrand knew it.

"We need horses, sir," said Captain Fallon.

Torbrand agreed, but he was reluctant to countenance horse theft.

"Do we have any friends in these parts?" asked Moranne.

"I would have said yes," answered Sir Caspin, "but I'm not so sure after Langley."

Prince Asger was listening to the exchange intently. There was a very slim chance, but a chance nonetheless. "Uncle," he said, trying to form the words. "Uncle Bamlee."

"The mad duke?" blurted Biorn, forgetting himself.

Fortunately, the prince was accustomed to the gossip and scandals surrounding the black sheep of the Fierdman family, and he took no offence. He nodded, laughing heartily.

"Would he help us?" asked Sir Torbrand.

Asger remembered his eccentric uncle with great affection. He was always there when the king ignored his disabled son or raged in anger when the young prince fell from his crutches or struggled with his words. Bamlee had patience and grace, but his strange ways and the eventual scandal saw him leave Cynstol for good, never to return.

"Will help," said Asger confidently.

With few other options, Moranne reluctantly agreed with Torbrand that it was worth a try. The prince only knew that his uncle lived near Langley, but luckily Sir Caspin knew the area well. The Fierdman estate was just ten miles north and close to their route. An early autumn nip was biting in the air, but the sun was shining low in the east, and the company was in good spirits. They headed north, following Caspin's lead.

The harvest of wheat and corn was long past, and the fields of burnt stubble were all that remained of the summer bounty. Sacks of flour now stood in stilted barns, ready to supply Grenfold with bread throughout the unpredictable winter. Crows squawked from their perches on brush fences, and starlings swooped overhead in chirping flocks. There was something familiar about the land.

Jem could sense the faintest echoes of a distant memory but nothing tangible. The gently undulating hills and the smell of the air sparked an impression he couldn't quite retrieve.

"What's wrong?" piped Hayden. The squire's son could tell when Jem was having one of his visions. His green eyes sparkled, and Jem focused far ahead through the landscape.

"I'm not sure," mumbled Jem, "but beyond that hedge is a stream with a narrow stone bridge."

Sure enough, as they clambered over a five-bar gate into a neighbouring field, the scene was precisely as Jem described it. Hayden looked at Jem shaking his head. Neither of them knew what it meant, nor did they notice Moranne watching them intently.

"This is a mistake," she whispered under her breath. Only Moranne and the dryads knew the significance of Duke Fierdman's estate, and all would keep their council.

Without Cal and Slitan, the mission became closer, and the unlikely friendships continued to blossom.

Biorn and Bresne had become friends since the first oni encounter. They often travelled side-by-side, sharing Biorn's family stories in Fawnham and Bresne's life in Cempess. Sword training and eating together helped unify the oretta and the captain.

The relationship between Gamin and Isen was restrained. They seldom spoke but often walked together, helping the recovering Sefti. The other female warriors teased *Ice* Stanhamur, but she remained impassive, never losing her composure. Isen's calm manner contrasted with Brenna Gunborg, who'd volunteered to mind the prisoner. Zonta would often snarl and snap, refusing any attempt at conversation.

Ostro and Carina were natural friends and knew each other well from Suncin. The core group of Lunn, Gron, Hayden and Jem shared many jokes, but the squire's son would often be found wandering with the dashing Cierzon. The attraction seemed mutual, and no one commented, even though the likes of Gron and Gamin were committed Freans.

Of the others, Cuyler and Yuka were inseparable soul mates, Brea and Ellen were best friends, while the mysterious Sax preferred his own company. Only the energetic nymphs kept themselves apart. Chakirris often conversed telepathically with the prince, but the enigmatic creatures could rarely be glimpsed skipping through nearby fields.

There is a large house ahead, said Chakirris in Prince Asger's mind.

The prince gestured to Moranne and Torbrand, who brought the company to a halt. They decided quickly to minimise the risk by sending a small group to the house while the rest remained out of sight.

Prince Asger, Sir Torbrand, Oretta Brimwulf and Lady Moranne continued ahead, leaving Sir Caspin in charge. If they didn't return within the hour, he had instructions to continue northwards to Numolport.

Moisture remained in the air and mud underfoot as the sun dipped past noon. The fields were well-tended; Moranne spotted a couple of farmhands harvesting potatoes. However, the stately line of poplars marked the main path leading to the duke's residence. It led, arrow straight, from the Green Road further west, to the doors of Lenturi Manor. Long abandoned by the Lenturis, one of Grenfold's most renowned families, it was now the residence of the remaining Fierdmans outside the capital.

"So what was the great scandal?" asked Tiam. The Cempestre were ignorant of any affairs outside of Deapholt.

Moranne and Torbrand looked at each other, but the knight couldn't tell this tale. It was too close to his feelings for Ellen.

"It was nothing, really," said Moranne. "The duke was supposed to marry the daughter of the Earl of Gosta, but he didn't love her."

"What happened?"

"He married his serving wench," blurted Torbrand. He could just imagine how his father would react if he didn't marry into his class.

"A lovely girl named Lilly," added Moranne. "He was shunned by Cynstol society, so he returned to Tudorfeld and never set foot in the capital again."

"Good for him," said Tiam.

Prince Asger said nothing but chuckled to himself as his horse picked its way along the rutted path.

Lenturi Manor was a part stone, part timber construction which had been the country residence to fifteen generations of the Lenturi dynasty, including seven kings. Mylos Lenturi III had been the last, deposed in a bloodless betrayal by the cruel Tyborg Fierdman. General Kemin Lenturi was the Queen's Battalion commander, but he had moved his estate to Middcroft to be nearer the garrison.

A pair of tall towers reared up on either side of the main gates and marked the start of a wide rectangular wall circling the inner estate. Bright green vines wrapped around the stones and weaved through the battlements in a scene which conjured memories of Deapgate. Many might have considered the estate to be in poor repair, but nature's encroachment lent the site a magical air.

The gatekeeper, dressed in simple sackcloth, was very relaxed. With tanned skin from outdoor life and a wrinkled brow which resembled a ploughed field, the middle-aged man agreed to take them straight to the house. They tied Asger's horse outside and followed the man through the wide oak doors. They opened onto the scene of a close-knit village rather than a duke's estate. A broad wooden bridge crossed a broad section of a local stream where many peasants were fishing.

There were few decorative features on the grounds. Most of the land was ploughed, planted with crops, or home to cows and pigs. Fourteen small, round croft huts were dotted around the fields, and peasants pulled potatoes or tended to the animals. Every person tipped the brim of their hat, and children smiled as the prince rode by.

"We don't get many visitors," said the gatekeeper.

Everyone seemed bright and happy, unlike most crofters who struggled on the land and could barely pay their rent.

The expansive, double-fronted house spread out before them, but it was poorly maintained compared to the surrounding farmland. Dark green vines twisted around its towers, and bright lichen patterned the stone. It reminded the prince of Deapgate, but no dread surrounded it.

Sir Torbrand ascended the crumbling steps, but the gatekeeper had turned left and led them out along the stream towards a wide field of mature potatoes. They ducked under a gnarled, five-hundred-year-old oak, which dipped its roots into the water. As the path turned back around the house, they could see a small, decked area where several figures sat around a long table.

"Bam, sir," called the gatekeeper. "We has visitors."

Seven people sat at the table, enjoying a late lunch in the afternoon sun. They all wore the peasant garb of white linen shirts with brown sack-cloth trousers. However, one grey-haired man in his late sixties wore a multi-coloured velvet cap perched on his large ears. His face burst into a joyous smile when he noticed Asger leaning on Torbrand's arm.

"Asger, my dear boy!" boomed the duke, climbing to his feet. He launched towards the young prince before Asger could say anything, and flung his arms around the lad. "It's so good to see you again."

Bamlee's eyes twinkled like a teenager, and his face radiated warmth, scanning the prince from head to foot. He appeared more like a friendly innkeeper than an extended member of the ruling house.

"You've grown into a tree," he laughed. "I remember when you sat on my knee, and we shared stories of dragons and ogres." He patted the prince firmly on the back and turned around shouting. "Lil, it's Asger!"

Even in her mid-fifties, Duchess Fierdman was a naturally beautiful woman. Her face had the same permanent smile as her husband, and her long grey hair cascaded freely over her shoulders.

She took the prince's hand and kissed him tenderly on the cheek.

"You look tired, my love, sit with us and have some raspberry wine," she purred.

"My lord, we need your help," interrupted Sir Torbrand. He had little time for pleasantries and always liked to come straight to the point.

"Steady on, big fella," chuckled the duke. "There's no lords here. You can call me Bam or nothing at all, and this is my wife, Lilly, but she prefers Lil. Now sit yourselves down and tell me how I can help."

The peasants on the property were from Lilly's family, or they were relatives of those who had served the Lenturis over the years. The duke and duchess had no children of their own but considered these people to be family. They ate together, worked together and even dressed in the same humble manner. Torbrand had never seen a member of the aristocracy choose to live in such a humble way.

The farmers returned to the fields, leaving the five to talk. Lady Moranne took the lead, telling the duke about their mission to stop the Stans from joining Corvus, and then Sir Torbrand detailed the nature of their party and how they'd recruited from far and wide.

"You have a female ogre?" noted the duke. "Fascinating. I've never seen a female."

"She's not very friendly," suggested Tiam.

"I bet she's not," he laughed. "And you have nymphs with you? I've heard many tales, but I've never seen one." Both the duke and duchess seemed intrigued, but the Pillars of Freanism were very clear. "Don't worry about any of that religious nonsense," he bawled, "I'll have none of those damn priests here. We're all creatures of the earth. Now you go and bring your friends here, and we'll have a feast fit for a prince."

Tiam departed to get the rest of the company, and Moranne took the opportunity for a private word with the duke. Together, they walked along the stream until they were out of earshot.

"What's that about?" asked the prince, but Sir Torbrand had no answers. He shrugged as they both watched Moranne and Bamlee, deep in conversation. Moranne's body language was threatening, and the duke seemed angry, but when they eventually returned, he was back to his gregarious self, although he wouldn't look at her.

"Something I should know?" queried Torbrand.

Moranne ignored him and sat beside the stream, watching the mallards bustle from bank to bank, hoping for table scraps.

It was midafternoon by the time the whole mission had assembled at Lenturi Manor. The duke had agreed to lend them eighteen horses from his estate, including two strapping shires, under the condition that they attended a feast and stayed the night. It was too late to travel, so Moranne and Torbrand reluctantly agreed.

All the Fay Legion members were welcomed with open arms, including the suspicious dryads and the scowling Zonta.

Jem's hug was more prolonged than any other. "Jem, my dear boy," gushed the duke. "I've heard so much about you. So brave and strong. I want to know all about your visions."

"Lady Moranne told you?" asked Jem, surprised.

"Shush!" cautioned Bamlee, holding a finger to his lips. "I'll speak to you later."

44 FEAST AND FLIGHT

Jem found his way to the large, square kitchen, where flames leapt from the rusting iron stove. He turned and followed the spiral stair, which wound upwards to the north wing. From there, he walked along the panelled corridor to a door that opened onto a high viewing platform. Jem gazed northwards into the darkening skies, where Numolport lay and Stanholm beyond. He'd been here before. Sensing every doorway and remembering every colour as if he'd walked these passages a hundred times. It wasn't possible.

Stooping back through the doorway, he gently closed the narrow portal behind him and retraced his steps. He proceeded halfway down the hallway, but something tugged at him to stop. A panelled door on the left was slightly ajar. He touched it gently, and it swung inwards to reveal a small bedchamber.

A generous window looking east over the estate gave the room a bright and airy feel. The double bed looked comfortable, and a wide oak dresser had been covered in small ornaments. They comprised roughly carved horses and an intricately detailed, black statuette of a smooth, bald woman, arms outstretched as if begging.

"Ah, you've found your room," boomed the duke, standing in the doorway.

"My room?" asked Jem.

"Well, if you want it," said Bamlee smiling. He walked into the small space and followed Jem's gaze towards the east. "Lilly's family lives in the south wing, but this room has been empty for many years."

"Who lived here?"

Bamlee picked up the small, black ornament and sat on the bed, tracing its curves. "This room belonged to a lad named Will. He lived and worked here for many years."

"Where is he now?"

The duke sighed, remembering Moranne's words from earlier that day. An oath was an oath. "He left suddenly," replied the duke. "We don't know why, but I always hoped he would return."

"Was he in trouble?"

Bamlee burst into laughter and slapped Jem on the back. "In trouble?" he chuckled. "Will was *always* in trouble, and I'll wager he's in trouble still."

Jem wanted to know more about the mysterious Will, but the duke told him the feast was almost ready and he should join his friends. Looking back at the familiar room, Jem followed the duke down into the main hall where the others were waiting.

The reception room of Lenturi Manor ran from the front to the back of the expansive building. Doors and wooden staircases on the left and right gave access to the north and south wings, home to the duchess' family. They would also provide overnight accommodation for the mission. The hall was adorned with paintings of the Lenturi dynasty, lit by hundreds of home-made candles. It had once been the scene of opulent balls and regal parties, but now it served as the communal dining room where the duke and duchess dined with their family and tenants.

There were no manor staff as such. The tenants cooked evening meals in return for free farming rights to the land, and the promise that they could stay indefinitely, even after the duke's death. It was a generous form of altruism that neither the prince nor knights had ever seen. It was closer in concept to the communal village of Cempess.

"Please, sit anywhere," beamed the duchess, as she took a seat at one end of the table.

Bamlee and his wife didn't believe in formality, and neither did they believe in servants. All the steaming food had been set on the table for self-service. There were golden rabbit pies, roasted chicken legs, a rich-smelling venison stew, baskets of seeded sourdough bread, huge bowls of hot buttered potatoes and all manner of seasonal vegetables. The farmers dined in the kitchen tonight, but the fourteen-year-old Tom was sitting beside the duchess as her favourite.

Both the duke and duchess had dressed for the occasion but humbly by Cynstol standards. The duke wore a blue velvet jacket over a ruffled white shirt, while the duchess sat radiant in a purple ball gown with a black floral pattern.

"You look stunning, my lady," said Gamin, sitting nearby. However, his eyes were fixed on Isen, sitting opposite.

"Call me Lil," said the duchess defiantly, "but I think *this* fine warrior has your heart." Lilly winked at Oretta Stanhamur.

The dryads weren't familiar with feasts or eating at a table. They tentatively took their seats and looked uncomfortable, fiddling with the alien spoons.

"Use your hands, my dears," said the duke, taking his seat at the opposite end of the table. "I often do."

Prince Asger was sitting to his right, with Chakirris and Sondrin on his left, but his eyes were on Jem. Moranne's gada sat between Sondrin and Carina, directly opposite Hayden and Cierzon. He was still grappling with the manor's familiarity, but the arrival of Brenna and Zonta silenced the room.

"She can't eat with us," said Tiam.

"It's too dangerous," agreed Moranne.

Bamlee Fierdman was having none of it. He stood at the head of the table and called for Brenna to bring Zonta to him.

"Welcome, my dear," he said. "I've never met an ogre—"

"Oni!" spat Zonta defiantly.

"Please forgive me," said the duke, smiling. "I would love for you to join our feast, but you must promise not to hurt anyone. Can you do that?"

Looks of horror reflected from the banquet table, and Zonta was confused. "Trust me?" she asked.

"An oath is an oath," replied Bamlee. His eyes bored a hole into Moranne as he spoke.

"Promise," said Zonta.

Tiam and Sir Torbrand rose to protest simultaneously, but the duke silenced them with the flat of his hand.

"Don't forget I'm a duke, although I only use my rank on exceptional occasions," he laughed. "I outrank everyone in this room except perhaps the prince and Lord Andain here. Now please remove Zonta's bindings, and let's eat."

Brenna carefully removed the ropes binding Zonta's hands, half expecting the oni to lunge at her in anger; instead, she rubbed her wrists and stepped back in fear.

"We won't hurt you," said Oretta Gunborg. She could scarcely believe her own words. Yesterday she wanted every oni dead.

Zonta tentatively pulled out a chair next to Ellen and looked down at the clean earthenware bowl and curved metal tool before her. Although the oni did cook their food, it was eaten by hand from small wooden bowls.

Once everyone was seated, the duke climbed wearily to his feet. He cleared his throat and admired the twenty-nine faces at the table before him. Visitors from the capital were rare, and other races were unheard of in these parts. His chest puffed with pride as his eyes finally rested on his wife's smiling face.

"You are all welcome to our home. It has been many years since I last saw the prince, and I'm so proud to have you with us, Your Highness." He bowed to the prince, then looked across at Cierzon and the dalfreni. "It's been too long since I last met members of your fair races, and I regret that you are still forced to live in the shadows. I would like to apologize for the small-minded actions of folk in these parts. All of you are welcome here at any time."

He extended the same welcome to the dryads and the Cempestre, but his demeanour changed when his attention turned to Moranne.

"Many friends go, and some friends return," he said, "but my doors are always open to those we love."

Jem looked up to see that Bamlee was looking directly at him.

"Now let's eat before it gets cold," he bellowed, flopping back into his high-backed chair, seemingly exhausted.

"What was that about?" asked Tiam.

Moranne shrugged; she knew precisely what the duke meant. He was playing a dangerous game.

Lunn was the first to grab food, opting for a chicken leg and roast potatoes. He also made up a plate for Sefti, who sat beside him. Something about the slight, blond warrior made the giant soldier very protective. There was nothing sexual; Sefti seemed to bring out a nurturing side in the colossal man that no one had seen.

The others quickly followed, pouring flagons of mead and taking hunks of bread. A low babble of excitement circled the room, as the men and women served themselves from large trays placed along the table's centre.

Hayden couldn't help watching Cierzon as he looked from left to right. His hair bobbed and reflected the candlelight like twinkling stars.

"I had a farmhand like you," said the duke. "Be careful in these parts."

"What happened to him?" asked Hayden.

"Better not to know," interrupted Sondrin. She couldn't shut out images of the young man being stoned to death in the centre of Langley.

The duke nodded. "Always close the curtains."

"Is there anywhere safe?" said Jem.

"Only Alfheim," noted Cierzon. "I don't care what my father says. Hayden will always be welcome."

Hayden felt a hand rest upon his leg beneath the table. His heart skipped, and he just caught his breath. Tears pooled in his eyes, and he looked away, trying to hide the emotions stirring in his chest.

"I mean it," whispered Cierzon, his jade eyes lit like jewels.

Brea noticed the encounter and smiled. It was in stark contrast to the awkward silence to her left. Ellen Hildebill and Sir Torbrand Linhold were drawn together like the moon's pull on the ocean. It ebbed and flowed but never met like the celestial and earthly.

They sat directly opposite one another, snatching the slightest glimpse when the other turned. Torbrand spoke with Moranne, his brother and even the quiet Jilliad to his left, but not one word to the strawberry blonde swordswoman with a silver band in her hair. He wanted to hold her tight, caress away every taint of the vile Slitan and take her far away, but he dared not. She couldn't dare to dream nor have any hope of a future. It was impossible.

"Your mate?" blurted Zonta.

Oni males often treated their mates with disdain. Zonta didn't pick up many human subtleties, but she could tell something was bubbling beneath the surface.

Ellen shook her head vigorously and sighed in resignation.

"You're not eating," she said, changing the subject. The oni female was pensive, watching others eat while she eyed the beef stew hungrily.

"Masters first," she replied. That was a lesson she quickly learned when she saw a female beaten to death for daring to eat before her mate.

"You can eat when you want," said Brenna. She dragged the steaming stew towards them and ladled a generous amount into Zonta's bowl and her own.

The oni observed as Brenna lifted her spoon and used it to gather some of the creamy dish. She blew on it gently and ate from the utensil. Tentatively at first, Zonta mirrored Brenna and took a small amount of food. She chewed it suspiciously and swallowed.

Like a child walking for the first time, a broad grin erupted across Zonta's face, exposing the sharp, glistening fangs. She turned first to Ellen and then to Brenna. "Good!" she shouted so loudly and aggressively that some of the company reached for their swords, while others dropped their food, and a plate smashed somewhere in the kitchen.

There was silence for a moment, and then the duke roared with laughter, followed by Lunn, Gron, and most others.

"Don't worry," said Brenna quickly. "They're not making fun of you."

"I make joke?" asked the bemused Zonta.

"You make joke," confirmed Bresne.

Oretta Fixen sat beside Biorn, watching her warriors enjoying the meal. It made her long for Gunnar's arms, keeping her warm through the Deapholt winter.

"This food reminds me of home," said Biorn. "Nina makes the most wonderful rabbit pies."

"You'll be home soon, I'm sure," beamed Bresne, but something in the captain's demeanour worried her.

"I'd love you to meet my wife; she's such a gentle woman."

"I'd like that very much," said Bresne. "We'll be there together."

Biorn was staring into the distance, through Sax, to a dangerous path ahead. He knew there'd be darkness and death before the journey's end. He was sure of it, Jem could see it, and Moranne could feel it like a gathering storm.

"What do we expect of Numolport?" asked Sir Caspin, pulling Moranne from her thoughts.

"Trouble," she replied. "The port is only slightly less religious than Langley. We'll need to be careful."

"Let's just enjoy the meal," ventured Tiam. She was watching some of her warriors and studying the contrasting characters.

Cuyler and Yuka had nothing but love for each other, sharing private jokes and finding any excuse to touch. Something which Isen and Gamin never did. The bowman worshipped the statuesque axe wielder but dared not voice his feelings in public. So besotted was he, that he would never risk embarrassing her in front of her friends. Their relationship was restrained and unspoken, if it existed at all.

The dryads, too, made little sound, but they spoke continuously. Sondrin was warming to the humans, even joining some banter, but Jilliad remained cautious. They'd witnessed their numbers dwindle, and the dominion of men expanded. Their leader's plan was risky and could spell their doom, but what choice did they have?

You'll make a strong king, said Chakirris into the prince's mind.

He enjoyed the connection they'd made but wondered how many of his thoughts remained secret.

None, came the answer, accompanied by a cheeky smile which flashed across the nymph's face.

"We have a king," replied the prince, out loud.

"An idiot," added the duke. "He lets the priesthood rule the land, puts a fool in charge of the Green Order and thinks your moronic brother will make a great leader."

"I think that might be treason," said Ostro.

Both the prince and duke laughed heartily.

"Oh, it's good to have you here once more," chimed the duke. "Don't wait so long next time."

Jem was aware that Bamlee seemed to be including *him* in that comment. *But I've never been here*, he thought.

You've been to many places, Jem Poulterer, came an unexpected answer.

Jilliad gave him a wry smile from across the table until Chakirris shot her a dark look. *Sister, it's not our concern.*

"What isn't?" said Moranne from the centre of the table.

The dryads often forgot that she had the gift of silent speech. They could mask their thoughts from her, but they needed to concentrate.

"The food isn't army rations," volunteered Gron.

"Thank you for this bounty," added Tiam. "You're so generous."

The duke and duchess smiled and nodded in recognition. "It's the least we can do," said the duke. "If the Stans invade with Myrik, it will be a massacre. I wish the king had seen sense and granted farm rights to King Ramon."

"He never asked," said Asger.

"Ha!" chuckled Bamlee. "Is that what they told you?" He shook his head in resignation. "If Pythar would leave his jewel-encrusted palace just once, he might understand how desperate these people are."

The prince couldn't argue. His father surrounded himself with fawning acolytes, who fed him the distorted picture of a contented land, praising his name. It was easy to see how the Frean church could ascend to fill the power vacuum.

"You'll need all the power of the alviri to stop Myrik," continued the duke. "Did you know he almost took the capital five hundred years ago?"

"How do you know this?" asked Caspin.

"I can read!" he laughed. "There were once many books depicting the first dark war, but the Frean church had most of them burnt. Something about worshipping false gods."

"Sounds familiar," quipped Brea.

"Do you still have the book?" added Jem.

Bamlee nodded with a wink.

"Let's not depress our guests, dear," said the duchess calmly. "You have a hard road ahead, so please enjoy yourselves tonight."

The evening continued in a similar vein. The duke skirted controversy with his views on the Frean church, the monarchy, and even the metalworking skills of the alviri. It was a refreshing change for all of them to speak so freely, and Jem enjoyed listening to the heated debates circling the table.

Bamlee was especially interested in the dryads and the way they survived. He knew about their ability to charm and referred to them as fair folk from the age of galdur.

"What is the age of galdur?" blurted Hayden. It was a phrase that Moranne had used, but none of them had questioned it.

The duke finished taking a deep draught from his flagon of mead, wiped his lips and let out a sigh of contentment. "Ah, my young gada. The age of galdur was the age before men. The time of magic."

Moranne huffed and rolled her eyes, but the duke wasn't finished. "The alviri ruled Weorgoran; they were at peace with dryads, naiads, seelie and even the oni."

"Naiads and seelie?" scoffed Gron.

"Mermaids and fairies," laughed Biorn.

"There's no such thing," said Caspin defiantly. "Old wives' tales and stories to scare the children."

Bamlee shook his head and laughed a deep rumbling chuckle. "My dear knight, this land was full of wonderful creatures before the humans took it for their own. It's true; the seelie have gone. They were too trusting of us, but the naiads are still here, in fewer numbers, but they endure in the waters around Brencan."

It was very subtle, but the prince noticed Chakirris and the other dryads nodding at the mention of Brencan. He knew little of the sunken isle besides its reputation as a ship's graveyard.

"Alright," said Caspin, baiting the gregarious duke. "From whence did we humans come?"

Bamlee smiled and threw up his hands. He'd reached the edge of his knowledge, but Moranne was on hand to answer the young knight.

"The humans you know as Jakaris were first; they arrived from the west. They lived in harmony with the fair creatures until different humans arrived from the south. Both races had fled from hardship or destruction, but the new humans never really trusted the Jakaris and hated the seelie and alviri."

"Now I know you jest, ma'am," laughed Sir Caspin. "Of all the ships that have explored in all directions, none have ever returned. There's nothing there!"

For just a moment, she looked around the table of expectant faces until her face slowly creased into a wide, beaming smile, and she exploded in laughter.

"You nearly had us there, ma'am," roared Gron, as the others convulsed and banged the table.

Moranne didn't drop her wide grin, but there was no jest in her words. If humans knew what lay beyond these sheltered shores, they would live in mortal fear.

Moranne and the duke continued to regale the assembled company with tall tales of dragons, wyverns, manticores and all manner of strange beasts. Eventually, eyes drooped, the drink took effect, and fatigue pulled the party towards sleep. They thanked their kind hosts and made their way up the creaking staircase to the north wing of Lenturi Manor.

The nymphs chose to sleep under the trees near the stream. Prince Asger, Moranne and Sir Torbrand had their own chambers, while the rest slept in pairs.

Sir Torbrand's room was on the third floor, at the very end of the building. The floorboards moved underfoot, and everything sounded as if the manor was breathing. He opened the door to see a small room with a dormer window reaching out as the roof sloped down. He ducked to enter the small doorway and turned to close the door.

"Evening," said Brea. She stood leaning against the door frame with twinkling eyes and a mischievous smile, which often meant trouble.

Torbrand sighed. "You should never creep up on a soldier." The fatigue was making him even more irritable than usual. "I didn't thank you for the fight against the oni," he smiled. "Using the terrain like that was clever thinking."

"I learned a lot hunting deer," she beamed. "Shame some of us is still so thick." The smile didn't drop, although Torbrand didn't appreciate it tonight.

"Remember to whom you speak—"

"Or you'll what, big man, hit me?"

He turned to ignore her, but she wasn't finished. "Have you spoken to her since the wolves? Have you even asked her how she is?"

"I can't," he said solemnly.

"You won't."

"I can't!" he raged. "You don't understand!" He opened his arms, grasping for her comprehension.

"Oh, I understand perfectly," she rasped. "I don't know what she sees in ya, but Ellen loves you. But you..." Brea sighed and turned, ready to walk away. "You only care about how it looks."

"How dare you," blasted the knight.

Brea was already walking down the hall to find her room.

Damn you, Brea, he thought; her words stung him like white nettle. When he woke, he thought of Ellen; she filled his dreams when he slept. He couldn't shake her, but worse still, he didn't want to. He kicked the door shut, and it banged, echoing through the entire north wing.

Jem looked back along the corridor, but the sound came from above. He lifted the latch, and the door swung inwards, revealing the same room he'd stood in earlier. Everything was the same, except for the bed, where a thick, brown book lay on the pillow.

It was bound in frayed dark leather, but the title was just visible on the spine.

The Lenturi Dynasty by Evelin Lenturi.

Some of the pages had deteriorated, and a few were missing. Jem noticed a black feather halfway through the book, used as a bookmark. He opened the crusty tome at the marked pages and began to read.

45 THE BATTLE OF KELBY

The trees of the Northwood bent and cracked as the red stampede poured forth.
A wall of ogre hatred from the beasts of mountains north.
No warning call nor bugle's sound did save old Kelby's home,
For fists of iron and clubs of stone did flay the flesh and crush the bone.
A woman's scream, a child's tear, and streets which ran with blood,
Were all that remained of the Grenfold town which broke before the flood.

Myrik laughed at human fear; the puppet master's plan drew near.
For simple creatures killed in his name and played for him his evil game.

"No!" she cried, though her heart did break. "The crown was never yours to take.
I'll stop your march and send you down to the underworld that is your home."
Although a witch, her heart was pure. She rode out and past the castle's door.
Her power flashed before her eyes, but Elara's gifts were no surprise.
For Rana, too, screamed a song of hate and rode once more through Cynstol's gate.
Friends no more but witches still; they raced as one, a demon to kill.

First Legion men in helms of steel were killed by friends or forced to kneel and grasp their own battle-weary knives, to thrust them down and take their lives.
Blood everywhere; on every stone; on every blade of grass; on every soldier kind
Who took his life with Myrik's hand inside his mind.

Through this grizzly graveyard did the witches toil, over twisted bodies and bloodied soil.
But the mountain men with curving horns stood fast. They would not let the women pass.
"You die today," they howled. "We'll split your souls," they growled,
But Elara and Rana stood strong. To doubt them would be wrong.

With sceptres high, wreathed in emerald fire, the witches screamed a spell of dread.
A tidal wave of power spread forth, and twenty ogres lay still and dead.
Clan creatures being simple beasts, were filled with fear and doubt.
In panic, they fled into legion knights who snuffed their red lives out.

Still, he stood, his will unbent, his sceptre was high, but it's power near spent.
Myrik laughed in maniacal glee, "You will never know the power in me!"
Rana, filled with anger and bile, ignored his words and mocked his smile.
It may have been forbidden love, but she would never forget Aludra, her love.
Such love; so much love. Rana cursed Frea above and blasted out a spear of light which threw Myrik down with power and spite.

His sceptre dropped, and power diminished; he knew his grab for the crown was finished.
In agony, he heaved, but Rana's knife was unsheathed and held above his darkened heart.
But no. "No!" cried Elara. "He's just a boy. He must be tested, tried, not destroyed."
"Stand aside," shouted Rana. "Stand aside, you bitch, for I will end the evil beast and too the evil witch."

*All was still, and all were quiet as Rana's sceptre sparked, but
Aludra's gentle words did echo, touching her stony heart.
"Without her, we'd be gone," she said, inside Rana's thoughts.
To love all creatures, foul and fair, was the lesson she had
taught.*
*With tears and words of angst and pain, Rana lowered her
sceptre and sobbed as the rain fell in torrents to wash the land;
free of the blood which stained their hands.*

*His sceptre secured, and his power ebbed; they looked around at
the fields of dead.*
*Never again would this war be fought. They had their demon, or
so they thought.*
*But before the hanging trial could start, he escaped his bonds
deep in the dark and ran for all his life was worth to hide
somewhere within this earth.*

*Rana was broken, her will was snapped, the trial to end his life
was scrapped.*
*With Aludra gone and nothing left, she flew from Lyften to her
death.*

*The Kelby battle ended, Mylos sat on the throne, the army was
rebuilt, and the ogres had gone home.*
*But in the darkness and the night, a warlock schemed to regain
his might.*
*He hated the witch for his life spared and plotted her downfall
and utter despair.*

*As to whence, Elara has gone, the secret to keep is mine alone,
For when evil Myrik rises again, it will end for good the
dominion of men.*

"The Battle of Kelby", by Prince Timur Lenturi.

༄

Jem looked back over the fields of potatoes and turnips to the hedges of hawthorn and copper beach. Somewhere over the lush farmland, in a distant hamlet, was the weathered, inviting Lenturi Manor and the tiny room where he'd read an ancient book.

It took the small hours to drag his weary eyes shut and let the book fall from his grasp onto the polished floorboards, but not before he'd read the same passage over twenty times. The story was real; he could picture Moranne and Rana confronting Corvus as if they stood in the field before him.

He looked forward towards the head of the column where Moranne, Asger and Torbrand rode. All three of them seemed deep in thought. Moranne's eyes stared through the horizon to some distant point ahead, Sir Torbrand's mood was dark, and his head faced downwards, while Prince Asger stole glances at Chakirris, who shared her mount with Sondrin.

Jem kept his distance, but he was keen to speak with Moranne. Unfortunately, she seemed to sense the simmering questions he had for her; she turned away and feigned interest in some of the Cempestre or spoke with Carina in hushed tones.

Most of the company were riding with companions, including Lunn who rode with Sefti, and Brenna partnered with Zonta; both pairs were on mighty shires. They couldn't ride their mounts too hard with such weight, but they still made faster progress than walking. Moranne hoped they'd reach Numolport by nightfall.

All were sad to leave the warm embrace of Lenturi Manor and its generous hosts, but some of the company had changed. Sir Torbrand had reverted to the distant, aloof knight who strode into Cynstol Castle's ballroom many weeks past. He pointedly refused to speak to Brea and didn't look at Ellen as they prepared to leave. Even Caspin received the cold shoulder while they rode northwards. Only Hayden seemed to be genuinely happy. Sat behind Cierzon on a stunning bay, they were wrapped so close that they seemed to be embracing. Sometimes sharing a whispered word and laughing at a shared joke, none who saw them failed to be touched by their intimacy. Even the stout Gron, sharing his ride with Ostro, found time to smile at the young gada and his six hundred-year-old companion.

Plodding through cultivated fields and across narrow streams was slower than taking the Green Road, but they couldn't risk attracting too much attention. The few farmhands and peasants they saw would run from their path to cower behind hedges or rickety barns. Just the sight of Zonta was enough to strike fear into the hearts of simple folk, although the whole company was beginning to resemble a travelling circus.

They wound mostly through the heavily cultivated lowlands, but occasionally they would cut through small strips of woodland and over shallow, unplanted hills. Most of Tudorfeld sloped northwards at a shallow angle until it peaked as a rough coastline of grey cliffs and jagged rocks. The whole area seemed safe and stable; there was little fear of bandits, and any threat from Salamas was distant. Only the Stans gave any cause for concern, but their minor incursions had all been dealt with swiftly. The north coast presented few landing opportunities, and the Green Order was disciplined and effective. Moranne feared their complacency.

The sunshine which bathed the party near the manor now receded; a bank of wispy, grey clouds was rolling in from the west. A thin mist carpeted the distant, undulating landscape, and the faintest hint of rain lingered in the cool, damp air.

They stopped several times to rest the horses and enjoy the food they'd received from the duchess. It ranged from game pies and strips of cured ham to crunchy apples and seeded sourdough. The bounty even included a leather pouch of mead passed around the camp with gratitude.

With every day, the team grew stronger and tighter. Even Jilliad felt more relaxed and sat closer to the others, raising a smile at Gron's bad jokes. Now unbound, Zonta tried to participate in the banter, but her vocabulary was weak; she mostly watched as the others laughed. Wherever she stood, Brenna would be close.

The tall, scarred oretta had become Zonta's full-time minder and watched her closely wherever they went. Tiam decided the oni was of little danger without her weapons, tied to one of the horses. She rode freely, and they would only bind her at night. Neither Moranne nor Sir Torbrand knew what to do with her. Handing her to the Green Order would result in her death, but letting her go could endanger others.

"Should have killed me," mumbled the oni when she heard Tiam discussing her fate.

Brenna's hatred of the clans was well known, but her approach to Zonta was gentle. She made sure the oni was well fed and tried to widen her vocabulary. Zonta never smiled, but a fragile friendship was gradually forming, even if she did insist on calling her Cempestre captor *Brenda*.

"B-r-e-nn-a," the oretta would say slowly, but it didn't seem to sink in. Or it was possible "she makes joke," as Tiam put it.

The relationships between Cuyler and Yuka, Hayden and Cierzon, and the fatherly love displayed by Lunn for Sefti were open for all to see, but one blossoming relationship was hidden. Chakirris and Prince Asger spoke continuously through their minds but seldom rode or sat together.

My father hates me, said the prince. *I've seen him willing me to fall from my sticks.*

Your father does not deserve you, replied Chakirris. *We have toiled in Deapholt for hundreds of years. We rarely conceive, and even then, our offspring only live to become food for wolves, tunnbroccs or snakes, or crushed under oni boots.*

Chakirris enjoyed sharing her burden with someone other than her sisters, and the prince relished a free-flowing conversation with an equal, free of his father's contempt or impatience. The prince looked back once more to the glowing nymph and her smooth alluring frame, but he was rewarded with only the faintest nod.

Outcrops of rock broke through the earth like giants escaping a tomb of soil, and shale cascaded down the hills from frost-damaged granite walls. The terrain was changing as they slowly neared the largest port in Grenfold. The coastline bulged northwards here, but the sharp cliff edges made landing a ship difficult. Fortunately, the alviri engineers had an ingenious solution, and Numolport was the result.

Sir Caspin knew a shallow valley which ran parallel to the Green Road, so they carefully traversed the rock-strewn bottom and climbed slowly up and out of the north end. A green, mossy bank fell downwards before them towards a narrow coastal path which skirted the cliffs.

Sir Torbrand called the column to a halt, near an abandoned barn, just over the hill's brow. It was built against the grey rock. Although some roof slates were missing, it would still provide shelter if the weather turned.

"Why are we stopping here?" asked Tiam.

Moranne and Sir Torbrand had discussed a new plan after Langley, but they hadn't shared it until now. "We can't just walk into the port," replied Moranne. "The dalfreni, dryads, Zonta and even Lord Cierzon could be seized or worse. Sir Torbrand and Sir Caspin know the garrison commander, so we'll just go forward with the humans first."

"I see," said Tiam, annoyed that she hadn't been consulted.

"The fair folk will stay here with Sax, Jem, Hayden and Brenna if you permit it."

Oretta Brimwulf didn't feel as if she had much choice. The decision had already been made. "Alright, I agree," she said reluctantly.

Sax, Brenna and Chakirris would lead the remaining party and wait for Caspin to return for them once safe passage had been secured. The rest would head for Numolport immediately.

"Listen carefully," said Sir Torbrand. "If you don't hear from us by sundown tomorrow, assume the worst. Return to your homes and release Zonta near Deapholt."

"Return to our homes?" asked Jem. Denbry no longer felt like home, and he had too many questions for Moranne.

"Look after yourselves. That's an order," replied Torbrand.

Taking all the horses but leaving food and supplies, Sir Torbrand led the human party down the hill to join the coastal path. Turning west, they stayed away from the local village of Clifftown and plodded gently along the stony road. It wandered back and forth between rocky outcrops and small copses until it rose over a bluff revealing the cliff edge and the sea below.

The placid Lower Straits separated the mainland of Grenfold from the grey isle of Stanholm. The distance was a mere forty miles between the closest points of Numolport and Gulward, a trade route for gold, silver and precious stones of every kind in its heyday. Stanholm's bounty had gradually diminished until the ships of wealth reduced to a trickle, and food became a bigger priority for the Stans. The fall in trade had also affected the people of Numolport; fewer merchants walked its streets, and the trickle-down of wealth slowed to a drip.

"What's that noise?" asked Yuka.

The sound was constant and unseen as thousands of gallons of water plunged over the Tudorfeld cliffs into a gorge.

Their first sight of the town was a line of black and white painted buildings which skirted the Green Road. Many beams were split, and some of the daub renders had flaked away, giving the dwellings a look of neglect and decay. The sign of the Red Dragon Inn creaked wearily in the wind. Its painting was so faded that it was just a merge of muddy colours.

A few townsfolk stared at the odd party, then sniffed and returned to their toil, but the children begging for coins revealed a town in crisis. Some skipped along with the Cempestre calling for coppers, but others had grown weak and sat beside the grey houses with arms outstretched.

"I thought Cynstol was bad," lamented Brea.

The sound of the Hiwness River dominated the town as it rushed behind the buildings, but it was the Foss Keep that commanded the horizon. Four round towers, capped with Green Order flags, peaked above the dwellings. Like an iceberg, the town masked the bridge-town's true extent to anyone approaching from the south.

"How is this a port?" asked Tiam.

"You'll see," said Sir Caspin, smiling. He'd been to the northern town many times, but the sight of its engineering marvel always took his breath. The city might be known as Numolport, but the bridge itself was named Bruborg. As they passed the last crumbling building before its eastern gate, the scenery fell away to reveal a substantial, half-castle, half-bridge construction perching impossibly behind the falls.

"The ingenuity of the alviri," said Moranne beaming.

The bridge's size was staggering, but the entire castle, built upon its single span, was at least as big as Deapgate in its prime.

The relentless flow of the River Hiwness had worn a wide gorge in the cliffs, and the resourceful alviri used this to build a port where none should exist. Using each side of the canyon as a platform, they constructed a bridge-town spanning the land drop on wide stone pillars, allowing the Hiwness to flow beneath to a sheltered harbour. They then tunnelled down through each clifftop, creating a wide shaft in the rock on both sides. By diverting part of the river through buried channels, they could use the water's weight to power two elevators at each end of the bridge. One would be used for goods, while the other would carry the local fishermen.

"Now I see!" exclaimed Tiam. The eastern side of the bridge-town lay before them, and she could see over the cliffs to the harbour below. Many longships and some fishing vessels were moored along the two quays, just visible through the arch.

"Moranne and I will do all the talking," said Sir Torbrand. He looked stiff and nervous, exchanging concerned looks with his brother.

The gate was known locally as the Tally Gate, owing to the gold and precious stones which would pass this way. Its opposing western entrance was the Burgate, designated for the fishermen and peasants who worked in the harbour. A small rectangular tower was situated just inside the entrance. The two iron wheels and paddle air-break, peeking from its top, revealed the Tally Winch machinery; one of the two alviri wonders carrying goods and people to the quays below.

Scrolled ironwork wove between the bars of the gates, propped open to allow merchants and fishers to enter unhindered. The road rose over the bridge, ending in the keep, which sat at the arch's centre. Two guards eyed the party suspiciously as they passed. Torbrand tipped his brow in recognition, and the silver-helmed guards bowed, but their expressions were serious.

No words of recognition, thought Caspin. Sir Torbrand was well known in the Green Order, and Sir Caspin wore his rank in his armour. The two guards had barely acknowledged them.

"Something don't smell right," whispered Brea.

Torbrand said nothing, but he felt it too. There was a wariness to the guard's demeanour and a feeling of nervousness in the air. "Stay close," he said.

Fish stalls and small shops lined the walls. Merchants would weigh the gold and diamonds in the market's heyday, but the brokers and traders were gone, leaving boarded, empty frontages and a ghost-town air.

Some townsfolk looked up and frowned at the sight of armour-clad women with swords at their sides. Bruborg Abbey stood just beyond the keep, acting as a magnet for all devout Freans in the area; its spire stood in judgement over the town and harbour. Torbrand was right to leave the others behind.

The rising road led them to the arched doorway of the Green Hall. An imposing, grey stone monolith housing a contingent of the Green Order and the local commander. The two guards wordlessly acknowledged the knights and opened the oak doors, swinging inwards, creaking on rusted hinges. A walled courtyard lay within, with a corral along one side where the party tied the horses. The square was ringed by a high, wooden walkway, allowing archers to keep watch, and several doors lay directly ahead; otherwise, the area was empty. The heavy doors banged shut behind them, leaving the party alone.

"Very friendly," said Tiam. "You boys must be popular in these parts."

The brothers exchanged looks once more, but Caspin was shaking his head. Something *was* wrong.

"I'll find the commander," replied Torbrand, starting for the largest door ahead. He brushed the dust from his armour, ready to greet the captain when the door suddenly opened.

Three armoured men entered proudly - all wearing the oak tree insignia of the Green Order and similar armour to Torbrand and Caspin. The leader wore a captain's garb, identical to Biorn, but his breastplate was the same polished steel as his gleaming helm, and his gauntlets looked new. He stopped just in front of Sir Torbrand and removed his helmet.

"Welcome, sir," he said stiffly, bowing his head in deference. He had long, thick black hair and a well-groomed beard; his stature was similar to Torbrand's. "I am Captain Rufus Drytenhold, Commander of the Bruborg garrison."

"It's good to see you," replied Sir Torbrand. "We're on a mission to Stanholm on behalf of the king. We need supplies and a ship to get us to Gulward." He deliberately omitted mention of the fair folk waiting just outside the town.

Rufus fidgeted while the knight spoke, looking over his shoulder as if others might be listening.

"Is anything wrong?" asked Moranne.

The reply came unexpectedly from the doorway behind the captain. "Everything is well, my lady," boomed the voice of General Cymel Marl, striding wilfully into the square. "However, I'm afraid your mission has ended." He stood before Torbrand, waiting for the soldiers to respect his rank.

"Sir, we have still to visit Stanholm," insisted Torbrand.

Cymel was enjoying the upper hand. "I'm sorry," he said. "The plans have changed; your journey ends here."

"But—" began Prince Asger, stuttering, but the general cut him off.

"General Benton and I spoke with the king after you left. We convinced him we had a better plan."

"A better plan?" howled Moranne.

"Yes, my lady," he replied, relishing the moment. "I've deployed the entire Green Order and most of the Queen's Battalion on the coast. When the Stans attack, we'll wipe them out for good and take Stanholm."

"You're insane!" she protested. "Corvus will cut you down!"

Cymel paced towards her in defiance and looked down on Moranne like a parent scolding a child.

"Oh yes, *Corvus*. If he even exists, which I doubt, he's just one man. He's no match for two armies."

"But, sir," gasped Sir Torbrand. "They could attack from anywhere."

His words were lost. The main doors opened behind, and a host of soldiers poured in. Trampling boots echoed around the parade ground and the terrace above. Thirty archers positioned themselves, with their bows trained on the company; the finest Green Order soldiers surrounded them with swords drawn.

"Welcome all," boomed the general. "You've done an excellent job, Sir Torbrand, but we'll handle things from here."

"Stop this!" shouted the prince.

"I'm sorry, Your Highness," said Cymel, with false contrition. "The king's orders were clear. I am to stop Lady Moranne's mission in any way I see fit."

"Don't test me, Marl," she spat.

The general was unmoved. "If you even touch your magic wand, one of my men will kill one of your party. Don't test *me*, my dear." He pulled himself up to full height and bawled his orders across the square. "Your men will report to Captain Drytenhold for reassignment. The women will be confined until I can spare men to escort them home." He peered at the bewildered faces and shook his head. "No elves, I see."

Sir Torbrand looked across at Captain Fallon and then at Sir Caspin. They all served in the army, and they'd all sworn the same oaths.

"They wouldn't join us, sir," he said, hoping the half-truth would mask the lie.

"As expected," sniffed the general. He turned to his captain and called him forth. "Please escort the prince, Lady Moranne and my knights to the keep, arrange billets for the men and take the women below."

"Below?" blurted Torbrand. "You can't!" His eyes flicked to Ellen.

"You must be tired, Sir Torbrand," said the general. "I'll forgive that outburst, but don't forget to whom you speak."

"I'm sorry, sir," he offered, but his head was down, and his mind was filled with dark thoughts. He would never take Cymel's place with any utterance of insubordination. The mission was lost.

"I have a hundred men here," said Captain Drytenhold. "Please put down your weapons."

"A hundred, you say," mocked Brea. "You'll need more to make it a fair fight."

Torbrand was shaking his head, and Biorn was urging his men to comply, although the Cempestre wouldn't go quietly. Isen punched a soldier sending him reeling into a wall before three others managed to subdue her. Brea spat her contempt, and Bresne simply met Biorn's gaze as she was bundled through a door and down stone steps into the heart of the bridge. Captain

Fallon watched while Cuyler and Yuka were yanked away, then looked to his men.

"Remember who you are, lads," he said, trying to maintain some dignity.

In truth, any pride he once had in the Green Order seemed to evaporate with the glowering general. Cymel grinned in satisfaction before striding back through the arched doorway, chuckling as he went.

With the women gone, Torbrand faced the Green Order captain shaking his head. "What happened?" he asked.

Rufus was reluctant to answer, but Sir Torbrand outranked him, and they were once good friends. "The general arrived a week ago and took over; there's nothing I can do, sir."

Torbrand nodded in resignation. Rufus was a good soldier. "Please look after my men; they've been through a lot," he said, scanning the ashen faces of Gron, Lunn, Gamin and Biorn. "Treat the women well; they deserve our respect."

Captain Drytenhold nodded in agreement, but the general had already sealed their fate.

46 BRUBORG

Drip, drip, drip echoed the sound like waking torture. Drip, drip, drip tapped away at Tiam's thoughts, causing her muscles to clench like a coiled viper, ready to snap at anyone who spoke. The slow tap of water on the stone was like a clock ticking away on life.

The cell was cold, damp and dimly lit. A narrow, horizontal slit just above head height allowed a thin twilight beam to pierce the gloom; an oil lamp swinging in the corridor above provided only a meagre background glow. At eight-foot-square, there was barely room for the two rough beds and putrid tin pail. There was no door as such; a hatch in the steel grate above gave the only access. Brea and Tiam had been forced to descend by ladder, which was then withdrawn.

Numolport's cells were located on the lowest level within the two pillars of the bridge. The stonework was five feet thick at this point, and below was solid stone forming the massive base of the town. All the women were locked in the east pylon, sharing two per cell. Sefti shared with Bresne, Ellen with Yuka and Cuyler with Isen.

Tiam was Cempestre born. Any domination by men boiled her blood, making the veins throb in her temple.

"Calm yourself, love," said Brea. "They'll let us go eventually." She sat upright on one of the beds watching Oretta Brimwulf pace from one side of the tiny cell to the other, clenching and unclenching her fists.

"Shut up!" she spat, in no mood for calming words.

Brea was unperturbed, sighing in disgust. "We has a saying in Caynna," she said. "The sleeping hunter gets the deer."

Tiam laughed, shaking her head. "Well, I'm *so* glad they put me in here with you and your great words of wisdom. Thanks!"

Ready with a withering reply, Brea decided to leave her be. It was going to be a long night.

※

The Foss Keep extended for three levels above Bruborg's bridge-town, but a further two, down into the bridge itself. Another two levels could then be reached via a pair of towers that leaned out from the north wall. It was an unusual design, and very easy to become lost in the narrow tunnels and twisting stairs. Access to the harbour could only be gained through one of the two winches on Bruborg's surface. Escape would be difficult.

Moranne pondered their predicament from her room on the west side of the top floor, overlooking the harbour and the foaming sea beyond. Red upholstery, woven with silver threads, adorned all the best rooms in the keep. The fires were well stoked, and the beds were soft and luxurious. While it was good to relax in the duck down once more, she couldn't help thinking of the Cempestre trapped below.

The sumptuous room adjoined an ornately decorated lounge, which she shared with Prince Asger. Alviri and Stanish weapons hung from the walls, along with embroidered drapes showing the winged form of Frea. Torbrand and Caspin were accommodated on the lower levels, while Biorn and the soldiers were billeted with the garrison.

Moranne paced back and forth across the large chamber, watching as the flickering firelight danced on the weapon's steel. She would need to face Corvus alone. Her thoughts darted back through time to the small boy with dark dreams and deeds. Dane warned her, but she didn't listen. She could still see his smile beaming above her on the grassy bank, but the sound of knocking broke her from the spell.

"My lady," urged a familiar voice, accompanied by knocking from the lounge door.

"Come in, Caspin," she replied. Their paths had crossed many times since he was a teenager, and they'd been friends ever since.

He entered quickly and closed the door carefully to avoid making a sound. "I'm being watched," he whispered, making his way across the room, but avoiding the windows. "I'm in the lower west tower, and Torbrand's in the east. They split us up. I don't know what to do."

"You have no choice," she said.

"That's what my brother says, but we can't let this stand." He took her hands, pleading for guidance. "I saw those wolves in the forest, that was no ordinary attack, and then there's Jem."

"What about him?"

"His visions, ma'am," begged the knight. "He's seen things which will come to pass. Terrible things."

She sighed and sat near the fire. Jem's power grew daily, and soon he'd know the truth. Without guidance, he'd be drawn to a confrontation which would be his end. They were fortunate that the general had forgotten her gada.

The door to Prince Asger's chamber slowly creaked open, revealing the prince leaning on a pair of new walking sticks. He was clean-shaven and fresh-faced, having enjoyed his first bath since Cynstol. While he looked healthy and refreshed, it was the look of determination which captivated both Caspin and Moranne.

"I have an idea," he said, shuffling into the room until he stood swaying before them.

A few green blades stood like spears above the snow. Naked tree branches dripped as the white blanket slowly melted. Every drop made a gentle tap as it landed in the snow, forming a ring of small holes beneath each tree. Each breath was a puff of disappearing steam, and his fingers ached in the cold, but Captain Biorn Fallon was smiling. He recognized every turn of the path and every rise and fall of the Middcroft borders. The River Cwen burbled through the glassy ice clinging to its banks and the icy stone bridge before him.

His heart beat a little faster. He knew how the land spread out over the bridge. His house was humble by a captain's standards, but it was all he needed for his wonderful family. Nina would run through the vegetable beds to greet him, his son Biorn would want to know about his adventure, while little Brenni would hug him until he could hold back the tears no longer.

The house's grey, slate roof peaked over the bridge, followed by the second floor's smashed windows. Biorn stopped. His breath failed, and his chest heaved. Every window was broken, and the door lay in splinters.

"Nina!" he cried, running towards the house.

His heart thumped heavy against his chest, and tears started to well as he raced frantically through the crunching snow. Skidding down the path, he kicked the door fragments aside and dived into the chilling house.

"Nina!" he screamed again, but there was no reply.

Barrelling down the hallway, he barged into the kitchen door, flinging it open, so it crashed against the wall.

"Nina—"

She wouldn't answer, but she was there. Her legs lay flat across the terracotta stone floor. Biorn moved gingerly around the table until he could see her lying lifelessly, with the curved blade of a Jakari sword protruding from her back. A vast pool of dried blood spread out from her body. He knelt and pressed her cheek, but she was as cold as ice.

With his vision blurred in a rage of tears, he ran through the house, but his children were gone. He howled in pain and cursed all the gods and his weakness when she needed him most.

"I'm sorry," he sobbed. "I'm sorry." Then the knocking began.

It pounded in his head, begging to be heard, so loud and insistent that he covered his ears, but it was just as loud. It increased some more, and now there was shouting.

"Who are you?" he cried. "Leave me to grieve."

He punched the air with his fist, and something smashed nearby.

Biorn's eyes snapped open; his breathing was short, and his heartbeat was so strong it throbbed in his neck. His skin ran with sweat which stuck to the bedsheets. He stared up at the panelled ceiling of his quarters; a nightmare.

The small room was modest by a captain's standard, but at least he wasn't billeted with the rest of the Green Order.

"Captain Fallon, sir," came the insistent voice behind the door, interspersed with knocking. "Captain, sir."

"Come," answered Biorn. The relief cascaded over him like a warming blanket, just a nightmare.

The door opened quickly, and Gada Rilling stepped inside and stood stiffly to attention. He looked down at the broken mug on the floor and then at the perspiring captain.

"Prince Asger wants to see you, sir. He's waiting in the officer's lounge."

The captain waved him away and quickly washed and dressed. He was still shaken by the nightmare and wanted to see his beloved Nina again as soon as possible.

The officer's lounge was a small room on the second floor of the Green Hall. A large window looked out over the bridge walls to the Hiw Falls cascading over the land drop and into the gorge. The room contained several high-backed chairs and a table with a brimming jug of mead. The lone figure of Prince Asger sat in a corner chair; he smiled as Biorn entered and stood to attention.

"You wanted to see me, Your Highness?"

Prince Asger gestured for the captain to sit and asked the gada to pour them a flagon. When they were both seated with a drink in hand, he requested Gada Rilling to leave them alone.

"Sir?" asked Biorn. He'd spoken to the prince many times since Cynstol, and he'd become familiar with the patience needed to allow Asger to express himself.

"Must thank you for all your work," replied the prince. "You are a brave man."

Biorn thanked him, but he sensed that the prince wanted something. He took a sip of the sweet liquor and placed the flagon on the table.

"You are free to go back to the Order, but I have a question," continued Asger.

"Ask it, sire."

The prince looked around as if they might be watched and leaned forward to whisper. "Will you help us?"

Biorn didn't need to know more; he knew what the prince was asking. The sight of a cruel Jakari blade in his beautiful wife still seared his consciousness. His answer was immediate.

"Yes, sire."

Asger smiled and offered his hand in friendship, but they could all still hang even with the prince's endorsement.

"Your men?" asked the prince. He already knew they'd follow Biorn anywhere. Gamin would do anything for Isen. Lunn felt like a father to Sefti, and Gron would go wherever Lunn went.

"You'll have them," replied Biorn.

There was a rough plan, but it relied on a lot of luck.

The route from Moranne's room took Caspin to one of the keep's towers, where a spiral staircase led below the street level. He emerged in a long corridor spanning the bridge from west to east. There were no discernible windows, but it was dimly lit by a line of small, brass oil lamps hanging between locked, panelled doors. These opened onto several main chambers used by knights, generals, the mayor and some of the wealthiest merchants in Tudorfeld. Numolport was once an affluent, exclusive address, but as the golden river became a stream, the lustre fell from its gates. Many of its dwellings now stood empty.

A small corridor on the left reached out to the western front tower, but as Caspin turned the corner, he collided with a young man hurrying to his post.

"I'm so sorry, sir," gasped the soldier. He crouched to retrieve a dropped ledger, but a crease of recognition furrowed his brow as his eyes looked up into Caspin's face. "Is it you, sir?"

Orange light flickered over the lad's face, reflected from the warm-coloured stone, but his features were unmistakable. The short dark hair parted from a high forehead, and a thin face and bead eyes reflected the oil lamp's hue.

"Rike?" said Caspin, trying to focus. "Gada Shepherd?"

"Its Private Rike Shepherd now, sir."

The sheep farmer's son had been Caspin's gada when the knight had only twenty years himself.

"How long has it been?" gushed Caspin. The smile bursting across his face was genuine. The two had been inseparable in the Queen's Battalion.

"Seven years, sir."

Caspin grasped him by the shoulders and embraced him firmly. "It's so good to see you."

There was genuine affection between the knight and his former apprentice. Caspin treated all his men more like friends than subordinates, unlike his stern brother. Rike and Caspin spent many happy evenings in the taverns of Faircester or the brothels of Gosta. Caspin recommended that the

Queen's Battalion give him a commission, but the lad's hard work led him to be granted a place in the Green Order.

"This is fate," beamed Caspin. "I need to speak with you."

Rike promised to attend Sir Caspin after his duties were complete. He believed they would be reminiscing about their time in the Queen's Battalion, but Caspin had other ideas.

The Linhold brothers had rooms in the forward towers, but the arch split them. While Torbrand had a higher floor on the east tower, Caspin was relegated to the west pylon's bottom floor.

Looking down through the vast, arched window, he could see the river rolling past and an array of ships moored in the harbour. Less sumptuous than Moranne's chamber, it was still well-appointed as befit his status. Red velvet curtains bordered the windows, and the same colour covered the bed and the indulgent chaise. He inspected the dents and scrapes on his knight sword and remembered his father's words when it was handed to him on his twenty-first birthday. "Don't dishonour the Linhold name."

Never a positive word nor any show of affection. Earl Normin Linhold took every opportunity to remind Caspin of his place, firmly behind his illustrious brother. He could have borne the rejection like a scar and treat Torbrand with contempt, but it wasn't his way.

"Come!" he shouted when Rike tapped on the door.

"You wanted to see me, sir?" asked the private. He stood to attention in front of the door, but the broad smile gave away the closeness they enjoyed.

Caspin paced in front of the window with his hands clasped behind his back. Everything was now a gamble. "It's delicate," he replied. "I know we go way back, but I need to know I can trust you."

Rike was unfazed. They already shared many secrets, like the time they stole Commander Mirgan's best mead. "You can always trust me, sir."

"Even if it means going against the general's orders?"

Rike looked down for the merest second, but his answer was final and heartfelt. "I has you to thank for my career and, begging your pardon, I counts you as a friend. You has my loyalty as long as I breathe, sir."

"May Frea bless you," said Caspin. He embraced his former gada and slapped his shoulders in friendship. Insisting that Rike took a seat, he stood in front of him, with his hands on his hips, and made his request. "I need a boat which will hold thirty, and a captain who won't ask any questions."

"Consider it done, sir," replied Rike.

The cold, silver light of the crescent moon rippled on the waves of the Lowker straights, climbed the cliffs and reached out to the abandoned barn where they slept. Most of the party lay beneath the crumbling roof. The dryads relaxed in nearby bushes that hid the building from the path below. They would not let their guard down completely and slept so lightly that they could be fully alert and to arms in seconds.

Her duty was to keep them alive and find mates, but Chakirris felt something new and personal. Unnerving and foreign, it filled her mind and scared her more than a charging tunnbrocc or black wolf in the Deap. She wanted to know he was safe, but the distance was great, and she couldn't feel him. Maybe if she concentrated, he would hear her and know how much she missed him.

She closed her eyes and focused on his long dark hair, the lop-sided mouth and the twinkling eyes.

Asger, can you hear me?

There was nothing but darkness and silence. A distant owl screeched, and another hooted in response. All else was still.

My prince, she projected into the gloom, pouring all her will into the thought of his clumsy gait, but a full and faithful heart.

I'm here.

Her heart skipped, and her eyes flashed open.

We're in trouble, he continued. *I need your help.*

47 PLOTS IN THE DARK

Jem woke to Hayden's overly cheerful voice, as usual. His laughter echoed off craggy rocks and the barn's stone, a private joke shared only with Cierzon.

"Are you ever quiet?" ribbed Jem.

Hayden was too entranced by the white-haired alviri to hear any of his friend's jibes.

"Love," said Sondrin. The orange glow of her face appeared around the barn wall like a sunburst.

"It's a good thing he was left here," agreed Jem. "The sound of his pining would have been unbearable."

The dryad nodded sagely. Same-sex love was widespread in her kind, but the need to procreate was too strong to rule men out wholly.

"I've no idea what I'm doing here," complained Jem. "With Hayden, it makes sense, and Sax knows the port, but I should be with the humans."

Sondrin looked down at the visage of a young man. He had powers not yet discovered and dangerous destiny. She disagreed with her sister; he needed to know.

"You're not h—"

"Sondrin!" shouted Chakirris.

It was rare for the nymphs to vocalise any conversations, and the startled Sondrin looked visibly shaken. *I'm sorry, but the lad should know.*

Soon enough, Chakirris cautioned. "Now," she commanded, returning to speech. "I need to gather everyone together. We have orders from the prince."

Ostro was practising his impressive staff-twirling skills while Carina rolled her eyes, and Sax sharpened his blades. It didn't take long to assemble the group in front of the weathered farm building. Chakirris stood with her hands on her hips, waiting for the others to settle. She looked every inch the seasoned leader, holding her head high, she gazed at the expectant faces and then appraised them of the situation.

"Officially, the mission has ended. The human men have been ordered back to the army, the warrior women are in prison, and Wickona is being watched. The stupid general intends to fight Myrik and the Stans with his puny, human army."

"Some things never change," said Carina dryly.

"Are we going home?" asked Hayden hopefully.

Chakirris nodded. "If you wish. You are all free to go."

"What about the mission?" asked Jem. "Corvus is coming, and people will die." He still pictured the crofters and the Supbry fortune-teller being hacked to death by Jakari warriors.

The nymph smiled thinly. Chakirris rarely showed any emotion, but something about the plan excited her. "Prince Asger is inviting volunteers for a new mission under his name."

"Let me guess," said Hayden. "It's the same mission, but we all hang when we get caught this time."

Chakirris said nothing; the prince would be unable to protect them from his father or the hawkish generals.

"I'm in!" shouted Jem.

"You have my staff," added Ostro.

"And my sword," chimed Carina.

Hayden turned to Cierzon, but the alviri lord was already smiling.

They all agreed except for Sax, who sat against the wall playing with one of his throwing knives.

"What say you, Knives?" asked Jem.

He looked up, but his face was a portrait of resignation. "I have nowhere else to go," he said solemnly. He slid the knife back behind his coat and looked into Chakirris' eyes. "You have my knives."

With the mission assembled, Chakirris described the rough plan. "We'll split into three teams. Sondrin will lead Jem and Hayden, I will take Cierzon and Ostro, and Jilliad will form a team with Carina, Brenna and Zonta. We will sneak into Numolport under darkness before enacting the plan at midnight. There are many things which may go wrong."

"We can always improvise," smiled Ostro.

"Make sure you all know your roles and the fall-back plan," said Chakirris. *I hope you know what you're doing, my prince.* There was no reply, but she had faith in him.

The party dispersed to break camp, leaving Chakirris alone, looking out towards the port. After a couple of minutes, she noticed a tall shadow falling past her feet.

"Brenna, what is it?"

Oretta Gunborg stood beside the towering Zonta, who looked down at her minder as if Brenna was now her master. Respect formed between the two after the oni discovered the Cempestre's strength, controlling their destiny without men.

"Zonta has a request," replied Brenna. "She would like to have her axe and helm."

Chakirris studied Zonta for a moment and probed her thoughts. She could see the horrendous life as a warlord's mate and the compulsion to escape, but there was something else. She wanted to be part of a bigger plan, not just out of duty. An emotional tie had formed with Brenna, and it was more than respect. Something more substantial was growing.

"You wish to join the mission?"

"Join," grunted Zonta in agreement.

"Do you swear an oath to serve the prince and not to harm any of us?" Chakirris already knew the answer before the oni's limited intellect processed the question and formed a reply.

Zonta looked down at Brenna, and something passed between the two without a smile or any visible emotion. "Swear," she said softly.

The company was complete.

A thin layer of dust lay over the cabinets and empty bookshelves. It rose beneath their feet as they entered the room, and it clung to the cobwebs which hung in the corners like stringy hammocks. The chambers of Bryant Gimcyn had been empty for a couple of years from the moment the diamond shipments had stopped. Situated almost directly above Bruborg's keystones, it was spacious, consisting of two interconnecting rooms. Plenty of space for a conspiracy.

"Are you sure you weren't followed, ma'am?" asked Caspin. He looked nervously towards the door but only saw Lunn's wide beaming grin behind Captain Fallon.

The prince was already seated in front of the grimy, arched window. He smiled as each conspirator entered, but one person was absent, leaving a tall, imposing void.

"Torbrand?" asked Asger.

Caspin shook his head. "I tried to talk with him, but he told me to forget the mission. He's a loyal officer."

"Alright!" interrupted Moranne. "Are we all agreed on the plan?"

They all nodded, but some of the men were unsure of their roles. The prince had shared all the details with Moranne and Caspin. He asked the knight to go through the details once more.

"Lunn, Gron and the captain will break into the armoury to retrieve our weapons. I will get the prince to the quay, and Lady Moranne will free the Cempestre."

"I volunteer to help Her Ladyship," blurted Gamin. His mind was never far from the statuesque Cempestre warrior.

Caspin smiled. "Of course."

In reality, Gamin had not shared a kiss nor barely a word, but Isen was his world. He was accustomed to the ribbing and secretly enjoyed every moment that placed him with *Ice* Stanhamur.

"What about the boat?" queried Moranne.

Caspin nodded. Rike had arranged everything. "Captain Barda Blake has a longship on the East Quay, but there is a small catch."

"What kind of catch?"

"He wants a diamond," said the knight, sheepishly.

"A diamond?" she retorted. "None of us have that kind of money!"

"Leave to Sax," said the prince, smiling.

Moranne hated leaving the details to others, but she dared not question the prince. He seemed to be enjoying the plot.

"Is there any chance we can warn the Cempestre?" asked Biorn.

"We could warn them through the dryads with their mind powers, but the plan works better if no one expects us."

"And what about the body count?"

"No dead," replied the prince. They all agreed that lethal force must be the last resort.

"Very well," said Moranne. "You all know your duties; just be ready for the signal."

"What signal?" rumbled Lunn, looking bewildered.

Caspin laughed, sharing a knowing smile with the prince. "You'll know it when you see it."

Two old knight swords were mounted on the wall above the solid oak desk; arranged in a diagonal cross, behind a shield bearing the Green Order crest. Sir Torbrand knew every dent and every scratch on their grey surfaces. His eyes had been running over them for ten minutes while he stood in General Marl's office, waiting for his superior to look up from his papers. That was after Cymel had already delayed him for two hours in the antechamber.

Torbrand didn't look down, sigh or show any outward sign of irritation. A knight he may be, but duty was his first call. The general had anointed him as the natural heir, and he dared not jeopardise the years of careful planning, strategic partnerships and quid pro quo favours done on his behalf to secure the role. Earl Linhold had bet everything on his eldest son, and it was Torbrand's duty to deliver.

"Knight Commander," drawled the general, looking up from his papers. The ledgers of Green Order expenses were not a pressing task, but he enjoyed displaying his rank and making his subordinates know their place. "What may I do for you?"

"Sir," replied Torbrand stiffly. He was trying to remove all traces of emotion from his voice. A skill practised throughout his unhappy Faircester childhood. "I'd like to make a representation on behalf of one of the female prisoners."

"I see. And which one of the Cempess wenches would this be?"

A ripple of distaste passed through Torbrand's mind, but he remained as impassive and impenetrable as a statue. "Do you remember the swordswoman from Grenborg?"

The general pretended to run through his mind, struggling to recall the detail. Finally, he held up a finger as if he'd struck the critical memory. "The clown!" he laughed gleefully.

"Her name is Ellen Hildebill," countered Sir Torbrand. He ignored Cymel's attempts to unsettle him. "She's the daughter of Corporal Raffus Hildebill."

"Is she really? Raffus was a good man."

Torbrand had practised the speech several times in his head, but he knew how it would sound to the general.

"Sir, Lady Moranne told us it was a priority to recruit her for the mission. I needed to make the woman a promise before she'd join us."

"What kind of promise?"

"She asked for a commission with any army branch, and I agreed."

"Do we have a clown vacancy?" roared the general.

Torbrand could see what was coming, but he plunged headlong into the fire like a moth darting about a flame. "As a soldier, sir," he corrected. "I thought she could join the Burland Guard."

The colour was already flushing in Cymel's face as he rose from his chair to stare Torbrand in the eye. "A soldier?" he scowled. "I don't care what you've promised this Grenborg whore, but we do not have *girls* in the army."

Torbrand felt his hands tighten and a pulse of hatred in his temple. For the briefest moment, he envisaged grasping one of the ancient swords and running it through the general's gut.

"I made a prom—"

"Sir Torbrand!" interrupted the general. "Remember who you are. The mission is over, and your work is done. You did what you needed to do. Now stop acting like a first-year gada." Cymel sank back into his chair, indicating that the meeting was over. "If there's nothing else, you are dismissed."

The knight stood for a moment watching the scales tipping above the general's head. On one side stood his career, his father's acceptance and life with a vacant debutant, while on the other sat a beautiful woman beneath the shadow of a noose.

"Sir," he said courtly, then strode from the room a little shorter than when he arrived.

48 FIRE AND WATER

The black new moon was perfect, casting a veil of darkness over Numolport, Bruborg and the lapping quays below. A few torches lit the bridge's arch, and lamplight flickered behind the windows, but otherwise, the town was near invisible.

Private Wilf Ancra peered through the swirling iron of the Tally Gate, but there was little to see past the small patch of path illuminated by the gate's torches. He thought he'd seen a shadow passing by, but the light often played tricks, and he shook the vision from his mind.

"Anything there?" shouted Private Merf Merebrim. He leaned against the north wall, stifling a yawn. Two guards were posted at each gate and took turns to watch the north and south sides overlooking the quay and Hiw Falls, respectively.

"Nothing, Merf," replied Wilf. Probably just a fox, he thought.

I'm no fox, Wilf Ancra. The voice was smooth and demure like a caress.

"Who said that?" shouted Wilf, whirling back to stare into the gloom.

"Who said what?" countered Merf.

"Are you playing ragging games again?"

The guards often played pointless guessing games or gambled on the next breed of gull to swoop over the walls.

I know a good game.

"Who are you? Show yourself," commanded the flustered guard.

"Who are you talking to?" howled Merf.

Wilf ignored him and tried to focus past the gate. The voice seemed to come from all around him, but she must be out there somewhere. As the torches bent and flickered, they caught a shape. It seemed to pulse in and out of existence until a face gradually formed. A sculpted, naked body soon blinked into view as the woman slowly approached. He wanted to shout out, but the vision might fade. The torches picked out a mottled green skin, woven with wisps of brown, wound around her arms and draped over her breasts.

"Who are you?" bawled Merf. He, too, could now see the sinewy naked form of Chakirris moving stealthily towards the gate, like a cat stalking a sparrow.

We can all play this game, Private Merebrim.

Merf span round to see a shining silver hand curling suggestively around one of the gate bars. A youthful woman's face soon emerged, smiling seductively between the railings; thin brown rings wrapped about her face like the glistening bark of silver birch.

"What in Frea's name are you?" he pleaded.

His mind was already falling into her spell. He said nothing as Wilf unlocked the gate and pulled it open. He felt only calm when Ostro dragged him to the ground, and Cierzon tied him tightly and gagged him with sackcloth.

"Too easy," grinned Chakirris.

"Can you now please put some clothes on?" laughed Cierzon.

Chakirris nodded and faced the west. *Your turn, sister.*

Sax's team had started earlier. With help from Sondrin, they managed to sneak Jem and the noisy Hayden into the centre of Numolport's town. Past a tackle maker and behind a large storage shed, they found the River Hiwness running beside a short wood-plank jetty. It was easy to steal a small boat and paddle to the opposite bank with no townsfolk in sight.

They waited just out of sight from the Bur Gate until the signal came from Chakirris. Sondrin's skills were twice those of her sister; she bewitched the two guards with no other help, leaving the men to quickly bind and gag the hapless soldiers.

"What now?" whispered Hayden while Sondrin poured herself back into the skin-tight leathers and bustier.

"Follow me," replied Sax.

The first fifty yards on the west side of the bridge was a mirror of the east. Small shops, fish merchants and actuaries lined the two walls, but there was no sign of life. Bruborg was deemed low risk, so only the Foss Keep was fortified. No soldiers patrolled the bridge or looked out from its arch.

"Stay low," whispered Sax, aware they could be seen from one of the keep's towers. Hugging the shop frontages, they made their way gingerly towards the goal.

With its spire pointing above the wall, the abbey of Frea's Light stood half as tall as the keep. Its tower pointed west to mark Father Lygen's origin, and its length backed up to the keep with which it connected. Sax led them just past the base of the tower, along its flank to where a low arched door recessed into the grey stone exterior. "Keep watch," he said, grinning.

Sax opened his coat and reached inside to retrieve a narrow leather bundle. It was tied with thin strips of leather, which he loosened so that it unrolled with the chink of metal on metal. Several short, delicate tools sat in small pockets. Some were pointed, others were blunt, and a few curved into intricate shapes. He withdrew an implement with a hooked end and a second pointed tool and began picking the abbey door's lock. Working with a clockmaker's slow, particular skill, he carefully turned the objects until a faint click signalled the door was open.

"You're a man of hidden talents," said Jem.

Sax winked.

That's not all you hide, added Sondrin; no one heard it but *Knives* Stulor. The grin dropped from his face, and he shot her a dark look.

The door creaked open into a small room. A candle still burned on a worn desk revealing spare chairs and shelves of religious books lining the walls. A collection of green velvet Frean robes hung on a wooden rack.

"Bring the candle," whispered Sax.

Hayden picked up the candle as instructed. Another arched door stood on the opposite side, but this one was unlocked. They carefully crept through and stayed low against the wall in case anyone was still around.

The abbey's main hall was ringed by large stained-glass windows showing Frea and Father Lygen holding a tall staff, dim in the low light. The chamber width was filled by four columns of deep oak pews facing the tower, where a nine-foot, golden effigy of Frea stood. One oil lamp still burned near the dais, revealing the goddess in all her winged glory. She was naked except for a sash draped over her torso, which ensured her modesty, but her wings were visible, extending outwards for six feet on either side as if she was in flight.

Jem thought he'd been to the Frean church many times back in Denbry, but the statue was alien to him. Everything about it seemed to be severe and oppressive. Even her dead-eyed stare over the heads of the congregation appeared cold and aloof. Few commoners had encountered a diamond, the highest of all the currency, but the sparkling gem in Frea's crown was the largest stone they had ever seen. Enough to feed five hundred orphans and help all the grieving war widows.

"That's obscene," ventured Jem.

"I'm glad you think so," agreed Sax.

He took a small, narrow knife from his jacket, grasped it between his teeth and jumped up the statue, clutching her wing so that he could hang on with one hand.

"This is desecration," whispered Hayden. "What are you doing?"

Sax took the knife in his free hand and started to prise the stone from its mount.

"Jem! Somebody stop him," implored the squire's son.

Freanism ran deep, even for those it suppressed. Many would take their own lives before being cast as sinners or guilty of forbidden love.

"Frea despises you," said Sondrin. "Your love for the alviri lord will see you dead at her hand."

"We're just friends!" he protested.

None of them believed him. Even Sax looked down from his perch with a raised eyebrow.

"I'm happy for you, but you owe her nothing," said Jem, gesturing to the statue.

They were right, and he knew it. Hayden was still staring at the flagstone floor when Sax pulled the diamond free, dropping it to the stone. It skittered across the surface, spinning over the cracks until it came to rest directly beneath Hayden's gaze.

"Pick it up," ordered Sax. "And start taking the oil lamps down."

"Why are we doing this?" replied Hayden. He didn't know why he was there or what they should be doing.

"Maybe you should have listened to the briefing," laughed Jem. "Rather than staring into Cierzon's eyes."

Sax and Sondrin were already scurrying from wall to wall, gathering as many of the brass oil lamps as they could carry.

"Douse the drapes, then throw everything else onto the pews."

Jem and Sondrin were already throwing the oil onto the long, velvet drapes that hung between the windows. Each bore the image of Frea or Father Lygen in gold stitch on a jade green background.

"Come on, lover boy," teased Jem.

Hayden examined the shimmering gemstone in his palm. There would be no going back to Dunstreet after today. He was the squire's son no more.

"Hurry!" shouted Sax.

The earthy smell of tallow filled the air. It dripped from the bottom of the drapes and glistened on a few rows of seating. Sax picked up the candle to light one of the drapes when Hayden grabbed his shoulder. "I'll do it," he said flatly.

Jem and Sondrin looked at him with surprise, but Sax simply handed him the candle and nodded.

"Frea!" bawled Gron as he hit his head on the underside of Gamin's bunk. A shrill bell rang, and one of the corporals was shouting orders. "All hands to the abbey!" he boomed.

Soldiers fell out of bunks and collided with each other as they stumbled in the dark, trying to drag on their leggings and fasten belts. The barracks dormitory slept one hundred men in a windowless room at the rear of the Green Hall. The smell of sweating bodies and unwashed leather was a pungent assault after the wide-open lands of Tudorfeld. The four men of Moranne's mission wouldn't miss the confined quarters.

"What's going on?" asked Gamin. His head appeared below his bunk as Gron rubbed his bald head.

"The signal," came the baritone response from Lunn, who stood behind them. His axe was already strapped across his back, and he wore a grin from ear to ear.

The men quickly dressed and snatched their weapons. In the confusion, they could slip through one of the side doors without being seen by the corporal. Once outside, they raced across the central courtyard. Voices barked orders, and men ran in all directions, but no one paid them any heed. They headed for the far right corner, where a guard stood before a pair of locked, rusting gates.

"What do *you* want?" asked the guard gruffly. All the soldiers knew about the failed mission and the soldiers who'd ridden into town with warrior wenches.

"We need axes," blurted Gamin. "The captain sent us."

The guard looked them up and down with his chin rippled into a rictus of doubt.

"Which captain?" he countered.

"*This* captain!"

The guard turned to see the tip of a knight sword resting against his side. He followed the rough hand, over the leather cuff guards, to the lean arm and shoulder guards of Captain Biorn Fallon.

"Take his keys, then bind him, and if he as much as squeaks, kill him."

Gamin grabbed the key chain and opened the gates allowing Gron and Lunn to bundle the hapless guard inside. The small armoury contained a large number of battle axes, as well as swords and bows of every kind.

They found the Cempestre weapons thrown in a corner beneath a pile of sacks. Gamin weighed Isen's bearded axe in his hand. It was light and well balanced, but there were dents along its blade where she'd cleaved oni skulls and dark stains on the shaft. They placed the weapons, bows and quivers into a large sack tied to Lunn's back over his axe. "Why is it always me?" he rumbled.

"Because you're built like an ox," laughed Gron.

Biorn locked the armoury gate and held onto the keys. Thick grey smoke poured over the Green Hall walls, billowing in patches as it swirled around the courtyard. The captain looked up and smiled. An orange glow filled the sky, flickering as the fire below lit each cloud of smoke.

"We need to move," he said.

Biorn unlocked the main gates, and they rushed through, almost colliding with Chakirris and her team.

"Well met, Captain," she said, tipping her head in respect.

Biorn didn't expect the dryads to acknowledge his rank, but Chakirris had immediately recognized his stature and turned command over to him without a word.

"Thank you," he replied. "We need to push; it won't take long before they know what we're doing. I'm the only one here who can operate the winch. The rest of you need to go below. Gron knows the way."

With the orders given, Gron led Chakirris and the leading company back into the Green Hall, where they headed for the stairs, leading them to the lower levels.

Biorn made for the Tally Winch room. They would need to open the sluice gates to empty the water from the lower carriage and allow the upper carriage to descend. It would take too long to wait and needed to begin immediately. He only hoped the others could make it in time; otherwise, they'd be stranded.

"Need any help?" said Carina, poking her head around the door. Jilliad was smiling just behind.

Biorn was about to respond when he noticed the brooding shape of Zonta behind Brenna, wearing a heavily spiked helm and brandishing her broad axe.

"Is that safe?" he mused.

"No kill," grunted Zonta, in her flat, monosyllabic style.

"Well, that's a relief," replied Biorn. "You can all act as the rear guard. Take up positions across the bridge."

His dreams were filled with the lush lands of his Tudorfeld estate. Retirement was going to be very comfortable. Unfortunately, someone knocked frantically on his chamber door and didn't seem to be going away.

"What is it?" bawled General Marl.

Gada Ike Ingram hadn't yet learned the art of discretion. Cymel would soon change that. The young man burst into the room, almost tripping over the fur rug until he stood gasping for breath with sweat pouring from his brow. Over three hundred steps connected the first level of the bridge with the Foss Keep's highest floor.

"Well?" growled the general, reaching sleepily for his uniform.

"Sir! The abbey's on fire."

"The witch!" spat Cymel under his breath. "Find Drytenhold and tell him that the witch is trying to escape with her wenches. Tell him to use all possible methods to stop her.

The general yawned loudly and looked out of one of his generous windows, already glowing orange with a flickering flame. He had one other desire but dared not utter it out loud.

If the prince dies too? So be it.

Stone and Sceptre

When guards opened the doors to Moranne and Asger's chambers, they found them already gone. Moranne had visited Bruborg many times over the centuries and was more familiar with its labyrinthine corridors than many of the stationed soldiers. Spotting the first glow from the abbey's stained glass windows, she knew it was the signal and immediately left the room to collect the prince.

The guard outside her room would never remember what had happened. In fact, he couldn't remember anything from that day. Every movement and word was blank, as though a hole now existed in his memories.

"How many know?" asked Asger as they negotiated the winding stairs.

Moranne shook her head. Few humans knew of her gifts, and it would only scare them. She'd seen enough Frean lynch mobs to understand how the simple folk tended to react.

A few soldiers whirled past, but their orders took them to the abbey, which was now a raging inferno as the flames reached the timber roof. Moranne led Asger back towards the vacant merchant's chamber where the conspiracy was hatched. She looked both ways to ensure they weren't watched, then knocked twice.

"It's Moranne," she whispered, as quietly as she could.

A short pause, then the sound of a bolt sliding, and the door slowly opened inwards. It revealed a candlelit room which appeared to be empty. She slowly crept inside and looked back to see Sax, Jem, Hayden and Sondrin hiding behind the door.

Sax had a knife in his hand, which he returned to a pouch inside his jacket. "Were you followed?" he asked.

Moranne shook her head. "I don't think so, but they must be on to us by now. Where's Caspin?"

"I'm here," he chirped from the door. He was fully dressed in freshly laundered and polished armour. Even his sword gleamed in the half-light. "This is Rike," he said, introducing the young soldier behind him.

"Come here, private," commanded Moranne. "I have a vital mission for you."

He hurried forward and bowed as low as he could. "Of course, ma'am."

She retrieved a small note, tied with a wax seal, from her cloak and passed it to the young soldier.

"This is a vital message bearing the prince's seal. I need you to take it to Sir Torl Radborough in Cynstol. Don't give it to anyone else, just Sir Radborough. Understand?"

Rike nodded and tucked the note inside his waistcoat.

"Frea's speed," said Caspin and hugged the young lad. "A horse is waiting by the Tally Winch, and the gates are open. Stop for no one."

Rike saluted his friend and raced from the room with his footsteps echoing along the corridor.

"Time to go," said Sax.

They needed to cross the arch to the east side, where hopefully they'd meet some friends, but by then, the whole bridge would be swarming with soldiers.

Chakirris and her group met no resistance as they barrelled below the Green Hall. The steep steps wove back and forth until they reach the first level below the bridge. From here, they doubled back east along the corridor until they came to spiral stairs leading below. Two merchants opened their doors to investigate the commotion but retreated quickly when the green-skinned dryad raced towards them, hissing her contempt.

Gron noticed the walls had become rough and unfinished, with wads of mortar bursting between the massive stone blocks. They were deep within the east pillar at the dungeon level.

"Leave the guards to us," he boomed, lifting his mace to swing it against the jail's battered door.

The latch flew inwards and splinters shot in all directions. Gron kicked the door with his boot, and it swung open, pulling from its hinges.

"What the—"

The first guard dropped his flagon of mead. Such was the shock that he had no answer when Gron stampeded into his chest. He flew back into a second guard, and both crumpled into a heap.

A third man emerged from a side room with his sword aloft, but Ostro's staff connected with his head, and he flew into the wall dropping his weapon with a clatter.

"You'll hang for this, elf," he cursed.

Ostro accidentally let his staff slide down to hit the guard between his legs.

"I'm a dalfreni, you thick human," he said, ignoring the howls of pain.

"Keys!" shouted Chakirris.

Lunn ripped the large ring of keys from the guard's belt and tossed it to Gamin. "Over to you, lover boy," he grinned.

A low, square, iron gate opened onto a narrow stone walkway, forming each cell's walls. Gamin took one of the oil lamps and peered into the first cell. An iron grid covered each with a square gate in the centre. He surveyed two sleeping shapes, almost filling the tiny box. The first appeared to be Oretta Brimwulf, and the second already had her grey eyes open.

"You took yer time," chided Brea.

Gron and Lunn used the prison manacles to restrain the three guards, while Cierzon and Ostro helped Gamin unlock the cells and drop the wooden ladders.

Tiam was the first out, stretching her limbs after the confined space. She watched as her warriors started to appear and noticed that Chakirris seemed to be in command.

"What's the plan?" she asked, blinking in the lamplight.

"There is a new mission," replied the dryad quickly. "The prince leads us onto the stone isle. Will you come?"

Oretta Brimwulf looked across at her warriors now emerging from the cages. Each nodded in turn as her eyes rested on them. Whatever this quest had become, they would see it through to the end.

"We're in," she said. "Now, let's get out of here."

The last to be freed was Isen. Gamin reached down and took her hand, helping her negotiate the narrow opening and find her footing on the ironwork roof. She pulled herself up and looked down at him.

"Thank you," she said formally.

"Kiss later!" shouted Brea. "We're leaving."

The young archer looked into her eyes. Whatever it took, he would be worthy of her.

Gron had untied the sack, scattering the weapons over a table in the guard's room. Brea slid the small hunting knife back into her belt, and Ellen weighed her sword as if reuniting with an old friend.

"Where's Sir Torbrand?" she asked, "and Sir Caspin?"

Chakirris looked up and knew the truth would hurt, but the warrior needed to know. "Caspin is with us, but his brother is not."

"Sorry, love," added Brea. "He knows his duty."

If Ellen was saddened, she didn't show it. Nodding in recognition, she fastened her sword belt and stood ready to do her duty. "Let's go," she echoed.

Chakirris ensured they all understood not to use lethal force, and they started to retrace their steps back towards the surface. The group spread out along the narrow passages and cramped stairs. Weapons scraped the walls, clattering as they banged against the brickwork, and ran headlong upwards.

A soldier appeared before them but fell backwards when he noticed their strength. Lunn grabbed him and threw him into an empty room.

"I think they're onto us," he boomed.

Other soldiers soon spotted them, but their numbers were small. Many ran away, but others tried to stand their ground until Gron swatted them with his mace or Ostro clouted them with the staff.

"Quicker!" screamed Chakirris.

Bresne, acting as the rear guard, heard sounds behind them. Boots ran on the cold stone, and metal armour rattled through the tunnels. "They're coming!" she shouted.

The group ran. Tripping over steps and bouncing from wall to wall, they struggled with the winding stairs. If the soldiers cut them off, there would be no escape. Gron and Lunn were starting to flag.

"Come on, old man," mocked Sefti. She grabbed Lunn's hand and dragged him forward.

"Cuyler, Yuka, cover the rear!" shouted Brea.

The two archers complied immediately and dropped back behind the men. They might be avoiding casualties, but nobody was willing to hang.

"I see them," called Yuka. She slotted an arrow and fired a warning shot which ricocheted off the wall and flew past a soldier's head.

They sprinted so quickly that they almost collided with the prince's party, waiting on the first level beneath the bridge.

"Do we have everyone?" asked Sir Caspin.

Chakirris nodded, and they proceeded together. There was no time for pleasantries. Jem and Hayden took the prince's arms and helped to pull him onwards. He was positioned in the centre to protect him from skirmishes in front or behind.

"We've got more company!" shouted Cuyler, as she and Yuka let more warning shots fly rearwards.

One more flight of stairs would see them burst into the Green Hall. They turned the last corner and looked at the steep climb to freedom. They scrambled up the stairs until Chakirris pulled them to a halt near the top.

The group spread out across the passage to see the silhouette of a tall warrior. He wore a high Green Order helm with a round shield on his left arm. His right bore a long broadsword, held upright and ready to strike. A solid, wide stance made him a wall, blocking their way.

"I can't let you leave," he boomed.

The voice was familiar and robust. It commanded respect from all who heard it and belonged to the heir to a fortune.

"Torbrand!" shouted Moranne. "You can't stop us."

"It's my duty to try," he countered.

"I command," said Prince Asger.

The knight shook his head. "I serve the king," he said. "I'm sorry, Your Highness."

He remained still but slightly swayed as he shifted his weight from left to right, ready to strike.

"I don't have time for this," said Moranne under her breath. She reached inside her cloak and grasped the sceptre. A green mist swirled in her eyes, and a halo of power danced over her arm. She readied to pull it free and blast the knight into oblivion, but a hand stayed her intent.

"I'll deal with this," said Ellen. She reached down and clasped the hilt of her sword, sliding it free, so it glinted in the orange glow and threw a shard of light across her eyes.

"Ellen," snapped Brea.

The swordswoman ignored her. She gradually climbed towards the granite figure ahead, taking each step with a slow, deliberate movement.

"Come no nearer," warned Sir Torbrand.

Still, she advanced.

With three more steps, he'd be within striking distance, and within four, her sword could slash his chest open.

"Ellen, don't make me hurt you."

"You made a promise," she retorted.

"I know," he said, "I'm sorry, but I have my orders."

With the next step, she clasped the sword with both hands and slowly brought it to stomach height. Her arms and legs tensed as she readied to unleash all her strength.

"Tor, can't you see what's happening here?" cried Caspin. He had never used his brother's nickname in public but saw he was about to make a terrible mistake.

"You swore the same oath," said Torbrand. "Don't throw your life away."

"I'm not," retorted Caspin. "I serve my king by saving his life and the lives of all those I love. I believe in Lady Moranne, and I know you do too."

Ellen raised the sword to head height with the next step and held it ready to lunge or parry. Gamin joined Cuyler and Yuka as they sent volleys of shots into the corridor below, holding off the advancing soldiers.

"Ellen, don't," said Sir Torbrand softly. He could strike her now, but his sword remained still.

"Stand aside or engage," she returned. She knew Torbrand had held back in Grenborg; he could kill her this time if he wished. His arms rippled with tensed muscles, ready to unleash a massive, fatal blow.

"Stand aside," commanded Tiam. "You can't beat all of us. We will pass."

Ellen's blade was now within reach. The tip caught the reflection from Sir Torbrand's shield; it flickered across his face and revealed the sharpness of her steel. They stood facing one another, neither willing to make the first move. Torbrand had never looked more muscular and handsome, his dark eyes smouldering under the polished helm. Those same eyes studied every crease and mark on Ellen's fair face. Prison grime was smeared across her visage, but her beauty shone through. *Frea! She was beautiful.*

"For bastard's sake, just kiss her!" tutted Brea, rolling her eyes.

He couldn't hurt her. He would never hurt her. Slowly he lowered the sword until it rested at his side. "Take care of yourself," he said.

"You too."

Sliding to a halt at the top of the stairs, Brenna Gunborg almost collided with the armoured knight.

"Stop hanging about!" she shouted. "The winch is almost ready, and we have soldiers coming from the bridge."

Torbrand stood aside, and the party raced past him as fast as Prince Asger could go.

"Join us," pleaded Caspin.

The elder Linhold brother looked down and shook his head. He dared not allow Caspin to stare into his eyes lest the inner turmoil spill out. Even knowing that Ellen would be lost and his family fractured, the sense of duty was so strong it ripped his emotions from their liberal centre. He could only watch as those he called friends ran forward without him.

The escapees crossed the courtyard quickly and plunged through the gate where Zonta was waiting.

"No kill," she repeated as if she needed to keep reminding herself.

The pace was too frantic for anyone to ask why Zonta was dressed in full battle garb. Charging through the doors and out onto the bridge, they could hear the soldiers approaching. Several archers had taken up position on either side of the Green Hall and were firing across the road.

"Get down!" screamed Jilliad from somewhere ahead.

They crashed to the floor just in time to see two darts streak overhead and hit two of the archers. They both looked down at the wooden bolts embedded in their chests, then crumpled to the floor, motionless.

"Are they dead?" asked Jem.

"Asleep," snapped Chakirris. The dryads had spent the previous day looking for valerian roots. They boiled it into a concentrated paste and mixed it with a tiny amount of the bohun upas to produce a potent sleeping toxin which could knock out a human in seconds. They couldn't make much; it was a weapon of last resort.

"Keep moving," urged Moranne. More archers and soldiers were arriving and pouring out of the Green Hall behind them.

More darts whizzed past as Jilliad fired from a position beside the Tally Gate. Biorn stood at the winch door urging them onwards while Carina provided suppressing fire with her bow. Water from the Hiwness plunged through the Tally Winch gully and fell into the bucket below. It was almost full, and the upper bucket would soon be ready to descend.

Sir Torbrand watched the scene from the Green Hall doors and breathed a sigh of relief. They were going to make it; Ellen would live.

"Fools," laughed General Marl.

Torbrand removed his helm and looked at the general. He was smiling; the creases in his weathered face were revealed like fissures in a mountainside.

"They're plunging into a trap," he continued. "My finest archers are already on the West Quay. They'll be cut down like slaughtered pigs."

The knight looked out at the escapees nearing the winch, then back at Cymel's laughing face. Soldiers were yelling, and Caspin was screaming over the melee. He never thought this day would come. His father would disown him, his mother would cry, and his neck might snap at the end of a rope. It was too late; he loved her from the first moment in Grenborg and every stolen look since.

With all the might stacked in his broad shoulders, Torbrand swung his arm back wide and punched the general square in the face. The impact carried so much force that Cymel flew backwards into the wall and crumpled unconscious into a clattering heap of armour.

"Hold your fire," shouted Torbrand, then he ran.

His legs pounded the distance quickly before any of the soldiers realised what had happened. He could see the winch wheel was starting to move. The elevator was descending already. *Come on*, he urged himself, taking great gulps of air and willing his strength onwards.

The prince's mission had already gone, crowded into the small rectangular bucket which would lower them slowly to the quay. It had sunk below the bridge, but he could see the rope that held it. Leaping blindly into the shaft, he reached for the rope and grabbed it with one hand. He flailed back and forth, grasping wildly into the air until he could wrap his legs around the cord and hug it tightly.

"I think it's raining knights," laughed Brea.

"Room for an idiot?" answered Torbrand as he slowly lowered himself to the carriage. The shaft was pitch black, with no windows or lamps and only the faintest light from either end. He jumped down into the bucket and turned instantly to Moranne. "It's a trap, ma'am. Marl has archers hiding on the West Quay."

Moranne looked at the shadowy faces and tried to think. The quay was exposed; they wouldn't make it; then she recalled the events of Cempess.

"Jem, do you remember how you felt when you saved the little girl from the tunnbrocc?"

"I think so," he said, looking bemused.

"Tell me."

He thought for a moment and pictured himself grabbing the girl and holding her tight. "I wanted to protect her with all my heart."

Moranne nodded. There was only the slimmest chance that this would work; if it didn't, they were all dead. "I want you to protect us with all your heart."

Jem nodded. "I will... if I can."

"Carina," she said, turning to her daughter. "We'll need your sceptre and everything I've taught you."

The carriage took five minutes to descend, but it felt like forever. Caspin had checked on the boat earlier to ensure it was ready and assured Moranne that Captain Blake would wait for them.

The harbour consisted of two long quays which reached out into the Lowker Straights. Other than a few small sheds and coils of rope, there was nothing on deck and no cover from the opposing quay; only boats would give light cover. Just one vessel was moored on the East Quay, and it was at the far end.

"It's been nice knowing you, scroats," cackled Brea.

They huddled inside the winch doorway and looked out at the open quay.

"Remember," said Moranne to a bewildered Jem. "You need to concentrate for the whole time. Don't pay attention to anything around you. Just protect us."

Jem nodded but still had no idea what was to come.

"Zonta, there's going to be some magic, but it won't hurt you," said Brenna, explaining as if to a small child. She remembered how the oni could be easily scared by anything they considered supernatural.

"Brenda protect," replied Zonta gruffly.

Moranne held her sceptre aloft with her right hand while Carina grasped hers with her left. Jem then clasped each of their free hands, forming a circle facing outwards.

"Everyone, stay as close to us as you can," said Moranne. "The light won't hurt you." She looked down at Jem and Carina, more proud than she could say. "Ready?" they both nodded. "One, two, three—"

Jem concentrated as hard as he could while Moranne and Carina let out an ear-splitting scream which echoed through the winch shaft; it blasted out across the quay, forcing dread into the hearts of the hidden archers.

Moranne's eyes burned bright green, as did Carina's, but Jem's eyes exploded into such a bright light that they illuminated the entire elevator shaft. A beam of jade light punched through the winch door like the sun's rays through a storm.

"Concentrate!" shouted Moranne.

The two sceptres exploded into life, and a blade of green lightning sparked from each orb. The streams twisted and crackled in the shaft, dancing along the walls and snapping at the empty bucket.

"Frea!" gasped Lunn.

"Jem, you can do it," said Moranne.

He imagined his arms extending so they could hold all his comrades. In his mind, he became a giant, picking up his friends and clutching them to his breast. *I will protect you all.*

The two beams started to writhe together, twisting and snapping until they wove together and formed a flickering archway.

"Now," said Moranne. "Pour your whole heart into that space."

Jem's mind flicked through every member of the mission. The mysterious Moranne, the brave Cempestre, gallant knights, hardy soldiers, Brea the comedian, Ellen the clown, Hayden the hidden artist, the fair forest folk and the monstrous oni with a heart of gold. *My friends.*

Like an exploding star, the green band convulsed and then blasted outwards until it formed a dome of green energy which completely enveloped them all. It flickered and swirled like an oily slick on a summer pond.

"Quickly," shouted Moranne, "It won't last long."

Led by Caspin, they tentatively moved out of the winch room like a hiding crab. The harbour water reflected the orange glow from above, where the abbey blazed out of control, its flames licking the Foss Keep and threatening nearby businesses. No arrows came. Perhaps it was a bluff.

"Stay close." Moranne didn't know how long Jem could sustain that much focus. If his shield were as potent as Aludra's, they would only have a few minutes.

Eventually, they were free of the rock face and roughly a quarter of the way across the dock when the first salvo hit.

"Incoming!" shouted Cuyler.

They all ducked instinctively, but no arrow pierced the shield. The first few shots erupted into a shower of splinters as they hit the pulsing barrier, but others ricocheted off into the cliffs or embedded into the boards at their feet. Having given away their positions, the Green Order archers fired freely. They were hidden on the decks of several military vessels lining the West Quay.

"Can we return fire?" asked Jilliad.

"Yes," replied Moranne. "The shield will not harm your darts."

The dryads possessed only a few sleeping darts, but every bolt hit home. Two archers fell back with the first round and a further few with the second.

"I needs me one of those," grinned Brea, as she eyed the small crossbow in Jilliad's hand.

"I'll make you one, if we live," she smiled.

More arrows splintered against the wall as frustration mounted on the opposite bank. The archers now stood in plain sight, struggling to land a single shot.

"Almost there!" shouted Caspin. He could see the longship ahead with its captain and first mate hiding beneath the side.

"Jem!" called Moranne. "Look over to the ship. You need to include the crew in your protection."

Jem's blazing eyes could see Captain Blake and his younger first-mate cowering beneath the ship's side. He focused on their features and added them to the swirling line of faces which ran through his mind like a torrent cascading over a waterwheel.

Arrows still flew from the far quay, but they also rained down from above as archers took positions along the bridge.

"Don't waiver!" ordered Moranne, and then she called out to the ship's captain. "Don't be afraid; the shield will protect you."

Captain Blake nodded as if he understood, but he had half a mind to throw himself overboard and take his chances.

No harm will come to you. You're under the prince's protection, pulsed into his mind. The captain felt a wave of calm spreading over him like a warm, dry blanket on stormy seas. Chakirris smiled at the prince. She'd never used her powers this way, which felt good.

Finally, they reached the longship and started to climb aboard while maintaining the close formation.

"Cast off!" shouted Caspin. "We have little time."

Sax waved the large diamond, and the captain bolted into action. The ship was a classic longship design with one large square sail and fifteen benches arranged along its length. Each bench was accompanied by a matching set of oars allowing the wind power to be augmented for speed or in calm conditions. A single square cabin stood at the ship's centre, useful as a dry grain store or as the captain's quarters.

The first mate unfastened the rope and pulled it in, then he and the captain grabbed an oar each and started to push the ship away from the dock.

"Half of you grab an oar," shouted the captain, "and the rest of you keep down."

Moranne, Jem and Carina protected the rowers as they lifted the long wooden oars and slotted them into the round rowlocks on each side. Arranging themselves in the front of the ship, they began to row haphazardly.

"Together!" howled the captain, rolling his eyes. "Landlubbers," he spat under his breath.

The shield was starting to flicker, and Moranne was beginning to tire. Jem and Carina showed no sign of weakness, but she knew the barrier was collapsing. "Row!" she barked.

Lunn had so much strength that the ship immediately lurched away from the dock. All the men and most of the Cempestre were now pulling on oars and trying to keep time. Sondrin and Jilliad used their last sleeping bolts as the rippling shield started to flash in and out of existence. They were still within longbow distance, even though the ship was now free of the harbour and heading into the open sea. Five archers stood at the end of the West Quay and drew their strings back for one last shot.

One arrow bounced off the shield; two went astray, another fell short, and then the shield blinked out. Moranne's power had gone, and every reserve was spent. She only felt the impact but not the pain. She looked down to see a shaking arrow protruding from her left shoulder. Her vision blurred, and vertigo swirled as her body began to fall until the world turned black.

Sir Torbrand caught Moranne in his sturdy arms and gently laid her down. Focus on the tiny ship was still to move as far away from Numolport as possible.

Jem's mind was elsewhere. Fatigued from channelling the earth power, he swayed back and forth at the stern. Something was pulling his gaze back to the smouldering Bruborg, and it wasn't fear of pursuers. An ancient hatred boiled on the northern shore. It was anger and pain in equal measure, but it had no form, only the focus of pure revulsion. Jem tried to pierce the veil, but the presence blocked all attempts to connect.

The island of Grenfold gradually receded, as did the feeling of dread. Denbry lay many miles away to the southwest, where Ned and Ada dwelled beside the Sile, and Cynstol was like a distant dream. The stone island would bring new challenges and perhaps more of the truth, but one aspect of Jem's life had changed forever: he was a chicken farmer no more.

49 THE WATCHER

Many of Bruborg's lower rooms were empty, but one was occupied. Only a short distance from the chamber where Moranne and the prince conspired to escape, the tiny room was always in darkness. No oil lamp lent its orange hue, and no candle flickered against its walls. The occupant entered by night and left by night. No one would recognise the hooded figure, and no one would live to describe what they'd seen.

When smoke wafted past the windows and the shouting began, it was time. The door made only the faintest creak as it opened; the mysterious person was almost invisible against the bridge-town's darkened passages. Stealing quietly along the tunnels, every footstep represented a decade, and each breath was a memory. The pain seared like a cattle brand; it was present at dawn and raging by dusk. A plan hatched in turmoil and sealed in despair; it was the simple catalyst for Elara's movements and that of the runt. Like throwing a pebble into a pond, the ripples could touch a lily pad or disturb a sleeping frog. When a boulder slid from the frost-damaged slopes of the Mur, its path may be unknown, but its destiny was inevitable.

The rectangular sail of the Kelly Ray slowly slid into the gloom and sank beneath the horizon; the spreading halo of the morning sun painted the waves with its fiery glow. Despite numerous buckets of water and howls of rage from the general, the Abbey of Frea's Light still smouldered, dropping its ash like an early dusting of snow.

The green eyes watched every movement of the fugitives as they ran to freedom and saw a barrier of writhing green light transport them to the safety of a ship. Eyes shrouded in darkness from a black hood, eyes unseen by anyone from the shadows beneath the Foss Keep, had finally witnessed the fruits of a long-made plan. Elara had slumped back into the arms of a tall knight, and the lad was at her side. It was a picture the watcher had seen many times; it was a haunting image which ignited only hatred and spite. No one aboard the longship would find peace on Stanholm.

The runt saw something, but his powers were no match. He would not pierce the shell; the lad was a passenger in a story of her writing, collateral from a selfish union of folly.

The dark figure looked towards the sky and remembered when natural pleasures were shared, before the nightmare images resurfaced. A friend was everything, the single reason for living, until the day when love died and turmoil returned. A green light flashed beneath the hood, but no one saw the brief glimpse of a face twisted at birth and hardened against the world.

The witch would pay. Everything she knew and everyone she cared for would turn to ash; before she would also pay the ultimate price.

The dark figure pulled the cloak tightly around a slim frame and retreated into the shadows.

50 THE HEALER

The boy stood with his pointed ear against the door, struggling to hear the words through tiny gaps in the wood. His hair was dark and spiky, framing an innocent, smooth face. With just seven years, he could almost be mistaken for a human but would never pass as an alviri. He knew his mother's voice, but the man's tone was cultured and eloquent.

"I am sorry, Rose, my dear; you cannot stay." The male voice had a melodic lilt that hung in the air like falling leaves. Every line was uttered as if the speaker had ruminated before spilling forth.

"I have nowhere else to go. You can hide us, surely?" In contrast, the woman sounded coarse, with the burr of a country dweller.

"I'm sorry—"

"You can't turn us out," she pleaded.

"I'm—"

"I have nothing. We have nothing. Please?"

"I have arranged passage to Suncin. You will be fine amongst *your kind*."

"He needs a father. He's your son. Don't that mean nothing to you?"

"I'm—"

"Sorry? Sorry? It's me who's sorry. Sorry I ever fell for your lies."

"I have five gold coins for you—"

"Is that all your son's worth?"

"I'm sorry."

Every muffled word echoed through his consciousness and drove a knife through his heart. Marin knew every aspect of his mother, but the man was a stranger. He'd never seen his father in all his seven years, and even now, the door remained locked.

Hiding in an abandoned house near Hagall was all the young lad had known. This life would continue until one day when they would walk free, and his father would be at his side. Marin imagined him as a tall, severe alviri with crystal white hair and magic in his fingers. He sometimes glimpsed other fair folks from the windows before his mother would usher him away.

A shadow slid in the gap beneath the door, and he heard voices once more.

"It is over, Rose; you cannot stay here. I can help you if you leave now, but you will leave with nothing if they find you."

There was a pause; Marin thought he could hear his mother crying. "Come with me. We can make a life together," she begged.

Stone and Sceptre

The man sighed as if he'd grown tired of the exchange.

"My place is in Alfheim—"

"But, your son—"

"I don't love you."

A long stride of boots on stone echoed through the room, and a door slammed, rattling in its frame. The sound of sobbing echoed in the small chamber until it became the lapping sound of water, and Marin's mind felt the rise and fall of a ship sailing on a calm sea.

Sax blinked awake and looked up into the severe faces of Ostro and Carina looking down at him. They appeared ghoulish in the flickering light of a single oil lamp hung near the ship's mast. Both sets of eyes bored into his face as if he might be able to read their thoughts. He knew exactly what they wanted. He'd hidden behind Sax Stulor's mask for thirty years. Questions about his parents were parried, and jibes from other soldiers were ignored. When his lack of ageing threatened his undoing, he'd request a transfer, and when he felt alone, he held onto the certainty that one day he'd confront his father.

"We know you can help," said Carina.

Sax said nothing; others were watching the exchange. The arrow still protruded from Moranne's shoulder, and blood trickled from her back onto Sir Torbrand's clean leather. He cradled her in his arms, keeping the arrowhead from resting against the ship's boards.

"That needs to come out," said Brea, "but we don't know how much she'll bleed."

"Please," begged Chakirris.

Sax tried to ignore her, but Caspin noticed the conversation, and some of the others were taking an interest.

"What's going on?" asked Caspin. "Who can help?"

"We're all fugitives now," sighed Cierzon. "What do you have to lose?"

Knives seldom lost his temper or displayed much emotion, but the Alfheim lord had cracked the skin and irritated it like a rash.

"What do I have to lose?" he stormed. You have the sunny Alfheim waiting for you after this, but what do I have? The noose or the slums of Suncin. I'm not sure which is worse!"

Caspin was bemused. Looking first at Cierzon and then at Sax. "What's going on?" he repeated. "Somebody, please tell me."

Sax looked into his hands, but the answers weren't there; all eyes were on him; he knew his cover was blown. It didn't matter what happened next; he would never be Marin. Not until the day he stood face-to-face with his father. Standing in the centre of the longship, he looked over at the pale body of Lady Moranne.

"I'm sorry, sir," he said, addressing Caspin. "I'm not who you think I am."

"So, who are you?"

The words hadn't passed his lips since the moment he'd picked up the small utility knife, which changed his life.

"I'm a dalfreni."

The men and the Cempestre stopped rowing, and even Torbrand watched from the small covered area near the mast.

"That's impossible," gasped Caspin.

"He don't have the ears," shouted Gron. "He's having us on."

Sax ran his hands through his long dark hair and gradually lifted a section above his ear. The shape was human, but something was different at the top. Where the upper ear should be turned, it was flat. Pointed ears would protrude through long hair, but rounded ears might not.

"You're a cutter," said Carina. "I'd heard the rumours, but I've never seen it."

"You cut your ears?" howled Hayden.

Sax nodded. "I'd do anything to leave that place."

Caspin was incredulous. "You knew?" he bawled, looking first at Ostro and then at Carina.

"We knew," said Chakirris. "He's a healer."

"A healer?"

"He saved Gamin and Sefti," said Sondrin. "He also helped all who were hurt in the wolf attack."

"Is this true?" asked Sir Torbrand.

Sax nodded. It was all true, and his time in the Green Order was done. He stood and looked back over the stern into the black beyond. An orange glow illuminated the Tudorfeld cliffs and the arched face of Bruborg. The abbey walls stood, but the roof was a crumpled mass of embers burning within the husk. His life as *Knives* Stulor lay in the ashes of Frea's light.

"We'll need a bandage," he said, stepping over the benches to where Moranne lay peacefully. The arrow had just missed her lung, but she was tired from using her powers; any blood loss could be fatal.

Removing a small sharp knife from his coat, Sax turned Moranne onto her side and cut the arrowhead away, removing any stray splinters from the square end. Sir Torbrand and Jem held her tightly while Sax yanked the arrow quickly from her body. She didn't stir with the pain or make a sound as they bound her in some spare sail linen. They lay her on sackcloth, then backed away. A red spot spread over the linen where the blood oozed from the wound.

"Stay back," warned Sax. He pulled back his sleeves and knelt beside her. "Juldra, give me the strength."

He spread his palms to hover above the wound and closed his eyes. The power immediately flowed as if he was pulling it from the ship's boards. It fizzed in his legs, crept through his body and coursed down his arms. Starting as a dim glow around his fingers, a pulsing ball of light gradually formed between his hands and Moranne's body. It beat in time with her shallow heartbeat until it flickered out after a few minutes. He slumped against the side of the boat in exhaustion.

"It's done."

Jem looked down at Moranne's face and noticed it fill with colour in front of his eyes. Her cheeks reddened, the frown smoothed from her forehead, and the hint of a smile appeared on her lips.

"That's incredible," he said. "How long does it take?"

"The wounds will heal in a day," replied Sax wearily. *At least the ones you can see.* He could feel something deep within. She hid it well, but he knew from his own buried feelings: the echo which would haunt the small gaps of silence when you were alone or when the tasks of life didn't occupy every ounce of your mind. It was the feeling of loss.

"We owe you a debt of thanks," said Sir Torbrand. He stood over the dalfreni healer with his hand outstretched. "If I live to take my father's place as earl, there's no one I'd rather have at my side."

"Aye!" boomed Lunn, quickly followed by all the other men.

Sax took the knight's hand, but Torbrand didn't shake it. Instead, he pulled the soldier to his feet and embraced him like a brother. *Knives* was dependable and loyal. He didn't just perform through orders or duty; he acted because it was the right thing to do. Torbrand's eyes met Ellen's, and he eventually released the dalfreni and walked out into the centre of the ship to address the company.

"I deserted you when you needed me most. I'm sorry." His voice was low and humble. "If you have me in your company, I promise I will endeavour to be worthy of your trust."

There was quiet in the ship for a moment as the men and women looked at each other.

"Sit down, ya big jessie, of course we'll 'ave ya!" yelled Brea.

The ship erupted in laughter, and Lunn slapped Torbrand so hard on the back that he almost pitched over the side. The knight beamed at the loyalty around him, but the smile on Ellen's face meant the most. Her blue eyes were wide and sparkling in the lamplight. Torbrand could feel her pride in him.

"Alright!" shouted Captain Blake. "That's enough of that. I suggest you all get some sleep. There's a fair wind, and we ain't being followed."

Barda Blake was rough in every way; he was short, and his arms were ribbed with the muscles obtained from rowing and hauling on ropes. A combination of advancing years and a craggy, pock-marked face gave his skin the appearance of his ship's barnacled hull. The gnarled face was obscured by a thick, grey, unkempt beard which climbed his cheeks almost to his beady grey eyes. He wore a thin leather tunic with half-length arms and a pair of loose brown breeches tucked into his long socks. A dull, blunt cutlass with dents along the blade hung from a rope belt.

"And another thing," he added. "While you're on my ship, it's my rules. If I tells ya to do something or Koll here gives you an order, you does as we tells ya. Otherwise, it's a long swim home."

Koll Brenting smiled. The first mate knew the captain's bark was worse than his bite. With only a year ahead of Gamin, Koll had Stanish red hair and a clipped goatee beard, which framed his naturally smiling face and crystal blue eyes. He was tall and gangly compared to the captain and made light work of the rigging.

With oars stowed, the Kelly Ray was a quiet ship, cutting the water with minimal wake and little noise. Originally a Grenfold war vessel, it now served as a merchantman, shuttling wares along the coast between Silmouth and Numolport. It was one of the last longships, replaced by the twin mast clippers that circled the green isles. Work had been scarce since trouble flared with the Stans, and the captain welcomed his payment. He felt the diamond's facets in his pocket and grinned at his shambolic crew.

"Fighting wenches!" he huffed under his breath. "Elves and ogres!"

Use those terms again, and it is you who will be swimming!

Barda turned to see a pair of brown eyes staring at him through green features; the gleaming teeth were formed into a smile. He shuddered and lowered his head.

The dryads attempted to sleep, as did most others, but Gron, Lunn, Brenna and Zonta decided to keep rowing. Captain Blake informed them that ten was the minimum number of oarsmen, but it didn't stop the four from pulling.

Lunn was balanced by Zonta, while Gron sat across from Brenna. They quickly became competitive, daring the other to cease rowing first. Zonta even smiled a little as she matched Lunn's pace, stroke for stroke. She'd begun to panic as they stepped onto the boat, but Brenna held her arm and guided her gently to a bench. The oni were naturally fearful of water, but she felt as if she could confront anything with Brenna at her side.

Jem watched them straining against the black water, but his thoughts were elsewhere. It was *he* who summoned the shield of earth power, channelled through Moranne and Carina. Something bound them together, but they were too different. Moranne was from nobility, Carina was a dalfreni, and he was the son of a chicken farmer. *She's not who you think she is.* The words of Princess Vena and Alize Berlain echoed through his mind. Even Sondrin had tried to tell him something; the nymphs knew more than they would say.

A nagging ache of doubt had plagued him since Deapholt, but it was now coalescing around Lady Moranne. It wasn't chance that brought her to Denbry with his apprenticeship, and it wasn't for the love of Grenfold that she pursued Corvus. *Could she really be over five hundred years old?* Every move was calculated, and each word was weighed for its meaning. They were on a mission together, but Moranne was chasing a personal quest that only *she* understood.

Jem didn't notice her eyes slowly open and look up to the stars or read the worry that passed through her mind as they neared an ancient foe.

Stanholm

51 SILENCE

It was midmorning when Jem finally opened his eyes to the grey sky. A veil of rain hung in the air, and thin mist hovered over the waves. He could see the ship in all its weathered glory. The Kelly Ray was ninety-foot long with boards of brown stained pine, curved into a symmetrical profile. The prow was carved into the likeness of a dragon's head, although half the face was missing. The stern curled into a tail. A wide, billowing sail spread across the centre, decorated in simple vertical, blue stripes.

Lunn, Gron and Brenna were collapsed in a snoozing heap towards the stern, but Zonta still rowed resiliently opposite Biorn. Others also pulled against the lapping water, so Jem took one of the benches alongside Hayden and slotted an oar into the rowlocks. He watched Cierzon just ahead and then matched his pace, dipping the heavy wood into the foam and pulling back.

Captain Blake stood on the prow, watching the dim sun through the grey. He could tell the time without any clock and navigated at night by the stars. Numolport to Gulward was a straight north run of some thirty-seven nautical miles; it should be visible soon. He peered into the mist, but there was no light shining through the shifting curtain. *Something was wrong.*

"Is everything alright, Captain?" asked Sir Torbrand. He was rowing with Caspin near the front and enjoying spending time with the men.

"There's no sign yet," he replied.

Two tall towers marked the mouth of Gulward's harbour. The harbour master ensured that fires were lit in the mist and fog, but the horizon was just a streak of grey. The ship might have been blown off course, but Barda had made this trip hundreds of times in the past and never missed his mark.

A dread was starting to descend on the ship like an approaching tide. It touched Moranne, Cierzon and the dalfreni, but the dryads felt it the most. The horizon was empty. No weak minds divulged their secrets or opened doors to the dryad's powers.

"We're off course!" cried Jilliad.

Koll looked horrified, but the captain didn't flinch. He knew exactly where they were, but he felt it too. Fishing vessels should be crossing their path, and sailors should be exchanging colourful curses. The Stans didn't stay in port for a little mist.

"What's that?" said Hayden, peering over the prow. Something was floating towards them on the starboard side. It looked like a tree branch or a couple of bobbing barrels.

"Oars up!" shouted the captain. He looked down into the murky depths, but it was a shape he'd seen many times before. It floated along the hull and passed beneath the oars as the party watched in horror.

The man's body was face down, but his Stanish red hair was visible, spread in the water and trailing a thin slick of blood from an unseen wound.

"Pirates?" whispered Ellen.

The captain shook his head; there were no brigands in the Lowker Straights.

"Land ho!" yelled Koll, breaking the captain from his thoughts.

Barda raised his eyes over the prow, and his keen vision could see the twin towers of Gulward's harbour emerging through the mist-like gravestones. No fires burned on their tops and no light trickled through the harbour mouth. Gradually the harbour walls spread out on either side; as if they were shooting across the horizon until the craggy coastline of Stanholm appeared on each side.

The men and women pulled in the oars and stowed them along the ship's centre. A gentle breeze allowed the Kelly Ray to glide through the harbour mouth and onwards to the longest quay in all the islands. Gulward's harbour made use of the natural bay but extended it by creating a vast, circular port and a curved gangway. The northeast side funnelled into the River Jarn, where much of the precious metal would be offloaded, but opposite the harbour mouth lay the grey city of Gulward.

Leaning inwards on either side, the twin towers loomed, pale and stark. No guards patrolled the walls or watched from the arrow slits, and no one scurried along the quay servicing the many vessels.

"Where is everyone?" whispered Hayden.

The port was silent but for the gentle water lapping on the ship's hull. Warships lined the docks on both sides, the intelligence had been correct, but not a soul patrolled the decks or watched their arrival from the shore. Ghostly shadows moved behind the flotilla, but it was only the shape of rigging, dancing like a phantom.

"Be ready," warned Biorn. "It could be a trap."

No fires burned in the town, and no smoke rose from the chimneys of the houses and businesses which hugged the north harbour wall. Fishmongers' stalls stood empty, and ship supply yards remained in darkness.

"I don't like the look of this," echoed Captain Blake.

He steered the vessel straight towards the quay's north side, where the buildings broke into a wide-open square. Stray dogs loped between the buildings, and crows squawked from the rooftops, but there was no sign of the Stanish inhabitants.

"Archers, be ready to cover the swords," barked Brea. All the archers complied without question. Brea's skill with the bow and excellent tactics had made her the archers' leader, and Sir Torbrand was happy to let her take control.

"Men with me," added the knight. He included the Cempestre, dalfreni and alviri sword wielders, who didn't seem to mind.

"Women and fair folk to the fore," croaked Moranne. She was still too weary to stand quickly, so she sat against the hull and watched the ghostly banks with concern. "Corvus could be here. The men must not engage him." She looked around and noticed that Zonta was standing near the stern with Brenna. Moranne asked the others to help her walk ashore.

Koll furled the sail, and Captain Blake used one of the oars to steer the Kelly Ray towards the quay. The other ships gently knocked the boards and forced water to splash up, spilling over the walkway to drip back into the harbour. No one spoke. The hush was like the sound of midnight, but the hazy sun signalled noon. The captain and first mate jumped from the ship and tied it to the quay while Brea and the archers covered them.

Barda hadn't been to Stanholm for over a year, but he knew the harbour master well. The stern official would stride purposely from his shack to inspect any new ship arriving, but nobody stirred. Maybe it was a holiday or a town meeting. There were too many warships. Where were the soldiers?

The dryads were the first over the side. They didn't mind the ocean but more earth power coursed through the land, and they didn't stay still for long. Tiam led the Cempestre swordswomen next, and the others cautiously followed. A long stone ramp climbed up from the dock towards the land. It should be busy with traders and fishermen, but the only movement was a group of warriors with swords drawn, creeping low against the harbour wall.

Chakirris reached the top first. She slowly looked above the wall until she could just see the street level. The sea mist swirled over the cobbles, but it thinned and parted as she peered over the grey stone. Moist air folded back, and she saw the first shape, rising above the ground, then the second and a third. The nymphs had guessed, but she wanted to be wrong. Letting the miniature crossbow drop to her side, she climbed to her feet and looked out across the town square with the first tear moistening her cheek.

"What is it?" said Jem.

One by one, the company ascended to the top of the wall and stood looking out over the town square. Some dropped the weapons to their sides, others just shook their heads in disbelief, but Hayden fell to his knees and covered his face, sobbing into the leather of his cuff guards.

Jem placed a hand on his friend's shoulder and rose slowly, allowing the scene to unfold. It filled the large town square and beyond, up the main road and down every side street. There were bodies everywhere; men, women, children and the elderly. No one had been spared. Streaks of blood spattered the buildings and ran in rivulets through the cobbles. Some appeared to have died at their own hand, but it was the women and children, hacked limb-from-limb which created the grisly scene, like a Deapholt nightmare. Whole families lay together bound in blood, while others were butchered merely going about their business. An overturned basket of potatoes and a dropped barrow of firewood lay beside the twisted bodies of homemakers with their bloodied children.

For once, Brea was lost for words. Biorn had seen the horrors of war but never a scene of such cruelty. Brenna and Zonta helped Moranne up the ramp, and she joined the silent vigil surveying the carnage. It was worse than she feared. If only she could have seen King Ramon and warn him of the danger; now it was too late. "Corvus," she said flatly.

Caspin gazed at her dark expression. He'd heard the story but couldn't believe it. "How could one man—"

"One man can control a million with the right words," replied Chakirris. "Myrik can force a hundred to do his bidding with just his will."

"Frea!" gasped Gamin. He reached out and grasped Isen's hand, and she took it without thinking.

"There are no gods here," countered Moranne.

"Bad," added Zonta. The oni were cruel and bloodthirsty, but even *they* would not butcher unarmed women and children needlessly. It was considered dishonourable.

"Very bad," echoed Brenna.

They struggled to grasp words befitting the evil before them, but Jem had seen it. Jakaris killing crofters, the knight wading through a distant swamp, or the frenzied soldiers who hacked Aludra to death in front of her lover. The words of "The Battle of Kelby" replayed in Jem's head:

> *A woman's scream, a child's tear, and streets which ran with blood,*
> *Were all that remained of the Grenfold town which broke before the flood.*

All of this had happened before, but Corvus had endured five hundred years in exile. Plenty of time to hone his plans and learn from his mistakes. Aludra and Rana were dead. Who could oppose such evil?

"We must turn back," advised Captain Blake. "I can take us to Silmouth."

Moranne was shocked by the barbarity, but she knew what must be done. "No, Captain," she replied. "We must find Corvus and stop him. We go to Stanburg."

"You're mad!" cried Caspin, forgetting himself for a moment. "Can you see what death he's wrought? We are too few; we can't defeat an evil this great."

"I'm afraid my brother is right," added Sir Torbrand. "We need the Green Order and the Legion; this is too great for our small band."

Green lights flashed in Moranne's eyes, and she pushed Brenna and Zonta away. "Have you heard nothing?" she raved. "Corvus is clever and cunning; we must discover his plans. He will cut through the army like a knife cuts the bread."

"She's right," exclaimed Jem. "I've seen it."

"He has the sight," chipped in Hayden, wiping the tears from his eyes.

Caspin nodded as did the dryads. Even Biorn and the other fair folk knew there was something special about Moranne's gada. The Stanholm capital, Stanburg, lay a hundred miles northwest past the foothills of the Corona Mountains and through the barren Silver Valley. It would be quicker and safer by sea, but they might miss Corvus if he was still on the island.

"I won't command my men to go," said Torbrand. "We're outlaws now, and the dangers are too great."

Tiam nodded in agreement. The Cempestre warriors had volunteered for a diplomatic mission, but the stakes had risen.

"I will go with Lady Moranne," announced Jem.

"As will I," added Carina.

Moranne smiled. They would always make her proud.

"I'll go wherever Jem goes," chirped Hayden.

"And I'll be with you," added Cierzon.

Isen looked at Gamin and realized she was still holding his hand. He didn't even need to ask. "We'll be with you," he said, speaking for them both.

"I'm not letting the kids have all the fun!" shouted Brenna. "Count me in."

"With Brenda," growled Zonta.

"Until the end," stuttered the prince.

One by one, each member of the company pledged their allegiance until Caspin, Torbrand, Tiam, Barda and Koll remained. Sir Torbrand looked at the other two leaders and smiled. There was no way they'd allow their warriors glory without themselves. "I'm sorry, Captain," he said, addressing Barda Blake. "We will need you for the return journey."

"I ain't going no further," replied the captain, "and neither is Koll."

Moranne's eyes flared bright green once more as she regarded the grizzled sea captain. "There's ten gold coins each for you, and all you can find on the way. I'm sorry, but you have no choice."

He weighed her up for a moment, but he'd heard many tales of the witch, and he'd seen the power she wielded on the Numolport quay. He'd play along, *for now*.

Slowly they started to move into the town, stepping carefully around the bodies and trying to stop their hearts from bursting. Many faces were twisted into expressions of horror, but one word seemed frozen on the lips of every corpse: *why?* There seemed no sense to the killings and no plan, just a frenzied explosion of evil on a scale none of the party had experienced.

"Search the houses for food," commanded Torbrand, "and see if you can find us some horses."

It seemed disrespectful, but the dead didn't need the salted ham, aged cheese or fresh vegetables which lined the larders and gardens of the Gulward homes. Many dwellings revealed further horrors; the older man butchered as he sat in his rocking chair before the fireplace, and the baby slaughtered in its crib. Hayden ran out into the square to vomit, unable to cope with the stench of death and the sight of such despair.

Koll bent down to inspect the silver necklace around the neck of a young woman, but Caspin shot him a dark look. "Only what we need," he said sternly. They couldn't bury such a quantity of bodies, but they would show as much respect as they could.

The mist rolled away behind them as they carefully picked their way through the city. It revealed the grey, barren Skutel Mountains that filled the corner of the island to the west. They were home to the copper mines furnishing the islands with most of their currency; the seams having long since ceased their flow of ore.

The foothills of the Corona Mountains peaked above the houses to the east. The most extensive mountain range, in all the islands, covered most of Stanholm. It spread out in a granite wasteland from the towering active volcano, Mount Dracas, at its centre, to the sea on all sides but the west. Although little grew on the snow-covered slopes, the range hid treasures of silver, gold, diamonds and many other precious stones. Most of the outer slopes had been mined bare, but the inner areas were too challenging to explore.

"Many have died trying," said Captain Blake, as he noticed Jem peering up into the icy peaks. "Few will venture near Dracas."

"Why?" asked Jem.

"Freezing weather that can turn in an instant, no roads, no food, and a dark power which dwells in the east."

"Dark power?"

"Ignore him," said Caspin, "it's just a volcano."

The captain raised an eyebrow in defiance, but he wasn't about to argue.

The company proceeded cautiously through the town in a wide line. The men plundered the houses and businesses, while the others formed a vanguard across the street, moving slowly forward. The town square ended in a line of inns and businesses. Small paths spurred off in all directions, but the main road turned left towards the northwest. The Silver Road led to Silfren and onwards to Stanburg, Buckmin and Steen in the far north. The majority of the Stanish population lived in these areas on the east coast.

They turned the corner to be met by the same scene. More bodies littered the street or slumped against the sides of buildings. One man still held the sword he'd plunged into his chest, while another was frozen in agony as he reached out to retrieve his severed hand.

"What's that?" shouted Yuka. The archer had spotted something moving on the cobbles ahead. A hunched, ragged shape swayed a little in the centre of the road.

"Identify yourself!" yelled Caspin.

The shape stayed close to the ground and appeared to be rocking back and forth. Slowly the party crept forward, and the figure was gradually revealed as an older woman. She was dressed in shabby, blood-stained clothes and hunched over a body on the cobbles. She was whimpering as she rocked, and the black shawl over her head flopped back and forth, revealing the deep furrows in her brow, and warts peppering her hooked nose.

"Hello," said Bresne. "We won't hurt you."

The woman ignored them, continuing to rock with her arms around her knees. Eventually, the company encircled her and stared at the body she mourned. A young lad, no older than Gamin, was dressed in army uniform. His hair was brushed back, and fresh flowers had been laid all around his lifeless form.

"I'm so sorry," said Bresne, kneeling to take the woman's hand. She stopped rocking and slowly looked up into Bresne's compassionate face. "What's your name?"

The woman stared through Oretta Fixen, trying to piece together a coherent answer, but the words wouldn't come.

"He's so brave," she croaked. "My grandson's in the army." Her cheeks were streaked in white tendrils where tears had washed the grime from her weathered face.

"What's his name?" prompted Bresne.

"Private Chert Norite, of the King's Guard," she proclaimed as if she'd said it a dozen times, and each instant with so much pride.

"Who did this?"

The woman shook her head and just kept repeating: "He's so brave." Either she didn't know what had happened or the trauma had turned her mind.

"This is useless," said Moranne impatiently. "We need to go."

The others looked at Moranne with distaste, and Jem ignored her. He slowly dropped to his knees beside Bresne and put his arm on the older woman's shoulder. "Your grandson *was* a courageous lad; you should be proud."

The woman looked up, and the thinnest smile parted her cracked lips as she remembered the young Chert when he first arrived home in his polished uniform.

Jem noticed that Moranne was fidgeting, but he fixed the old lady with his calm green eyes and knew there was only one doorway into her heart. "He deserves to rest with Frea," he said quietly. "Would you like us to bury him?"

"We don't have time—" began Moranne.

Prince Asger silenced her with his hand.

The older woman's eyes glistened as tears welled once more and she nodded so slightly, that it was barely detectable. Gron, Lunn, Isen and Gamin needed no further cues. The four soldiers immediately disappeared to find spades, a mattock and a bed sheet to cover the broken body.

The City's Frean church was only a short distance further up the road, so they carefully wrapped Chert's body. Lunn, Gron, Gamin, Jem, Hayden, and Biorn hoisted him onto their shoulders and strolled up the street. Bresne and Brenna helped the older woman to her feet, and Prince Asger leant her one of his crutches. She was malnourished and frail, stumbling over the granite stones and coughing as the cold, moist air hit her lungs.

A Frean bishop's body lay across the doorway to the church and other blood-spattered corpses draped over the pews and against the altar as people had sought sanctuary in the hallowed hall. The company took Chert's body through the church and out into the cemetery at its rear. The ground was hard and stony, but Lunn, Gron and Isen made easy work of the shallow grave, which they positioned beneath a crimson-leafed sorbus tree. Of all the men, Gron was the most devout Frean; he knew a few words which he spoke over the grave, while Moranne seethed with silent fury.

"Goddess Frea, please take the soul of young Chert Norite to your bosom. Guide him through the garden of peace and protect him in the kingdom of paradise. May he live forever at your side and enjoy the fruits of eternal life in the halls of your palace."

"So be it," they all said in unison.

The older woman watched as the gravelly earth was piled onto the shroud, and Chert's body disappeared beneath the grey soil. The tears dropped, robbing her body of more moisture until the deed was done, and she turned to Jem with her withered hands clasped in prayer.

"Thank you," she said.

"Can we leave now?" blustered Moranne.

Jem wasn't done. "No!" he replied sternly, to her surprise. "You'll wait one minute!" He turned to the older woman and met her glistening eyes. "Please tell me your name."

The woman wiped the tears from her cheeks and looked up into Jem's green gaze. "Ruby," she croaked.

Jem leaned forward and held out his hands. "Take my hands, Ruby," he said. "I won't hurt you." Without hesitation, she reached forward with her parched, withered hands and held the warmth which ran down his arms and tingled in his smooth fingers. "Don't be afraid," he added. "You're going to show me what happened." Jem closed his eyes.

Although he still didn't fully understand the visions, Jem tried to imagine standing in the centre of the street but with a sense of impending dread. He cleared his mind of all thoughts and let his consciousness wander as if it strode through the Gulward streets and peered into the family homes. At first, there was nothing, but he could feel a force travelling from Ruby's hands, pass into his palms and begin to tingle in his arms. It started to blanket his body, but as it pulsed through his head, his thoughts became dark, and his mind went blank.

Suddenly Jem's eyes snapped open, and he stood in the town centre. The sun shone over the Corona Mountains, and his senses were filled with a hundred aromas from the market. The smell of fresh fish wafted pungently from large wooden crates, and aged ham hung above a butcher's shop. A group of soldiers relaxed in front of one of the taverns, watching the pretty maids walk by, while housewives bustled from store to store and little children played with hoops and balls. Like Denbry on market day, the town was rich with life. It took Jem back to simpler times, transporting eggs around the hamlet and walking nonchalantly along the River Sile.

The scene was perfect in its detail and could have portrayed any Grenfold town and the folk who toiled to live each day. Jem turned to see the harbour alive with soldiers and fishermen, shouting and cursing in colourful prose. He felt himself smiling with the ruddy-cheeked trawlermen. All was as it should be, but another sound was pulling his gaze back towards the square.

Jem could hear hooves clattering on the cobbles, but not from the shire horses that pulled the carts of vegetables and firewood. It was distant, frenzied and echoed through the lanes and passages which crisscrossed the town. There was more than one rider, as the sounds overlapped. Gradually some of the townsfolk noticed and turned to look north. With a blur of bay and grey steeds, three riders careered around the corner and broke into the centre of the square. People threw themselves clear, and a barrow was knocked over, spilling its cargo of firewood.

The three men were soldiers, although Jem was unsure of their rank. The first rider wore a gleaming gold helm and appeared to be the leader. He quickly removed his helmet and addressed the crowd.

"My name is Sir Halvor Gabbro. You must listen to me," he commanded. "Gather a few belongings and go into the mountains. You must do it now. Death is approaching."

The people looked at each other in bewilderment. "What's happening?" shouted some. "Why should we leave?" cried others.

Sir Halvor spun his horse and looked over the puzzled faces. He'd seen it with his own eyes but still couldn't believe the witchcraft which had created such fury. "If you stay, you'll die," he bawled. "Get to the mountains; there isn't much time."

With the click of his heels, he turned his horse, and the three riders sped off towards the mouth of the River Jarn. They disappeared behind the houses as they followed the waterway into the hills.

The soldiers on the docks and scattered around the town immediately obeyed their orders. They hauled large kit bags onto their shoulders and followed the three riders towards the mouth of the Jarn, leaving the bemused townsfolk in shock. Some took to horses and followed the soldiers, but others simply stared in disbelief. A few anxious mothers ran from shop to shop trying to find their children, while young wives searched for their husbands at work on the docks or drinking in the taverns.

Folk made for the River Jarn, while some aimed for the Skutel Mountains. Some stood in the square, arguing over the knight's message. One group of men remained seated outside the tavern, reckoning that the soldiers were drunk, while other families went home and shuttered their windows.

The town was at least half full when the first sounds of fury bounced off the city walls and rolled through the alleyways like a rockfall. There were shouts and screams mixed with the desperate snort of exhausted horses ridden near death. Then the panic started.

People ran through the alleyways, trying to escape the unseen force. Some tripped and fell, while others scooped up children and ran for their lives. The sound of steel on stone and metal on bone brought gasps of horror as a wall of hate flowed through the city, killing everyone in its path.

Chert Norite had been desperately trying to find his grandmother. She wasn't at home or in the market. He raced along the lanes, colliding with other townsfolk and careering over fences and through the gardens.

"Ruby!" he yelled as wild-eyed locals screamed past.

Emerging onto the Silver Road, he finally saw her. She was frozen in fear, helplessly scanning the horizon for her grandson while people ran in all directions around her.

"Gran!" he called, running to grab her. He pulled her across the road and into a neighbour's house. He pushed aside a table where the cellar door was located and hauled the wooden door open. "Get in!" He looked back through the door and noticed a little girl standing in the road, crying for her mother.

"I'll be back," he said. "Open the door for no one." He slammed the thick door shut and ran back out into the street.

Private Norite barely reached the girl when a wall of blood-soaked men slid and tumbled around the corner. Most wore military uniforms, but others were simple townsfolk; even a few young boys and lads no older than fifteen made up their snarling number. Their blazing green eyes were wide with the barbarity wrought by their own hands, and their limbs swung wildly like thrashing beasts. The force pushing them onwards spared no life. Men and women were butchered in seconds and trampled underfoot. Doors splintered under axes, and windows were smashed.

Chert pulled his sword and swiped at the first soldier, but four were on him at once, and he vanished beneath a frenzy of blood and steel.

Jem gradually opened his eyes. His vision seemed to last an hour, but his eyes had been closed for mere seconds. "Your grandson was very brave," he said, wiping the moisture from his eyes.

Ruby nodded and turned to kneel at Chert's grave.

"They were trying to kill the soldiers," said Jem. "You'll probably find dead soldiers along the river." He pointed back towards the harbour where the River Jarn poured its glacial waters into the sea. "There are few survivors."

"That doesn't make any sense," said Biorn. "Why kill your own invasion force?"

Moranne didn't have an answer. *What was Corvus planning?* "It's even more important for us to go north," she said.

"Right!" said Sir Torbrand. "Men! Get us those horses. We'll meet on the edge of town, where we'll eat before we set forth."

"Wherever you go," added Moranne, "take a woman or one of the fair folk with you. Remember that Corvus can control any human man."

"If I see him, he's dead," spat Hayden.

52 SILVER

The Rocker Box Tavern was located at the far northwest side of Gulward, on the Silver Road, just as it entered the city. None of the Stanholm towns possessed barrier walls, gates or protective towers. It was a small island with a tiny population and a low crime rate. While once it was a prime destination for wealthy merchants, it had gradually morphed into a barren rock as each gold seam ran dry and gemstone mines were abandoned.

The three-story stone building was one of the oldest in Stanholm; Moranne had stayed there during many visits. She sat on one of the benches outside and looked up at the rough, grey, flint exterior. She'd gazed many times through the window panes at the bustling harbour below. King Ramon was a stubborn man; he never listened to her.

Gron had found a small cask of mead and a bottle of mapulder, which he was passing around the company. The tavern's interior was strewn with bodies; everyone decided to sit outside.

A circuit of the town had revealed several stables filled with starving horses, but a few decent mounts stood in stony fields to the west. They managed to saddle enough for every rider, with two more sickly animals as pack horses. They cut the rest free.

"Tis a shame we can't bury them," said Gron as he looked down the road at the bodies. "It don't seem right."

"It ain't right," agreed Biorn, "but they lie where they fall. We protect the living, not the dead."

Jem had been watching Moranne since the funeral. Her demeanour had changed; it happened back at Lenturi Manor. Every step towards the mission's goal seemed to darken her mood, making her anxious and impatient. Gone were the smirks of disdain and jokes at Hayden's expense. Many others had noticed the change and steered clear of her ire.

"The lady?" asked Hayden. He was with Cierzon as usual but always stayed close to Jem.

"I think she knows more than she says," replied Jem. Questioning your patron was unheard of, but they were all fugitives now. Her hold on him was slipping.

"Yes," agreed Cierzon. "Her mind is a walled cell."

The others enjoyed the bounty they'd found in the Gulward homes along with a small glug of mead. Most of them had barely eaten since the Numolport escape, although the stench of death suppressed some appetites.

Sir Torbrand sat with his brother and the prince, but his eyes were fixed on Ellen. He couldn't keep his oath, and he couldn't tell her. Being near made him want to hold her; he kept his distance.

"You know what I thinks," grumbled Brea.

Ellen loved the experienced huntress, but her words of wisdom fell on stony ground. "I don't care," she replied. "I can't help how I feel."

"Hey, love. I don't enjoy emptying me bowels, but I can't help that either."

Even Jilliad and Sondrin laughed at Brea's outrageous statements. The dryads knew the minds of all those in the company except Moranne. Not only did she have the gift of silent speech, but she could shield her thoughts from prying minds. Chakirris was nervous. She knew some truths hidden in plain sight, but Wickona held another agenda deep within.

"Watch her," she ordered Sondrin.

None of the Cempestre had been this far north; Deapholt seemed a million miles away. They hadn't bargained on becoming outlaws, but their company was solidly behind Oretta Brimwulf. Tiam surveyed her warriors with pride; she smiled to see Bresne enjoying Biorn's company, and Isen sat silently with Gamin. The most surprising relationship was the bond forming between Zonta and Brenna. The hulking red presence followed Oretta Gunborg everywhere she went, like a puppy.

"You can go anywhere you please," said Brenna, but Zonta would stare at her impassively.

"Brenda," she would reply gruffly. Often followed by "no kill."

It was late afternoon when they decided to push onwards. The sun would soon be dipping behind the Skutel Mountains, but no one wanted to stay another moment in the open grave of Gulward. Sax and Gamin loaded any leftover food onto the packhorses, while Gron and Lunn helped the prince into his unsupported saddle. He could ride conventionally, but it was an effort and strained his back. "Fret not," he told the two soldiers. The scale of suffering all around had brought him low. His father's policies had led the Stans into desperation and the embrace of evil.

The Silver Road meandered through the Skutel Mountains and the Corona Range valley. It was grey and stony, like the landscape surrounding them. There were farms and planted fields on the way, but the crops were thin and weak. The coarse, volcanic soil contained few nutrients, and extensive farming had robbed it of any life and structure. Stanholm's nickname of the stone island came both from its history of gem stone mining and the nature of its rocky, unyielding terrain.

"Who would choose life in such a rancid land?" asked Cuyler as they rode past a large, dilapidated farm. There was no sign of life; the family had either died in the fields or fled into the mountains. The mottled grey farmhouse leaned against rough outcrops of rock and appeared cold and harsh. The company's mood was dark; few spoke, alone in their thoughts of the Gulward atrocity.

When night fell, and the path was dark in the scant light of the crescent moon, they made camp in a large hay barn. Still, their words were few. It seemed disrespectful to make merry in this land of dread. None of the company slept well in the draughty farm building, and the night watch rotated quickly.

"Any of *your* kind on this rock?" asked Hayden. He and Cierzon sat on the barn roof, looking at the stars. The dryads were scattered around the area, sleeping lightly; they seldom showed themselves at night.

"None," replied the alviri lord. "We feel most at home amongst the green of life. We once lived on these islands, but humans took the trees."

But for a few dry, spiky bramble bushes and the occasional pine, there was little vegetation. Fields for grazing cattle and root vegetable plantations took up most of the semi-fertile soil.

Moranne had the company woken early the following day. She was desperate to reach Stanburg as quickly as possible. Convinced that Corvus had taken the throne of Stanholm, she assumed that King Ramon was dead, along with most of his family. The sun was barely a sliver of light glancing over the Corona Mountains, and the air was chilled. A thin veil of frost kissed the pastures, and a ring of mist wrapped itself over the mountain peaks, but the disparate company continued their journey along the Silver Road.

A few clear, twisting streams cascaded down the mountainsides and ran beneath them through solid bridges and ancient tunnels. The harsh nature of the land held a simple beauty, but the company only wished for home. The Cempestre and the fair folk longed for the humid paths of Deapholt, while the men dreamed of the green lands of Middcroft, Tudorfeld and Burland. Denbry was a distant memory, but Jem would never miss its claustrophobic embrace.

Around noon, Sondrin spotted Stanholm's only extensive woodland. Peridot Forest was smaller than Bearun and tiny in comparison with Deapholt. Fallow deer and grey wolves were its principal inhabitants. Tunnbroccs couldn't burrow through the stony ground, and the oni had never crossed the Lowker Straights. It gave the dryads a brief glimpse of home, but the column did not stop.

The pine forest began on the northern slopes of the Skutel Mountains and poured into the valley before it faded towards the Silver Road.

"They are watching us," said Chakirris.

"Who?" questioned the prince.

The nymphs could feel the fearful eyes following them along the road. "Humans," replied Sondrin.

Some had fled from nearby farms, while others had run from Gulward and Silfren. Slowly they'd return home to continue the harsh Stanish life when all signs of danger had receded.

"What evil now!" shouted Tiam from the front of the column.

Moranne, Torbrand and Caspin rode forward to her position. The path curved to the northwest, but they followed Oretta Brimwulf's gaze over the road's eastern edge, where the Corona foothills edged their route. A dense, black stream of smoke climbed over the slopes and faded into the grey sky. No one spoke. Their course was northwards, and each member knew they hadn't seen the worst of Corvus' hand.

Leaving the forest behind and sweeping closer to the mountains, the terrain became severe and barren. Large, splintering outcrops of rock appeared on each side of the path, leaving piles of frost-sheared shale beneath their feet. The road rose and fell with each left and right turn. Constant was the column of smoke that hung over the landscape, becoming broader and darker as they approached. Occasionally it would billow as its fuel moved and cast a foreboding shadow on the horizon. Hearts grew heavy with every step towards the smoke. Moranne had been this way many times but had never dreaded placing each step that brought her closer to him.

They cleared a final stump of near-black granite, and the land fell away before them. Silfren revealed itself through the smoke, but it was the inferno raging before the town that stopped the company dead. A raging pyramid of fire stood as tall as an abbey's steeple. It snapped and flashed, coughing out great clouds of smoke.

"That smell," said Hayden. "What is it?"

The warriors knew it well but hesitated to say. The smell of burning flesh was hard to forget and haunted anyone who experienced it.

"It's a pyre," said Captain Fallon. "I can see bodies."

"Frea!" whispered Gron.

The party looked forward to resting but approached the town with mixed emotions. The road declined quickly, and the horses struggled for footing on the gravel surface. Silfren buildings had a similar stone construction to Gulward, but most were single-storey. A single Frean abbey marked the town entrance beside a small gatehouse, but all of it shimmered in the heat haze from the pyre. The bodies appeared, stacked atop firewood, old carts, doors and furniture. The Stans remained invisible behind the fire and hidden in the stone dwellings.

"Look sharp, lads," commanded Biorn. The men put their hands on their swords, and the archers readied their bows.

A group of some fifty people approached, but it became clear that they posed little threat as they neared. Most were farmers with spades and axes or tradespeople carrying carving knives and cleavers. All of them were filthy, desperate and tired from building the pyre. But the four nearest men were soldiers, one with rank.

"Stop there, strangers!" he shouted.

Sir Torbrand halted the column and dismounted to meet them. The man was dressed in similar garb to Jem and Hayden, but his breastplate carried the diamond mark of House Scoria. His long hair and short beard were ginger red, and his sad, blue eyes were tired and bloodshot. Blood and grime marked his glistening brow. "I'll know your business, sir," he said, recognising Torbrand's rank.

The knight held his hands high as Caspin and Moranne dismounted behind him. "We're on a diplomatic mission to see your king," he said. "We mean you no harm; we just need some rest."

"They have elves!" shouted one of the farmers.

"And a ... thing!" cried another as he saw Zonta towards the back of the group.

"I am Lady Moranne of the King's Council, and this is Prince Asger Fierdman," said Moranne, gesturing to the prince. "Who may I be addressing?"

The soldier looked across at his colleagues, then bowed in respect. "I am Corporal Tufa Mudstone," he said stiffly. "These are the last of my men."

"I'm sorry, Corporal," said Sir Torbrand. "We travelled through Gulward, and it's the same."

The corporal shook his head, and the townspeople gasped and cursed in hushed tones.

"My brother lives in Gulward," said Tufa. "He has a wife and three children."

"I'm sorry. I hope they made it out." Torbrand could offer no better words of comfort. From the scale of the massacre, it was likely that most of the town was dead.

"Might I ask about the strange... I mean, unusual, er—"

"You mean the fair folk," corrected Moranne.

"We have a common enemy," continued Torbrand. "The one responsible for turning man against man is a powerful warlock." Moranne grimaced at the mention of the arcane name, but she knew the knight was trying to use terms that simple folk could understand.

"Horse dung!" shouted a stout butcher. "One man killed half a town? We saw the soldiers with our own eyes."

"Twisted by Corvus," proclaimed Moranne. "Your king was seduced and used."

"King?" cried a farmer. "The harvest fails, and our cattle die. He sits on his golden throne and laughs. A thousand curses on that house of filth!"

"Aye!" chorused the men.

"When our families return, he hangs," said the farmer.

Corporal Mudstone looked to Sir Torbrand. With the army diminished and so many dead, the king was done. If he survived the lynch mobs, there would be few safe hiding places. "They think we might turn on them," he whispered. "They fear us."

"I speak," said Prince Asger. Lunn and Gron had helped him from his mount, and he leaned against the axe wielder while Gamin retrieved his crutches from one of the pack horses. "Make vow," he croaked, "help rebuild, will I." Moranne echoed his words for those unaccustomed to his speech. "Never divided again." He slumped against the crutches with the exertion of forcing out his words.

"Our prince struggles with every step," said Sir Torbrand, hoping he hadn't misspoken. "Yet he toiled with us through dale and forest, faced a horde of Red Caps, stood against vicious black wolves and led us through an army of mountain clans. I trust this man with my life, and I will stand by his words!"

The townspeople had seldom heard such speech. Many dropped their weapons, and a few bowed their heads.

"You have my sword, Prince Asger," said the corporal.

"And ours," added one of his men.

Although the Silfren men couldn't fully trust the green-skinned nymphs or the fair forest folk, they welcomed the prince's mission into the town. Past the terrible sight of burning bodies and the sickening fumes which stung the eyes and clung to the throat, the flint-clad buildings of Silfren bore the scars of death. Blood stained the cobbled streets and sprayed across the walls, where peaceful lives had been extinguished with no mercy. The surviving men and their families had watched the carnage from the mountains above, unable to comprehend the pointless butchery. Women and children remained, sheltering in the cliffs and caves above, too frightened to return. Winter would cut through the highlands soon, and they'd need to harvest what pitiful crops remained, but sorrow had stained the land, and the families would struggle in the biting Stanholm cold.

Relatively unscathed was the Gilded Leaf Inn, which stood at the centre of town. It was near empty when the horde crashed against the community; the innkeeper and his wife did not see another day. Their blood stained the flagstone floor leaving two patches which no one would walk over.

Gron examined a large cask of mead behind the bar, but nobody had the stomach for ale. Corporal Mudstone found them more stocks of ham, cheese and bread before the company spread out around the building to find a place to sleep. Moranne and Asger had good rooms, the Cempestre took most of the rest, but the men, alviri, dalfreni and dryads were content to use rugs and benches around the bar and lounge. Biorn and Bresne remained vigilant at one of the upper windows, but they enjoyed the company, swapping tales of oni skirmishes and encounters with bandits in truth. Another night of restless sleep awaited.

Moranne watched the last pink glow of day sinking into the western horizon. The ocean was too distant to see from here, but she felt its cold waves lapping against the rough rocks of Stanholm, like the hands of dead children tugging on her jacket. "Tell us a story," they'd shout as she arrived in Silfren's square, but this tale was too dark for any bairn. Misted glass panes reflected only her pale, furrowed features, but she felt a dark presence behind her. The weight was more than any Stanish rock, but she'd bear it until the end.

"What have we done," she whispered, but Dane was just a phantom, flitting through her troubled thoughts. She pulled the curtains shut and turned towards the bed. The spry silhouette standing in the doorway stopped her dead.

"Who is *we*?" said Jem. His deference was slipping, and his manner was emboldened.

She stood regarding him for a moment, then removed her jacket and placed it over an adjacent chair. "Having trouble sleeping, my *gada*?" she said, emphasizing his rank. Steorra hung prominently at her side, glinting in the candlelight.

Jem didn't move. Moranne could just see a sliver of green reflecting beneath his unkempt dark hair. "What have you done to me?" he growled through gritted teeth. "What happened in Numolport?" Jem could still see the dome of shimmering light about them.

Moranne reached down beneath her blouse and withdrew a silver necklace with a leaf pendant. She ran the shape through her fingers and remembered the day she received it.

"You have gifts, Jem. I can help you to see them."

"And Carina?"

They were alike in many ways, but Carina could control her powers like the arm controlling the hand.

"Her gifts are strong," said Moranne.

"Why does she have a sceptre?" said Jem. "Why am I here?"

Moranne slipped the necklace's clasp and placed it on the table. The candle's flame was flickering to a breeze from the window. She could feel the green fire beginning to burn in her own eyes.

"I've always liked you," she said. "I thought you deserved a better life— "

"Lies!" spat Jem.

Jade fire sparked across her face, and she turned to stare at him. Her eyebrows furrowed in anger, and Jem could see her fists clenched at her side.

"Don't push me—"

"Or what?" he goaded. "Maybe you'll lead us to a forsaken land to be hacked to death by friends and foes."

"I'm warning you—"

"Just as you did to Aludra and Rana."

Thin green lightning arced over her arms and flared in her eyes. She lunged wildly at Jem, grabbing him by the collar of his tunic and pushing him through the door; her strength was coursing from the earth power in her body. He stumbled across the second-floor landing until he crashed into the bannister and leaned over the drop with her weight against him.

"You'll never suffer the way I suffer every day," she raged. "You'll never understand the sacrifices I've made. You've seen a mere crack in my life, and you think you know me?"

Jem could feel her warm breath on his cheek and the shaking in her body through the very floorboards beneath.

"How dare you!" she exploded. "Without me, you'd be—"

"Just a chicken farmer?" he blasted, beginning to push against her. "Mia Tunland knew something, Alize warned me about you, and even Princess Vena told me not to trust you. You're a liar!"

"Without me, you'd be dead—"

"What in Frea's name is going on?" shouted Caspin. Neither of them had noticed him leave his room to investigate the noise.

"No concern of yours!" snapped Moranne, finally releasing Jem's collar. He brushed his tunic down and glared at her defiantly. "Go to bed, gada," she ordered, "and don't ever say *no* to me again."

Moranne was alluding to the incident with Ruby, but Caspin wasn't entirely convinced that was the origin of the conflict.

Jem thought to push her further, but now wasn't the time. He nodded curtly to Sir Caspin and retreated over the landing, down the stairs and back to the wide rug where he would sleep beside Gamin. Moranne had told him everything he needed to know.

53 THE ROAD TO RUIN

The jagged, snowy peaks of the Corona Mountains were wreathed in low cloud and vapour from the sleeping Mount Dracas, but light crept forwards. It slid along the western tips, plunged into the valleys, and reached across the shale slides to the plain, where a group of disparate riders toiled northward. The horses snorted their disapproval with large plumes of steam that hung in the cold air and wafted behind like a trail. Every step away from Silfren saw the grass thin a little more, the soil grow harder, the wind become harsher, and the temperature drop to a chilling low. Winter was embracing Stanholm and would soon bring its snow from the blinding peaks into the lowlands' brush.

Hayden didn't understand why the capital would be situated so far north, but the history of this land originally included three large islands. Prosperous was the relationship between Brencan and Stanholm until a fissure opened beneath the smaller island, causing it to sink and become a collection of islets and an impenetrable swamp. Some blamed evil spirits, while others blamed the sinners and fornicators of the once-liberal island. The truth of this geologically unstable area was lost on the simple folk of the north. Now the sunken isle remained as a reminder to puritans of the dangers of apostasy.

The biting cold air suited the mood of the company very well. Everyone had witnessed the angry storm that flared between Jem and Moranne, but none would mention it openly. Hayden looked back towards Jem, who rode with Captain Blake and Koll at the party's rear. His head was down, lost in dark thoughts, while Moranne sat at the head of the column in equal silence. Whatever sparked the confrontation still simmered beneath the surface, just waiting to be fuelled. All of this seemed so far from the sleepy simple life of a squire's son in Dunstreet; drinking with friends while pretending to flirt with barmaids, hunting fallow deer in Geg Woods, or just walking back to the stables while the evening sun danced through Ham's hair. Hayden pulled the coat close around his neck and shivered. "Curse this place," he whispered to himself.

Cierzon detected even the quietest words while frost winds whistled about them. He looked up and smiled, the same heart-melting visage which made Hayden want to fall into his arms. Where the Scirmann's groom had been a beautiful boy, the alviri lord was a man. His fighting skills, refined manners, wit and wisdom had matured over six hundred years. That he even looked at

Hayden made the gada's heart beat faster, but something more was growing. They both felt it, but neither dared to give it life.

"Don't wait, lads," said Brea cryptically. She'd been watching them fondly since Suncin, a feeling she wanted for Ellen too, but her tall knight was as impassive as the granite rocks behind them. Any love in his soul was buried behind a towering wall of duty, but events in Numolport showed that even the thickest barrier could crack.

Hayden didn't see Cierzon wink in reply or the smile on Ellen's face. Even Gron accepted the young gada. He'd always considered himself a good Frean. "Any man prepared to die for me is a friend," he'd say to Lunn. Far from Langley's lynch mobs and his father's disapproval, Hayden felt safe, but trepidation took over where fear once dwelled. A single, loving kiss with the stable boy sealed his fate, but he'd never given himself to a man. The alviri lord was proud and confident. What did a Burland coward have to offer?

"You're no coward," whispered Cierzon, "and you have more to offer than you know."

Often forgetting that some alviri could read minds, Hayden blushed, but secretly he was happy that Cierzon didn't seem repulsed by the thought.

"Man with man?" grunted Zonta. Same-sex relationships didn't exist in the clan culture. Any oni even discussing the possibility would find an axe in his back.

"I think it's sweet," replied Brenna.

Zonta shuddered. The only *sweetness* shown to her by Kagel was the time he decided *not* to beat her when she failed to prepare his meal quickly enough. The female rivalry was too strong to allow any bonds to form, and affairs with other males never happened. She'd never known love; she waved goodbye to her only same-sex friend at thirteen when a jealous female murdered Shand. Zonta looked down at the long matted hair of Oretta Gunborg, tied with hemp string into a ponytail; it swept back and forth across the katana strapped to her back as her mount traversed the pot-holed road. Brenna was closest to a friend; she seemed less feminine than the other women, except Isen, and more like an oni female. Only the alviri girl's blade spoiled the picture. "Need axe", Zonta would say, smiling behind her fearsome fangs.

However much the party whispered, gestured or changed their facial expressions, the dryads heard it all. Except for Moranne and Cierzon, the tree nymphs read every thought. They knew Captain Blake was trying to devise an escape, Sefti reminded Lunn of the elder sister he'd never spoken of, Ellen and Torbrand were breaking their hearts together, and Bresne looked at Biorn the same way she once smiled at her late husband. They couldn't prevent the cacophony of thoughts which whirled around them, begging to be heard; the by-product of an evolution which had made them successful hunters and survivors in the darkest forests.

While Chakirris and Sondrin were committed to the mission, Jilliad was still unsure. *We can't defeat Myrik*, she said into her sisters' minds.

Not without help, agreed Sondrin.

They both looked to Chakirris, who rode silently beside Prince Asger. The sisters spoke frequently, and she knew their feelings well.

I'm committed to this mission, and I believe the prince, she replied, *but you're right. Myrik has become so strong we will not defeat him without help.* She looked west, remembering back along the centuries to a time when the world was different. There was still a chance. She'd keep her counsel for now, but a dangerous idea was starting to form.

Moranne, too, was deep in thought. Jem's words had cut her deeply. She could still remember that grey winter's morning in Cynstol when a young gada burst into her Lyften Tower room. Not pausing to grab her coat, she leapt through the door and raced up the winding staircase with fear in her heart and dread clouding her vision. The cold stone walls blurred past so quickly that she couldn't even remember how she found herself on the walkway circling the tower's top level.

"Don't come any nearer," said Rana. She sat on the ornately-carved stone balustrade, legs dangling over the side. Foaming waves crashed over jagged rocks three hundred feet below.

Moranne could see her old friend past the tower's curve on the opposite side of the building. She had her head lowered, looking down into the abyss. Her straight, short hair was thick and matted, and her clothes were creased and dirty as if she'd been sleeping rough.

"She was my friend too," said Moranne, grasping for words. "This isn't the way—"

"Friend?" cried Rana. "She was my whole life. I've never been with another."

The day that Aludra introduced Moranne to her soulmate was a day long past these weathered isles to simpler times before the fall. The two had been inseparable for three thousand years, unheard of in their kind.

"Don't leave me alone," pleaded Moranne.

"You'll never be alone. You love these simple creatures."

"Please, Rana! We can find him again; together!"

"Ha!" she laughed. "*You* know we'll never find him, and he'll never die."

Moranne tried to move forward, but Rana detected every movement.

"Not a step further!" she shouted.

"I can't do this alone," begged Moranne, "I need you!"

Rana turned for the first time with a smile of clarity and puffy eyes which had cried their last tear. "You knew the risks, but you were too selfish to care. Ally saw the best in people, even you."

"I was lonely."

"So you cursed us all."

"I'm sorry!" yelled Moranne.

Rana turned her back and gazed over the Grey Sea to the blurred horizon and Inseld Island beyond. "You used us," she said. "I'll never forgive you." The image of Aludra hacked to death beneath a wall of Corvus' puppets haunted every moment of her tormented life. *Fly, my love.*

I'm coming.

With a slight flick of her wrists, Rana pushed herself off the edge and disappeared from view. No scream nor breath of wind, just an empty space where Rana had sat. Moranne couldn't move. Frozen in shock, she gasped, holding her breath until the grief flooded her mind, and she exhaled in anguish. Barely facing the truth, she grasped for the balustrade and followed it to the spot where Rana had been. She looked down into the foaming ocean, but the body was gone, already claimed by the crashing waves.

Jem's words were cruel because they were true. She hid behind her role as a royal advisor or storyteller to inquisitive minds, but painful memories surfaced every day and grew as they journeyed north. She couldn't look back at him nor give him the answers he craved. Jem was in danger, and she had put him in harm's way. Maybe it was a mistake to have pulled him from that simple life; perhaps he should have remained hidden.

"Is everything alright, my lady?" asked Caspin. He could bear the silence no longer.

She couldn't help replying with a smile. Caspin had a good heart, and they'd always been friends since the day she met him, aged fourteen, in Faircester. She told some of her tall tales, and the young lad wouldn't stop asking questions. "Where do elves live? What's a wyvern? Who are the clans?"

"I'm fine," she replied. "The horror of this place affects us all, even me."

"You know you can tell me anything?"

She knew he meant it, but some burdens were not easily shared. "I think it's you that needs help," she replied, changing the subject.

"Me?"

"Why is an eligible young knight like you still unattached?" she said mischievously.

"You sound like my mother."

"Well?" she teased. "I know you're popular with the ladies."

Caspin rolled his eyes. He differed from his brother in many ways, but in one, they were the same. The dizzy ladies of Middcroft left him cold. He craved strength and maturity.

"Brenna's a fine woman," he whispered.

"A little old for you," smirked Moranne. "I'm not sure you're her type."

"A knight?"

"No," she grinned. "A man."

Caspin seemed puzzled for a moment, but he looked back down the column and noticed Brenna trying to teach Zonta a few more words.

"Well, ma'am, maybe I could take *you* for a drink when this is all over," he said cheekily.

"I'll take us all for a drink if we live through this."

Although Moranne's spirit had lifted, she avoided Jem for the rest of the day and the following morning. She wanted to progress to Stanburg as quickly as possible, but it was too far for a single journey, so they camped in an empty farmhouse and continued early the next day.

The terrain was familiar, but the temperature was plummeting. Frost peppered the thin grass and clung to the rocky outcrops punctuating the road. It crusted the fronds of the few pine trees and hung in the air. None of the riders was fully equipped for such a climate and used sackcloth and sheets to wrap themselves. Only Zonta and the dryads seemed immune. When billowing darkness filled the horizon, it blanketed the party in a twisted relief.

"Another burning town," mused Brea. "I really love this island."

The fires were long extinguished, but the hot, smouldering beams sent wisps of grey smoke to the clouds hovering above the city. It spread out over the sea and moved west with the prevailing breeze. Stanburg was gone. The picture was similar to both Silfren and Gulward. Dead bodies littered the streets, and blood stained the walls, but a scorching fire had also raged through the town, destroying every home. A few shacks near the docks had survived, but there was no sign of life.

Stanburg City stood on a corner of land between the wide Marglen River to the north and the cold waters of the Blusker Channel to the west. Its past was dominated by trade with Brencan, but the curving harbour now served as a fishing port. Monuments to ancient rulers looked down onto the streets of carnage, where every soul had perished. In some places, the bodies of entire families lay in bloody piles, and in others, whole squads of soldiers had slaughtered themselves. Swords still protruded from twisted bodies, and axes lay embedded in the spines of poor wretches cut down from behind.

The party couldn't help looking down at the grim sight as their horses picked carefully through the streets of blood and death. Hayden felt tears pricking his eyes, and even Biorn gasped back the emotion. Soldiers would see the worst of human cruelty, but this was beyond anything he'd ever endured.

"Heads up," said Sir Torbrand. "We have a job to do."

Moranne was already looking above the smouldering ruins to the gold which flashed through the smoke. The others would only see the resplendent palace when they rounded the last corner of town.

"Is that real gold!" gasped Gamin.

The rest of the party were too speechless to comment. Only Moranne was familiar with the gleaming towers of Obsidia Palace, and it still beguiled her whenever she saw it.

A long, arched stone bridge crossed the icy Marglen River, but every gaze was on the smooth, white limestone of the palace towers, capped with bulging, gold-covered domes. Unlike the castles and walled cities of Grenfold, Obsidia Palace had no boundary wall. Instead, its sixteen round towers were interconnected, forming a single, giant structure. Some were as large as Cynstol's Keep, while others acted as watchtowers. Each one was crowned in gold which shone in the few rays that cut through the grey sky.

"We're lucky," noted Torbrand. "The drawbridge is down."

"Define lucky," mused Tiam.

Obsidia stood on a tall outcrop of rock which overlooked the harbour. The east side was guarded by a deep stream spanned by a drawbridge. A steep mountain sealed the north.

"It's a good defensive position," replied Sir Torbrand, ignoring Tiam's concern.

"Real gold," said Gamin once more, unable to grasp the opulence.

"Yes," replied Moranne. "It's real gold, and the red dot you can see in each spire is a real ruby."

"Frea!" gasped Gron.

The palace's majesty grew as they crossed the bridge, turned left at the Buckmin Crossing and headed for the gate. Two narrow towers stood on either side of the gate tower, but no archers leaned out from the arrow slits, and no guards stood to greet them. The massive oak doors were inlaid with tarnished silver scrolls, but they stood open, flat against the inner walls.

The party halted on the creaking drawbridge, peering into the impressive entrance.

"Where did it go wrong?" asked Caspin.

"Let's find out," replied Torbrand.

With hands on swords, they proceeded inside.

54 OBSIDIA PALACE

Ashen skies covered the Cynstol Keep, the scurrying town below and all the lands of Caynna, but the misty rain clinging to his window held Sir Torl Radborough's attention. Tiny droplets ran together until they formed larger ones which tumbled down the glass, leaving streaks in their wake, much like Moranne's ambitious mission. He opened the creased scroll and read it once more:

> Dear Torl,
>
> The mission now includes Cempestre, alviri, dalfreni and other fair creatures you would not believe. We've ventured as far as Numolport, ready to cross to Stanholm, but Cymel came before us. He imprisoned the Cempestre, and he barred us from completing the mission. Cymel holds some insane notion of defeating the Stans in battle with help from Kemin Lenturi.
>
> The man is a fool. Corvus would not risk a direct strike against Tudorfeld. I do not know his designs, but he's had three hundred years to scheme them.
>
> We have a plan to break out of Bruborg and proceed to Stanburg. If you receive this letter, we have been successful.
>
> I will try to write once I've met King Ramon, but be prepared for war. Do everything you can to recall the First Legion to Cynstol and stop Marl from committing all the troops to the north.
>
> Please see that Private Rike Shepherd is rewarded for his bravery.
>
> Your trusted friend.
> Moranne.

Torl carefully rolled the scroll back into a tube and secured it with ribbon before pushing it into one of his robe's deep pockets. He paced across his chamber and pulled open the door.

"Tino!" he boomed.

A door creaked open below, and scurrying steps echoed up the winding stairs as Gada Crayber leapt upwards as fast as he could.

"Get me an audience with the king," he continued. Curse that man, he said to himself. General Marl knew his hawkish manner played well with the king, but he wasn't here now.

Take care, my friend.

―⚯―

Moranne peered through the wide gates to Obsidia, half expecting Prince Pancel to be striding forth to meet her. He'd make a much better leader than his proud father. Handsome, kind and measured, everything King Ramon wasn't. The two dead guards slumped on either side didn't fill her with hope. Both had killed themselves with their swords.

The Blanca Tower housed curving stables on both sides and a further floor accessed by a shallow sloping ramp. All the stalls lay open, their former occupants having been ridden to death on the Silver Path to Gulward. The party decided to use the empty stables with an adequate supply of hay and plenty of room for the horses to rest.

"The servants' quarters are above," said Moranne. "Can I suggest we start searching for life?"

Sir Torbrand agreed. He split the company into five groups to fan out across the palace and meet in the central courtyard. They were a mix of men, women and fair folk in readiness if Corvus still stalked the halls. Chakirris led the first group, which included Prince Asger. They would slowly patrol the ground floor while Moranne, Torbrand, Caspin and Tiam would lead teams on the upper floors, the basement and the main living area, known as the Gold Tower.

"Be on your guard," warned Sir Torbrand. "You've seen what Corvus can do. Take no chances."

They nodded their understanding and slowly pushed forward into the palace.

Detailed carvings of two snarling dragons adorned the double doors leading to the Great Tower. They stood slightly ajar and opened easily as Gron and Lunn pulled them back.

"My eyes!" gasped Hayden.

A mirror-polished marble floor spread forth in every direction to meet the distant curved walls of the grand hall. A green onyx statue of a distant king stood at the hall's centre, looking out at other busts and paintings lining the wall. Two curving marble staircases swept up each side to a first-floor gallery. Carved, twisting limestone pillars supported the mezzanine and domed roof. Some were adorned with carvings of strange creatures or veined alien leaves.

Although no torches or lamps were lit, the tower was bathed in light from a circle of square, panelled windows above. Light spilt down the stairs and bounced off the smooth floor. Only the drips of blood and broken bodies soiled the splendour.

"The courtyard is through there," said Moranne. She pointed to a pair of arched doors on the opposite side of the hall.

"We meet there at dusk," added Sir Torbrand. "Watch yourselves."

Two groups stayed below, and the three others climbed the sweeping stairs before splitting up to search the other wings and upper floors. All the walkways were finished in pink and grey-seamed marble, but every room was different. Walnut cabinets lined a double-height library, all stuffed with curling, leather-bound books. The drawing room had a polished oak floor dotted with tightly stitched armchairs. The opulence was as dramatic as the bodies draped over the four-poster beds or slumped over padded chairs, throats cut. Women died hiding their eyes; servants fell, running for their lives, while soldiers and guards thrust their own weapons into their chests. Every passage held a new horror.

Jem sighed in relief if they found a room free of the dead. His team was led by Caspin and included Hayden, Cierzon, Sondrin, Brenna and Zonta, who lumbered after Oretta Gunborg like a hunting dog.

"Are either of you picking anything up?" asked Caspin.

Both Cierzon and Sondrin shook their heads. There were murmurs, but sometimes it was hard to pick out specific voices, with many now on the mission.

"I can feel the horror like an echo," confessed Cierzon.

Sondrin silently agreed. Jem felt it too, but he resisted letting it enter his thoughts. He'd seen enough.

Room after room and staircase after carved staircase, the life of Obsidia was gone. The sight of innocent servants was the saddest, cut down just earning a humble wage in the king's service.

"This is hopeless," sighed Hayden. "It's a tomb."

"We have our orders," said Caspin.

All of them spoke in hushed tones out of respect for the fallen behind every wall.

"Bad," grunted Zonta. "No honour."

Two scullery maids, no older than fourteen, lay caked in blood together, slumped against a polished oak dresser, hand in hand.

Gada Scirmann could take it no more and fell to his knees, covering his face to hide the tears. He remembered sweet Signy and the night they danced until dawn. "No sense," he sobbed, repeating it until Cierzon placed a hand on his shoulder.

"I think we're done here," pronounced Brenna.

Zonta and Sondrin nodded in agreement, and even Caspin was forced to concede it was hopeless. He knelt to take Hayden's hand just as running footsteps echoed on the marble behind them.

"Anyone?" shouted Sefti. "Brenna, is that you?"

The diminutive swordswoman careered through the chamber door and slid across the polished wood, knocking over a vase and slipping to the floor beneath the oni.

"We've found one!" she babbled. "A live one, in the kitchens."

"Who?" asked Sir Caspin.

"We don't know. He's in a bad way, a *really* bad way." She struggled to catch her breath while climbing to her feet, brushing the dust from her leggings.

"The others?" queried Jem.

"You're the first I've seen. The man's very weak; Sax is helping him."

Caspin looked to his team, but Brenna was already taking the initiative. "We'll complete a sweep out to the edge of the Gold Tower," she said, referring to herself and Zonta.

"Meet you in the courtyard," confirmed Sir Caspin. He watched them disappear towards the giant Western Tower. "Now lead the way."

Sefti led them to one of the small side towers and down a winding stone stairway that directly spiralled through all the floors to the sub-basement. Long, glazed skylights allowed just enough of the approaching dusk to illuminate the hallways, which curved towards an expansive inner room.

Life below stairs was immediately less glamorous as the marble turned to slate, and gold door handles became brass. Doors were made of unvarnished boxwood, and no view of the sea could be seen through the grubby skylights. The round theme continued with bespoke curved workstations against the walls and a cast stove with two round doors. Pans hung from meat hooks around the room, cheese crumbs littered the tables, and ham bones lay on the floor beside smashed jars and empty tins of dry biscuits.

A single wide column at the kitchen's centre buttresses the ceiling where Tiam, Yuka and Cuyler looked down at a shape slumped against the cold stone. The man was in his sixties with a grey beard and a deeply lined forehead, but his appearance was so dishevelled that he looked like a pile of sacks. His black coat was ripped and stained, and his leggings hung around his knees where he'd tried to drag himself around the floor. His right leg was shackled to a long rusting chain, wrapped about the column and secured with a lock. The sight was pitiful, but the smell was awful, and his whimpering was wretched. He was muttering the same thing repeatedly, but it was too quiet, and the group struggled to decipher it. Jilliad tried to read his thoughts, but his mind was awash with pain.

"Myzon, myzon, myzon..." murmured the man, struggling to see Sax and Jilliad knelt beside him.

"Is that a place?" said Torbrand.

"Maybe a Jakari word?" mused Jem.

"We don't know," replied Tiam. "We think he's been here for a while. He's been eating what he can reach. Who knows what horror he's seen."

"I do," answered Moranne.

She entered with Lunn and Carina. The others parted to let her through, and she kneeled in front of the shaking older man. Drool hung from the corners of his mouth, and food clung to his beard, but his bloodshot eyes flickered with recognition.

"It's not Jakari," she said.

He stopped shaking and looked into her jade eyes. "My son," he said slowly, his voice quivering with every hushed syllable.

Moranne grasped his filthy, gnarled hand, cut from the broken jars. "I'm sorry," she whispered. "He was a lovely boy."

The Gold Tower housed the throne room and military briefing chambers where Moranne and her team had found the dead body of Prince Pancel, along with many of the lords and ladies of the court. Blood streaked every surface, a record of the violent frenzy.

Tears cascaded over the cracks in the man's face and his nose ran into them, dripping onto his filthy jacket.

"This is King Ramon Scoria," said Moranne. "Lunn, find something to break the chain."

"The king?" gasped Hayden.

Yuka encouraged him to take a few sips of water, and Sax brought a pale of water to help clean his face. His hands shook, and he struggled to focus on the faces around him, but Moranne was like a fixed point; he was trying to say something to her.

"Where's Corvus?" she said directly, but Ramon wasn't listening.

"They're gone," he said weakly.

"Ramon, where's Corvus?"

"She's not dead."

"My lord, please focus," said Moranne impatiently. "We need to find Corvus."

"He took her."

"Who did he take?" interrupted Jem. Moranne shot him a dark look, but he was unrepentant. "Who did Corvus take?"

"My wife and my beautiful Ana." More tears flooded his face and shook his body in grief. "He took my wife and daughter."

"Where to?" harried Moranne.

The king shook his head and simply replied: "promise me."

"We don't have time for this!" she blustered.

"Find them," he countered. "I'll tell you everything. I swear it."

Moranne looked up into the faces of Jem, Hayden, Caspin and Torbrand, who'd joined from searching one of the guest wings. The knights were practical, military men, the others were honourable and compassionate, but Jem's heart was so strong it could be his end. *Just like his father*.

"Alright!" she protested. "I swear we will do all we can to find and rescue Queen Yasmin and Princess Anatase, but we need to know the truth quickly."

With further sips of water and a hunk of cured ham, the king started to gain a little colour on his haggard face. Lunn and Gron soon arrived with a farrier's hammer and chisel they'd found in the stables and quickly set about removing the chain. The cuff had cut the king's leg where he'd strained to reach food hung about the kitchen. It was already infected.

He struggled upright with help from the two swarthy soldiers and slowly limped up the connecting tower and into the southern guest wing's lowest level. They helped him onto a velvet chaise and gathered around to hear his story.

"King Ramon, the past is the past," said Moranne. "Please tell us everything so we can stop him and save your kin.

The king took a small swig of the mead Gron carried with him and scanned the expectant faces. When his eyes rested on Jem, he seemed puzzled for a moment. He looked back and forth between Moranne and Jem but couldn't fathom the connection, eventually shaking the thoughts from his head.

He cleared his throat and reached into his blood-stained robe to retrieve a small scrap of parchment. After carefully unfolding it, he offered it to Moranne.

"I was desperate," he began.

The harvest failed for the second year running, and crime was rising. King Ramon's subjects became increasingly restless, taunted by the gleaming golden towers in their midst, while they struggled for survival. The gold and silver had gone, and diamond finds had slowed to a trickle. Winter was approaching, and the barns contained little food.

"It came on a clipper," said the king. "The captain said it was given to him by a young lad."

Sir Sigil Dalcite had carefully unrolled the leather package, revealing a gleaming sceptre identical to Moranne's. A parchment note was wound tightly around the handle.

When all is desperate and gone is time,
Journey to Brencan, a warlock to find.
Hold forth the sceptre to place in his hand,
And take ye once more the bountiful land.

A. friend

While the Stans did have spies throughout Grenfold, neither the king nor his advisor knew of any sympathisers.

"We paid no heed for a while," said the king, "but the situation worsened."

"Tell us everything," prompted Moranne.

Ramon was reliving the poor choices he'd made, but she needed all the details. He looked uncomfortable, continually shaking his head, but there was nowhere left to hide.

"They plotted against me," he stuttered. "The nobility wanted me dead."

A volunteer mission led by the king's most trusted knights was dispatched to Brencan in the hope of finding the mythical warlock. Only one man returned.

"Welcome, Lord Corvus," stated the harbourmaster. Jim Skarn spotted the small clipper a hundred yards from the harbour mouth. He tried to call for assistance or run to the port guards, but he couldn't move. His limbs were not his own, and his mouth couldn't form the words, but when the strangely dressed man came near, he found himself gushing in deference.

"Thank you," replied Corvus. His sharp features were creasing into an exaggerated grin. "Please escort me to the palace."

The morning mist was starting to clear, allowing thin beams of sunlight to illuminate the bustling port. Fishermen readied their nets, and guards sat on the harbour wall keeping an eye on proceedings so close to the palace. None paid any heed to the thin stranger, dressed in oversized warrior garb, as the harbourmaster led him towards the seat of power. Sir Faege Aplite's boots were much too large and rustled as Corvus walked, but he held his head high and ignored any questioning looks.

The palace guards lowered the drawbridge without a word and opened every door. They, too, found their bodies acting as if in a trance, their hands grasping handles and ushering a vagabond through the palace. The Great Tower doors opened onto the courtyard with its central pool and beds of climbing roses clinging to the inner walls of the guest wings.

Corvus smiled politely and nodded at the pretty ladies of the court, walking demurely in their velvet robes, recoiling from his ungainly clothes and syrup grin. A few would remember the tall, unkempt man, but none would live to recount the tale.

King Ramon was in conference with Sir Sigil, Prince Pancel and one of his generals when the doors swung open to reveal a thin man with angular features and shoulder-length black hair. His eyes were narrow green slits, and dark goatee stubble clung to his chin.

"What's the meaning of this?" barked Sir Sigil.

The harbourmaster accompanied the man, but the vagabond dismissed him with a wave, and the double doors slammed shut behind him. "Guards!" called the advisor, but no one came.

Corvus surveyed the room and inspected every man standing around the large table. It contained an inlaid map of the four islands, with various objects identifying troops or ships.

"I received your invitation," he purred, lifting the pulsing green sceptre for all to see.

"You're the warlock?" exclaimed the king. He straightened his mink and velvet robes, allowing the light to sparkle from his small, golden war crown.

"I prefer Lord Corvus," grinned the man. "Warlock is so... old."

"How do we know?" said one of the generals. The words had barely left his mouth when he found his hand reaching down to his sword. He unsheathed it in a single smooth movement and swept it to his own neck, stopping just as it drew a thin bead of blood.

"I'm not sure, General Manzonite. Would you like a demonstration?"

"Let him go," ordered the king. "You've made your point."

"Have I, General?"

Dorf Manzonite couldn't nod or move any limb, locked inside a puppet body. He could only stare down at the sharp blade and beg silently for his life.

"I agree," said Corvus, releasing the general, "and I accept your apology."

Dorf's sword dropped from his hand and clattered on the marble floor. Breath shuddered from his chest as he wiped a stream of sweat from his brow.

"Will you help us invade Tudorfeld?" asked the king bluntly. "The Grens have a much larger army and a difficult coastline to attack."

Corvus ignored the king for a moment and walked around the chamber until he could look out of one of the tall, arched windows. Only the western reaches of the Corona Mountains could be seen from the palace. He would need to go much further east.

"I'll need fifty men," he said flatly. "There's something I need near Mount Dracas."

"That's madness!" boomed Sir Sigil, "Nobody can survive that journey."

The sickly grin returned, reflecting from the window into Corvus's green eyes. "That's the deal," he said.

Corvus was accommodated in the best chamber within the East Guest Tower and furnished with a new set of bespoke, tailored clothes. He ordered a long, black, close-fitting coat with silver filigree and plush velvet leggings. It made him look tall and severe.

With a new, gleaming knight sword at his side, he departed early the next day, leading fifty riders and eight pack horses along the river Marglen as it rose steeply into the Corona foothills.

There was no word for two months until the doors opened one day, and Corvus stood before the king, sceptre glowing in his hand.

"I have returned," he crowed. "Yet I hear no fanfare in my honour and no feast in my name."

"What have you gained?" asked the king.

"The upper hand, you weak-minded fool."

Corvus' words poured into the room like oozing oil.

"How dare you—" began Sir Manzonite, but events stole his words.

Two guards strode purposely into the room behind Corvus. Their faceguards were down, and blood dripped from drawn blades. The general backed away, fumbling for his sword but one of the guards struck him down with a single blow.

"Stop! What are you doing?" cried the king.

Side doors burst open on each side of the chamber. Prince Pancel was dragged into the room through one, while Queen Yasmin and Princess Anatase were herded through the other.

"Father!" called the prince, "what's happening?"

Two guards pushed him to his knees and forced him to face the king. The queen and princess screamed as they were thrown down before Corvus, but he simply laughed. Bloody soldiers now ringed the room. There was no escape.

"Like the moth, your father danced too close to the flame," Corvus explained to the women. "He thought I was helping him. Poor human fool."

Corvus took a sword from one of the soldiers and offered it to the king. Ramon felt a strange calm pouring over his body, and his hand reached out to clasp the sword hilt.

"Kill him, father!" shouted Pancel.

The king tried to take control, but his limbs were possessed. His arm pulled back to strike, but his will was gone. *No!* With all the might in his body, he fought the pull, but Corvus' eyes burned bright, and the sceptre crackled with power.

"Please, father!"

With a single thrust, the king drove the sword into his son's chest. The queen screamed in terror, but the moment was gone. The lad gasped his last breath of incomprehension, then fell to his side.

"That's such a pity," mused Corvus, tutting loudly. "Your army is too small and weak to take Cynstol - but thank you for the hospitality."

"Let my wife and daughter go," sobbed the king as he looked down at his dead son. "You don't need them."

Corvus smiled at the two women wailing over Pancel's body. "Well, I'm afraid I do," he said. "They'll make excellent slaves when I give them to the Jakaris."

"Please, take me!" pleaded the king. He dropped to his knees and grasped at Corvus' coat.

"Oh, that's very noble, but I need you for something else."

"What more?"

"When the witch comes, and she *will* come, tell her I'm going to destroy her and all her weak little human friends." He gestured for the guards to drag the queen and princess from the room. "Oh, and there is one more thing," he said. "Tell her I know the runt lives, and he'll never be strong enough to face me."

***

The room was silent but for the sobbing of King Ramon. His body convulsed with every breath, and he shed more tears to join the river, which wouldn't end. The night was falling, but Moranne could still see the peaks of the Corona range through the windows, pink in the dying embers of the day. The man of myth was finally described in all his majestic horror. Jem looked at Hayden, and the Cempestre looked at each other, but no one could form words that would fit the harrowing tale. Even Zonta's monosyllabic stabs were absent.

Moranne looked down at the crumpled letter bearing the words which launched a doomed mission. "*A. friend*" stared back at her and picked at an ancient memory, but the fragment was too small, and any insight remained locked out of reach. When she eventually turned to face the company, her face was ashen. "I should have seen this," she said. "I've been a fool."

"Don't blame yourself," countered Sir Torbrand. "*None* of us saw this."

"No!" said Moranne. "Jem told me about the Jakaris killing the crofters in his dream. I thought it was a possible future, far ahead. I was wrong."

"Why would the Jakaris help Corvus?" said Caspin. "They have no love for him."

Moranne nodded. Corvus had been smart, very smart. With over three hundred years to forge his revenge, he'd devised the only plan which could work.

"He's woken the wyverns."

"The what?" coughed Biorn.

Jem remembered Moranne telling the story of a shepherd boy back in Denbry. *A wyvern has two legs, a barbed tail and vast wings.*

"Old wives' tales," scolded Captain Blake.

"Oh, they're real," said Moranne, her eyes flashing green. "The Jakaris believe they're the manifestation of Stanin, the dragon god."

"That's insane!" howled Hayden.

"As insane as a winged golden goddess?" she retorted. "The Jakaris believe humans are the spawn of Stanin."

"Ma'am," pleaded Torbrand, "I don't see the connection."

Moranne clenched her fists. She sometimes forgot how little the humans knew of the world around them.

"The last wyverns are named Vindraco and Aldnari. They have slept in peace on Mount Dracas for thousands of years but always return to the same hunting ground; Salamas. The Jakaris will believe that we have sent the wyverns to kill them."

"Why would they believe that?" asked Caspin.

Corvus had been clever. "Because, my dear knight, Corvus will possess the highest Rajuni priests, and those priests will incite the people into a holy war against the east."

"Really? Are they so easily led?" Caspin didn't understand religion but spoke for most of the company.

"The Jakaris are more devout than Freans and are a kind, passionate, loving race. They live in close family units, and it is one of the greatest privileges to be invited into their home," said Moranne.

"I still don't understand," said Caspin.

Moranne sighed. It was the one aspect of Jakari life which always scared her. "The priesthood interprets the ancient texts, and not even the emperor will question their word," she said. "The Jakari people will believe everything they're told or be too afraid to voice dissent. Add a couple of wyverns eating their children, and they'll *want* to believe it."

"Frea!" gasped Gron.

"How many Jakaris are there?" queried Tiam.

Moranne turned back to look through the window once more as the mountains stood as black silhouettes against the fiery sky. "More than all the other humans of Grenfold and Stanholm combined with every alviri and every clan."

A small door on the ground floor of the Gold Tower opened out to a narrow bridge. It plunged over the cliffs and arched over to a tiny islet four hundred yards from the coast. King Ramon loved to gaze at the stars and had an observatory built on the narrow rock. The short tower was capped by an opening roof which allowed the telescope to view the skies above.

Sir Torbrand sat on a small bench, looking out at the dark waters of the Blusker Channel. The rocky Calder Island lay northwards, Brencan was to the west, but tomorrow they'd be travelling south, hoping to avoid imprisonment. He felt powerless in the face of Corvus' evil, but lives depended on him. There was always a responsibility; to his men, the Green Order, his mother, his father, and to Faircester. He looked up at the cloudy night sky and wondered if the king ever saw anything in the stars.

"Copper for them," joked Ellen. She stood behind him and followed his gaze into the night.

He looked around, and for once, he didn't make an excuse to leave. Patting the bench, he gestured for Ellen to join him. She sat against the tower and put her feet on the guard wall.

"Bit chilly out here, sir," she said.

"Hmm," he agreed. "It suits my mood." It was rare for Torbrand to express any emotion, but he was beginning to drop his guard.

"We've put the king in a guest room; he seems like a broken man."

"He's lost everything," agreed the knight.

They sat, staring into the darkness together, each alone with similar thoughts and wanting to enjoy the company. Then Torbrand remembered his oath.

"Ellen, I need to talk to you about something."

For the merest moment, Ellen believed that Torbrand was about to expose his heart. True feelings that they both shared and hid in plain sight. She held her breath, hoping his words would match her thoughts, but it wasn't to be.

"I can't keep my word by giving you a commission," he continued, in his deep brooding voice.

She felt the air burst from her lungs and the hope drain from her heart. "I understand," she said, holding back the bubbling emotions. "Many of us won't live to see the spring."

It was a strange comment, thought Sir Torbrand, but the evil in their midst weighed heavily.

"Please excuse me, sir." Ellen turned quickly to avoid showing her tears and ran across the bridge to find her room, leaving the tall knight watching her go.

Cursing the cold air, he yelled his weakness into his thoughts. *You're a fool, Torbrand.*

Most of the company had found rooms in one of the two guest towers, where the majority of chambers were free of grisly scenes. The dryads decided to sleep inside for once, with Chakirris insisting she must take the bedroom nearest the prince. Everyone found a room, even Zonta, who wanted to share with Brenna. They discovered a suite with interconnecting doors, which seemed to keep her happy. Although from a proud warring race, she was afraid of this new world and felt uneasy around the humans, like a wolf away from its pack.

"I suppose I better get some sleep," said Hayden.

He and Cierzon sat in the library where an open fire bathed the bright walls in an orange glow, spilling over the polished oak floor. There were many dusty, bound books from ancient scholars and distant monarchs, but their wisdom had been lost to King Ramon.

Hayden pulled a guard across the fireplace and started to walk towards the East Guest Tower, but Cierzon was right behind him. "It's a pity you couldn't find a bedroom in the West Tower," he mused. "There were plenty."

"The ladies took them," replied Hayden, looking back at his friend. "Goodnight, Cierzon."

Gada Scirmann continued walking towards his room, but he noticed the alviri lord was still following. "You know my room is large enough for two," he said.

It was the moment he dreamed of but feared in equal measure. Hayden stopped, mesmerized by Cierzon's emerald blue eyes. "It's—"

"Say nothing," said Cierzon.

"But—"

"Shh!" Lord Cierzon placed a finger on Hayden's lips and took his hand. "We are like leaves which fall from the tree. We bend and fly in the wind for a while until we eventually meet the ground."

Death was all around them; it littered the halls and lurked behind many palace doors. In time, it would hit the Fay Legion again.

"I'm scared," blushed Hayden, "I've never—"

"Shh!" the lord said once more. "Take my hand, don't question yourself."

Hand in hand, they circled the spiral stairs in one of the connecting towers until it opened onto Cierzon's floor. A few bodies still lay slumped in the arcing corridor, but Hayden's thoughts were elsewhere. Nerves fluttered in his stomach and buzzed in his fingers, but the warmth from Cierzon's hand pulled him along until they stopped at the chamber door.

"Is this what you want?" asked Cierzon.

Hayden looked once more into the alviri's beautiful fair face. Cierzon already knew the answer, but it was time to say it out loud. "Yes," he said. Hayden reached for the door handle, and together they stepped inside.

Just two rooms occupied the top floor of the West Guest Tower; each chamber included richly upholstered chairs and a chaise arranged around a sculpted marble fireplace. The drapes and furniture all matched in a deep crimson, embroidered with the diamond of House Scoria. Marble, onyx and obsidian sculptures stood vigil on short oak tables. The luxury was jarring when contrasted with the Stans' fate, and Sir Torbrand had no time for it. Often more at home sleeping rough under a tent or in the box-hewn bed of a sweaty barracks, he threw his clothes on the floor and collapsed into the soft, feathered bed.

Too much had happened since his arrogance spilt out in King Pythar's audience chamber back in Cynstol. The mission would be simple, leading a group of girls to Stanholm, but he'd failed just miles from the capital, and she was known as 'the clown'. The thoughts ebbed and flowed until fatigue conquered his restless mind and draped the realm of dreams over his cut and bruised body.

Images started, receded and reset as the dream played tricks and repeated his past conflicts. Green Order campaigns clashed with colourful balls and sent him reeling through the halls of Faircester Castle until he lay once more in the bed of his youth. A wisp of cool air blew through his dream, and somewhere a door creaked shut with the lightest pressure on its latch. It left a benevolent presence like a guiding light or a guardian standing vigilant at his side. Torbrand's consciousness tried to wake him, but his dream was filled with wonder. The gentle scent of jasmine filled his mind, and warm, bare skin pressed against him. His eyes flicked open, but he didn't move as a soft, searching hand caressed his shoulder and wrapped around his chest to pull him close.

"Say nothing," said Ellen, her warm breath stirring the hairs on the back of his neck. "Give me this night, and I'll trouble you no more."

Torbrand placed his mighty hand over hers and held it tight. He gave his reply as loudly as he could. He said nothing.

55 SHERATAN

The warmth of summer gave way to the chill of autumn, but the swaying pines stood fast. Winter could be cruel in the Sahabal Mountains; it was a race against time. Sheratan could feel the beads of sweat forming on his forehead before they ran together and trickled down his neck or dropped onto the log. At least the short dark hair couldn't flick it into his eyes. He hacked another keyway into the long timber, just a few feet into the end so it would mate at the cabin's corner. Porrima would enjoy seeing his smooth, taught body, spotted with sweat at the end of a hard day. She didn't care about the male stench or the filth crusting his arms; she said he looked "magnificent."

They longed for their own home, and maybe children might follow. A plateau midway up one of the mountains provided a perfect backdrop for a home away from danger. Jakaris feared the north-western peaks, and wolves hunted in the lower climbs. Beside a clear mountain stream, with a backdrop of woodland, and plenty of wild goats and sheep to hunt, the location was ideal. With a skin colour closely matching that of the Jakaris and a good grasp of the local dialect, Porrima and Sheratan could blend into this stunning country; it was perfect.

Sheratan stopped to inspect the woodworking joint and look at the cabin walls, which now stood five feet tall. A porch, doorway and several window apertures were easily visible. It was taking shape; they could be happy here.

A twig snapped somewhere behind, and he whipped around instinctively.

"Porri?" he laughed. She was seldom subtle.

There was no response or movement in the trees, just a mild wind blowing the branches, so they bobbed back and forth. Sheratan returned to his work, but he could feel a presence nearby.

Another snap, but this time it was nearer and followed by a second.

"Who's there?"

Other than Porrima living in their tent further down the mountain, there was nobody for miles. Deer and a few grizzly bears would circle the lower slopes, but both were wary of humans and usually kept their distance. He reached for the sceptre hanging from his belt and grasped it in readiness. His principal gifts were sight and voiceless speech, but he could issue a bolt of deadly energy when in danger.

More movement, but this time it was to the left. Sheratan turned to see a branch springing back and forth, but no one was there.

"Show yourself!"

With power pulsing through the sceptre, he could feel it now. Someone was close and watching him. It wasn't Porrima; it felt younger.

Put down the sceptre and walk away. The threat shot through Sheratan's mind. He knew the voice from somewhere, but it was deeper and more menacing.

"Who are you? What do you want?" he shouted as his heart pounded. With the axe in one hand and the sceptre in the other, he scanned the woodlands, but still, there was nothing.

Put down the sceptre, repeated the voice. *Your powers are weak; you don't need it.*

He knew that voice, but it had been many years. Flailing wildly, he turned left and right, trying to locate the source, but it seemed all around him.

Porri, I'm in trouble. He tried to call out, but the tent was too far away, even if his thoughts could connect with her at such a distance.

Another twig snapped closer this time. Sharatan's heart raced as he circled the cabin.

Last chance, old man. Drop the sceptre and go!

Sheratan stopped with his back against the cabin. His breath was short, and his eyes darted from left to right. There was something about the voice and those words. "Old man." Only one person used those words about the streaks of grey in his tightly curled hair.

He peered around the end of the cabin, and the young man stood before him.

"Corvus!" he yelled.

The young lad's hand was already thrusting forward with the hunting knife. Sheratan convulsed, dropping both the axe and sceptre as he grabbed for the knife, but it was already piercing his stomach. He tried desperately to fight back, but Corvus stabbed him again, and again, and again until Sheratan's cream tunic ran with blood. He slumped to the ground against the crimson-stained logs.

Corvus stood over the crumpled body and wiped the knife on his tunic. "This could have been easier," he gloated, bending down to retrieve the sceptre. His eyes immediately blazed green as he clasped the silver rod. "I'm going to have a lot of fun with this." He wandered from the camp without another word and disappeared into the trees. Sheratan watched as the life drained from his body.

Porri, my love, I'm sorry. Corvus has killed me.

Jem's dreams were dark, as were those of the Cempestre and most of the men, but Torbrand smiled in his sleep. It was uncharacteristic, but the feeling flooded his body. He could see Ellen standing on the banks of the Cwen with flowers in her hair and wearing a white dress edged in blue. The sun shone, and bees buzzed back and forth over the clover flowers. He reached out to take her hand, but someone ran up behind him.

"Torbrand!" shouted his father.

Torbrand turned, but the earl was nowhere to be seen.

"Torbrand!" he shouted once again.

The knight tossed and turned, trying to shout out, but the dream held him tight.

"Torbrand!" The footsteps were getting louder now, almost on top of him. "Sir!"

The door to the knight's room burst open, and Gamin skidded to a halt at the end of the bed.

"Sorry, sir, but someone's fallen," he gasped, trying to catch his breath from the long climb.

Torbrand rubbed the sleep from his eyes and tried to steady himself as his heart beat through his chest, shaking his whole body.

"Slowly," he said. "What's happened?"

The young archer took a moment to compose himself and straightened his back. "Someone's fallen from one of the towers. I don't know who, but there's a body in the courtyard."

Sir Torbrand looked across to the space in the bed beside him. There was an indentation in the pillow, and the covers were pulled back, but no sign of the fiery-haired swordswoman. *Give me this night, and I'll trouble you no more.*

"Ellen!" he gasped.

Torbrand leapt from the bed and grabbed his leggings, which took too long. Ignoring the boots, he snatched up a shirt and careered from the room, with Gamin running after. The knight's bare feet slapped on the cold stone of the stair tower; he stubbed his toes against the wall and scraped his knuckles, but he felt nothing. Only fear drove him, and the churns of his stomach feared the worst. "Please," he begged.

Some of the others were making their way down, but Sir Torbrand pushed them out of the way. He was frantic, shoving Cuyler against the wall and ploughing between Hayden and Cierzon, walking hand in hand.

"Get out of the way," he screamed.

He tried to see through the arrow slits, but the view to the courtyard was too steep. Only halfway down the stairs, the panic possessed him; Gamin was now far behind.

"Please, Ellen, I can't...."

His father was laughing, his mother was parading a catwalk of dizzy suiters, and General Marl dangled the noose. It couldn't be for nothing; *I can't face life without you*. Finally reaching the bottom, he shoved the door so hard that it crashed against the wall, straining on its hinges. "No!" A group of bodies stood like a wall around his love, conspiring to shatter his private grief. He pushed past Brenna and Sefti and jabbed at Lunn until he moved aside. They all looked down in silence, and he couldn't bear it but forced himself to gaze at the spreading pool of blood beneath the twisted naked body.

"Poor bastard," said Brea, shaking her head.

King Ramon lay face down against the flagstones, with his dented crown still in place. He'd fallen or, more likely, jumped.

"Where's Ellen?" yelled sir, Torbrand. "Where is she?"

"I've not seen her," said Brea.

Torbrand grabbed her by the coat and yanked her forward, screaming into her face. "Tell me where she is!"

"I'm here," came a voice from behind.

With tears welling in his eyes, Torbrand ran to Ellen and wrapped his granite arms around her. All pretence was gone, and the mask was shattered.

"Don't ever leave me," he begged, holding her so tightly that the breath was forced from her lungs. "Promise me."

She pulled his face from her shoulder and clasped it in her hands. "I promise," she said, fighting back her own tears.

"Thank Frea for that!" chuckled Brea to herself. Even the jovial huntress knew when to respect the dead. She winked at Ellen, who was rubbing the moisture from her eyes.

One by one, the company arrived in the courtyard to see the sad end of King Ramon Scoria. Few were surprised, but it highlighted the horrors they'd already encountered on the rocky isle and their eagerness to leave. Moranne said nothing when she emerged with the prince. She knew Ramon's sanity had been hovering on the brink. He couldn't escape the image of his son, murdered by his own hand. The trauma would destroy many more Stanish lives before the memory of Corvus' massacre faded into the dust of history.

Seeing that Ellen and his brother were sharing a tender moment, Caspin took charge. Lunn, Gron, Zonta, Brenna and Isen would bury the king and Prince Pancel on a small patch of land north of the palace while the others used some of their provisions to prepare a hot breakfast.

"Where's Captain Blake?" he shouted, noticing that both Barda and Koll were missing.

"I have them!" replied Sondrin as she and Jilliad bundled them into the courtyard and pushed them onto the floor. "They were in the harbour trying to escape."

"The creature's lying!" howled the captain.

"We was only looking," claimed Koll.

Caspin smiled. "The dryads can read minds. Apparently, you both think very loudly."

"I never agreed to this," retorted Barda. "Dead Stans and unnatural creatures."

"And women," added Koll.

"You'll both be richly compensated," replied Moranne.

It didn't take long to give a Frean burial to the king and his son. Gron offered a few lines from the sacred texts, but few of the warriors stood by. A hoar frost dusted the coarse grass and clung to the fronds of pine trees as winter slowly crept into the lowlands. The men and women were happy to hurry back to the palace, where the Cempestre had lit a fire in one of the reception rooms.

Breakfast was toasted stale bread with honey and strips of ham which they'd saved from Silfren. It wasn't much, but they needed to reserve supplies for the onward journey.

Moranne looked about the room at the stout hearts who'd battled into the far north of the known world. It was a mercy that only two lives had been lost, and the remaining company had bonded so well. The divisions that separated the different races and sexes were now gone. Isen sat stoically with Gamin, Lunn shared a joke with Gron and Sefti, Cuyler, Yuka, Hayden, and Cierzon swapped stories. Biorn, Bresne, Brenna and Zonta laughed together, and Jem watched Ostro go through his daily training. Only Sax was silent, sitting alone with his thoughts.

The king's advisor climbed wearily to her feet and waited until the throng had quietened. "I'm very proud of you all," she said. "I stood in front of the great and good who doubted we could work together, let alone make it this far, but here we are."

"A pox on 'em!" shouted Brea.

"We've battled the powers of darkness and our short-sighted masters, trying to reach our goal, but we failed—"

"Hang on," interrupted Caspin.

"No, my friend. We have failed in our mission to stop Corvus from corrupting the Stans. Right now, he marches to Salamas to build an army who will attack from the west."

"Need to warn," said Prince Asger.

"I agree," replied Moranne. "We must sail for Silmouth and send word to Cynstol and all the other fortified towns in the west."

Jem started to speak, but Moranne ignored him and continued. "I thank the Cempestre and our fair friends, but you are free to go when we make landfall."

"Ma'am—" began Jem, but still she spoke over him.

"I take full responsibility for this mission and the breakout from Numolport. None of you needs to face the court-martial."

"Ma'am—" Jem said once more, now on his feet.

"Captain Blake will choose a good ship from the harbour and can keep it as part payment."

Jem looked at his friends in horror. They all thought the same thing but were too frightened of her power.

"I suggest Sir Torbrand goes to Faircester to raise the Queen's Battalion," she continued.

"Ma'am, please—" begged Jem.

"The prince and I will—"

"Let the lad speak!" shouted Captain Fallon, from the back of the room.

Bresne looked at him as a wife who might be surprised by her husband's integrity.

The room was silent as Moranne stared at Jem, daring him to utter a single word in defiance. The light filtered through the high windows as the sun touched the Corona Mountains' icy peaks. It placed slim rectangles of light on the opposing wall, which gradually rose in pace with the anger coursing through her veins.

"I know Corvus is raising an army," said Jem waving his cup of water towards the windows, "and I know we need to warn the capital. But—"

"But what?" she fumed.

Jem didn't want a confrontation, with all the death in their midst, but often the rains brought a storm.

"We made an oath," he said.

Everyone could see the tension on her face as the veins throbbed in her forehead and she clenched and unclenched her fists.

"*I* made an oath," she corrected, "and that oath died with the king."

"But the queen and princess could still be alive," said Jem. "We have a duty to try."

"He has a point," interjected Biorn.

Moranne flushed red, and her voice became harsh. *We don't have time for this.* "Our duty is to all the men and women of Grenfold who will die if we don't raise the alarm. I'm sorry, but we can't help them."

"This isn't right," protested Jem.

"I'm sorry," she repeated.

"It's too dangerous," added Sir Torbrand, coming to her aid.

Jem was shaking his head in disbelief. "It was an oath; it doesn't matter that he's dead!"

"We could split the company—" began Caspin.

Moranne finally snapped. "Enough!" she raged. "We leave for Silmouth in one hour. Pack your things and head for the harbour!"

Jem didn't wait for further humiliation. He threw his earthenware cup against the wall, smashing it into a hundred pieces. Giving a cursory look to his comrades, he turned on his heels and stormed from the room, slamming the door behind him.

"Has honour," said Zonta under her breath.

A grey mist filled Jem's mind as he strode through the palace. He'd never felt truly alone, even as the Burland orphan deserted by his love-struck father. He wanted to know more, but the truth was closed to him. Uncle Ned and Aunt Ada would never speak of his mother and father. Moranne knew the truth but buried it so deep that a flicker would not crease her face. Jem couldn't see his parents in his dreams, but he saw others. People with strange powers and quirky ways in lands he'd never visited; it was more than just the sight.

The horses snorted and whinnied as he passed the stables. They seemed to sense that a storm was brewing, following the Burland gada in their midst. Jem swept past them and out through the main entrance onto the drawbridge. It rattled and echoed beneath his feet until he stepped from the end onto the stony road, but as he continued down towards the port, the wooden planks echoed once more.

"Don't you walk away from me, Gada Poulterer!" raged Moranne.

He didn't turn, though her words pierced him, and he clenched his fists in defiance.

"You think you're just going to sail off to Salamas? Don't be a fool!"

Still, he strode forward, increasing the pace and trying to throw doubt into the chill wind. He could find a small boat, follow the coast, and cross during daylight. He could do it.

"You'll be dead by noon!" she chided.

Finally, he stopped where the road started to descend to the town, wreathed in a light, frosty mist. "Why do you care?" he spat back. "The lies pour from your mouth like water!"

"How dare you—"

"You might break every vow, but I do not!"

He turned to continue, but her hand grabbed his arm and spun him around.

"I've paid the price for my mistakes. You have no idea what I've done for you—"

"So tell me!" he screamed.

Jem's eyes were starting to pulse as anger tapped the earth power coursing through his veins.

"You know your life," she said. "I choose you because—"

"I have these gifts? Why? I know nothing about my parents, yet see places I've never been! Why do I not see Ben and Asmeen?"

"I don't know," she replied, shaking her head. He was piecing together the fragments. She'd underestimated him.

"You lie!" he stormed. "Every word is a lie. They all warned me about you, but I didn't listen." He snatched away and continued to walk towards the port, but she matched every step.

"Ever piloted a sailing boat?"

Jem ignored her.

"Ever navigated by the stars?"

Moranne was right, and Jem knew it. He'd be dead by morning or adrift on the open ocean, but the anger was too strong to stop now. "Jem, stop this madness! That's an order!"

When he stopped and slowly turned to face her, Jem's eyes were flickering with a green flame, and he could feel the power surging in his stomach. All the lies and half-truths were tumbling in his mind to mix with the visions which seemed so real. Measuring every step, he walked back towards her until he was just feet from his mistress.

"Jem, I know you're upset," she continued, trying to strike a conciliatory tone. "But it's too dangerous to follow Corvus into Salamas. You must realize that?"

The ocean breeze swept her hair back, making her look beautiful and deadly. Her eyes sparkled with intent, but Jem's were raging.

"I resign my commission," he said gruffly.

"I won't release you," she countered.

"I don't care," he snorted. "When we return to the mainland, I'll be gone."

"I forbid it!" Her eyes flared, and she threw down her arms as if placing an invisible marker on the ground. "Jem!" she tried once more. "Salamas is too dangerous. You can't go alone."

"So come with me," he countered. "Let the knights do battle; keep your word."

"It's too late. The queen and princess will be dead. I can't risk your life for them."

Jem shook his head. "It's my life to risk."

"Think of your friends: Hayden, Gamin and the others," she pleaded.

"They agree with me!" he blustered. "They're too scared of you to speak out, but I know what you are. You're a twisted witch with your own agenda. You're no different to him."

The reference to Corvus ignited in her eyes, and she reached for her sceptre. With it grasped in her right hand, she grabbed his tunic and pulled him close. "How dare—"

"Are you going to strike me down?" he said, pushing her back. He could see the lights dancing in her eyes but waved them away. "I thought not!"

"Bluffs and lies," he continued. "You come to Denbry and choose me by chance? Lie! Are my powers a surprise to you? Lie." Eyes in the palace were on him as he paced around her. "You were there when Aludra died, when Rana died and when Corvus was defeated, yet he endures still."

"What are you saying?" she spat.

"I don't know, ma'am. I can't separate the truth from the lies."

"I'm telling you. You cannot go to Salamas."

"Why?" he snapped.

"You must not face Corvus alone." Her voice was beginning to crack as he receded from her grasp.

"I have powers."

"You're no match for him, and you know it."

"I'll find a way."

"You must not go!" she screamed.

"Why?"

"Because…"

"Just tell me. Don't keep lying to me!"

Moranne slumped onto an outcrop of rock bordering the road and looked down into the pebbles which marked its surface. Every secret killed her a little, but it was the only way. Nobody could ever understand her pain or the burden she couldn't leave behind. Where once he was weak, he was now a man. She traced the shape of his face in her mind and saw how closely it matched. It was almost as if he stood before her once more.

"I cannot let you face Corvus alone… you're my son."

Eyes from Obsidia saw the king's advisor confronting the chicken farmer from Denbry. Some would know the whole story, some would glean fragments, but most would know nothing. A bridge had been crossed. The two individuals stared through each other like statues, daring each other to crack their stone and make the first move. A cold wind whipped about the two glacial figures locked in emotional turmoil.

Somewhere in the west, a pair of narrow green eyes creased inwards to a grinning smile.

End of Part One

Acknowledgements

It's impossible to complete this novel without acknowledging the extraordinary contribution of my wife, Lisa. Her support, proofreading and editing went beyond my hopes and helped me shape a dream into reality. Thank you for everything.

I would also like to thank the following:

My friends and family who have supported and encouraged me along the way.

Anto at Icarus Games for your excellent map drawing tutorials (https://www.youtube.com/@IcarusGames).

Phil Barthram, creator and custodian of the old English translator (www.oldenglishtranslator.co.uk).

Damonza, for taking my brief and creating such fantastic cover art.

Author's Note

Thank you so much for reading this, my second novel. I hope you've enjoyed reading it as much as I've enjoyed its creation.

The ideas behind the Nifaran Chronicles germinated over twenty years before the first publication. What if a conflict could be more than simply good versus evil, and how could a diverse company of characters exist in a medieval world? The warm reception to my first book, Zero Magenta, persuaded me it was time to finally realise my dream of authoring an original fantasy.

The second part of the series will chronicle Jem's journey as he discovers the truth about his past and the origin of the Nifarans.

I have advanced plans for parts three and four. Hopefully, it won't be a further twenty years before these become a reality.

I would love to hear from you, and please feel free to engage on social media; let me know what you think and perhaps share your theories.

Happy reading, and always remember your difference is *your* power.

John Howes

Printed in Great Britain
by Amazon